1634
THE
BAVARIAN
CRISIS

**For a complete list of
Baen Books by Eric Flint,
please go to www.baen.com.**

1634
THE
BAVARIAN
CRISIS

ERIC FLINT AND
VIRGINIA DeMARCE

.1634: THE BAVARIAN CRISIS

This is a work of fiction. All the characters and events portrayed in this book are fictional, and any resemblance to real people or incidents is purely coincidental.

A Baen Books Original

Baen Publishing Enterprises
P.O. Box 1403
Riverdale, NY 10471
www.baen.com

ISBN 10: 1-4165-4253-1
ISBN 13: 978-1-4165-4253-7

Cover art by Tom Kidd
Maps & charts by Gorg Huff

First printing, October 2007

Distributed by Simon & Schuster
1230 Avenue of the Americas
New York, NY 10020

Library of Congress Cataloging-in-Publication Data

Flint, Eric.
    1634 : the Bavarian crisis / Eric Flint and Virginia DeMarce.
        p. cm. — (The ring of fire series)
    "A Baen Books original"—T.p. verso.
    ISBN-13: 978-1-4165-4253-7
    ISBN-10: 1-4165-4253-1
    1. Thirty Years' War, 1618-1648—Fiction. 2. Time travel—Fiction. 3. Europe—History—17th century—Fiction. I. DeMarce, Virginia Easley, 1940– II. Title.

    PS3556.L548A6175 2007
    813'.54—dc22

                                                                    2007023561

10 9 8 7 6 5 4 3 2 1

Pages by Joy Freeman (www.pagesbyjoy.com)
Printed in the United States of America

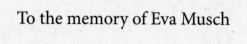

To the memory of Eva Musch

Contents

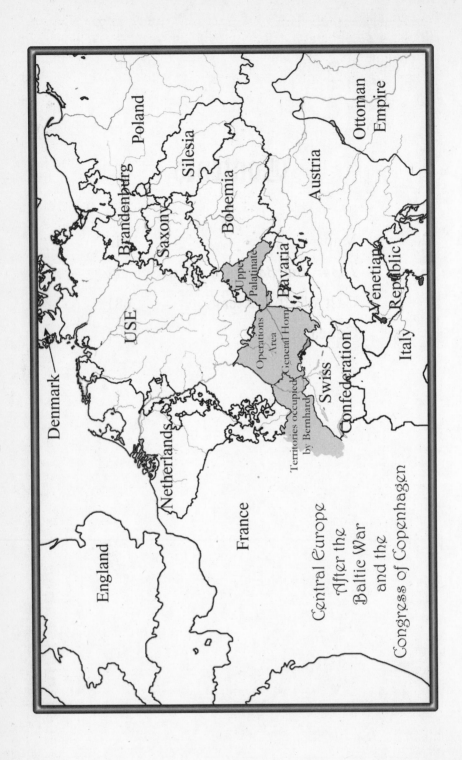

Denmark

England

Netherlands

France

Poland

Brandenburg

Saxony

Silesia

Bohemia

USE

Upper
Palatinate

Bavaria

Operations
Area

General Horn

Territories occupied
by Bernhard

Austria

Swiss
Confederation

Ottoman
Empire

Venetian
Republic

Italy

Central Europe
After the
Baltic War
and the
Congress of Copenhagen

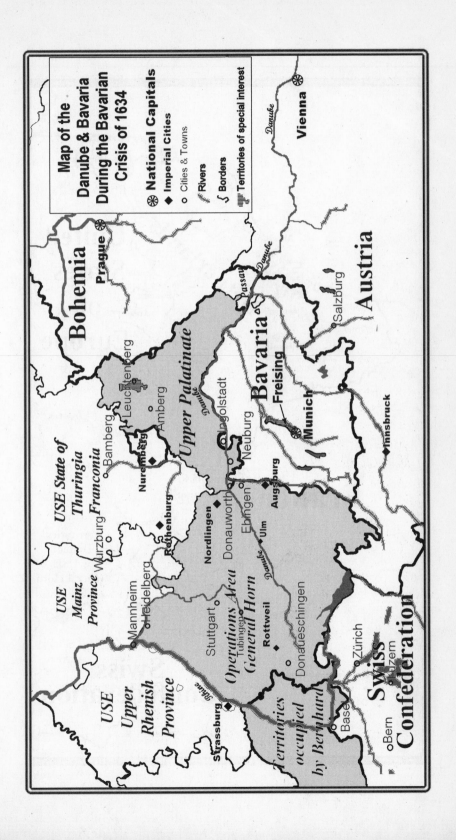

Map of the
Danube & Bavaria
During the Bavarian
Crisis of 1634

⊛ National Capitals
◆ Imperial Cities
○ Cities & Towns
〜 Rivers
ᔓ Borders
▥ Territories of special interest

Bohemia

⊛ Prague

Leuchtenberg

USE State of
Thuringia
Franconia

Bamberg ○

◆ Nuremberg

Amberg ○

Upper Palatinate

Danube

○ Ingolstadt

Neuburg ○

USE Mainz
Province

○ Würzburg

◆ Rothenburg

◆ Nordlingen

Donauwörth ○

Ebingen ○

Danube

◆ Augsburg

Bavaria

Freising ○

Munich ★

Passau

Salzburg ○

Austria

⊛ Vienna

Danube

▼ Innsbruck

USE
Mainz
Province

Mannheim ○

Heidelberg ○

Rhine

Stuttgart ○

Tübingen ○

Ulm ◆

Operations Area
General Horn

Rottweil ◆

Donaueschingen ○

Danube

USE
Upper Rhenish
Province

◆ Strassburg

Territories
occupied
by Bernhard

Basel ○

Zürich ○

Luzern ○

Bern ○

Swiss
Confederation

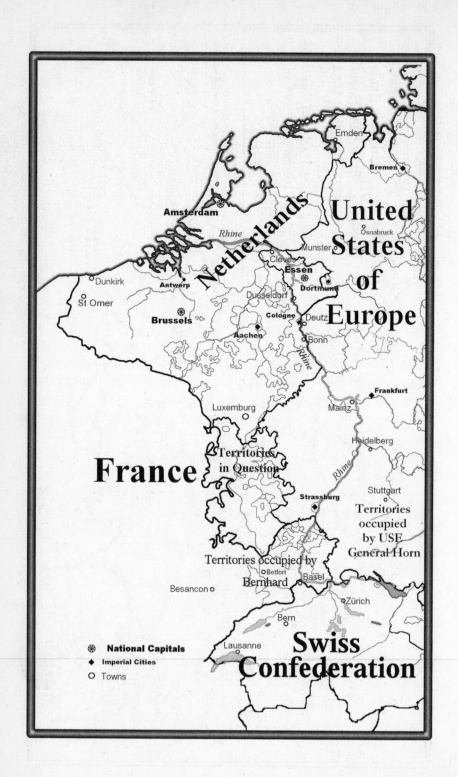

January 1634

To me alone there came a thought of grief

Munich, Bavaria

Duke Maximilian of Bavaria kneeled by the side of the bier upon which his late wife's body lay in state. "Nobody else remembers," he cried out. "The rest of you only recall how she was these last years—an ill old woman, tired, discouraged and heavy in spirit because she had not given Bavaria an heir."

He banged his forehead against the stone pedestal upon which the bier had been placed; then turned to the chamberlain who was standing behind him. "Only I remember what she was like when she came to Bavaria as a bride. I am the only one who remembers what it was like. She radiated merriment; she was so lovable. Under God, she was the greatest blessing of my life. So virtuous! So pious! I have lost the most wonderful wife that any man ever had. Her price was truly above rubies!"

He turned back to the bier. "O, My God, how have I offended You? In what way has my service to You and to the Church failed, that You have so bereft me? Elisabeth Renata, may God take you directly to paradise. You never did anything that would require you to remain in purgatory. Elisabeth Renata. My wife."

Turning again, he called for a pen and paper—and a knife. The chamberlain moved to the door; a silent servant brought the supplies rapidly. Slashing the ball of his thumb, the duke

1

accumulated a little puddle of blood on the floor, with which he wrote—wrote shakily, with numerous blots, not just because of his agitation but because blood, coagulating so quickly, does not make the best of inks. "To Mary, Queen of Heaven, Patroness of Bavaria," he began. Finished, he turned. "Bring me the golden box on my writing desk—the one with the mirror on the top."

The servant slid away, returning swiftly with the box that the duke had requested. Maximilian opened it and placed the paper inside.

"This is my vow. Take it to the pilgrimage shrine at Altötting. My worldly life is over. Others may shoulder the burden. I shall abdicate and retire to a monastery. Until I am reunited with my duchess, my days will be devoted to fasting and prayer."

Duke Albrecht of Bavaria looked silently at the privy council. The councillors looked back, in equal silence.

"My brother is still at Duchess Elisabeth Renata's bier. There is certain urgent business that cannot wait until he can bring himself to turn his attention to it," Albrecht finally commented. "First, however, let us each say a silent rosary for the peaceful rest of the late duchess. I cannot regret the pneumonia that took her. For more than a year now, the physicians have told us, the crab, the cancer, has been attacking her from within. She was strong. She would have had a hard death, otherwise. As we pray, let us thank God for His infinite mercies."

Part One

January 1634

The glory and the freshness of a dream

CHAPTER 1

Pietas Austriaca

Vienna, Austria

Maria Anna should have been meditating upon the bloody wounds as displayed upon the crucifix. She had just come from early mass. Instead, the archduchess of Austria was humming *Edelweiss* and thinking about the upcoming morning of birdwatching that she had scheduled with her beloved stepmother. Birdwatching would be followed, inevitably, by being poured into yet another elaborate court dress. Today, however, the afternoon concert promised something special.

She heard a slight protest behind her as she strode down the corridor toward her own quarters and, feeling a twinge of guilt, slowed down. Maria Anna tended to walk in a brisk manner when her attention wandered. She was a young woman and, thanks to that same stepmother, physically vigorous and in better health than most members of European royal families. Female members, for a certainty.

Alas, the same could not be said of her chief attendant, Doña Mencia de Mendoza. Doña Mencia's spirits were certainly perky enough, but her body was that of a woman nearing sixty and she had rheumatic knees, to boot.

Doña Mencia caught up with her. "Sorry," Maria Anna murmured,

5

glancing down at the older woman. "I'm afraid I was quite caught up by that marvelous music."

"There's the whole afternoon to look forward to then, Your Highness," Doña Mencia replied, smiling. "You really don't have to rush to meet it."

"It's not likely to top *The Sound of Music*," Maria Anna pointed out.

Doña Mencia kept smiling, but didn't argue the point. She'd never say so, but the archduchess was quite sure that her attendant shared her own musical tastes—as unconventional as those tastes might seem, to some people in the Austrian court. Not, of course, that anyone was likely to criticize her for it. There were advantages to being the eldest daughter of the Holy Roman Emperor, after all.

One of those advantages was the quality of the musicians who appeared in the court. Claudia de Medici, widow of Maria Anna's uncle Leopold and regent of the Duchy of Austria-Tyrol for her minor sons, had sent her troop of musicians (all fourteen of them—Duchess Claudia had been economizing since she was widowed) to Vienna to cheer the spirits of Maria Anna's papa. What with the problems in Bohemia and the ingratitude of Wallenstein, the spirits of Ferdinand II, Holy Roman Emperor, were currently in dire need of being cheered. Yesterday, Claudia's musicians, with the assistance of many persons borrowed from the Vienna court personnel, had performed the most marvelous *commedia* that Maria Anna had ever seen.

She had to restrain herself from striding again. Turning her head, she commented to Doña Mencia, "Such beautiful music! How amazing that those American heretics brought along such a magnificent tribute to the Austrian spirit. So morally uplifting. The Baroness Maria was so admirably pious. The marriage must have been morganatic, of course, but that is all right, since the baron had plenty of legally acceptable heirs from his first marriage. Not quite the *opera* that Mama so loves, but very close. How can they trump it, as they have promised to do?"

Edelweiss, Edelweiss. Maria Anna's hum expanded to a whistle.

Discovering that she had overshot the doorway to her own apartments while meditating on yesterday's play, Maria Anna maintained her dignity by managing to give the impression that she had intended to drop in on her younger sister all along.

Cecelia was eating pancakes topped with fruit preserves, and making no visible progress toward getting into riding clothes.

"Up, lazybones!" came the serenely illustrious and highly well-born sisterly admonition.

"I'm not going." Archduchess Cecelia Renata snuggled back down into her pillows. "You may think it's refreshing and invigorating, but I say it's cold out there. If you and Mama want to freeze your ears off, be my guest."

"Sloth is a deadly sin," retorted Maria Anna with a grin.

It was not really said in jest. Not that Cecelia was particularly slothful. It was just that, well, a younger sister ought to follow her older sister's lead. Cecelia's tendency to have a mind of her own—well, to be more than a little pigheaded—and direct her undoubted energy into her own projects was a constant irritant to Maria Anna, if for no other reason than the personal aggravation it often caused her.

An Austrian archduchess *couldn't* go anywhere unaccompanied, of course. Mama was often occupied with court functions. If Cecelia would only agree with Maria Anna's ideas, sometimes . . .

"Oh, all right. Stay here, then. But tomorrow morning it's tennis and you *are* getting up for that. The courts are walled and when the sun shines on the brick, it should be warm enough even for you. No excuses."

Maria Anna headed into her own apartment. There, instead of a maid waiting with her riding habit, she found a dressmaker, with full train of assistants, waiting with the costume she would be wearing this afternoon. Even Maria Anna's good humor sagged a little at the sight.

"It needs one more fitting. Unquestionably! Without any doubt. It must be done, Your Highness!"

Thus spake the redoubtable Frau Stecher, the court's chief seamstress. Maria Anna managed to suppress a sigh. The young archduchess' life had been filled with *it must be done!* followed by *it is your clear duty!* or *it is God's will!* for as long as she could remember. Obediently, she stood for the fitting.

"Ach," said Frau Stecher. "Where are my tack pins? Susanna, go get them. A round box, light blue enamel, with an iris on the top. It should be on the far end of the cutting table." One of the assistants rose from where she had been holding a hem, curtsied, and backed neatly out of the room. The girl was new, Maria Anna remembered, the most junior of Frau Stecher's senior apprentices. She, too, had arrived last week with the group sent from Tyrol by Duchess Claudia, with the highest recommendations—daughter of Claudia's own seamstress, stepdaughter of the head court tailor in the Tyrol. At eighteen, she had already acquired all the fundamentals for a successful career in luxury and couture clothing, but would benefit from two or three more years of experience at an even more distinguished court. All the proper flourishes for a letter of recommendation. The Vienna *Hofstaat* had been delighted to add her to its personnel roster.

What is her name? the archduchess asked herself. *Oh, yes. Allegretti. Susanna Allegretti.* Unlike many highborn ladies, Maria Anna was punctilious about knowing the names of all of her staff.

After all the challenges associated with tack pins had been resolved, Maria Anna did manage to get into her habit and out the door, where the empress, Eleonora Gonzaga, was waiting for her. As she curtsied, Maria Anna's mind went back to *The Sound of Music.* There were probably people who thought that her stepmother wasn't an equal match for her father the emperor, either. When Papa had been simply archduke of Styria, Carinthia, and Carniola, no one had thought it amiss that he'd married Maria Anna's mother, who was a sister of the duke of Bavaria. That was equal enough. But by the time he'd married Eleonora Gonzaga, he was already Ferdinand II, king of Hungary, king of Bohemia, Holy Roman Emperor—and she was just a collateral relative of the duke of Mantua.

But the Jesuits said they were both faithful, virtuous, and religious; that they would be happy together, so the match went through. *Lucky for him; lucky for us,* Maria Anna mused, not for the first time. She always thought of her stepmother as "Mama," and—now that she had seen that marvelous American play—she knew that Eleonora Gonzaga had blessed the House of Habsburg as much as Maria had blessed the von Trapp household.

Curtsey completed, she gave her stepmother a hug and an enthusiastic kiss on both cheeks. Maria Anna adored the pious, childless, woman who, as that young, orphaned, Mantuan duchess, had come to Austria from a modern education in an Ursuline convent. Eleonora Gonzaga had dug her stepchildren out of the clutches of Spanish-model court protocol, and, in line with the best and most progressive Italian views on bringing up children, took them outdoors to run in sunshine and rain, dig in the gardens, hike, ride, and, yes, birdwatch.

There was no doubt about it, Maria Anna realized. She herself, her brothers, and her sister were now the most abundantly healthy young adults the Habsburgs had produced in a long time. Papa himself proclaimed to anyone who would listen that, "Under God, it is to Eleonora's care that I owe my continued life and such health as I have."

And he was quite right!

Doña Mencia de Mendoza and her rheumatic knees did not join the birdwatching expedition. Doña Mencia had come from Spain three years before, in 1630, in the entourage of the Infanta Mariana, Maria Anna's sister-in-law, wife of Maria Anna's brother Ferdinand.

Almost at once, she and the older of the two archduchesses had liked one another. She had found it no hardship whatsoever to transfer to Maria Anna's household, even though working for that energetic young woman was sometimes strenuous. If she weren't doing it, she thought with some amusement, another equally elderly woman would be. What was the function of a chief attendant if not to squelch, when necessary, the youthful exuberance and ebullience to which even Habsburgs were sometimes prone?

Blessed with two to three hours of quiet time, now, she wrapped those aching knees in tubes of toweling loosely stuffed with dried beans that her maid had warmed in front of the fire and settled in to catch up on her correspondence. First, from her mother in Spain. Doña Elvira was not far from her eightieth birthday. If not immortal, she appeared to be giving immortality a good chase. The contents were predictable: land and finances, estates and household, grandchildren and great-grandchildren. Not to mention a new recipe for melon relish.

Duty done, Doña Mencia proceeded to a long letter and thick packet of attachments from her brother, Cardinal Bedmar.

Oh, my! Alfonso would be having an interesting year, what with having been assigned to represent the cardinal-infante's interests in Venice while the *Americans* were there! Her next letter should be addressed to him in Venice.

Doña Mencia leaned back, anticipating a good read.

Duchess Claudia's *Kapellmeister*, Johann Stadelmayr, had just completed reading a short biography of a great Austrian composer named Franz Joseph Haydn. This had been located, the master of musicians explained to the audience, in a great compendium of knowledge called an *encyclopedia*.

Everybody in the audience realized, without question, that this compendium must have been located by someone who had been sent to visit the pestilential ally of the misbegotten Swedish king and the miserably ungrateful Bohemian rebel. The music master tactfully refrained from saying so, of course. But the dates of birth and death that he had listed for the composer made it impossible to doubt that *someone* from the court of Tyrol, or hired by the court of Tyrol, had been to this Grantville.

It probably hadn't been the music master himself, however, Maria Anna thought. He didn't speak much German, so he had read the biography in Italian. That was fine with the Viennese *Hof*. Everybody in the upper levels of Austrian society spoke Italian. In Tyrol, it was the official language of the court. Maria Anna usually spoke Italian herself, by preference. Her German was fluent but it was also an Austrian dialect; it had never been considered necessary to provide her with formal training in the language. She had learned French and Spanish, of course—those were only prudent preparation for the countries into which she would most probably be married. She had a working reading knowledge of Latin, but didn't find it easy to produce Latin compositions.

Most of the music was instrumental. For the final piece, however, the singers who had presented *The Sound of Music* yesterday—and who, by popular demand, would present it again on Thursday, on Saturday, and three times during the following week—returned to the stage. The manager of Duchess Claudia's musicians was explaining the custom of the "national anthem" as it was called, and that the loyal, outstanding, and pious Haydn had composed such a "national anthem" for Austria. Unfortunately, they had not yet found a copy of the words that were properly sung to this anthem and it appeared that they might not be available. However, they had found a score for "Austria" in which the music had been used as the setting for a *Te Deum* written, apparently, by an Englishman. In any case, the author was one Christopher Idle. The manager descended from the podium. The music began.

After the introductory measures, the hairs on Archduchess Maria Anna's arms stood up. Halfway through, the hairs on her head were trying to do the same. For the sheer glory of the thing!

Throughout her afternoon eucharistic devotions before the reserved Host, the melody continued to replay itself in her head. Perhaps a bit guiltily, she assured herself that it was, after all, a hymn.

"I want to know," Maria Anna said firmly to Father Wilhelm Lamormaini, S.J., her father's confessor. "It is a reasonable question."

"How can you expect me to find out?"

"There are Jesuits in this Grantville. Write them. Ask them. Do these words in English, set to this music by Haydn, this *Te Deum*, mean that in those later days, England had been returned to the fold of the Church? And, if so, how? When? By whom? Through what means? And, if not, why was this man writing a *Te Deum* in English? Using Austrian music?"

Father Lamormaini looked at the archduchess rather cautiously. He understood the political motives that had caused the emperor to delay arranging marriages for his daughters. However . . .

Maria Anna was twenty-five years old. By this time, she should have long since been transferred from the authority of a father to that of a husband. She should have been too busy bearing and rearing babies to fret her mind about philosophical and political problems. But, having been permitted to reach adulthood and maturity while still unmarried, she was showing an unfortunate tendency to think for herself and to ask disconcerting questions.

Caution was unquestionably the best tactic.

"In this Grantville itself, as I understand it . . ." Father Lamormaini began.

"Yes?" The undertone was impatient.

So. Speed up the response somewhat. "The origins of this town were from the continent of North America. The settlers who came were from all parts of Europe, and were permitted to retain their faith upon settlement. The country became confessionally mixed, as in the case, for example, of the Imperial City of Augsburg. As we know, there are Catholics there . . ."

"Considering," interrupted Maria Anna with clear exasperation, "that their priest has been sent as head of the United States of Europe's delegation to Venice, I think we may presume that. Please answer my question. Had England, which is here in Europe, been returned to the Church?"

"To the best of my knowledge . . ." Father Lamormaini started again.

"Upon what is your knowledge based?"

"Reports."

"Thank you, Father." Maria Anna nodded. "Now, please, what do these reports say about England?"

"The entire country had not, as a unit, been returned to the fold of the Church. However, it had granted freedom of worship with no civil disabilities to Roman Catholics and had a fairly large number of citizens who belonged to the Church." Father Lamormaini's face expressed distaste for the next statement. "However, it was forbidden for the monarch to be Catholic."

"And in this *America* or *United States*? Was it also forbidden there for the *president* to be a Catholic?"

"Well, of course, their *president* was not properly a monarch. He was elected."

Maria Anna frowned. "What is wrong with that? My father was elected. God willing, my brother will be elected, and my nephew after him. So have all the Holy Roman Emperors been elected. So are bishops and abbots. And abbesses. So is the pope. Since God is omnipotent, He can certainly ensure that the electors follow his will when they make their choice."

Again, the emperor's confessor found himself wishing Maria Anna had been married off at a *much* younger age. Wherever the archduchess's train of thought might be going—he could anticipate at least three possible goals—Father Lamormaini found it worrisome. Each of the possibilities he envisioned somehow managed to be more unnerving than the others, which was a remarkable logical achievement.

"Was it forbidden for this *president* to be a Catholic?" Maria Anna had not lost track of her original thought. As usual. In a way, Father Lamormaini was proud of her tutors. They had been Jesuits, of course.

"Ah, no. It was not forbidden," Father Lamormaini said uncomfortably. "It is my understanding that on one occasion a Catholic had been elected to that office. Once. Out of about forty men chosen over a span of almost two and a quarter centuries. In a country with a population that was almost one-quarter Catholic. Though it is only fair to say that at the level of the provinces, the 'states,' Catholics held a higher proportion of the offices."

By 1634, one of the proudest and most useful possessions of the Jesuit Order was a 1988 *World Almanac and Book of Facts*. Friedrich von Spee had found it in a box at a yard sale and sent it to Rome immediately.

"Was it forbidden, either in England or this America, for the Church to own property? To hold Corpus Christi and other public processions? To establish religious orders? To instruct children in schools?"

"The Church was permitted to carry on all those functions. Indeed, I understand, in America the constitution was written in such a way that it prohibited the civil administration from interfering in them."

"Do you have a copy of this document?"

Father Lamormaini did. However, he had no intention of corrupting the young archduchess' mind with it. "I am not in a position to provide you with a copy, Your Highness."

Maria Anna appreciated the diplomatic wording of his answer. She'd really just been probing Father Lamormaini, as she often did, to discover the limits she would be officially permitted. As it happened, she already had a copy. In fact, she had read it many times. She wondered if Father Lamormaini realized just how many copies were available in the world as it now was in the year 1634. It seemed like half the presses in Europe were printing them by the thousands. Sometimes spiritual advisors, even Jesuits, were just so . . . unworldly.

She reminded herself, as firmly as possible, that that was after all their job. To draw people to God, especially those in positions of power. At least, that was what they were supposed to be for.

So, her reply was also carefully worded. "I will not press you to get one for me."

She paused. "I do have another question, though. Father Lamormaini, I know that you were one of Papa's advisors who most strongly supported having him issue the Edict of Restitution four years ago. True, this defended the rights of the Church to its temporal goods, to its worldly property. But by demanding that the princes of Germany restore all of the . . . things . . ."

She waved her hand expressively at the top of the table at which they were seated, its golden and bejeweled crucifix, its mother-of-pearl-inlaid box of writing materials, its globe of the world. "By demanding restoration of all of the real estate—which is a form of material things—that the German princes confiscated during the Reformation, back to the way things were in the year 1552, some say that it really caused the intervention of the king of Sweden. He would scarcely have come to defend the free exercise of religion by the Calvinists and sectarians, I should think. The Lutherans like them little more than the Holy Church does. It was the provisions in regard to material things that really, some people say, restarted a war that otherwise might have ended on endurable terms."

She picked up a piece of paper and wrote a line on it: *What does it profit a man, if he gains the world and loses his soul?*

She handed it to him. "Is it more important that the Church regain all the temporal worldly goods that she once held? Or that she be free to practice her faith unhindered in Protestant territories? If these were placed before a Catholic ruler as a choice, which way should he go?"

Father Lamormaini swallowed. "I am not your confessor," he pointed out.

"I'm not asking you to provide me with guidance, Father," Maria Anna answered impatiently. "I'm just asking a simple question. A question for people who live in a world where you can't have exactly what you want—not all of the time; not even most of the time. That's just as true for emperors and archduchesses as it is for shopkeepers and peasants. So. Which one is more important?"

After the archduchess left, Father Lamormaini heaved a sigh of relief.

"We *must* get her married off," he muttered to himself. "To the right man. And the sooner the better!"

"Doña Mencia," Maria Anna asked. "Would you do something for me?"

"Of course, if it is within my capacities."

"Would you please write to your brother, Cardinal Bedmar, and ask him this question: 'Is it more important that the Church regain all the temporal worldly goods that she once held? Or that she be free to practice her faith unhindered in Protestant territories? If these were placed before a Catholic ruler as a choice, which way should he go?'"

"Certainly, Your Highness."

Doña Mencia personally saw her letter placed into a diplomatic pouch within the hour.

Not, however, into the diplomatic pouch going out from the imperial chancery to Venice—although that, also, contained a nice, chatty, letter from Doña Mencia to her brother, covering nieces and nephews, great-nieces, great-nephews, and a new recipe for melon relish. She felt quite sure that the emperor's intelligence agents would try to decipher it. She wished them great joy in their attempts, for it contained nothing other than what she had written on the surface. There was not one veiled reference or cryptic allusion, much less a code. She hoped, with considerable relish that was not made from melons, that someone in the imperial intelligence office wasted hours and hours and hours on it. And on the one she would send the next week. And the week after that.

This other letter, however, went into the pouch that had come in from Brussels and would be returned there by Cardinal-Infante Don Fernando's own courier. Brussels could send it on to Alfonso. Among the attachments to Alfonso's letter had been a sealed certification from the infante authorizing her to use his pouch at her own discretion.

CHAPTER 2

Prudentia Politica

Brussels, the Spanish Netherlands

Don Fernando, often known as the "Cardinal-Infante," was the younger brother of King Philip IV of Spain by birth and, by virtue of his own martial accomplishments, the effective ruler of most of the Netherlands. All of it, actually, except Amsterdam and the small rump of less than two provinces still held by the Dutch rebels under the prince of Orange, Fredrik Hendrik. But the uncertain expression on his face as he lowered the letter made him seem even younger than the twenty-three-year-old that he was. So, at least, it seemed to Pieter Paul Rubens, watching him—but since Rubens was acknowledged throughout Europe as one of the great portraitists of the day, his assessment was reliable.

The young Spanish prince was, indeed, very unsure of himself. All the more so, perhaps, because he knew as a gifted military commander that uncertainty was a deadly thing in the middle of battle. Still, at least for the moment, Don Fernando was uncertain.

"He has a somewhat unsavory—well, certainly interesting—reputation, you know."

Rubens smiled thinly. "I think, were Cardinal Bedmar still here in person, he would urge you to abandon the qualifying 'somewhat'—but would also point out that his reputation is only unsavory among his enemies. Spain's enemies."

The smile broadened. "To almost anyone, of course, he is interesting—including you. Which, may I remind Your Highness, is the very reason you decided to send him as your unofficial envoy to Venice. So why the sudden doubts about his capabilities?"

Don Fernando shook his head, folded up the letter from Bedmar and handed it back to Rubens. He leaned back in his chair in the salon of his headquarters. "It's not Alfonso's capabilities that concern me, Pieter. It's . . . well. His loyalties."

They were now treading on treacherous ground. Rubens paused, while he chose his words carefully. It would be tactless in the extreme to make too much of the fact that Bedmar's loyalty to Spain was precisely what the young Spanish prince was worried about—since his own loyalty was now highly questionable.

Best to avoid terms like "loyalty" altogether, Rubens decided. "Alfonso has grown weary of what he regards as the blind feck-lessness of Spain's ministers, Your Highness. I think you may rest assured that his thoughts run in tandem with yours."

A quick smile came and went on the cardinal-infante's face. "That was very nicely put, Pieter. Have you considered taking up a career—just as a sideline from your painting, of course—as a diplomat?"

They shared a soft laugh. When it was over, Rubens shrugged. "What I said remains true. I really do not think that Your Highness needs to entertain any doubts with regard to Cardinal Bedmar's discretion. In any event"—he waggled the letter in his hands—"he has nothing much to report of any interest, beyond the usual machinations of the Venetians. The American delegation hadn't yet arrived in the city when he sent me this."

Now, he smiled a bit ruefully. "I'm afraid you probably have a lot more to fear from my own . . . well, not indiscretion, exactly. Still, it's not always easy to explain why I'm seeking a portrait of someone like Anna Katharina Konstanze Vasa or Anna de Medici or Claude de Lorraine—to say nothing of the two Austrian arch-duchesses, Maria Anna and Cecelia Renata. Taken one at a time, I believe my explanations have not aroused any suspicions. But should any competent spy"—what he meant was *Spanish* spy, but he left that unsaid—"happen to discover that I'm seeking portraits of *all* of them, I'm afraid . . . Well, to use that American expres-sion, there will be hell to pay."

"I can imagine! Given that there could be only one plausible reason that you'd be seeking portraits of every eligible Catholic princess in Europe." Don Fernando gave Rubens a sly smile. "Of course, I suppose I could claim that you were obviously intending to do away with your wife Helena and marry one of them yourself."

Again, they shared a soft laugh. And when it was over, Rubens shrugged again. "I don't actually think there's much risk involved, Your Highness. I've been dealing entirely with artists, not diplomats."

"Yes, I imagine they wouldn't be as prone to suspicion."

Rubens burst into much louder laughter. "To the contrary, Your Highness! I can assure you that artists are obsessive about their suspicions—far more so than diplomats. The up-timers even have a word for the attitude. 'Paranoia,' they call it. But the suspicions run along professional channels, not those of matters of state. Each and every one of the artists from whom I've either bought a portrait or commissioned one is absolutely certain that I intend to do one myself based on their work—and then sell the end result for ten times what they would have gotten."

He cleared his throat and added, perhaps a bit smugly, "Which, indeed, I could, were I so inclined."

Don Fernando scratched his chin. "Perhaps that explanation . . ."

"No, I'm afraid not," said Rubens. "One or two portraits, yes. But seven?" He shook his head. "No capable spy—not one, at least, with any knowledge of art—would believe for a moment that I'd delve that extensively into what is, after all, neither a lucrative nor a prestigious field of portraiture. At the risk of immodesty, I am an artist who gets commissioned by royalty to paint them in person—and I turn down far more commissions than I accept. I do not have to paint portraits at secondhand in the hopes that I might be able to sell them at a later date. One or two I could explain, with not much difficulty, as a matter of specific personal interest. For seven portraits, there can be no logical explanation beyond the one that involves affairs of state."

The Spanish prince was still scratching his chin. "Only seven? I'd hoped . . ."

"You will perhaps recall that I warned you, Your Highness. I'm afraid that today—and this won't change for years—we have a shortage of eligible Catholic princesses who would suit you for a bride. Even that figure of 'seven' is stretching the matter. Two of the ladies involved—Claudia de Medici, the regent of Tyrol, and her older sister Maria Maddalena—are really a bit too old. Maria Maddalena is reported to suffer from very poor health, as well."

Don Fernando finally stopped scratching his chin. "I've met Claudia. She seemed quite capable and she's not *that* much older than me. Somewhere around thirty, I believe."

"Yes, you're right—and if you were a prince in a different position, with one or two brothers whose children could provide an heir in the event your own wife did not produce one, she'd be quite suitable. But a thirty-year-old woman—yes, you're right about her age—is really a bit too old, when the entire dynasty will of necessity have to depend entirely on your own offspring."

He cleared his throat again, but before he could speak Don Fernando waved his hand. "Yes, yes, I see the point. Not that my brother Philip wouldn't be delighted to provide me with an heir—but that would rather defeat the whole purpose of the enterprise, wouldn't it?"

His eyes narrowed slightly. "So . . . I need a wife who's no older than her mid-twenties, and in good health. Of the remaining six, which do you think are the best prospects?"

"Best, in what terms, Your Highness? In an ideal world, there's no question—the two Austrians, especially the older sister. By all accounts, and I've collected quite a few, they are both in good health—even very vigorous health, by the standards of most highborn women—and both of sound mind. The older daughter Maria Anna even has something of a reputation for her intellect, if not the younger. And"—here he suppressed a smile—"they are also quite comely."

Don Fernando scowled. "I don't care about their looks. Well. Not much. I need a wife who'll produce children."

The prince's pronouncement was in the finest tradition of capable royalty. It was also complete nonsense. Don Fernando was a *very* vigorous young man and he was no more indifferent to the comeliness of women than any other twenty-three-year-old male in good health. Given his training, of course, he never ogled such women. But Rubens had not failed to notice the prince's rapt interest whenever a woman as beautiful as—to give just one recent example—Rebecca Abrabanel came into his presence.

Don Fernando would never pursue the matter, to be sure. He was far too self-controlled for such foolishness. Leaving aside the fact that the Abrabanel was married, and apparently faithful to her husband, she was a Jewess. So, the prince made no advances, and did not ogle. But he certainly . . . *observed*.

Privately, Rubens understood perfectly well that he had to find a bride for Don Fernando who would be sufficiently attractive for the prince to spend enough time in her bed to succeed in his royal duties. Dynasties died out for many reasons, and the ill health or infertility of the wife was only one of them. Lack of interest on the part of the husband would do just as well to wither a royal line.

But Rubens left all that unsaid. Like any vigorous and capable twenty-three-year-old prince, Don Fernando was also sensitive about his youth. He would not take kindly to the suggestion that he was not, actually, a wise old Nestor.

So, he went back to the subject at hand. "As I say, those two—especially the older sister—would be the ideal one from your point of view. However, they are also the daughters of Emperor Ferdinand II. Who is, ah . . ."

"A religious fanatic," stated the cardinal-infante curtly. "To the point of bigotry."

"Well . . . yes, unfortunately. So I can see no likelihood that he would ever agree to such a match. Given that, under the best of circumstances, it would cause a severe strain to be put upon the Habsburg dynasty across Europe—to which he also belongs. He'd view it as a capitulation to the Dutch Protestants. Who are not even Lutherans, but Calvinists."

Don Fernando made a face. "I find it hard to see where a marriage to an Austrian Catholic would constitute a 'capitulation' to Dutch Calvinists. But . . ." He sighed. "Yes, I can see where he would view it that way. By producing a fissure in the solid ranks—not so solid as that!—of the Habsburgs, the premier family of Catholicism, I would indirectly be giving succor to the enemy of the true faith."

He raised his hand and almost clutched his blond hair, as if he might pull it out by the roots. "Aaaah! Am I the *only* member of my powerful and widely scattered family who studies those up-time books, and is capable of drawing intelligent conclusions from them? Are all other Habsburgs village idiots accidentally wearing royal finery?"

He lowered the hand and glared up at Rubens—or rather, glared at the world, with Rubens just happening to be in his line of sight. "Is the lesson so difficult to read, in those up-time histories? *Every* dynasty that survived—some of them even prospered—did so by abandoning the attempt to enforce religious beliefs and behavior. Am I not right?"

"Well ... In Europe, certainly." Pieter did not add what he could have, that all those dynasties had also survived because they abandoned their attempts to rule as well, and satisfied themselves with simply reigning. Rubens knew that Don Fernando even understood that himself, somewhere in the recesses of his mind, but was not really prepared to accept it yet. And perhaps never would be, though he lived to the age of eighty.

The prince slapped the armrest of his chair with exasperation. "Yet they won't give it up! No matter the cost!"

He shifted the glare about the room, transferring it momentarily from one portrait to another hanging in the salon. They were all portraits of Habsburgs, and they covered every wall. There had been a lot of Habsburgs, over the centuries.

Then he looked back at Rubens and, with the same exasperation, waved at a nearby chair. "Oh, sit down, Pieter. Surely we can dispense with royal protocol at such moments."

Rubens made no move toward the chair. "Actually, we can't, Your Highness. In the absence of a meal or some such acceptable—"

"There's only the two of us!"

The artist glanced meaningfully at the three servants and two soldiers who stood not so far away; the servants, next to the table holding wine and other refreshments; the soldiers, by the entrance. Except for Don Fernando's last outburst, they'd been speaking softly enough that neither the servants nor the soldiers could have understood the conversation. But they were not blind. And, almost certainly, at least one of them was accepting pay from some foreign spy—including Spain, as they now must, in the category of "foreign."

Understanding the meaning of the glance, the prince sighed and sagged a little in chair. "Damned silliness," he muttered. "And I can assure you that once I—"

But he broke off that line of thought, with the self-discipline to be expected from a grandson of Philip II. Instead, he levered himself erect in his chair. Stiffly erect.

"Very well, Pieter. We'll continue as before. Are you sure your correspondence with Alfonso is in no risk of interception?"

"Not entirely. But the cardinal is a circumspect man, whose letters can always be interpreted innocently. And for those occasions when they can't, he will use his sister in Vienna as his intermediary. She can communicate with us through your aunt Isabella. The archduchess and Doña Mencia are old friends, so no one will think it odd that they have an extensive correspondence."

Don Fernando smiled. "The formidable Doña Mencia. I met her several times, you know? I was very young, at the time. She quite intimidated me."

And that, too, Rubens decided to let pass without comment. As it happened, he maintained his own correspondence with Doña Mencia also. He would not have described her as formidable so much as very shrewd. Of course, he had the advantage of enjoying the same years of age that she did, rather than encountering her as a lad.

It was all he could do not to sigh himself. Doña Mencia was now the close attendant to the older of the two Austrian archduchesses, and she seemed to have discerned already—such a canny woman!—Rubens' strategy, even though he had said nothing directly to her at all.

So he presumed, at any rate. For there could only be two explanations for Doña Mencia's constant praises of Maria Anna, archduchess of Austria and the Holy Roman Empire. The young woman's intelligence; her physical vigor; her courtesy and consideration for others; her exceptionally thorough education; even her beauty, if the old woman was to be believed—and she probably could.

The first explanation was that Doña Mencia understood and supported the goal of Rubens and his patron Don Fernando. And felt strongly enough on the subject of her mistress Maria Anna that she pursued the subject despite knowing full well herself, as she must, how impossible such a match would be under the circumstances.

The second explanation was almost frightening. What if Doña Mencia *hadn't* discerned Rubens' purpose? What if her depictions of Maria Anna were simply those of an enthusiast?

Almost frightening. For Doña Mencia was indeed very astute. As astute and experienced as any elderly and widely traveled noblewoman in Europe. Her assessments of people were generally superb, in Ruben's experience.

In which case . . .

The continent of Europe actually possessed the closest thing that ever existed in the real world to the silly American notion of a "fairy tale princess"—and there was no chance at all that Rubens' patron Don Fernando could wake her from her sleep. In the real world, if not the up-time fables, the wards and barriers that guarded princesses were far denser and thicker and mightier than paltry magic. At bottom, entire armies stood in the way—real armies—not the spells of witches.

So it was. Rubens was not a man given to whimsy, outside of his art. He put all thoughts of Maria Anna aside. Her sister too, for that matter, since the barriers were the same.

"I think the best possibility is Anna de Medici. Second best would be the Polish girl, the Vasa, although she's only fifteen. Failing her, the Lorraine."

None of the three were actually very good, in his opinion. The de Medici was certainly the best, but the drawback was that her father was simply the grand duke of Tuscany. Her lineage was suitable, both in terms of blood and faith—but there would be little in the way of a powerful alliance to come with the marriage. The daughter of Henri de Lorraine was rumored to have an attachment to one of her cousins, which, if true, would be awkward at best. As for the Polish princess . . .

Again, Rubens suppressed a sigh. He suspected he'd be doing a lot of that, in the future, as he pursued this matter.

The one portrait he'd managed to obtain so far of the seven eligible princesses was a portrait of Anna Katharina Konstanze Vasa, half-sister and first cousin of the king of Poland. It was possible that the artist had botched the assignment by making her less attractive than she actually was—but it was not likely. As a rule, artists bent the stick as far as they could in the other direction, when doing portraits of any wealthy patrons, much less royalty.

So, she would be unattractive at best, and possibly downright ugly. She seemed to have inherited the Vasa beak of a nose in addition to the Habsburg lip. Worse still, from what Rubens could glean from the maddeningly spotty historical records of the up-timers, he thought she might have died at the age of thirty-two, in that other universe. That might have been due to an accident, of course, which could be avoided in this separate existence. But there was also the possibility of exceedingly bad health.

Maria Anna lived to the age of fifty-five, long past her child-bearing years, and might well have lived longer given up-time medical . . .

But that was pointless. "I'll do the best I can, Your Highness. Under the circumstances."

The prince nodded heavily, then his expression brightened. "And there's always that, we shouldn't forget. Since whatever other lessons brought by the Americans my family chooses to ignore, there is one that they simply can't."

"I'm not quite following you, Your Highness."

Don Fernando was actually grinning now, and quite cheerfully. "Circumstances. They change, you know. That is the one thing you can be absolutely sure and certain that circumstances will do."

❖ CHAPTER 3 ❖

Femella Minima

Vienna, Austria

Maria Anna stood patiently as Frau Stecher adjusted a pair of sleeves. Since sleeve adjustment involved the ability to move one's arms, she occasionally got to change position. Sometimes, she was even allowed to tickle the bare toes of her nephew Ferdinand, who was precociously propped up in a little padded chair, carefully watched by both his noble *Aja* and a more common nursemaid to make sure that the heir of Austria didn't topple over and harm himself.

"Frau Stecher." Doña Mencia entered the room. "Can you please go to the empress. There is a problem with the dress for this afternoon's audience and she is quite determined to wear this one and no other. It appears that the lining is not appropriately attached. This must have been done improperly when the dress was taken apart to be cleaned and then fastened back together. Her maids are with her. Take your seamstresses; it must be repaired and there isn't much time."

"Certainly. But, Susanna, you stay here and hold those sleeves in place." Frau Stecher curtsied and vanished with the remainder of her staff.

Maria Anna looked behind her. Then she looked down. The top of Susanna Allegretti's head barely reached above the archduchess's

25

shoulder—not that the young seamstress was abnormally small. She was short and thin, but no court dwarf. Maria Anna, by contrast, was a stately, unusually well-grown, woman. Her dressmakers truly appreciated this. Gorgeous clothing displayed so much better on a statuesque form. Not to say, a buxom form. It was like the difference, for an artist, between the constraints of a miniature and the opportunities offered by a large canvas.

"This could take the whole time until Mama goes down to the audience. Are you really going to stand there holding sleeves up while they are gone?"

Susanna's eyes sparkled. "Not unless Your Highness truly wishes it. But, if not, we should set a spy in the corridor to tell us when they are coming back."

"Lena," Maria Anna said to the governess. "It's time for our baby to eat, anyway." She stopped, picked up Ferdinand the Most Recent, as her delighted brother called his son and heir, and gave his neck a bit of a nuzzle. "Mariana will be waiting for him."

The archduchess thought, with all due respect to the Blessed Virgin and Her mother Saint Anne, that it would be quite nice if the Habsburgs could more often name their daughters something more—distinctive—than Maria Anna. Or Anna Maria. Or Anna. Or Maria. It had been kind of Ferdinand's wife to retain the Spanish form of her name for written purposes but, spoken, they were still the same. It was confusing. At least, when someone referred to Cecelia Renata, there was only one of them in the family. This had been true with great-aunt Caterina Micaela, too. Surely, a little more imagination in the family nomenclature would do no harm.

But. "Please take him back to the nurseries. And send us a maid to stand behind a statue in the corridor and be our spy. I intend to sit down." Which she did, inviting Doña Mencia to do likewise.

Susanna, of course, remained standing.

"You come to us from Duchess Claudia, don't you?" the archduchess asked.

"Oh, yes," Susanna replied. She had grown up as a court servant, so was less disconcerted by this situation than she otherwise might have been. Still, she realized that nervousness was going to make her talk too much. Everyone, especially her mother, assured her that talking too much was one of her major failings. "I was born in Italy, before she married Duke Leopold. But we came to Tyrol with her and have been there ever since. Except, of course, that my mother sent me back to Ferrara when I was thirteen, for my training. I was at the court there for five years before I came back to Bozen, and was only there for a year when the duchess was so kind as to send me here, to Vienna."

"So," Maria Anna asked, "do you have any acquaintance among the musicians that the duchess has also sent to us?"

"One of the lute players is my cousin; well, he's the son of my aunt's husband, by his first marriage. My stepsister's husband's younger brother is apprenticed to the music librarian. He isn't here, though; he stayed home. I know all the musicians, though. We make their costumes. And re-make them, alter them, fit them to newly hired musicians. It's a lot easier to make a costume smaller than it is to make it bigger."

"But the musicians are men. Don't the tailors have to do that?"

"Not for the court servants. All of us work on whatever job has to be done. I love to work on velvets, but satins are so slippery. There really should be two people assigned to each satin garment; one just to hold the pieces in place."

"I suppose." Maria Anna sighed. "Do you know which among them went to this Grantville in the Germanies? One of them must have. To get the music." She whistled the first two phrases of the scales from the song in the play.

"It wasn't one of them. It was one of the cloth merchants in Bozen who supplies the duchess' court who sent an agent there. The agent looked around, of course, to find other things that he thought would be profitable or of interest. He thought that the music would be, so he hired one of the Italian musicians in town to copy as much of it as he had time and money for. Now Duchess Claudia has sent a half-dozen people, but they aren't back yet. At least, they weren't back yet, when we left for Vienna."

"Ah. That is too bad. I had thought perhaps that I could speak with someone who had been there."

"You can," Susanna answered cheerfully. "None of the musicians have gone there, but the cloth merchant's agent is in Vienna. He's the regular factor here. The other was just a temporary assignment. Exploratory. Their firm supplies a great deal of the cloth that is used for the imperial household. Not the luxury goods, such as these." Susanna waved the brocade sleeves in the air. "Ordinary cloth, for the servants, or the uniforms the guards wear when it isn't a ceremonial occasion. It comes into Bozen from Augsburg; then they re-ship it all over. A lot goes to Venice and Naples, but it also comes this way."

Maria Anna turned her head. "Doña Mencia. I do not believe that I have ever spoken to a cloth factor. Do I have reason to speak to a cloth factor? Or to visit a cloth warehouse?"

"Not that I know of," she replied.

"But I can probably think of one," she added.

Doña Mencia and Archduchess Maria Anna got along very well, indeed.

The solution occurred to her even before the spy reported the return of Frau Stecher. "Perhaps we would like to put on a pre-Lenten masque to entertain the children. The maids can be the players; we will be part of the audience. You will need to arrange for costumes."

Susanna succumbed to what, in any court, could be a fatal temptation for a servant, resulting in instant disgrace or dismissal—speaking without having been invited to do so. "I saw a good one in Ferrara, at the girls' school in the Ursuline convent. It was about Jesus saying, 'Let the little children come to me.' With songs."

Even such a gross transgression of etiquette could be pardoned for sufficient reason. Archduchess Maria Anna deemed the reason to be sufficient.

Frau Stecher, when she discovered that her apprentice had not continued to hold the sleeves in place throughout her absence, was not happy. Her unhappiness was not ameliorated by the archduchess' interrupting the scolding to say that it had been her own decision to take off the sleeves and sit down. Frau Stecher was even less pleased when she discovered that her apprentice was wanted by the archduchess to accompany her on a visit to a cloth warehouse. Particularly since that specific cloth warehouse was owned by a company that provided major competition to Frau Stecher's brothers.

Maria Anna found that the cloth factor was a very understanding man. When the purpose of the costumes was explained to him, he suggested that they simply be made of draped lengths of cloth, such as were shown in many paintings of the ancient world, worn over the actors' regular clothing; then, after the masque, the archduchess could present the lengths to the maids who took part as their Easter gifts. This had great appeal to a young woman whose allowance was quite limited. It was scarcely surprising that she consulted him several times during the rehearsals for the masque. Everyone agreed that the antique-style costumes were very effective.

Susanna found that being simultaneously highly favored by the archduchess and in deepest disgrace with her mistress required some delicacy in her behavior over the next few weeks.

"Naturally, I know which choice Papa would consider right."

Maria Anna was talking to her one-year-older brother Ferdinand who was, since the unexpected death of their older brother Johann Karl in 1619, heir to Austria.

"Everyone knows the vow he took at Loreto. And that he changed the words of their song, the ones that go, 'and take they our life, goods, fame, child and wife, they yet have nothing won' into, 'so take your bodies, property, honorable reputation, child and wife and get out' as a theme for handling Austria's Lutherans. Papa swore that he would rather rule over a desert, would rather eat bread and water, would rather go begging with his own wife and child, would rather allow his body to be hacked into pieces, than to tolerate heresy. He meant it. He enforced that in his own duchies from the time he came of age in 1598, expelling the Protestant preachers and closing the Protestant schools. He allowed a week for those who would not convert to wind up their affairs and emigrate."

"No one," Ferdinand said rather ruefully, "will ever say that Papa does not have the courage of his convictions. However, I do wish that he could see his way to a sufficient compromise with the Imperial Estates that they would go ahead and elect me as King of the Romans. It's going to be a real mess if Papa dies without that and the whole election is thrown wide open. That hasn't happened since Charles V—and think what that election cost us."

They looked at one another. Whatever his theological intransigence, Emperor Ferdinand II was, in private, a truly loving father. A father who was by no means well. According to the *encyclopedias*, a scant four years from now, he would die.

"I don't think that he's going to be willing to compromise on religion to advance your political interests," Maria Anna answered.

"Since he became emperor, he has tried to enforce his principles not only in the hereditary lands but also throughout the lands of the *Reich*, throughout all of the Germanies. You're going to have to decide how to handle it. If you make promises to the electors now that hinge on future contingencies, they could limit what actions you can take later. And there's no guarantee that the electors would keep their word when the time came, either."

In spite of Father Lamormaini's theological views on the proper role of women being entirely domestic, Austrian archduchesses were not trained to be clinging vines. Their education was designed to prepare them to join the long tradition of Habsburg daughters and sisters who served their fathers and brothers as regents in various parts of Europe. They were prepared to carry their share of the family business. Margaret of Austria. Mary of Hungary. Margaret of Parma. Aunt Isabella Clara Eugenia.

Maria Anna found it more than a little annoying that Papa had not gotten on with the rest of the project of qualifying her to be a Formidable Habsburg Regent. He had given her the education, true. Like her brothers, somewhat to Father Lamormaini's distress, she had received formal debate training and all. Papa had also provided her with the political training as well.

But there were a couple more prerequisites. First, she needed to get married. Second, she needed to be widowed. Preferably, to be widowed quite promptly, being childless, if she wished to govern a Habsburg principality. However, a short marriage that produced a surviving son would, in a pinch, do the trick and make her regent of her late husband's lands, although it also would put her in the position of having to govern in the child's name and practically guarantee a forced retirement in middle age, just as she reached the height of her powers. Although, then, she could govern a Habsburg principality.

Maria Anna sighed. Papa was more likely to choose her husband on the basis of current political advantage than the prospect that her groom would die in a timely fashion.

CHAPTER 4

Bavaria Sancta

Munich, Bavaria

Duke Albrecht of Bavaria, as he fingered his rosary, thanked God for his brother's long and happy marriage. Thirty-nine years it would have been, next month, since Elisabeth Renee of Lorraine came to Bavaria as a bride and accepted the Germanized name of Elisabeth Renata. He, himself, had been not quite eleven years old, then. And it was true. As a new bride, she had brought a light-hearted spirit into the rigid Bavarian court, which had been anything but light-hearted under the rule of their father.

Duke Wilhelm "the Pious" had attended mass every day, when possible several times a day. He had also devoted four hours daily to prayer, one to contemplation, and all his spare time to devotional reading. He had received holy communion every week, and twice a week during Advent and Lent. He had taken part in public devotions, processions, and pilgrimages. One ambassador had called Bavaria a monastery in their father's day. It had not been just the court, or even Munich, either. His father had turned Bavaria itself into a monastery, as far as could be done. In 1634, it was far different from the half-Lutheran society it had been in the 1560s.

In the past half-century, Bavaria had been Catholicized: it was a land of saints and shrines, healing images and miraculous relics, pilgrimages and processions, the daily routine of its people marked by the tolling of church bells and recital of litanies. People who would not conform had been forced to leave. Nearly twenty years ago already, Father Matthaeus Rader, who was still teaching in Munich, had published his *Bavaria Sancta*—Holy Bavaria. It was a really hefty tome, praising the duchy's historic and sacred destiny, listing its saints and martyrs, its holy monks; its pious rulers, culminating in the current members of the House of Wittelsbach.

The rulers of Bavaria knew, well enough, that making Bavaria a Holy Land was far too important to be left to the church alone. Their intent was to create a Catholic state. In addition to the privy council, which administered secular affairs, and the treasury, which ensured financial stability, the dukes had formed the *Geistlicher Rat*, the ecclesiastical council. As much as any Lutheran prince's consistory, it supervised and disciplined the duchy's Catholic clergy through regular visitations; it controlled the Catholicism of all the state's officials by issuing certificates documenting annual confession and communion as strictly as the Church of England did under Elizabeth; it funded new Catholic schools, new Catholic colleges, new houses of religious orders, especially the missionary and educational ones, such as the Jesuits and Capuchins for men, the Ursulines for women.

Elisabeth Renata. Maximilian had insisted on having her—no "crook-backed Habsburg bride" for him, he had proclaimed. So she had come, slender and elegant. Not a frivolous spirit, never. Her life had been untiringly devoted to works of charity. But she had performed them out of sheer love of God and others—not from a sense of grim duty. "Hail Mary, full of grace."

Albrecht's mind wandered. Maximilian's marriage had been so ideal—a pattern of that prescribed by God for a Christian couple. Except that there were no children. No pregnancies. After some years, their father, Duke Wilhelm V, concluded that her childlessness was the result of some spell that witches and heretics, and possibly also Jews, had cast upon his oldest son's wife. Perhaps, his father had thought, God had permitted the young duchess to be bewitched because he had not persecuted the heretics zealously enough. Perhaps, even during his great campaign against them in 1590, he had shown too much mercy, had demonstrated too little firmness in exterminating the witches who ruined harvests, who destroyed cattle and crops, and who brought pestilence, plague, and sickness into Bavaria. Or, on the other hand, perhaps, Duke Wilhelm had persecuted the heretics in his realm so zealously, had shown so little mercy in burning the witches, had served the cause of Christ so plainly, that the bitter hatred of the Devil had descended directly on himself and his family. There had been prayers to break the spell; there had been devotional exercises. Duke Wilhelm had brought the general of the Barnabite friars, Michael Marrano, to Munich. He was a celebrated expert in removing spells from princely personages.

All to no avail. Elisabeth Renata had remained childless.

Which turned Duke Albrecht's thoughts to his own marriage. By that time, the Estates of Bavaria had already forced their father to abdicate. That happened two years after Maximilian's marriage. Father had built too much—palaces, churches, Jesuit colleges. He had contributed generously to Catholic missions in China and Japan. There had been accusations of extravagance; threats of an impending state bankruptcy. Maximilian had assumed rule in Bavaria. By then, their father's piety had gotten for Munich the name of the "German Rome" for its advocacy of Counter-Reformation piety. The two brothers between Maximilian and himself had already been placed in the clergy. Philipp Wilhelm, who had been made the bishop of Regensburg the same year that Max married and a cardinal of the Church two years after that, was already dead. Ferdinand had been, and still was, archbishop and elector of Cologne.

So. Albrecht must marry. He did. He had been twenty-seven, at the time; his bride Mechthilde, four years younger. The marriage had been followed by—four years of childlessness. He added in a couple of additional prayers for their first child, Maria Renata, who had died at the age of fourteen. Then God's mercy had prevailed. They had four sons; three had survived. Karl Johann Franz was a little rash and reckless at the age of fifteen, but surely he would become steadier. Maximilian Heinrich, twelve; Sigmund Albrecht, ten. Both intensely intelligent and promising; all carefully educated for the responsibilities which, he and Maximilian believed, were due to fall upon them.

Mechthilde was the younger of the two children of Landgrave Georg Ludwig of Leuchtenberg, imperial privy councilor and president of the Imperial Aulic Council. He had been a tireless supporter of the Catholic cause, although his struggle with the tendency of his subjects to sneak across the borders and go to Protestant church services in the Upper Palatinate had worn him thin. He had also been rather well known for demanding and frequently getting a salary three times higher than anyone else would have received for doing exactly the same job.

Leuchtenberg had long been a nuisance, from the viewpoint of Bavaria. Albrecht's marriage to Mechthilde had brought the possibility that, should her brother die without heirs, the last non-Wittelsbach principality in the region of the Upper Palatinate could be incorporated into Bavaria's ever expanding boundaries.

Unfortunately, that eventuality did not appear likely at present. Her brother Wilhelm Georg was still alive, even though his health was very shaky, and he had two surviving sons. Too bad that the youngest Leuchtenberg boy had died at Halberstadt eighteen months ago, but he had died in the service of his emperor and his church. Those were the risks that went with being born into the nobility.

He would need to talk to Mechthilde. To listen to Mechthilde.

Their rosaries completed, the privy councillors were looking at him. He called the meeting to order.

Magdeburg

Landgrave Hermann of Hesse-Rotenburg hated politics. Unfortunately for him, however, his older half-brother Landgrave Wilhelm of Hesse-Kassel was one of Gustav Adolf's primary allies in Germany. That gave Hesse-Kassel, for all practical purposes, the nomination right to at least one of the cabinet posts under the new prime minister.

So, Wilhelm had nominated his younger brother Hermann as secretary of state. And, of course, Hermann would do his duty, as a good Calvinist should. He was working morning, noon, and night to be an honor to his brother's choice and ensure that the Emperor Gustav Adolf had no regrets about agreeing to find a place for Calvinists in the new government.

But he didn't have to like it. Hermann was only twenty-seven years old. He yearned for his home, for the newly-married wife who had stayed behind to run the place, for his study, and for his project of producing a complete physical geography and topography of Hesse.

The prime minister looked at him impatiently. "Hermann," Mike Stearns said, "will you please sit down?"

Embarrassed, suspecting that this was a concession to the prosthesis that he wore in place of one foot—not because of a respectable wound obtained in war but because of a birth defect—the landgrave sat. He wished that his brother had nominated someone else. But there wasn't anyone else. Of the surviving sons of Moritz of Hesse, he was the oldest after Wilhelm himself.

As he watched his secretary of state take a seat, Mike Stearns sighed. Arnold Bellamy back home in Grantville; Hermann here. Why did diplomacy seem to produce so many stiff-necked, stiff-backed, and thoroughly uptight types? Not that either of them was dumb, just . . .

God, how he missed Ed Piazza.

"Let the briefing begin." He hated these third-person down-time formulas of speech, too.

Hermann gestured at Philipp Sattler, who was serving as Gustav Adolf's personal liaison to the prime minister. Sattler, an experienced diplomat, was originally from Kempten, which gave him a considerable advantage in understanding the crazy quilt that was the political geography of the Germanies south of the Main river. Sattler had been brought in mainly to deal with Swabian issues, but was doubling as the Bavarian expert as well.

Sattler started out. "Bavaria has fifty privy councillors, more or less. Most are administrative functionaries, with only minor influence. If you will forgive me, I have prepared summaries only on those whom I consider to be of political importance."

Mike snorted. "You are forgiven. Even better, you are commended. Go on."

"The chancellor is Dr. Joachim Donnersberger. He has been the most important political official in the duchy, the supreme court chancellor, since 1599. That means, naturally, that he isn't by any means a young man any more; he'll be seventy next year. He's a commoner, from a prominent Munich family, with a law degree. It's probably about time for the dukes to put a seal of approval on those long years of service by raising him to the nobility and changing his name to von Donnersberg, but they haven't done it yet. Don't count him out on grounds of age—he's been at Duke Maximilian's right hand ever since he took over the administration of Bavaria from his father."

Mike nodded. "I think that I get the picture."

"Just about equally influential, you have Duke Maximilian's confessor, Father Adam Contzen. He's a Jesuit, in his early sixties, originally from Jülich. He's been a Jesuit since 1591. Duke Maximilian places unlimited confidence in the Jesuits, so he tends to push the limits that their order places on them just a little further than he ought to. He requires the Jesuits at his court to provide him not just with spiritual and political advice, but also with diplomatic services."

"What's Contzen's position, then, when he hands out political advice?"

Sattler laughed. "Ah, Herr Stearns, you are very lucky. In 1620, Father Contzen wrote a nice long treatise, *Ten Books Concerning Politics*. Sometimes translated as *Ten Books on Political Economy*. I will, of course, be happy to summarize it for you. Possibly the most famous sentence is, '*Hymni Lutheri animos plures, quam scripta et declamationes occiderunt.*'"

He paused, probably recalling the warning he must have received that the up-timers rarely had a decent foundation in the classical languages. "That is, 'Luther has murdered more souls with his hymns than with his writings and sermons.' This does not mean in the least that he doubts the effectiveness of other Protestant writings and sermons in murdering souls. Throughout the 1620s, he was the leading spokesman for the Jesuit extremist party in Bavaria. The zealots, as they were known."

"A delightful man, I am sure," Mike muttered.

"He is a religious bigot. However, I want to be fair. It is no service to you if I show you only a caricature of the men with whom you will be dealing, Herr Stearns."

Mike nodded.

Sattler continued. "The *Ten Books* also lay out the obligations of a ruler to his subjects. The ideal Christian commonwealth. In the book, he advocated tax reform; freeing the peasants from excessive burdens while placing tax levies on objects of luxury; that the state should itself own certain industries for the purpose of enhancing its revenue. Maximilian invited Contzen to become his confessor largely as a result of that publication. The parts you would consider good as well as those you would not like."

Duke Hermann interrupted. "What about Richel?"

"Bartholomaeus Richel. Also a commoner, a lawyer. He has been Donnersberger's deputy since 1623. Before that, he was chancellor of the diocese of Eichstätt. He left because of a slightly difficult episode. His wife Maria, a member of the patrician Bonschab family, was burned as a witch in December 1620. Richel transferred to the service of Bavaria very quickly after that—not a bad move in view of the fact that six other Bonschab family members were burned as witches in Eichstätt between 1617 and 1627. That included the town's mayor, Lorenz Bonschab, and his wife and daughter. Being related to the Bonschabs, even by marriage, was not exactly a career-enhancing item on a man's resume in Eichstätt."

"No kidding," Mike said. "Why did Duke Maximilian hire him?"

"He's very competent. And his wife was dead." Sattler's expression was sour.

"What is concerning Landgrave Hermann, I think, is that Richel was Maximilian's emissary to Ferdinand II last year. He was right in the middle of the attempt to assassinate Wallenstein, egging Ferdinand on. Richel served Maximilian very well during his term as ambassador in Vienna. From what we have been able to learn, his correspondence supplied Munich with large quantities of very useful information, which Maximilian has been using to gain additional leverage with the pope against the Austrian Habsburgs."

"I keep reminding myself of that," Mike said. "Not to regard the powers that were in the Catholic League as some sort of a monolith against the Protestants. They are just as fractious among themselves as Gustav Adolf's German allies. Okay, Donnersberger, Contzen, Richel. Anyone else I should know about?"

"It's a little questionable, but perhaps Father Johannes Vervaux. Duke Francis II sent him down from Lorraine to Munich just two years ago with a recommendation. He became confessor to Duchess Elisabeth Renata, Duke Francis' sister. I say that it's questionable because now that she is dead, it's hard to tell whether he will be keeping his position on the privy council or will be looking for another job. We will have to wait and see. He is just as much a Jesuit as Contzen, but almost a generation separates the two men. Vervaux is in his mid-forties and he did not join the order until 1618. A full generation separates their spiritual formation. It isn't that he is less devout than Contzen; just that their modes of expressing that piety diverge widely, from what I hear."

Mike looked at Hermann. "Is there anything that we can do about the Bavarian situation, one way or the other?"

"Not barring direct military intervention. Which we cannot possibly afford when everything needs to be focused on the League of Ostend. Diplomatically, not a thing."

"Then, I guess, we just tell Francisco Nasi to keep on top of developments as best he can. And let me know if anything changes."

Munich, Bavaria

Duke Albrecht looked around the table. He had not invited the functionaries this morning; the men facing him would be the ones whose opinions guided the setting of Bavarian policy.

If, indeed, his brother could be brought to think about policy. Duke Albrecht glanced toward the door. A servant silently signaled that Duke Maximilian was again closed away in the chapel.

In the privy council chamber, the discussion rose and fell. Could the duke be persuaded not to abdicate? Should he be? How would an abdication impact the problems in Bohemia? How would it affect the League of Ostend's efforts against the Swede?

Chancellor Donnersberger was inclined to think that the duke should be allowed to abide by his choice. It was far from unprecedented. Emperor Charles V, himself, had abdicated and spent his last years in a monastery. Every man had the right to take thought for his soul.

It was Contzen, at the last, who was adamant. "An abdication by the man who for so many years has been the general and guiding force of the Catholic League must necessarily have an adverse impact on efforts against the Swedish heretic. It will be perceived as a sign of weakness, and will undermine the church's efforts to reclaim souls. The effect on public relations will also be horrible; we must dissuade him from this at all costs."

CHAPTER 5

Dux Christianus

Munich, Bavaria

"So you would have me break my vow to God?"

Duke Maximilian looked around the council table. Three weeks after the duchess' death, this was his first return to the chamber.

Contzen's views aside, almost all of the privy council, his staff and advisors, had—after some reflection—been appalled by Maximilian's decision to withdraw from secular life. Contzen's position was based on a very strong belief that the duke was more valuable to the Church as head of the Catholic League than in a monastery. For most of them, however, the tipping point had been the almost universal perception of bureaucrats that a change in bosses (followed, inevitably, by a change in personnel on the staff) is a catastrophe. They had immediately started to cast around for ways to persuade the duke to abandon his decision.

Within the past two hours, depending on the individual, Maximilian had been told that he had a duty to stand by Ferdinand II against the problems that Wallenstein was causing him in Bohemia, that he had a duty to attempt to expel the heretical Swedes from the Upper Palatinate and once more take up the cause of restoring its population to Catholicism, that various prior treaty obligations could be interpreted as requiring him to defer carrying out the most recent vow until he had completed them; that, in fact, he must not abdicate.

"Albrecht?" Maximilian looked at his brother.

"I will not attempt to constrain your conscience." Duke Albrecht considered himself to be in a very tight spot. He would, after all, from a worldly perspective, be the primary beneficiary of Maximilian's decision to retire.

"Dr. Donnersberger?"

Joachim Donnersberger's decision had not been easy; at heart, he still believed that the duke should follow his conscience. Still, there had been so many occasions over the years when Duke Albrecht had intervened with the privy council on behalf of the less progressive party. Donnersberger was strongly committed to Father Contzen's views on the proper nature of governance. Peace could exist only where there was one universal Catholic faith. But, once that one true faith had been ensured, once there was harmony within a realm, rulers had duties to their subjects. Donnersberger was not yet quite willing to give up the dream of an ideal Christian commonwealth. Reluctantly, he replied, "Your Grace. Bavaria still has need of you."

"Richel?"

"You cannot abdicate, Your Grace. Not without taking upon your conscience the guilt of once more plunging the Austrian lands into chaos and permitting the rampant spread of heresy. Wallenstein has proclaimed free exercise of religion; the walls of the ghetto are down. We need your decisiveness, your unswerving dedication, the power of your convictions."

"Father Contzen?"

Adam Contzen laid two pieces of paper upon the table. "Your Grace, if I may. These are copies, sent me from this Grantville, from the *encyclopedias* of the men from the future."

Duke Maximilian frowned.

Encyclopedias, Duke Albrecht thought, *the wondrous encyclopedias.*

If the future had learned nothing else from the Jesuits, he mused wryly, it had learned the Art of Extraction that they taught so painstakingly to their students—how to go through a nearly unmanageable body of material, reduce it to its essence, and take notes with marginal indices that enabled one to find the needed reference again without immense waste of time. The books of the up-timers were all very well, but Father Contzen had complained to him more than once that finding something in them was like searching for a needle in a haystack. Which book might have it, if, indeed, any book had it at all? But the encyclopedias, all of them: alphabetically arranged, with cross references at the end of one article indicating where the researcher could find related material in the compendium. Not just the great one, the *1911 Britannica*, which they guarded so carefully, but all of them—the later *Britannica* editions, the *World Book* and *Americana*, *Columbia*, and *Funk and Wagnalls*, old and new, large and small. Some more useful than others, but each one a treasure trove.

Duke Albrecht had been told that Father Kircher devoted all the time that he could spare to encyclopedias. But more, there were a half dozen other young Jesuits, five of them from the English College and thus able to handle the language more effectively, whom the order was subsidizing to spend their days sitting in Grantville's libraries. Once they translated their valuable discoveries into Latin, of course, the information was available to every man of learning in Europe.

"If I may?" Contzen repeated. Maximilian nodded his head.

"These are two short biographies of the life that you lived in that world. In that world, you did not abdicate."

"Perhaps, in that world, I had not taken a vow to enter a monastery?"

"There is not sufficient detail here to tell us whether you did or not."

"What became of the rest of my life?"

"You took a second wife, who bore you sons. The elder succeeded you as duke and elector. You defended the Catholic cause to the end."

Duke Maximilian bowed his head.

Duke Albrecht sat, his face impassive. Why hadn't anyone brought this to his attention earlier? What would his wife Mechthilde say to this—that all her efforts in bearing and rearing their children were to be made irrelevant to the future of Bavaria?

He wondered if he could get a copy of those biographies from Contzen. Or from someone else.

Duke Maximilian looked up again. "Father Vervaux?"

Johannes Vervaux looked at the duke, making sure that his face hid the pity that he felt. It did not do to pity Maximilian of

Bavaria. "Your Grace. Reluctantly, I concur with Dr. Donnersberger. Bavaria still needs you, at whatever sacrifice of yourself."

"Thank you, gentlemen. I shall now retire to my meditations. Please be assured that I will take the advice of each of you into account." The duke rose, the councillors rising with him. As he prepared to withdraw to his oratory, Duke Maximilian asked, "What did I name my sons?"

He did not ask, "Who was my second wife?" That, apparently, was a matter of complete indifference to him.

There was nowhere in Munich that Duke Maximilian's decision to delay his abdication was greeted with more relief than in the convent of the "English Ladies" or "Jesuitesses," formerly the Institute of the Blessed Virgin Mary. The dozen or so members in the Munich house—forbidden, at present, to designate themselves as nuns or even as sisters—waited for a signal from Mary Ward to begin their after-supper devotions.

Mary Ward—*not Mother Mary Ward, they were not a religious order any longer, she had to remember that*—waited, her hands folded quietly in her lap. She was nearly fifty. In the almost thirty years since she had left England in pursuit of a religious vocation, she had been as far south as Rome and as far east as Bratislava. She and her sisters had founded schools for girls from Liege to Naples in the Spanish lands, from Cologne to Vienna in those of the Holy Roman Empire, farther east in the Habsburg possessions. She had tried the traditional contemplative convent life of the Colettine Poor Clares and found it not to be her vocation. After a year spent with her family, assisting people in need and people who were experiencing difficulties with their faith, she had returned to the Netherlands with a group of other young Catholic Englishwomen she had gathered around her. She had developed the concept of a new kind of women's religious order whose members would be able to travel, to work and live among the people who needed their services most, wearing not a habit but the ordinary clothing of the laity, living according to the Jesuit rule.

The difficulties, most of them, had arisen there. Since long before the days of Chaucer's pilgrim prioress, the idea of nuns "gadding about" in public had irritated ecclesiastical conservatives. Ideally, for them, not only would a nun never leave the walls of her convent, but no lay person would ever enter within them, either. It was the only way to control the dangerous females of the species: immure them.

The Council of Trent had declared that all religious orders of women must take solemn vows and observe strict enclosure. Pope Pius V had confirmed this resolution. Given how many other declarations of Trent were observed more in the breach than to the letter in the first third of the seventeenth century, it was astonishing how many members of the College of Cardinals, how many officials in the Holy Office, insisted that this one could not be breached in the least.

Mary Ward nodded. "Let us pray. Sister Winifred, please lead us. Sister Frances, please provide the tones for the chant."

Against the background of the familiar evening prayers, her tired mind wandered. In 1615, she had requested papal confirmation of her institute; the hearings process had outlasted two popes and continued into the tenure of a third. The Jesuit rule specifically prohibited them from undertaking the *direction* of women's orders. But Father Muzio Vitelleschi, General of the Society of Jesus, found that there would be no objection to, and much to be gained from, the establishment of a parallel but unconnected institution. During the next ten years, in spite of the opposition of clergy who objected to the idea of a women's order directly subject to the pope rather than under the authority of the dioc-esan bishops, she had established several branches in the Spanish Netherlands (with the patronage of Archduchess Isabella Clara Eugenia), the Germanies (with the approval of the archbishop of Cologne), Naples, and Perugia. In Rome itself, there had been—well, now there was again, thanks to the Barberini—a school for poor girls. But in 1624, the Congregation for the Propagation of the Faith issued its ruling: accept enclosure or the institute would be dissolved. One by one, the schools in Italy closed; many of her sisters had entered other, more conventional, orders.

In Munich, however, Duke Maximilian and Duchess Elisabeth Renata were among the most sturdy of the Catholic rulers in supporting the idea of unenclosed orders of women who could teach and perform works of charity. In 1627, Mary Ward had come to Munich. The duke assigned them a house, appropriately enough on Paradise Street, and they opened a school. At the duke's rec-ommendation, Ferdinand II invited the English Ladies to Vienna, where they opened a school for girls. Its success had demonstrated that she was right—that this order met a need within the church. The girls' school that they opened in the imperial capital attracted four hundred sixty-five pupils the first year.

On July 7, 1628, the Holy Office had declared the institute disbanded because of its refusal to accept claustration. Mother Mary Ward had met with the nuncio in Vienna, then with the nuncio in Munich. In May of 1629, Pope Urban VIII had granted her an audience; early the next winter, she defended her foundation before a commission of the College of Cardinals—speaking in Latin. She returned to the house on Paradise Street. In the background, the ecclesiastical bureaucracy continued to carry out its assignment to disband the order's houses. The schools in the Netherlands were closed; also the one in Cologne. Because of the efforts of the inspector whom Mary Ward sent to the Netherlands to reopen the school at Liege, the case was transferred to the Inquisition. The charge: disobedience.

Well—it was true. Winifred Wigmore's actions had been imprudent at best and insubordinate at worst. Her own defense of her sister in Christ had been intemperate. In January 1631, Urban VIII issued a bull "definitively" abolishing the institute; she herself had been "imprisoned" by the Inquisition in Munich, albeit that imprisonment consisted of a stay in the infirmary at the Poor Clare convent, with a sister from her own order to keep her company, her meals delivered from outside, and lax enough supervision that the lunch baskets included notes, incoming and outgoing, written on napkins with lemon juice serving the place of invisible ink.

In March of 1632, she went to Rome once more; met with the pope once more. In that other world, the *encyclopedias* said, the pope had furnished her with a residence in Rome, where she and her companions lived on a modest income that appeared from somewhere deep in the recesses of the Barberini family's revenues.

In this world, he had sent them back to Munich, where under Duke Maximilian's patronage they had reopened their school, but as lay teachers. It was not what Mary Ward wanted; she wanted recognition that the institute was a religious body. But it appeared to be, for the time being, all that she could get. It certainly appeared that the English Ladies would never become, formally, a Papal Institute.

Cardinal Francesco Barberini had suggested, tentatively, in a private conversation before her return, that they might possibly be reconstituted as a diocesan order that fulfilled the same function. Serving only in those dioceses where the bishops wanted them; not in those where their existence would be an irritant. Yes, he knew that was not what she had wanted. It was not as prestigious as being a papal institute; nor would it provide the leaders of the order with the same independence. But, then, it was widely recognized that humility was good for the soul. One diocese at a time; it would be possible to insert in the document allowing such foundations a clause that the bishop must guarantee to respect their rule and would not subsequently attempt to impose enclosure. Furthermore, should a successor wish to withdraw his approbation of the foundations, the ladies would be allowed to transfer to another diocese—with their property.

Cardinal Francesco had suggested that this experiment might preferably begin with dioceses some distance from Italy and Spain. There was, of course the example of Vincent de Paul and his Daughters of Charity in France. Cardinal Francesco, with whom Mazarini had shared the delightful story of the original name of the Catholic parish in Grantville, had laughed at that point in the conversation. Mary Ward had wondered why.

The murmured litany came to its end. "Now," Mary Ward said, "let us each say an additional rosary for the soul of the Duchess Elisabeth Renata." If her own rosary included a petition that some benefactor might appear to substitute for the generous charity that the late duchess had extended to the English Ladies and their school, she did not say so.

On the other hand, there was nowhere in Munich that Duke Maximilian's decision to delay his abdication was greeted with more disappointment than in the apartments of Mechthilde of Leuchtenberg, Duke Albrecht's wife. Nor anywhere that it was greeted with more fury.

Duke Albrecht had been afraid of that.

What he said was, "Don't count your chickens before they're hatched. Face it, Tilda. It's as good a principle as any for taking life one day at a time."

"I will not see my sons shunted into insignificance! I have endured for more than twenty years now, living in Bavaria as a dependent of the court. Maximilian has never assigned you an *appanage* of your own. We have been nothing but upper servants, all our lives. I have *endured* it for the sake of our children. Who will now be tossed away. Nothing for you, nothing for them!"

"Maximilian has no intention of breaking up Bavaria into something that resembles the absurd little Saxonies and Anhalts. Primogeniture was put in force in 1506. There hasn't been an independent territory for a Bavarian cadet line since Kunigunde of Austria forced her older son to create one for her younger son in 1516, no matter what their father's will said. That was more than a century ago. And Ludwig X had the grace not to marry."

"Don't ever dream that I don't know what she asked the Estates, then. 'Isn't my younger son as nobly born as his brother? Didn't I bring him forth from the same womb, set from the same seed?' The Estates, the *Landtag*, agreed with her. They awarded him a third of the duchy. You are Maximilian's full brother: same womb, same seed. What is it that brings him to rule and you to be no more than any one of the others on his council—men who have no more nobility than can be garnered by attending a university and getting a law degree?"

"Power," Albrecht answered tersely. "Unified, Bavaria is a strong force within the empire. Break it up, and each part will be no more than, say, one of the pieces of Baden or of Hesse."

"Power," said Mechthilde. "Do not doubt for one moment that this means that our sons will have none."

They looked at one another.

Part Two

March 1634

In a thousand valleys, far and wide

CHAPTER 6

Commoditas Maxima

Vienna, Austria

Maria Anna had not been a party to the discussions in her father's council. Why would she have been? She smiled a little. Was salt ever a party to discussions about tariffs? Did anyone tell a case of wine or bale of silk what the seller and buyer were planning?

She couldn't sit down. There weren't any chairs in the anteroom. Even if there had been, it would be contrary to protocol for her to sit on one of them. She ran her rosary through her fingers. That was acceptable etiquette. Twisting her fingers would not be acceptable. In any case, she wasn't willing to have her ladies-in-waiting observe her uncertainty.

She already knew it would be Bavaria. No one had told her so, but she had observed which diplomats were spending the most time with her father and his advisers. Nothing was happening in the war right now, nor was planned to happen in the war next summer, that would require so much consultation with Uncle Max as head of the Catholic League. So she knew, but not quite in the same way that she would know very soon.

She had not been a party to the negotiations, either. Did it occur to anyone that sheep should be consulted as to their preference when it came to transhumance pasturing that crossed the borders of kingdoms?

She told herself firmly that everything would be well. Well enough. As well as a reasonable person could expect.

Ten *Ave Marias.* Then, for each large bead, instead of a *Pater Noster*, count a blessing.

First blessing. Bavaria was Catholic. She was not being sent to marry a heretic and live in a heretical country, as had happened to Henrietta Maria of France. Her husband's subjects would not hate her for her faith. Nor martyr her for it, although, of course, if it proved to be necessary, she would have the duty to glory in martyrdom. Overall, though, she would prefer not to be a martyr. At least not until she was older. Quite a bit older. In any case, it did not now seem that it would be necessary.

Second blessing. She knew from the up-time *encyclopedias* that she had, in that other world, borne sons. Heirs for the duchy. She was not barren. The marriage would be fruitful. She would not be scorned as a sterile wife. Not, at least, if things occurred in the same way. Of course, the physicians would have ascertained, before the negotiations began, that Uncle Max was still capable of copulation. That wasn't something that could be assumed when a man was sixty years old. He would be sixty-one in a couple of months. A year older than her mother, his sister, would have been if she had not died almost twenty years ago.

She glanced up from the rosary. Doña Mencia was watching her, a concerned expression on her face. Maria Anna smiled reassuringly.

Third blessing. She paused, trying to bring a third blessing to mind.

The door to the council chamber opened. She looked up, expecting to be summoned into the presence of Ferdinand II, Holy Roman Emperor and her papa.

It was not the doorman, however. Father Lamormaini emerged, briefly greeted her, Doña Mencia, and the younger ladies-in-waiting, and walked away.

She returned to her rosary. Third blessing. She had not died in childbirth. Or, maybe, she would not die in childbirth? *These strange verb tenses.* Thanks to this strange miracle of Grantville, she was going—would go?—into marriage knowing that she was capable of giving life to a son without sacrificing her own. This was a great comfort and source of confidence. Something that most prospective brides could not know. Her fingers paused a moment while her busy mind focused on the realities of life. Unless the prospective brides were widows with children, of course. Many brides were widows with children.

Fourth blessing. She drew a deep breath. Uncle Max was sixty years old. Of course, the *encyclopedias* said that he had lived another eighteen years in that other world of God's creation. But eighteen years was not so bad. In eighteen years she would be in her forties. In her prime. Ready to assume her responsibilities as an adult member of the Habsburg family.

Father Lamormaini returned and reentered the council chamber. She smiled again, bending her face down so that none of her maids-in-waiting would notice the irreverence. Even Jesuits were not angels and were subject to calls of nature. Another reminder that all men, from the highest in rank to the lowest, were the children of Adam and Eve. Her fingers moved steadily through another decade of the rosary.

Fifth blessing.

The door opened again. This time, it was the doorman.

"It's fine, Sissy. It's fine." Maria Anna hugged her sister.

"But I'll miss you." Cecelia Renata was clinging to her. "I know I haven't been the best sister, and I know I'm stubborn and contrary, and I know I don't always do what you want me to, but we've always been together. Always. We've never been apart, not since I was born."

"Well, then . . ." Maria Anna paused. "We know that I survived the first eighteen months of my life before I had your company. I have been apart from you, so it should be easier for me to be alone. That is a blessing. And you won't be all by yourself. You get to stay here, with Mama and Papa. With our brothers and Mariana. At least for a while. Until . . ." Maria Anna didn't need to speak the end of that sentence.

Cecelia Renata nodded. They had read the very little that the *encyclopedias* had to say about her life, too. *At least for a while. Until it was her own turn to become a commodity in trade. A far less fortunate commodity than Maria Anna, if the future remained as it had been. Cecelia Renata's marriage to the Polish king Władysław IV in 1637—only three years from now—had not apparently been a happy one.*

And she had died young, too, only six years later—although the encyclopedias did not explain the cause. Perhaps it would all be different in this universe.

Cecelia Renata lifted her chin. "I'm not as brave as you are. But I'm brave enough."

"Oh, Sissy. I'll miss you, too. So much."

"It is certainly time she was married," Father Lamormaini said. "Married to a man with the proper personality to keep her mind from straying along unsuitable paths. Not that I am saying that the archduchess is frivolous or in any way perverse. She is a pious young woman. She is just . . ." He paused. "Too curious. Too interested in new things."

Ferdinand II leaned back in his chair. "It is a great comfort to me that Duke Maximilian has such a strong mind and will. He can guide her in the direction she should go. She has reached the age where a husband can direct her much more effectively than a father can."

The Bavarian ambassador did not reply at first. Then, slowly, he said, "Your Majesty, I am not sure that you can count on the duke's directing her. Or, from what I have gathered that you hope for, from my earlier conversations with your confessor, controlling her intellectual development."

Lamormaini breathed in sharply. "Can't he?"

The envoy looked out the window. "Say, rather, *will* he? The death of Duchess Elisabeth Renata has affected him deeply. You already know that the duke was . . . reluctant . . . to remarry. I am not betraying any diplomatic confidences by telling you that. He may not take the trouble to provide her with the loving guidance that a wife has a reasonable right to expect from her husband."

Ferdinand II stood up, choleric as usual at being forced to listen to anything he didn't want to hear. "Then an immediate marriage will benefit the duke, as well, in more ways than providing him with sons. Take his mind off his troubles, and all that. I have no patience with melancholia." He leaned over, rubbed his right calf, and limped out of the room, followed by the chancellor.

Lamormaini frowned after him, worried. The emperor's legs had been bothering him for months, aching whenever he sat for too long or tried to move quickly. He turned back to the ambassador. "Were you implying that Maria Anna might come to dominate the duke?"

The Bavarian shook his head slowly. "No. Not precisely."

"What, then? Can't he direct her? Control her?"

The ambassador shrugged. "He could have. If he were still the man he was ten years ago. If he were even still the man he was a year ago. As I said to the emperor, 'Will he?'"

Lamormaini rubbed his temples. He was starting to feel a headache coming on.

"It's all right, Doña Mencia. At least, you will be coming with me. And staying in Munich. Papa insisted on that, so I won't be surrounded by strangers right away. I'm counting that as another blessing." Maria Anna waved her rosary.

"Do you have a full decade of blessings, yet?"

"Almost. Nearly." Maria Anna jiggled her rosary, pulled her skirts up, and sat down on a hassock, dropping them behind her. Frau Stecher had been harping again on the amount of work that was involved in pressing her everyday clothing while the dressers and seamstresses were so busy putting together a new trousseau, so she had been avoiding chairs the last few days. There just wasn't any way to keep from wrinkling fabric if a person sat down in a chair. "I've also added that at least Uncle Max won't ever take a mistress—well, the odds are really against it, since he was faithful to Tante Elisabeth Renata for all their lives. So I won't have that problem to contend with, the way most of the French queens have done."

Doña Mencia de Mendoza nodded.

"Nor *mignons*, the way Anne of Austria has had to do in France. And the English king's Danish mother did."

Doña Mencia winked. "Is that one blessing or two?"

Maria Anna put on a serious face. "One, I think. At least, I don't know of any kings who have had both mistresses and *mignons*. That's not the same thing as a king just having a favorite. Nobody has ever accused the count-duke of Olivares of being a *mignon*. Just a really close adviser. I think." She looked across the room. "You know more about the Spanish court than I do. Mariana wouldn't ever say anything, of course, even if she knew otherwise. She's very loyal to her brother."

"The count-duke is King Philip's close adviser and favorite. Only." Doña Mencia's tone of voice was firm.

"That's . . . reassuring."

Doña Mencia decided not to mention Philip of Spain's various mistresses. None of them were quasi-official court figures the way French royal mistresses tended to be.

Maria Anna stretched her arms. "It will be easier in Bavaria, then, from all that I've heard, than it is for some new wives. Strict and formal, of course. Uncle Max has political and military advisers and he's very close to Uncle Albrecht, too, but . . . not anything else."

"Nothing else. Not even a rumor of anything else."

"And Uncle Max has an excellent library."

"True."

"And a wonderful art collection."

"Yes."

"There are beautiful churches in Munich."

Another nod.

"Excellent preachers, too. And I'll have my own confessor. How many is that?"

"How many what?"

"Blessings. 'No mistresses or *mignons*' is the fifth. Library is the sixth. Art is the seventh. If I can count churches, preachers, and my own confessor separately, that would make the decade. Is that quite fair? Aren't they really just one, altogether? And don't they really all belong under my first blessing, that Bavaria is Catholic? That at least I am going to a Catholic principality? Maybe these are just . . . subheadings."

"Don't create unnecessary scruples," Doña Mencia warned.

"I won't." Maria Anna nodded. "I'll try to think of more, different, blessings, though. For instance, since Leopold Wilhelm is bishop of Passau, I will see one of my brothers after my marriage. At least occasionally. That makes an eighth separate blessing. I only need two more."

CHAPTER 7

Miles Bellicosus

Amberg, the Upper Palatinate

Gustav Adolf's regent in the Upper Palatinate and his general assigned to the same principality were having a private discussion.

Duke Ernst's private secretary, Johann Heinrich Böcler, was seated behind his employer and taking meticulous notes. He sat in on all of his employer's meetings, at least those that he knew about, and always took careful notes—perhaps even unnecessarily extensive, given that they included marginal comments. But Böcler had been born in the utterly insignificant little town of Cornheim in Franconia, son of a Lutheran pastor and grandson of a high school principal. Today, in March of 1634, he found himself in a plum post that most twenty-three-year-olds could only dream of obtaining. So, better to err on the side of caution.

Thank you, Professor Bernegger; thank you, historical faculty of the University of Strassburg; I pledge upon my honor to be worthy of your trust. He intended these notes not only for the duke's current use, but also as the basis for a history of the exciting events of this great war which he hoped would, some day, make him as immortally famous as Caesar or Livy, Suetonius or Tacitus.

Böcler pursed his lips primly and invented yet one more shorthand substitute for the . . . *colorful*—not to say blasphemous and scatological—terms that peppered General Johan Banér's vocabulary.

Böcler was a bit of a prig. His father and grandfather would have been proud of him.

"If I don't get out of this godforsaken Upper Palatinate, my troops will mutiny. They are fighters. I have no talent for keeping the men happy when they are in quarters doing goddamned near nothing. Or, at least, not much." Banér slammed his tankard of beer down on the dual-purpose breakfast and card table in the conference room in Amberg castle, which was serving the regency of the Upper Palatinate as a capitol building.

Duke Ernst of Saxe-Weimar had been serving as Gustav Adolf's regent in the province—the *Oberpfalz* or Upper Palatinate, as contrasted with the Rhine or Electoral Palatinate—since late the previous summer. Technically, he was governing in the name of young Karl Ludwig, the rightful ruler, who was in polite and comfortable imprisonment in the Spanish Netherlands at the moment. He had been appointed by Gustav Adolf and was, as everyone knew perfectly well, managing the region on behalf of the USE. That he was acting for Karl Ludwig had been retained as a polite fiction, however. It was also a useful one, particularly since the USE did not choose to recognize Ferdinand II's 1628 transfer of the Palatinate's electoral vote to the other branch of the House of Wittelsbach in the person of Duke Maximilian of Bavaria. In a pinch, if Ferdinand II summoned a diet for the purpose of getting his son elected as King of the Romans, Duke Ernst could challenge, on behalf of Karl Ludwig, Duke Maximilian's right to vote, which could tie it up in procedural wrangling for a long time. Long enough, perhaps that Ferdinand might die before the electors designated his son as his successor.

Well—a man could always hope.

Duke Ernst knew that Banér had his men constantly practicing innovative tactics involving fighting retreats and winter campaigning. He looked at his colleague reproachfully.

"General, you are fully aware of why you and your regiments must remain stationed in the Upper Palatinate. Your presence here is necessary to guard against any Bavarian incursions across the Danube. Even more, the threat caused by your presence along the Danube keeps Duke Maximilian's troops tied in place, so that he cannot bring them to the assistance of the Austrians against Wallenstein in Bohemia—nor to the League of Ostend against whom our monarch is waging war in the Baltic. Your task here

is not the one which you have just described as 'doing nothing.'"
His face grew a bit tight. "Accompanied, I fear I must say, by a
blasphemy that is not acceptable in polite discourse, and which
I do not propose to repeat."

He decided an additional remark was called for here. "Moreover," he added, "your troops *are* being paid. Not as much as they
might like, but regularly. That appreciably reduces the immediate
risk of mutiny."

"Appreciably! Immediate! You know, Your Grace, you have
some adverb or adjective just dripping with pious cant that puts
a condition on everything you say," Banér said, all but sneering
openly. "The whole Upper Palatinate is an overused cesspit as far
as I am concerned! Particularly since my troops, during this winter
of 1633–1634, are neither quartered upon the townspeople, whose
stores they could eat up, nor allowed to exact more than very
limited and rationed contributions, which my *honored regent* does
not permit them to collect themselves—with whatever supplements
they might bring in during the process—but is obtaining through
contractors with the souls of stiff-necked, constipated bookkeepers
and accountants. *Calvinist* bookkeepers and accountants. *Walloons*,
most of them. Or *Genevans!*"

"The *honored regent*, as you call me, feels obliged to point out
that Frederick V of the Palatinate and erstwhile Winter King of
Bohemia, whose political ambitions were the immediate trigger of this great war, was a Calvinist—whether you like it or I
like it. As is his son Karl Ludwig; so far, at least. It seems only
reasonable, therefore, to employ at least a moderate number of
Calvinists in the administration of the province. If I engaged
only fellow Lutherans in this region, it would cause hard feelings
unnecessarily."

He leaned back in his chair and continued, in a somewhat
milder tone. "The Upper Palatinate is not only that which you
rendered so unacceptably as 'an overused cesspit.' Although there
are times that I too have been tempted to consider it almost
ungovernable—if only because there are three sets of legal claimants, duly but separately appointed or authorized by its former
Lutheran, Calvinist, and Catholic rulers respectively, to almost
every piece of property within its borders. Nonetheless, it has
industrial resources that are crucial to the technology of the
up-timers. That are, therefore, crucial to the war effort being

waged by Gustav Adolf. Who is, if I may remind you once more, your king as well as my emperor, the emperor of the USE. The presence and protection of your troops is necessary if we are to restore the mines to full production. Otherwise, a raid from Austria or Bavaria could destroy the infrastructure once more, just as effectively—and just as fast—as Tilly and Mansfeld, between them, destroyed it during this past decade."

Banér, alas, was nothing if not stubborn. He was none too heavily burdened with respect for his superiors, either. "If the king—or, more likely that tight-assed young Torstensson—wants the artillery that might be manufactured from the ore produced by the Upper Palatinate's mines, smelted with the Upper Palatinate's charcoal, and processed in the Upper Palatinate's hammer-mills, then"—here his fist slammed the table—"it should be that fucking Torstensson's troops who get stuck with the hell-designed duties such as protecting mines, assholes, smelters, latrines, hammer-mills, and chamber-pots."

He planted his hands on the armrests of his chair, leaned back, and glared at Duke Ernst. "While real cavalrymen get on with the process of fighting battles."

The two men, odd couple though they might be, had learned a lot from one another in the past several months. They had conducted variations on this conversation so frequently that Duke Ernst didn't even pause.

"We have to consider the problems presented by the other Upper Palatine territories, as well, especially Leuchtenberg. Duke Maximilian's brother is married to the sister of the landgrave of Leuchtenberg. Her brother and nephews fled into Bavaria when we came through on our way to Regensburg."

Banér snorted. "Of course we fucking occupied the whole region! There's really no practical way to conquer part of the squares on a game board and pass by the others."

Duke Ernst ignored him and looked at Böcler. "For your notes. Wolfgang Wilhelm is the duke of Pfalz-Neuburg. He married Duke Maximilian's sister in 1613 and converted to Catholicism in the expedient hope that it would enhance his maternal inheritance expectations in Jülich and Cleves. He's been in Düsseldorf for years now. For our purposes, even though his Bavarian duchess has been dead for five years and he has remarried, he's still basically Maximilian's client. Especially since he's got the Bavarian duke's brother, Archbishop Ferdinand of Cologne, looking over his shoulder."

The young secretary nodded gratefully. He was learning fast, but he still was nowhere as close to being on top of the political developments of the past quarter century as his employer, who had been born to the job.

Duke Ernst was still dictating. "Wolfgang Wilhelm, seems, for the moment, to have no immediate intentions of undertaking military action to reclaim those parts of his Neuburg lands that are up here, north of the Danube, intermixed with those of the Upper Palatinate. That's probably because Gustav's main theater of military operation this spring and summer will be against the League of Ostend in the north and thus uncomfortably close to Wolfgang's lands on the lower Rhine and Düsseldorf itself. However, his local administrators are still in place in the Neuburg lands south of the Danube and he has filed a complaint against us with the Imperial Supreme Court on grounds that we have 'unjustifiably dispossessed' him of the north-Danubian lands that interpenetrate those of the Upper Palatinate."

Böcler mentally thanked his father for making him learn shorthand, because Duke Ernst wasn't even pausing between sentences.

"And, I expect, whether the acknowledged emperor of the Germanies be Swedish or Austrian, Lutheran or Catholic, in Magdeburg or Vienna, the imperial chamber court will hear the case. But what is immediately important to us as we sit in Amberg is that most certainly, given the slightest chance, Duke Maximilian will seize upon Wolfgang Wilhelm's grievances as an excuse to invade the Upper Palatinate, citing noble defense of the unjustly dispossessed as the *casus belli* of a just war."

Banér chimed in. "You can add to your notes that Duke Wolfgang Wilhelm of Pfalz-Neuburg is a son of a bitch—or would be, if his mother hadn't been a perfectly respectable woman. Still, he qualifies as a son of a bitch even though his mother was impeccably virtuous. His character has the kind of son-of-a-bitchiness that overrides such minor impediments. He—"

"What do you think of his brothers—the Lutheran dukes of the Junge-Pfalz? August at Sulzbach—well, he died a couple of years ago, so it's his widow as regent—and Johann Friedrich at Hilpoltstein?" Duke Ernst interrupted Banér's spiel with some apparently genuine curiosity. These cadets of the Pfalz-Neuburg ruling house held *appanages*, independently-administered lands that checkerboarded with those of the Upper Palatinate. Böcler knew that he dealt with them, or, at least, with their officials, on an almost daily basis.

"Honestly?" Banér asked. "I think that the 'ruling high nobility' of all of these crappy bits and pieces of the Palatinate would be a lot improved if someone did to them what the kings of Sweden did to their own nobility two generations ago. Namely, chop off their shitting heads. And keep chopping until the ones left alive become useful servants of the crown instead of hopped-up would-be-independent rulers. The Danes started that bloodbath method, I'll admit, the fucking bastards. They had all four of my great-grandfathers killed for being Swedish patriots. If I have anything to say about the peace settlement after the war, I'd be sending plenty of Danes to the chopping block, believe you me."

The general was in full tirade mode, now. Obviously recognizing the signs, Duke Ernst just settled back in his chair. There'd be no way to interrupt him at this point, until the choleric fellow got it all out.

"But whether it was shithead Danes who came up with the idea or not, it's still a good idea. Our native Vasa dynasty—my kinsmen, mind you—later had all sorts of petty kinglets and would-be kinglets and the like nicely shortened. You herd a hundred or so of these miserable Palatine *Freiherren* to me and I'll do you the same favor. Turn this running asshole of a place into something that looks like a country instead of this little mini-state here and that little mini-state there."

"Oh," Duke Ernst said. His tone was carefully noncommittal.

Böcler had been taking shorthand "a mile a minute" as the up-timers put it. After the, "Oh," there was a pause, during which his mind wandered. He wished he knew what Duke Ernst was thinking. Although the Wettin family were natives of Thuringia and Saxony rather than of the Palatinate, there was little doubt in Böcler's mind that it probably fell into Banér's category of should-be-choppees. Particularly Duke Bernhard of Saxe-Weimar, of course, given that he was a traitor who had taken service with the French.

But the other Saxe-Weimar brothers were, more or less voluntarily, serving Gustavus II Adolphus because he appeared to offer the best option available to them as former Protestant rulers.

Wilhelm had even abdicated his title as duke and become plain Wilhelm Wettin in order to run for the House of Commons in the USE's new Parliament. Even so, they were still nobles by upbringing and temperament. This was always clear to Böcler, considering that he himself certainly was not.

While Wilhelm and Ernst had agreed rather gracefully when the up-timers "slid" Saxe-Weimar itself into the New United States, Wilhelm had been more than compensated—from the gritty standpoint of economics—by Gustav's giving him the Eichsfeld to administer. Ernst, through his long-standing betrothal to the little heiress of Saxe-Altenburg, had prospects for a prosperous future as well, presuming that she survived for a few more years and reached marriageable age. Plus, their brother Albrecht had stayed home to cultivate their remaining economic interests and private property in what had once been an independent Saxe-Weimar.

"Oh," the duke said again. Whatever he might have been thinking after Banér's diatribe, he introduced a change of subject-matter. "You asked for this special meeting," he said. "What is the topic?"

Böcler snapped to attention, pencil at the ready.

"I want to take Ingolstadt," Banér said baldly. "Letting the Bavarians keep a garrisoned fortress on the north bank of the Danube is a boil on our rump. And a danger to Horn's flank in Swabia. Which means that it's a threat to the king. I'm sick of it. And my men damned well need something more to do. I'm tired of having half my available men just sitting there, investing it. That bridge, the way the piers are built, is practically indestructible. Even when we manage to get rid of the planking temporarily—which, believe me, is not easy—we know perfectly well that it's being reprovisioned almost every night by those fleets of little boats that run through those multiple channels of the river to the south. And if you want us to keep the Bavarians off Wallenstein's back and make sure Maximilian is too busy to invade the Upper Palatinate this summer, a major campaign at Ingolstadt will give them something else to think about—actually pull Max's troops to the west, probably. A fair number of them, anyway."

"I am sure," Duke Ernst said judiciously, "that the fact that we hold Regensburg is just as much of an irritant to the Bavarians as their possession of Ingolstadt is to us."

Banér glared. He was not by temperament favorably inclined toward an evenhanded, fair-minded assessment of the rights and wrongs of the military situation. From his standpoint, the ideal situation would be for Sweden to have every military stronghold in the Germanies firmly within its grasp.

"If you take all the rest of your regulars—or most of them—to Ingolstadt, what do I do about the rest of the borders?" asked the duke. "I'm still not so sure that we were smart to take that neck of hill and forest running down from Regensburg to Passau, just because it was north of the Danube and just because we could, right then, since the Bavarians were in full retreat after we took Regensburg. Admittedly, it's one of the few things that we've done that actually helps Wallenstein—giving him a fairly secure south-western border against the USE rather than against the Bavarians as far down as Passau. But it's not an easy place to patrol. Plus the whole river, from Donauwörth to Passau. That's two hundred fifty miles by itself. Not counting the twists and turns."

Duke Ernst assumed a righteous expression—one that came to him rather easily because of extensive practice.

Banér's countering expression was closer to "Gotcha!"

"Hill and forest, you say? Then use your oh-so-valuable hill-billies and foresters. River bank, you say? Then use your precious river rats and their barges. Don't look so sanctimoniously at me, Duke. I know what you've been doing, training whole squads of non-soldiers to patrol the regions they know best. And you've been doing it because you fucking well believe that the first chance I have, I'm going to pull out of this twice-damned, thrice-cursed, totally-abandoned-by-God place and get my men back to my king and his war in the Baltic, which is where I belong and where I might, just might, have a chance to get a fucking promotion. Which is what I *am* going to do. For a general, it is a thoroughly career-destroying move to be stuck in a backwater where nothing is going boom. Be grateful that I'm solving Ingol-stadt for you first."

Banér drained his tankard and stood up without the regent's permission.

Duke Ernst was used to that.

The general slammed the door on his way out.

Duke Ernst was used to that, too.

As Böcler duly noted in the margin. Of course, the clean copies of the minutes that he submitted to the duke never included his marginal notes.

CHAPTER 8

Idea Boni Principis

Duke Ernst rested his forehead upon his hands. Being a Lutheran, he did not believe in purgatory. He did, however, suspect that purgatory would not have been a necessity for even a Catholic, presuming that said Catholic was upright and God-fearing otherwise than in the matter of being a Papist, who was assigned to work with Johan Banér. Banér provided purgatory on earth.

Nonetheless, he admonished himself, he could not let his distaste for the man impede him from performing his duties. He had a job to do. Clearly, with young Karl Ludwig being a minor, there had to be a regency. The USE had certainly not wanted to see Ferdinand II establish an imperial regency for the boy. Which he might have tried, if he could have persuaded Don Fernando to transfer custody when he first captured the Winter King's widow and children.

But, worse, Don Fernando might try some version of what the Spanish had done to William the Silent's oldest son. They had abducted him to Spain when he was fourteen, converted him to Catholicism, and kept him, basically, as a hostage against his father and brothers for fifty years. Only the mercy of God had granted that his marriage had been sterile—Fredrik Hendrik did not, right now, need to contend with Spanish-sponsored claimants from a senior line of the House of Orange.

If Don Fernando tried hard enough, with tutors, with the

insidiously seductive plays and spectacles, with gestures of friendship, feigned or genuine, Karl Ludwig, at sixteen, might actually become a convert to Papistry. *God preserve us all. Then how could the king reasonably refuse to reinstate him in his lands?*

So, Gustav Adolf had sent him here, telling him to work with the cadet, Protestant, counts of Pfalz-Neuberg to set up a system that would be terribly hard for a hotheaded young count Palatine to mess with if the Spanish and imperials succeeded in converting Karl Ludwig and in a few years sent him to claim his hereditary property.

Lifting his head, he turned. "Just what we don't need," he muttered to Böcler. "A young bigot on the model of Maximilian or Ferdinand II, planted on the north bank of the Danube and both banks of the Rhine."

Böcler seriously wished that he had been able to take notes on whatever train of thought that had led Duke Ernst to that comment. But now the duke was saying, in his normal tone of voice, "Please prepare a memorandum for General Banér, reminding him that John George of Saxony has employed Heinrich Holk. If John George should, for some reason, decide to send Holk's men south toward us, rather than east toward Bohemia, the general and his regular troops will have plenty to do. Especially if, at the same time, Maximilian should decide to come north or Ferdinand should decide to come west."

Then he spoke rather shortly. "Find Zincgref," he ordered.

After a half-dozen false starts—Julius Wilhelm Zincgref was not in his own apartments, not in the breakfast room, had not been seen by the clerical staff, and the like—Böcler finally found him in the exercise room, watching Erik Haakansson Hand work out.

Zincgref spent a fair amount of his time doing that. Hand, or more precisely, Hand's mother, was a cousin of the king of Sweden. Illegitimate, to be sure, an acknowledged daughter of Eric XIV by one of his mistresses. Zincgref, who harbored a passionate desire to produce a best selling neo-Latin epic poem glorifying the Lion of the North, spent a great deal of time trying to learn more about the omens of greatness that must have clustered around the monarch in childhood.

Hand couldn't seem to think of many. He was only a year or so older than the king, about forty, so his memories of the glorious ruler's infancy were, not surprisingly, rather vague. He had grown up in Germany as a page in the court of one of the dukes Mecklenburg; then learned his trade in the lifeguard regiment of Maurice of Nassau; then started as a lieutenant in the Smålands infantry in 1615. Captain in 1617; major in 1628; colonel of the Östergötland infantry in 1628. In 1631, he had been with the king at Breitenfeld and at the crossing of the Lech; at Alte Veste, he had commanded a full brigade, the Östgöta, Jönköping, and Skaraborg regiments, against Wallenstein. He had been severely wounded, left behind as dead or dying, in the fall of 1632 when the Swedes swept past Ingolstadt, into the Upper Palatinate, in pursuit of the Bavarians.

He had survived. He spent most of his free time, when he wasn't training the men who were training and would train the Upper Palatinate's local militias, in the exercise rooms, determined to regain as much function as possible. It seemed unlikely that he would serve his king in the field again. Today he was talking to Zincgref about his family and about service: his brother Knut, killed in Russia in 1614; his brother Arvid, killed in action at Riga, in Latvia, in 1621. His brother Jan was still alive, though, as were his three brothers-in-law.

"They haven't managed to do us in yet," Hand was saying.

Böcler had been unable to determine, thus far, whether Hand regarded Zincgref's persistent questioning as a nuisance or a way to pass the time. Surely, Böcler thought, it could not be interesting to spend hour after hour with one's right hand in a grip attached to a heavy bar, suspended from the ceiling on chains, which one was trying to move back and forth. But the curve of the bar, marked upon the wall, was longer this morning than it had been last week. In pulling it toward his chest, Hand had gained an inch; in pushing it away, nearly two. Some day, perhaps, the colonel would be able to straighten his right arm again.

While his secretary was out of the room in search of the elusive Zincgref, Duke Ernst crossed his arms on the table and put his head down. He had already been up for six hours, which equaled the number of hours that he had slept the night before.

There was a lot to do in the Upper Palatinate after a dozen years of war and devastation. He was quite prepared to do it: to reorganize, to reconstruct, to locate settlers for abandoned lands and try to find businessmen who were willing to invest in a place that had proved to offer a very chancy return. He would not do it with the political flair of his brother Wilhelm, perhaps, but he was willing to do it. In fact, he rather enjoyed the challenge of trying to create a model administrative system, without having to deal with co-regents. He and his brothers had governed Saxe-Weimar as a committee.

Even without an outright military invasion going on, he spent a lot of time thinking about how he would cope if Banér and his army weren't there. Basically, Duke Ernst was of the opinion that General Banér tended to be too impatient. The nature of the war, thus far, was such that if a man stayed in one place, particularly in a strategically located place such as the Upper Palatinate, the war would come and find him. He thought that he might be able to manage to hold, at least. Not with the genius of his brother Bernhard—damn his arrogance and ambition—but to *hold*, long enough for somebody else to come to the rescue. That would have to do. He was willing to try.

His head was pillowed on the printed edition of the full transcript of the minutes of the Rudolstadt Colloquy. He had read it, all of it, several times, along with the C.F.W. Walther speech. The king of Sweden expected him to turn a province full of cynics—people who under the provisions of *cuius regio* hadn't had a full generation as Catholic, Calvinist, or Lutheran for the past century—back into devout Lutherans. The Peace of Augsburg, made between the Holy Roman Emperor and the German princes in 1555, had established the right of the ruler in each principality of the Germanies to determine the religion of his subjects—well, within the limits of whether that religion would be Catholic or Lutheran. Calvinism had not been included, much less the sectarians. Unquestionably, in the eighty years since then, the rulers of the Palatinate had changed their minds more than most, and several had, contrary to the 1555 agreement, become Calvinists and determined that their subjects should be Calvinist as well.

In the abstract, it would be desirable for all the subjects and residents of the Upper Palatinate to be Lutheran, of course. Duke Ernst had no doubt of that. Lutheranism was right, and the doctrinal positions of other faiths, where they differed from Lutheranism, were wrong. The basic principle was quite clear to him. But accomplishing Gustav Adolf's goal was simply impossible.

At least, it was impossible without employing the ruthlessness that had marked the enforcement of Catholicism by the version of the Counter-Reformation that Maximilian and Ferdinand II had imposed in Bavaria and Austria-Bohemia. Should he quarter Banér's troops on Catholic subjects who were unwilling to become Lutheran, as Maximilian had quartered Bavarian troops on Calvinists who were unwilling to become Catholic? At a minimum, that level of repressive action would seriously interfere with both economic reconstruction and military security. Not to mention that the American up-timers who were so important to Gustav Adolf's plans would be sure to raise a storm of protest.

Ernst asked himself what he *was* willing to try. After all, everything should be done decently and in order; that was the fundamental principle of existence. What was decent and orderly? The Lutheran counts of the Junge-Pfalz, the younger brothers of Wolfgang Wilhelm, were suggesting a parity arrangement, by which they would tolerate the practice of both Lutheranism and Catholicism, with a shared use of church property.

How did one translate the principle of decency and order into practice without driving even more people out than had already been driven out? Especially when the current rightful ruler, acknowledged to be so by Gustav Adolf, was a Calvinist—a member of a church that had never been included within the provisions of the Peace of Augsburg. In that, the *Junge-Pfalz* had it easy—they weren't trying to design a polity that would encompass Calvinism. Especially, how did one establish a system of ecclesiastical polity that embodied the principles of decency and order when the rightful, and currently Calvinist, ruler, under the emperor of the USE, might become a Catholic—a member of a church that *was* one of the signatories to the provisions of the Peace of Augsburg?

Would it be wrong of him to do his experimenting with the up-time "no established church" idea on somebody else's subjects? That is, on those of young Karl Ludwig? There was no point in making a universal principal of it, of course. The king of Sweden would have no reason to institute such an order in his own lands; they were solidly Lutheran. For that matter, until these latest developments, the Wettins would have had no reason to try it with the both solid and stolid population of Lutherans in their Thuringian lands. But should he try it on this inchoate mix of Calvinists, Lutherans, and Catholics, few of whom really knew what they were any more and all too many of whom appeared to be willing to lay claim to any ecclesiastical allegiance that might bolster their wide variety of property claims?

Perhaps he could try it. But not without money. General Banér was constantly nagging him for more money to support the army, but everything else that needed to be done required money, too. The mines, for example, had continuing problems from the destruction wreaked by Tilly and Mansfeld in the 1620s and early 1630s. They needed pumps; they needed to reopen the shafts when the pumps arrived; they needed transportation to bring the ore out. As manager of the elector's very large share of the joint stock company that financed the iron mines, a major part of his economic development work would be to get them back into full production.

There were reasons that Bavaria had been so greedy for the lands of the Upper Palatinate. Always, historically, these hills had furnished the financial basis for the wealth of the Palatine electors. They had produced raw materials—above all, iron. Amberg, the administrative residence, was also the center of a landscape that had, for centuries, been marked by mines and smelters. Before the war, its economic ties had extended not only into Bohemia, but also into the great mercantile cities: Regensburg and Nürnberg prime among them. The principality had traded iron for Bohemian tin; had prepared the ore for export as pig iron; had produced multiple types of wrought iron and cast iron products, as large as ship's anchors, exporting them to Venice and other ports. When he had arrived, these were gone; all gone. Mansfeld's marauders; Tilly's plunderers. Iron production had fallen to almost nothing by 1632.

His first major project had been to find out just what the resources were. It wasn't that the prior rulers hadn't kept records. Most certainly they had. But in the nearly fifteen years of war-driven chaos, they had all become obsolete; many files had been damaged or destroyed, burned or stolen; the men who knew how the indexes worked and what all the symbols meant had been driven out during the years that Maximilian of Bavaria held the country. People listed as landholders were frequently fled or dead. Businesses that were listed on tax assessment lists had been burned or smashed, the walls fallen into the basements; their owners also, very often, fled or dead. He scarcely had enough personnel to keep track of the real estate transactions; every piece of property needed to be reassessed; thousands of titles needed to be cleared. For the past six months, his staff had been crossing the territory; questioning the former *Amtmaenner* and Bavarian *Pfleggerichter* when they could be found, distributing questionnaires.

There was a knock on the door. Duke Ernst lifted his head and said, "Enter." Böcler came in with Zincgref. Duke Ernst did not underestimate himself, but he knew his limitations. Hardworking, conscientious, serious, and competent, "willing to do it" and "willing to try," were qualities that some people—in fact, quite a lot of people—found to be ultimately boring. He had hired a public relations man.

Zincgref was having trouble getting with the program. Neo-Latin poetry—that he could furnish almost with a wave of his hand. Admonitions to patriotism and bravery in German—a cinch. A blistering anti-Catholic polemic in either language—be my guest. A product of the late humanist circle at the University of Heidelberg, he had fifteen years of experience as a propagandist for the Palatinate, after all. But . . .

"Do I understand Your Grace correctly?" he asked carefully. "You want me to write an inspirational poem, in German, by tomorrow? It is to be called *Der Fragebogen*? It is to persuade the residents of the Upper Palatinate of the value of filling out questionnaires completely and fully? And it is to be amusing, so the people will willingly read it? Will, in fact, recite it out loud to one another in taverns and inns?"

"Precisely," said the regent.

Böcler included a summary of the instructions in his notes.

CHAPTER 9

Corona Conflagrens

Grantville, State of Thuringia-Franconia

It was Ash Wednesday. Athanasius Kircher, S.J., substituting for
Father Larry Mazzare at the parish of St. Mary's, had made a place
in his schedule, on one of the busiest days of the church year, for the
three women. When Bernadette Adducci had called for an appointment, she had asked specifically that it be on Ash Wednesday. Not,
as the up-timers normally asked, for an appointment on a certain
day of the month. She had referenced the liturgical calendar.

He had made it his business to find something out about each
of the three women who would be coming. Between running the
parish, even with three curates to assist, and teaching at the high
school, he did not know Father Mazzare's parishioners as well as
he should. It had been—impressive. It appeared that among the
up-timers, families of the middle classes, ordinary businessmen
and sometimes even manual workers, educated their daughters
as carefully as the down-time high nobility. Granted the absence
of Latin and Greek—one always had to make allowance for the
absence of classical languages among the Grantvillers.

He looked out the window. The three women had arrived.

"Miss Adducci, Miss Constantinault, Miss Mastroianni," he said,
by way of a greeting.

Kircher noticed that Bernadette Adducci had a book in her hand. Presumably one of her own, that had not been wanted for the state library, or that she had needed for her daily work. Kircher refreshed his mind. In her mid-forties, she worked for the police department as their "juvenile officer" specializing in transgressions by, and against, children. She had an advanced degree, not in any field that was a subject of university study in his day, but she was a *magister. Magistra?* The word fell strangely on his ears. Her brother, Tony, the state treasurer, he knew fairly well.

She handed him the book. Over a hundred pages. Several entries on each page; for each a picture of a woman in a habit and short description. Women's religious orders as they had existed in the United States of America in—he flipped to the front—the 1950s. A half century before the Ring of Fire occurred. The three women sat quietly while he looked at it.

Finally, Miss Adducci spoke. "I entered the Daughters of Charity founded by Vincent de Paul when I was twenty years old; I left, not because of any scandal, when I was thirty-three."

She had not said, "Saint Vincent de Paul." Did she think that Larry Mazzare would not have shared the original name of Grantville's parish with his assistants?

Her next question confused him. "Have you read any of Simon Jones' detective stories?" He assured her that he had read several.

"There was—is—a series that I love. An elderly nun who was a detective. Sister Mary Theresa Dempsey. I can lend you a couple of the books, if you might possibly have time to read them. I mostly borrowed them from the library, when I was working in Pittsburgh, but I bought a few in paperback that the library never got in."

Kircher noted the wryness of her smile. She was continuing. "There was one young nun in that house, among the elderly women. In one book of the series, she remarked that when she entered the order, one of her relatives had commented that she was 'climbing aboard a sinking ship.' The women's religious orders in the United States were a sinking ship. It happened in a half century, between when that was published"—she gestured at the book in his hand—"and the time the Ring of Fire happened."

He maintained his silence. After a pause, she continued.

"Do you want to know why?"

He nodded.

"I can't answer for everyone. In part, probably, it was that there were other opportunities—the same reason that fewer women were going into elementary school teaching and nursing. But. I entered the order wanting to give a hundred percent of what I was capable, or more. By the early 1980s, though, so few young women were entering that the superiors seemed to be afraid of frightening them away. They never seemed to require more than eighty-five percent. Oh, I might have found it somewhere else. I could have asked for a transfer. In Calcutta, I am sure, Mother Teresa could have found a sufficiently strenuous job for me. But I was American; it was selfish, perhaps, but I didn't want to go so far from my family. So, what did I do? I left the order and went into social work. In social work, I assure you, Father Kircher, a person can give more than a hundred ten percent for a lifetime and still see a gaping black hole of unmet needs before her."

Kircher wondered idly what a "black hole" might be. A pit, perhaps? An abyss? Miss Adducci appeared to have said all that she intended to say. Miss Mastroianni gestured, an understandable request for permission to speak. He had noticed that many of his students used the same one and she was a teacher, a woman about thirty. He nodded.

"We've never had a house of sisters in Grantville, Father Kircher. The town could use one, now. Not the kind you're used to; women enclosed inside walls. Not contemplative. The active kind that Bernadette is talking about. All we're asking is that you think about it. If you could look at the book—see what sisters did? There's so much that we could do."

Kircher's fingers met one another. He placed his chin on them. "And the three of you are doing nothing now?"

One of the other women rose. Miss Constantinault; just appointed the chief of staff of the state court system for all of the state of Thuringia-Franconia, trained as an administrator and, to some limited extent, in the law. She looked at him sharply and said, "Not as a group—not as a unit. And not," she pointed to the "AMDG" motto on the wall of his office, "to the greater glory of God. That's why I came along. Because that is why we should be doing things."

"I will," he heard himself saying, "look at your book. Carefully."

The three women rose. "We know that you have a lot to do today," Bernadette Adducci said. "That is all we ask. Shall we plan to meet again after Easter?"

✧   ✧   ✧

"There is no reason why I should not go now. There are many reasons that I should go now." Veronica Dreeson looked at her husband. Not mulishly. She did not want to look stubborn. She wished to look calmly determined. She wanted an expression of serene dignity. Her prematurely wizened face strained with the effort of assuming one.

All her life, at need, Veronica Schusterin, *verw.* Richter, *verh.* Dreeson, had been willing to argue with others when it was needed. Last fall, in Magdeburg, the abbess of Quedlinburg's approach to life had struck her as a blinding revelation—the elegance of it. The abbess almost never argued with anyone, because she simply assumed that no one would contradict her wishes and acted upon that assumption. Even amid the sorrow of her grandson Hans' death, Veronica had filed away in her mind the general usefulness of this approach to getting one's own way. If one could manage it.

Another tactic. "I have a letter of recommendation from the king of Sweden himself. Or," she added conscientiously, "at least one with his signature on it, though that may have been added by one of his secretaries. It introduces me to his regent in the Upper Palatinate. It requests him to assist me in obtaining a resolution of our just claims to Johann Stephan's property. So, clearly, I should go while the regent whom he named is still holding the office."

Then, to clinch the deal, she added, "We need the money." She sat quietly. Henry could not argue with that.

Henry was doing what he called "cogitating." Ronnie let him cogitate. He knew the truth as well as she did. His salary as mayor was not large; before the Ring of Fire, when it had been only what they called a "part time" job, his salary had not existed at all. He once had a pension, a *Social Security*; it was gone. Fortunately he had saved money for his retirement; like any city councilman down-time, his civic service had been premised on having sufficient income to "get away from the office" and serve the public good.

The savings had come through the Ring of Fire, but they were gone. Oh, if there had been only the two of them, with his salary, her business, and the little coming in here and there from the real estate, there would have been plenty.

There were far more than two of them. Gretchen, amazingly

enough, was famous now. But fame, especially fame gained by giving speeches urging other people to revolt against their superiors, did not pay many bills. At the beginning, Jeff and his friends had helped. But Jeff, Gretchen, and, presumably, Jeff's pay from the army, were now in Amsterdam, far away in the Netherlands. If Jeff's pay was not arriving in Amsterdam *via* letter of credit, Veronica did not have the slightest idea how the two of them were paying for their food, and rooms, and replacing shoes that wore out, and all the other necessities that came with prolonged travel, but it wasn't something that she could do anything about.

Jimmy was in Amsterdam too, presumably with his pay also arriving there. Eddie was a captive in Denmark; she didn't know where his pay was. Not in the Dreesons' bank account, certainly. She hoped that the navy bookkeepers in Magdeburg were saving it for him. Larry and Hans—she blinked quickly—had died bravely. But they weren't being paid any more. Neither of them had had legal dependents.

The other children, from Annalise on down, were still in school. She felt her face tightening into a slightly grimmer expression, in spite of her efforts to remain tranquil. What was more, Annalise would *stay* in school. Annalise, no matter how much she protested the matter, was going to college. She *would* be a member of the first class of the new women's college at Quedlinburg. And her grandmother would, somewhere, find the money to pay for it. Veronica had learned a lot, these last months, about the cost of *tuition* at such a school for the daughters of the elite and wealthy, the patricians, the great merchants, and the nobles. It was only reasonable that her dead husband Johann Stephan's property, if anything were left of it, should pay for his granddaughter's education.

The question of who would pay for the education of the other children as they grew older, and how, could rest for the moment. If Gretchen and Jeff returned from Amsterdam—that was an *if*; she would not delude herself that it was no more than a *when*—then she could give that problem back to them. If they did not return . . .

She looked across the room at Henry. He shifted in his chair. His hip was bothering him again, she could tell. If Gretchen and Jeff did not return, she hoped that the schools would be doing very, very well in another ten years. She would need every *Pfennig* of the income from her business.

Veronica leaned over the side of her arm chair, reaching into her widely recognized tote bag. *Come to Mardi Gras in New Orleans*, it proclaimed, with a large picture of a harlequin in costume. "I have an answer from the lawyer to whom I wrote earlier. It is going to be complicated. I want to retrieve anything that I can. I want to ensure that whatever is sold is sold for the maximum price. At least, for the most I can get. The economy is recovering very slowly south of the Thueringerwald. After all, Henry, it is peaceful there now. It is likely to remain peaceful there throughout the summer. Everyone says that this year's action will be to the north. In the Baltic. Where the king of Sweden is."

Magdeburg

"We *will* open the normal school next fall." Mary Simpson, sitting in the conference room of the Magdeburg offices of the Leek family's new down-time IBM corporation (manual typewriters and mechanical adding machines), put only the slightest emphasis on the word "will." "Teacher training is a project that we just have to get started."

Vanessa Clements nodded; so did Livvie Nielsen. Carol Ann Washaw, who was trying to acquire a library for the project, looked more doubtful. She was universally addressed as "Tiny" by the Grantvillers, a nickname which derived not from her present comfortable girth but rather from the size of the preemie she had been back in 1934.

"There isn't any money to open the normal school next fall." Carolyn Rush, Ben Leek's daughter and office manager, shook her head. Carolyn brought a lot of perspective to this project—fifteen years as an administrative aide in the Marion County public school system on top of an undergraduate degree in American history. "Normal schools just aren't glamorous. You can excite the upper nobility and rich merchants about opera, about ballet, libraries, even about these new women's colleges at the *Damenstifte*. Those have eye appeal. What's the prospect of getting them excited about re-treading hundreds or thousands of middle-aged widows and one-legged or one-armed soldiers into grade school teachers? Zilch."

Mary Simpson shook her head. "There are some. I just need to talk to the right ones. Preferably, in person. Look, Carolyn, you have been working on this long enough now to have gotten over the idea that all of the down-time wealthy get their kicks out of being oppressors of the oppressed."

"I still don't think that we're going to get money for this one, Mary. Definitely not any tax money." Carolyn shook her head. "Even a lot of the people back home in Grantville think that it's the wrong way to handle the problem. Once we get past the crunch of these first few years, they're thinking of college-age kids; of full university educations, like the medical school in Jena. A lot of them *lived* through the years when the school reformers forced women who just had the two-year normal school degree out of the system. There are women in Grantville who *were* forced out of the system that way. They see it as a step backwards; not just gearing down, but giving up and saying that we're not going to make it; admitting that we really won't be able to make this work."

Vanessa spoke up. "It's not, really, a lot different than the teacher training program they're starting at the middle school, now that they've finally faced up to the fact that their existing teachers aren't immortal and they'd better start getting some new ones into the pipeline."

"Notice that they aren't calling it a normal school. There's a lot in a name," Tiny answered.

"Well, then." Mary smiled sweetly. "Think of another name. That's the next assignment for the marketing department. That's you, Livvie. Community college; teachers' college. Pick it. Just make sure that the curriculum stays aimed at turning out grade school teachers, K–8. And plan to open on a shoestring. Get Otto Gericke to let you use any unfilled space in the new building for the Magdeburg *Gymnasium* next year. Admit more people than he gives you space for, to show that the demand is there. While you do that, I'm going to find some money. Real money."

"Where do you intend to get it?" Carolyn raised her eyebrows.

Mary smiled. "From the Wettins; or, at least, through the Wettins, since it appears that we can't get it from parliament. Through the right Wettins. I've been talking to Wilhelm Wettin's uncle, Duke Ludwig of Anhalt-Köthen. He's been very much involved with education reform projects for twenty years or more. Some of them went all the way up to the *Reichstag*, the Imperial Diet."

"And he," Carolyn pointed out, "couldn't ever get any money appropriated for them, either."

"He says that Wilhelm might be some help, at least with the publicity. The two of them can get the members of their *Fruchtbringende Gesellschaft*—in spite of 'by their fruits ye shall know them,' why does a name like "Fruit-bearing Society" strike me as hopelessly absurd?—to write letters and poems and such. Newspaper articles. Create a favorable attitude among the intellectual elite." Mary Simpson was not easily swayed.

"Intellectual elites are not noted for having large amounts of excess capital to donate to worthy causes." Carolyn smiled, but it didn't take the sting out of her words.

"They're tutors to the children of people with excess capital; private secretaries to people with excess capital. Atmosphere helps, too. It will contribute to creating the *milieu* in which the normal school becomes a charity with eye appeal."

"Let's create a *milieu* in which we have enough money to pay the faculty their first month's wages." Carolyn had a relentless sense of the practical.

Mary pulled another letter out of her purse. "Yes, let's. I just heard from Veronica Dreeson. This summer, she is going to the Upper Palatinate to try to retrieve anything that she can from her first husband's estate. The regent there, Duke Ernst, is Wilhelm Wettin's brother. Everything that I've been able to find out about him says pretty much one thing. For all his life long, the slightest whiff of chalk dust acted on him like the aroma of Chanel No. 5. He was attracted to proposals for educational reform the way moths are attracted by mating pheromones."

"Let me guess," Carolyn said. "Ronnie Dreeson is afraid that if she goes on this trip by herself, Duke Ernst will want to keep her in Amberg to discuss early childhood education rather than letting her get on with the project of getting her money back. She has invited you to come along and talk schools."

"Precisely. And I'm going. I told my husband John that there's absolutely no reason to expect any problems. Everybody says that the action this year will be to the north, against the League of Ostend."

Grantville

There wasn't any more chaos or racket than was customary in a grade school, but it was seven o'clock in the evening rather than the middle of the day. Keith Pilcher paused in the corridor. There were tutoring sessions in the library; after-care in the gym, and some group was holding a meeting in the cafeteria. There were third-quarter parent-teacher conferences going on in some of the classrooms; in the art room, there were high school girls conducting craft projects for the children whose parents had to bring them along to the conferences because they couldn't find, or couldn't afford, sitters. There were no pipe cleaners; no one was manufacturing crayons yet; but the paper mill in Badenburg now collected the water with which the Stones' dye works cleaned out its pots. Colored construction paper had made a comeback and there was plenty of glue.

Maxine's classroom was at the far end. She had left for school before dawn this morning; he had dropped the kids off on his way to work an hour later. Now she was leading a whole squadron of middle-aged German women in . . . "You put your *left* foot *in*, you put your *left* foot *out*, you put your *left* foot *in* and then you *shake* it all about." Traditional methods of teaching foreign languages had been sacrificed to Grantville's acute need. People learned to speak English painfully slowly when presented with books and rules; they learned English, at least enough to function on a daily basis, remarkably fast when put through nursery rhymes, simple songs, children's games, and other group activities in which any one person's occasional mistakes were neither apparent nor humiliating. "And that's what it's all *about*." Maxine finished dancing the hokey-pokey, saw Keith at the door, tossed her shocking pink plastic whistle to Dionne Huffman, and said, "take it from here."

Dionne looked like she still had enough energy to keep going for a couple more hours. She washed the whistle with soap and water at the sink, shook off the excess, said, "All right, everybody," and popped it into her mouth. Its shriek quieted the room. "I'm a little *teapot* . . ." The class was back into shape in less than five minutes.

Keith shook his head as he draped his arm around Maxine's shoulder. Unlike Dionne, he thought, his wife looked worn out. They passed through after-care, collected Megan and Joshua, and headed for home. He had stopped at Cora's to pick up something for supper; starting to cook a meal "from scratch" at eight in the evening was not a bright idea when people had to be up by five or six the next morning. Cora was into creative cooking again, but at least it wasn't zucchini quesadillas. It was some kind of whole-grain barley salad with bits and pieces of vegetables in it, marinaded in oil and vinegar. Weird; not bad, though, with the rye bread from the bakery. Cora's results varied.

The kids went to bed right after supper. They got their homework done in after-care, these days. Keith cleared off the dishes; there were rarely any leftovers to worry about. Maxine was still sitting at the table; he walked up behind her and she lifted her head, resting it against the buckle of his belt. He looked down. Maxine had hated it when her favorite "autumn copper" hair coloring had run out and she had discovered that the hair under it wasn't just the plain mousy brown that it had been when she started using the tint back in high school, but had gone at least half gray. Keith didn't mind; he thought that Max looked fine this way. Thelma had given it a cut that was sort of short and perky. That was the best that he could describe it. She was too skinny, though. She'd always been thin, but now she was way too thin. Probably because she danced the hokey-pokey with German housewives for three hours after school every day. She didn't need what was coming next.

"Max," he said. "Ollie's sending me on that trip."

She turned, buried her face in his stomach, and moaned.

"Hey, honey, it's to your credit, 'cause you made me go and sing German nursery rhymes night after night."

Maxine moaned again.

"We've got to have more iron. We've got to. For guns; for rail; for all the other stuff that will help us hold against the League of Ostend. Every machine shop, up-time and down-time, needs more steel than it's getting, and it doesn't matter how much steel-producing capacity we build up unless we have the raw material for the mills. The mines around here are producing just about as much ore as they can, as fast as they can, with the technology we've been able to give them so far. We've got to get some of the old mines that were destroyed in the war back into production, and that means the Upper Palatinate. That's where the next nearest chance to get our hands on more iron is. At least, the nearest that's pretty securely inside the USE."

Maxine squeezed her arms around his substantial waistline.

"Come on, honey. It's just a business trip. We have a lot of stuff to offer them. Pumps and stationary steam engines to run the pumps. A bit of explosive to open the closed shafts. Improved rail design for the carts, to bring it out faster. I won't be running into any trouble."

Ed Piazza started for home, saw who was on the bench outside his office, and grinned. "Leopold. I didn't know that you were in town."

"I wasn't until this afternoon," Leopold Cavriani answered, leaping up to shake hands. "Be flattered; this is my second stop. The first was to entrust my oldest daughter to the Reverend Wiley and his wife. Idelette is almost seventeen, now. This spring and summer, she will learn your language and ways; the next two years, she will go to school. Then, if all is well, she will train in the office of a businessman. Probably with Count August von Sommersburg's factor. The count has a permanent office here in Grantville, now. His factor has been among you Grantvillers long enough that he is willing to have a daughter of a business partner as one of his apprentices. At least, he says so now. If he does not say so then, why, we shall be flexible." He grinned himself.

Flexible. Flexible could be the Cavriani motto, Ed mused. Aloud, he asked, "So what is our friend the noble concrete bandit up to now?" Sommersburg was not only making a mint from the slate quarries that he owned on the Schwarza river above Grantville, but was also up to his neck in cement, concrete, and related construction projects in Magdeburg.

"Diversification," said Cavriani happily. "Quite a lovely word. I like it almost as much as 'facilitator.'"

"Diversification into . . . ?"

"Mining," said Cavriani. "Mines involve moving so much rock, you know. The count is financing one of your entrepreneurs in an effort to obtain more iron supplies from the Upper Palatinate. That will involve a lot of rock, of course. The count hopes to develop ways in which to make a profit from the by-products of a mining enterprise. By-products that the miners themselves find uninteresting. Waste products."

"'Waste' products that down-time miners find uninteresting, but that might, just possibly, find a market in up-time technology."

"Possibly, just possibly."

"Well," Ed said, "come on home with me for dinner. I'm sure Annabelle can find something extra to put on the table."

As they went down the stairs, Ed asked casually, "Which entrepreneur?"

"Ollie Reardon. He is far too busy to go to the Upper Palatinate himself, of course. He will be sending one of his trusted co-workers. A man named Keith Pilcher. I haven't met him yet. I'm looking forward to the trip. We will be stopping in Nürnberg to pick up my son Marc. He is coming with us. This should be an excellent chance to give him his first real experience in negotiations. A routine matter, to be sure, but he will have a chance to meet some influential people, both up-time and down-time. And the Upper Palatinate seems to be settling down very nicely under Duke Ernst. He can get a first-hand view of how rapidly we can hope for economic reconstruction to proceed once a region is no longer a war zone."

"Bernadette," Maxine Pilcher asked, cornering the juvenile officer in a booth at Cora's during lunch. "What is this all about?"

Bernadette looked at the newspaper. Maxine's attention was fixed on a legal notice which stated that Mrs. Veronica Dreeson had appeared before Judge Maurice Tito with a petition for the legal emancipation of her granddaughter, Miss Anna Elisabetha Richter.

"What is that woman up to now?"

"Don't hope for scandal," Bernadette answered. Grantville had been considerably enlivened for the past three years by occasional flare-ups when the divergent educational philosophies of Ronnie Dreeson and Maxine Pilcher came into conflict. "It's no Hardesty-type case. I'd call it a bit risky, but it's perfectly prosaic and she probably knows the girl better than anyone else does. Annalise is going to be running the St. Veronica's schools this spring and summer."

"Annalise is what? Seventeen?"

"She just had her seventeenth birthday. Last week, in fact. Ronnie petitioned to have her emancipated so that she can make binding contracts. And she's providing Annalise with a full power-of-attorney to handle all of her affairs while she's gone."

"Gone where? And why not Henry?"

"As they headed out of the courtroom after Maurice granted the petition, I heard Ronnie say, 'ask Henry if you have any questions, but remember that he's a very busy man, so don't bother him unless you have to.' Which is, I presume, why Henry isn't being stuck with the schools. On top of everything else that he has to do."

"But," Maxine asked, "where is Ronnie going? For so long, anyway? I know that she travels around to visit her 'schools.' They're springing up all over the place, like mushrooms." She grimaced. "Or toadstools." She grinned. "Toad-schools. But she could visit them all and still come back to town, in between. Magdeburg is the farthest away."

"She'll be gone *much* longer this time. Not day trips, not week trips. She's heading off to the Upper Palatinate to see whether she can get anything from her first husband's estate. There are a whole batch of Grantville people with business there this spring, plus the Voice of America is sending back a batch of newly trained down-time radio operators to Duke Ernst, and Mary Simpson is going. There's no reason to expect any trouble, of course, but Admiral Simpson and Mayor Dreeson apparently thought that it would be better for the ladies to travel with some military escort. And, of course, Ollie was just as happy to include..."

Bernadette had been about to add, "Keith and Mr. Cavriani." And to ask, "hasn't Keith mentioned it to you?"

Clearly, he hadn't. Bernadette realized why.

"Ooooooh, nooooooo," Maxine howled. "Keith is *not* traveling with *that woman*."

CHAPTER 10

Bella Gerant Alii

Magdeburg

"What we need, Prime Minister," Landgrave Hermann of Hesse-Rotenburg began the morning briefing, "is to send someone to Basel. Margrave Georg of Baden-Durlach's son Friedrich is running the government-in-exile there. He requests an envoy from the USE."

"Surely," said Mike Stearns, "this didn't need to come to me. Send him an envoy."

"He specifically requests that the envoy be an up-timer. His father saw, for himself, some of the up-timers at the Rudolstadt Colloquy. The son now wants to see an up-timer, or more than one, perhaps, for himself."

"Remind me why this is worth our while. We don't really have enough up-timers, or at least not enough who can find their way through the protocol of a down-time court, to waste them on the vanity of every minor princeling in Europe."

Hermann gestured at Philipp Sattler, their expert on Germany south of the Main. Which was not quite the same world as Germany north of the Main.

"The location of Baden-Durlach is strategically important for General Horn's campaigns in Swabia. Basel itself is important because . . ."

Sattler's lengthy, accurate, important, and dull assessment of the importance of Baden-Durlach and Basel droned on for quite some time. Finally it ended.

"Let me think about it," Mike said. "What else?"

"There is little else of significance that I see in today's pouch," Landgrave Hermann said. "There is an official announcement of the planned Austro-Bavarian marriage; that was expected enough, and should not change any alignments."

"Frank," Mike said at dinner that evening. "It's driving me nuts. We absolutely do not have a single up-timer we can spare to soothe the vanity of this guy. But we have to find someone. Someone whose rank won't insult him."

"Yes," said Diane Jackson. "Yes, you have someone. Like you sent Becky, like you sent Rita. Because these *dinosaurs* see them as related to someone important. I don't need to be here. When do I see Frank? While he is awake? One hour of the day, perhaps twice in the week? French I do speak. The man expects something strange, probably. How is *he* to know that the rest of you aren't Vietnamese?"

"Diane!" Frank exploded.

"It is true," she answered stubbornly. "You do not need me. In Grantville, I was helping. Here, there are plenty of secretaries to read the letters you get in French. I am," she said firmly, "a fifth wheel. Use me. All you have to do is write out what I should say. I can say it for you."

"Diane," Mike started. "It's just that we don't want to send you into that mess down in Swabia. The front between Horn and Bernhard has been awfully fluid; for nearly two years now, between them, they've been turning the countryside into a wasteland. It's a sideshow, I suppose, to the Baltic, but for somebody in it, it's a damned dangerous sideshow."

"You think," Diane asked, "that I have not seen dangerous?"

Mike and Frank looked at one another. Finally, "Who could we send with her?" Mike asked.

"Tony Adducci—young Tony, that is. That will be another appeasement to their damned rank-consciousness, considering that his father is secretary of the treasury for the State of Thuringia-Franconia. With an up-time radio, since that's his MOS. No radio, no go," Frank said firmly. "And a full company of down-time bodyguards, at least. If things blow up in Swabia, we're pulling you out of there, Diane." Frank reached across the table and took her hand. "I need you more than Bernhard of Saxe-Weimar or Turenne does. Even if you have only been seeing me a couple of hours a week while I'm awake."

Diane blushed.

Officially, Ed Piazza was in Magdeburg for a meeting of Parliament. As a head of one of the component states of the USE, he had a seat in the upper house, and would until they got around to adopting a constitution that provided some other form of representation. He could hardly wait for the elections.

Even though Mike might lose them. Wilhelm Wettin wouldn't be all that bad. Though, of course, Ed thought, grinning as he looked at the decor in the prime minister's office, it would require some redecoration. The incredible paintings of Stearns with Gustavus would be shipped to some outer corridor if Wettin moved into this room.

Mike, who had no qualms whatsoever about maintaining a "kitchen cabinet" with which he felt comfortable alongside his official set of appointees, had set apart two hours.

After providing Mike with a rundown on everything that he had heard from Venice, a lot of it along backchannels, Ed paused. Then, "There's a lot of the Italian peninsula beyond Venice, you know."

Mike nodded.

"Some of it's Spanish."

Mike nodded.

Ed continued. "I don't want to pry, but the general rumor is that you have something bubbling away that involves the cardinal-infante in the Spanish Netherlands. Nothing specific, of course."

"Can I nod to half of that? Agreeing only that there is a general rumor to that effect," Mike asked.

"Certainly." Ed suddenly looked a little more serious. "Would you be interested in background on some possible developments—not certain ones, by any means—that might soon drive a wedge, at least temporarily, between the papacy and Spain and, perhaps, provide Urban VIII with a little more room to maneuver?"

"Rumors, of course," Mike said.

"Rumors, certainly," Ed agreed. "Let's start with Naples."

Mike could make one very definite statement. "Naples is a

long, long, way from here; the USE hasn't been doing anything in Naples at all."

"That doesn't mean that things aren't happening in Naples that may have an impact on the USE. It's not the good old butterfly effect, again. Call it the 'spaghetti effect,' if you want to think of it that way. You have a pot of water on the stove, simmering away. Drop in one strand of spaghetti—just one—and all of a sudden the pot boils over in a roiling upsurge and you have a mess all over the top of your stove. Sorry, Mike, but we've dropped in the spaghetti, whether we meant to or not."

"So tell me, what is going on."

"First, there's the actual piece of spaghetti, in the form of the *Encyclopedia Britannica* article about the Portuguese revolt of 1640. I know definitely that at least one copy of that is floating around in Naples. Probably more."

"Definitely?" Mike raised his eyebrows.

"From Leopold Cavriani. Definitely."

"Why is it causing trouble in Naples instead of Portugal?"

"'Instead' probably isn't the right word. Perhaps, 'as well as,' but I don't have anything current on Portugal," Ed answered. "In that world, the world that wrote the encyclopedia, the duke of Osuna—the third one—who was stirring up trouble in Naples died in 1624 and his son, the fourth duke, didn't follow up. In this time, however . . ."

Mike raised his eyebrows. "Yes."

"Would it give you a clue if I said that the fourth duke's mother is a granddaughter of Hernan Cortes?"

"The Mexico Cortes? Implying a certain inherited adventurousness?"

"Yes, that Cortes. Anyway, through his paternal grandmother, this Osuna the Fourth is also a cousin of João of Braganza—the man who will end up on the throne of Portugal six years from now if things go the same way here that they did in our old world. Osuna's somehow gotten hold of the article."

"Heaven forbid," said Mike, "that our friend Leopold should have put a copy in the mail when he was in Grantville last year."

"Heaven forbid," Ed agreed piously. "Anyhow, he's apparently thinking, 'If João can do it, why can't I? King of the Two Sicilies? Now that has a nice ring to it.' The Spanish aren't happy, as you can imagine."

"Ed, where *do* you dig up all these connections?"

"Count Ludwig Guenther's librarian, mostly—royal genealogies are his hobby. With some assistance from Cavriani."

"Okay. That explains a lot. Is this project of Osuna's going anywhere?"

"It probably wouldn't by itself, but when it's combined with all the other factors, it could. Conditions in Naples—not just the city but the whole Spanish viceroyalty—have been wretched for years. Antonio Alvarez de Toledo was there from 1622 to 1629 and actually tried to do something, but the crisis, both commercial and monetary, has kept rolling merrily along. His successor, the duke of Alcala, has taken some measures to try to solve the problem of grain supplies and storage for the city itself. That's been popular enough. However, there have been a series of bad harvests. The famine situation is pretty grim."

Ed grinned suddenly. "But they've recently invented a mechanical pasta machine that is about to make the cost of spaghetti, ziti, and many of the other staffs of life affordable to the average man. SoTF has sent formal enquiries about opening trade relations."

Mike frowned a little. "Now that we have the USE rather than the CPE, a union rather than a confederation, what is the State of Thuringia-Franconia doing conducting its own foreign policy?"

"Foreign policy?" Ed gestured. "Heaven forbid, once more, I assure you. Just a modest venture into a mutually profitable field of economic development. No different at all from the trade relations that we are opening with Genoa. Until such time as the USE adopts a constitution that specifically says we can't, we can."

"Spaghetti diplomacy," Mike groaned. Then, "Why Genoa?"

"Jeans," answered Ed. "Everybody's jeans are wearing out. Genoese sailors wear work pants made of cotton denim. Obviously—"

"I don't," said Mike, "even want to know about this. Really."

"All right, then. Back to Naples. We've covered Osuna, so that brings us to the second guy: Dom Giulio Genoino. He's a priest—a scholar, a political theorist. And, I think, a lawyer. I figure that he's about seventy years old, but he's going strong. He has interesting ideas about equity in taxation. He's been in jail for his ideas, which include wanting the voice of the people on the city council to be equal to that of the patricians. Even without the Committees of Correspondence, there's a lot of agitation going on there. The question is whether it will just be one more rebellion—people rioting, attacking the prisons, attacking the armories, lynching a few unpopular persons, and then being put down by the Spanish military. Or if something actually comes of it . . . Which it might, if Genoino somehow links his people up with Osuna the Fourth. Anyway, that's part of why the Spanish and the Curia aren't exactly on speaking terms at the moment, because for various reasons, Urban VIII isn't doing anything firm to oppose Osuna the Fourth."

"Why not?"

"I honestly don't know. Then, thirdly, there are the Albanians."

"What are Albanians doing in Naples?"

"They've been there for a hundred fifty years, at least—exiles."

Mike groaned. "Don't tell me about it, please don't. Is there any spot on the map of Europe that isn't harboring exiles from somewhere else?"

"The short answer is, 'No.' Shall I proceed?"

"Yes. But I don't want to hear it."

"Scanderbeg. Famous Albanian hero. His son turned the Albanians' holdout against the Ottomans over to Venice in 1474. Venice turned around and sold it to the Turks. The Albanian nobility took off for refuge in Naples. Some of them, like the Arianiti family, have been very prominent in the Imperial diplomatic service; others have burrowed in. The Kastriotes heiress married into the Orsini, for example, which pulls a whole complex of the Italian nobility into having interest in what the Albanians do. Anyway, the Albanians have decided that this would be a wonderful time to try to get Skopje back, and they're throwing almost all of their resources into mounting a flotilla. Think Cubans in Miami. If it goes out, we'll have a Balkan crisis on our hands, of course."

"We don't need a Balkan crisis," Mike protested.

"You can't avoid having a Balkan crisis," Ed answered quite serenely. "Cavriani tells me that this falls under the rubric of predestation. There is always a Balkan crisis. If we had arrived five hundred years ago, there would have been a Balkan crisis. If we had been thrown five hundred years into the future, there would have been a Balkan crisis, too. It's a given. So, think about what this means."

"It means that there will be a lot of small boats in the Adriatic Sea."

"At the most elementary level, true. But factor in the word, 'crusade.' For the guys down at the Curia, 'crusade' has the same ring as 'The South will rise again' for the Sons of the Confederacy. It causes emotional reactions in the most improbable sort of people. Think of Pius II, for goodness sake! Aeneas Scipio Piccolomini, the ultimate secular humanist—say 'crusade' and he started to drool. If the curia doesn't excommunicate Osuna or take some kind of action that could give his more wavering supporters a religiously acceptable excuse to leave his camp, the Spanish will have to focus mainly on him, which means that the Albanians will have enough wiggle room to launch their little fleet."

Mike winced. "It doesn't make sense."

"No, it doesn't make sense. Some things don't, but that doesn't make them any the less real."

"We don't need a crusade on top of everything else," Mike protested.

"It will," Ed answered cautiously, "be a small one. I think."

"How is Cavriani involved with the crusade?"

Ed's answer came as something of a relief. "Not at all, I think. He is, after all, a Calvinist. They're having the crusade on their own. Next."

"More?"

"More," Ed agreed cheerfully. "Now, to move on to the fourth factor, there's Tommaso Campanella. He finally—or, at least, in combination with Dom Genoino—probably gets us to what the Cavrianis are messing about with."

"Who's he? Campanella, I mean. Never heard of him."

"Well, Campanella's a Dominican. He has been for the past fifty years or so. He's a philosopher. He's probably a heretic. At least, the Inquisition has been trying him for heresy of one form or another for the last forty years. You will note, however, that he's still alive to cause trouble. If nothing else, the man has a genius for attracting influential supporters, climbing right up the ladder from local feudal lords in Naples to the Orsini again to the Medici Grand Duke of Tuscany in Florence to Maximilian of Bavaria to the Austrian Habsburgs—the late Rudolf and our beloved Ferdinand II both. At this point in our old world, up-time, he was in Paris under Richelieu's protection."

"Richelieu. All we need is Richelieu. Why is Richelieu supporting a Neapolitan heretic?"

"Supporting is the exact word for it, at the moment. Richelieu is paying Campanella's bills. I think you'll enjoy the reason, but I'm not quite ready to get to it yet. I need to run through some other stuff, first. Unlike Galileo, it isn't Campanella's natural history that has kept him in hot water with the Inquisition. He started thinking about political theory. He wrote things about the authority of the Catholic church. He wrote things about the role of the Spanish monarchy in Italy. He developed all sorts of plans for reforming society. Starting in 1599, he got involved in political conspiracies in Calabria. That's the general area outside the city of Naples itself. This landed him in prison for thirty years, but it didn't keep him from writing. What's more, he got involved with Osuna the Third. Remember Osuna the Third?"

"It was inevitable, I suppose," Mike said.

"Well, of course—once you get to know the people," Ed agreed.

"Ed, how on earth do you keep track of all this? Starting from ground zero, so to speak?"

"It's really no different from being a high school principal—not from being a good one, at least. You have to know the cliques, the inherited animosities, the buzzwords. The main difference is that I don't have the level of personal acquaintance, now, when I'm sorting all these things out. But the *principle* is the same."

Mike groaned at the pun. Ed grinned and continued.

"Anyhow, in 1626, Campanella was moved to Rome. Urban VIII let him out of prison in 1629. Keep in mind, all this time that Campanella's been in the Inquisition's prisons, he's been living on a church pension and using the money to appeal to important politicians for support, so what did Urban have to lose?"

"Oh, no. Not the Barberinis, too!"

Ed Piazza smiled blithely. "Oh, yes. The Barberinis too. Anyway, as of 1629, Campanella got out. Then, this year, he got himself implicated in the new conspiracy in Naples. He may not actually have been involved to start with—probably wasn't—but the people doing it were certainly inspired by him. It looked like it was back to the comfortably cushioned dungeons for Tommy, but up-time the French ambassador, Noailles, helped him escape from Italy. He stayed for a few months with Peiresc and Gassendi in Aix-en-Provence, doing mathematics, and then he went to Paris under Richelieu's protection. Mike, I tell you, this guy is connected. Up-time, he was received at court by Louis XIII. Down-time, he's just in the French embassy in Rome. Every antenna that I have wiggling out of my head says that pretty soon he'll be publishing books that substitute France for the Spanish Habsburgs as playing the lead role in his grand schemes of political reform."

"Why should the Spanish Habsburgs care?"

"That brings us full circle. Campanella's supporters in Naples have apparently linked up with Osuna the Fourth. That's one thing. However, they've also linked up with simmering popular revolutionary movements in Palermo and Messina. Also with Genoino's people in Naples itself. Osuna's gotten the idea that he can display himself as the strong protector of the common man against the exploiting feudal landlords. The peasants in Bari, Puglia, all over Calabria, in the Abruzzi, the people in Salerno, seem to think the idea has something to be said for it. 'S funny, Mike, how much the history textbooks left out because they needed to arrange things in nice neat units with topic headings like, 'The Rise of Absolutism.' The bits and pieces are almost all in the encyclopedia, once I find out the names and dig them up. This crazy century is full of popular revolts, in Switzerland, in Lisbon, in Russia, in Upper Austria, all over. And just by being here, by demonstrating that one of them succeeded, we're speeding them up. They're coming faster. More spaghetti. Did I think to mention that someone in Sicily has invented the pasta press? Spaghetti's getting cheaper and more abundant, becoming the food of the people ... But I digress."

"Have the Committees of Correspondence, the CoCs, gotten that far? To Naples, I mean?"

"It's not just Gretchen's CoCs by any means. Sometimes I think that it isn't her propaganda in favor of revolutions that's having the most effect. No matter how much it may have slipped the minds of the people who wrote the textbooks, the European common people didn't need to be introduced to the idea of revolution. And their rulers know it, since the events of the 1580s and 1590s are a bit more recent in their memories than they were in ours. Gretchen and Spartacus don't really have to stir up revolutionary sentiment; it's already there. They're tapping it and molding it, but they're not creating it."

Mike nodded. "The real effect of the Committees of Correspondence is in their practical manuals on how to run a revolution effectively. It's the organizational side where modern ideas are going to make the most difference, I think."

"But, to get back to the topic. The curia doesn't want to oppose Osuna because he's distracting the Spanish from sitting on the Albanians who are going to have a crusade, so they're tacitly letting this revolutionary tie slide through. The Spanish Habsburgs have said furious things in the diplomatic correspondence. At least," Ed said primly, "that is what I am told."

"Do I dare to ask who told you?"

"I would prefer to consider it a privileged communication."

Mike waved his hand. He had heard the same thing himself, from Don Francisco Nasi. But Ed did not have Don Francisco at his disposal. Of course, there were a lot of Don Francisco's cousins in Grantville. Samantha Burka, Ed's good right hand during his tenure in the Department of International Affairs of the New United States before it became the State of Thuringia and then, since the February elections, the State of Thuringia-Franconia in the USE, had just married whom? He'd remembered to send a letter with his felicitations, he was sure. Yeah—she had married Diego Nasi.

"In any case," Ed was saying, "the distractions that Spain has in the southern part of the peninsula, just now, means that they are putting less pressure on the grand duke of Tuscany. Which may have some impact on how Urban VIII decides to handle the whole Galileo matter, though nobody can be sure."

"Galileo has a lot of public relations appeal," Mike said, "but that's out of our hands. Grantville isn't going to be involved in it, one way or the other."

"As far as we know at the moment," Ed answered.

"Ed, stop going all diplomatic and cover-your-ass on me."

"I'm holding to my position," Ed said. "But Naples, I think, is the key. The problems in Naples will also mean that the Spanish are in such a pinch that they can't divert any kind of actual force against Don Fernando up in the Netherlands if he decides to try for some kind of *appanage.* The idea of quasi-independence for the Netherlands isn't something that's going to appeal to Philip IV, or to Olivares in Philip's name, since they 'know' from our encyclopedias that they're staring comparable events in Portugal, Catalonia, and Andalucia in the face, while having one start in Naples right now. Or, at least, pretty soon. But nobody knows which way Don Fernando is going to jump. And, at least, since he's in the church, even if he did decide to carve out a piece of the pie for himself, it would escheat back to Spain eventually."

"Why," Mike asked, "do the Cavrianis care?"

"To be quite honest," Ed answered, "I don't have the vaguest idea." He drank his cold coffee.

"But at least Leopold is going off to the Upper Palatinate to try to make a profit from rocks this summer. That should keep him safely out of any immediate messes."

The next morning, when it was too late—Ed was already on his way back to Grantville—Mike said out loud over breakfast, "Wait a minute. We got distracted. Ed never got back to saying what Richelieu wants of Campanella."

He found himself juggling twenty-seven different balls that day. He forgot to make a note to ask Ed about Tommaso Campanella.

Part Three

April 1634

And lovely is the rose

CHAPTER 11

Iuventus Speratus

Grantville

"It certainly is nice that so many people came to see us off, isn't it?" Veronica Dreeson looked at the crowd with pleasure. "It is a great compliment to Henry, I am sure. And to John, of course."

Mary Simpson, already mounted, looked out over the crowd. She preferred to ride in formal costume—jodphurs, coat, and bowler—even in the seventeenth century. The Grantville tailors were by now used to getting odd orders, but this... Leonhard Kalbacher had just looked at her sketch, sighed, and gone to work with his measuring tape, thanking his lucky stars that the boots and hat were someone else's problem. Mary Simpson's stance on horseback was a tribute to what a young ladies' finishing school could achieve when it deemed a skill to be truly life-essential.

"Mostly people from the city government," she confirmed. "Some from the army; they are probably friends of the men who were being trained as radio operators for Duke Ernst. There are a couple of school classes."

Veronica leaned around Mary's shoulder for a better look. She sat on her mule with all the grace of a sack of rye draped over the back of a donkey for its final trip to the grist mill. Riding was not a skill that seventeenth-century urban women ordinarily needed. She was less than happy about the decision that the

97

group would go on horseback. Overall, she would much prefer to have walked. It wasn't so far to Amberg, after all—certainly less than two hundred of the up-time miles. She had told them that she would rather walk.

It was much too far, they said.

"I walked from Amberg coming here," she had replied, "and to many other places in between, when we were with the mercenaries."

They had tried to put her on a horse in spite of it; the mule was a compromise. True, they had offered the use of a wagon, but that would have been just as uncomfortable and even slower, not to say, more expensive. It would have been cheaper to walk. And probably, given the personality of this mule, just as fast. This was one animal that would never die of overwork.

"They are the classes that Keith Pilcher's children are in," she identified them for Mary. "And the class taught by his wife. She is the thin woman, if you haven't met her. The shorter woman next to her is Lena Buehlerin. She is married to Lambert Felser. He is a tinsmith from the Upper Palatinate. His apprenticeship was interrupted by the war. Ollie Reardon hired him. He is going with Keith, to assist him. To translate, if it is needed. They have married since they came to Grantville. Before, they did not know one another. She is from Baden-Durlach. Her first husband was a mercenary. One of those killed at Badenburg."

"Can you identify everyone in town?" Mary asked.

"Oh, no, probably not all. But because Henry is the mayor, I have come to know most, certainly. That is Mary Lou Snell. Her son Toby is with us. She is very glad that he is being sent on this duty. Because there is no fighting. She was afraid that they would send him to Swabia."

A tall boy, one of Jeff's friends, was waving from the back of the crowd. She waved back. "Off to Amberg," he yelled. "Have a nice time in your home town."

"*Ach*," she called back. "Amberg is just where we were living; where Johann Stephan had his business. My real home town is several miles beyond there. An easy day's walk, farther up into the hills."

"What's it called?"

The boy was closer now and she remembered his name. "Oh, Matt," she said. "It is just a little, tiny place. No American would ever have heard of it. It is called Grafenwöhr."

She had no idea why half of the crowd, especially the middle-aged men, broke out laughing so hard that they threw their heads back. A couple of them howled. But it was nice to have everyone in such a fine mood for the start of their trip. It was a good omen.

Veronica marked off the days of the trip; from Grantville to Badenburg to Arnstadt, that was one day; from Arnstadt to Suhl, a second. They stopped there for two nights and a day, so that the men could talk to the gun manufacturers; she had been grateful for the rest. Then the only part that might have problems, from Suhl to Coburg; through Lichtenfels to Bamberg. Franconia was uneasy; the elections were an object of concern. But, no problems; they spent the morning in Bamberg, since some of the men had business with the people in the SoTF's administrative offices there. Veronica rested. Mary wanted to go see the cathedral and a statue called the "Bamberger Reiter"; she said that they were very famous. The administrator sent two men to go with her. In the afternoon they made a very easy day to near Forchheim. The next day, even before the midday meal, Nürnberg came in sight. The road was busy all the way, full of horses, wagons, and people. After all, it was a main trade route. But none of them were fleeing, so it was quite different from what she remembered from three years ago. There were no wandering troops of mercenaries. She noticed that some of the burned villages were even being rebuilt.

Nürnberg

The bottom half of the door was closed, to keep wandering cats and dogs out of the shop, but the top half was open to the morning sun. Standing at the clerk's counter, Marc Cavriani was bouncing up and down on the balls of his feet.

Jacob Durre smiled at the boy's impatience. He had enjoyed having this one to train. He knew the family well. His own wife was a cousin of Marc's mother. The boy looked like his mother's family rather than like the Cavrianis. That meant black hair, with a curl that fell into the middle of his forehead if not strictly restrained, and the bright blue eyes of northern Italy. Marc's face was a little full, rather than thin like his father's; his nose was slightly pug rather than aquiline like his father's; his build was generally rather more square than angular. He had great endurance for such things as distance hiking, but he was never going to be a sprinter—his legs were too short.

They were expecting Leopold to arrive today. This would mark the end of Marc's two years in Nürnberg. Now, for the first time, he would be going with his father on a trading expedition, even if only a very short one, no farther than Amberg. His *père* wanted him to observe the negotiations between the up-timers and men who controlled the iron cartel. Jacob knew that Marc was looking forward to this, very much. Negotiations were a valuable skill.

"Boy," he called. "Get back to work. There is no point in going out to look. You could miss them on any street or block. Your father knows where you are. Wait. Exercise patience. If you do not, I will send you out to the mill on the Pegnitz to weigh spools of wire for the shipment going to Ulm, and you will not see him until tonight."

Marc went back to work quite cheerfully.

That was a good thing about him, Durre reflected. Marc not only worked quite hard and conscientiously, most of the time—at least as much of the time as anyone could expect from a boy of eighteen—but he also displayed irrepressible good temper while doing it, even in the face of balances that refused to be reconciled for hours and shipments that did not arrive on schedule but rather were delayed for weeks and nobody knew just where they were.

Which was just as well, because it was past the noon sun before Leopold arrived. Marc ran out into the street, Jacob following him more sedately. He kneeled properly, as a son should kneel to his father; then leaped up and kissed him on both cheeks. The two started to chatter in French; then switched to Italian; then back to French.

That evening, Leopold Cavriani sat back to assess his son.

Marc was right at the end of the bumptious stage of development, when young men have amounts of energy that are seemingly inexhaustible and utterly exhausting to everyone around them—amounts of energy they manifest by making noise, jumping up and down, digging their elbows into one another's ribs, and overturning the furniture. That would, however, be cured with time. He had been in Nürnberg, in training with Durre, a metals broker who also had considerable skills as a metallurgist, ever since he finished secondary school when he was sixteen. He was a commercial trainee, not a craft apprentice. His time had been focused on mining and metals—with specific attention to the items in those areas that could be most profitably sold to people who were tinkering with up-time technology. Instrument-makers in Augsburg, for example. Or Venetians. Or, of course, to the up-timers themselves.

"Well, Jacob," he asked over their wine. "What do you think of him?"

Durre pursed his lips. "He will take after your cousin Giuseppe, I believe, in his willingness to try almost anything that might be legal somewhere, under some interpretation of the statutes, if it appears that there might be a profit in it. He is not averse to risk."

Leopold considered this silently. He was not really surprised. Marc had the ability to charm the gold out of a miser's safe when he put his mind to it. If that could be channeled constructively, it should prove invaluable to Cavriani *Frères* in the future. If. Marc had been an irresistibly cute child—not to mention the oldest child and the only boy in a family of four sisters. But he didn't try to slide through life on that basis. Almost all of the reports from his tutors had commended him for effort. Somewhere underneath his veneer of adulthood, Leopold suspected, Marc still had the casual—not vain, but just "never needed to think about it"—assumption that, for all practical purposes, to see him was to love him. For all of Marc's life, everyone he really cared about had loved him dearly, cherished him carefully, valued him highly, instructed him conscientiously, and maybe even indulged him just a bit. But not excessively. Cavriani prided himself on that. It had been hard to resist the temptation to spoil Marc.

Durre waved his hand. "Do not worry that he will use his charm to defraud a widow out of her mite. As far as two years of observation can reasonably inform me, I am prepared to say that Marc is equipped with a conscience."

Leopold's lips quirked. "You know me all too well, Jacob."

"I've been very pleased with his conduct. Also his acquaintances. The best friend that he has made is some years his elder. The man is a Lutheran, named Georg Philipp Harsdörffer. He has ambitions to write epic poetry, but aside from that, the contact is a very good one. The family is patrician; very old and solid. He is an academic; he studied first at Altdorf; then at the University of Strassburg under Professor Matthaeus Bernegger."

Leopold considered this. It was not the custom of their family, usually, to attend a university. Only if someone didn't seem really suited for the work and the elders felt that he should be found a somewhat more sheltered vocation. Therefore Marc did not have the kind of education that would make him a natural associate for a classicist. He had fairly decent Latin from his secondary school training, but very little Greek—scarcely more than the alphabet and a memorized proverb, here and there. A would-be epic poet seemed an improbable choice of friend.

Modern languages were a different story. He had grown up speaking French and Italian, of course. These two years in Nürnberg, he had become reasonably proficient in the local Franconian dialect of High German. His *Swietzerdietsch* was fine, but in Spanish, he could barely get by. No Dutch at all, yet. Leopold had originally planned to send him to the Netherlands next, but then decided to postpone that posting until matters settled down somewhat. Marc had no English, either. England did not seem to be a good idea right now, so it would probably be Grantville. Leopold wasn't certain, though, now that Idelette was there. Commercially, the town was an exciting opportunity, to be sure. But scarcely exciting enough for him to place two children there at once.

"Harsdörffer is valuable how?" he asked.

Durre smiled. "You are looking for contacts for working with Duke Ernst?"

"Yes, of course."

"Of course. Nürnberg is also interested in seeing the mines in the Upper Palatinate return to production. The shortage of raw materials is handicapping a lot of the city's industry: many of the mills along the Regnitz and Pegnitz rivers are running at far under capacity, not because they do not have orders, but because they do not have the raw material to fill the orders. As I have said, Harsdörffer studied with Bernegger at Strassburg. As did Duke Ernst's private secretary Böcler. As did Duke Ernst's publicist Zincgref. Marc has personal letters of introduction to both of them in his hands already."

Leopold smiled cherubically; Durre smiled back.

Vienna

It was a Lenten breakfast, of course. The map of Europe might be littered with churches that had their "butter towers," built from the money that the wealthy and self-indulgent paid for dispensations to eat dairy products during Lent, but the imperial court observed the fast meticulously.

Maria Anna slowly finished her first slice of dry bread. Next to her, Cecelia Renata was eyeing a bowl of porridge without milk. No eggs. No bacon. No cheese. For six weeks, the courtiers of Vienna would eat no better than ordinary farmers. More amply, undoubtedly, than farmers would eat in times of war and high taxes, but no more luxuriously.

She glanced toward the center of the table. Papa had been to mass before breakfast. He always went to mass before breakfast, so he could take communion. He had taken only one slice of bread. In his own person, he observed Lent not only meticulously but rigorously. Until the feast of Easter arrived, he would not eat more amply than an ordinary farmer, even.

There wasn't any conversation. Mama had warned them. Papa needed peace and quiet while he read diplomatic dispatches. A courier had arrived very early this morning and his secretary had brought the most urgent ones to the breakfast room immediately.

Maria Anna took the first bite of her second slice of dry bread, chewing slowly. Hearing a sputter, she looked up. Mama was on her feet, pushing against Papa's back. His glass of water—there was never wine in his water during Lent—was tipped over on the table.

The secretary dashed forward from his position behind Papa's chair and snatched the dispatches out of the path of the spilled water. Maria Anna and Cecelia Renata both jumped up to help Mama, each taking hold of one of Papa's upper arms and supporting him as he leaned forward. The butler who served breakfast was running out of the room, screaming for help, screaming for the emperor's personal physician.

Mama kept pushing against Papa's back. He coughed and spat a chunk of unchewed bread onto his plate; then collapsed into his chair.

By the time the physician arrived, the Holy Roman Emperor had recovered, although he was still red-faced. Ferdinand II had not choked to death at breakfast. Not today.

"What happened, Mama?" Cecelia Renata asked anxiously, as soon as the footman closed the door to the empress' private apartments.

Eleonora Gonzaga sighed and dropped into the chair that Doña Mencia pushed forward for her. "Your father was so startled at some of the news in the dispatches that he strangled on his food."

"What news?" Maria Anna was standing with her arm around her sister-in-law Mariana's shoulder. "What was there that upset him so badly? Has something major gone wrong? Has the League of Ostend lost a battle?"

The empress shook her head. "In some ways, it may be worse than that."

"How could it be?"

"In the Spanish Netherlands—"

Both of the archduchesses perked up with interest.

"—we are informed that the cardinal-infante has not only been negotiating with Fredrik Hendrick—"

"Everybody knows that," Maria Anna pointed out. "At least, everybody who cares."

"—but has also held a personal meeting with Gretchen Richter," the empress finished, ignoring the interruption.

"There had been rumors of that, already, so it shouldn't have upset Papa so much to hear it again."

"This time there is more. There is a reliable report that the regent herself, Isabella Clara Eugenia, has asked that a meeting be arranged between her and this . . . young woman."

"Young agitator," Mariana said. "Young revolutionary."

"She is that," the empress agreed. "But your Tante Isabella has expressed a wish to meet her, nevertheless. According to the dispatch, she is coming to Brussels, with her husband."

"The man who torpedoed a Spanish warship and sank it?" Mariana frowned.

"Mariana was very displeased." Maria Anna crossed her arms in front of her chest and leaned against the mantel.

Cecelia Renata plopped down into the pillows on her bed.

"You can scarcely blame her," Doña Mencia replied.

"Do you have to be so reasonable?"

"It's part of my job. I note that you have just pointed out that your sister-in-law was displeased. With whom, do you think? With the young man Higgins, for destroying the ship. Or with her brother and aunt, for meeting with the destroyer's wife? Or with the wife for upsetting the political order of things, first in the Germanies and now in Amsterdam? Now that you are to be the duchess of Bavaria, you must accustom yourself to being precise in your analysis of political events."

"Mariana was probably somewhat displeased with all of those things. And very displeased by the combination of them."

Cecelia Renata stretched. "Oh, please do sit down, Doña Mencia. Your knees must be killing you. I think it would be fascinating to meet *die Richterin*."

"Papa would be unlikely to agree with you, Sissy. You're old enough to remember how much trouble the Fadinger revolt caused him, just a couple of years ago."

"Probably not. But it sounds like Tante Isabella agrees with me."

That brought the conversation to a temporary halt.

"She must be very different from Papa," Maria Anna said a few moments later. "It would be interesting to meet her." Then, shaking her head, she threw up her arms in a dramatic gesture. "What? What? Did I just agree with my sister about something?" She brought the back of one hand to her forehead. "What have I done?"

Doña Mencia smiled.

"But . . ." Maria Anna paused. "But it was the cardinal-infante, Don Fernando, who met with her first." She looked at Doña Mencia. "Did you ever meet him? What is he like?"

"I saw him quite frequently when I was at the court in Madrid. He is a clever young man. Although I have not seen him for nearly four years, I have not been . . . surprised . . . by his successes in the Netherlands."

Maria Anna hopped up onto the bed next to her sister. "Tell us more."

CHAPTER 12

Exercitium Religionis Privatum

Mary and Veronica begged off from going to church on the perfectly valid grounds that neither of them was at present of the Reformed, or Calvinist, religious persuasion. Mary wanted to go sight-seeing; Toby Snell, who was not a church member of any variety, said that he would be delighted to escort her. Veronica wanted to lie down in her room. Preferably on her stomach.

Keith decided to go with the guys. He had a vague recollection that his own denomination, the Disciples of Christ, had split off from the mainstream of Calvinism somewhere along the line, and thought it might be interesting to see the service. He didn't mind that this involved getting up at five o'clock in the morning. He got up at five o'clock every morning. By six, they were outside the gates of Nürnberg.

"I don't deny that there have been tensions," Durre was saying. "To be perfectly honest, both the Lutheran city council of Nürnberg and the relatively few Reformed whom they have accepted as citizens of the city over the past seventy-five years or so were used to Calvinists who were prosperous businessmen. Very prosperous businessmen from the Netherlands and France, for the most part; merchants, silk manufacturers, dyers, goldsmiths and bankers, other businessmen with substantial fortunes. That was what made them acceptable as citizens of a Lutheran polity." He shrugged expressively. "The city council has always been cautious, of course. It is responsible to a Catholic emperor, who could use any toleration of 'sects' not permitted by the Peace of Augsburg to deprive the city of its independence. It's not paranoia—think of what Maximilian of Bavaria did to Donauwörth on a similar pretext. So Nürnberg hasn't permitted a Calvinist congregation to be founded in the city."

"Isn't that a bit inconvenient?" Keith Pilcher asked.

"In the last century, it was a three-day trip to places in the Upper Palatinate where we could worship. Not legally, of course. And if Nürnberg's Calvinists had their children baptized by Reformed clergy in the *Oberpfalz*, they were fined."

Keith contemplated a three-day trip to church while Durre kept talking. Keith thought that the man could have probably made his fortune as a tour bus guide if he'd been born up-time.

"But that was in the last century. The last twenty years, it got easier for us. Jacob Geuder, a member of one of Nürnberg's patrician families, had a fight with the city council. He renounced his citizenship, bought a couple of little estates called Neunhof and Heroldsberg that conveyed him the status of an imperial knight, and took service with the elector Palatine. He and his wife Sabina Welser accepted the Reformed faith. Their palace, Neunhof bei Lauf, which is where we are headed, is only four hours northeast of the city. Since Geuder died, his son has maintained a Calvinist minister and held services in his palace at Heroldsberg as well. He's not home right now, however. He's serving in the Swedish army. Frau Sabina continued to host them at Neunhof as well, until she died two years ago. She was tenacious in defending the right of her 'guests from elsewhere' to take part in them, insisting that as members of the free imperial knighthood, they had the right to private exercise of religion."

Durre smiled reminiscently at his memories of Frau Sabina's tenacity. Her defense of *exercitium religionis privatum* had been a wonder to behold. Then he added, reluctantly, "Of course, it could be said that the Geuder family has been less than generous in allowing the same privilege to their Lutheran subjects. We'll be able to see the castle from just around this bend. It's still quite a long distance by road from here, though."

Keith looked up at the castle with interest. When he heard

"castle," he still thought, automatically, "pile of dank gray stone." This was a three-story house. Big, all right, but a house. The bottom floor was painted red, with the shutters trimmed with red and pink zigzag stripes; the middle floor was painted pink, with the shutters ditto; the top floor was a positive explosion of gables and *Fachwerk* beams painted red, with the stucco in between them painted pink. There was a lost commercial opportunity for Grantville right in front of him. Whoever built this place would have paid a fortune for pink plastic lawn flamingos.

In a way, he was sorry that Mrs. Simpson had missed it. If she wanted to see sights, this was certainly a sight to see.

"The city council protested, of course," Durre was continuing. "But considering that in 1609 it had entered the Protestant Union along with the Calvinist elector Palatine, its position was not as strong as it might have been. Considering that the elector's regent in Amberg was Geuder's boss. But with this business in the Upper Palatinate these last few years, things have changed. Most of the people who took exile were professionals: administrators, clergy, teachers, physicians, apothecaries. Not independently wealthy, most of them. People who gain their livelihood, primarily, through being paid by someone else. They brought some money with them, true. Most of the Palatines who had no money at all couldn't even afford to emigrate. Plus, there's a limit to the ability of other Protestant territories to absorb refugees. Bayreuth took some; so did Ansbach; a few, mostly clergy, went to Leiden. Most stayed where they were and accepted Maximilian's forced conversions. But I don't mind saying—it's been a challenge for those of us who make money to make enough of it to support the refugees who did arrive in Nürnberg until they could find some way to support themselves. Sometimes there have been four hundred or more on our charity rolls. And, because they have little money, the council has been very sparing with granting them citizenship rights, which makes it even harder for them to find work."

Durre gestured exuberantly.

"So that's where we are. Still no proper congregation with elders and presbyters in the city or its outlying villages; no minister of our own. And," he smiled, "a refreshing four-hour trip to church. Isn't it nice that it's spring?"

✧   ✧   ✧

"Herr Durre," Keith asked rather cautiously, a while later. "Did you say that the boss guy who authorizes these church services is away from home?"

"Yes."

"It looks to me like there's a bunch of bully-boys in the road who think that going to a Calvinist church is the wrong idea."

Durre looked. "Oh," he said. "That has to be Georg Seyfried Koler von Neunhof. Or his men, to be more precise. It's not likely that he's with them. He's a Lutheran, and the co-possessor of patronage rights over the churches in Beerbach and Neunhof. That means, he thinks that he ought to have the right to appoint a clergyman of his choice rather than the Geuders' appointing a clergyman of their choice. He would not dare to try this if Frau Sabina were still alive."

"Do they normally duke these things out on the public roads?" Keith asked.

"There's no duke involved here," Durre said. "What's important jurisdictionally is that these are imperial knights, directly subject to the emperor, with no intervening authority. That's why the landlord of something that looks like an estate of a few hundred acres with a small village on it can exercise the *cuius regio* principle."

"Jurisdictionally," Leopold Cavriani added, "they are independent of Grantville's administrators in Franconia. Because the knights are mostly Protestant, this region near Nürnberg was not included in the king of Sweden's assignment of authority, any more than Nürnberg itself or Ansbach and Bayreuth were."

Lambert Felser, who had garnered his English vocabulary on the floor of Ollie Reardon's machine shop rather than from literary works or books on political theory, intervened with an explanation of the alternative meaning of "duke." Once he had managed to convey the essential meaning of "duke it out," Durre averred that they did indeed "duke it out" on the roads and in the streets. Unless, of course, they had resorted to lawsuits. Normally, however, people employed both methods.

To Keith's relief, the party had paused during this discussion rather than proceeding onward toward the manor house. He noticed that the riders securing the road had already pulled a couple of wagons containing families to the side, barring them from going any farther.

However, the riders—armed riders—were now coming toward them. Durre started to move forward slowly. Like everyone else, Keith felt obliged to follow.

Except, apparently, the Cavriani kid. Rather than moving along the track—it could scarcely be dignified with the name of a road, being two ruts with grass growing between them—he kept sidling his horse a little towards the right, while holding the reins in his left hand. Not much, with any step.

Marc didn't like the idea of the families in the wagons being here. Not when two bunches of men, one that had all of them with guns and the other of which had several of them with guns, were looking at one another belligerently. As the group with Durre advanced, Marc managed to move a few feet to the side of the road. With his right hand, which Koler's oncoming men could not see because it was hanging down at his side, obscured by his body and the saddle, he made urgent scooping motions, as if he were dipping water. One of the drivers got the idea. With the guards away from the boundary stone, it was time to leave for church. What were a few more hoofbeats when a dozen mounted men were riding toward another dozen or so mounted men? The two wagons started to creep slowly forward. Slowly, at least, until they were past the border and onto the Geuder land; then their pace became quite brisk. Not to say expeditious. From the back of one, a boy turned around and waved.

Marc started side-stepping back towards the rest of the group, carefully not looking toward the departing wagons. He didn't keep a horse of his own, of course. There was no need to, in Nürnberg. This was a rental; an elderly gelding of no particular distinction who now demonstrated that he didn't like sidling to the left. He tossed his head; snorted; turned his head; tossed his head again. Marc started to control him; then realized that something could be gained from this. He assumed the nervous expression of a city man who put very little trust in even the best of horses. He also slipped his feet almost out of the stirrups, loosened his grip on the reins, and gave the stupid beast a sharp pinch with his right hand.

He landed hard. Koler's men guffawed. Rubbing his seat dramatically, Marc gestured for permission to go catch his horse. The lead rider, noting that the young idiot from Nürnberg wasn't carrying anything more threatening than a dirk, waved him on.

The horse, now that nobody was asking him to side-step to the left was just standing there, looking dumb. He was that kind of horse. Marc remounted and requested that he step to the left again. The horse demurred. Marc and the horse fussed at one another.

By this time, everyone was laughing. Except, of course, Jacob Durre and Leopold Cavriani, both of whom were just smiling with considerable satisfaction, since they knew perfectly well that the money that Marc's father had laid out for expensive riding-masters had not gone to waste. By this time, the wagons were out of sight, around a bend in the road. Marc made a demonstration of getting the nag under control and moved back toward the rest of the group by turning him around to the right and ceremoniously riding him all the way around the back of the others, wearing a chagrined expression as he did it.

Inwardly, he was much relieved that he had gotten away with it. At eighteen, he still had in some ways the mind set of the younger Marc who had gotten his growth spurt considerably later than many of his contemporaries. From thirteen to sixteen, he had found himself obliged to outwit the school bullies rather than outfight them. Oh, he had read stories, just like anyone else, in which the smaller man won the fight. The problem with those stories was that somehow, always, most conveniently, the larger man was a slow, awkward, clumsy, poorly trained oaf, while the smaller man was deft, quick, and much more skilled.

How convenient this arrangement must be for the authors! In the real world of the armsmaster's studio in which he had learned to fight, he had discovered by way of the scientific method that if one man was four inches taller and twenty pounds heavier, while both were more or less equally skilled, the smaller guy would get whomped nine times out of ten. And, based on his observations of the sad example of his classmate Franco Neri, if the smaller guy was the one of the pair who was awkward and slow, he would get whomped ninety-nine times out of a hundred.

Overall, therefore, Marc's preferred response to oncoming batches of muscle was still to evade them, if possible. He had no illusions. He had received the amount of training in personal arms that any young middle-class merchant would receive—which meant, basically, that he owned, and knew how to use, a sword and pistol as well as the dirk that he usually carried, and could probably take care of the average mugger. That was what the armsmaster had been hired to teach the students at his school, so that was what he taught them. Purveyors of copper wire and undyed fustian were rarely called upon to display more martial skill than that, nor would they have the time to maintain a higher level if they did learn it. Effective swordsmanship took a lot of continuous practice.

Marc knew perfectly well that he could not withstand a professionally trained fighter for any length of time—especially not when the fighter was wearing armor and carrying a gun. Koler's men were doing both. Marc was wearing his best doublet, suitable for a church service. He had a distinct feeling that this was not the best place to undertake heroic actions, if they could possibly be avoided.

Marc would have been surprised to learn that the sergeant in command of Koler's guards brought a rather different perspective to what he had observed. He was feeling rather glad that the kid was such a dolt; otherwise, he could have been a problem, as large and well-built as he was.

Marc wasn't given to spending much time either at the gym or looking into the mirror; his apprenticeship with Jacob Durre had kept him very busy the past two years. His only real awareness that he had changed quite a bit between sixteen and eighteen was derived from Frau Durre's constant complaints that he kept outgrowing his clothes. He hadn't thought about it much.

Not, at least, until he had gotten off his knees outside Herr Durre's shop last week and discovered that he had to lean down a bit to kiss his father's cheeks rather than going on tiptoe and reaching up to him.

Leopold Cavriani looked up the road, behind Koler's men. He cleared his throat and said, quite politely, "Excuse me, sir."

The sergeant looked at him. "We have our orders from *Ritter* Koler. We don't want trouble. Just turn around and go back to Nürnberg. That would suit us nicely. This is a local problem, between the two knights. No problem of yours. No need for you to get involved."

"We have recently come through the Catholic sections of Franconia," Cavriani remarked. "As you may have heard, there is a certain amount of unrest among the peasants, there."

He might as well have been commenting on the splendid weather.

The sergeant nodded.

"I get the impression," Cavriani continued casually, "that the unrest may be spreading into this portion of Franconia as well."

The sergeant knew better than to be tricked into looking away, but he motioned for one of his men to take a glance in the direction in which Cavriani was looking.

"About two hundred men coming, sir, at a fast guess."

Cavriani would have estimated fifty. But they did have guns, and a dozen or so were mounted. On clodhopping draft horses, but mounted, which would give them some momentum in a pinch. It wasn't as if the sergeant and his men were riding the pick of the breed, either.

The sergeant wheeled his horse with a curse.

"Damn. They're from right around here. I recognize several of them—the ones who are close enough. Odds are, I'll recognize all of them. *Ritter* Koler didn't give us any warning of this."

Durre motioned his whole party to move to the side. This wasn't their fight.

The leader of the oncoming peasants announced that they had a petition to present to *Ritter* Koler in regard to the annoyance that this silly dispute between the Lutheran and the Calvinist lords was causing the residents of the affected villages.

"I have no authority to receive such a petition," the sergeant replied.

"Don't expect that you do. Hadn't really planned to rebel today, anyway."

Cavriani caught that "today." He found it very interesting.

The farmer continued. "But the weather's nice for it. Just take us to *Ritter* Koler. Take us inside the castle. You can do that. Tell him that we've got an honest complaint that he needs to listen to. We'll give him the petition and go home, if he agrees to look at it and give us an answer next court day."

"What's your gripe, this time?"

"You are." The farmer waved at the riders. "It's a big nuisance having soldiers on the road. Another bunch have gone up to talk to Geuder's steward. All we want is for them to use a little common sense. Instead of sticking guards at the boundary stone, the Geuders should let their Lutheran subjects walk to the nearest

Lutheran church and Koler should let the Calvinists in his villages go up to the church on Geuder's land. It's Sunday, anyway. It's not as if we would be working if we didn't go to church."

He paused.

"They are our lords, but they do not control our consciences."

Leopold Cavriani smiled cherubically, fingering the toy ram he now carried in the inside pocket of his doublet.

Marc had the nervous thought that if another group of unhappy farmers was up at the Geuder's castle, he might not have done the families in the wagons much of a favor by motioning them to go on. But no—there they were, coming back down the track, none the worse for wear. The wagons plodded past the boundary unhindered. He looked at his father.

"I think," Leopold said, "that it might be excusable to skip church today." As the sergeant and the farmers argued, Durre's party turned around and followed the wagons back toward Nürnberg.

CHAPTER 13

Familia Restorata

The three women had been debating the matter for several months. Their late brother, unlike themselves and their husbands, had remained in Amberg during the Bavarian occupation. He had converted, at least nominally, to Catholicism, as had his wife and children. As had their stepmother. After the plundering of Amberg, when they never heard from any of their brother's family again, they had assumed that they were dead. And mourned.

Until the Battle of Wismar. When the newspapers reported the family and relationships of the dead hero, Hans Richter. Then they had mourned Hans again. And argued with one another, what to do.

Now, she was in the same city. Their stepmother, whom they had long thought to be dead.

"Do you think," Hanna asked, "that she will think that we come to see her now only because we, too, can claim a share of Papa's property if she gets it?"

"Why *are* we going, if not for that?" Margaretha asked. She was the oldest.

"Because our nephew and niece are suddenly famous, so we know who she is?" Clara suggested.

"Or," Hanna interjected, "because sister Elisabetha's widower, Elias Brechbuhl, is an accountant. Here in Nürnberg, he has barely eked out a living, that is true. But he knows where a lot of the Upper Palatinate's bodies are buried. Financially speaking, that is. I still think that it would be a good idea if Elias went with her. We can try to persuade her of that. Lorenz is willing that we should take Elisabetha's children, if Elias goes."

Her sisters looked at her. Once upon a time, before the war, Hanna's husband Lorenz Mossberger had served as chief clerk to an *Amtmann*. As an exile, he barely made enough to feed his children as a private notary, serving mainly the Calvinist community. His offer to take in three more children was very generous.

Margaretha looked down uncomfortably. Her second husband, a prosperous shopkeeper and Nürnberg native, would have been much better placed to make such an offer. But he hadn't made it. Nor had she suggested it to him.

As the wagons headed back towards Nürnberg, their debate continued.

Eventually, they reached consensus. This very evening, before she left the city, they would attempt to contact the woman who had once been married to their father, Johann Stephan Richter, and who was now married to the mayor of the notorious Grantville. She should at least be given the opportunity to meet her namesakes, the three little Veronicas. Only three, not four. There had been four little Veronicas once, but half of Elisabetha's children had died.

At worst, Hanna pointed out, she could only refuse to see them.

By supper time, Veronica felt considerably restored. Naps were excellent things. She joined the rest of the Grantvillers for supper in the public room of the inn. Keith Pilcher was making a good story of the day's adventures. Especially of his thoughts about plastic flamingoes.

Veronica still thought that Maxine Pilcher's philosophy of education was the height of foolishness. She was rather getting to like the woman's husband, though.

The host approached the table. "Gracious lady," he said, addressing himself to the grandmother of the famous Hans Richter. He paused, waiting for her permission to continue. He had already expressed, several times, how profoundly he was honored by having the heroic pilot's grandmother lodge at his establishment. Was he going to do it again? Veronica was on the verge of becoming annoyed.

"There are three women here who ask to speak to you. They say that they are your stepdaughters. That they live as exiles in Nürnberg."

Veronica grasped the edge of the table with both hands. She needed the support. It was never safe to hope.

"Please," she said. "Please." She was not sure whether she was addressing the petition to the innkeeper or to God. "Please ask them to come in."

CHAPTER 14

Exercitia Futilitatis

Vienna, Austria

"What can it mean, that they are undertaking this mission?" Lamormaini was not the only political advisor in Europe asking himself that question.

The news that the wife of Grantville's mayor and the wife of Gustav Adolf's up-time admiral were on their way to the Upper Palatinate had caused great consternation in many European capitals, not only Vienna. There wasn't a city in Europe in which the policymakers believed that Veronica Richter was primarily preoccupied with the needs of her own household, family, and business. It was appallingly naive of those up-timers to assert that Admiral Simpson would permit his wife Mary to undertake such a journey for the purpose of getting money to open an institution for the training of teachers for village schools.

What a manifest absurdity! It would have been utterly simple-minded of any responsible man to accept such transparently ridiculous reasons at face value. Which left, of course, the problem of deducing the *real* significance of the trip.

The only capitals where the trip received minimal attention were those of the north and west. The ladies were, after all, traveling in the opposite direction. In the dispatches from London and Copenhagen, Stockholm and Paris, it rated scarcely more than a passing mention. In those from Spain and Italy, it was barely noted.

Lamormaini himself believed that the visit by the wife of Grantville's mayor might portend a renewed attack on Bavaria, given the instability that Duke Maximilian's misguided attempt to abdicate had introduced into the political situation there. Although, in that case, it was not clear why the admiral's wife was included in the mission. Bavaria, after all, like Thuringia and the Upper Palatinate, was land-locked.

He started to cast around for alternative explanations.

"Isn't it frustrating?" Archduchess Cecelia Renata asked her older sister. "Two of the women from the up-time are going to be so close to us, really. It isn't that far from Vienna to Amberg. And yet, we won't get to see them for ourselves."

"They are scarcely zoo exhibits, imported from Asia or Africa for you to view," Doña Mencia de Mendoza said dryly.

"Your Highness," said Frau Stecher. "If you would be so kind as to raise your left arm to shoulder height."

"Well, yes." Cecelia pretended to pout as she lifted her arm. "But really, aren't you even curious?"

"It is hard not to be. Yet, really, they are not our proper concern," Doña Mencia answered.

"Thank you, Your Highness. That will be sufficient," Frau Stecher said. "Now, Archduchess Maria Anna, if you would be so kind."

"If the up-timers keep changing the world," Maria Anna commented as Susanna Allegretti helped her slip into an inside-out bodice that was bristling with pins, "they may be. Our proper concern, that is. Because we, Papa and Ferdinand, of course, Uncle Max, and whoever it may be that you marry, are the ones who must keep control of the changes, if they are not to destroy everything. So Ferdinand says. Bavaria is even closer to the Upper Palatinate. Maybe, some day . . ."

Turning to Doña Mencia, Maria Anna continued, "Cecelia is not alone, you know. I also wish, sometimes, that I could see them for myself."

"Remember your proverbs, Your Highness. Remember your proverbs. Beware of what you wish for. You may get your wish."

❖   ❖   ❖

"Both of the archduchesses," Frau Stecher reported. "Both of them, I found, displayed a most unseemly interest in the up-timers."

Her contact thanked her gravely.

Father Lamormaini, upon reading the report, sighed. *Whoever it may be that you marry.* Thank goodness, Maria Anna was to be married soon, and to Germany's most reliable supporter of the Catholic cause. That was a relief. He could stop worrying about her. She would be someone else's responsibility. Now to think about Cecelia Renata's marriage. To the right man.

Brussels, the Spanish Netherlands

"We are, after all, in the middle of a war," Don Fernando mused to his advisers. "I suppose it is too much to hope for that the lovely Grantville ladies who are now in Amsterdam would be willing to explain the significance of this trip to us."

There was general consensus that it was far too much to hope for.

He tried asking the delegation that came from Grantville to discuss the disposition of the funds in the Wisselbank. But they said only that, as far as they knew, Veronica Dreeson was going to settle her first husband's estate and Mary Simpson was looking for funding for the normal school in Magdeburg.

That was no help at all.

Don Fernando and his advisers didn't spend much time considering the matter, though. At the moment, they were far more interested in the doings of Bernhard of Saxe-Weimar, down in the Franche-Comté.

"And you're certain about this?" Don Fernando asked his advisers. "Bernhard took his forces no farther north than Schwarzach on the Rhine?"

Miguel de Manrique waggled his hand back and forth. "Well, not quite. Bernhard himself went no farther than Schwarzach, true. But he did send three of his cavalry companies toward Mainz."

One of the other officers snorted. "Amounts to the same thing. They're still in no position to come to the aid of the French and Danish armies outside Luebeck."

Manrique shrugged. "True enough. The gist of it all, Your Highness—and, yes, we believe our reports are accurate—is that it appears Bernhard plans nothing more than a token gesture. Just barely enough to deflect his employer Richelieu's wrath."

Don Fernando nodded. Then, rubbed his chin thoughtfully. "There's another interpretation, you know. Perhaps Bernhard is acting according to secret orders from Richelieu. The cardinal might be planning to betray his Danish allies, the same way he did the Dutch at Dunkirk."

The cardinal-infante and his officers contemplated the possibility for a moment. Then, almost simultaneously, they all shook their heads.

"No, too complicated," said Don Fernando. "Even for Richelieu."

Leipzig, Saxony

Duke John George was uneasy. He had been uneasy ever since he took Heinrich Holk into his employ after Holk and his army had been driven out of Prague. He needed Holk's troops as a barrier against Wallenstein, but they were all too likely to turn against his own people. He had felt the need to hold them along his own borders with Bohemia; however, the people of those borders were sending petitions against their presence—and the petitions were becoming increasingly sullen in tone.

He had considered sending Holk south—not *authorizing* him to operate in the Upper Palatinate, of course. Authorizing him to do something about Leuchtenberg might work. It would involve crossing part of the Upper Palatinate, of course. During the crossing, Holk and his men could forage there. Not in Saxony.

The discussion continued around the conference table. Now this. The woman—the wife of Grantville's mayor. If they were sending her to Amberg, it could only mean that the Swede was intending to provide significant reinforcements to Banér. If the Swede was intending to provide significant reinforcements to Banér, it must mean that he was very confident of success in the north. If he was very confident in the north, he must have data that John George did not. If he had that confidence, where would he turn next? To the south? To the east? Which way would Banér move, if he were reinforced? Against Ferdinand? Or north, against Saxony?

May it please God in heaven, to the east; not to the north. Not toward or through his poor Saxony. Not again.

They had best hold most of Holk's troops where they were for the time being. And deal with those increasingly sullen petitions the best they could. Perhaps with just a few companies to make a feint towards Leuchtenberg?

Prague, Bohemia

"One thing I *am* sure of," Judith Roth said, "is that if Veronica Dreeson says that she's going to Amberg to settle her first husband's estate, then she's going to Amberg to settle her first husband's estate."

She made that pronouncement in the great salon of the mansion that she and her husband Morris owned in Bohemia's capital. Being as Don Morris was one of King Wallenstein's central advisers, the salon was frequently occupied, of an evening, with a significant percentage of Bohemia's movers and shakers.

Everyone else in the room begged to differ.

The grandmother of Hans Richter, the hero of Wismar, would not go on so insignificant a mission.

The grandmother of the revolutionary, Gretchen Richter, would not go on so insignificant a mission.

The wife of the up-time admiral really could not be so concerned about the education of teachers that she would leave the national capital of the USE and devote three months of the year to a trip to a much less significant regional capital.

The speculation continued. There must, certainly, be a deeper underlying significance to this trip. Perhaps it portended a major effort of the USE on behalf of Wallenstein; perhaps it indicated that the USE feared that Wallenstein's situation was precarious and this was an effort to persuade the regent to release Banér's troops for use in Bohemia; perhaps there was to be a coordinated revolutionary uprising in Bavaria and Austria, led by the Committees of Correspondence.

Judith raised her eyebrows and sighed. She thought that she had an advantage over the others. She had actually met both Veronica Dreeson and Mary Simpson. Numerous times, in fact.

"They are," she said, "really quite single-minded. Both of them. Trust me."

The others shook their heads pityingly.

Munich, Bavaria

"Why," Joachim Donnersberger asked, "are they coming? Clearly, it can scarcely be about a bit of property in the Upper Palatinate. There is no way that they can expect us to believe that. The Dreeson woman's first husband had a small printing business, not a great mercantile concern."

Contzen and Vervaux looked at one another. The willingness of the Jesuit Order to draw its recruits from all social classes gave many of them a perspective on property rather different from that of the urban patriciate or the nobility. "It may be," Vervaux suggested, "that the amount is not insignificant to her."

The remainder of the privy counselors sublimely ignored this absurd idea.

"At least," Richel interjected, "we do have observers in place. We will know, as soon as can be, what she really spends her time doing. What both of them spend their time doing. If we can get someone else into the household of the Swede's cousin, we really should. The true intent must be that they are bringing instructions for him. Or for Banér, which amounts to the same thing."

"There is now," Duke Albrecht said, "a concentration of Banér's troops around Ingolstadt. Whatever the instructions the women are bringing, clearly they are so private that the Swede is unwilling to risk the possibility of a disloyal operator of their 'radio.'" Not, he thought, that this was excessive caution on Gustav Adolf's part. There would soon be at least one radio operator in Amberg who was willing to transmit information to Bavaria on the rare occasions that he was alone in the room.

Breaking the codes was another matter altogether.

Duchess Mechthilde had a private conversation with her brother, the landgrave of Leuchtenberg. More accurately she tried to, for Wilhelm Georg's mind was no longer fully reliable. She would have liked to have called in his sons, but one was at Ingolstadt and the other in Vienna. Or should have been in Vienna, if he had not been sent to accompany Ferdinand II's heir on a tour of inspection of fortifications in Hungary.

Although the family had fled from Leuchtenberg and the Swede's regent in the Upper Palatinate was now administering it, this did not mean that a significant portion of the population was not loyal to the landgrave and resentful of the usurper. Mechthilde thought that something ought to be done. Duke Maximilian had clearly lost his edge; Bavaria was being run in his name by the privy council. The privy council had no more nerve than the average committee. If something was to be done in the Upper Palatinate, it would be up to Leuchtenberg, but she had no way to do anything. It was frustrating.

Amberg, the Upper Palatinate

The Swede's regent of the Upper Palatinate was equally puzzled. "Why is she coming?"

"Why not?" Duke Ernst asked. He threw up his hands. "Tell me why I should be surprised."

In 1628, Duke Maximilian had demanded that all residents of the Upper Palatinate either become Catholic within six months or leave the country. Just in Amberg, the capital city, about ten percent of the citizens had left.

Duke Ernst continued. "Within the past two years, we have received letters from exiles in Regensburg and Nürnberg. That was to be expected, of course. Those are the nearest major Protestant cities. But there have also been letters from Basel and Geneva, from London and Edinburgh. If the former denizens of Amberg have gotten that far from home within the past five years, why should some of them *not* have gone to this Grantville?"

Turning toward Böcler, he held out his hands, as if in supplication. "But why does it have to be the wife of their mayor? Why does it have to be Hans Richter's grandmother? Why couldn't it have been some perfectly ordinary person? And why the admiral's wife?"

Böcler had no answer. In his heart, however, he could not have been happier. He could hardly wait for his duties to be over so that he could go back to his own room and insert the outline for a new chapter in his projected *historia*.

This was going to be much more interesting than the originally announced arrival of a trade delegation to discuss iron mining. Not that the economy wasn't important, of course. But it was hard to narrate economic matters in such a way that they kept the reader's interest. Intrepid ladies, on the other hand, offered fascinating possibilities.

Grafenwöhr, the Upper Palatinate

Kilian Richter, while not giving a single thought to Mary Simpson, had a pretty clear idea why his sister-in-law Veronica was coming back. The prospect of her return did not make him happy.

During Maximilian of Bavaria's occupation of the Upper Palatinate, Kilian had collaborated, quite enthusiastically, with the Bavarians. Quite remuneratively, too. Part of that remuneration had consisted of the property of his late, and much older, half-brother, Johann Stephan Richter.

Johann Stephan was most certainly dead, after all. He had died long before the war started. It had been a tragedy that his widow, son, daughter-in-law, and grandchildren had disappeared without a trace in the turmoil of the war. Truly, a tragedy. Kilian had told everybody so. However, he had pointed out to anyone who would listen, given the nature of mercenary forces, one could only assume the worst, so one could only be grateful for the blessing that they had not died heretics.

As for Johann Stephan's other children—they were irredentist Calvinists, every one of them. They had gone into exile, all four of Kilian's nieces, their husbands, and their children.

Clearly, he had been the only proper heir, and Duke Maximilian's officials had proved to be quite cooperative. Kilian had filed a petition requesting that his nephew Anton's family be declared dead; the authorities had issued the declaration. Legally, without the slightest doubt, Veronica was dead, as were the rest of them.

Therefore, Kilian had found the furor over the Battle of Wismar distressing. It had upset his digestion quite a lot. It appeared that his nephew's family was alive. Well, his nephew Anton certainly *was* dead, killed the day that mercenaries had raided his shop in Amberg. According to the newspapers, no one knew what had become of his wife. That was the only moderately good news in the whole thing—not that, at the time, Kilian had not done his very best to ensure that no one found out what had happened to the woman. He had more than sufficient reasons to be sure that she, too, was dead.

Young Hans *was* dead now. Spectacularly dead. Good riddance. But Hans' sisters were alive. So was that shrew Veronica, who was on her way to the Upper Palatinate this very minute.

And the Bavarians were long gone. Probably all gone to hell.

He needed a lawyer. His mind went at once to Augustin Arndt in Amberg, who had served him so well in getting title to the properties in the first place.

Amberg, the Upper Palatinate

At breakfast in the Amberg Collegium, Jakob Balde asked his fellow Jesuits not "Why are they coming?" but, rather, "Why are we here?"

The Amberg Jesuits asked one another that question fairly often these days. They were not suffering from existential *Angst*. They were quite sincerely bewildered.

During the Bavarian occupation, in 1629 and 1630, Duke Maximilian had taken a whole section of the city of Amberg by the power of eminent domain, razed the existing buildings, and turned the land over to the Jesuits for the building of a huge *Collegium*. The construction had begun with every expectation of success. There were many Bavarian bureaucrats in the Upper Palatinate who would send their sons to be educated there. The quality of the education would act as a magnet to city councillors and rural nobility alike; within a generation, the re-Catholicization of the rulers would be accomplished and a loyal band of alumni would extend the Catholic Reformation further among the population.

Now, however, the Bavarians were gone. Although there were still some Catholics in the town and the territory, they had lost most of their political influence and many were fighting for their property against claims by Protestant exiles. The *Collegium* was half-finished, undersubscribed, and nearly bankrupt. They wondered why Duke Ernst had not finished the job and thrown them out. Or, if he happened to be feeling less nice about it, thrown them into prison.

Instead, they were here. Not only those who had been in Amberg when the Swede conquered the Upper Palatinate, but those who had been thrown out of Sulzbach by Count Wolfgang Wilhelm's brothers. So why were the Jesuits still there?

Duke Ernst also sometimes asked himself that question. But, until he made up his mind whether or not he was going to experiment with "religious toleration" at Karl Ludwig's more or less permanent expense, he was keeping his options open. That involved letting the Jesuits stay until such time as they might realize that their cause was hopeless, pack their bags, and go.

Balde was the youngest. He had arrived from Munich for the opening of the school in the fall of 1632, all of five weeks before the Swedes came thundering into the Upper Palatinate after Alte Veste. He had been here ever since. With so few students, he had a great deal of time to write. So he wrote poetry, in modern Latin. That was his metier. And did research.

So this morning he added a postscript to the usual question. "It seems possible that we may not be here for much longer."

"Duke Ernst has decided to expel us?"

"Not as far as I know. But I have been reading the real estate records of the eminent domain proceedings."

The others looked at him blankly.

"We are eating breakfast on the very site that was once the print shop of a man named Johann Stephan Richter."

He waved the newspaper at the others. "The rest of the building is on the land of others, but this dining hall, right here, marks the location of the business of Johann Stephan Richter. Whose widow is this Veronica Dreeson. Who, we are told, is coming to Amberg to settle her husband's estate."

Balde, although a Jesuit for a decade already, was only thirty. Young enough to laugh about things.

"Not that she will have much use for a half-built *collegium* on a muddy construction site."

Magdeburg, USE

Well—there was *one* capital that accepted the announced reasons for the journey. His own. Mike Stearns was rather enjoying the reports coming out of the diplomatic pouches, which so clearly demonstrated that the rest of the world did not understand that Veronica Dreeson was a walking embodiment of the Law of Unintended Consequences. Which was a universal. Nor that Mary Simpson embodied the Principle of Single-Minded Fund-Raising. Which was possibly, but not probably, uniquely up-time. Combining the two of them, however, had a remarkably synergistic effect.

He hoped that they had a successful trip.

CHAPTER 15

Rosa Mystica

Rome, Italy

Easter would be on April 16 in this year of 1634. The penitential routines of Lent were already upon them. The Golden Rose, the Rose of Virtue, had been blessed and dedicated, as always, on *Laetare*, the fourth Sunday in Lent.

Laetare. If you looked at it another way, it was the third Sunday before Easter: the Sunday during Lent when the penitential purple was replaced by rose-colored vestments, signaling hope and joy. The Sunday during Lent when the Mass opened with the command, "Rejoice." *Laetare*: rejoice that there is love after hate, joy after sorrow, and fullness after famine.

When the jeweler to the curia had delivered this year's rose, Cardinal Antonio Barberini the younger had looked at it, phrases from Isaiah floating through his mind *There shall come forth a rod out of the root of Jesse.* And: *A flower shall rise up out of his root.*

"Lo! How a rose e'er blooming." The hymn of Marian devotion had been sung in the Germanies for well over a century, at least. Some of the printed versions had more than twenty verses. In Antonio's view, Michael Praetorius's modern arrangement from his 1609 *Musae Sionae* was the most magnificent setting of the tune:

Das Roeslein, das ich meine,
  Davon Jesias sagt,
Ist Maria, die reine,
  Die uns das Bluemlein bracht;
Aus Gottes ew'gem Rat
Hat sie ein Kind geboren
  Und blieb ein' reine Magd.

The rose that I am thinking of,
  Of which Isaiah speaks.
Is Mary, the pure,
  Who bore the little flower.
By God's eternal counsel,
She bore a child
  And yet remained a virgin.

The rose was truly golden—an ornament of the purest gold that could be made to hold the shape the artisans gave it—a thorny branch with leaves and several flowers. The largest rose sprang from the top of the stem; the others clustered around it. There was also a ruby at the center of the rose, its color reminding the observer of Christ's blood. Depending upon the state of the Curia's exchequer, the rose blessed in any given year might be larger or smaller, more or less bejeweled with diamonds, but always beautifully made. If no one was deemed worthy to receive it, it was kept in Rome. The blessing ceremony occurred every year, but the same rose was re-used until it was given away. Then a new one was made.

Originally, the rose had been given to men and women, cities and monasteries, persons and institutions, without distinction. Since the beginning of the century, the rose had been sent only to queens and princesses. A militant church had started to bestow blessed swords on kings and princes. The duty of carrying the rose and giving it to recipients who were not in Rome at the time of the ceremony fell to cardinal legates, to nuncios, and to other high church officials.

Now, nearly a month later, Cardinal Francesco asked, "Who's getting it this year?"

"The Austrian archduchess, Maria Anna," Antonio the younger

answered. "Uncle Maffeo recognizes quite clearly that marrying Maximilian of Bavaria represents a service to the church that is far beyond the ordinary call of duty."

Everybody else in the room stared at him.

Part Four

May 1634

There hath passed away a glory from the earth

CHAPTER 16

Quaestiones Diplomaticae

Vienna

"Half of Don Fernando's tercios only? And only as far as Grol?" Maria Anna raised her eyebrows. "That's in Gelderland. Eastern Gelderland, but they still haven't moved very far toward the Elbe."

"The chancery can safely rely on the reports it has received—as far as they go. It is hard to disguise troop movements. In the nature of things, large bodies of armed men on their way from one place to another are easy to see. Not to mention to hear. And to smell."

Doña Mencia's late father had been a soldier as well as governor of the Canary Islands. Her brother, Cardinal Bedmar, had been a soldier as well before turning to an ecclesiastical career.

"Particularly in a country as densely populated as the Netherlands," she continued. "Just as we knew very rapidly that Admiral Simpson had moved the king of Sweden's ironclads down the Elbe and passed Hamburg successfully. I am sure Don Fernando knew about it several days sooner than the news reached Vienna. It just was not something that the USE could hide. So he moved his troops toward the theater of war."

"But not into it. I need to know more." Maria Anna turned around impatiently. "Not just what Papa chooses to tell me. When he has time. Of course, he's very busy now."

Doña Mencia nodded. Important-looking men, dressed all in black, with solemn faces, had been hurrying in and out of the emperor's audience chamber for a week.

"And Father Lamormaini won't tell me anything at all."

Cecelia Renata propped her feet up on a hassock. "Why do we need to know more?"

Maria Anna frowned. "Why hasn't he sent them beyond Grol? Is it really because the archbishop of Cologne is refusing reasonable terms for letting him pass through Muenster . . . ?"

Her voice trailed off and then picked up again. "I know that it's Ingolstadt that has to be Uncle Max's main concern right now, but . . ."

She was thinking on her feet. "The archbishop . . ."

"*Nota bene.*" Cecelia Renata made a face. "Our *uncle* Ferdinand, as distinguished from our papa Ferdinand and our brother Ferdinand and our nephew Ferdinand. And those are just the ones who are still alive. It doesn't count our great-uncle Ferdinand, our great-grandfather Ferdinand, or the original Isabella's husband Ferdinand of Aragon, way back when they caused all these problems with the up-timers to start with by sending Columbus off to America."

" . . . is Uncle Max's brother," Maria Anna continued, sturdily ignoring the interruption. "Uncle Max is the head of the Catholic League. So Uncle Ferdinand should be a pillar of support for the League of Ostend in northwestern Germany. It's unlikely that he would refuse to cooperate with Don Fernando without Bavaria's tacit consent, at the very least. One of the best things for Bavaria, I would think—"

She looked at Doña Mencia quizzically, "—would be a huge victory for the League of Ostend in the North, so the Swede would have to pull Banér and Horn out of the south with their armies. Away from Ingolstadt. Away from Swabia. So why won't the archbishop grant passage to Don Fernando's troops?"

Cecelia Renata digressed again. "Given how badly Uncle Ferdinand wants to become a cardinal, it's unlikely that he would refuse to cooperate without Urban VIII's tacit consent, either. Not unless he's arrogant enough to think he can make the pope angry and still end up wearing a red hat."

"He is well known for his contentiousness and prickly pride," Doña Mencia commented mildly.

"In any case . . ." Maria Anna looked down at her sister. "Given that I will very soon be the duchess of Bavaria, I need to understand what is happening." She paused. "That's *need*, not just *want*, Sissy."

"We could buy some newspapers," Cecelia Renata suggested. "They might have more information. Especially if we can find some that Papa's censors haven't approved of."

"How are we going to manage that? Do *you* know how to buy a newspaper? Or where? Neither of us can scarcely wander out into the streets alone looking for one."

Doña Mencia leaned back. She had her own confidential sources of information in the Netherlands, but she wanted to see if the archduchesses could make satisfactory progress without her help.

"It came to me while I was standing there for a fitting," Maria Anna said to Doña Mencia a while later. "That I didn't know how to buy a newspaper and neither did Sissy, since merchants usually bring the things we might want to purchase to us. But Susanna Allegretti probably does, and she's able to move about in the city. I thought about asking her to stay behind a few moments when Frau Stecher was ready to leave, but that would just have made more trouble for her. So if you could tell *your* maid Guiomar to find Susanna and ask her to get us some newspapers? When she has the chance, of course. She won't be staying with us in Bavaria. She's employed by the imperial court. She will have to come back and work with Frau Stecher for a year or two more. So I don't want to get her in a lot of trouble."

Maria Anna reached through the slit in her skirt for the pocket that was tied around her waist. "Here's some money. Will that be enough? What do newspapers cost?"

"It should be enough." Doña Mencia thought it would be quite a bit more than enough, but then she had never personally purchased a newspaper, either. She had bought books, though. Right in the shops that sold them, rather than having them delivered. But that was many years ago, when she was visiting her brother Alfonso in Venice.

"Your Ladyship?"

Doña Mencia blinked. The May sun reflecting from the rosy brick walls of the empress' private garden had led her—misled her?—into a brief nap on the marble bench. She looked around quickly. Maria Anna was safe on the other side of the enclosure, digging in the dirt next to the empress and dropping flower seeds into the trenches she made.

"Your Ladyship?"

"Yes, Susanna."

The girl held out several items rolled up like ancient scrolls. "I have the newspapers."

"Ah. Oh, yes. Thank you."

"And the change."

"I think . . ." Doña Mencia glanced at the empress. "I think it would be better if you brought them to the archduchess' apartments privately. There is a formal dinner this evening. So—tomorrow morning, please, right after breakfast."

"Salt water isn't good for the seeds, you know," Eleonora Gonzaga said gently.

Maria Anna put her spade down. "I know, Mama. I didn't mean to drip on them. I just thought, all of a sudden, that this would be the first time that I won't be with you here, in the summer, to see our flowers bloom."

Susanna Allegretti stood quietly in Archduchess Maria Anna's bedroom, her face blank. She wasn't wincing. That, she assured herself, meant that she was getting better at being a court seamstress. She wanted to wince. The two archduchesses had newspapers spread out all over the tapestry coverlet on the bed. Smearing ink on it. Undoubtedly smearing ink on it.

She had gotten some of the newspapers she had brought them at the Thurn und Taxis post office. But the others, the uncensored ones, she'd obtained through unofficial sources—two apprentices of the cloth factor who had provided costumes for the play they put on before Lent. Those, especially, had smeared ink all over her fingers. Not, luckily, on her clothing, although it was on the inside of the tote bag she had used to carry them back to the palace. As soon as she could, she would have to turn the bag inside out and clean it if she didn't want to ruin other things.

The archduchesses weren't even thinking that someone would have to clean that tapestry coverlet.

Why would they? It would be a maid or laundress who cleaned it, not either of them.

If it could be cleaned at all. That ink had boiled linseed oil in it and was nasty stuff to get off.

She opened her mouth nervously and then closed it firmly. It wasn't her place to ask two archduchesses of Austria to take the newspapers off the coverlet.

It wouldn't do any good to put the newspapers on the floor, anyway. It was covered with a Turkey carpet, just as expensive and just as hard to clean.

"There's nothing in the papers about the negotiations between Don Fernando and the archbishop." Maria Anna twisted her mouth with annoyance. "Well, nothing except guesses. What they call these 'opinion pieces.'"

"Duke Bernhard has not sent his troops to the Elbe to join with the rest of the French army, either. Like Don Fernando, he has moved out some of his units. Three cavalry regiments. Some distance. But only part way north from Swabia, along the left bank of the Rhine toward Mainz." Cecelia Renata looked up. "How do the newspapers get all this information so fast, now?"

"Radio, I expect," Maria Anna answered.

"It would be nice to have a radio," Cecelia Renata said wistfully. "I've read about them, these 'crystal sets.' Ordinary villagers in the USE have them now and can listen to the Voice of America."

"You're not going to get one." Maria Anna, ever practical, squelched that hope as soon as it was born. "Not, at least, unless someone smuggles one into Austria for you. You'd have to hide it. Papa would have apoplexy and your confessor would have a stroke."

"I'm not sure how far a person can hear with them, anyway. But I'd be willing to try." Cecelia Renata, as usual, was not repentant. "There is a radio in Amsterdam, although it belongs to the USE embassy and not Fredrik Hendrik. They use towers. Tall towers. From Amsterdam, reports go to Magdeburg, I assume. And to the Swede, wherever he is at the moment. That is rapid. Almost at once, or at least as fast as the operator can send this 'Morse Code.' I need to learn more about how that works."

"What is this 'Morse code'? A cypher?"

"I suppose it could send something that had been cyphered." Cecelia Renata looked thoughtful. "But from the *encyclopedia*, it seems just a way of sending the letters of the alphabet by way of these radios. Maybe it is not always encyphered. Stearns' administration does not seem to be as obsessed as some regimes I will not mention with keeping everything a secret."

"Don't say that to Mariana. She loves our brother Ferdinand and is very loyal to him, but she still will not listen to a word against Philip IV."

"Magdeburg is crawling with spies. Grantville is, too. So then just a courier from Magdeburg or Grantville to here? A week once the newspaper reporter learns the information?" The tone of Cecelia Renata's voice made the statement into a question.

Doña Mencia shook her head. "There is radio in Nürnberg, too, now. Even in Amberg. Although the one in Nürnberg belongs to the city council and the one in Amberg to Duke Ernst. Still, your father has agents there, so the newspapers do too, I am sure."

"Agents?" Cecelia Renata giggled. "Say 'spies.' I said 'spies.' You mean 'spies.'"

"Agents," Doña Mencia said firmly. "Especially in Amberg. Not that it probably makes much difference how loose Stearns' people are, since obsessively-secretive administrations tend to be leaky as sieves also. Just think of the French. I was astounded that they managed to keep the League of Ostend a secret until the Battle of Dunkirk last year. So . . . it really just needs a courier from Amberg to Vienna. Much less than a week, by way of Passau."

Doña Mencia bit her upper lip. Should she or shouldn't she? "I have received letters from Brussels, also."

"Isn't your brother, Cardinal Bedmar, still in Venice?"

"Yes. Alfonso writes regularly. He has been observing the USE embassy with great interest. The ambassadress is a Moor, you know. But I have letters from Brussels, as well. When we were both much younger than we are now, before the infanta's marriage to Archduke Albrecht, I had the honor to serve as her lady-in-waiting for several years. She was gracious enough to give me her friendship."

Maria Anna narrowed her eyes. She had not been told about that part of her chief attendant's past.

Doña Mencia continued. "We do correspond regularly. She wrote me a very interesting description of her interview with Gretchen Richter. Gretchen Higgins as those up-timers would have it. Ridiculous thing, to call a woman by the name of her husband! Absurd, even. A person's surname is properly determined by the provisions in her parents' marriage contract."

"And you didn't *read* it to us?" Cecelia Renata wailed.

"I relent. Now that you know I have it, I will share it with you."

"Doña Mencia, you're an angel on earth."

"No, Your Highness," that lady replied after a brief, meditative, pause. "No, I am not. Not an angel. But . . ."

"But what?"

"Because of that old friendship, with Isabella Clara Eugenia's approval, I receive letters from some of her close advisers as well. Occasionally from Rubens. More recently from Alessandro Scaglia."

"The Savoyard? She has taken him into her confidence?"

"Not without questions from some other members of her circle, but yes. He tells me that Don Fernando received Señora Rebecca Abrabanel—please observe that she is not sufficiently stupid to call herself Rebecca Stearns; indeed, she is not stupid at all, from what I hear—for a formal dinner at his quarters. That was two days after the tercios moved out to Grol. Rubens was there also. So was Scaglia himself. And . . ."

"Tell!" Cecelia Renata jumped off the bed, scattering newspapers. "Tell!"

"Gretchen Richter and her husband also."

"Splendid," Maria Anna said. "Yes. Tell. But what I *really* need to know is why those tercios have only moved as far as Grol."

Susanna Allegretti was quite certain that she should not have been present at this conversation. It wasn't just that she was small and standing quietly. It was that she was a servant. Great lords and ladies tended to forget that servants were there.

The archduchesses were lucky that she was trustworthy.

She took a private vow to be worthy of their trust. Forever. Even though, really, they did not realize that they were trusting her.

CHAPTER 17

Honoris Causa

General Banér's siege lines, outside Ingolstadt

Dane Kitt and Mark Ellis understood one another very well. They had started kindergarten together and graduated from high school together. Both of them were solid students, but not brilliant. Both came from the kind of family in which reasonably good behavior and reasonably good grades were not regarded as negotiable. Both of them had decided to live at home and commute to Fairmont State to save money. Dane had majored in mechanical engineering and Mark in civil engineering. They were both third year students when the Ring of Fire hit. They had even talked, sometimes, of starting their own firm some day—one that would specialize in projects for rural areas and small towns, the kind of things that the big boys turned up their noses at.

Neither of them wanted to be here, attached to Banér. All the more so since the Swedish commander of Gustav Adolf's military forces in the Upper Palatinate had recently decided to bring most of his army out of their billets in order to besiege the Bavarian fortified town of Ingolstadt. Boring and unpleasant garrison duty might be, but at least it was reasonably safe. This probably wouldn't be, as time went on.

No high-flying heroics for them, thank you; no dramatic romances with down-time women. The previous year, Dane had married Jailyn Wyatt, one of the WVU girls who had been at Rita Stearns' wedding. Mark was engaged to Stephanie Elias, the younger daughter of Grantville's second dentist. What they really, really, wanted was for Gustav Adolf to win this stupid war, so they could go back home and live a normal life.

For which reason they were throwing themselves heart and soul into the winning of it. Mark just had more trouble getting the down-time military types to pay attention to him. Terry Johnson, his mother, had been ingesting all sorts of things that she shouldn't while she was producing him and his twin sister Mackenzie out of wedlock. No one knew for sure if that was the reason, but in spite of everything that his Aunt Amanda and her husband Price Ellis had done after they adopted them, the twins had ended up being pretty unimpressive physically.

Dane's folks, on the other hand, had chosen his name because he looked like a Viking when he was born. He still looked like a Viking—a sort of thin and weedy one, not a Hagar the Horrible type. Dane had played basketball. So, people around the camp paid more attention to him than they did to Mark. Even if General Banér had once remarked, "Why did they have to name you fucking Dane? Why not Swede?"

Hearing some sort of ruckus outside their tent, Dane unwound himself from where he was sitting, which was a gray metal folding chair with thin yellow vinyl cushions on the seat and back and a matching card table with a yellow vinyl top. He had liberated both from his late Grandma Sadie's bridge club supplies, packed them into his baggage when he was sent to Amberg, brought them along to Ingolstadt, and insisted that he couldn't possibly fight this war without them.

Given the kind of fighting that he did most of the time, he might have been right. Back home in Grantville, his parents were working frantically on aviation and associated things, sort of but not exactly parallel to what Jesse Wood and Hal Smith were doing. He was supposed to figure out whether anything they had developed so far might give Banér just that little edge that he needed to bring this siege off successfully.

To this point, the answer was "no." By seventeenth-century standards, Ingolstadt's fortifications were quite impressive. Any reasonably sized fleet of World War II era bombers could have reduced it to rubble in half an hour. For that matter, if Admiral

Simpson's ironclads could somehow be brought down to the Danube, he could have done much the same in the course of a single day's bombardment, with those absurdly powerful ten-inch guns. Dane and Mark had once reduced themselves to a fit of semi-hysterical laughter conjuring up ways that might be done. The least implausible scheme had involved using giant fleets of dirigibles to hoist the ironclads out of the Elbe and drop them into the Danube. Some of the same dirigibles could then be used to keep the ironclads from running aground in the Danube.

Remembering that conversation, Dane muttered to himself. "Blue Danube, my ass." He'd never seen the Danube, back up-time—he'd never traveled anywhere outside the United States—but whatever state of pristine blue riverness it had enjoyed in the late twentieth century, it enjoyed none of it in the here and now.

It wasn't really even "a" river, to begin with. At least in this stretch of its course, the Danube was usually divided into several branches. It meandered across southern Germany like a watery braid, not a single well-defined stream. Each and every one of which braids—tributaries, branches, whatever they were called—was muddy brown.

"What was that?" asked Mark, getting up from his own folding chair. He'd brought one also, of course.

Dane was moving toward the tent entrance. "Blue Danube, my ass," he repeated. "We ought to be doing something useful, like reinventing the Army Corps of Engineers."

Mark smiled. "Isn't that the truth? A lot of American rivers were just as messed up, originally. So much for the glories of pristine nature, huh?"

Dane had now reached the entrance and was moving the flap aside. "What's the commotion out there?" he wondered.

Mark came up to join him. The sound of General Banér's unlovely voice raised in anger was clearly audible. Clearly recognizable, too. They'd both gotten very familiar with that sound.

Outside, in the distance, they could see the walls of Ingolstadt. In the foreground, standing in front of some sort of bizarre apparatus, they could see Banér hollering at Duke Ernst and waving his arms about.

If the Swedish general's normal state of mind was choleric, that of the German administrator of the Upper Palatinate was serene.

He was responding to Banér's protest with his usual expression of imperturbability.

Well . . . "serene" wasn't quite the right word. It just had the advantage of brevity. Dane and Mark had both gotten to know Duke Ernst rather well since they'd arrived. This particular one of the four Wettin brothers who had once been the rulers of Thuringia was almost diametrically the opposite of the youngest brother Bernhard, by all accounts they'd heard, so far as his personality and view of life were concerned. Where Bernhard was driven by personal ambition, Ernst was driven by duty. Where Bernhard's ego required constant personal gratification, Ernst's seem to require nothing beyond his sense that God approved of his actions. Where Bernhard did not suffer fools gladly and suffered personal insult not at all, Ernst seemed oblivious to such issues.

Not exactly "serene," but awfully close. And the word was a lot handier to use than *calm and unruffled in the face of adversity, certain that he was doing his duty both in the eyes of Lawful Authority and the Creator.*

"What the hell . . ." Mark was giving most of his attention to the weird contraption, not the two men quarreling. "Jesus, Dane, that's a *catapult.*"

Dane looked. Sure enough, that very moment, the contraption went into operation. What he'd taken at first glance for an earth-moving scoop turned out to be the propulsive arm—whatever that was called—of the artillery device. A moment later, the arm *whanged* into a restraining crossbar and a small crate of some sort was flung over the walls of Ingolstadt.

"Damned impressive range," Mark murmured. "Hey, Mike and his guys used something like this to toss napalm onto the Wartburg. D'you think . . ."

Dane frowned, considering the idea. "Well . . . I don't know. The Wartburg was a real castle. Lots of stuff in it that could catch fire." He gestured with his chin toward Ingolstadt. "I suppose we could burn the town itself down, but I can't see where napalm would do much good against stone and earth berms. And the duke wants the town kept as intact as possible. So does Banér, for that matter. He wants to be able to station his troops in Ingolstadt, when and if he takes it. Can't do that if the place is all in cinders. Still . . ."

He and Mark looked back at the Swedish general. Banér was still in full protest mode. Arm-waving, red faced, voluble, the works.

Such an unlovely sight. Not to mention sound.

Dane shrugged. "Let's think about it some. Beats getting in the middle of *that*."

He led the way back inside the tent.

"—the king hears about this—"

"His Majesty gave me clear instructions to foster the true Lutheran doctrine here," Ernst interrupted Banér. He gestured toward Ingolstadt. "Since it will obviously take you months to reduce the will of yonder Catholics, I see no reason I shouldn't see to their souls and their moral conduct in the meantime."

"—be royal hell to pay—*Vasa* hell, I remind you—"

"Oh, nonsense. And what do you care if I fling some religious tracts and self-improvement pamphlets into Ingolstadt?" A bit uncharitably, Ernst added: "It's not as if either you or your soldiers have been clamoring for the items."

"—beside the fucking point! Catapults are *military* equipment—"

"I had them made myself, out of my purse, not yours."

"—in charge of all military affairs, not you—"

"Spiritual uplift is a military concern?" Ernst finally had something of an expression on face, with his eyebrows climbing. "In that case, General Banér, I must regretfully inform you that you and your officers have been sadly remiss—"

"—last time the Vasa temper cut loose, noble heads rolled!"

The duke shrugged. "Send a letter to the emperor in Luebeck, then, if you will. I will await his response quite calmly, be assured."

All the more so, he thought but did not say aloud, *since I have already sent Gustav Adolf several letters myself, warning him of your plans for an independent campaign against Ingolstadt.*

In one thing, if nothing else, all four of the Saxe-Weimar brothers had imbibed the same milk. They were all experienced practitioners in the art of political maneuver.

"—could probably have paved the streets of Stockholm with the skulls, if the king's grandfather had been a pagan."

"Which he certainly wasn't," concluded Ernst firmly. "Gustav Vasa was a good Lutheran. Hence—"

He gestured a command. The catapult fired again.

❖   ❖   ❖

Two days later, in the chambers of a nearby tavern that Banér had sequestered as his headquarters for the duration of the siege, the Swedish general was in a much calmer mood. In fact, he was as close to "serene" as the man ever got.

Which was not close at all, of course. Still, Duke Ernst knew the signs. Now that the energetic and very-difficult-to-repress if not exactly irrepressible Banér was finally back in action in the field, he was a lot more content than he had been as what amounted to a garrison commander in Amberg. Furthermore, despite appearances, the Swedish general was very far from a buffoon. There was actually quite a keen military mind in there somewhere, beneath the choler and the dramatics.

Banér laid down the report he'd just summarized for Ernst and leaned back in his chair at the table. "So. Duke Bernhard did *not* send his regiments north to join de Valois at Luebeck. In my assessment"—he waved a contemptuous hand at the report—"unlike that of this over-intellectual spy, this only signifies that the man isn't stupid."

Duke Ernst nodded. "Over time, people have called my youngest brother Bernhard of Saxe-Weimar a lot of things. Arrogant. Inconsiderate. Ambitious. Rude. 'Stupid' was never one of them."

Banér grunted. "Nobody ever called him 'incompetent' either."

Ernst leaned back in his chair also, and contemplated the situation. To the best intelligence that Sweden and the USE had been able to collect, Bernhard had responded to Richelieu's repeated prodding by sending part of his troops sort of halfway toward the north. He had left most of his infantry in the Franche-Comté and taken himself, Friedrich von Kanoffski, and their picked companies north through the Breisgau, settling for the past couple of weeks into the monastery buildings at Schwarzach on the Rhine—not that he wouldn't be heading back to Besançon pretty soon, most likely. He'd set up his administrative headquarters there. Bernhard had sent Caldenbach, Ohm, and Rosen, with the rest of his cavalry, toward Mainz, apparently to provide a screen against any moves that Gustav might be contemplating there. Or, possibly, to make the USE nervous about the possibility that he might launch raids in the direction of Thuringia.

He spoke that last aloud. "It certainly isn't impossible that Bernhard's men could get as far as Fulda, or do a *razzia* against the towns in the Werra valley on the south face of the Thueringerwald."

Banér scowled. Not in displeasure; that was simply his usual expression when he was thinking. "I've worked with those captains of his, Duke. All three of Bernhard's cavalry units facing Mainz have something in common. They can move very fast when they need to. Maybe Bernhard does intend to send at least a token force to support the French regiments outside Luebeck. But then again—maybe that isn't what he intends. Fast is fast, no matter what direction it might be headed."

The general was tactful, for a wonder. He did not add the obvious coda. *Since your brother has proven himself to be a traitor, who's to say he's not planning to betray Richelieu as well?*

Ernst was thankful for Banér's courtesy in leaving all that unsaid. Not because he really cared about the issue of family honor, though. He and Wilhelm and Albrecht, by their own unswerving loyalty to Gustav Adolf since he landed his Swedish army in the Germanies in 1630, had done more than enough to still any suspicions that the Saxe-Weimars as a whole were untrustworthy.

He simply didn't want to get into another argument with Banér. The Swedish general didn't really understand Ernst's youngest brother. True, Bernhard was almost satanically ambitious. But he was not actually that quick to treason, nor was he the conscienceless and amoral man that most people took him to be. From Bernhard's viewpoint, he had not betrayed Gustav Adolf in the first place. Rather, the Swedish king had betrayed *him*.

Ernst did not agree with that viewpoint, but he had no trouble understanding its logic. There were times, now and then, in the darker places of his soul, when the same resentment surfaced. Between them, the Swedish king and the American up-timers had dealt roughly with the Saxe-Weimar dukes. With their status and prestige, at least, if not their personal selves.

Yes, Bernhard could be ruthless. And, yes, he had the sort of arrogance that made it very easy for him to interpret events in a way that satisfied his personal code of honor and ethics. But that was not the same thing as the absence of honor and ethics altogether. Once satisfied that his course of action was acceptable—to himself, at any rate—Bernhard would proceed according to that same code. The youngest of the four Saxe-Weimar dukes was not only competent and capable, he was no more prone to pointless cruelty or gratuitous misconduct than any of his older brothers were. He was quite a devout Lutheran, actually, in his own way.

All that said . . .

Ernst looked out of the second-story window of the tavern onto the landscape below. Already, Banér's engineers and soldiers had turned the once-fertile fields surrounding Ingolstadt into a nightmarish landscape of trenches and fieldworks.

There was no report, anywhere, that Bernhard had ever sworn an oath of loyalty to the French. Not, at least, the sort of personal oath he had once sworn to Gustav Adolf. He had simply agreed to accept employment from them as the commanding general of a mercenary army.

Ernst was reminded of an American witticism of sorts he'd once heard, from one of the UMWA men who still provided Mike Stearns with the backbone of his regime. One coal miner explaining to another the words he'd spoken to an employer who had angered him. *Fuck you, buddy. I was looking for work when I walked in this door, so it's not as if I'm any worse off on my way out.*

Yes. It was quite possible that his brother was planning to betray Richelieu. He wouldn't think of it that way, of course.

Hearing movement, Ernst looked back into the room. Banér had sat back upright and was leafing through some of the other reports on the table.

"But Bernhard's not my problem," he said. "He's Horn's problem, and the problem of Nils Abrahamsson Brahe in Mainz. So let's get back to the siege here at Ingolstadt. I've got a report that just came in from one of my cavalry units. It seems that some of Maximilian's troops are—"

CHAPTER 18

Dramatis Nuptialis

Vienna

There had been a great spate of diplomatic activity, Maria Anna knew. Requests for the issuance of ecclesiastical dispensations for multiple lines of consanguineal and affinal relationships between the prospective bride and groom had gone from Vienna to Rome by the fastest post possible, accompanied by letters from the nuncio. Undoubtedly, similar requests and letters had been sent from Munich. After some very brief vacillation on the part of the pope—or, possibly on the part of the cardinals and other curial officials, which had scarcely been surprising, since Cousin Philip's ambassador would almost certainly have been pressuring for a delay—they had received word. The pope would do all that was necessary and would do it as quickly as possible.

Thus, today's audience, for Papa to announce a wedding date: July 15.

Thus, today's mass, to give due thanks to God.

Papa upon his throne in the *Hofburg* was far more impressive than Papa at the breakfast table with crumbs in his beard. The principal public audience chamber, which went under the name of the *Ratstube*, which made it sound rather like a cozy little room, was really quite large. The throne was at one end, with a canopy or pavilion above it. This had curtains, which were withdrawn to reveal Papa's presence. The court marshal, holding the sword of state, stood on his right. The chamberlain stood to his left, reading out the items on the agenda. He carried the symbols and introduced foreign representatives; it was his right to determine the sequence of the audiences. The right to determine the order in which those present would be heard gave him great power.

Also on Papa's right, but on the side wall, was a smaller throne with a smaller canopy. The heir to the throne sat there when he was present, but Ferdinand was not present. He was inspecting fortifications against the Turks. There was a chair for Cardinal Dietrichstein. He was old, he was not well, and once the protocol people were persuaded to think of it the right way, being a Prince of the Church, he was a prince. So he got to sit.

Everyone else in the room stood, the men bareheaded in deference to the emperor. They also all wore heavy cloaks over their formal court dress. May or not, the high-ceilinged room was as cold as a wit— *Oh, no. We don't think those words.*

If Papa looked impressive, the palace in Vienna was truly not very grand. The geographer Merian, in his book that described the Germanies, had said that it was "not particularly splendidly constructed, and rather small for such a mighty and supreme potentate." Long ago, Maximilian I, the founder of Habsburg greatness, had preferred to reside at Innsbruck and even at Augsburg. Of course, so long ago, the *Vorlande*, the scattered Habsburg possessions in southwestern Germany, had been comparatively more important. That was before Hungary and Bohemia had come to the family. More recently, Rudolf II had preferred Prague. Vienna was, really, a provincial capital that Papa had pressed into service as an imperial seat of government—not that he did not still travel, to Linz and to Graz, to Pressburg and to Prague, taking the court and its major officials with him. Sometimes he took all of the court. With family, officials, councillors, chaplains, choristers, and pages, that was about five hundred people to move from one residence to another. The high steward supervised the people, but the master of the horse controlled the horses, wagons, and carriages, which sometimes made travel an interesting experience.

Maria Anna waited. The family members were to accompany Papa on a procession from the audience chamber to church. The *Hofburg* was not like the Spanish Escorial, with the great church as the center of the palace. In Vienna, unless using a small private chapel, the imperial family walked to church in public, just like anyone else.

In Munich, things would be much more grand. Uncle Max was only a duke, not an emperor, but he kept a court almost twice as large as that of Vienna. The *Residenz* in Munich was far more modern and elegant than the imperial palace in Vienna.

It was too bad that Uncle Max could not come to Vienna for the wedding, she thought. The more of her time that had been taken up with wedding preparations, the less opportunity she had for study. It had become more and more difficult for her to obtain information. If it hadn't been for Doña Mencia, she would have had miserably little.

Doña Mencia, however, somehow, was obtaining copies of material from the up-time *encyclopedias*. Things were not the same; truly they were not. In some ways, it was the small things, rather than the great ones, that made this most real. In that other world, true, she had married Uncle Max. But in that world, Tante Elisabeth Renata had lived for one more year. In that world, the cardinal-infante had not gone to the Netherlands and defeated the heretic house of Orange there. In that other world, he had brought an army from Spain, via Italy, and had joined with the Austrian army led by her brother Ferdinand. Outside of the imperial city of Nördlingen, they had won a great victory over the Swedes. Papa had been so proud of Ferdinand that he had cried tears of joy.

Here, of course, no one had defeated the Swedes, yet. Their king, who led the armies of the heretics to achieve impossibilities, was not dead. Ferdinand had not achieved a great victory; Papa was not angry with him, but not especially proud of him, either—no more so than usual. The Catholic cause was not ascendant and secure.

Therefore, Uncle Max refused to come to Vienna for the wedding. He must, the Bavarians had said, remain at home, ensuring the security of the Danube frontier against the Swede's regent and general who were occupying the Upper Palatinate and actively besieging his jewel fortress at Ingolstadt. The Bavarian diplomatic correspondence said that the duke had decided that he should not go so far from his army. He must remain available if needed to defend the cause of the Catholic League.

So Maria Anna would be married in Munich, not Vienna. If all was well at Ingolstadt, the duke would meet her at Passau and escort her from there to the Bavarian capital. *Somehow,* she mused, *it would have been a little easier to be married at home.* Turning her head slightly, she smiled at Doña Mencia, who was standing just behind her.

Doña Mencia had also, as it chanced, been thinking of the differences between the *was* and the *is.* Thank God for the dispatches from Brussels. She had quite deliberately been focusing the archduchess' attention on the interesting discrepancies between the broader history narrated in the *encyclopedias* and what had happened since the spring of 1631.

She hoped that no one else had filled Maria Anna's ears full of the disturbing reports from Munich. The ones about Duke Maximilian's indifference to the marriage, and his plain statement to his privy council that if they wanted him to marry the girl, they could bring her here, because he saw no reason to take the trouble to go there. The ones which said that Duke Maximilian was not concentrating his attention on the threats from Duke Ernst and Banér; the ones which said that he left his chambers only to go to the chapel, and the chapel only to go to his chambers.

Another man moved forward to present his petition. Mentally, Maria Anna called up the wreath of blessings upon which she was still focusing her morning devotions. She hadn't added any new roses to it for quite some time. She thought hard about blessings.

Munich, Bavaria

Although Duke Maximilian showed no interest in the arrangements for his forthcoming marriage, numerous other people were quite determined that Bavaria should not be disgraced by a shabby welcome for its new duchess. Many of the interests coalesced: Duchess Mechthilde, the city council, the Jesuit *collegium.* Among the various other items offered to celebrate her arrival in the city, there would be a play.

A play in Munich was not a modest undertaking. Long since, they had spilled out of the confining space of the courtyard of the Jesuit college and took place in the huge *Schrannenplatz* in front of the cathedral. It was not uncommon for a play to have one hundred fifty or two hundred actors with speaking parts; the costumed extras for crowd scenes could range from a thousand to more than fifteen hundred. They had huge painted sets; multiple special effects with waves and shipwrecks, guardian angels descending from heaven, music, and fireworks. They were in Latin, of course. For more than fifty years, however, it had been the custom to print German-language programs for the spectators that summarized the plot development of each act, pointed out the moral of the story, and sometimes even translated crucial passages of the major speeches. It was Father Matthaeus Rader, still teaching at the collegium, who had had that idea. The first such program had been printed in 1597 for the dedication of St. Michael's church. Although for the past fifteen or more years he had been concentrating on a three-volume collection of the lives of Bavaria's saints, he agreed to accept responsibility for the overall supervision of one more event.

There wouldn't be time to commission an entirely new play for the wedding and have new music composed and rehearsed. Why, the wedding celebration this year between the son of the king of Denmark and the daughter of the elector of Saxony (heretics all) had required two years of preparation. Three months was quite hopeless for that. They would need to revive an existing play.

Of all the well-known Jesuit playwrights, one had taught for a time in Munich before being called to Rome to serve as a papal censor—Jakob Bidermann. Bidermann, like Father Drexel, the court preacher, was one of Rader's former students. Rader suggested one of his works with, perhaps, a new and topical poetic introduction and epilogue.

The whole committee agreed that this would work. But which play? The most famous was the *Cenodoxus*. It was powerful, undoubtedly. When it was first performed, the actor who portrayed the protagonist had been moved to join the Jesuit order and more than a dozen Bavarian court officials had taken leave from their ordinary duties in order to make a retreat and perform Saint Ignatius Loyola's *Exercises*.

Mary Ward, who had been drawn into the committee on the presumption that her school would supply the many flower-petal-scattering girl children who constituted part of any celebration, remarked that this was not, perhaps, precisely the effect that one wished to achieve during a wedding celebration.

Josephus? Not quite right. *Philemon the Martyr?* Umm, no, not this time. *Jacob the Usurer?* Off-topic.

Patiently, Duchess Mechthilde let the discussion proceed along its inconclusive way until everyone was getting tired and would welcome a decisive intervention. They should make the play a compliment to Duke Maximilian, she suggested. A compliment to his generalship of the troops of the Catholic League. Of all of Bidermann's plays, the best for this purpose would be . . .

Of course! Why hadn't they thought of it in the first place. Some time during the week before the wedding, Munich would put on a spectacular performance of *Belisarius, Christian General.*

However, Father Rader had insisted, there should be a new poetical prologue and epilogue that specifically referenced the wedding. That could certainly be achieved within the allotted time. Who? Well, young Balde would be the best choice.

"But," one of the city councilmen sputtered, "he's in Amberg. In the Upper Palatinate. Imprisoned by the heretics."

"He isn't imprisoned," Rader answered. "And the mails are going through. By somewhat roundabout routes, at times, but going through. The house of Thurn and Taxis is most ingenious. It shall be Balde."

Once this had been decided, all of the committee members took up their tasks with little additional discussion; most of them had taken part in the staging of a dozen or more plays of this type. There are many advantages to fielding a veteran team.

Duchess Mechthilde saw no reason to remind them of the play's full title. Not that her brother-in-law deserved to experience derision or misery. As far as Mechthilde could find out, based on the information she received from servants and various other informants she had placed judiciously here and there among the court personnel, Maximilian truly did wish to retire to a monastery. So, he clearly deserved all the assistance that she could give him in attaining his desire.

The misfortune was that there were others who were hindering his pursuit of that laudable and praiseworthy goal. Those others—yes, they did deserve whatever adverse fate could be brought to bear upon them. Munich would be performing *A Tragi-Comedy of the Rise and Fall of Belisarius, Christian General, who Fell from the Highest Happiness of Fame into the Extreme Mockery of Misfortune under Emperor Justinian, about the Year of Christ 530.*

CHAPTER 19

Disciplina Militaris

Luebeck

Gustav Adolf, king of Sweden and emperor of the United States of Europe, was in a very good mood this day. Word had just come from General Torstensson that he and his army had reached the Wardersee, thereby cutting off the French line of retreat from the siege of Luebeck. And Admiral Simpson's flotilla of ironclads would be entering the Bay of Luebeck very soon now.

That was perhaps just as well for General Johan Banér, reflected the emperor's aide, Colonel Nils Ekstrom. Had Gustav Adolf been in a bad mood, he might well have reacted to the dispatches sent from the Upper Palatinate by Duke Ernst quite differently.

Banér could be . . . aggravating. Even at a distance, much less in person. At least, at a distance, you could pretend he was sober most of the time. And you didn't have to listen to his constant profanity and blasphemy.

Gustav laid the dispatches down on the desk in his office in the city's Rathaus. "Well, why not? Johan's capable in the field. He might even reduce Ingolstadt, which would be a very nice development."

Ekstrom cleared his throat. Before he could utter words of caution, however, the emperor waved his hand. "Yes, yes, I know," he said. "The odds of that happening are not so good. But they're not impossible, either, and simply the attempt will keep the Bavarians preoccupied. Which is all I really need at the moment."

"The Austrians—"

"Are not likely to take advantage of Banér's withdrawal of troops from the border," Gustav interrupted. "Not with Wallenstein allied to us and sitting close to their northern territories. Relax, Nils. It's safe enough, I think."

Ekstrom felt compelled to complete his duties. "That still leaves Bernhard of Saxe-Weimar."

The emperor thought for a moment, and then shrugged. "Yes, but I can't see where that's a problem either. General Horn has enough men in Swabia to keep Bernhard from doing anything prodigious, so to speak—a term which would certainly qualify any attempt on his part to march into the Upper Palatinate. Horn's not perhaps the most imaginative and daring commander you could ask for, but he's never careless. Besides . . ."

For a moment, Gustav tapped his big fingers on the desktop. "Besides," he continued, "I think Bernhard is now looking mainly to his own purposes. If that's the case, why would he undertake such a risky gamble? Even if it were successful, he might advance the interests of France and Bavaria—but only at the expense of half-destroying his own army. No, I can't see it, Nils. Everything we can determine about Bernhard's actions leads me to believe his principal motive, at least for the time being, is simply to keep his army intact, and in place."

He left off his finger-tapping and picked up the dispatches. "So, we'll allow Johan his independent campaign at Ingolstadt. Send a reply to that effect to the duke, if you please."

"He'll be somewhat exasperated, you realize."

Gustav Adolf grinned. "Well, of course. It's in Ernst's nature to be exasperated, just as it is in Johan Banér's to be exasperating. That's part of the reason I thought they'd make a good match."

The Breisgau

Bernhard of Saxe-Weimar was in a foul mood, as he had been for days. What made the situation all the worse for his officers was that the young Saxe-Weimar duke's irritation had nothing to do with the general political and military situation, which was developing quite favorably. It was simply due to indigestion.

Bernhard, unfortunately, had a rather delicate stomach, perhaps inherited from his mother. It often flared up when he was on campaign and making do with field provisions. To make things more difficult for his aides and adjutants, his pride usually got in the way. What sort of daring cavalry commander can't go on campaign without getting an upset stomach? Any expression of sympathy was likely to trigger off an explosion of rage.

So, Friedrich and his associates had been treading carefully of late, around the duke. They'd been riding back and forth across the countryside for weeks. Not because they were trying to accomplish anything but simply because Bernhard had thought it prudent to act as if they were. Perhaps, after getting reports of their activities, Cardinal Richelieu might be fooled into thinking that Bernhard was contemplating—energetically, most energetically—a daring mission to come to the aid of the French army outside Luebeck.

Not likely, of course. It was exceedingly hard to fool the canny prelate who was the effective ruler of France. But, if nothing else, Bernhard had calculated that those reports would go unquestioned by Richelieu, however much they might cause him to seethe inwardly— for the good and simple reason that the cardinal's own position was now precarious. Very soon, in Bernhard's estimate, the French army at Luebeck would be coming to a disaster—and when it did, France's simmering factional disputes would come to a boil. Outright civil war was by no means impossible, and major unrest was a certainty.

The king's younger brother Monsieur Gaston and his sycophants would be laying many charges at Richelieu's feet—nailing them to his door, more like. One of them was sure to be the accusation that he had squandered money on that useless Bernhard of Saxe-Weimar and his mercenary army in the Franche-Comté, which had played no role at all in the Ostend war.

Under the circumstances, Richelieu could hardly admit that his opponents were quite right!

Which, indeed, they were. The last thing Bernhard and his close associates intended was to see their preciously assembled army battered into pieces in an all-out campaign against the Swede and the American technical wizards who had provided him with such a fearsome array of weaponry.

No, no. They'd have a much better use for that army soon enough.

Ingolstadt

There had been a time when Johann Philipp Cratz von Scharf-fenstein had been thankful to have the position of the commander of the Ingolstadt garrison bestowed upon him by the duke of Bavaria. Unfortunately, through no fault of his own—Wallenstein's malice was to blame, as well as the fecklessness of the authorities of Lorraine—the Rhenish count's military record as a professional soldier was . . .

Well. Undistinguished.

His enemies, of which he had many, would no doubt have used a less neutral term. But they were motivated by spite and envy, usually combined with ignorance.

It was hardly Cratz von Scharffenstein's fault that, while he'd been in Wallenstein's service, his troops had committed some depredations upon the populace. Mercenary troops were always rough on civilians, including those they were hired to protect. Any professional officer knew that perfectly well. Wallenstein's anger had simply been the naiveté of a man who was really just a lowly merchant who'd applied his talent for avarice to military affairs. And a nasty bastard to boot. He was not a genuine soldier, like Cratz himself.

The complaints of the Lorraines had been even more absurd. Was Cratz a baker or a tailor or a saddler, obliged to keep meticulous and finicky financial books because he lived on the edge of destitution? An officer and a nobleman, by nature of the very temperament that made him suited to his position in life, of necessity had a sanguine attitude toward these things.

They'd been incredibly unreasonable. Had even dissolved his regiment!

Thereafter, there'd been almost two years of penury, while the imperials dilly-dallied about employing him. That was Wallenstein's malevolence at work, of course. And didn't it serve the emperor right, that in the end it would be Wallenstein who betrayed him? While Cratz von Scharffenstein took his services to the Bavarians.

Even with Tilly's recommendation, before the old man's blunder at the Lech that cost him his life, the best Cratz had managed to get was a garrison post. Still, by then he'd been thankful enough. If nothing else, being the military commander of a walled and fortified city like Ingolstadt made it exceedingly difficult for his creditors to pester him.

Cratz von Scharffenstein was no longer thankful, however. Garrison duty was boring, and provided little opportunity as a rule for an officer to distinguish himself. On the positive side, there were many avenues for enrichment that were far superior to the measly salary his Bavarian commission brought in—and it was usually not dangerous work.

Usually.

Alas, "usually" was a term that could be quickly buried when an enemy commander like Johan Banér was in the vicinity, damn the drunken Swedish pig. How did a man who consumed as much liquor as his reputation said he did manage to be so energetic at the same time?

Gloomily, Cratz pushed aside the scout reports on the desk in his headquarters. It was just more of the same. Banér's men here, Banér's men there, the Swedes seemed to be everywhere.

That done, he eyed another little stack of papers on the desk. Even more gloomily. Those were the latest dispatches from General Franz von Mercy, the man whom Duke Maximilian—God knows what he could have been thinking—had chosen to place in command of Bavarian field forces in the vicinity of Ingolstadt.

Cratz was tempted to shove those aside as well, but . . .

Cavalry scouts and their captains could be ignored, safely enough. Generals couldn't, even if—there was this small ray of light—Maximilian had not been mad enough to place von Mercy in command of the garrison as well.

So, sighing, he picked up the first one. As he expected, it was . . . vigorous . . . in tone. Urging Cratz to do this and do that and do the other. And who was to pay for all this? Even assuming there were enough hours in a day, days in a week, and weeks in a month.

He set that dispatch aside, for the moment. Picked up the next.

This one was even worse. Beneath a short note from von Mercy "strongly recommending" that the measures in the attached report be applied, the report itself had been penned by von Mercy's subordinate, Colonel Johann von Werth.

Cratz von Scharffenstein lapsed into the vulgar patois of his Rhenish upbringing for a moment. Of all the officers in Bavarian service in or near Ingolstadt, the one he detested the most was Johann von Werth.

Jan van Wierdt, to call the arrogant ass by his right name. He was no more of a genuine nobleman than the simpleton corporal standing guard just outside the door. Unfortunately, by sheer good fortune, van Wierdt *had* "distinguished" himself in the recent wars. Much the way a peasant might blunder across a buried treasure.

Von Mercy thought most highly of the bastard. Still worse, so did Duke Maximilian. Cratz had even heard that the duke had once remarked that van Wierdt was as good a cavalry commander as Pappenheim. Which was absurd on the face of it, of course.

Reluctantly, Cratz began reading the report. His gloom grew by the minute.

The Swedes are doing this and that and this and that and the other.

We must do this and that and this and that and the other and yet another.

Just reading the damn thing was exhausting.

Brussels, the Spanish Netherlands

Stiffly, in the manner of a stern young prince bound and determined to be faithful to his duty, Don Fernando resumed his seat. Then, stone-faced, he gave the portraits one last quick examination.

"Anna de Medici, then?"

Rubens inclined his head. "All things considered, Your Highness, I think she would make the best choice. Now that the rumors of Claude of Lorraine's involvement with her cousin have been confirmed, she's obviously out of the question. Claudia de Medici and her sister Maria Maddalena, as we already discussed, are too old. The Polish girl is only fifteen, and . . . ah . . ."

"Ugly," the prince grunted. He gave her portrait a glance. Then, gave the portrait of Anna de Medici a glance that was only slightly less brief.

That was odd, in a way, since the de Medici girl was actually quite attractive, even if you allowed for a certain amount of artistic license by the artist who'd done the portrait.

Rubens knew the reason, and had to suppress a sigh. As impossible as it might be, for political reasons, Don Fernando had concluded that either of the Austrian archduchesses would make a good match. Especially the older one, Maria Anna. The arrival of their portraits had simply solidified his opinion. Both young women were very attractive.

It was true enough—had the world been other than it was. A marriage with one of the Austrian Habsburgs would bring real power and influence, unlike a match with the Tuscan girl. But with Ferdinand II still on the throne in Vienna, there was no chance that he'd agree. Not even to a match with Cecelia Renata, who was still at liberty, so to speak.

With Maria Anna, of course, there was no chance at all. She was already betrothed to Maximilian of Bavarian, and the wedding was supposed to take place in July.

"Shall I begin the negotiations with the Tuscans?" he asked the prince.

After perhaps half a minute, the answer was "Not yet."

Rubens was not surprised. Nor was there any point in arguing the matter for a while. Don Fernando could do "stubborn" as well as any Habsburg who ever lived, when he was of a mind.

"Very well, Your Highness."

On his way out of the cardinal-infante's chamber, Rubens made a mental note to himself. *As soon as possible, hide the portraits of the Austrian archduchesses.*

❖ CHAPTER 20 ❖

Et Ferrum Ferentes

On the Golden Street

By the second day, they were about thirty miles northeast of Nürnberg.

"It's enough to make you sick." Marc was looking at the smashed ruins of a hammer mill. His time with Jacob Durre had provided him with some sense of the effort and money it would take to rebuild it.

Mansfeld and Tilly, the Bavarians and the Swedes. Every army that came through the Upper Palatinate for the past dozen years had been acting on the same presumption. If they could not keep a grasp on the wealth of the region themselves, they would at least destroy as much of it as possible, so the enemy could not benefit from it either.

"There must have been really a lot of iron being processed," Keith commented. "It's one thing for someone to tell Ollie so, and for him to send me off to see about getting the place back into production. It's something else to see these wasted smelters for myself. How much were they turning out, annually, before the war?"

"Before the war?" Leopold Cavriani looked reflective. "I wish that Durre could have come with us. He would know better than I do. A geographer with a sense of the poetic described the smelters and hammer-mills as 'strung along every stream in the

161

Upper Palatinate, like pearls on a necklace.' Especially, in addition to the Pegnitz here, along the Vils and the Naab."

"Funny way to describe the mess and pollution that they must have made," Mary Simpson commented. "Look at the size of those slag piles."

"Iron was pearls," Leopold answered. "Pearls in the sense of wealth. How many? More than two hundred fifty, I am sure. But no matter how carefully they have managed these forests—the peasants of the Upper Palatinate are forbidden to keep goats, you know, because they are so destructive of the wood if they get loose—there have been constant shortages of charcoal. Without fuel, the smelters have to stand down."

"Why didn't they use coal?" That was Toby Snell, with a question that just came naturally to a Grantville boy.

"I don't think there's any around here," Keith answered. "None suitable for metalworking, anyway. If they could get a railroad through, from here to Grantville . . ."

Leopold resumed his interrupted lecture. "The Emperor Charles IV's *Goldene Strasse*, his 'Golden Street' from Prague to Nürnberg, the one we are riding on and will continue riding on as far as Sulzbach, was built because of iron, too, not gold. Not by Charles IV, originally. It existed long before. He just improved it, and rerouted parts of it through his own lands."

Cavriani looked thoughtful. "It should have been the *Eisenstrasse*, the 'Iron Street.' For four hundred years, at least, it has been iron, in this region. Probably for much longer than that; I don't know, but that is when the records that I have seen begin. About four centuries ago. Occasionally, however, farmers find pots and iron tools along here that are far, far, older—things from the time of ancient Rome and even before. Look around you. God never meant the thin soil on these hills to grow grain. It is the ore beneath them that made the fortune of the electors Palatine. The up-timers speak of the Ruhr. Throughout the middle ages, the Upper Palatinate was for the Holy Roman Empire what the Ruhr became for the German Empire so much later."

He grinned. "Oh, the Rhine Palatinate is a fine place. Lovely, scenic, civilized. But the wealth that supported that culture, that ancient university, the great library that was stolen from Heidelberg and taken to Rome a few years ago, was wrested out of these hills by men with picks and shovels. This second part of the Palatinate was the center of the south German iron trade. Mining and processing, both. If the iron isn't brought back into production, nothing else that Duke Ernst can do will help in the long run. In these hills, it is iron or poverty. The proverb runs, 'Dig iron or eat stones.'"

He gestured. "It goes on far beyond what we can see here. The *Montanbereich*. It is about a hundred of your up-time miles long, from Sulzbach and Rosenberg in the west, it runs northeast almost all the way to the border of Bohemia. These little towns, even those no bigger than a large agricultural village in other parts of Germany, received their city charters in the fourteenth century because of iron."

"You can pretty much tell that," Keith commented. "Everyone in Grantville keeps talking about the importance of industrializing. Around Thuringia, I've not seen anything like this. Some around Suhl and Schleusingen, Schmalkalden, but that's on the south side of the mountains. Just how much of the work force was already out of agriculture down here? Before the war, I mean?"

Cavriani thought for a moment. "It isn't like northern Italy or the Netherlands, of course, so it's hard to compare. It isn't 'urbanized,' as you say. Mining is a rural occupation and so is ore processing. Only the producers of finished goods live mainly in the towns. Or near them, since the forges also benefit from having a source of power from the streams. But probably, of adult men, one out of five; in some places, such as along the Pegnitz River here, or along the Naab, which flows south into the Danube, one out of four, worked in mining or metals."

"Looking at this, I can see why Herr Durre and the other metalworkers in Nürnberg are so worried." Marc was returning to his first thought. "It isn't just that they are short of materials for making wire and such. Even though, if they can't get raw materials for the metals trades, it will soon no longer be a proud and wealthy city. It's the arsenal, too. It's a manufacturing arsenal. Without iron, without *enough* iron . . ."

Approaching Amberg, the Upper Palatinate

"It was not an easy time," Elias Brechbuhl told Mary Simpson. The widower of Veronica's stepdaughter Elisabetha shook his head. "Nor did the Bavarians intend to allow any Protestants who remained in the city an easy time." He had been talking about the year 1626. "In September—I recall very well that it was the fifteenth of the month—they held a Catholic mass, a *Te Deum*, in the main parish church of Amberg to celebrate the Catholic victory over the Danes. And the school children were forced to attend it. That was the day that I decided to go into exile. Whatever the hardships it would bring upon Elisabetha and the children. For in only two more years, my oldest son would start school. And they would have schooled him into a Catholic. I could not permit it, not on my conscience."

He reined his horse in, pausing to look up at the walls of Amberg.

Veronica drew up her mule next to him. "Yes, I remember that day. Hans was at that service. He was in the Jesuit school. The damned Bavarians had closed the *Pädagogium*, the Calvinist school, already, three years before that. It was the year before he started his apprenticeship with his father." She sat, looking up at the walls.

Brechbuhl looked startled.

Veronica glowered. "I will say it. *Die verdammten Bayer*. If you don't want to hear it, you don't have to listen."

Brechbuhl turned back to Mary Simpson. "This is the first time that I have been back. Margaretha's first husband was already dead; he was killed by Bavarian troops almost three years before that day. She came with us, as did Lorenz and Hanna. Clara and Matthias weren't married yet and she was living with Margaretha. So she came with us, as well." He smiled. "A year later, there was Matthias at our door in Nürnberg. I think she had given up hope, but by waiting longer, he was able to salvage more money from the sale of his father's house and business than if he had left so quickly. But then, a bachelor is not as constrained as the head of a household. It is easier for him to take some risks."

Keith Pilcher frowned. He wasn't Catholic, but he had gotten to know some of the Jesuits who were working at St. Mary's in Grantville and liked them. "What do you mean by 'schooled into a Catholic'?" he asked.

"The Jesuits in Amberg accepted any boy who turned up at their door, without a charge in money. That," Brechbuhl said, "I will grant them. Protestants as well as Catholics. Oh, yes, they *wanted* the Protestant families to send their sons. Not just pupils whose parents could not pay the full fees. They accepted boys with no coats, boys with no shoes, and gave them bread to eat. But there are other ways to impose a cost. On the soul, if not upon the purse. The year that Gustav Adolf landed, 1630, that would have been, I received a letter from a friend who had stayed. He said that the schools had been dismissed in the morning, the day before he wrote, so that the children could attend the burning of the books that the Bavarians had confiscated from the Lutherans. 'So that they could some day tell their descendants about it.'"

"You were right, you know," Veronica said. "To leave, if it was so important to you that your children not be schooled as Catholics. Somehow, it did not make that much difference to us. The first time we were plundered, by Mansfeld's 'Protestant' troops in support of the Calvinist Winter King, we were still good little Calvinists ourselves, just as the elector declared that his subjects should be. So, my stepson Anton figured, how could becoming Catholic make it worse? We delayed as long as we could; that's true. We did not leap enthusiastically into the arms of the damned Bavarians, the way Johann Stephan's brother Kilian did. He threw himself upon their breasts, practically, when they first occupied Amberg in 1621. But in 1628, when Duke Maximilian declared that we must become Catholic or leave, we became Catholic."

Nodding at him, she continued. "It isn't as if Johann Stephan brought up his children the way your father brought you up. He didn't suffer fools gladly. Even though he died long before this war started, he had more than enough of the back and forth between the Lutherans and the Calvinists. I can only think what he would have said about adding Catholics to the stew. After one of the changes, when the ecclesiastical visitor complained of his apparently minimal familiarity with the doctrines and teachings covered on the questionnaire, he replied, 'It may be that I do know the answer. I'm just not sure which one you are looking for this time.'"

"Ah," Brechbuhl said. "Yes. I do believe that I heard that story from my father." He smiled. "And many others about Johann Stephan. The various religious changes generated a lot of jobs for printers. Just think of how many copies of the *Mandatum de Non Calumniendo* were needed when one of the electors decided that the Lutherans and Calvinists had taken their theological disputes to a far from genteel level of rhetoric. 'Thou shalt not insult one another.' Indeed, think of all the pamphlets that led to the issuance of the mandate. Such controversies must be very profitable for the printing trade."

Veronica also smiled. More grimly. "Gretchen had not been confirmed as a Calvinist. The ministers and teachers were exiled first; she wasn't old enough for confirmation when they left. Although she accepted the conversion like the rest of us, she was no longer exactly a child, so she has never really been instructed in the teachings of any church at all. Hans was confirmed as a Catholic. He was obliging enough about it, but he was, I think, a little too old when they started teaching him. He was ten. He didn't really take it all very seriously." She blinked. "He reminded me of Johann Stephan, in many ways."

Then she looked directly at Brechbuhl. "Annalise has no clear memory of having been a Calvinist, ever. She is Catholic, Elias—truly a Catholic, instructed as one and content to be one. So few years, barely six, between the oldest and the youngest, to make such a difference. The years of childhood are very short. We are working in common, now. Someday, maybe, you will have to decide if you will let your children know a cousin who is truly a Catholic. But it isn't something that we need to face today. Or even tomorrow."

Brechbuhl looked down.

She shook her head. "In 1628, we were plundered again. As Catholics. This time by some of Tilly's 'Catholic' troops in a land that was now 'Catholic.' Nor did our obedient change of confession move Duke Maximilian to protect us from his allies. That is when Anton was killed and his wife taken. And we were taken."

She looked directly at her stepdaughter's widower. "I intend to get Johann Stephan's property back, Elias. I *will* get it. Enough to send the Catholic granddaughter of a Calvinist publisher to a down-time college teaching up-time subjects headed by a Lutheran abbess. That much, the damned Bavarians owe Anton's family. Do not expect me to handle things the way I would have done ten years ago. I am not the respectable widow of an established printer any more. Nor am I entirely the wife of the mayor of Grantville. I have seen and done things that even Elisabetha and her sisters, with all the hardships of exile, have not and did not. I am an old hag of a camp follower also, Elias. You will do well not to forget that. Just as people will do well, as time goes on, to remember that Gretchen was a young camp follower. These things do not leave a person the same."

Amberg, the Upper Palatinate

Duke Ernst had been polite about making the acquaintance of most of the party from Grantville. Not that he wasn't interested in seeing the up-timers for himself, but he was, after all, a very busy man, with many demands on his time. He suspected that he faced extended conversations with Mary Simpson and Veronica Dreeson. The appointments were on his calendar. He would do his duty. But after their first conversation, he had been utterly enchanted to make the acquaintance of Keith Pilcher. If they were not kindred spirits, they had, at least, a common appreciation of straightforward facts.

"Böcler," he said. "Get me my notes."

"Buckler?" Keith asked, looking after the secretary's retreating form.

"No," Duke Ernst said absently, following the direction of his guest's gaze. "Böcler."

Keith made a note to himself to ask the kid how to spell his name.

Turning back to Keith, Duke Ernst said, "We do, of course, have the materials from before the war. The Palatinate has been very well-governed. We have plenty of inventories and surveys. But they are terribly obsolete, because of the destruction. My first project has been to determine just what the current status is. However, here is what there was before the war."

Keith nodded. "It's always good to have a base line for comparison."

"You do realize," Duke Ernst asked, "that not all of this area properly belongs to the Upper Palatinate?"

"I didn't know it," Keith answered. "But I think that I could have guessed. We've seen a lot of that sort of thing since we landed in Thuringia. It really complicates life."

Duke Ernst, obviously proud of his increasing command of modern English, said "Tell me about it," and beamed. "The Upper Palatinate proper, the lands of the young elector Karl Ludwig, is in two main sections, northern and southern. Between them are part of Pfalz-Neuburg, then *Amt* Vilseck, which belongs to the bishop of Bamberg and is a great nuisance to your administrators there since it is quite detached from the remainder of the diocese, and, of course, Leuchtenberg. Although we are, currently, administering Leuchtenberg, since the landgrave fled from Pfreimd into Bavaria when the Swedish army arrived in the vicinity."

He cocked his head. "You will have become used to the word *Amt*, I think, for a local administrative district. Here, though, it is called a *Pfleggericht*. There is very little difference in the functions. Amberg is in the southern main part of the Upper Palatinate, along with Pfaffenhofen, Haimburg, Rieden, Freudenberg, Hirschau, Nabburg, Neunburg vor dem Wald, Wetterfeld, Bruck, Retz, Waldmünchen, Murach, and Treswitz-Tenesberg. In the northern part, you have the districts of Bernau, Eschenbach, Grafenwöhr, Holnberg, Kirchentumbach, Auerbach, and Hartenstein. Plus, just so things don't become too neat, the treasury *Amt* of Kemnat, the *Landgericht* Waldeck and a little free lordship called Rothenberg. Which is not the imperial city of a similar name, which is in Franconia. Plus, there are little exclaves to the west, intermixed with the jurisdictions subject to Nürnberg."

As all the place names went rattling past his ears, Keith recognized one familiar word. "Mrs. Dreeson says that she comes from Grafenwöhr. We all caught that. God, that was funny. In our day, it was a *huge* center for army maneuvers; Americans by the hundreds of thousands trained at Graf. Does this mean that if she wants to go up there, she actually has to go through some spot that doesn't belong to the Upper Palatinate? That isn't under your control?"

"There are some *Pfleggerichte* belonging to Pfalz-Neuburg in between. Pfalz-Neuburg was set up by Emperor Maximilian in 1505; it belongs to a cadet line of the Palatinate. The mother of the first counts was the daughter and heiress of Duke Georg of Landshut and most of it was taken from his lands, not those of the Palatinate. It's divided currently into three parts. Like Gaul. The largest belonged to Wolfgang Wilhelm—the one who married Maximilian of Bavaria's sister and turned Catholic for the sake of an inheritance on the lower Rhine. Then there are two smaller sections belonging to his younger brothers, who remained Lutheran, August and Johann Friedrich. Well, August's widow, now that he's dead. On behalf of Gustav Adolf, I have been working quite closely with Johann Friedrich and his widowed sister-in-law. And fairly successfully. The king, ah, emperor, decided that they should co-administer Wolfgang Wilhelm's former lands, since they are both Lutheran. Gustav Adolf doesn't wish to seem greedy."

Duke Ernst grinned. It made him look like a leprechaun. "Also, it is really more convenient in a way, since there is a nice Pfalz-Neuburg enclave on the south side of the Danube which Maximilian would most certainly gobble up if the king, ah, emperor, claimed it, since General Banér is currently besieging Ingolstadt. It makes a rather nice base of operations for some things. From our perspective, that is. From Maximilian's viewpoint, I'm sure that Neuburg and its hinterland are as great an irritant to him as Ingolstadt is to us. Except that they are not half as well-fortified. Few places are as well-fortified as Ingolstadt."

Duke Ernst looked up, an idea seeming to strike him. "I don't suppose that your administration in Franconia would be interested in trading Vilseck to the Upper Palatinate in exchange for something that we may have that is closer to their administrative center? I would certainly be happy to explore the possibility."

Keith was a bit taken aback. This was out of his league. But they had come through Bamberg on the way down, so he had a name handy. "You could always drop a note to Vince Marcantonio. He's the administrator there. He'll have to buck it up, through Steve Salatto to Ed Piazza. But I expect that they would be willing to talk about it." *That*, he thought, *should be safe enough.* "Don't expect an answer right away, though. Steve and Vince sort of have their hands full at the moment, what with . . ."

"Oh, yes," Duke Ernst answered serenely. "The peasants and their ram. Peasant revolts are always time consuming while they are happening, but things eventually settle down. Böcler, draft a letter please, for my signature, to Herr Marcantonio. I'll expect to have it in the morning."

He returned his attention to the statistical survey of the Upper Palatinate. "According to the survey done in 1609, the *Montanbereich* had four hundred twenty-eight employers in industries connected with mining and related industries. The mining was mainly iron, but also tin, lead, and calamine, the ore that you call zinc. The related industries were ore processing, and the manufacture of metal goods, mostly wrought iron up to and including something the size of ship anchors."

He paused. "And, of course, transporting these. It takes certain specialized wagons, heavy horses, and skilled drivers to get something the size of a ship's anchor from here to Venice."

"I can see that," Keith agreed.

Duke Ernst continued. "These businesses directly employed 10,550 miners and other metal workers. With dependent family members, this meant that 36,400 people out of a population of 180,000 in the region were directly supported by mining and metalworking."

Keith did some rapid calculations in his head. Dividing 428 employers into 10,550 employees did not come out to a bunch of little one-master shops with a journeyman and a couple of apprentices. Assuming that there had been some little shops, and there were bound to have been, the rest had been big businesses by down-time standards.

Duke Ernst was marching through the statistics. "That does *not* include those who worked in transport, with a network that ran into Hungary, northern Italy, and all through Germany. The Upper Palatinate's teamsters were widely known. The exemptions from toll and tariffs that the emperors granted to them go back to the fourteenth century in many cases. Back to the time when the *Goldene Strasse* received its privileges."

Keith wished that he could have brought the guy a battery-operated laptop. With a spreadsheet program. He'd love one. "Must have given them a bit of an advantage, trade wise, getting their stuff to market without all those add-ons."

"Oh." Duke Ernst smiled a little smile. "Yes, of course. It was much resented by the robber barons. And not always enforced during times of turmoil. But the principle was well established."

He leaned over, turning a few more pages in the ledger. "A lot of the 'agricultural' workers were also doing things other than growing food, such as working in the charcoal industry that supported the metal processing industry. Again, according to the 1609 survey, 310,000 measured meters of wood were cut in the *Montanbereich* that year; there were 1,460 charcoal burners who were counted as industrial workers, but also the 1,100 woodcutters and 1,950 people working in 'side jobs' associated with charcoal manufacture who were counted as agricultural. The regulations for managing the forests to maintain the supply of charcoal go back to the late 1300s: replanting, banning of goat-keeping, and the like."

He stood up. "Then the war came."

Keith nodded. It always seemed to come back to the war.

CHAPTER 21

Mulieres Intrepidae

Amberg, the Upper Palatinate

The trade delegation had taken quarters in an inn, at Cavriani's urgent recommendation. Over the past century, there had been numerous episodes of serious tension between the metals cartel, the *Hammerinnung* comprised of the owners of the mining enterprises, smelters and mills, and the various other businesses that transformed metal into finished products, and the rulers and their officials. Episodes caused, largely, by the suspicion of the owners that the rulers of the Palatinate would be quite happy to impose monopolistic controls on the iron trade, to their own profit. Which, indeed, they would have been. The counts of the Palatinate had been mercantilists before mercantilism, so to speak. It would be bad, Cavriani insisted, to give a first impression that the Grantville delegation was directly sponsored by the regent.

Moreover, the innkeeper subscribed to several newspapers. Everybody in the delegation waited anxiously for the latest installment of the eagerly expected, distant but very important, spring season soap opera that Keith Pilcher called, "How to Squash the League of Ostend Like a Bug," starring Gustav Adolf, Lennart Torstensson, and John Simpson with supporting roles to be taken by Mike Stearns and . . . well, who knew. Perhaps the USE would have some new heroes in the next couple of months.

The ladies were another matter. Duke Ernst had naturally insisted on providing them with quarters in the Amberg *Schloss*. At his own expense. And, when he discovered that they had somehow managed to travel without a bevy of maids, with attendants suitable to their station. Chambermaids. Ladies' maids.

Mary Simpson thanked him very graciously.

While Mary was thanking him, Veronica managed to put on her abbess of Quedlinburg face. Then she thanked him, too, thinking dourly that she was going to have to use that face and voice more often than she wanted to this summer. She had practiced, since that reception in Magdeburg. She had watched the way that women such as Mary and the abbess did it. She was not dumb; she was not yet too old to learn new tricks. If they were useful.

One of the chambermaids at the *Schloss*, Afra Forst, still had family in Pfreimd. Augustin Arndt, Landgrave Wilhelm Georg of Leuchtenberg's agent in Amberg, was able to use this leverage to persuade her to report to him everything that she observed about the up-time women.

It was no secret that Arndt was the landgrave's agent in Amberg, of course. He was a lawyer. His function was to represent the financial and political interests of the exiled ruler to the current government. That was quite normal. It would be peculiar only if Landgrave Wilhelm Georg had not employed an agent. That would have created a great deal of suspicion, indeed.

The regent and his officials assumed that Arndt spied when he could and sent reports to the landgrave. What else could one expect? He watched them. They watched him—when they had time, of course. The gathering of intelligence on the level of the local bureaucracy tended to be a business in which the two operative sentences were "That's not my job; that's his job" and "Who's paying for this, anyway?"

Several of the people who had been watching Arndt when they had time were now at Ingolstadt with General Banér. Keeping an eye on Herr Arndt was fairly low on the regent's priority list.

Right now, Arndt was operating on the basis of old instructions from the landgrave. For the past eighteen months, all he had received were the payments on his retainer. Those came more or less regularly, transmitted by a steward. As long as they kept coming, he would continue to send reports.

Kilian Richter's ties to Arndt were not of any interest to the Amberg authorities. Richter was not a citizen or resident of Amberg, nor did he any longer own property there. The man had entered some, not much, a few years back, but promptly sold it. His interests lay miles to the north. His connection with Arndt was not the obvious one of employer and agent that linked Arndt to Leuchtenberg. Who cared now that Richter had used the attorney's services once before, for a short time, several years ago. Every practicing lawyer had multiple clients.

Arndt was not especially happy that Richter, when he had first read the newspaper reports of "that harridan Veronica's" planned trip to Amberg, had contacted him again. But it shouldn't involve any adverse consequences for Arndt, himself. It was only natural, after all, that Richter would be hiring a lawyer in the capital to defend his property claims.

Duke Ernst was more impressed by Veronica Dreeson's letter of introduction than she had been herself. That was, indeed, an original signature. Or the initials, at least, had not been scribbled by an adjutant. GARS. *Gustavus Adolphus Rex Sueciae.* The king of Sweden, emperor of the United States of Europe and the prospective head of the renewed Union of Kalmar meant seriously that he himself, Ernst of Saxe-Weimar, should personally lend assistance to the grandmother of Hans Richter, the hero of Wismar. A postscript indicated that Prime Minister Stearns agreed that it would be a good idea.

The woman was chatting along. " . . . and the town is so changed that I scarcely recognize it. My stepson-in-law Elias and I have walked around some, and we actually lost our way twice. We had to take a line of sight on Our Lady's to get back on streets that we recognized. That huge half-finished building on the former site of St. George's church—why, it spills way over the boundaries of the original lot. They've even moved one of the city gates to make room for it. There must have been at least a dozen houses along the wall, there. All gone. Including . . ."

Duke Ernst nodded politely.

"Including *our* house. The one where Johann Stephan had his print shop. We lived upstairs." Temporarily losing her abbess of Quedlinburg face and voice, Veronica glared at him.

Duke Ernst winced. That "huge half-finished building" was the

Jesuit *collegium.* He knew a great deal about it. The moving of one of the city gates in 1630 had serious technical implications for the defense of the city of Amberg. He and Banér had spent a great deal of time looking at the plans. General Banér had been, profanely and blasphemously, of the opinion that, from a military standpoint, a bastion of Catholicism directly adjacent to the city wall was a really bad thing. Banér had been right, but political considerations had prevailed. He had, thus far, allowed the Jesuits to stay in the building next to the wall. Under careful surveillance, of course.

He looked back at Veronica. Perhaps Job had a point when he asked God why he did these things to people. Surely, of all the houses in Amberg, the Jesuits could have chosen to build where some other owner had his lot. Almost *any* other owner.

"Ah, Mrs. Dreeson. It is the Jesuit school."

"When I left Amberg," Veronica said firmly, "the Jesuits were holding masses at Our Lady's. They had Latin school in the St. George's *Pfarrhof* until 1626, but in 1627 they had just closed down the Calvinist school at St. Martin's and the Jesuits moved their school into it. That was far more convenient, I'm sure, right in the center of town."

"Perhaps it was more convenient. Nevertheless, the year after you left Amberg, the Jesuits traded the St. Martin's site again, for St. George's. I understand that the trade involved considerable debate at the time. There was a great deal of building activity during the last years of the Bavarian occupation. They meant for Amberg to be the center of a mission effort for the reconversion of the entire Upper Palatinate to Catholicism. There were visitations by high officials of the order. By early 1631, the Jesuits were running seventeen missions out of Amberg. They hired an Italian architect from Passau to complete a design. One of the—ah, results—of the Ring of Fire was that Duke Maximilian interpreted it as a signal that he should redouble his conversion efforts. In Amberg, that meant his construction efforts. In May of 1631, that spot by the wall was a construction site; the demolition had been completed, but little had been built. When we, the Swedes, took Amberg at the end of 1632, we found what you now see—unfinished, but the start of a great *collegium* on the model of those in Bavaria, half-completed."

"And the section on top of Johann Stephan's lot is?"

Duke Ernst glanced behind him. Böcler came forward with a fistful of drawings.

"The section on top of your late husband's lot is . . ." Duke Ernst leafed through a couple of pages, then put his finger down. "The dining hall."

"So," Veronica said at lunch, "it seems that I must beard the Jesuits in their den. In the company of Elias and my lawyer, of course."

Keith and Cavriani were off somewhere, talking about iron at what was undoubtedly tedious length. A very high percentage of Amberg's male population appeared to be interested in discussing iron.

Duke Ernst was tied up at the moment with administrative affairs, and Herr Böcler, of course, was with him and tied up as well. So, they were being hosted by Gustav Adolf's cousin, Colonel Hand, and the public relations man, Zincgref.

Veronica glanced at the cousin. She almost wished that she could have brought Annalise along. Even with the injured arm, exposure to this man might distract her from that silly infatuation with Heinrich Schmidt. Too old for her, of course, but distracting. Tall, blond, lanky. Well . . . Swedish. Mary's comment had been that Erik Haakansson Hand would have looked right at home on a ski jumping team at the winter Olympics. Veronica had no idea what either ski jumping or the winter Olympics might be, but she did get the general idea that Mary, also, thought that Hand merited compliments on his appearance. Zincgref did not, but, then, he was also married, so it made little difference.

Hand offered to accompany her to visit the Jesuits. Veronica accepted graciously.

"I suppose I need to arrange an appointment first, rather than just dropping in. I'll send a note. Herr Böcler kindly furnished me the name and address of the rector."

"Who is he?" Mary asked.

"Father Hell. Father Caspar Hell."

Mary looked at her, almost choked on a bit of salad, and collapsed into helpless laughter.

"Why are you so concerned with the Amberg property?" Hieronymus Rastetter, Veronica's lawyer, asked her. "It is, after all, really the smallest part of your late husband's investments. The properties that he inherited around Grafenwöhr are considerably larger."

"And they are," Elias Brechbuhl added pointedly, "still bringing in an income. Unlike a lot from which the building has been razed. Uncle Kilian just took the one-time payment for that and ran with it, so to speak."

"I have no intention of forgetting the Grafenwöhr property," Veronica said forcefully. "Nor, do I intend to forget what you"—she nodded at Brechbuhl—"have discovered about the way that Kilian has handled it."

Elias Brechbuhl had been very busy amid the tax records of the Upper Palatinate for the past several days.

"But, I think, we need to know more before we make any definite moves in Grafenwöhr. Things that we can't find out here in Amberg. The most complete records will be there, in Grafenwöhr itself. We need to check the town's own books."

"They have a new young man as the town clerk, *Gerichtsschreiber*," Rastetter said. "You may know him, Brechbuhl, or at least his father. Nicholas Moser, the name of father and son alike. His father is settled in Bayreuth; that is where they went into exile. The boy has only been there a few months, but he seems very competent and conscientious, not to say clever as well."

Elias nodded. The older Nicholas Moser was a prominent man among the Palatine exiles.

Veronica ignored the interruption. "And we need to *talk* to people, Elias. The way my brother-in-law Kilian had your Elisabetha and her sisters excluded from the inheritance was straightforward enough. He declared on oath that they were heretics who had chosen to go into exile, and that he was the next heir. Which they were; which he was."

Brechbuhl nodded. So did Rastetter.

"But us. Anton's children and their mother and I."

She paused for a moment.

"I have read the copy of his petition, the one that you"—she waved toward the lawyer—"got for me from the chancery. The one in which he petitioned to have us declared dead."

Rastetter stroked his beard.

"It says nothing to the effect that we disappeared in the turmoil of war and that our whereabouts were unknown. It should have. He filed that petition less than a year after we were taken from Amberg. Why was Kilian so sure that we were dead?"

"Yes," Rastetter said gravely. "Yes. That question has occurred to me too, on occasion, since I received your first letter from Grantville. It is not as if mercenaries always kill their captives. Often, true, but it is not universally the case. It concerns me."

Kilian Richter was also meeting with his lawyer. "You could," he suggested, "file an allegation that the woman and her alleged step-grandchildren are imposters."

Augustin Arndt just looked at his client. "If she had appeared two years ago, I could have done that. Immediately after they surfaced in this Grantville. I could even have made it sound plausible. Camp followers from nowhere, emerging in a town that claimed to be from the future. At a minimum, it would have caused a significant delay in the proceedings. A delay during which you could have continued to collect all the income from the property."

"So why can't you do it now?"

"Because I have no desire to look stupid. The woman is famous now. I understand that she arrived with a personal letter of introduction from Gustav Adolf. Hans Richter is even more famous. He is the reason why she arrived with a personal letter of introduction from Gustav Adolf. The allegation would be thrown out as frivolous."

Kilian gave him a sour look.

Arndt went on. "Additionally, she is here with Elias Brechbuhl, who will undoubtedly be filing claims on behalf of his children and sisters-in-law. We can scarcely allege that the Nürnberg exiles are imposters. The paperwork already on file indicates that you have known where *they* were all along and that you merely based your possession of the properties upon the provisions of Duke Maximilian's various edicts in regard to landholding by Protestants. It is my duty as counsel to bring to your attention that these provisions are no longer in force. Although Gustav Adolf's regent has not automatically invalidated all claims to property made by Catholics, he does *not* give them precedence over claims by Lutherans. Or by Calvinists."

"You know," Kilian said. "This could get to be a problem."

"You are understating the dimensions of what you are facing, Richter," Arndt replied.

Kilian looked at him. "If you do not come up with a way to manage this, it will not be what *I* am facing, but rather what *we* are facing. Remember that, Arndt. I do. You were there. If I go down, I will certainly take you with me."

Arndt flinched, remembering the "mercenaries" he had employed on Richter's behalf, several years before. His life would have been so much simpler now if another group of mercenaries, real ones, had not interrupted their work.

Duke Ernst found his first conversation with Mary Simpson considerably more relaxing than that with Veronica Dreeson. They talked about education. They talked about cultural patronage. They talked about the cost of education and cultural patronage. Finally, they talked about money. Most of it was quite familiar ground. Any member of the higher nobility was constantly besieged by requests to extend patronage.

The concept of a normal school was not familiar. It was a fascinating idea, that of training teachers specifically for village schools, rather than leaving them to be taught, catch as catch can, by a miscellaneous patchwork of junior pastors, sextons, widows, impecunious students who had run out of money halfway through the university, former shoemakers with good intentions and a little learning, failed theological students, or any combination of the above.

What would the curriculum for such an institution be?

The appointment ran overtime.

He had Böcler schedule several more appointments.

Money would be a problem. He was not, personally, a wealthy man. He would have to think about money.

Art and culture, however, he could provide at very little cost. Amberg was really a quite beautiful town. It had benefited greatly from its years as the official residence of the various counts and regents. He sent Mrs. Simpson on a guided tour, conducted by Böcler, and settled down to work his way through his inbox.

Augustin Arndt was enciphering his latest report to Landgrave Wilhelm Georg. Usually, he saw no reason to bother. Not that he had a great deal of news. It was the absence of news that bothered him most. He stated frankly that he was afraid that he must be missing something. Even with a woman inside the *Schloss* itself, he was getting only information to the effect that the women from Grantville appeared to be doing only things that were in accordance with the overtly stated purposes for their being here. Carefully, he reported on their clothing; on their hats. Indeed, thanks to his informant, he reported on Frau Admiral Simpson's underclothing. He also included a careful description of her jodhpurs. He hoped that the information might be of some use; it was all that he had been able to obtain.

Similarly, he said, the men in the alleged "trade delegation" were, in fact, meeting extensively with those people with whom one would expect them to meet if they were here to investigate the revival of iron mining and the metals industry. According to the under-cook at the inn where they were staying, who had it from one of the waiters, the men, with several citizens of Amberg, had devoted a full evening to discussing how, in the days of their grandfathers, Amberg had broken the Wunsiedel monopoly on coating sheet iron with tin. There was also some discussion of how the Amberger had been able to defy the efforts of the count to channel all exports through one market that he controlled, continuing to use several different ones.

The mentions of tin had included Bohemia as a source for importing tin. Arndt was glad to be able to include that, given the current political excitement surrounding Wallenstein, the new king of Bohemia. It might be of at least some minimal interest to the landgrave. The rest of his report, goodness knows, was dull enough.

He became so involved in thinking about the interesting recent events in Bohemia that he forgot to mention the last item the cook had reported to him. There had been discussion of cartels and the unjust way in which the big owners tried to squeeze the smaller men out of the business, even though the purpose of an *Innung* was to assure all members a fair share of the trade.

Caspar Hell offered to meet with the woman—Dreeson, the up-timers called her, even though it was her husband's name, Balde told him—in his office.

She replied, through her lawyer, that she preferred to meet in the dining hall and to have all of the Jesuits in Amberg present to hear her statement.

The Jesuits thought about that for a couple of days. They didn't have a lot of information on which to proceed. Amberg, isolated as it now was in Swedish-controlled territory, had become something of a backwater in the order. True, the mail arrived. But it did not contain anything that their superiors would mind having fall into the hands of the Swedes, which meant that the contents of the bag were usually quite dull. Welcome, of course. But unexciting.

Private couriers were, for all practical purposes, impossible. The location of the *collegium*, so advantageous in a Catholic city, meant that in a city with a Protestant government, the regent's guards were able to observe every single person who came to their doors. Since they did not really wish to endanger any of their students or parishioners, and were quite sure that every one of themselves was watched every time he ventured out into the town, their communications were very limited.

The regent had told them, rather nicely under the circumstances, to give Our Lady's Church back. It was Lutheran, now; the Lutherans seemed quite happy to hold services in a *Frauenkirche*, dedicated to the Virgin Mary, as long as it had already been a *Frauenkirche* before the Reformation. The Calvinists were using St. Martin's. Father Hell was grateful that, only a few weeks before the Swedes arrived, the bishop of Regensburg had consecrated a chapel for the new *collegium*. It wasn't attracting many lay people; those Catholics who remained in Amberg seemed doubtful of the wisdom of public attendance at mass.

The school was still drawing students, though. Lots of them. Poor boys, mostly, from families that could not afford the tuition at the other schools. Quite ordinary boys, mostly. Brilliant boys, a few. All worth the effort of teaching them.

The revenues that Duke Maximilian had assigned to support the *collegium* had been diverted to other uses by the Swedes. In the absence of tuition-paying students, they would soon be bankrupt.

The library, however, had been left intact. They had managed to purchase a rather nice library while the revenues were still coming in. Wonder of wonders, it had been neither burned nor expropriated to compensate for the books that had been taken from the Protestant schools during the Bavarian occupation. It was housed on the second floor, above the dining hall.

Father Hell didn't know what the reestablished Calvinist and Lutheran schools were doing for books. Perhaps Duke Ernst had given them money to buy new ones.

At the end of a couple of days, they had no more information than when they started thinking.

Balde urged his superior to meet with the woman on her terms.

The rector refused.

Balde suggested the possibility of bringing to the attention of the woman's lawyer the fact that the site had been sold to Duke Maximilian's agents in a manner quite legal at the time, which meant that her grievance in the matter of title should be more properly directed against the seller, who was—he rechecked his notes from the real estate records—one Kilian Richter.

Hell agreed to that.

Balde once more suggested, tentatively, that it might be useful for them to meet with the woman on her terms.

The rector refused again.

Balde shrugged.

On behalf of Frau Veronica Dreeson (*geb. Schusterin, verw. Richter*), her attorney, Hieronymus Rastetter, filed a title suit simultaneously in the municipal court of Amberg and the courts of the Upper Palatinate against both the Jesuit Order and one Kilian Richter. The filing was accompanied by a cloud of witnesses, or, at least, a very long list of witnesses who should be deposed. Not to mention a cloud of sealed, stamped, and notarized documents.

It was the kind of thing that could drag on for years. If somebody appealed it to the imperial level, it could drag on for generations. Consequently, nobody got very excited.

Arndt reported the filing of the lawsuit to Landgrave Wilhelm Georg of Leuchtenberg. He didn't bother to encipher this letter. Lawsuits were public documents.

Eric Haakansson Hand was just as glad. It had taken his code specialist several tedious days, during which he could more profitably have been working on something else, to decipher the previous one. Not that Hand hadn't enjoyed the description of Mary Simpson's jodhpurs. But, having seen the garment for himself the day the Grantville delegation arrived, being worn by its owner, it hadn't come as news. The underwear had been more entertaining.

Idly, he wondered why on earth the landgrave wanted to know.

✧　　✧　　✧

As requested, Böcler prepared a summary of his first impressions of the Grantville delegation.

Practical men. Intrepid women.

Overall, Duke Ernst concurred.

"But," he added, "we cannot spend all of our time thinking about the up-timers. Take a letter to General Banér, please."

Eric Haakansson Hand spoke. "Before we adjourn, please, one more thing."

"Yes?" Duke Ernst raised his eyebrows.

"We should get together all the information we have in regard to the duke of Bavaria's forthcoming marriage. Just to have it at hand. There's no reason to expect that the event itself will directly affect the Upper Palatinate in any way. The Austrians will be bringing the archduchess to Passau, we understand. The duke will meet her there and they will make a ceremonial procession to Munich, where the wedding will be held. It may pull a few of Maximilian's troops away from Ingolstadt, but Banér doesn't think that he will move many. Munich is far enough inside Maximilian's borders that he doesn't need a heavy garrison there."

The regent nodded. "Just in case. But it's hardly one of our main problems, right now." Duke Ernst paused. "Just in case, though. Put the *Grenzjaeger* on alert, Hand, starting the day that the Austrians are to arrive at Passau. And ask the Danube boatmen to keep an eye out for any suspicious activities. Bavaria is, after all, just across the river."

CHAPTER 22

Ferrum Redux

Amberg, the Upper Palatinate

"The production levels were?" Keith asked.

Lambert Felser was assisting his boss and Duke Ernst's secretary Böcler with translations. Keith's German was not bad, but he apparently found Böcler's accent, which was *Fränkish* modified by study in Alsace, difficult to follow. For his part, Böcler was devoting some time every day to the study of English, rising an hour earlier than was customary for him, but he found that his progress was slow.

Böcler pulled out a copy of the 1609 survey. Everything appeared to go back to the 1609 survey.

"It is all listed by the individual *Ämter* or *Pfleggerichte*, of course. But for the general area that was administered from Amberg and Sulzbach combined, that is, the whole *Montanbereich* and not just the part in the Upper Palatinate proper, this lists eighty-eight thousand five hundred tons of iron ore that year. Of course, that doesn't count the lead and the tin."

Böcler turned. "Herr Pilcher, if you don't mind—I am by way of being a historian. There is something that is important, I think, if you wish to hear it."

"Go ahead."

"There are those who will tell you that the mines are nearing exhaustion. I do not believe that this is true. The 1609 production levels for ore were not as high as those of 1475; that is accurate. But, neither were the levels in the past century. In 1545, there were eighty-eight thousand tons mined; in 1581, eighty-six thousand tons. In 1609, production was holding steady. More importantly . . ."

"That's fine, go on."

"For those years, the production of the Sulzbach region *was* going down, but the production of the Amberg region was going *up*. From forty thousand tons to forty-four thousand tons to forty-seven thousand tons. The remainder was accounted for by other administrative jurisdictions. The production of sheet-iron was also holding steady: twenty-six thousand tons in 1581; the same in 1609. If we can trust the figures, the production of rolled iron was also holding steady. Even though the number of mills had gone down somewhat from 1545, the production was stable. And the number of rolling mills went up again between 1581 and 1609. Only by three, but it went up. The number of sheet mills remained the same. And the number of masters whose shops produced finished products was going up steadily."

Böcler swallowed hard. "That is what the 1609 survey tells us. Then production dropped. Dramatically. In the next decade. By 1618, there were only a third as many hammermills in operation as there had been in 1609."

Keith looked at him sharply. "By 1618? But . . . everyone I've talked to so far, including Duke Ernst, blames the production drop on the war. That was *before* the war seriously affected the Upper Palatinate."

Böcler nodded, almost anxiously. "I doubted it, at first. Because everybody is starting with the 1609 survey and saying that the decline has been caused by the armies marching through. And that certainly hasn't helped; the various armies have destroyed a great deal of the infrastructure. But I went back and checked, over and over. We don't have anything for 1618 as convenient as the 1609 survey. I had to look at lots and lots of different records. I've gone over the numbers, again and again. Many of the mills and forges that the armies destroyed had already been abandoned; many of the mine shafts that they collapsed were no longer being worked."

"You are telling me," Keith said, "that no matter how the

cartel-masters badmouth the situation, the problem is not with the invasions. It is with the system. Do you have any idea why this happened?"

"No. But I can tell you one thing. I have tried to get more information. The masters of the *Hammerinnung* don't want to talk about it."

Keith rubbed his jaw thoughtfully. "They certainly didn't mention it to me, I can tell you that. So. They were already cutting production back then. And they do not want to make serious investments now. I've just been assuming that they've been frightened off by the destruction that the war brought, and that they were going to keep telling me that the investment wasn't likely to be worthwhile until there appears to be some prospect of a durable peace. You *are* saying, basically, that the main drop came before the war? And that you can prove it?"

Böcler nodded.

Keith clapped Böcler on the shoulder. "You're a good man, Charlie Brown."

Böcler made a note to himself. *Identify Charlie Brown.*

Leopold Cavriani was reaching the same conclusion as Böcler, but on a different basis. He had spent the past weeks, when they weren't actually in negotiations, riding through the countryside with Marc, looking at the local dog mines, or opencast mines (better described as holes in the ground), and forges. The active mines were still producing ore; good ore, some of it; twenty percent iron ore. Few of the big smelters had been rebuilt; fewer of the mills. But Marc could smell iron. That was one thing he had learned from Jacob Durre. Up the valley of a little side-stream, they had found a local landowner with a half-dozen employees, water held by a homemade dam turning a homemade wheel, and a forge with seven hearths.

"Little things," the head smith said apologetically. "Not like it was when I was an apprentice. But men still need tools and nails; women still need spits and skillets. I can't do anchors, and wouldn't have a way to ship them to Venice if I could. But I can do chains. Everybody needs chains. Everybody needs shovels. We peddle our things; take them to the fairs."

"If you wanted to expand, what would you need?" That question was from Marc.

"What could we use? Let me tell you, we could use a pump. Not just to pull the water out of the shafts, though that would be a help. Even more, to pull water upstream when the creek is running low. Run the same water over the wheel three or four times and keep the trip hammer moving faster. Not waste it by the bucket."

The smith pointed to a spot in the stream, just below the mill. "That's where our pond was, with the creek dammed up. We had a pump, before the war. Brought in from Nürnberg. It's one thing that I haven't been able to figure out how to rebuild, and I sure can't afford to buy another one."

Marc asked a question.

"Ore?" The man laughed. "There's plenty of ore. If we had the men to mine it and work it. Not endless ore, of course. Sometimes a seam runs out. But there's enough ore on this one little creek to keep ten forges the size of mine busy for ten of my lifetimes."

Cavriani had been to Sulzbach, too. Sulzbach, on the Pegnitz, was more closely tied to Nürnberg than Amberg was. Jacob Durre had contacts there.

"The main problem?" The old man had repeated his question. "I'll tell you the main problem, all right. The larger masters in the *Hammerinnung* made their money before the war. Enough money that they rose into the lower nobility and married the daughters of imperial knights. Had sons whose mothers taught them that working with their hands was beneath their station."

He snorted and held out his own hands. Burned and scarred, sometimes one scar partly on top of another. "I rolled sheet iron all my life and took the wounds from it. As many as the average cavalryman will ever take. But it is less honorable to take wounds in making something than destroying it. So they think, in any case. As my wife taught my sons. Much to my regret. If I had my life to live over, Herr Cavriani, that's the first thing I would do differently. When my father chose a knight's daughter for my wife, I would tell him no."

He winked. "Just a word to the wise, you know. If you're thinking of marrying off that fine son of yours over here"—he nodded at Marc, who blushed a little—"don't pick a daughter of the nobility for him. Don't even pick the daughter of a merchant who wants to *buy* a title of nobility. Not unless you want useless grandsons.

Take it from an old iron man. They've built themselves fine castles, a lot of them. But soon they will find that without the money coming in from iron, they will be eating stones off their expensive tableware. And not even be able to blame it on the armies, if Gustav Adolf manages to bring this war to an end. They could have rebuilt most of it by now. If they had the will."

"So iron could be as profitable as before?" Marc asked.

The old man frowned. "The profits—how much you gained on the basis of how much you had to spend—were changing, even before the war. I wasn't in the mining end of it, but I heard the mine owners complaining. It was becoming more expensive to get the ore out of the ground. More digging, deeper shafts; that meant more pumping, more transport costs to bring the ore up. They were still making profits, but not at the rate they had a century earlier. But if you can't get the mines back into operation, there's not much point in asking the mills and forges to rebuild. That's where you have to start."

"Presuming that someone could provide the ore, do you know," Cavriani asked, "of any smelters or hammer masters of an age that they would be willing to risk the effort to rebuild? Or would they be held back by the other cartel masters?"

The old man's laughter was like a bark. "Hell, man, I'm not dead yet. If you could break the *Innung* and find me some capital, I'd rebuild my own mill during the time that God has left to me."

He picked up his mug, drank deeply, and put it down again. "And leave it to the men who built it with me. Not to the fools who are my sons."

"Is he alone?" Keith asked. "Or are there others who think like him? That may be crucial."

When Ollie answered Keith's letter, he put it a little differently.

Even if you break the cartel, they aren't thinking about the tonnages that we'll be needing for major industries if we go for nineteenth-century technology. Not the amounts of raw iron that we'll need for the railroads. Not even for the telegraph lines. But if, with just basic help with things such as pumps, they can get back to their 1609 capacity pretty quickly and supply the needs that they were supplying then—after that, the production from any new mines that we open up can be directed to new industrial development. We won't be backpedaling, trying to meet the old requirements as well as the new ones.

Once they've gotten to that point, using what they know and using men who already know how to do it the old way, we can talk to them about immense increases in production.

But, right now, see if you can get them back to supplying Nürnberg and Venice with what they need. Right now, both cities are our allies. They're starving, economically, because of the iron shortage, and we don't have any miracles for them. Twenty years from now, maybe. They need the iron yesterday. See if you can get it for them tomorrow.

If production goes up beyond that level, Grantville and Magdeburg will be happy to take the surplus. If any. Struve-Reardon Gunworks could certainly use an expanded supply. That's why I sent you. But, the more I think about it, talking to Mike, we just can't afford, politically, to grab every bit of iron in sight for ourselves. Not even if we pay for it. See about setting up partnerships, if you can, that run from Amberg through Nürnberg up to us. Tie these border regions of the USE into our network.

Keith hadn't been just been sitting while he waited for Ollie to answer his report. He looked at the pile of notes he had taken. Five years ago, if anyone had told him that he would be sitting here—sitting anywhere at all, up-time or down-time—feeling happy about something he had read in a law book, he would have laughed directly in the guy's face.

With Böcler's help, he had been digging into the laws that covered mining in the Upper Palatinate. Böcler had given him a good start and a capsule history. The earliest sets of laws that covered mining around here—at least, the earliest that anybody had kept—were in Amberg's collection of city ordinances, the *Bergrechtssätze*. They'd been there for at least a couple of centuries; then were dropped out in the 1550s. Böcler said that they'd basically been superseded, so he hadn't taken time to look at them. Some of them had been taken over into the rules and regulations of the *Hammerinnung* itself; that was basically a government-licensed, ah, something. Not a corporation, because it wasn't incorporated. But the counts had approved the rules and regulations, so it must have had some kind of legal status. Finally, there were several codifications of the *Bergordnungen*, the mining laws that the counts themselves had issued, with changes and amendments. The latest of those was the 1594 edition, so that's what Keith had been reading.

It had been real nice of them to write these in German rather than Latin. German, Keith could pretty well handle now. As far as he was concerned, Latin just sat there on the page and looked pretty. If they'd been in Latin, he'd have been dependent on Böcler's having free time, or would have had to find someone else to write out a translation. As it was, reading the laws sort of gave him a grasp on how things worked. Or, at least, on how things were supposed to work. There was almost always a considerable difference between a bunch of regulations and the way they got implemented. Safety rules, for example. As it was, he thought it might have been helpful to have a lawyer looking over his shoulder. On one side. And someone who had been there and knew how it really worked looking over his shoulder. On the other side.

And they might even owe old Duke Maximilian the Horrible of Bavaria one vote of thanks. Even a small cheer. In 1626, he had dissolved the *Hammerinnung*. Mainly, of course, because so many of the owners had been Protestants who had gone into exile. Partly, because he'd been pretty pissed to discover that where he was expecting to annex a wealthy territory, a money mine, which really it had been shortly before the 1620s, he had gotten a poor one.

Plus, of course, he had gotten the Palatine's electoral vote. Maybe that had made it worthwhile for the old man, but he had still been pretty pissed. He'd followed up the 1626 edict by nationalizing the Amberg mines in 1628; a conquered province was a conquered province, after all. At that point, production had plummeted to just about nothing. The Bavarian officials had all sorts of excuses—wood shortages, local unrest. Duke Ernst was still trying to sort through the fall-out from that one.

The *Hammerinnung* had been a real, honest-to-goodness, cartel.

Keith would never classify himself as the world's greatest brain but, by golly, he knew conspiracy in restraint of trade when he saw it, and he saw it right here. It had tried to set up a monopoly. It had done a pretty effective job. It wasn't any guild; it was an organization of owners. Mine owners, smelter owners, hammer mill and rolling mill owners, covering the process, top to bottom. The regulations really focused on how all of those interacted with one another. Officially, nobody was required to join. It just wasn't possible to do business successfully unless you did. It was intended to restrict competition. Well, the guilds did that too, but you had guilds of weavers and dyers, cloth finishers, and the like. No single guild, as far as he knew, had ever really tried to control every step of fabric manufacture from the time the sheep was born until the finished piece of wool cloth was shipped out.

Presuming that nobody had been dumb enough to revoke Duke Max's edict since 1626—nothing that anyone had said so far indicated that it had been revoked—then, legally, the cartel was gone, no matter how often the cartel men appealed to its sacred regulations when he talked to them. Which meant that it would be a lot easier to open a path for the few masters who wanted to rebuild and start over than he and Cavriani had been expecting.

He would have to check, though, about whether or not it had been revoked. Nothing that anyone had said to him before today had even given him a clue that the edict had ever been issued, either.

As for rebuilding the mills and hammers whose former owners weren't interested, not to mention the fact that not one of those laws really contained any provisions that protected the workers . . . The best way to manage that would take some thinking about.

Preferably by Duke Ernst and Ollie, or even Mike; not by Keith Pilcher.

He closed the book. It was about time that he got some supper and went to bed.

CHAPTER 23

Difficultas Laborque Discendi

Vienna

Maria Anna rested her chin on the heel of her hand, her elbow on the table, while she watched her younger brother.

Leopold Wilhelm had collected a half-dozen different chess sets and spread them out. On the basis of the latest news, he was replaying what had happened. At Hamburg. At Luebeck Bay. At Copenhagen. At Ahrensbök. Since his ambitions were not nautical, he was devoting at least eighty percent of his time to Ahrensbök, proclaiming to anyone who would listen that even he, at the age of twenty, with no practical military experience, could have done better than the French generals.

She smiled. Leo had made it very clear that, in his opinion, de Valois had learned nothing by living an additional thirty years.

Then there was the Wietze raid. Turenne.

He grumbled something along the lines of, *if only Papa would let me into the field . . .*

"Yes, Leo," Maria Anna murmured soothingly, for the fourteenth or fifteenth time. She knew as well as the rest of them that the youngest of the family had minimal interest in the ecclesiastical career for which Papa had destined him when he was only five years old. Leo's enthusiasms ran in the direction of armies. And art.

In practice, of course, a "career in the church" meant that he already held a lot of bishoprics, but had not taken any vows. The family was reserving the right to change its collective mind, in case Ferdinand did not produce surviving male heirs.

Sometimes great families did change their collective minds. Think of Claudia de Medici in Tyrol, who had sent them the wonderful music from up-time. *Could that have only been in January? It seemed so long ago. Much more than four months.*

Claudia's father had been a cardinal before he resigned and married. Her second husband, Uncle Leopold, Papa's younger brother, had been a bishop before he resigned and married. In fact, he had been Leo's predecessor as bishop of Passau and Strassburg. Now Uncle Leopold was dead, but he and Claudia had given the world four young Habsburg heirs.

There was nothing to say that, some day, Leo might not be called upon to marry and take up a secular life.

Still, she knew, at present he found his circumstances— constricting. Not that he wasn't pious. Not that he didn't live in such a manner as to avoid scandal. At least, in another year, he would enter the Teutonic Order. Some day, after the death of the incumbent and coadjutor, he would become grand master. That had been agreed upon when he was eleven, the same year, 1625, that he succeeded to Uncle Leopold's two dioceses.

Looked at one way, the Teutonic Order was just another ecclesiastical benefice, among the pluralities he was accumulating. Looked at in another, it would give him a reasonable chance at military action. But it hadn't happened yet.

Maria Anna frowned, considering the frustrating difficulties of learning what one needed to know from the libraries in Grantville. It was a lot of work, even for Jesuits who were used to doing that sort of thing, and often very slow to produce results.

The *encyclopedias* said that in 1639, another five years, Ferdinand had entrusted Leo with command of the imperial army and he hadn't done a shabby job of it, either. At least, he'd had enough sense to listen to more experienced advisers. Plus he had become regent of the Netherlands after Don Fernando. Not to mention that he had been in charge of the ceremony when Queen Kristina of Sweden converted to the Catholic church after her abdication.

All of which she—and he, and Ferdinand, and Doña Mencia—knew, not because the world had remembered Leopold Wilhelm von Habsburg as an archduke of Austria, not because the world had remembered him as a general, not because the world had remembered his efforts to advance the Counter-Reformation and support the Jesuits, but . . . Leo was remembered only because he had—would have?—the sense to employ a painter named David Teniers, whom its *encyclopedias* did remember, as the purchasing agent for his art collection. The author of the article about Teniers had been gracious enough to include a paragraph about his patron.

It had taken the researcher they employed a really long time to find any information at all about her younger brother's future.

She shifted her position a little. She had been watching Leo for quite a while and was starting to get stiff.

Teniers had made a career of painting peasants. That was the source of his lasting fame. A humbling thought. She should ask Doña Mencia to ask her brother Cardinal Bedmar to find out more about Teniers. He lived in Antwerp, after all.

She looked back at Leo. *Actually, that other world had not done too badly by him.*

He nodded his head in response to her most recent soothing murmur and returned his attention to the chess sets.

"Right before your wedding, too," Cecelia Renata contributed that evening. "I can hardly believe it. Such a terrible defeat. Such horrible, absolutely disastrous, omens for a marriage. Have you checked your horoscope?"

Maria Anna grimaced. She had a horoscope, of course. A very elaborate one. It had been drawn up immediately after her birth and updated regularly. No important person would attempt to go through life without the guidance provided by a horoscope. Astrologers were among the better-paid court personnel, once one got below the ranks of the nobility.

"I don't need a horoscope to tell me that the Habsburgs came through it all relatively unscathed," she answered. "Spain was not directly involved this time. At least, not heavily. Perhaps our cousin in Madrid learned something from the way Richelieu sacrificed Admiral Oquendo's fleet the last time. And Don Fernando . . ."

She stopped. They were alone. As alone as they ever were most of the time. Papa had returned to his audience chamber after supper, the constant parade of solemn-faced men dressed all in black having redoubled since the news of the League of Ostend's various disasters in the north reached Vienna two days earlier. Mama had gone to her apartments to rest. But. Not only Doña Mencia was here, but also Cecelia Renata's chief attendant. And also. She glanced at the servants who stood by the door.

She was not certain that it would be entirely prudent to continue. Rephrase that. She was certain that it would not be prudent to continue. Father Lamormaini knew too much about what occurred in her private chambers. Someone—someone close to her retinue—was reporting to Papa's intelligence officers.

At least her trousseau was finished. Finally. Frau Stecher and the seamstresses had gone into packing mode. Which meant, unfortunately, that she hadn't seen little Susanna for several days.

She would discuss Don Fernando's astonishing level of non-participation with Doña Mencia when they were in private. They actually were in private, sometimes. Doña Mencia slept in her room, after all. An Austrian archduchess did not spend her nights unchaperoned.

Of course, a maid slept on a cot at the foot of her bed, also, in case she should need something during the night. She could always need something during the night and send Magdalena on an errand.

So she looked back at her sister, grinning, "The only thing my horoscope predicts is that I will make a splendid marriage. That's safe enough, of course. If a daughter of the Habsburgs survives long enough, and does not become a nun, it's the only kind of marriage she's likely to make. Yours says the same thing." She pursed her lips. "Of course, it does not say that I will be marrying Uncle Max six weeks from now. Or anyone else, specifically, at any precise time. No more than yours predicts exactly who you will marry. I sometimes suspect that the motto of court astrologers is, 'Vague is your friend.'"

"It's obvious that the up-timers *had* better libraries." Maria Anna was afraid that the tone of her voice was a little sulky. So be it. "The books that they *do* have in Grantville mention them. The Library of Congress, in their own United States of America. The British Museum. The *Bibliothèque Nationale* in Paris. There was a great library in Florence." She paused a moment and glared at Doña Mencia. "A great library in *Vienna*."

"If God had chosen to send Vienna back from up-time, we would not be here ourselves, but somewhere else," Doña Mencia pointed out.

"I wish you didn't have to be so reasonable." Maria Anna tossed her head. "At least, not reasonable all the time. Perhaps God could just have sent the library. Right here, next door to the *Hofburg*, where we could use it ourselves instead of depending on the Jesuits."

Somewhere under her breath, Doña Mencia muttered something about spoiled brats who wanted eggs in their beer. Aloud, though, she said, "There was a great library in Munich, also. Since a certain archduchess will be leaving Vienna in less than a week, while she is wishing for the moon, she might devote her efforts to expressing a desire that God had chosen to transfer the Munich library, instead. Or send up a prayer that he had deigned to move all the libraries she listed to Munich, conveniently close to the *Residenz*. While she is coveting the possession an up-time library that exists nowhere in this world, she might as well make a thorough job of her exercise in futility."

While it was not a direct reproach, it had that effect. Maria Anna apologized.

Doña Mencia accepted the apology gracefully.

As she said her final rosary of the evening, Maria Anna was glad that Doña Mencia had not been offended. The terrible news in regard to the League of Ostend had burdened everyone's spirits, but that gave her no right to be rude to her attendants.

Of course, it was the terrible news about the League of Ostend that so burdened her, she assured herself. Not the thought that in six weeks she would be married to Uncle Max. That was just one of the duties that went with her station in life. One of the unvarying duties. Even if the League of Ostend had won great victories at Hamburg, at Luebeck Bay, at Copenhagen, and at Ahrensbök, in six weeks she would still have become duchess of Bavaria.

Some circumstances did not change. She submitted herself to the will of God.

Part Five

June 1634

Those shadowy recollections

CHAPTER 24

Tempora Jucunda

Vienna

Every item that had personalized her apartments, made them her own, was gone. Packed, some of them. The rest placed into storage. Some day, a daughter of her brother Ferdinand and his wife Mariana would live in these rooms. Until then, they would stand empty except for the bed, chests, and chairs.

Maria Anna walked over to the window and stood watching as the carriages that would take the court to Passau for the ceremony transferring her to Bavaria lined up on the streets below. The wagons were waiting outside the walls. The servants had finished the job of loading the baggage the day before, but things were moving slowly. A woman, the wife of a chancery official from the place of her carriage in the cortege, lost control of a wiggling lapdog. A groom grabbed it before it could spook the horses, thank goodness. A team out of control could have delayed everything for hours. It seemed that every additional minute since breakfast just made her more melancholy.

She turned back in toward the room, fingering her rosary. "Did you manage to get any news this morning?"

Doña Mencia reached into her satchel. "No newspapers. I suppose that Frau Stecher has kept little Susanna too busy to go find any for us. The private secretary to the ambassador from the

Spanish Netherlands sent me correspondence that arrived in the diplomatic pouch yesterday evening. Someone delivered it while we were at mass. It doesn't contain much that we didn't already know. There's a list of all the prominent people who are or will be taking part in the Congress of Copenhagen called by Gustavus Adolphus. The official sessions have started. The preliminary official sessions, at least. There's a lot of discussion of Prince Ulrik's heroic actions. They've caused a great deal of excitement."

"It must be nice for the nobles to be able to find and talk about at least one heroic prince among all the heroic commoners in this campaign." Maria Anna's voice was flat. "What do they say about the Norwegian whose designs and ideas let the prince be heroic? Or what Oxenstierna thinks about the Swedish king's agreement to negotiate with the Danes?"

"As for the Norwegian, it depends upon who is writing the dispatch. Oxenstierna is said to be less than pleased. Both with heroic Danish princes and heroic commoners." Doña Mencia paused, trying to think of something that would distract the archduchess. "Many of the participants were brought in the up-timers' airplanes. Scaglia is there as an observer and was able to observe the planes land and take off again."

"Don Fernando sent an observer to Copenhagen? Was permitted to send one? Isn't that a little . . . odd?"

"He was invited to do so by the USE ambassadress. By Rebecca Abrabanel."

"With the Swede's permission?"

"Presumably. Although one hears that the Stearns administration often acts on the maxim that it is easier to ask for forgiveness after a *fait accompli* than to obtain permission in advance. We live in very interesting times."

"But Don Fernando himself is not going to be in Copenhagen?"

"That would be a little . . . excessive . . . under the circumstances. Whatever people expect, whatever people speculate, he has not yet made a formal break with Spain. Although—it is said that Rubens has collected portraits of all the eligible Catholic princesses. Not, it is to be presumed, just on a whim."

"Before my betrothal to Uncle Max, I would have been among the eligible ones."

"Indeed, your portrait is among those in Brussels. Presumably, Rubens ordered one before your betrothal became official. Which is interesting, since it indicates that Don Fernando must have been contemplating his next move for several months before the rumors began to circulate."

Maria Anna went back to the window. She wished that the steward would send someone to summon her. There was nothing left for her in the *Hofburg*. She might as well leave right now. But people entered the carriages in a certain order, defined by protocol. It would never do for the emperor's daughter, much less the emperor, to sit waiting while lesser mortals ran back into the palace for forgotten items or grooms repaired a bit of harness that broke at the last minute. She would be called third from the last. Then Mariana, baby Ferdinand, and her ladies-in-waiting. Then Papa and Mama and their personal attendants. After that, her wedding procession could start on its way.

She placed one hand on the drapery. "Talk to me, Doña Mencia. Tell me a story. 'Once upon a time . . .'" She laughed softly. "But leave out the fairy tale ending, please."

Besançon, in the Franche-Comté

By the time Bernhard of Saxe-Weimar ended his faked maneuvering in the Breisgau and brought his forces back to his administrative center at Besançon, there was more news from Paris. Some of his aides thought Bernhard had acted precipitously, even rashly, to have ended the maneuvers immediately after receiving the first reports of Torstensson's crushing defeat of de Valois' army at Ahrensbök. But the newspaper accounts from Paris that awaited them at Besançon made it obvious that he'd gauged the situation correctly. Bernhard was basking in the sunshine of a bold move that had turned out quite well, and all but sneering at his more timid associates.

Richelieu had summoned Marshal Turenne and his cavalry to Paris. That was a sure sign that the cardinal was now completely preoccupied with France's internal situation. Well . . .

Mostly preoccupied. Richelieu was quite capable of handling several matters at once, and doing them all very competently. But it really didn't matter if he did manage to devote some time to gauging the situation with Bernhard in the Franche-Comté. What could he do about it, really, beyond sending stern missives?

The only capable army he could rely upon at the moment was Turenne's, and he needed Turenne guarding Paris and the royal palace at the Louvre.

Bernhard clapped his hands. The gesture was simply one of satisfaction; indeed, exuberant satisfaction. Not only was the political situation developing very nicely, but his indigestion had ceased as well.

"Who says plans never work the way they're supposed to?" he demanded, smiling slyly at his chief aide, Friedrich von Kanoffski.

"Not I," replied von Kanoffski. Unlike some others, Friedrich had had the sense to keep his mouth shut.

Bernhard nodded. Then, after a moment, said: "I believe I've been a little testy of late." He cocked an inquisitive eyebrow.

Friedrich shook his head, making sure to maintain a solemn expression. "I can't say I noticed, Your Grace."

Amberg, the Upper Palatinate

"I suppose there's no way to restrain General Banér now," said Duke Ernst. He leaned back in the chair in his office and studied the mass of papers on his desk. "As if I didn't have enough to worry about already."

Colonel Erik Haakansson Hand chuckled and shook his head. "After the news of Ahrensbök? Not a chance. Johan was champing at the bit already. He's jealous by nature, and of no other of my cousin's generals is he more jealous than Lennart Torstensson. Johan Banér is looking at his thirty-eighth birthday, in a couple of weeks, and Lennart just turned thirty-one. Now, the upstart Torstennson has the great victory at Ahrensbök under his belt—and to make things worse, he was the commander-in-chief at the battle, not simply serving under my cousin. So now Johan is determined to match the feat—come as close as he can, at least—by seizing Ingolstadt from the Bavarians."

"But it's silly, Erik, even in those terms. Ahrensbök was a decisive victory, one of the very few such in the annals of war. Even if Banér succeeds in reducing Ingolstadt, it wouldn't come even close. To be sure, having a Bavarian enclave north of the Danube is a nuisance to us, but that's all it is. Especially since we have our own enclave south of the river at Neuburg."

Colonel Hand shrugged. "What difference does it make? For good or ill, Gustav Adolf made it clear that Johan could operate as an independent commander down here. You simply can't restrain him, any longer."

Duke Ernst sighed. "True enough. What do you recommend I do?"

"Since you can't stop him, you may as well do what you can to see that Banér succeeds. I don't quite agree with you, anyway, that Ingolstadt is simply a nuisance. So long as the Bavarians have a bridgehead north of the Danube, they'll pose a continual military threat to the USE. Seizing Ingolstadt would improve our strategic situation considerably."

As the chief administrator of the Upper Palatinate for Gustav Adolf and the USE, Duke Ernst was not inclined to argue the point. In truth, he'd be a lot happier himself if he didn't always have to keep a wary eye on Ingolstadt. These things were unpredictable. Sooner or later, Duke Maximilian was bound to dismiss the fortress' garrison commander, Cratz von Scharffenstein, and replace him with someone who was less slothful, if not necessarily less avaricious. An energetic and aggressive commander of Ingolstadt's forces, combined with the already-aggressive Bavarian cavalry under the command of von Mercy and von Werth, could present a real problem.

So . . . Colonel Hand was undoubtedly right. If Johan Banér was determined to press the matter, best to give him all the assistance possible.

"There are the mercenary units in Franconia," he mused. "I know for a certainty that Steve Salatto and Scott Blackwell would like to get rid of them. Given the situation with the Ram Rebellion, mercenary units of that nature are more trouble than they're worth. Ten times better at stirring up animosity among the populace than they are at squelching it."

"True. And what's better still, after Ahrensbök I think it's quite likely the emperor would agree to freeing up some of Torstensson's units and sending them down here."

The duke winced. "They'll be CoC regiments, Erik. CoC-influenced, at the very least. Hardly the sort of troops that would please Johan Banér."

"Fuck Banér," said Colonel Hand bluntly. "That's simply the price of his own ambition. He can't take Ingolstadt unless he can neutralize the Bavarian cavalry—and he doesn't have cavalry as good as that commanded by von Mercy and von Werth. He doesn't have captains who can match them, either. The regiments from Torstensson's army could make the difference, especially if you can persuade my cousin to release one of the flying artillery regiments. By all accounts, they were quite effective against the French cavalry."

Duke Ernst thought about it, for perhaps a minute. Then, nodded. "As you say ... Well." He was not about to repeat the crude expression aloud, even if in the privacy of his own mind the sentiment *fuck Banér* came quite frequently. Even easily.

"We'll do as you recommend," he said. "Would you do me the favor of composing the message to the emperor? I'll have it sent out over the radio this evening."

"It would be my pleasure, Ernst. The truth is, I'm tired of those Bavarian bastards at Ingolstadt myself."

Mary Simpson had had an appointment to see Duke Ernst today, right after breakfast, to further discuss the prospects of fund raising for the normal school. She'd been looking forward to it, since Ernst Wettin was a man who positively loved the subject of education. In a happier world, he'd have been the Secretary of the USE's department of education—which still didn't exist, unfortunately—instead of the administrator of a province under military occupation. He was certainly competent at the task, but it was not one that really suited his temperament.

But the meeting had had to be cancelled. Just when the flurry of political and military activity triggered off by the news of Ahrensbök had seemed to be dying down, news came to Amberg from Düsseldorf of an event that was probably even more important to the Upper Palatinate, if not to the world as a whole. It seemed that Duke Wolfgang Wilhelm and his son and heir, Philip, had gotten themselves killed in the course of a stupid attack on the Republic of Essen while the duke was pushing his claims to his maternal inheritance of Jülich, Berg, and parts of Ravensburg.

Westphalia would have to take care of itself now that Torstensson had so thoroughly trounced the French at Ahrensbök, but it would make a huge difference right here in the Upper Palatinate that the heir to Pfalz-Neuburg was no longer a nephew of Duke Maximilian of Bavaria, but rather an infant. Duke Ernst and most of his advisers, including Colonel Erik Haakansson Hand, had been closeted for two days discussing the matter.

So be it. Mary would see to rescheduling the meeting with the duke in due time. Meanwhile, she could relax in the comfort of the inn, savoring the knowledge that her husband John had come through the hard-fought naval campaign in the Baltic. Without so much as a scratch, so far as she could determine from the newspaper reports. He was certainly alive and not seriously injured. All the accounts agreed on that.

Her companion at the breakfast table did not share her insouciance, however. Veronica Dreeson slapped the newspaper down on the table. "Arrested! What was that idiot boy thinking?"

She glared at Mary. It was one of those glares that was not simply rhetorical. Ronnie wanted an answer.

What to say . . . ?

Reading between the lines of the newspaper stories—and all the newspapers were dwelling on this one; no, slobbering over it—the situation seemed clear enough. It was obvious that Eddie Cantrell had been nabbed *in flagrante delicto*—by the girl's father himself, to make things perfect—while engaged in activities with the daughter of the Danish king that the newspaper did not precisely delineate but were not hard to imagine.

"I suspect he wasn't thinking much at all, Ronnie," Mary said, as mildly as possible.

It was going to be a long day.

Amberg, the Upper Palatinate

"Elbow room," Keith Pilcher exclaimed.

Leopold Cavriani raised his eyebrows.

Keith put his newspaper down. "Did anyone ever tell you about Daniel Boone?"

Leopold nodded a yes; Marc nodded a no. Keith turned toward the boy.

"He was a frontiersman. Not to start out with. His father was a settler in Pennsylvania, a weaver, with a big, comfortable house. All the amenities, like Huddy Colburn puts in the ads when he's trying to sell a house. A spring for fresh water, a cold room for keeping food fresh. Plastered walls. It's a park, now. Well, it was a park, then. Daniel Boone's birthplace, that is. Maxine dragged me to see it once."

Leopold raised his eyebrows again.

Keith looked back toward the older man. "I do have a point, here. Well, George Boone's little boy Daniel didn't take to amenities. He headed out to the frontier and he pretty much kept moving. Western North Carolina. Kentucky. Missouri. That's where he died, out in Missouri, on the other side of the Mississippi River. As far away from where he was born as . . . oh, as Muscovy, where Bernie Zeppi has gone, is from here. Maybe even farther. And when I was in fourth grade, we had to memorize a poem for a school program. I've forgotten most of it. Heck, I never learned most of it—I was just in the chorus that recited the refrain after the soloists went out front and gave a verse.

"Every time he made a move, it went: 'Elbow room,' said Daniel Boone."

"So?"

"So that's what Gustav has gotten for us. He's bought us a year, Cavriani. You and Count August, Duke Ernst, Ollie and me, and all the iron people here. He probably thinks that what is important is that he beat Denmark and got his little girl betrothed to that prince, but I know better. We've got a year of elbow room before the next crunch comes down. A year to get things going again.

"Now we've got to get these guys to roll up their sleeves and show some elbow."

CHAPTER 25

Enchiridion Chirurgicum

Amberg, the Upper Palatinate

Breakfast at the inn was usually when the men talked over what they had read in the newspapers—the war in the north, what Wallenstein was doing in Bohemia, anything that had been heard from Venice or Rome. Supper at the inn was when they compared notes on the day's work. What each of them learned separately was of far more use after it had been combined with the information that the others had collected. The reluctance of the mine owners to invest, for example, which they had made very clear, made a lot more sense in the light of what the Cavrianis had learned about cost/profit ratios and what Keith had found out about Bavaria's nationalization of the mines and the resulting uncertain legal status.

"But," Keith summed up, "I think it can be done. Not as fast or as easily as we were hoping. Duke Ernst is going to have to cut some knots. And hit some kind of a balance between total control and letting the entrepreneurs run wild with no supervision at all. It's not as if our—the SoTF's, I mean—laws are in effect here, covering labor relations and pollution and such. He's going to have to think about that, and some of it may have to go all the way up to the king, ah, emperor, for approval. I just hope that won't drag out too long. Otherwise, new technology will help a lot—stationary steam pumps for the big operations. Capital will help a lot, too—low cost loans for the smaller operations to buy the traditional pumps."

Marc started to open his mouth; then closed it again.

Keith waved at him. "Go ahead, kid. If you've got something to say, then say it."

Marc looked at his father. "I'm, ah, here to watch. To observe. To learn. Not to say things."

"Say it, and I'll decide whether it was worth saying." Keith wasn't entirely joking.

"Well, sir, I don't think you're going to get younger men for the rebuilding of the metals trades once you have the ore. Not skilled workers, I mean. Oh, you can get plenty of unskilled workers. Ex-soldiers. Servants, even, from farms and towns, if they're strong enough for the work. Especially if they want to get married. The mines and mills and smelters never tried to limit their men's marriages, the way towns and farmers do. Oh, they had barracks for the unmarried guys. But there's no need for miners to 'live in' the way servants do. And it's out in the country, not short on space the way walled towns always are. So the men can marry, build cottages; their wives can garden, keep chickens, cook for the unmarried men, do laundry. It works fine for them, as a system. They'll find that kind of worker. But skilled? I don't think so."

"Why not?" Keith was listening a little harder now.

"The whole *Montanbereich* has not really been working for fifteen years. That's . . . well, it's *almost* as long as I've been alive. The conditions described in the 1609 survey—that's several years *longer* than I've been alive. That's too long for a man to wait for a new job. They've left, if they could. I bet, if you look, you'll find them in mines and forges all over Germany, all the way to Silesia and Lusatia. In Austria and Bohemia. In northern Italy. Which means that they haven't been training apprentices here in the Upper Palatinate for that long, almost. So you're not going to find many younger masters and hardly any trained journeymen. Not even apprentices about to become journeymen—not except for just a few places, like the one Papa and I found out in the country. Plus, Duke Maximilian forced out a bunch more of the skilled workers who were Protestant, mostly grown men who naturally took their sons with them. Some have come back, but not many to stay. They've just come to get what they can and cut their losses. Then, of the ones who stayed in the 1620s, others have died of the plague and other epidemics since then. No, Herr Pilcher. I think, I really think—for the processing and finishing, it will be old men and untrained boys, at least to start with. That will slow things down. People may start to come back when things get going, but not . . . not right away."

Keith pursed his lips. "I'll file that away to think about. And mention it to Ollie."

Leopold Cavriani smiled to himself. His son had noticed this, thought about it, presented it clearly. He would have to compliment Jacob Durre.

The waiter appeared with food. Quite a lot of it. They dropped business for eating. Especially Marc. His capacity for food astonished the rest of them.

Toby Snell was with them, for a change. Like Mary and Veronica, he was living in the *Schloss*. Not, by any means, in such luxurious quarters. He was sleeping in a cot in a small room on the top floor, next to the array of large blue bottles and connecting wires and stuff that constituted a down-time radio room.

He started talking about his girlfriend, back home. Dawn. Not, he pointed out, his fiancée. Half-seriously, he lamented that even if she did agree to marry him, he was never going to be able to live up to the images on the romance novels that she read by the jillion.

"You'd think," he finished, "that fate would have done us guys a favor. That eventually, after the Ring of Fire, the things would have worn out. But no. What do the down-timers do? Reprint them! Complete with woodcuts of all the hunks on the covers."

"If you get her to say 'yes,'" Keith answered, "the rest of it is easy. If, that is, she's romantic *enough*."

Toby was inclined to listen. Keith's wife was a member of the same book club that Dawn had joined a while back.

"The hard part is having a wife who sees you the way you are. Hey, having one of those and keeping her in love with you is something of a challenge. If she notices that your hair is sort of thin on top"—he pointed to his own head—"and you're sort of sloppy about pruning the weigela bushes and sometimes you don't get around to taking out the garbage when she asks you to, how do you explain it? If she compares the waist size on your last set of briefs with the waist size on your new set of briefs, how are you supposed to persuade her that things aren't settling, so to speak? A realistic wife—that would be a problem."

Marc was listening with fascination.

"But a member of the Romance Readers book club. Hey, Toby, it's a cinch, if you do the husband business at a sort of minimum level. Basically, I mean, don't get hauled home sodden drunk very often. Usually get there for supper on time and call when you can't. Remember her birthday and anniversary with flowers. Which isn't that hard, in spite of all the jokes. I keep Max's birthday and our anniversary written on a note card on my machine. So, you see, just do that much. Your wife's imagination will take care of all the rest. You see, she really *wants* to have a romantic, hunky, husband. So she'll festoon you with all sorts of desired heroic qualities that you . . . ummm . . . may not actually have, like tinsel on a Christmas tree, and cheerfully ignore the fact that middle age is not just creeping up on you but has already arrived and taken up squatters' rights on your midsection."

Marc would have been happy to listen all evening, this being completely beyond anything he had thus far encountered in his rather sheltered Calvinist existence.

"You mean?" Toby was asking.

"Yup. Just don't deliberately disillusion the little thing, and she'll do all the rest of the work that needs to be done so she can have a Great Romance. Happily ever after. Guaranteed recipe, the old 'Pilcher special.'"

Toby pulled a little spray bottle and soft cloth out of his breast pocket and started to polish his glasses.

"Where did you get the cleaning fluid?" Keith asked.

"Just vinegar. Like everything else. Some vinegar manufacturer in Badenburg must be making a fortune out of Grantville, the amount of the stuff that we use. That's where the crocks full of it come from. McNally says it won't hurt the lenses and these little spray bottles last and last." Toby cocked his head. "Speaking of lasting, how long have you and Max been together, anyway?"

Keith thought about it. "Well, Mom brought Lyman and me back from Detroit the summer after she and Dad divorced. That would have been, um, '83. I started high school in Grantville as a sophomore. And I took Max to the Halloween dance that year. That was our first date. We got married the summer of '89. So it sort of depends on how you figure it, I guess."

"You really never dated anyone else?"

Keith shook his head. "We pretty much figured out that we'd be getting married some day on the second date. But Max was a year behind me in school and we didn't want to frazzle her folks. Old man Maddox was an okay guy, but Max's mom could be a real PITA sometimes. Plus, I knew that when I turned eighteen, Dad would stop the child support, just as soon as he legally could. So I graduated and moved over to Fairmont, got a factory job and started on my A.A. in night classes. Kept right on, summers and all, so it only took me three years. Max graduated the next year and commuted to State; we got married between her sophomore and junior years."

Keith grinned. "Want some advice from a wise old man, Toby? Ninety percent of marriages that go on the rocks land there because of that 'first you say you do and then you don't' business like the song says. Pretty soon it's 'gloom, despair, and agony on me.' He's down at Tip's having one too many and she's at the county seat talking to a divorce lawyer. If you want to be married to Dawn, just make up your mind that you're married to her, and then stick to it. And if you don't really want to be married to her for good, don't marry her in the first place."

Toby thought that this sounded altogether too simple. Leopold Cavriani, though, was nodding in approval; Marc was watching his father.

The conversation meandered on. Eventually, Lambert Felser asked if anyone else had heard mention that there was a lot of sickness going around.

"Not a lot," Keith answered. "But Tanzflecker didn't show for the meeting today. Nadelmann said that one of his children died last night."

"One of the radio techs is sick," Toby contributed. "He didn't feel well enough to get up this morning. I mentioned it to Mrs. Simpson and she came upstairs. Then she went and talked to Jake Ebeling and hauled Bill Hudson upstairs to look at him."

Jake was the military liaison from the up-time contingent in the USE military to Duke Ernst. Here to teach and to learn. Spent most of his time with Hand, the Swede. Bill was Willie Ray Hudson's grandson, trained since the Ring of Fire as an emergency medical technician. He was teaching and learning, too. Those two, with Dane Kitt and Mark Ellis, made up the whole body of up-time military assigned to Duke Ernst. The trade delegation had scarcely seen them since they'd been here. Kitt and Ellis weren't even in town. They had gone to Ingolstadt with Banér. Plus three "civilian advisors," one of whom, Bozarth, the UMWA man, was down in Regensburg schmoozing the city council, while the other two, Glazer and Fisher, were someplace out of sight doing something that no one had bothered to tell the trade delegation about. Probably something that no one was going to tell a trade delegation about.

"Plague?" Leopold Cavriani asked. It was the first thing that always came to mind. There had been plague in the entire Upper Palatinate since February 1632, when a passing army unit left a couple hundred infected soldiers behind; Amberg had been particularly hard-hit the previous winter.

Keith shook his head. "The local doctors say that it isn't. And, honestly, they ought to know. They can't cure plague, but they sure see enough of it to recognize it when it comes along."

Mary Simpson made the diagnosis first, long before Bill Hudson had finished leafing through his manuals. Through the admiral's old friendships in the Netherlands, she knew people at the World Health Organization who had worked for the international center for vaccination when the disease made its way through the former Soviet republics in the early 1990s.

Diphtheria.

The down-time physicians concurred. It was the "strangling angel of children." They had, all of them, seen it before. All too often.

"It's a kid's disease," Toby said, when Bill told him. "You get your DPT shots and that's that."

"They don't have DPT shots here," Bill pointed out. "And we don't have any magic bullet to cure it. Oh, yes, it's bacterial rather than viral. My little pamphlet says that it can be treated with penicillin. Or with erythromycin. Neither of which I happen to have available."

"Oh."

"Try to get through to Grantville tonight, will you, Toby? I know that reception in these hills has been driving you guys crazy, but please try. If not tonight, then tomorrow morning. Keep trying. Get me one of the doctors. What I have is chloramphenicol, and not much of that. Ask them if it works on diphtheria. If it doesn't, there's no point in wasting what we have; I'll save it for something it does work on. If it does work, well . . . ask them if they can send some more. Please."

"People don't really *die* of it, do they?"

"According to what I have here, it was a major killer, right up through the end of the nineteenth century. There aren't going to be DPT shots for a long, long, time. I've put your tech into quarantine. Let's hope that it doesn't spread too fast. What about you? Are *your* shots up to date? When did you get your last DT shot?"

Toby didn't have the slightest idea. "Last time that I had to get one, I suppose. That would have been, uh, when I started high school, maybe?"

"And you're twenty-five now? So, about ten years. Well, let's hope that you still have antibodies." Bill stomped off, looking glum.

He was feeling frightened. That's about how old his shots were, too. He was just a year younger than Toby. Of all the up-timers in Amberg, only two had their immunizations up to date when the Ring of Fire hit. Keith Pilcher was one of them, because of the nature of his job. He had to have tetanus shots, being a machinist, and diphtheria vaccine came with it. Mrs. Simpson was the other one, partly because she traveled so much; and partly because she was just naturally one of those super-picky people who kept everything up to date. Jake's last shot was before his and Toby's.

And there were a lot of down-timers who had never had diphtheria. Including, he found out, Mrs. Dreeson. She'd had a lot of stuff, but no diphtheria. Duke Ernst, yes; Böcler, no; Zincgref, yes; Hand, no; Brechbuhl, yes; Leopold Cavriani, no; Lambert Felser, no; Marc Cavriani, no. The "no" list went on and on. Not a virgin field, but bad enough.

Like the out-of-date immunizations, he hoped that the immunity gained from childhood exposure would last for the ones who'd already had it. Diphtheria was one of those things you could get again, once the antibodies wore off. Strangling on the swollen membranes in your own throat wasn't a pretty way to die. Not that there were very many pretty ways. It hit children hardest, mainly because their windpipes were smaller, more quickly closed off by the membranes.

The pamphlet talked about complications, too. *Severe heart and nervous system complications which develop after two to six weeks and can lead to collapse, paralysis, coma and death* in about five percent of the cases. He guessed that real doctors found that sort of information fascinating. And stuff about possible long-term complications for people who survived. He'd worry about those later.

And he was supposed to identify carriers? Not! At least, he could tell the down-timers that there *were* carriers and ask them to look for patterns. If person X's visit to a household is regularly followed by an outbreak, quarantine him, too. And tell them what the incubation period was. If he could convince them that it was contagious and that's how it was spread.

Oh, damn.

If he ever got out of the army, he was going back to Grantville. And going to work for Tom Stone. Let the other guys go to med school. He was going to make the medicines. Somebody else could deliver the doses.

Caspar Hell's voice was steady. "I have closed the school because of the epidemic. Too many children are quarantined, or their parents are afraid to let them come, for us even to try to hold classes."

None of the other Jesuits disputed that.

"We will offer the *collegium* to the city as a quarantine hospital. It is the largest suitable building. Those diagnosed can be brought here and we will nurse them. That may offer some hope, at least, that uninfected members of their families will escape exposure. Otherwise, the young *medic*, as they call him, tells us that whole families will die, one after another."

None of the other Jesuits disputed that, either. Most of them had seen it happen, when families, the sick and the well alike, were quarantined together in their own houses.

Duke Ernst accepted the offer of a lazarette with gratitude.

Hand crossed "espionage centered at the *collegium*" off his list of things to worry about for the time being.

Bill Hudson's hopes sank. He had kept wishing for a magic bullet. That someone could dispatch a 4x4 from Grantville with a batch of a lifesaving drug. Instead . . . as best the medical personnel in Grantville knew, chloramphenicol would not work on diphtheria. They didn't know just why. Diphtheria was a gram-positive bacillus, which chloramphenicol was effective against as a *class*. In short, it did work on the class of bacteria but they couldn't find anything in their searching that specifically said that it would work on *C. diphtheria*—on this specific organism. It probably wouldn't hurt someone, if he tried it on them as an experiment, Doc Adams had radioed. But they didn't have any evidence that it would help.

Jakob Balde found it odd, having so many strangers inside the private portions of the *collegium*. There were usually students, of course. The few boarding students, however, had now been confined to their own quarters on the other side of the building, where the infection had not entered yet, and to the care of one of the cooks.

The Jesuits were not the only ones who volunteered to nurse. The older up-time man had been here, almost from the start. He wasn't squeamish, either. An up-time woman had volunteered to come, but Father Hell had drawn the line at having that. So she worked in the city, with the young *medic*, who insisted that he was not a full-fledged physician. Doing something that she called triage. The arriving patients were marked: those who, God willing, would benefit from nursing; those who, barring a miracle of God, probably would not.

The other men who assisted the Jesuits in caring for the sick had only one thing in common. Chosen by Duke Ernst and the up-timers, they had all had the disease before and survived it. And, of course, a second thing: they were willing to come. Duke Ernst had not forced them, other than some of his own direct subordinates and some of the city employees. A few Catholics—there were not many Catholics in Amberg any more. Several Lutherans, several Calvinists. A Jew, just a peddler passing through the city. Two Swiss men who listed no religion when they arrived, which probably meant that they deserved burning for heresy. Jakob Balde, now in charge of the hospital, had chosen not to ask them for details.

Duke Ernst had not closed off the city; which was the reason the Jew and the two Swiss were here. One could not quarantine a city for every little disease that came along. For plague, yes, but not for diphtheria. Life had to go on.

Three deaths; five deaths; nine deaths. The count went up every day.

Father Hell among them. Also Oswald Kaiser, one of the lay

brothers, a cabinetmaker who had been working on finishing the interiors of some of the rooms.

Balde, in the company of the regent, continued his tour of the sickbeds. And pulled the sheet over the face of another child.

None of the rest of them would have believed that Keith Pilcher could stand up to Veronica Dreeson until he did it. Over his dead body, he announced, was Veronica going to be involved in the care of the sick.

"Because," he said, "you never had diphtheria and if you die on us here, everybody back home will blame it on Maxine's not liking you. They'll say that because the two of you don't agree about whether four-year-olds ought to learn conversational Latin, I didn't take care of the old woman. And I'm not going to put Max through that. You've got Henry waiting, you've got Annalise to send to school, you've got a dozen of Gretchen's kids who depend on you. So you're not going to go out and die of something on my watch. Like it or lump it."

He might not have made it stick by himself, but Mary Simpson agreed with him. As did Bill Hudson, Duke Ernst, and just about everybody else. Hand volunteered to keep an eye on her.

They couldn't precisely lock her up. She continued to investigate the situation with the Grafenwöhr properties. Elias couldn't help her; he was one of those at the hospital, caring for the sick. She continued to meet occasionally with Rastetter, her lawyer. Until his family became ill and he closed his office temporarily.

"Hey, Toby," one of the down-time radio techs asked. "Why aren't you eating?"

"I don't really feel like it, Franz. I'm getting a sore throat."

"Where's Lambert Felser?" Marc Cavriani asked. "I don't think that I've seen him the last couple of days. Is he taking time off because Keith is busy at the hospital?"

"I'm not sure," Eric Haakansson Hand answered. "I don't think that I've seen him around, either."

"I'd better," Marc said, "check his room."

Felser wasn't there. The chambermaid at the inn said that, the morning before, she had come to clean and found him sick. So, according to the instructions that had been given to all the innkeepers, she told Hans from the stables to take him to the quarantine hospital. Had she told anybody? Well, no. She hadn't known whom to tell. Herr Pilcher, his master, was, like the others who cared for the sick, sleeping at the hospital.

Balde made his rounds. More than seven hundred people were lying ill in the *collegium*, today. They were calling for more volunteers to care for them. For more people who had already survived the disease.

Three more of the Jesuits were among the ill.

There had been only about seventy deaths, though, so far. Most of them children.

A recurrence of the plague would have been far worse.

By the end of the week, the tide seemed to be turning. The patient count was under five hundred. Not, of course, all the same people who had been there the week before. The acute period of the disease did not last long; many of those still in the hospital were clearly recovering. Those who had family to care for them had already returned to their homes for convalescence.

Balde completed the day's entries in his ledger. The death toll stood at ninety-three, including one of the sick Jesuits. However, no more of the brothers had sickened. So far.

During the plague epidemic the previous year, there had been nearly five hundred deaths in Amberg. God had been very merciful this time.

Franz looked at his friend Toby. Then, had one of the stable-men load him into a cart and take him to the hospital.

Toby was likely to recover, though, Franz thought. He was a strong young man.

Franz, like the chambermaid at the inn, wasn't sure whom he should tell. Toby had been more or less the boss of the other radio techs. Franz wasn't really sure who Toby's boss was.

It wasn't as if he could just drop into the regent's office, even though he was living in the *Schloss*. Nor could he leave the radio room for a long time to go running around town looking for someone to tell. Finally, he just left a note on Böcler's desk and returned to the top floor. Someone had to watch the radio, now that Toby was no longer there to do it.

He looked at the familiar, comforting, scene with its blue Leyden jars. Tiptoeing across the room so as not to jar them, he lay down on his cot.

Keith Pilcher was the first of the up-timers to learn that Toby was in the hospital, when he came to bathe him. Of the radio techs who had come with them from Grantville, this left how many on duty? Keith racked his brain. One of the down-timers, the first one who had become ill, was dead. Three more had been here and recovered enough to be sent over to the convalescent ward, because there wasn't anyone to take care of them at the *Schloss*. Now Toby. That left one more. What was his name? Oh, yes. Franz. He ought to remind *somebody* that they were down to one functional radio tech.

Bill Hudson climbed up to the top floor of the *Schloss* and started to cuss a blue streak. It was one thing to say that the geeks were married to their work, but that didn't mean that all six of them had needed to have their cots crowded into one little room next to the array of Leyden jars. Not eight inches between them; they must have walked sideways to get into bed. Plus they worked together and ate together. No wonder they had infected one another.

He asked Franz whether he had diphtheria before. Franz went on the "no" list.

Two days later, Bill ordered Franz to the hospital. Until one of the recovering techs was well enough to come back to work, Amberg would be on a radio blackout. No one else had the vaguest idea how to work the thing.

He notified Jake Ebeling. And Duke Ernst.

CHAPTER 26

Occasio Rarissima

Amberg, the Upper Palatinate

Veronica sat in her room in the *Schloss*, looking out the window and tapping her fingers on the table. She had just finished breakfast, eating by herself, and reading the newspapers. It was old news, of course, by the time it reached Amberg. A week old, at least; more often two weeks old. Not that it would benefit her a great deal to have more recent news. She wouldn't be able to do anything about it.

Useless, useless. Of no use to anyone. Everybody else was busy. Useless old woman, shunted to the sidelines. Useless old woman, bossed around by the husband of that idiotic woman Maxine. Useless old woman, told what she could and could not do by the father of those two ungovernable children. He had it right, that old man in the Bible. *Vanitas, vanitas.* Everything was useless. *She* was useless.

She not only couldn't help others; she couldn't even help herself. Elias was busy; Rastetter's office closed. *Useless, useless.*

Until she got the wonderful idea.

What did they need next, in order to file suit for the rest of Johann Stephan's property? They needed affidavits from several people in Grafenwöhr. Since none had arrived at Rastetter's office, even though she knew that he had requested them using all the proper forms,

219

and since everybody else in the city of Amberg was too focused on the diphtheria epidemic to pursue the matter, that was something she could do. She could go to Grafenwöhr and get the affidavits herself, or at least find out why they hadn't arrived. Kilian being the kind of man he was, she wouldn't put it past him to be either intimidating or suborning the witnesses, or both, or worse.

Things looked different, once she had made up her mind. She packed a few essentials into the trusty and capacious canvas tote bag that had served her so well since her arrival in Grantville three years before, put on her sturdiest boots, and marched down the stairs. On her way to the gate, she stopped at a shop and bought a walking stick; at another and bought some bread and sausage. It wasn't as if it were far to Grafenwöhr; less than twenty-five miles, with a decent road to travel. It was a nice summer day, early in June. She was starting early and she could easily reach the town before dark.

And it was her home town. She had relatives there—relatives besides her detestable brother-in-law Kilian Richter. Her own family. Schusters and Kleins; Herders and Rothwilds. None of her brothers or sisters were there; she had written long ago to find out. Two nieces, Jakobaea's daughters, Magdalena and Margaretha. No one knew what had become of Hans Florian and his wife; they had left already in 1623. Casimir had died in Bayreuth in 1629. The family believed that his widow had still been alive a year later, and some of the children. Hanna Schreiner, Matthias' sister, had remarried last year to Wilhelm Bastl.

The Rothwilds were almost all fine people. Oddly, the only one who had gone to the bad, just about as far to the bad as a man could go, was Johann Stephan's own nephew, Johann, his sister Sara's son. He had gone all the way to the bad long before the war started. He wouldn't be around, though. The Grafenwöhr authorities had exiled him for good and sufficient reasons. She was surprised that they had not hanged him.

Sara's daughter, Magdalena, had been Wilhelm Bastl's first wife. Cousins. The comfort of kin. She wouldn't run into any trouble on a visit to her own home town.

She did leave a note. She put it under Mary's hair brush.

Afra the chambermaid noticed that Frau Dreeson was carrying the bulging tote bag. It bulged much more than it usually did when

Frau Dreeson left the *Schloss* to talk to her lawyer. She quickly
checked the room to see what the old lady had taken. More than
just papers. She slipped out the side entrance and followed the old
woman, saw her buy the walking stick, saw which gate she left
by, and ran to Augustin Arndt. More accurately, she had intended
to run, but she wasn't feeling very well this morning. She had a
bad sore throat, and it was getting worse. So she walked, but she
did get to Arndt's office. For one thing, she believed in earning
her money honestly. For another, her family had worked for the
landgraves of Leuchtenberg for a long, long, time. Since the days
of her father's grandfather, at least. The landgrave was her lord.

Arndt was feeling uneasy. Really uneasy. He wasn't sure, any more,
just what Kilian Richter's limits were, and Richter had threatened
him about revealing that . . . mess. He wasn't, thank goodness,
dependant upon Richter, but he thought that he had better keep
an eye on the old woman. He didn't want any fatalities—any more
fatalities, at least. He could justify a billing to Richter for having
Veronica Dreeson watched, especially if he didn't explain that in
his own mind the observation was for the purpose of trying to tell
whether his employer might be planning something that was not
at all prudent.

Maybe he could kill two birds with one stone. Even three birds.
It was always nice to have three different clients paying for the
same investigation. It improved his profit margin quite a bit.

He sent a note to a couple of men working in Amberg, Leuchtenberg loyalists like the chambermaid Afra Forst. Valentin Forst was
the woman's cousin and Emmeram Becker was also from Pfreimd.
He sent them instructions and money for expenses.

*Follow the Dreeson woman to Grafenwöhr. Keep an eye on what
she does and who she contacts. Keep me informed. Also, while you're
there, see old Karl Hanf the cooper about ore barrels—he is trying
to overcharge; see the barge builder Wilhelm Bastl about an order
that he hasn't completed (specifics from Herr Troeschler enclosed
with this note). I'll pay you at the usual rate.*

There was no need to tell them that neither of those tasks was
a job commissioned by the landgrave. That would have been a lie.
If the two men got the *impression*, however, that the landgrave
took an interest in Frau Dreeson and that Troeschler's delayed
deliveries were interfering with the landgrave's interests, well,

that would not be a problem. Those two were zealous Catholics. They always worked hardest when they thought they were serving Landgrave Wilhelm Georg.

After all, Arndt assured himself, he had been sending reports on Frau Dreeson to the landgrave and no one had told him to stop. Not that the landgrave had directly asked for them, but a man had to do *something* to keep earning his retainer. Arndt had no way of knowing, any more than Forst and Becker did, that nothing was of interest to the landgrave any longer and that the steward's remittances were just a standing order.

By early evening, Afra really was not feeling well at all. The head housekeeper at the *Schloss* noticed and sent her to the hospital.

Hand assumed that Frau Dreeson was having supper in her room. This did not surprise him. Those who had never had diphtheria were eating separately from those involved with the sick, on Duke Ernst's orders. He found Böcler rather tedious as a conversational companion himself. The young man would probably footnote a funeral sermon and attach notarized copies of the original documents on which he based his statements about the dates upon which the deceased had been baptized and confirmed.

Hand resigned himself to listening to a discourse on neo-Latin poetry. A quite extended one. It appeared that several of Böcler's friends practiced the art. Harsdörffer in Nürnberg. There was also Balde, right here in Amberg.

Hand perked up. "The Jesuit? The one running the hospital?"

"Yes, that one. Did you know that he was asked to write a new prelude for the play that will be performed for Duke Maximilian's wedding?"

It took only the most minimal display of interest to encourage Böcler; his latest information dump was off and running.

Grafenwöhr, the Upper Palatinate

It was good to be home. Very good to be home.

Veronica's arrival in Grafenwöhr caused a lot of excitement. For a change, not because she was Hans Richter's grandmother, but because she was one of the many who had been lost and was now found. Grafenwöhr had lost a third of its people in the past decade, and it did not expect to find many of them. Each one was a small miracle.

Especially one who brought news from the larger world outside. She was staying with her nieces, Magdalena and Margaretha Herder. Who, in turn, kept house for their stepfather, Karl Hanf, and Jakobaea's two boys, their half-brothers. Barbara had died as a baby, of course. Jakobaea and the two youngest children had died during the horrible *Schreckensjahr* of 1621, when Mansfeld's armies came through the Upper Palatinate. In private, the girls told her that they had no expectation that Hanf, the old skinflint, would ever dower them. Magdalena was nearly thirty; Margaretha a year and a half younger. They made the best of it. Anything they might have had coming from their own father had vanished in the confusion of the war and occupation.

"Damned Bavarians," Veronica snorted. She settled in to talk about Grantville. Gretchen and Jeff. Annalise.

Hans, of course. They wanted to hear about Hans. And airplanes. Magdeburg. The little Princess Kristina. Veronica had actually *seen* her? With her own eyes? What did she look like?

Nürnberg? She had come through Nürnberg? She had actually *seen* Margaretha, Hanna, and Clara to talk to? Tell us about their children. Is Matthias well? You mean that Elias is actually *with* you, in Amberg? Is he planning to come up?

The entire town of Grafenwöhr was buzzing with excitement.

There were some exceptions. Forst and Becker, Augustin Arndt's two agents, found it very, very dull in Grafenwöhr. They didn't ask Hanf and Bastl the questions themselves, of course—just delivered Arndt's message about Troeschler to a local lawyer and let him ask the questions. They needed to be inconspicuous, if they were to find out what lay behind the answers. Hanf protested that his charges were accurate. Bastl had a thousand excuses why Troeschler's barges were not finished. Business as usual.

Neither of them could understand why the landgrave would be interested in any of this, but since Arndt had deliberately omitted to explain to them that Troeschler's problems were distinct from those of Landgrave Wilhelm Georg, they had, just as Arndt hoped, gained the impression that there was a connection. And they were loyal Leuchtenberger. If their lord wanted to know, they would do their best to find out.

They also had to manufacture reasons to keep hanging around to watch Frau Dreeson for the landgrave, they thought, so they started to take an even deeper look into the manufacture of barges and barrels than they ordinarily would have done. After a couple of days, they took jobs as casual laborers at Bastl's barge-yard, which allowed them to spend a fair amount of time talking to some of the local boatmen.

It was a lovely visit, of course. But it wasn't getting her any farther in seeing about the affidavits. On the third day, Veronica went to the city clerk's office. Young Nicolas Moser was very cooperative, just as Rastetter had assured her that he would be. Very informative, as well.

On the fifth day, she called on her brother-in-law Kilian, wearing her very best abbess of Quedlinburg face. He did not seem excessively pleased by her presence. His wife hardly spoke; part of the time, she appeared to doze off. She didn't even ask about her relatives in Nürnberg, which was odd, considering that her brother Lorenz was Hanna Richter's husband and the third of Veronica's stepsons-in-law. She must have known that Veronica had seen them. In spite of her dereliction of interest, Veronica brought her up to date conscientiously.

Their daughter Dorothea sat, her hands folded in her lap. She didn't say a word. The boy, Hermann, was seventeen; a big young oaf. Oaf was the proper word. The youngest of the three children who survived, another boy, was a boarding student at the Jesuit *collegium* in Amberg and was being kept isolated with the other boarders because of the epidemic.

Veronica was very satisfied with how well she had controlled her tongue. She did mention a couple of her thoughts about intimidation and suborning of witnesses, along with the legal penalties for such activities. Just in passing, of course. Also that she was finding her research at city hall very rewarding, indicating that since her lawyer, Hieronymus Rastetter, and Elias Brechbuhl had laid the foundation with their work in Amberg, she had a clear idea of what to look for and was not wasting her time. She let him know that she would be resuming it the next morning. In another two or three days, she should have found everything that the lawyer needed. It had been a pleasure to combine work with a family visit.

It was *nice* to see Kilian squirm. Veronica was not even a little bit ashamed of herself. He sold Johann Stephan's print shop, didn't he? Not to mention some of the things that she had found here. Elias would be very interested.

Amberg, the Upper Palatinate

The day after Veronica's visit, Kilian went down to Amberg first thing in the morning, taking Hermann with him. He did not find Arndt particularly helpful. The man appeared to be seriously distracted.

He did manage to find his nephew Johann Rothwild, Sara's son. That was no problem, really. Rothwild worked as a bouncer at a really rough tavern in an old mining settlement a couple of miles outside the city walls and had for years. Johann could be a really helpful man in a pinch, Kilian knew. He had demonstrated that several years before. Johann and Hermann between them could probably take care of the worst of Kilian's current problems.

One of which, increasingly, appeared to be Augustin Arndt. He *could* just be afraid of what Kilian held over his head, but he could be starting to have a case of bad conscience, which was always dangerous. Kilian had checked his old records the night before. He had enough on Arndt to ruin him professionally, with rumors, if nothing else—but not, probably, enough to control him. He had no clear documentation that Arndt had anything to do with the group of "mercenaries" that night in 1628, much less that he had organized it and that Rothwild had dragged Anton's wife back to his office. The lawyer was wily. He had covered his tracks well.

Grafenwöhr, the Upper Palatinate

Dorothea watched her father and brother leave. Her mother was starting on her daily drinking, of course. She started at breakfast and finished when she went to bed, if she could get enough beer. Or if she could make it all the way to the bed. She had been like this for seven or eight years, now. Dorothea usually tried to limit what Mama could get. This morning, feeling guilty, she poured her a large stein of the strongest that Clara Schreiner brewed.

Last week, she thought that she had no hope. Yesterday, with Papa's strange sister-in-law's visit, she had started to hope again. She washed herself carefully, even her hair. First soft soap in the basin; then a rinse with rose water. A clean shift under her dress; a clean apron over it. She picked up a market basket; then put it down again. It was not market day. What reason did she have to be seen anywhere near the *Rathaus*, much less in it? Young women, unmarried women, rarely had business at the city hall. She opened the chest where Papa kept his business records and pulled out a handful of the ones right on top at random. They weren't in neat piles; she could certainly put them back before he and Hermann got home. He would never notice.

Mama was well on her way to being mentally out for the day. Dorothea refilled her stein with the strong beer.

Veronica was well on her way to tracking the handling of Johann Stephan's share of old Abraham Richter's land; Kilian's share was his own business. But Kilian been mucking around with Sara's portion also. How did he manage that? Sara had left children. Magdalena was dead, to be sure, and her only baby had been born dead. But Karl Hanf had told her that Johann Rothwild was still alive, she thought. Frowning, she moved to another ledger and lifted it to take it to the standing pedestal where she was working. When she heard voices in the outer office, she started to eavesdrop quite unashamedly.

Nicholas Moser was one of them. Well, he should be here. He was the city clerk, after all. The other? Who? Dorothea? Kilian's daughter?

"What on earth are you doing here, Thea? Your father—"

"He's gone to Amberg with Hermann, Nicol. Mama isn't going to notice anything today."

"You can't come here. Not here. Not while I'm at work."

"I need to talk to her, Nicol. Papa's sister-in-law. Please. She told Papa yesterday that she was going to be here today. I brought papers, see. So anyone who saw me come in might think that I was bringing something for Papa. I *have* to talk to her. If anyone asks, you can say that I was here to see her. There's no reason that anyone should think that I am here to see you."

"Thea."

Veronica sauntered out. "If she wants to see me, Herr Moser, please do let her come in. She is, after all, my niece by marriage."

Eyeing the physical tension between the two of them, she asked herself, "And what is she to you?"

Moser stepped aside from where he had been blocking the door to the back room where the records were stored.

Veronica looked at him. "You now. If you're worried because she's here, just open that front door to your office and do something where anybody who happens to glance in can see that you are busy doing what you are supposed to do. If anyone saw Dorothea come in, the gossip will be about the fascinating dissension among the Richter heirs and not"—her glance swept across both of them—"whatever the two of you have been up to that leads to desperate whispering when you should know perfectly well that someone else is close enough to hear even whispers." She pulled Dorothea into the back room.

Question one. She had been away from Grafenwöhr for a long time, and she had a lot of relatives. "How old are you?"

Dorothea looked a little startled. "Twenty-one, Tante Veronica. In May."

"Oh, yes. You're the one who was born the same year as Hans, then. Not a child, any more than he was a child."

At the word "child," Dorothea winced.

Veronica looked again. The crystal clarity of the complexion; the little brown rings under the eyes. She saw no reason to mince words. "How far along are you?"

Dorothea's eyes opened wide.

Veronica, from the back room, had been able to hear a whispered front-room conversation between two young people who called one another Nicol and Thea. Nicholas Moser was therefore perfectly capable of hearing a back-room conversation conducted in a normal tone of voice, even though he was supposed to be concentrating on his work in the front room. He came plunging through the door, abandoning all pretense of indifference to Richter family business.

"Thea?"

"Nicol, please. Go back. Do your work. Please. I need to talk to my aunt."

"But if . . ."

Veronica tilted her head. It was, at any rate, perfectly clear that neither of them had the slightest doubt who the father was. That was always a real advantage when it came to managing these things.

She did have to ask herself *how* they had managed it, though. Especially in a town this small. It couldn't have been easy for a newly hired town clerk, son of an inflexible and well-known Calvinist exile, a university graduate and possibly at the moment the most eligible bachelor inside the walls of Grafenwöhr, to avoid the eyes of Protestant parents of eligible daughters long enough to impregnate the Catholic daughter of an equally well-known Bavarian collaborator. It must mean that they had more ingenuity than either of them had demonstrated so far today.

Of course, it was only two hours past breakfast. Perhaps they "just weren't morning people," as Mary Simpson said of some of her acquaintances.

She looked at Moser gimlet eyed. "And just how old are *you*?" she asked.

"Twenty-four."

"Old enough, in other words, to know better. The pair of you."

"We didn't," Moser protested defensively, "know that it was going to happen *right then*. It's not as if . . ." His voice trailed off.

Veronica made up her mind on the spot. The instant she got back to Grantville, she would see to it that Annalise adopted up-time underwear, even though she did normally prefer to wear down-time clothing. Certainly by the time that Heinrich Schmidt got back from Amsterdam. If nothing else, it did require an amorous couple to pause in their pursuits long enough to deliberately remove the drawers. Which might, just possibly, give them time to think that they were about to proceed to a new stage in the expression of their mutual affection. And stop, if they were reasonably prudent people.

To Moser she said, "Close the front door." He did.

Back to the original question. "How far along are you?"

Simultaneously, they answered, "March fourth." From the expressions on their faces as they looked at one another, this must have been an epic day in their lives, roughly equivalent to the collapse of the walls of Jericho or the recent eruption of the volcano in Italy.

Oh, blast it. If they were that certain of the date of conception, it probably meant—just once. Recent ex-virgins, both of them. Just what every woman who is peacefully trying to collect affidavits for a property title lawsuit needs to have on her hands. A Pair of Star-Crossed Lovers, one of whom is a little bit pregnant. And, of course, likely to become more so in the immediate future.

Definitely likely to become more so in the immediate future. It was past the usual time when a woman might miscarry her fruit.

"You," Veronica said firmly, "are both utter and total fools."

Moser stepped farther into the room and put his arm protectively around Dorothea's shoulders. Then, got a little distracted by the scent of rose water in her hair. He remembered that scent. . . .

Reorganizing his mind, he looked at her terrifying aunt. Aunt-by-marriage. Terrifying wouldn't be a familial trait. That was a good thing, he thought. Women were supposed to be gentle and compliant. Everybody knew that.

The frightening old lady was holding her canvas tote bag out at them. It had a picture of a harlequin on it. And words. "Mardi Gras." That he knew; a Catholic superstition. Orleans he had heard of; it was in France. Where might New Orleans be?

"This does not," the formidable old lady was saying, "mean that I have much sympathy—any sympathy—with those stupid 'Harlequin Romance novels' that have become such a fad."

"I have one of the books," Dorothea said. "It is quite lovely to read. This girl is traveling alone on a road in Spain—"

"*Fools*," Veronica snapped. "I would not have believed that one of those pernicious books had traveled as far as Grafenwöhr. Stupid, stupid books. Infecting even my Annalise with ideas about *romance*. Sit down."

They sat.

"Can you boil water here?"

Moser blinked. "Yes, I have a small brazier."

"Do you have cups?"

"I have four cups."

Veronica reached into the tote bag. She should not be too hard on Annalise about her romances. All of them had learned vices in Grantville. "Very well. What all of us need right now is a good cup of coffee. Which, with your brazier and cups, I can prepare."

She made it black and she made it strong. It was clear that neither of the others cared for it much, which made no difference to her whatsoever. She wanted them awake and paying attention.

First things first. "Do you want to get married? I am quite prepared to list all the problems that it will bring for both of you, if you haven't bothered to think about them. And don't think that you have to say that you do, either of you. If you don't, either one of you, I can see to it that Dorothea and her child are taken care of. Family is family, after all, and she's not the first girl to find herself in this fix and won't be the last."

They wanted to get married. Problems and all. So they said.

"What you need, then," she said, "is money. How much do you have?"

Dorothea didn't have any. Moser still had most of his most recent month's pay.

"You'll need more. And a map of how to get to Grantville from Amberg. You do know how to get to Amberg, I presume? Grantville doesn't have any laws against Calvinists and Catholics marrying one another. Henry, my husband, is a Calvinist. I am, owing to the damned Bavarians, Catholic. And likely to remain one; changing again at my age would be more trouble than it's worth.

"And one final thing. You're *not* leaving Grafenwöhr until after I do. Do you understand me? *Not!* I'm willing to help Dorothea, but being left behind to deal with Kilian when he finds out that you have eloped is way above and beyond any duty I may have to her." Veronica glared at them fiercely. "Do you understand that?"

They understood.

"Go home, now." That was to Dorothea. "Go back to work."

Moser shuddered slightly. There had to be words that were more, well, descriptive, than just "terrifying."

Veronica walked back to the pedestal where she had left the ledger she was using. On top of the ledger lay the packet of papers that Dorothea had been holding when she came in. Without the slightest sense of shame, she started thumbing through them. Paused. Read more slowly. Decided that she had better consult Rastetter again, as soon as possible. Hopefully, by the time she returned to Amberg, his family would have recovered. She tucked the papers into her tote bag, inside one of her greatest treasures—a semitransparent blue plastic expanding pocket folder, somewhat larger than the average sheet of paper, with a flap that fastened with a snap. She really loved that envelope; she had no idea how she would manage St. Veronica's Academies without it. Rain or snow, she could go anywhere and the ink on her papers never smeared or ran.

She should, perhaps, have left it in Grantville for Annalise to use. But she hadn't. It was too useful.

She turned back to the ledger.

CHAPTER 27

Optiones Ineptae

Amberg, the Upper Palatinate

They had collectively kicked themselves. Mary had been so tired when she got back to the *Schloss* the night after Veronica left that she hadn't brushed her hair—just washed her face, brushed her teeth and then collapsed into bed. So she hadn't found the note until the next morning. It had been an object lesson on the dire consequences of sloppiness.

The other Grantvillers, Duke Ernst, Erik Haakansson Hand, her lawyer Rastetter—any of them or, if necessary, all of them combined—would normally have managed to stop her from taking off on her own, but they had been too distracted by the epidemic. Those who knew her personally were not really surprised that she had gone. She just wasn't accustomed to thinking of herself as a person of national, much less international, significance, even if the rest of them realized her importance. Her symbolic importance, at least. To some extent, as the wife of the mayor of Grantville, she even had actual importance.

Spilt milk. And, according to the report that the mayor of Grafenwöhr had provided to Duke Ernst, she was having an enjoyable visit with her family. So, as Keith said, they might as well relax a little. At least, there were no reports that the diphtheria had spread to Grafenwöhr.

✧   ✧   ✧

The epidemic in Amberg was definitely tapering off. Balde made his entries. Only two deaths yesterday. One a child. The other, Afra Forst, a chambermaid from Pfreimd who had worked at the *Schloss*. Catholic. No family in Amberg, poor girl. Frau Simpson, although not Catholic herself, had generously provided a stipend for a funeral mass. She said that the maid had cleaned her rooms, and those of Frau Dreeson.

Grafenwöhr, the Upper Palatinate

Kilian Richter and his son Hermann came back to Grafenwöhr together. Johann Rothwild came separately, bringing an associate remarkably like himself. Kilian had to find them a place to stay in a cottage outside the town. Johann was, unfortunately, *persona non grata* with the Amberg authorities.

That didn't mean, of course, that the two men couldn't enter the town during the day. Johann's face wasn't *that* well-known after several years of absence. Day laborers, looking for a bit of work; transients, perhaps. Those were common enough sights in any town. If they didn't stay too long, it shouldn't be a problem, Kilian thought.

What he did think was a problem was the disappearance of quite a few of his business papers from his chest. The last ones that he would want anyone else looking at. The old ones that he had pulled out to refresh his memory about just how much pressure he could put on Arndt.

So, not even papers he could explode about. He couldn't shout and slap his wife. She was scarcely the model of the frugal and prudent housewife. The odds were high that she had been so drunk that a military company could have marched through the house playing their fife and drum and she wouldn't have noticed them. Nor could he scream at his daughter. Why hadn't she been home?

He did ask her where she had been. She answered that she had gone to her godmother's house at mid-morning and remained there the rest of the day. So much for the possibility that she might have noticed someone lurking around. *Who in hell might have known about those papers?*

His daughter Dorothea's reply had the advantage of being

perfectly true. No matter that Tante Veronica had told her to go home, she hadn't wanted to spend the rest of the day hearing her mother snore. When she left the city hall, she had gone to her godmother's and had stayed there until it began to get dark. Kilian didn't think anything about it. Dorothea had spent a lot of time at her godmother's these past few years.

It had been a relief to Dorothea, although a little undermining to her general sense of self-importance, that apparently no one in town had taken any notice of her visit to the city hall. Not even the mayor and aldermen who, naturally, had offices in the building. And she spent so much time thinking of Nicol and their planned elopement that she forgot entirely that she had left her father's papers there.

If Dorothea had grown up in Grantville, her classmates would have been of the opinion that her head wasn't screwed on too tight. Or that she was a ditz. There were a lot of ways a person might describe Dorothea Richter, such as "sort of cute." No one would have included, "Really, really smart."

Nicholas Moser was working really, really, hard at not paying any attention to Dorothea Richter in public. This was in order not to arouse suspicion. He certainly did not want her father to guess about their planned elopement. This meant that whenever she was in sight, on the streets or in the marketplace of the town, he carefully looked somewhere else.

He had no idea who Johann Rothwild was. Rothwild had been banned from Grafenwöhr years before Moser was hired. He naturally had no idea who Rothwild's companion was, since the man had never been in town before. However, when he looked at places where Dorothea wasn't, he kept seeing them.

Seeing them, sometimes, in places where a couple of casual laborers had no business being. Sometimes near Dorothea.

Horrible visions crept into his mind. He was, after all, a Calvinist. Could Dorothea's father have guessed, in spite of all his precautions? The man was Catholic. Was he going to have Moser's beloved kidnapped and—the terms came with capital letters—Immured in a Convent? Being Immured in a Convent was, in Moser's mind, roughly equivalent to being Chained in a Dungeon. Or worse than being chained in a run-of-the-mill dungeon, since it would involve a Papist Plot.

The two men disappeared from the streets of Grafenwöhr for a couple of days. Moser relaxed a little. They must have moved on.

Then they came back. All of Moser's fears returned. They must have been making arrangements with a Wicked Abbess to deliver Dorothea as a prisoner.

Unlike Dorothea, Moser was "really, really smart" in the sense of book learning. Clever, conscientious, and competent in his work, just as Rastetter had said to Veronica. Cooperative and helpful to the people who came to city hall needing to receive or file documents. He was, however, somewhat deficient in the ordinary common sense department. Not to mention being, in this matter, a victim of his upbringing, complicated by a bad case of hormones.

In any case, he sat down and wrote a letter to Herr Hieronymus Rastetter, the Amberg lawyer who was working for Dorothea's terrifying aunt, expressing all his fears. He was a little doubtful about the wisdom of this. The aunt was, as she had admitted, Catholic herself. She might be in on the Papist Plot, however improbable that seemed on the face of it.

The lawyer, however, was not Catholic. He was a Calvinist, and a friend of Moser's father. He would be fully reliable. Moser told him everything he knew of the matter, without reservation.

Amberg, the Upper Palatinate

Rastetter had just reopened his office the day Moser's letter arrived. His family, thankfully, were all recovering. He had a huge backlog, so he put the letter on the bottom of his correspondence pile. When he did read it, ignoring all the nonsense about Immuring in Convents, the words Dreeson, Kilian Richter, and "two dangerous-looking men" practically shouted off the page at him. He grabbed his hat and headed for the *Schloss*.

Frau Simpson was there. He gave it to her. She took it to Duke Ernst. Or, more precisely, to Böcler, who took it to Duke Ernst. That didn't matter; the delay was approximately five minutes by her watch.

While they were waiting, Rastetter asked her if she had heard the news about Augustin Arndt—the lawyer representing Frau Dreeson's opponent in the lawsuit.

Mary shook her head. She had never even known the man's name.

"He was found dead two days ago."

"Will this epidemic never end?" she asked. "I had thought that it was pretty much over. I hope that a new chain of infection isn't starting up."

"He didn't die of diphtheria, Frau Simpson. He was found by a man who works for him, more or less regularly, as an agent and had come to the city to consult with him about some matter of business he had been handling on his behalf in Grafenwöhr. Arndt's throat was cut."

Mary looked at him. "Grafenwöhr?"

Rastetter never utilized profane or blasphemous expressions. He wished, right now, that he did.

After they had presented their concerns to the regent, Duke Ernst also commented, "I do wish that General Banér were here this very instant. He could say what I am thinking."

Hand did question Arndt's agent, Valentin Forst, the one who had found the body. However, there seemed to be no connection. The man was quite forthcoming about the matter he had been working on, involving ore barrels and barges, disputed payments and delayed deadlines—the ordinary routine work of a practicing lawyer. So Hand let him go back to Grafenwöhr.

Forst had, of course, omitted any reference to the landgrave of Leuchtenberg from his narrative. They hadn't asked him about Leuchtenberg. There was certainly no reason for him to volunteer the information.

Mary Simpson had been right. The epidemic was almost over, at least the part of it on which she had been working. There had been no new infections yesterday or today. There were still people sick in the hospital, of course, and numerous convalescents.

So, she said, she was going up to Grafenwöhr herself to see what was going on. At the very least, she could keep Veronica company and then make sure that she didn't walk back to Amberg alone. This was, Duke Ernst thought, basically a good idea. Naturally, she should not go alone.

"I wouldn't," Mary assured him, "even dream of it."

"Take Böcler. I will give him a letter of authorization, under my own signature, to investigate whatever is going on. A personal representative of the regent. Otherwise, talk to Hand. He'll find you someone else."

He turned and told Böcler to draft the letter.

Mary thanked him and went looking for Hand. Who, in turn, was talking to the Cavrianis.

Marc Cavriani knew perfectly well that he should stay in Amberg. Herr Pilcher had returned to the inn; the epidemic was tapering off; the negotiations were resuming. But at the thought of getting to go on a trip to Grafenwöhr with Mrs. Simpson and Böcler, he started to look wistful. Marc did "wistful" very well. He had, ever since he was three or four years old. Which his father knew perfectly well, but still found it hard to resist. So Marc didn't have to progress to "wheedle." Leopold actually suggested that his son be included. Marc went off to talk to Böcler about it.

Unlike a lot of people, Marc did not find Böcler boring. They were on first-name terms by now. Or second-name terms, or nickname terms, to be precise, since Böcler was named Johann Heinrich. Marc called him Heinz. Or, if he deliberately wanted to be annoying, when Böcler was being just a tad too meticulous, Heinzerl. It really annoyed a Franconian to have someone stick a Bavarian diminutive on the end of his name.

Who else? Well, Rastetter, of course. And his clerk. And Elias Brechbuhl. Anyone else? No, that was enough.

Hand didn't see any reason why they shouldn't go ahead and leave tomorrow morning. He thought that he would come himself, as soon as he worked through some of the things on his desk. Let him know if they actually found anything behind this—send a messenger and get a company of *Grenzjaeger* in return. It would be that simple.

It was a little awkward that Veronica was staying with family. She apologized that the Hanf house really was not large enough to receive six more guests. Nor could she, really, extend hospitality in someone else's home, even if it was.

Mary said that was fine. They would take rooms at the inn. Could Veronica recommend the best one in town?

The best was not by any means first class. Except, perhaps, from the perspective of the fleas.

Veronica joined them for supper. The inn's food was not gourmet. That was why she brought a basket with her in a laudable effort to ward off the danger that her friends might come down with food poisoning. The residents of the town were well-acquainted with the facilities available at their local inns. She recommended that they buy food at the market and live on sandwiches and fruit. Bread for breakfast at the inn should be all right; however, the butter was often found to be rancid.

All in all, the five down-time men concluded, Grafenwöhr offered fairly typical small-town lodgings for travelers—nothing comparable to the well-appointed establishments in cities such as Amberg and Nürnberg.

Two men watched them from a corner table at the back of the little dining room. One of them stayed.

The other went out after he had eaten, to see Kilian Richter, who was not happy to have Johann Rothwild show up at his house. If someone saw the two of them together, it might trigger memories about just who Rothwild was and why he wasn't supposed to be in Grafenwöhr. That would completely ruin his usefulness from his Uncle Kilian's point of view. Since he was already here, however . . . He called Hermann in to his *Stube* as well and began to explain his views on the best way to eliminate the nuisance that his sister-in-law Veronica had made of herself by coming to town.

By the time Kilian had finished talking to them, it was well after dark, which meant that the city gates were closed. Rothwild had to spend the night in town. Since he had told his companion to wait for him at the inn, that man had to stay the night in town, also. He begrudged the money for a straw mattress on the floor of the inn's common sleeping room, even if it would be covered by the expense money Rothwild had gotten from someone. "Blame it on the old lady," Rothwild said. "The guy holding the purse says that she's been making a nuisance of herself for quite a while."

In the morning, Rastetter and his clerk, Brechbuhl, and Böcler headed for city hall to talk to the town officials. And, just in passing, while they were there anyway, to the town clerk. Marc went to talk to a shipping company about the sources of the iron ore they sent out.

The basket that Veronica had taken to the inn the night before had given her an idea during supper. She had decided to show

Mary some of the places where she and her brothers and sisters had played when they were children. She wouldn't bother with a basket, though; a basket would be stiff and awkward to carry around all day. She stuffed their lunch into her trustworthy tote bag and they headed out into the country.

Veronica had her walking stick. Mary declined her offer to stop by the Hanf house on their way out of town and borrow another one. She was mildly embarrassed by her own refusal but, well, she had always prided herself on staying in shape. At her age, canes would become a fact of life soon enough; no sense in hurrying the inevitable.

Johannes Rothwild, his associate, and Hermann Richter followed the two women out the gate. Rothwild was rather looking forward to the day. He liked being paid to follow his natural inclinations.

Forst and Becker were long out of the gate. Arndt might be dead, but they still hadn't used up all the expense money he had advanced them. Even without Arndt, they could get the information to Landgrave Wilhelm Georg. When they got back to Amberg, they would just drop it in the mail.

It wasn't a problem that Bavaria was "enemy territory." The mail went out from the Upper Palatinate to Bavaria just as easily as the Jesuits in Amberg received communications from those in Munich. A person rather had to admire the House of Thurn und Taxis. Wars might come and wars might go, but the imperial postal system kept right on going. "Public, Regular, Reliable, and Rapid," as its advertising broadsheets read. Now that the USE had its own postal system, the bags just changed hands at the borders. The USE was, after all, using the same routes and methods, not to mention a lot of the same personnel. The Thurn und Taxis post-master in Frankfurt am Main, feeling that he had been ill-treated by the Habsburgs because he was a Protestant, had defected to Gustav Adolf and was *still* running the postal system.

But there had also been Arndt's job for Troeschler. Which had led them to some rather interesting information about graft, corruption, and kickbacks in the timber business. Arndt might be dead, but Troeschler would pay. They had both been boatmen in their younger days, which wasn't unusual. They had hired on with Bastl's barge-yard, representing themselves as casual laborers on their return from a seasonal job, happy to work for a few days and then punt a barge down the river in order to make some money on their way back home.

Mary and Veronica were thinking about having lunch in a pretty clearing by a big creek. At least, Mary thought it was a creek. It would have been a creek, up-time.

Veronica said that it was a river. The tiny stream that ran by Grafenwöhr itself was a brook, but they had followed the road about three miles south from the town and now they were looking at the river.

Just downstream, there was sawing and hammering.

"That's Wilhelm Bastl's barge-yard. His first wife was Johann Stephan's niece. Just below it is Karl Hanf's cooperage. That's where I'm staying, at his house. He makes ore barrels. Or made them, exclusively, back when iron production was higher. Now he'll make any kind of keg that anybody wants. Business is really off for both of them since mining collapsed."

Veronica turned around. "That's why there's a clearing here. They build the shallow-draft barges and rafts here, upstream, to float ore and pig iron downstream. They don't bother to bring them back—just sell them when they get to Regensburg or wherever they are headed. It was far busier when I was a girl." She pointed at the creek. "Look, you can see for yourself. The water is running practically clear. When I was a child, it was red-orange with the rust from the mines and slag piles."

"I really would not have imagined," Mary said, "that a creek this small could be used for navigation."

"This is the river," Veronica answered stubbornly. "There is an elaborate system of locks and dams, all the way down the river. There had to be, since the water was also used to power the triphammers, which meant that the barges had to navigate past the mill wheels and mill ponds. If you don't want to stop and eat right now, we can go further down, below the cooperage, I can show you the first lock that takes the barges over the rapids. It must still be working, since they're still building barges here."

It had been a lot easier for a child of ten or eleven years old to get out to the lock than it was for a woman of fifty-nine. It wasn't the fairly well prepared path that the workmen used. It was the back way that kids had used when she was growing up.

Veronica was starting to wonder if this had been a good idea. After all, they would have to climb back up.

They did make it down, at which time they decided by consensus to sit with their feet dangling over the water and eat lunch before they climbed back up. Alas, they weren't as young as they used to be.

The lock was filling up, gradually. A barge loaded with full barrels was tied up at the side of the stream, ready to go. Next to it, waiting for cargo, was an empty one. Thirty or forty years ago, Veronica said, the lock would have been crowded. They wouldn't have even bothered to open the gates for one barge.

They couldn't stay to watch the gates open, though. Veronica suggested rather firmly that when the lock got filled to three fourths, they should start to climb back up. Men would be coming down to untie the barge and punt it out. She remembered very well from her childhood that people at the barge-yard got really mad if they caught unauthorized people sitting down here dangling their feet over the water on a fine summer day. It would be rather embarrassing for the wife of Admiral Simpson and the wife of Mayor Dreeson to be hauled into court for trespassing on private property.

Johann Rothwild could hardly believe his luck. The two old women were out of sight and, because of the hammering and sawing upstream, out of hearing of anyone else. The one old lady had actually put her walking stick down while she ate. That had been the only thing that either of the fool women might have used as a weapon.

So. Knife them. Take anything valuable. Toss the bodies into the lock. Everybody would put it down to beggars or vagabonds or unemployed mercenaries, which amounted to pretty much the same thing.

Motioning his henchman and Hermann Richter to follow him, he started down the back way to the lock, which turned out to be just as awkward for them as it had been for Mary and Veronica. It was, after all, just a deer path. One of the branches that he had grasped to keep his balance broke with a crack and he slipped a couple of feet.

Mary heard the men first, but by the time she turned, they were already down to the bottom of the path. With their knives out.

Running. She got off two shots. Both missed. Aiming at running men with a short-barreled revolver was a chancy thing.

Rothwild cursed. Those shots would have been heard, even with all the sawing and hammering upstream. Someone was bound to come and investigate. They had to get this over and get out of here fast. Damn Uncle Kilian!

Veronica, contrary to masses of good advice and lectures delivered by Henry, Gretchen, Dan Frost, and a wide variety of other people, did not carry a gun. By this time, though, she was on foot with the walking stick in her hands. It was a long one, a shepherd's crook. Her grip was not scientific—two hands desperately grabbing the straight end. Against someone trained to fight with a cudgel, she wouldn't have delivered a single blow. It did, however, have a considerably longer range than knives. She got in one hard thwap against the shoulder of one of the men attacking them.

Unfortunately, it was the man's left shoulder; and he was obviously a brawler, used to taking blows. He didn't drop his knife. The weight of walking stick, held out awkwardly as it was, slid it from his shoulder down to the ground. As she struggled to bring it back up, entirely by accident, she caught one of the other men's legs with it—she recognized him suddenly; it was Hermann: what on earth was Hermann doing here?—and dumped him into the lock.

The third man kept coming. With a shock, she recognized him also. *Sara's boy; Rothwild.* The one who had gone to the bad. He had apparently stayed there, once he arrived. That was her last thought for the time being.

Mary scrambled to her feet and looked over. The biggest man, with his left hand, grabbed the walking stick about a third of the way down, pulled it from Veronica's grip and knocked her out.

After those first two shots, Mary had stopped herself from shooting again. No point in wasting the bullets. At closer range, she had better luck. Not, however, good enough luck. The first two of the four remaining bullets still seemed to have missed. She accidentally bloodied one man's hand; the bullet went on to scratch the side of his neck. The last one landed in his upper arm, breaking it just below where Veronica had smacked him on the shoulder. He stopped, bent over, looking nauseated.

The other man kept coming. She threw her gun into his face. He lost his balance, slipping on the slick grass, and fell forward heavily against her. He was tall; his knife went over her shoulder. Both fell. Mary, closer to the edge, went over into the lock, striking her head on a piling on the way down.

Forst and Becker, since they were supposed to float Bastl's barge full of barrels out, had already been halfway down the good path when the shooting started. They started to run. They saw the end of the picnic and panicked. Three attackers, counting the one who was now floundering his way over toward the edge of the lock. Only one really appeared to be out of the fight. They were unarmed themselves.

And the women. Foreign women.

Their own connections with the landgrave of Leuchtenberg would show up if there was an investigation. What if someone had intercepted Arndt's reports to the landgrave? They were Leuchtenberger. If they were caught at the scene, the Swedes would blame their lord for this assault on the two women. It would give the Swedes a chance to defame his character. And he hadn't had a *thing* to do with it. Neither had they. It wasn't their *fault*.

They didn't stop to talk. Becker disposed of the big man who had fallen on his face after knocking the one woman into the water, using the man's own knife. Just a simple stab through the neck while he was still half-stunned from the collision. Forst frantically wrestled two empty barrels from the waiting barge to the loaded one. Becker fished Mary out of the lock and dropped her into one of the barrels, bunging on the lid. Forst picked up Veronica, dropped her into the other barrel, and did the same.

They untied the barge and punted it out into the middle of the lock, waiting for the gate.

By the time the men from the cooperage got there, they were standing on the barge, not precisely calmly, but looking no more excited than men should who had just witnessed a fight. They waved urgently, motioning toward the two men on the bank and the one in the water.

"Fight," they yelled. "There was a fight."

At the far end of the lock, the gates opened.

CHAPTER 28

Maleficiae Abditae
Atque Perfidiosae

Grafenwöhr, the Upper Palatinate

Karl Hanf, who was not as young as he used to be, came huffing down the path from the cooperage after his men.

"What happened?"

"Two guys from Bastl's were already out on the barge. They yelled that there had been a fight."

Hanf took in the scene.

Two of his men, holding a very wet one. Who was Hermann Richter.

One of his men standing over another, who was injured. Seen him hanging around town lately.

Two more, rolling a very dead one from his face to his back. Familiar. Oh, God. That beast Johann Rothwild, the brother of Bastl's first wife.

"Go up the path. Bar it and don't let Bastl's men from the barge-yard come down here." That was to the two men who had turned Rothwild over.

He wished he had more men. It was taking two to hang on to Hermann. He'd have to risk the third man staying down. From the looks of the wound in his arm, that wouldn't be a problem. Not for a while, anyway.

"Run up and get some rope, as fast as you can. We're going to have to truss that one. Hurry."

Hanf moved; he would stand over the third man himself. And just in case . . .

He picked up a walking stick that was lying near the corpse. *Veronica's* walking stick?

He looked around. He saw something in the lock, floating next to the empty barge, which had kept it from going downstream when the lock opened. He fished it out, grabbing the handles with the crook. Veronica's tote bag.

And, on the grass, the remains of a picnic lunch.

He stood over the injured man, thinking. All they could get him for would be systematic overcharging on the barrels—pegging his costs at what they would have been if he were buying lumber at the set prices rather than stolen lumber. It was Bastl who was directly involved in the timber thefts, which was why he was behind deadline on Troeschler's barges. His main supplier had recently been arrested. And Bastl's former brother-in-law was lying here dead.

All they could get him for was overcharging. That would just be a fine. A stiff fine, hard to pay in bad times, but still just a fine. And he had an obligation of hospitality; Veronica had been staying at his own house.

The guy came back with the rope.

Hanf came to a decision.

"Tie them both up. The one with the bad arm, just tie it to his body; then tie his feet. When that's done, you two go up and help keep Bastl's men from coming down the path and trampling everything. And *you*"—he pointed to the man who had gotten the rope—"get into town as fast as you can and notify the authorities. I'll watch here."

The proper authorities, consisting of the bailiff, Thomas von Wenzin, and two of his men, came in a hurry. As did Böcler, Marc Cavriani, Rastetter, and Brechbuhl. The proper authorities had not been enthusiastic about this. However, it did make a significant difference to von Wenzin's thought processes that Böcler had a letter signed by the regent, with all appropriate formalities.

Böcler had drafted it himself. It said exactly what the regent had directed. He was fully authorized to investigate, in the regent's name, "whatever is going on." Böcler had already internalized one of the fundamental rules of the successful bureaucrat. Unless there is some compelling reason to be specific, be vague. He hadn't expected this, of course. But he was fully authorized to investigate it, now that it had happened. Before they left town, he had sent a courier to Hand. Now . . .

Marc picked up a piece of metal, half-buried in the grass. "This is an up-time pistol. I don't think that pistol is the right word for it, precisely. But it is a gun to hold in the hand. Easy to handle, for a small woman like Frau Simpson. Also, easy to hide."

Böcler nodded. He had seen a similar one. The up-timers had given it to Duke Ernst, who kept it inside his doublet. Always.

The Grafenwöhr bailiff looked dubious. The "handgun" was very small. It was hard to believe that it would shoot anything, but there had, indubitably, been shots.

Karl Hanf was singing a song about timber theft. Von Wenzin thought that its verses would tie Wilhelm Bastl to a man who had been recently arrested in Weiden. The bailiff would have to write the *Pfleggerichter* there. He didn't think that it probably had anything to do with what had been going on here.

The injured man was swearing that he didn't know a thing. Rothwild had hired him and he didn't know who had hired Rothwild. Von Wenzin thought that might possibly be true.

That left Kilian Richter's son. They'd better take him back to town.

Böcler and the bailiff agreed that they had probably seen everything that was to be seen here. Von Wenzin sent a couple of his men up to arrest Bastl. He'd worry about the paperwork when he got back to town. If he gave the man time, he would start destroying records as soon as he heard what had happened.

Hermann Richter, upon being interviewed under some duress, admitted that he, Rothwild, and the third man had attacked Frau Dreeson and Frau Simpson. He even admitted that his father had put them up to it.

He denied that the three of them had attacked the women with the intent of killing them. Von Wenzin thought that the judge could take that for what it was worth.

The utter absurdity was that Hermann insisted that, while he was in the water, two men whom he had never seen before, with whom he was in no way acquainted, and of whom he had no knowledge whatsoever, had shown up in the middle of the attack, picked up the two women, dropped them into barrels on the barge, and taken them away.

"That's ridiculous on the face of it," von Wenzin told him emphatically.

On the other hand . . .

The two women were not to be found. And, by Hanf's statement, not much time had passed between when the first two shots were fired and the men from the cooperage arrived on the scene. Plus, Hanf's men said that there had been a barge in the lock.

The absurdity was that Hermann Richter denied knowing anything about the other two. Questioning, duly authorized by the *Pfleggerichter*, resumed.

Kilian Richter, hauled before the forces of justice on the basis of his son's statement, reluctantly—very reluctantly—admitted to hiring Rothwild and his henchman to attack Veronica, and to having sent his son with Rothwild. He swore that he had no intention of any kind to cause damage to Frau Simpson. He also swore that he knew nothing at all about any other men or any barge.

The bailiff didn't believe a word of it.

The third man, reinterviewed rather emphatically, insisted that he didn't know anything at all about what Kilian Richter may have told Rothwild. He insisted that he had never seen Richter before in his life, did not even know his name, and had been recruited for the job down near Amberg by Rothwild only. He only knew that there was someone in the background who held the purse.

He did say that originally, when they started out in the morning, they had only expected to attack Frau Dreeson and not necessarily that very day. They had attacked when the second woman was there only because it was such a conveniently isolated spot. Upon being pressed, he said, "well, there was so much hammering and sawing upstream, no one would be likely to hear screams. Rothwild thought it was just sort of convenient to do it there."

The bailiff, fingering his beard, asked just why they had expected screams.

"Well, it was just in case. Actually, once we took a look, we hoped we could stab the old ladies in their backs while they were sitting down eating their lunch, without any trouble."

On the basis of that, the bailiff started reinterviewing Hermann. It was a long night in the Grafenwöhr city hall basement.

The only consistency between Hermann's version and the henchman's story was that they absolutely did not know anything about the barge or the bargemen.

Wilhelm Bastl, questioned without duress, knew a little about both, none of it involving any plans to kidnap women and put them on the barge. The two men were just casual laborers, he said—boatmen when they were younger, on their way home. They had only been at the yard a short time.

The bailiff did ask for the precise date when Bastl hired them. He didn't immediately identify as significant that it was a few days after Veronica Dreeson had arrived in Grafenwöhr.

Did Bastl know where they were going?

Not exactly, but he had heard one of them mention that he had been born in Pfreimd and had a cousin who worked as a chambermaid in Amberg.

That meant nothing to von Wenzin, either.

Böcler, Marc, and Brechbuhl were upstairs with Rastetter. They had all courteously declined von Wenzin's invitation to be present at the interrogations. As soon as they got back to Grafenwöhr, Rastetter had sent his clerk to Hanf's house to collect all the papers Veronica had there. The oldest niece, a mulish look on her face, had come back to the city hall with him, demanding to be given an itemized receipt on her aunt's behalf; staying until she got one; standing behind the clerk as he went through each item to make sure that he didn't leave anything out. Marc thought that Frau Dreeson must have looked a lot like that when she was thirty years younger.

Rastetter had gone through the papers from the house, sorting them into several piles. He found about what he expected, but nothing really exciting. At the moment, he was systematically investigating the contents of Veronica's tote bag. Most of it was damp. Not wet, because the canvas was sufficiently waterproof to have floated for some time, but damp. He spread the various papers out to dry; then turned to the more protected contents of the blue plastic envelope.

He wondered how she had gotten hold of Kilian Richter's private papers from years ago. Dealings with the lawyer Arndt. Not particularly flattering to Arndt's professional ethics, but now the man was dead.

Two things happened the next morning. Beyond, of course, the fact that most of the residents of Grafenwöhr ate breakfast and started work. And talked to one another; the whole town was buzzing with excitement about Veronica again.

Böcler, on the assumption that Hand would soon be arriving with a company of troops and could take charge, left at dawn to follow the barge down the river. There were, after all, only so many places that a barge could go. It was unlikely to grow feet and walk. His letter from the regent authorizing him to investigate "whatever is going on" would be of great use in getting information from possibly reluctant local authorities.

Being more or less local himself, even though most of the residents of the Upper Palatinate would certainly have defined Cornheim in Franconia as a strange town in a foreign country, he had the ability to both understand the people who were answering his questions and to move about comparatively inconspicuously. The last thing they wanted to do was start a panic. The mining and metallurgical communities of the Upper Palatinate were accustomed to having officious and comparatively youthful apprentice electoral bureaucrats with the seventeenth-century equivalent of clipboards wandering around the locks and tollbooths, poking their noses into everybody else's business and counting things. One more would not even rise to the level of, "what's *he* doing here?" One more customs official would just be a part of the scenery. Especially since they were all busy filling out Duke Ernst's *Fragebogen*.

Unlike any of the up-timers; unlike, even, Hand himself. Extremely tall Swedish colonels with obvious war injuries rarely manifested an interest in ore barges; nosy customs officials often did.

Nicholas Moser and Dorothea Richter eloped. They had, after all, only promised to delay until after Veronica left town, and Moser, by virtue of his job, had gained a pretty clear awareness that she had now left town. After all, he had spent the night in the basement recording the protocol of the questioning under torture. Thea's aunt had not specified *how* she was to have left town when she instructed them not to elope until after that. Moser didn't want to stay for the next stage, when von Wenzin took the evidence he already had and set out to get a confession from Thea's father. That could get sort of grisly.

Moser shuddered. Von Wenzin was just so matter of fact about it. He looked at the executioner and asked, "Wilhelm, are the tongs ready?" in the same dry as dust tone of voice as he usually asked, "Nicolas, have you finished the record copy of that affidavit?"

The elopement threw a red herring of major and distracting dimensions into the deliberations of everyone else, since none of them knew that it was one. Owing to his paranoia about Immuring in Convents, Moser had insisted that they not leave notes that might aid in a pursuit, so the Grafenwöhr officials wasted a great deal of time discussing the possible implications and potential ramifications of the disappearances of the town clerk and Richter's daughter. Rastetter finally made the connection, but it took a while. He was not inside the city government loop.

It slipped the lovers' minds, as they fled, that upon leaving Grafenwöhr, they were supposed to meet Dorothea's Tante Veronica in Amberg, where she would furnish them with a bank draft, because they didn't have enough money to get to Grantville. They forgot about it because they spent most of their time along the way discussing such things as Thea's noble effort to break their nonexistent engagement because of her family's appalling disgrace compounded by Nicol's equally noble determination to permit no such action. So, they didn't realize that they were running out of money until they got to Nürnberg.

Several things also happened that afternoon. Or didn't happen that afternoon, depending upon how one looked at it.

Leopold Cavriani, having left Amberg at first light, arrived. He didn't stay; just hired a couple of fresh horses, collected Marc, and started down-river, following the path that Böcler had taken.

Hand, who was supposed to be two hours behind them, didn't arrive at all. He hadn't even tried to get a company of regulars for this purpose. Banér had almost all of them over around Ingolstadt and there was no way he was going to strip the rest out of Amberg, leaving the regent himself with no decent security. He was bringing a company of *Grenzjaeger*, boatmen, and other competent trackers. They came up the road just in time to run into a party of foreign soldiers near Freihung and, not surprisingly, became distracted from their original aim.

A lively time was had by all. Hand sent a messenger to Grafenwöhr to let Böcler know that he was turning back to Amberg because of an unexpected emergency.

Kilian Richter's wife appeared at the city hall. She was feeling terribly hung over, but she was sober. Once the first clerk ascertained that she hadn't shown up to try to bail her husband out, she was shunted from room to room. She couldn't find anyone in authority to talk to. Finally, she stood in the corridor and shouted, "I want to tell someone what happened!"

Hieronymus Rastetter came out of the back room of the city clerk's office. He looked very official in his standard bureaucrat's robe and hat. He was followed by his clerk. She started to talk.

The clerk started to take notes.

"Kilian was terribly angry when Anton decided that his family would convert to Catholicism. With Anton's sisters gone, only his nephew had been standing between Kilian and Johann Stephan's share of their father's property. He'd been biding his time, waiting for Anton to go into exile also. When he heard that Anton had conformed, he swore fiercely. Oh, how he cursed and blasphemed."

"What about Augustin Arndt?"

Kilian's wife frowned. "I know the name, but not much else. Except I know he hired most of the bullies for Kilian. But I don't think he was there himself when it happened."

"Was where? When what happened?"

"Why, at Anton's shop, that night. The night that Amberg was plundered, Kilian sent a party of men disguised as mercenaries to Anton's shop. They were going to kill him, and his whole family, and make it look like the soldiers did it. They would have killed *all* of Anton's family. Him and his wife; Veronica; the three children. Except that they were interrupted by a group of real mercenaries and had to run away. They took Anton's wife with them when they ran."

She paused for a moment. "I guess it was real mercenaries who took Veronica and the children."

The questioning continued, faithfully recorded by the clerk.

No, she didn't know who all was involved. That Johann Rothwild had been there, she did know; Kilian had promised him a share of Johann Stephan's property, since he was Sara's son; later, Kilian somehow kept it all. She wasn't sure how that happened, but she thought that it had to do with the case that caused him to be permanently exiled from Grafenwöhr. They could look it up. Magdalena and Wilhelm Bastl should have gotten part of it, too, since Magdalena was a niece. But they didn't get any, either. Maybe they decided that they would rather be alive and didn't push it.

In any case, the men disguised as mercenaries had gone back to Arndt's office, where Kilian was waiting. It may not have been Johann Rothwild who had killed Anton Richter. But it was Johann who killed Anton's wife. She was sure of that. How come? Oh, because Kilian told her so. That was after the men had all come back to Grafenwöhr. Kilian told her that Anton's wife had been struggling and threatening Johann while he dragged her through the streets. How did Kilian know that, if he had been waiting in Arndt's office? She wasn't sure; she had never thought about that. But after they got to Arndt's office, Johann did kill her, right there. Arndt hid the body for a couple of days. Then, when the worst was over, he just brought it out and added it to the others that the cart was taking to the mass grave.

She sat there long enough to initial the rough copy of the notes that Rastetter's clerk had taken. She initialed every page. Then she said, "I guess I feel better now." Then, after fidgeting a bit: "Are you really sure that they aren't going to let Kilian out?"

Rastetter looked down at her statement, smiling very thinly. "You may rest assured that Kilian Richter will not be 'let out.'"

"All right," she said. "I guess, then, that I will go home."

"I think," Rastetter said, "that you had better stay until I can find the bailiff."

Böcler had gone; Hand had not arrived. It was all back in the Grafenwöhr bailiff's lap. Business as usual. He strode out.

Richter's wife was still sitting on the bench, her hands in her lap, rotating her thumbs around each other, when they came back with von Wenzin.

Amberg, the Upper Palatinate

By the time Hand wiped up the mess resulting from the skirmish by Freihung, he determined that these were a detachment of Holk's men, who claimed to be making a diversionary move through the Upper Palatinate on their way to cause some trouble in Leuchtenberg.

It only made sense for him to take his captives back to Amberg; it would have made no sense at all to take them to Grafenwöhr. He turned back, sending a messenger to tell Böcler that he would be delayed. In the ensuing discussions over the next couple of days, he and Duke Ernst reached the not particularly surprising conclusion that the second set of villains in the kidnapping, the ones who disposed of Kilian Richter's thugs, were probably employed by Holk in the service of John George of Saxony. It would only make sense, after all, that John George might be looking for hostages to hold against the USE.

The captured soldiers denied entirely any connection with ore barges or kidnapped women, but that was only to be expected. So Hand and the regent devoted extensive analysis to a mistaken premise and sent quite a number of their *Grenzjaeger* and other scouts to the north and east rather than to the south.

The whole episode left Duke Ernst, after he had interviewed a couple of the captured officers, feeling decidedly miffed with John George of Saxony. Which, in fact, John George deserved, even though he didn't have anything at all to do with the kidnapping.

On the Naab River, the Upper Palatinate

Böcler thought that he had a good identification of the barge. He would have loved to have it stopped, but, unfortunately, it was well ahead of him and nobody else could catch up to it any faster than he could. He was gaining a little, but not much, and was beginning to wonder if the damned barge was *ever* going to stop. It passed through every lock it came to. Where could it possibly be going?

✧   ✧   ✧

On the barge in question, Forst and Becker were feeling increasingly out of their depth. They didn't want the old ladies to die. They took the lids off the barrels every now and then, so they could get air. Once the women recovered consciousness, they dropped water into their mouths with a spoon. But when they came to locks and populated areas, they had to stuff up their mouths and put the lids back on or they'd scream. They'd tried that, several times.

The Naab was coming to an end. They were going to have to make up their minds pretty soon. They hadn't done anything, but nobody would believe that. The ladies had been out cold; they weren't going to testify that the men on the barge had valiantly rescued them from an attack by bandits, even if it happened to be true. One thing was sure, though. They did know that Arndt had been collecting information about the one lady for their lord, Landgrave Wilhelm Georg of Leuchtenberg. If they didn't want their heads cut off, they only had one choice. They would take the ladies to the landgrave, let him worry about it, and hope that he would provide them with *Schutz und Schirm* in return for their loyal service. Protection and defense; that was what a good lord owed his subjects.

They passed through another lock. And another.

The Cavrianis caught up with Böcler fairly quickly, since they hadn't had to stop and ask questions of tollkeepers or gate attendants. The three of them continued south as fast as the condition of the Naab's banks allowed them to. They couldn't go any faster on the river. If they were on a barge themselves, they would have to wait for the locks to open and close. Past Pfreimd. Why in hell, if the men were Leuchtenberger, hadn't they stopped in Pfreimd?

Past Schwandorf.

Past Burglengenfeld.

All the way to the mouth of the Naab, where it ran into the Danube. Where they found out that two idiotic bargemen, just a few hours before, had, without stopping at customs, shot their barge out of the river and crossed the Danube, presumably beaching themselves on the right bank above Regensburg. The barge had not appeared in Regensburg's waters.

All three of the pursuers, being stronger on brain cells than on biceps, sensibly refrained from doing anything really stupid, like trying to swim the Danube after it.

✧   ✧   ✧

Böcler entirely agreed that his first duty was to Duke Ernst. He would take the information back to Amberg.

When he arrived, his news caused great frustration among those intelligence analysts who had been assuming that John George of Saxony was the villain in the piece.

They realized now that it must have been Duke Maximilian. They started to develop new scenarios. Scenarios that involved Ingolstadt. Did Maximilian actually think that holding Veronica Dreeson and Mary Simpson hostage would get Banér to call off the siege? If not that, then what?

Hand called back the scouts he had sent to the north and east. Not that they hadn't gathered quite a bit of useful information while they were out. Taking a calculated risk, he practically stripped the border facing Bohemia of *Grenzjaeger*, sending them north to face against Saxony. He wished that he had more soldiers. If the king sent a regular regiment, though, Banér would appropriate it. In General Banér's world, internal security ran a very distant second to active campaigning.

"So where did the Cavrianis go?" the Swedish colonel asked Böcler.

Böcler's mouth fell open. Somehow, Cavriani had kept him so busy discussing all the things that he needed to bring to the regent's attention that he had forgotten to ask what the two of them planned to do next. He made a note to himself to be more thorough, next time.

Duke Ernst shrugged. The Cavrianis were not his problem: not his officials, not his subjects, not, really, even official members of the Grantville trade delegation. They were representing whom? Oh yes, Count August von Sommersburg. He could not be held responsible for every foreign merchant who passed through the Upper Palatinate.

Leopold and Marc followed the Danube upstream for some distance. Crossing right away, so close to Regensburg, Leopold explained, would most certainly have brought them to the attention of the Bavarian authorities, which would not have been a good idea at all. As it was, they would simply cross openly into the

Pfalz-Neuburg enclave rather than into Bavaria proper, in their own names and as exactly what they were: merchants from Geneva, bringing their horses, and an appropriate amount of baggage.

Cavriani Frères had a factor stationed in Neuburg, another in Pfaffenhofen. Veit Egli was originally from Constance and was a Catholic. Considering the location of this branch, it was far easier for a Swiss Catholic to go back and forth into Bavaria more or less freely than it would have been for a either a Genevan Calvinist or a local resident. Not that local residents did not make useful employees, Leopold pointed out. The factor in Pfaffenhofen, a man named Brunner, had relatives in Hohenwart and Reichertshofen; the cousin in Hohenwart had a brother-in-law in Schrobenhausen.

In any case, since they got to Neuburg first, Egli got the job of notifying a livery stable owner in Grafenwöhr that he had just *de facto* sold two of his horses (fair payment enclosed, see independent appraisal obtained by my employer; please send receipt). Marc had time to write to Frau Durre in Nürnberg and ask her to send him the clothes he had left in his room there, because they were taking a different route home. He included an entertaining, if rather sharply edited, version of their stay in Amberg with the request.

Using the firm's various resources, Leopold set his mind to two immediate projects. First, locating Mary and Veronica; second, getting them out of Bavaria. Those seemed rather obvious to him. For the time being, somebody else could worry about why they were there at all. Leopold Cavriani was a practical man.

CHAPTER 29

Tribulationes

Prüfening, Bavaria

Forst and Becker contacted Landgrave Wilhelm Georg of Leuchtenberg's steward, Petrus Sartorius, in Prüfening, which was as directly across from the mouth of the Naab as one could get and still avoid Swedish-occupied Regensburg. When they asked him for instructions, he told them that their lord was lying on his deathbed at the estate of *Freiherr* von Hörwarth at Planegg outside Munich and both his sons were both still away serving in the army.

"I know nothing at all about the landgrave's having taken any interest in anyone named Veronica Dreeson," Sartorius insisted.

Not that he would, of course, he thought to himself; he had never been involved in any way with the landgrave's collection of intelligence data or foreign activities, not even when the landgrave did such things. He no longer did such things. The landgrave's health had been shaky for the past several years; extremely bad for the past year; serious for the past six months. Sartorius' presence in Prüfening was for the purpose of looking out for the landgrave's surviving economic interests in his Swedish-occupied lands. Also, of course, to transmit money and occasional messages back and forth. And to keep an eye on Regensburg. Almost everyone in Prüfening was keeping an eye on Regensburg these days.

But still, he did not believe that the landgrave had been interested in Frau Dreeson. He was very firm about that. By now, he had decided Forst and Becker were harebrained idiots.

Unfortunately for the best laid plans of Forst and Becker—which were not, it had to be admitted, very good—the landgrave's mind was not well; he had become senile. All of his stewards knew that he had not taking an interest in anything or anyone for a long time. Sartorius made it plain that he wanted nothing to do with them.

This, of course, presented a problem for the bargemen. They still had the barrels.

Well, only two of the barrels. Sartorius had at least been happy to take charge of the ones filled with iron ore. He could find a use for it one of these days, he said.

Sartorius was also a cautious man. Although it did not seem probable on the basis of his reports, it was possible that the landgrave might recover his health. Divine miracles were never to be discounted. Should he recover, it might also be possible that he had indeed instructed his agent in Amberg—what was the man's name? Oh yes, Arndt. It might be possible that the landgrave had instructed Arndt to procure these women as hostages. If that did turn out to be the case—well, it couldn't do any harm for him to offer facilities to the women that they might relieve themselves. And, ah, clean themselves.

Sartorius assisted them to stand up; they were very cramped and stiff. He provided clean water; cold porridge left over from breakfast. The odd-looking one with her hair cut like a man's had a bruise and small cut on her temple; he provided the other woman with cloths to clean it, and a salve. He told a stableboy to clean the barrels.

Veronica cleaned Mary's wound from hitting her head on the piling. Then she took out her false teeth, washed them, and tucked them into the pouch gathered onto a heavy string that she wore around her neck, beneath her clothing. For the last two days, she had been afraid that one of the times when the guard pushed the rag back into her mouth to gag her, he would push them out of place and cause her to choke.

"This really sucks," Mary muttered. Then she half-giggled. "When I heard my son Tom use that expression as a teenager, I gave him quite the talking-to, believe you me! But I squirreled it away in my memory. It's got a certain catchy flair, and you never know."

Gingerly, she probed her head. "Yes, indeed. This really sucks."

Sartorius assured himself that this much assistance was all that anyone could possibly expect of him. He gagged the women and tied their hands again before he led them back down to the warehouse, which opened on one side to the river and on the other side to the street. In spite of the gags, they managed to make it quite plain that they did not want to be put back in the barrels. He had to assist the other two by holding the smaller one while they tied the legs of the one with short hair. It took all three of them to retie the second woman's legs; they used an extra length of rope on her.

Forst and Becker insisted on the extra rope. By this time, both of them felt that they needed a lord's protection badly. Sartorius' obvious nervousness had only reinforced their own suspicions. They, in fact, had concluded during the journey down the Naab that they had two unusually powerful witches on their hands; or, at least, one powerful witch and her assistant. Why else would the landgrave have been concerned about a little old lady? They were not sure about the other, but they intended to take no chances.

Particularly not since the steward had taken away the iron ore. Everybody knew that witchy powers did not work well in the presence of iron. Perhaps that was what had kept the witch under control on the trip down the Naab. Without that . . .

On the other hand, there was no way that they could possibly have hauled a cart heavy with iron ore over land. It had been hard enough to persuade the steward to advance them money to buy a donkey cart.

"Why do you want the donkey cart?" Sartorius asked.

"Well," Forst said, "if our lord is not available, then we need the protection of a lady."

"The landgrave's sister was in Bavaria," said Becker. "Somehow, we'll take these women all the way to Munich, and consult Landgravine Mechthilde."

Rather stiffly, Sartorius said: "Landgravine Mechthilde—who is known in Bavaria as *Duchess* Mechthilde, if you please, since she is the wife of Duke Albrecht—is not in Munich to begin with. As the sister-in-law of Duke Maximilian and, until his remarriage, the first lady of Bavaria, she is taking a *very* important part in the wedding procession for the duke and Archduchess Maria Anna, which this very day will welcome the archduchess in Passau. When the ceremonies there are completed, the procession will start on its way back from Passau to Munich. With, of course, the *duchess* continuing to play an important part."

Forst and Becker found this to be good news. This meant that their very own Landgravine Mechthilde would soon be much, much, closer than Munich. Which meant much, much, less hauling. If they could haul the barrels south to the Isar, they ought to be able to intercept the procession.

Even simple bargemen knew one thing. All formal processions moved very slowly. Their purpose was to let the people take a good look at the ruler.

CHAPTER 30

Conjurationes Atque Consilia

Besançon, The Franche-Comté

Bernhard of Saxe-Weimar smiled at Friedrich Kanoffski von Langendorff. "Not only has Cardinal Richelieu formally accepted my explanation that recent troop movements on the part of General Banér in Swabia made it impossible for me to send any significant forces as far north as Holstein—and no matter how furious he is after the catastrophe at Ahrensbök—he will have to acknowledge that it would have had no effect at all for me to send them, anyway. Not given that d'Angoulême had overall command."

Kanoffski shook his head. "The cardinal will eventually have to acknowledge it. That doesn't mean he is doing so right now, Your Grace. He is also, very soon, going to realize that aside from Turenne's cavalry, which is tied down in Paris, your troops in Alsace are the only intact body of effective soldiers under French command. Nominally under French command. He will have to wonder how long that will last."

Bernard tapped his fingers on the table. "In regard to de Guébriant. I think that we can go beyond making it clear to him that my offer of employment still stands. I think that we can afford to pay his ransom—anonymously, of course—without jeopardizing any of our other projects." Bernhard raised his eyebrows. Impressive, thick, bushy, eyebrows. "Don't you?"

"I'm sure of it. It would certainly be a pity for him to languish in USE captivity for years." Kanoffski rubbed his cheek. "Do you suppose that anyone has mentioned to Werth just how long the Imperials left *him* to languish in French captivity in that other world?"

"I doubt it. But there's no reason that someone shouldn't mention it to him. Just in passing, of course. And leaving out the fact that I'm the one who captured him in the first place."

"Of course."

Bernhard was still tapping his fingers on the table. "The fact that we have some more time, however, requires us to consider some possible future problems. I'm thinking in particular of the plague that is 'scheduled' for next year."

Kanoffski nodded, immediately understanding the reference. The previous winter, Duke Bernhard had sent a recruiter to Tuebingen, in hopes of acquiring the services of the mathematics professor, Schickard, for his projects in Besançon. After all, Schickard's father had been, and his brother was, public works director. The dukes of Württemberg were not, at present, in any position to construct public works and the university was not holding sessions.

Unfortunately, Schickard had gone off to work for the landgraves of Hesse. However, the recruiter had spoken to one of the other professors who had commented a little pompously, "Well, at least, since he's in Landgrave Hermann's castle in Rotenberg, Wilhelm won't die prematurely in the great plague epidemic that will sweep Alsace, Swabia, and Württemberg in 1635. That's a blessing, since we expect many great things from that brilliant mind."

The recruiter had come home talking plague. A quick examination of the up-time encyclopedia possessed by the duke revealed that the good professors at Tuebingen had the right of it. If all went as it did in that other universe, they would be faced with a major outbreak of the plague next year.

Duke Bernhard had perceived that such a medical emergency—right in his area of interest—might well have disastrous consequences for his plans. He had also heard that the up-timers had methods for combating plague that were measurably more effective than simple quarantine and movement restriction. He had been agreeable to Kanoffski's suggestion of attempting to hire an expert. The recruiter went to Grantville.

"We've gotten a response to our discreet queries in Grantville, Your Grace," said Kanoffski. "Do you recall the 'Suhl Incident' in January of last year?"

Duke Bernhard frowned. "Yes, although I can't recall many of the details. A mutiny by the local garrison, suppressed by the up-timers in alliance with the gun merchants of the city."

Kanoffski issued a soft, somewhat sarcastic grunt. "Whether it was a 'mutiny' or not could be debated. Indeed, it *has* been debated, and by the up-timers themselves. But the relevant item, from our point of view, is that one of the ringleaders of the so-called mutiny was himself an up-timer. A certain Lieutenant Johnny Lee Horton, who was killed in the course of the affair—and reportedly at the direct order of the American officer who led the suppression of the garrison."

Bernhard was still frowning. "And your point is . . ."

"Lieutenant Horton left behind a widow—also an up-timer, by the name of Kamala Horton—and their children. What's relevant is that, first, Frau Horton is quietly seething over the matter; secondly, she is now in straightened financial circumstances; and last but not least, she is herself a trained medical expert. What the up-timers call a 'nurse,' although the term has little in common with our own notions of such persons. She will have more medical knowledge than almost any doctor we could find, anywhere in Europe."

Bernhard's expression cleared, replaced by a thin smile. "In other words, by their treatment of this mutineer's widow, the up-timers in Grantville have created their own willing defector."

"Precisely. Our recruiting agent has spoken with her at some length, and she has agreed to move to Besançon and transfer her services—and her allegiance—to Your Grace. She and her children are expected to arrive here sometime next month. 'After school is out,' Mrs. Horton told our recruiter. 'I want them to finish up the spring semester.'"

Bernhard rose, clapping his hands. "Well, that's splendid. Well done, Friedrich."

Kanoffski nodded solemnly, being careful to hide any trace of a smile. There was an added benefit to the matter, but not one that he could raise directly with the duke. Bernhard's pride was even more sensitive than his stomach, and he would take offense at any suggestion that he was less than completely hale and hearty.

But the fact remained that his health was not and never had been as good as he liked to think. So...

If Wallenstein could have an up-time nurse watching over his health, why not Duke Bernhard? Particularly if the duke did not have to publicly acknowledge—or even acknowledge to himself—that watching over him would be one of the Horton woman's *other* responsibilities.

Kanoffski was rather pleased with himself. After all, when a man has decided to hitch his wagon to a star, it behooves him to make sure that the star continues to shine.

Amberg, the Upper Palatinate

"You don't expect General Banér to make any serious protest *at all*?" asked Duke Ernst, his eyebrows raised. "Not even when he learns that some of the reinforcements the emperor has agreed to send him to reduce Ingolstadt will be regiments from Torstensson's army? Which is to say, CoC regiments, for all practical purposes."

The duke's eyebrows climbed still farther. "Erik, I must point out that Johan's expressed opinion of the Committees of Correspondence—very pungently and profanely expressed, I might add, right here in my office, and on more than one occasion—can be boiled down to the proposition that the most suitable use for a CoC agitator's head is to serve as an adornment for a pike head."

"Oh, he'll issue a squawk or two, certainly. But I don't expect any worse than that." Colonel Erik Haakansson Hand grinned. "Ernst, I'm afraid your own modest degree of ambition—a very admirable personal trait, I'll be the first to say it—blinds you to certain realities. Johan Banér was already deeply jealous of General Torstensson's triumph at Ahrensbök. The news that recently arrived concerning General Brahe's successes have him positively spitting with fury."

Ernst frowned, trying to make sense of the matter. Gustav Adolf's commander in charge of the Swedish forces near Lorraine was Nils Brahe. He was not a general to miss an advantageous opportunity. Once the news arrived of the French defeat at Ahrensbök, he'd placed his forces on full alert. Then—probably as he'd expected, since Brahe was quite shrewd enough to gauge the complicated politics that fractured the French enemy—no sooner did he learn that Bernhard of Saxe-Weimar had withdrawn his forces facing Mainz back into Alsace and the Breisgau, than he'd made a dash to the border of Lorraine. Grabbing, in the process, much of the region that would now be incorporated into the expanding United States of Europe as the new Upper Rhenish Province.

But why—

"Oh," he said. Then, shook his head at the mentality involved. Leave it to Johan Banér to react with greater spite at a success by his *own* side in a war, than he would to one gained by the enemy—provided, of course, the enemy's triumph came at the expense of a different general than him.

There were at least three of the seven deadly sins at work here—Wrath, Pride and Envy. A good case could be made for adding Greed to the list, for that matter. Duke Ernst would fear greatly for Banér's soul, if he hadn't pretty much concluded that the general's incessant blasphemy had already condemned him.

So be it. He and Colonel Hand had decided to support Banér in his determination to seize Ingolstadt. Whatever this latest development might portend for the Swedish general's eternal fate, it boded well for the immediate future. At the very least, Ernst wouldn't be constantly distracted from his own duties by the need to play peace-maker between Banér and the reinforcements that would soon be arriving.

Ingolstadt

And now *this* insult!

Johann Philipp Cratz von Scharffenstein barely managed to keep from snarling openly at the insufferable man standing before his desk in the commandant's office, smiling down upon him.

The smile was perhaps the most insufferable thing about Colonel Wolmar von Farensbach, too, outside of the so-obviously-false "von" he was now adding to his name. The smile exuded a certain sort of smug condescension, barely this side of derision.

Still not confident of his ability to speak in a normal tone of voice, the commandant of the Ingolstadt garrison spent a few more seconds in a pointless study of the document Farensbach had handed to him upon being ushered into the office.

Document. Document. Cratz von Scharffenstein forced himself to use the simple and neutral term, in his own mind. Far better that, than to use any one of several other phrases which might have been equally well applied to the damned thing. Such as "veiled reprimand" or "insinuation of incompetence—possibly even disloyalty."

"I see." He finally managed that much. Then, waited a new more seconds before adding, "Well, then." A few more seconds, before adding: "Welcome to Ingolstadt, Colonel von Farensbach. I'm sure our officers will be glad to assist you in your . . . ah. Project."

The insufferable smile thinned, just slightly. Farensbach leaned over the desk and retrieved the document from Cratz's loose grip. "I don't object to 'project,' commander—so long as it is *clearly* understood that my authorization comes from Duke Maximilian *himself.* Make sure your subordinates understand that they *will* cooperate with my investigations."

With every stressed word, the bastard's smile flickered just that little bit more insufferably. Farensbach straightened up and looked down his nose at the garrison commander. "The duke was *most* emphatic in his orders. Which he gave to me *personally,* you understand, not simply in written form. Ingolstadt must *not* fall into the hands of the heretics—and *I* was the one he charged with the responsibility to see to it that *all* necessary security precautions have been taken."

He bowed, if such a miniscule movement of the head and shoulders could be graced with the term. "And now I'll be off. I must see to my duties *immediately,* you understand."

After he left, Cratz von Scharffenstein spent several minutes muttering curses, as many of them heaped upon Maximilian of Bavaria as his Farensbach creature. The duke's discourtesy to his loyal subordinates was positively outrageous!

Once he left the commandant's office, the smile vanished from Farensbach's face. True, the interview just passed had gone quite well. And, true also—his new commission from the duke himself as the chief of Ingolstadt's security was certain proof of it—Farensbach's embezzlements from certain of the Bavarian military accounts had gone undetected.

Well . . . embezzlements was an absurd way to put it, really.

Farensbach had simply lent himself money, unofficially, from accounts under his immediate control. With the full intention of paying them back, soon enough. Unfortunately, "soon enough" had not allowed for the possibility that the duke might send him out of Munich on this fool's errand to Ingolstadt.

Undetected—so far. But that wouldn't last, not with Farensbach no longer on the scene to oversee the keeping of the books. If he could return within a month, perhaps even two, things would work out well enough. But given the tense situation at Ingolstadt, with that maniac Swedish general Banér so obviously determined to press the siege, Farensbach might be stuck here for months and months. Eventually, the discrepancies were bound to turn up.

He'd have to think of something. If he didn't, the day would come when new soldiers would arrive at Ingolstadt bearing new orders—and that fat swine Cratz von Scharffenstein would be smiling evilly at him instead of the other way around. When he was led back to Munich in chains.

As he paced down the hall of the military headquarters, Farensbach's scowl was enough to keep anyone from approaching him while he chewed on the problem. Word had gotten out, obviously, concerning the nature of his assignment—and no garrison soldier in his right mind wanted to draw attention to himself.

All the better, all the better. No one, and certainly not the lazy garrison commandant, would be paying much attention to Farensbach's movements. More precisely, they'd be paying attention—but only from a distance. That would probably give Farensbach the leeway he needed, no matter what he decided to do.

And by the time he exited the headquarters and passed into the outer fortress, the decision had already been made. It wasn't as if Farensbach really had any other workable option.

So. Hopefully, the Swedish general's mania extended to his purse, as well. Safe and financially well-off was a far better prospect than simply being safe, after all.

Brussels, Spanish Netherlands

"No problems with the cease fire, then?" asked Don Fernando. "Not even from CoC irregular units?"

The Spanish prince's chief political adviser, Pieter Paul Rubens, smiled in response to that. His chief military adviser, Miguel de Manrique, chuckled aloud.

"No, Your Highness," he said. "Not any. From all accounts, the Richter woman maintains a ferocious discipline over her people. I'm quite envious, actually. I wish *my* troops were that obedient."

Don Fernando was not actually that pleased by the news. True, the absence of any incidents with Dutch CoC hotheads was an immediate blessing. But he could foresee a time in the not-so-distant future when he would find that same Richterian discipline a monstrous nuisance. Even now that he'd met the woman personally, it was sometimes hard *not* to think of her as a she-devil. She'd almost certainly maintain the same rigorous control over the CoCs when they entered the political arena.

But, that was a problem for a later day. For now...

One of Miguel's many pleasing qualities was his ability to sense when the prince needed a private moment. He bowed and excused himself, with some vague comments about business he needed to attend to.

After he was gone, Don Fernando slouched back in his chair. "Any word yet from the pope?"

"No, Your Highness," said Rubens. "But I really didn't expect to hear anything yet. You need to keep in mind—always—that once such a missive arrives in Rome, it's impossible to keep its contents really secret. By now, any number of Urban's advisers will be aware that you have presented the pope with a petition requesting his permission to relinquish your position as a cardinal of the church. No priest stays for long in such a position in Rome if he lacks brains. They will understand immediately that there can only be one logical reason for your petition—and at least one of those priests is certain to be in the pay of the Spanish crown."

He cleared his throat. "And at least one other will be in the pay of the Holy Roman Emperor. Who is not actually stupid, once you look past his stubborn bigotry."

The prince nodded. "Yes, yes, I understand. Soon enough, my brother will be seething with fury—and Ferdinand II is likely to be congratulating himself for having already married off his oldest daughter. That only leaves the younger, Cecelia Renata, as a cause for him to be caught in a Habsburg crossfire."

"You're most likely right, Your Highness. And what's to the immediate point is that Pope Urban is bound to hesitate himself, for a time. In the end, I'm confident he'll grant the petition—at which point *he* will be caught in the crossfire."

The prince grunted. "Why are you so confident he will? It would seem to me that if he refused, he'd get the best bargain of all. On the one hand, he avoids bringing down enmity on his own head—but he also must know that I'll go ahead and resign the cardinalship without or without his agreement to the petition. So he gains that benefit, as well."

Don Fernando sat erect. "I *don't* actually need his permission, after all. I never took major vows. I am not a priest, nor even a deacon."

Rubens shook his head. "You're thinking like a prince of a realm, Your Highness, not a prince of the church. In the end, the pope's power rests on his moral authority far more than it does on the dubious merits of that small army he maintains in the papal territories. That's been true for sixteen centuries. It would be worth far more to Urban to have it known that the newest branch of the Habsburgs asked—and received—his permission to found a dynasty than whatever temporary gains he might make from evading the issue."

He shrugged. "Besides, the Spanish and Austrian Habsburgs are already angry with him for having appointed Mazzare the cardinal-protector of the USE. This way, at least he gains the friendship of a new third branch of Europe's most powerful family."

The young prince pondered the matter, for a moment, and then sighed. "Yes, of course you're right. I suppose I'm just impatient."

He sighed again. "I don't know why, really. It's not as if I'm impatient to marry! Not given the choices left. It's too bad that . . ."

Almost hastily, he rose from the chair. "But that's pointless. What news from Scaglia, in Copenhagen?"

CHAPTER 31

Pompa Introitus

At the Passau Border, Bavaria

Maria Anna stood passively, submitting to the protocol that required her to be undressed in public. Why flinch at this? After all, when they reached Munich, she would be married. Her wedding night would have witnesses who would take proofs of her virginity; she would give birth to her children with fifty or sixty people in the room, taking official notice of the event. Which was certainly not as bad as the long-ago Constance, who had given birth to the future Emperor Frederick II in a tent with its walls up in the city's market square, just to make certain that those who might claim that she was too old for childbearing and assert that her child was an imposter could be confuted. The life of a ruler's wife was by its very nature a public one.

Mama stood behind her, receiving the Austrian garments in her arms. That did not mean, of course, that the glorious dress she had been wearing to cross the border would go to waste. Or even that it would be given to Cecelia Renata as a hand-me-down. The ceremony was largely a symbolic one. The seamstresses would check that the dress was still in good repair and pack it back into her trunks with the rest of her trousseau. Doña Mencia was standing behind Mama, waiting to take the discarded clothing from her hands when this part of the ceremony was over. Frau

Stecher was standing inconspicuously behind Doña Mencia, waiting to remove it from the pavilion.

There would be other occasions for her to wear the dress, she hoped. Duchess Mechthilde was starting to reclothe her. The new dress was also quite luxurious, the bodice covered with lace and pearls. It was very beautiful, if you liked black brocade embroidered in black.

She wished, with one last flicker of nostalgia, that Papa had chosen to marry her into the Spanish Netherlands. Then, she could have traveled a long way, seeing new things. Conditions in the Germanies being what they were at the moment, through Tyrol and Switzerland; then France and Luxembourg, she supposed. She would have gotten to see something different. Marrying into Bavaria was just like, well, moving next door.

Possibly Cecelia Renata would get to travel to the Spanish Netherlands. It was an open secret now, within the diplomatic community, that Don Fernando had privately written to Urban VIII asking whether a petition for laicization would be looked upon with favor. Maria Anna assured herself that she would not be envious of her sister if that happened. Envy was a mortal sin. She would not commit it. If she did unthinkingly commit it, she would repent of her error, confess it with contrition.

She had learned her German from the servants. She had no difficulty in understanding the ribald cries and shouts coming from the crowd outside the pavilion.

She was supposed to stand with her eyes modestly downcast throughout the reclothing. Quickly, she flicked them up. Uncle Max was not watching her.

What would she call him when he was no longer her uncle, but rather her husband?

Although Duke Maximilian was maintaining a passive indifference to the proceedings, this was not the case with any other person within the court pavilion. This marriage represented a crisis for every member of the Bavarian nobility, male or female; for every Bavarian government official, all male. If the Austrian managed to get pregnant, it would result in a shuffling of power structures and relationships at the Bavarian court that people had been setting up for nearly two decades. There was a great deal of curiosity; the courtiers pressed forward to view her.

✧   ✧   ✧

The next stage of the proceedings began. First, the prince-bishop of Passau stepped forward. Maria Anna looked at him affectionately. That was natural enough; he was her younger brother Leopold Wilhelm, just twenty years old. He had been a bishop since he was eleven. Like his older brother and sisters, he was the product of a Jesuit education. The pluralistic ecclesiastical offices that he held were a burden to his conscience already; more, undoubtedly, would be heaped upon him in the future in the interest of maintaining Habsburg political power. Papa's plans for him included the dioceses of Strassburg, Halberstadt, Magdeburg, Olmuetz, Breslau, the headship of the order of the Teutonic Knights. Although he was devout, determined to conduct himself in a manner that would cause no personal scandal, he would be more than delighted if he could get rid of them and go into a secular, military or diplomatic, career.

The canonical scandal of plurality itself was one that he could scarcely avoid. *The lands*, Maria Anna thought. *So much of what we do, that we call "defending the church," is directed at controlling the lands, the secular power and wealth that are in the hands of the church.*

Father Lamormaini had never really answered her question. If there must be a choice, was it more important for the church to hold its property or to care for the souls of its flock? The lands had not always been there. In the days of the early church, there had been no lands.

. . . the birds have their nests, but the Son of Man has no place to rest his head. The apostles had not been prince-bishops.

The prince-bishop of Freising stepped forward. Veit Adam von Gepeckh. He could scarcely have been excluded, no matter how furious Duke Maximilian had been in 1618 when the cathedral chapter elected him instead of one of the duke's brothers. Duke Maximilian had no qualms at all about violating canon law by heaping up a plurality of benefices when it came to his brothers, although he had presented himself as extremely concerned by the allegations that Gepeckh had fathered more than one child. He had brought charges; initiated investigations. The papal investigator, the bishop of Augsburg, had issued a finding that there was no bar to Gepeckh's consecration. Eventually, he had sworn to lead a model life henceforth if confirmed, admitting only by implication that his conduct thus far had not been ideal. Reluctantly, the duke had consented to the papal confirmation of his election. As far as anyone knew, Gepeckh had done as he had promised and become the very model of an energetic and reforming Catholic Reformation bishop, not to mention introducing major measures of economic reform into his territories.

It had been a lovely scandal while it lasted, though. And everybody present knew that Duke Maximilian had no intention of ever accepting the election of another prince-bishop of Freising who was not a member of his own immediate family.

Bishop Gepeckh was accompanied by the papal nuncio, Carlo Carafa. Maria Anna smiled at him. He had served as nuncio in Vienna in 1621; she had known him since she was a child.

The nuncio smiled back. He moved steadily. Scheduled events went on, even when the morning's dispatches, delivered by a non-stop relay of couriers and horses from Rome to Passau, brought news of an attempt to assassinate the pope. That was not public yet, here in Bavaria. He assumed that the duke had received a message from his Roman agent Crivelli, also, since a special courier had arrived for him this morning.

Father Johannes Vervaux, S.J., was standing behind his two charges. Within a month of Duchess Elisabeth Renata's death, his position in the Bavarian court had changed rather significantly. From being the confessor of an elderly woman, he was now the tutor of two very, very, lively boys; of three, on the comparatively rare occasions when the eldest was in a mood to receive some academic instruction. Karl Johann Franz was fifteen; he was far more interested in fencing and riding, gymnastics and other "knightly arts" than in intellectual matters. He was aching for the day that he received permission to serve in Bavaria's army. He would be sixteen in November; there would probably be no holding him back from a cavalry regiment once he passed that milestone.

The two younger boys showed much more promise, in Vervaux's opinion. Duke Albrecht and his wife had lost a child between Karl and the two younger boys; when he was nine years old, which often ached far more than losing an infant. Maximilian Heinrich was twelve; Sigmund Albrecht, ten. Both, whether Duke Maximilian's new marriage proved fruitful with a quiver of sons or whether Karl did eventually succeed to the duchy, would be destined to lives in the highest offices of the Catholic church. The elder, almost certainly, would follow in the sequence of Wittelsbachs who had become archbishop-electors of Cologne; for the younger, there was a wider range of possibilities.

Freising, perhaps. Duke Maximilian really wanted Freising in the family. Regensburg or Passau would be possible; if Bavaria managed a real coup, Salzburg.

It was, in any case, Vervaux's assignment to form and mold them in such a way that they would be a credit to their vocations. All too many political appointees to high church office were not, nor had been since the earliest historical records of the Church. Consequently, he did not consider his new post to be a demotion. He would grant that it might be so in the eyes of worldly men; it certainly was not so in the eyes of God. Nor, if he succeeded in his task of providing them a good spiritual formation, in the eyes of the Jesuit Order.

At the moment, however, his task was to see that they did not stand on tiptoe; neither squirmed nor wiggled, craned their heads, nor in other ways acted like boys. They were in the middle of a formal court ceremony. Their father, Duke Albrecht, ignored them, focused entirely on his role in the welcoming ceremony for Archduchess Maria Anna of Austria. Duchess Mechthilde, although carrying out an equally important part in the ceremony, flashed occasional glances their way, anxious to confirm that they were behaving themselves.

This was not surprising, considering that they were boys, and at the moment their mother was occupied with stripping Archduchess Maria Anna down to her shift, in order to re-clothe her in garments of Bavarian manufacture. It was difficult to keep boys from displaying an unseemly interest in something like that.

Vervaux smiled inwardly. It was difficult to keep even a middle-aged Jesuit from displaying an unseemly interest in something like that. The ceremony by which the archduchess was being transferred from the custody of her father to that of her future husband required a public change of clothing. The crowds who were attending, beyond the limits of the enclosure for court personnel, were making no effort to refrain from unseemly interest. He gathered his errant thoughts up and disciplined them. Surely, there were more edifying topics to which he could devote his consideration than the degree of dress, or undress, of the future duchess of Bavaria as she stood surrounded by her ladies-in-waiting.

Ladies. Yes. He would think about other ladies. Mary Ward's English Ladies. The Ladies who were "not Jesuitesses," since the Jesuit rule forbade it to accept the direction of women's orders. The Ladies who, nonetheless, were shielded from the Inquisition by Father-General Vitelleschi, even in the face of a papal bull dissolving them.

Since Duchess Elisabeth Renata's death, Duchess Mechthilde had assumed her role as their patron and benefactor in Bavaria. Well, officially, of course, Duke Maximilian was their patron. Effectively, however, it had been the duchess. Just as, in Vienna, Emperor Ferdinand II was officially their patron and benefactor, but effectively it was Empress Eleonora whose interest and support had shielded them, thus far, from publication of the papal edict dissolving their order. In almost every place where the Ladies had established a foundation, they had received very extensive patronage from women of the highest nobility. In England, Queen Henrietta Maria herself protected their activities in a Protestant land. In the Netherlands, they had been under the sponsorship of Infanta Isabella Clara Eugenia for as long as anyone could remember. That was in the face of the situation created by the fact that the court physician, Andrea Trevigi, had been a bitter opponent of the Jesuits and had tried for years to use the order's support for the Institute of the Blessed Virgin Mary to bring them down. Vervaux reminded himself that he should not be thankful that the man died last year (he would confess this thought).

That conflict had pulled in Carlo Carafa when he was nuncio in Cologne. Vervaux glanced up again. Carafa, now nuncio in Munich, was here today, awaiting his role in the ceremony. In Naples, great noblewomen had exercised enough influence on the Spanish viceroy that he had, supposedly, pressured Cardinal Buoncompagni into consenting to the reopening of the Ladies' school, in spite of the opposition of the Holy Office. It might be interesting to investigate what that constant support by great noblewomen signified. What was the attraction that the English Ladies exercised on them?

Would Archduchess Maria Anna, as duchess of Bavaria, continue her predecessor's interest in their endeavors? Her stepmother's interest was a promising omen, but was not, of course, a guarantee.

Would the new duchess be able to gain enough influence with her husband that she could establish a strong position at the court in her own right? Would her position enable her to provide such patronage? Almost involuntarily, Vervaux glanced up to see how the ceremony was progressing. Then he glanced back down again, placing his left hand rather firmly on Maximilian Heinrich's shoulder. He hoped that this was about as far as they intended to go in the matter of unclothing the archduchess in public.

That was really a very impressive bosom. Vervaux glanced at Duke Maximilian. He was standing next to his brother, richly clothed in brocade. Black brocade, embroidered with black. He had refused to put off his mourning for the Duchess Elisabeth Renata. For all the interest he was displaying in his intended and at the moment largely unclothed bride, he might as well have stayed in Munich.

Which he had wanted to do. It had taken the collective pressure of the entire privy council to persuade him to come to the border at Passau. Vervaux knew that he had risen before dawn, attended mass, devoted some time to private devotions, and then read dispatches that had been delivered by a special courier until it had been time for him to prepare for the ceremony.

From Ingolstadt, Vervaux presumed. He didn't know of anything else that was happening at the moment that would require a special messenger. The regular couriers delivered information to the duke twice a day.

Maria Anna had known that she was to receive the rose. She had not realized that it would be so beautiful. It was lying on a white satin cushion edged with braided gold thread; there were gold tassels dangling from the corners.

She knelt for the nuncio's blessing; rather, for the pope's blessing, delivered by the nuncio. Urban VIII had, for years, been a strong supporter of Uncle Max's efforts to see that the Catholic church should be restored in the Germanies. Sometimes, even, perhaps, the pope had supported Uncle Max so strongly that he hadn't shown enough appreciation of Papa's efforts. Not because Papa was less zealous than Uncle Max, but because Papa was a Habsburg and Urban VIII had quite a lot of conflicts with the Habsburgs in Italy. Even though those were Spanish Habsburgs such as Cousin Philip. There were layers upon layers of diplomatic complexity, even when it came to things such as restoring the church.

Maria Anna kneeled and bowed her head. She would continue to study hard, she promised God silently. She would master all of these complications. When her time came to be a regent, she would be prepared to serve Him to the fullest extent that lay within the capacity of the gifts of mind and body that He had given her.

Carafa prayed.

Maria Anna rose. Bishop Gepeckh placed the rose in her hands.

She held it out for Duke Maximilian to see. Waited. Prayed that he would not turn his face away from her in the presence of Papa and Mama, of the nuncio, of all these people.

Maximilian turned to Carafa, thanking the pope for bestowing this high honor on the Duchy of Bavaria and expressing his hope that Bavaria in turn would never fail in its duty to the church.

Involuntarily, contrary to protocol, Maria Anna clutched the rose against her body, hugging it against the black brocade dress. It gleamed in the sunlight.

Doña Mencia came forward and placed it back on the cushion.

The excitement of the day was not limited to the courtiers. Assigned a place as far away from the archduchess as a person could get and still be inside the roped-off enclosure, Susanna Allegretti stood on tiptoe. She had never been so thrilled in her life.

Behind her, a captain in Duke Maximilian's bodyguard, assigned to ensure the safety of the archduchess' household during the procession, checked his horse as it shifted restlessly. He glanced down, automatically noting the shape of the head, neck, and shoulders of the people inside the pavilion. He would not have risen to his present rank if he was not conscientious about his work.

CHAPTER 32

Festae Miraculique

Bavaria

Papa and Mama, Cecelia and Mariana, were gone, back to Vienna. The wedding procession moved slowly toward Munich, the days punctuated by the ringing of bells calling people to prayer, the dismounting of everyone in the procession in response to the bells, and the recital of the liturgical offices. In between, it moved through villages that offered pantomimes in honor of the marriage and towns that had decorated their market squares. Every mayor welcomed her; every Latin school had a teacher who had written a poem in her honor; some towns had organists or choir directors who had set the poems to newly composed music. There were allegorical pageants, some classical and some biblical. Always, there were children with flowers; always, there were prayers that this marriage might prove fruitful.

Every evening, they stopped as guests of one or another prominent nobleman. Maria Anna was beginning the process of learning all the names and connecting the names to the proper faces. Making polite conversation, she commented on the beauty of Bavaria's children, elegantly comparing it to the beauty of the flowers they gave her.

The courtier to whom she was speaking at the moment was Don Diego Saavedra Fajardo, a Spanish diplomat and literary figure who had been in residence at the Bavarian court for some time.

"I am most glad that the future duchess duly appreciates that children are one of God's greatest gifts," he said. "You know, perhaps, that one of the most severe of the witch burnings in Bavaria in the preceding generation occurred when it dawned on Duke Maximilian's father that his son's first marriage was going to be permanently barren."

Maria Anna stared at him. The Spanish courtier nodded solemnly. "Oh, yes. Duke Wilhelm decided that witches had hexed his daughter-in-law and set out to make them sorry. Which he certainly did."

The judiciary chancellor, Johann Christoph Abegg, was standing next to Saavedra. Quickly, she reviewed what she knew about the man. Another jurist—Uncle Max, like Papa, gave positions of great honor to the nobility but tended to rely upon his academically trained advisers when it came to administration. Abegg had been in his position since 1625; he could probably stay as long as he wanted to, if he didn't go too near to the edge. For a couple of years, he had teetered on that brink. In 1626, a relative of his wife, married to the town clerk of Eichstätt, had been executed as a witch. Many considered him to be an enemy of dealing firmly with the witch problems. On most matters, however, he was now neutral.

Casually, quite matter-of-factly, Abegg assured her that if she was not fertile, he expected that the pyres would burn again.

The geography of Bavaria made it somewhat difficult to go from Passau to Munich by land. True, the procession generally followed the course of the Vils, and would then cut across to the Isar at Landau. Still, the route involved crossing a number of small streams. Everything had been prepared in advance at the fords. For those that could not be conveniently forded by a procession of elaborately dressed people, ferries had been procured, but every ferry crossing ensured that the procession moved slowly. First a group of guards crossed; then the duke and his entourage, which, of course, included his brother's family; then the nuncio and the bishop with theirs; then Maria Anna and her attendants; then the courtiers and officials who were not in the duke's own entourage, with their wives; higher servants; lesser servants with the baggage; finally stablemen with remounts, followed by another troop of guards. Then the procession would re-form and move to the next village or town where a reception had been arranged.

By the time they reached Freising, of course, everybody was talking about the attempt to assassinate the pope. And that the pope had appointed an up-time priest, an Italian by the name of Mazzare, as cardinal-protector of the usurping United States of Europe. Cardinal-protector of a principality ruled by a heretic, by the Swede! How infuriating.

Duke Maximilian was not in a good mood. The privy council met every evening, cutting the ceremonial banquets short. Each meeting began with a rosary, thanking God for preserving the pope's life. No matter how—it appeared that it was a Scots Calvinist who had interposed himself between His Holiness and the gunman. Which was quite embarrassing.

Richel, it appeared, had successfully infiltrated an informant into St. Mary's in Grantville, in the guise of an apothecary who had come to learn from one of the up-time parishioners. The parishioner was another Italian, one Agostino Nobili. It was difficult to account for the presence of so many Italians in this up-time community; but, of course, Italians went everywhere. For the past three and a half centuries the peninsula had provided all of Europe with an unending stream of artists, architects, engineers, scientists, teachers, jurists, not to mention military commanders and common soldiers. If this town truly came from the future, there was no reason to presume that Italians would have ceased to be the intellectual leaders of the world three and a half centuries from now.

That aside, according to Richel's informant, this up-timer had a phrase that he used to describe himself. "More Catholic than the pope."

"It is possible, My Lord Duke," Richel commented, "that this is a signal to us. We may be entering an era in which the work of God must be carried out by the secular rulers who serve Him. In these last days, it may be, the papacy itself will be corrupted by demonic forces."

Duke Maximilian stroked his goatee. At the next evening's meeting, he omitted the rosary.

The council members were treading very lightly in the duke's presence. Each day, he rose well before dawn and withdrew to his oratory, heard mass, then withdrew to his oratory again before reading the dispatches and preparing for the procession.

Father Contzen heard the duke's confessions, of course. Anxiety showed on Contzen's face, no matter how he tried to control it. That made everyone else uneasy.

And the news from Ingolstadt was not good. General Mercy and Colonel Werth had made it very plain in their communications to the duke and his council that they expected that the Swede, now that he had achieved his great victories in the north, would be diverting additional resources to the support of General Banér. They urged Duke Maximilian to do his utmost.

Freising

Forst and Becker felt a profound sense of relief. When they arrived at Freising, the procession had not passed yet. It was due the following day, when there would be the most magnificent of all the receptions yet held.

Freising was not officially part of the duchy of Bavaria. It was merely surrounded and enclosed by the duchy of Bavaria. Its bishop was a prince-bishop, legally, if not *de facto*, an independent ruler. *De facto*, if not legally, dependent upon the duke, yet to some extent capable of conducting an independent foreign policy and exercising jurisdiction within his own lands.

Festivals and receptions were always chaotic, with too much going on for the local inspectors to keep track of. The two Leuchtenberger found out where the procession would pass. Placed the barrels on a corner. The landgrave's steward had given them a little money toward expenses. They bought some decorative bunting from a vendor who had set up his shop early, and flowers from a peasant woman with an apron full of nosegays. They bought all the nosegays, to re-sell; the peasant woman, delighted, made another trip to where she had parked her cart outside the walls and refilled her apron. By the time the men were done, they thought that their little flower stand looked fairly pretty.

The second man stopped a passing artist carrying his charcoals and chalks, ready to sketch visitors; had him write "Long Live Leuchtenberg" on the bunting. They would jump up and down; yell the slogan at the top of their lungs. If they were lucky, Landgravine Mechthilde would slow her pace and wave; maybe even pull up her horse. That would be their chance.

They sold nosegays for two hours, at quite inflated prices. By mid-morning, they had recouped their investment and made a little money. Nobody had asked to see their vendor's license. So far, so good.

The procession was here. The duke had already passed. That meant that the main attention of his guards was directed ahead, at whatever dangers might be coming next; not at what was already safely behind them. Becker gathered the rest of the nosegays into a small pile; Forst pulled the tacks that held the bunting from blowing off the barrels, reached underneath, and loosened the lids. Duke Albrecht was coming; the crowd was yelling his name. With his wife, their lord's sister, Landgravine Mechthilde herself.

Forst and Becker waved and yelled. "Long Live Leuchtenberg!"

She pulled up her horse and smiled at them graciously.

They tipped the barrels and rolled them in front of her.

The guards coming behind started to advance; people in the crowd started to scream; Duke Maximilian's guards half-turned to get a look at the disturbance.

So did the duke; then he turned his horse. The iron general of the Catholic League was not likely to be frightened by a minor disturbance during a civil festivity.

The two bargemen dumped the barrels out at the feet of Mechthilde's horse.

Maria Anna, quite aware of both the possibility that barrels sometimes held explosives and the certainty that not all subjects adored their rulers, had prudently reined in when the men started to roll them. Now, she pushed forward. What on earth? Two old women?

She and Duke Maximilian arrived on either side of Albrecht and Mechthilde simultaneously.

Forst and Becker started to explain. It was, from Mechthilde's perspective, a total farrago of nonsense. Her brother, an agent in Amberg, overcharges for ore barrels, delayed deliveries of ore barges, a mysterious attack on the two women when they were picnicking. The men said they knew that their lord had paid them to watch the one old lady, but they had not known what to do when the attack occurred. Then, when they crossed the Danube, the steward said that the landgrave was sick but they hadn't known that.

✧   ✧   ✧

Mary Simpson was gradually straightening herself out. Since the pause at Prüfening, she and Veronica had been back in the barrels for several days now. Not, it was true, without being provided with food and water. The bargemen didn't want them to die. However, ever since that break, they had been given food and water in the barrels. Always when the cart was in some location with nobody else around. With threats that if they tried to scream while their gags were off, there wouldn't be any more. They had eaten and drunk.

She got her legs unflexed; they were still tied together. Sat there, wiggling her feet and ankles, while people shouted over her head. Wondered if there was any way she could get up. Not without help, with her hands tied behind her back. Veronica was in the same plight, except worse. Her hands were not only tied, but her arms were roped to her body; her legs not just trussed at the ankles, but the ropes wound all the way up her legs.

They were both filthy, stinking, dirty. Mary was stiff. Every muscle in her body ached. She was furious.

It was safe to assume that Veronica shared her attitude.

Mechthilde was not in a very good mood, either. Impatiently, she motioned to one of her guards to release the women's ropes.

The two bargemen threw themselves between her and the smaller one—the one who was more tightly tied. They were screaming protests that the woman was a witch; that they had undergone many hardships after they captured this witch that the landgrave was interested in. That had been in Grafenwöhr. They had not known, then, that she was a witch, but she must be very dangerous; the landgrave must have been worried that she was plotting against Leuchtenberg. They had been watching her for a month, they said.

She had actually been living in the *Schloss* in Amberg, under the direct protection of the regent placed in the Upper Palatinate by the usurping Swede. Well, both of the women had, but they thought that this one was the main witch; the other was only her assistant. Surely, the bargemen insisted, there had been a plot against Leuchtenberg, which they had averted at great danger to themselves.

In the time between the incident at Grafenwöhr and this day, they had speculated so long and hard, and told one another possible variants of the story so many times, that they now believed it.

Duke Maximilian heard the words *Schloss* and Amberg and regent. He was a man who read the reports submitted by his intelligence agents with great diligence.

Tight-lipped, he issued his order. "Let the women be released at once." The guards complied.

Mary managed to stand up by herself; the guards had to assist Veronica. Her feet and legs were completely numb; her arms little better; her hands swollen; she felt miserable. The guards pulled out the rags with which they had been gagged.

Mary bit her tongue hard to get enough saliva into her dry mouth that she could speak again. She stood up straight and smiled. First, at the gray-haired and stiff-faced man in the black clothing. She wasn't sure where she was, but it was obvious that he was in charge here. Then at the woman the bargemen had been yelling at. Then at the man next to her; then at the second woman. She spoke in English.

"My name is Mary Simpson. I am a citizen of the United States of Europe, and have been abducted from within its borders while conducting legitimate personal business in the Upper Palatinate." She repeated the words in German.

The man in black looked down at her. Then, replied in German. "There is no United States of Europe. Its claimed emperor is an usurper of the rights of the Holy Roman Emperor. The Upper Palatinate, of which I am the duly recognized elector, is legitimately a province of the Duchy of Bavaria."

Mary's smile wavered slightly. She was rapidly figuring out where she was, although she still had no idea why she was there. "Hostage" was the first word that came into her mind. *John, whatever you do, don't let them give in to this. I've lived nearly sixty years. Tell Ronnie's damned Bavarians to go fly a kite.* Her smile steadied.

Veronica still couldn't stand by herself, but she had been opening and closing her hands. She managed to bend her right arm. Fumbled at the neckline of her dress. Pulled out the pouch; retrieved her teeth. Her mouth was dry. She put them in anyway.

Without them, she was just an old hag of a German camp follower standing here. With them . . .

"My name is Veronica Dreeson. I am a citizen of the United States of Europe and have been abducted from within its borders while conducting legitimate personal business in the Upper Palatinate." She was following Mary's words exactly. That was a relief.

A woman with a leather water bag hung around her neck came forward from the side of the street. She must have been selling water to the crowd. She had a ladle, and offered each of them a drink. The odds were one hundred percent that it had not been boiled; they drank it anyway.

The younger woman leaned down from her horse and gave a coin to the water seller. For a moment, Mary's admired her dress and her poise. Considerably more poise than the older woman to whom the bargemen had been speaking.

Mary waited for the man in black to make the next move.

Veronica opened her mouth again. "I am the wife of the mayor of Grantville, the city that came from the future. Hans Richter, who destroyed the Danish ship at Wismar, was my husband's grandson. Gretchen Richter, who organizes the Committees of Correspondence, is my husband's granddaughter. And you, whoever you are, are going to be very, very, sorry about this." She turned to glare at the bargemen who had brought them here.

Forst and Becker were already feeling very, very sorry. When asked, they did confirm the identity of the two women. The town authorities, pending future developments, had arrested them for vending flowers without a license. Landgravine Mechthilde was not doing anything about it. So much for *Schutz und Schirm* and unswerving loyalty to the House of Leuchtenberg.

The constable removed them to temporary quarters in the Freising jail.

"Let the women be taken into custody." That was Duke Maximilian speaking to the captain of one of his guard companies.

Bishop Gepeckh cleared his throat and brought up a certain matter of jurisdiction. This was, after all, the prince-diocese of Freising. With all due respect, the duke had no authority to order the women taken into his custody. It was also within the limits of Freising proper. The town had a city charter, which also gave it certain jurisdictional rights. It would be necessary to obtain a legal opinion. Preferably several. From the best universities. Eichstätt, certainly; Dillingen. Perhaps any disposition of this case should even be delayed until after the siege of Ingolstadt was resolved one way or another, so that the faculty of the law school there could offer its advice.

Duke Maximilian glared.

Bishop Gepeckh offered the hospitality of the episcopal palace in order that the issue could be discussed in greater comfort.

Duke Maximilian's steward reminded everyone that there was a procession scheduled. While, indeed, providentially, they were scheduled to spend the night at Freising in any case, it would nonetheless be prudent not to deprive the onlookers and vendors of having them complete the route. He muttered about both popular unrest and financial losses. It was not good to disappoint people who were expecting to be entertained, and had made preparations. There were greetings to be received; poems to be recited; flowers to be presented. An hour's delay was nothing; such things happened all the time. The people would wait. If the procession did not appear at all, however, problems could arise.

Maria Anna moved forward.

"Perhaps there is a solution, Uncle Max. Since the bishop has so graciously offered his hospitality to us," she smiled at Gepeckh, "I will offer to take these women temporarily into my household."

She nodded her chief attendant. "Doña Mencia can leave the procession now and take them to the quarters in the palace that the bishop has reserved for me. That way, for the time being, they will be in the custody of neither Bavaria nor Freising. And we can complete today's route as," she nodded again, "your steward has reminded us that it is our duty to your subjects to do. That will allow time for discussion of the jurisdictional issues by the proper officials this evening."

Duke Maximilian glowered. Then, grudgingly, agreed. Of all the things that he hated, an interruption to his scheduled routine came very high on the list.

Doña Mencia guided her horse to the side of the street, motioning the guards to follow her with the two women they were holding. She waited until the remainder of the procession had passed; then ordered one of the stablemen at the rear to bring a litter.

✧　　✧　　✧

Mary and Veronica had no idea who she was or, really, what was happening. But they were taken to quite luxurious rooms. Where there were maids. And tubs for hot baths. And beds.

Doña Mencia spent the afternoon sitting, watching over the archduchess' sleeping guests. Outside, she could hear the noise of the procession as it moved stage by stage along its convoluted route through the town. The odors of roasting pig and mutton, sausages on the grill, poultry on the spit, frying fish, and dried beef being boiled back to edibility came in through the open windows. The bishop had arranged quite a feast, both for his guests of high degree and for the townspeople. She heard hawkers crying their wares: "fruit for sale, souvenir programs, waffles, get your waffles here."

She sat there, watching. And thinking about the last letter she had received from her brother, Cardinal Bedmar, just before she left Vienna. He had been smuggled from Venice through the United States of Europe—by Gustav Adolf's own agents—so that he could directly advise Don Fernando in the Spanish Netherlands.

She thought about the implications of the attempt to assassinate the pope.

The implications of the appointment of the up-time priest as cardinal protector of those United States of Europe.

So many things, complicating Maria Anna's Bavarian marriage. Things that had not happened when Ferdinand II agreed to it.

And there was a personal note from Don Fernando stating that he still considered the option of a marriage with Archduchess Maria Anna to be the best one.

So much to think about. She had not mentioned Don Fernando's note to Maria Anna. It had been water over the dam.

But sometimes, Doña Mencia had heard, when there was an earthquake, the rivers ran backward for a time.

Sitting. Watching. Thinking.

Susanna Allegretti spent the afternoon sewing. She was, after all, still the most junior of Frau Stecher's apprentices, and therefore the one who was being deprived of the privilege of attending the feast outside.

She did not mind. She was hastily altering two of Doña Mencia's older gowns to fit the archduchess' guests. A woman from up-time!

And Hans Richter's grandmother! The Battle of Wismar had been in all the newspapers. This woman's grandson had flown in a machine in the sky! She would get to see them. Be in the same room with them. Help dress them when they woke up. She was so excited.

Every reporter who had been in Bavaria to cover the marriage ran for the Freising post office, scribbling madly as he went. Every observer for a foreign power did the same. The mail went out the next morning. A day to Munich; a day to Neuburg. Three days to Amberg; three and a half to Nürnberg; three or four to Venice and Vienna, in the summer. It would have been a week or more to Rome and Magdeburg; two weeks to Paris, the Netherlands, and Madrid.

It was still two weeks to Paris and Madrid. Venice, Nürnberg and Amsterdam had radio, now, though. From those three cities, it went almost at once to every other city that had radio, as soon as a transmission window opened up. First and foremost, to the new radio station in the capital of Denmark, where the Congress of Copenhagen was now well underway.

A lot of the stories were garbled. However, they left no doubt that Mary Simpson and Veronica Dreeson had surfaced in Freising, of all improbable places. Bishop Gepeckh was soon to be the subject of more discussion than had been the case since the day he was finally confirmed in office. In the cases of Mike Stearns, John Simpson, Henry Dreeson and Keith Pilcher, by people who had never heard his name before.

Part Six

July 1634

Shades of the prison-house begin to close

CHAPTER 33

Schola Patientiae

Freising

Even for the heir to the duchy of Bavaria, it was practically impossible for a man to have a private word with his wife in the middle of a formal wedding procession traveling through the countryside. True, the room that Bishop Gepeckh had assigned Albrecht and Mechthilde was quite luxurious, the walls covered with tapestries, heavy brocade hangings on the bed.

They were also sharing it with wall to wall cots. A personal attendant for each of them; their three sons, their sons' tutor, and a number of bodyguards. The bodyguards did not have cots and did a remarkably good job of staying awake throughout their shifts. All of which explained why the duke and duchess were sitting up in the middle of their bed, the hangings drawn closed in the middle of a hot July night, whispering to one another.

They couldn't even check silently to see if the guards were trying to eavesdrop. Every time one of them moved, the ropes that supported the mattress creaked.

There was a lot that they needed to talk about.

First, the situation with Leuchtenberg. Landgrave Wilhelm Georg's physician had written to say that his death was expected momentarily. Although he had lived several months beyond the reasonable expectations of his doctors, his time of grace was drawing to an end. The physician asked where the young land-graves might be.

The answer, for Maximilian Adam, was "somewhere south of Ingolstadt." Phillip Rudolf, unfortunately, was in Hungary, tour-ing defensive installations facing the Turks in the company of Ferdinand II's son. Duke Maximilian had not been happy when he took service with the Habsburgs. There was no way that he could get back before his father's expected death. There was no way that either of them could go to Leuchtenberg.

That meant that within the week, the subjects of the land-grave, enclosed as they were within the Upper Palatinate, would be free from their oaths of allegiance. Everyone had heard what the up-timers had done in Coburg when the duke died. They had oathed his former subjects to their "state constitution" before the Wettin heir could get there. It seemed likely that Duke Ernst would do the same in Leuchtenberg. Not that all of the landgrave's subjects had been outstandingly loyal to begin with. Some of them were, but for over a generation, even before the Swedes came, a lot of them had been inclined to cross the borders into the Upper Palatinate to attend Protestant church services. But having them oathed elsewhere would mean that they were released from all obligations of loyalty to their hereditary lord.

Mechthilde insisted that they were going to have to interrogate those two bargemen.

"They are in the bishop's custody, not ours," Albrecht said, forcing himself not to let his anger cause his voice to rise above a whisper. "I am furious with Wilhelm Georg for landing us in this pickle. Your brother is, for all practical purposes, a penniless exile living in Bavaria by Maximilian's grace. It was outrageous of him to have been conducting what amounted to an independent foreign policy without having consulted the duke and the privy council."

Mechthilde shook her head. "That's silly, husband," she whis-pered. "My brother has been sick for months and in no position to arrange any such plot. You know it as well as I do. For the past half-year, at least, although Wilhelm Georg has been present on earth, his mind has been quite vacant."

Reluctantly, Albrecht admitted that she was right.

Then what had led up to this? Mechthilde returned to the idea of interrogating the two bargemen.

Albrecht reminded her that they were in the custody of the Freising city authorities—not of Bavaria and most definitely not of Leuchtenberg.

"Then interrogate the women," said Mechthilde.

Even more reluctantly Albrecht pointed out that they were in the custody of Archduchess Maria Anna, who was still, in spite of the ceremony at the border, an Austrian, and would be for another fortnight.

Mechthilde was not in a good mood.

Neither was Duke Maximilian when he summoned the two of them into his bedchamber the next morning. Before breakfast.

Prudently, Mechthilde tried the truth first—that she knew nothing at all about it and was sure that her brother had nothing to do with it. Nor did his sons.

The duke clearly was not going to believe the truth.

So Mechthilde explained it all. Starting with the bargemen's presumption, she created an elaborate fiction involving secret informants, witch plots against her brother that had begun over a year before and sucked the mind from his body, involvement in the conspiracy by the highest authorities of the usurping United States of Europe who were sponsoring the witches, and accusations that Duke Ernst of Saxe-Weimar, the regent of the Upper Palatinate, was a warlock himself.

It was a good story, which had the additional merit of being somewhat more plausible than the truth. She concluded by demanding that the two witches be removed from the custody of the Austrian archduchess and placed in her own, stating that if they were allowed to be with the future duchess, they would certainly take the opportunity of placing an infertility spell on her.

In a last moment of inspiration, she stated that all the other things had probably only been done to give the two women that opportunity.

Maximilian just looked at the two of them. On the note pad in front of him, he scratched the date at which Landgrave Wilhelm Georg's illness had begun, the date of Elisabeth Renata's death, the date upon which the arrangements for his second marriage had been concluded, and the date, retrieved from the intelligence reports, upon which Mary Simpson and Veronica Dreeson had arrived in the Upper Palatinate.

He raised one eyebrow and dismissed them without further comment.

The women might be witches. He would not dismiss that possibility. But Mechthilde was lying through her teeth.

The Freising city authorities had already interrogated the barge-men, whose names proved to be Valentin Forst and Emmeram Becker. They had asserted under the most strict questioning (properly authorized by a judge, with the requisite number of witnesses, and a clerk present to record the testimony *verbatim*) that they had not been employed to observe the Dreeson woman until after the privy council had pushed him into agreeing to remarry. Both men were from the Landgraviate of Leuchtenberg.

Who would benefit most if the women were witches and they did successfully put an infertility spell on his niece?

For that matter, who would benefit most if they were not witches, but if a sufficient uproar could be raised now about their presence in Maria Anna's household that his niece was tarred with the "witch" brush? Enough of an uproar that the marriage had to be cancelled?

He had no wish to remarry. *Elisabeth Renata, my wife.* Neither, however, did he hold any grudge against his sister's daughter. Maria Anna could not in any way be blamed for being, at this moment, in Freising on her way to the Munich *Residenz.* It was not her fault that she had been sent to marry him. She was a good daughter, obedient to her father's wishes.

In another world, the *encyclopedias* said, the girl had borne him two sons and been a good regent. Perhaps she would do the same in this world. That was in the hands of God.

Who would benefit most if she did not?

Regretfully, he added his brother and sister-in-law to his list of people who were not to be trusted. He was sorry to do it, for he and Albrecht had been close since they were children. The list was a long one, however. There were very few people whom he *could* trust.

Bishop Gepeckh agreed that Duke Maximilian could take the two foreign women to Munich, as long as they remained in the custody of the Austrian archduchess. That was a purely face-saving provision, of course. He was, diplomatically and militarily, in no position to retain them against Maximilian's wishes, no matter what conclusion the legal consultants might eventually offer. Within ten days, Maria Anna would be married to the duke and they would be effectively in his custody. There wasn't anything that Gepeckh could do about it.

The wedding procession moved on to Munich. Mary and Veronica traveled under guard, but among the members of the archduchess' personal household. Compared to the past few days, they considered spending two more being carried in a sedan chair with its curtains drawn to be a restful interlude. They were also able to talk quite freely, given the general level of noise surrounding the procession.

Neither of them had the vaguest idea what had happened between the time they were attacked at the lock and the time they came to on the barge, which was disturbing.

Veronica's best guess was that Kilian Richter, who was well-known to be a Bavarian collaborator, had sent the three men who came down the deer path with knives to force them backwards toward the lock, where the bargemen, who were Bavarian agents, were waiting for them. So, they presumed, the instigator of the snatch must have been Duke Maximilian. They explored Mary's hostage theory at some length and concluded that it was the most likely explanation. Everything else that was going on was probably some diplomatic face-saving for the duke.

If they had a chance, the first thing they would do would be to smuggle out a message to Henry and John insisting that the reply from the USE to any concession that Maximilian demanded should be, "Keep them and be damned."

Then they took another nap. The litter was big enough and they were both still exhausted.

Maria Anna rose early. She was conscientious about continuing her regime of devotional reading, even within the excitement of the worldly activities that surrounded her. If she was currently choosing to read works published by the spiritual advisors of her future husband—well, she also needed to familiarize herself with the nature of the Bavarian court.

Father Jeremias Drexel, S.J., was certainly the most famous preacher in Munich, as well as its most famous author. Father Lamormaini had given her this book; had told her that in Munich alone, more than a hundred thousand copies of Father Drexel's works had been printed. This was one of the most recent editions, less than five years old. The *School of Patience*. Dedicated to Prince Radziwill, the great magnate of Poland. The illustrations were beautiful.

In the course of earthly existence, each person has his assigned role in the play, whether king or beggar, allotted to him by God. Yet none of them should forget, whether he is given the role of learned man or peasant, that it will last only as long as his temporal life endures. Each should play his part on earth well, so that the play may go on. If you have been assigned the role of prince, do not pride yourself in it, for it is only a part you are playing at the will of the director. If you are assigned the role of beggar, then play that person slyly and artfully. For, whatever the role, no one, in these times of crisis, will pass through life without sorrow and suffering.

What is life?

Life is a flower, passing smoke, a shadow, the shadow of a shadow, a bubble on the water, a piece of dust in a sunbeam, a bit of foam on the sea, a raindrop on the roof, an icicle, a rainbow, a spring day, the uncertain weather of April, one note in a melody.

Life is a wax candle about to gutter out, a sack full of holes, a broken pitcher, a decrepit house, a passing spark, a spider web, a treacherous fog.

Life is a thin thread, a helmet made of straw, a golden apple rotten at the core.

Life is a short comedy, a sleep, a frivolous dream, the parable of the wealthy man who built ever larger barns in which to heap up his riches, yet his soul was taken from him that night.

She read on, until Doña Mencia entered the room to remind her that it was time to dress for another day.

CHAPTER 34

Rumores Plurimi

Nürnberg

It took so damned much time to get news out, down-time, when a person needed to. There was nobody in the whole goddamned city of Amberg who could work the radio this week. Three of the techs *were* getting better; there was some comfort in that. But they sure weren't well enough to come back to work yet, Bill Hudson said, unless people deliberately wanted to put them in danger of complications and relapses. Plus a lot more words.

As soon as Böcler had finished briefing them, right up to the point when the ore barge disappeared across the Danube, Jake Ebeling got on a horse and headed for Nürnberg. Somebody who spoke English had to let Grantville and Magdeburg know what had happened—that Mrs. Simpson and Mrs. Dreeson had been kidnapped. The nearest down-time radio array that might be functional was in Nürnberg. If it wasn't working for some reason, he'd try Suhl. And if that wasn't working, he would have to ride all the way to Grantville.

He told Duke Ernst that he would send a messenger back and let him know which way things turned out.

The Nürnberg radio was working. Occasionally, things turned out just a little right. Getting permission to use it, since it had been paid for and was controlled by the city council, was another matter. Nürnberg was feeling touchy about its sovereignty. Unlike Ansbach and Bayreuth, the other major Protestant principalities in Franconia, it was still technically an ally of the USE, not a state within it. The city fathers were far from sure how long they could make this last.

He could probably have ridden to Suhl faster. Of course, he had no way of knowing that when he first presented Duke Ernst's letter at the *Rathaus*.

Amberg, the Upper Palatinate

Under other circumstances, Keith Pilcher would have been tearing out what remained of his thinning hair. He absolutely did not believe the way that things had turned out. He had been trying to keep Dreeson's wife *safe*. He might as well have let her die of diphtheria. Now half the old cats in Grantville would blame Max because she had been kidnapped by the damned Bavarians. And Mary Simpson with her. He could just imagine the cackle, cackle, cackle when the news got there. But he didn't have time to worry about it right now.

The patient count in the main ward was under a hundred, now, Jakob Balde noted. No new cases had been admitted in the past week.

Unfortunately, most of those remaining were very ill. They had developed what the up-time *medic* called "complications." These patients included Herr Snell and Herr Felser.

Herr Pilcher was very concerned. He had temporarily broken off negotiations with the iron masters and was staying with the patients, nearly night and day. The young "medic," as they called him, was visiting the remaining patients regularly. It was hard to determine why he did not consider himself to be a physician. Although he insisted that he was not really fully trained, even as an apothecary, he was giving some of the patients an up-time medication. He said, honestly enough, that he did not know whether or not it would be effective. He had chosen a group of patients to receive it and another, the same number, not. A "control group." Both were small. He did not have much of the medicine.

Balde thought that the real "control group" was much larger—all of those who were not receiving the medication. As he watched the ward, he picked up his spiritual reading. Drexel's *School of Patience.*

> The condition of mankind is miserable, from the moment he is born, howling and crying. O, the foolishness of those who believe that they were born for splendor. Do they not remember that when they were born, they were less capable than a four footed animal. That they had to learn to eat? Learn to walk? Learn to talk? How long did a nurse have to change the diapers of the man of highest rank on earth? Just as long as the meanest serf needed his diapers changed. Is the man of high rank not just as subject to illness and injury as the lowest? Doesn't he have to take medicine as often? He had to crawl as long, and is no more able to fly.

Balde paused and looked at the beds in which the patients lay. And yet, these up-timers were able to fly. Not of their own powers, to be sure, as a bird flew. But with the assistance of their mechanical marvels. What effect did this have on their humility before God? He directed his attention back to the book.

> What then is a man? He is a ball with which God bowls, a mirror of the temporary, an image of unsteadiness. Both Seneca and Scripture agree that he is in his own nature a thing of weakness, in need of the help of strangers, the prey of wild animals. Food for worms, a ship passing by, a guest for one day.
>
> Nonetheless, we miserable men compete for high titles and gladly listen when others call us "Gracious, Illustrious, Mighty, Unconquerable, Fortunate, Lucky, Eminent, Highest of the High." Splendid misery! What a terrible thing it is when a man forgets his true nature. *Vanitas, vanitas.* Without God, the mightiest man on earth is only a slave of death.

There were no mighty here, in the lazarette of the *collegium.* Only the ordinary people of the town of Amberg. Balde put the book down and stood up to make his rounds again.

Grantville, State of Thuringia-Franconia

What was worst, Henry Dreeson said to Ed Piazza, was that, according to Jake Ebeling, nobody knew where Mary and Veronica were. Other than "in Bavaria." Somewhere in Bavaria. Or who did it. Other than probably agents for Duke Maximilian. Or why. Especially not why. It was a very up in the air kind of situation, not helped by the unreliable nature of the radio transmission from Nürnberg.

Nürnberg? It appeared that the radio array in Amberg had gone out. Jake Ebeling hadn't said how or why.

Annalise was sobbing, saying that they should never have let Oma go.

Henry, more practically, said that there hadn't really been any way to stop Ronnie, once her mind was made up.

Maxine Pilcher had been on edge ever since Keith had written about the start of the epidemic. Nearly a month ago. Now she was furious. She was worried sick about Keith, so she was furious. Everyone else took it pretty much in stride. That was how Maxine reacted to things.

Today, she was on a tear. "Ebeling, damn him, didn't say a word about anyone else. There he was, gone all the way to Nürnberg and not one word. Not how Keith is; not how Toby is. Not a thing except about that damned Veronica Dreeson. Well, and about Mary Simpson, of course. They're all that the people in the government are thinking about. And it takes more than a week for letters to go back and forth."

Dionne Huffman brought her a cup of coffee. Not much coffee; lots of hot milk.

Finally, Maxine spit out what she was thinking. "With Rita and Melissa in the Tower of London and Julie's baby getting sick in Edinburgh and Rebecca and Gretchen besieged in Amsterdam— and now Mary Simpson and Veronica Dreeson kidnapped into Bavaria—the whole thing is getting absolutely ridiculous. Pretty soon, nobody is ever going to let any Grantville woman set foot out of the town again. It seems like every time one does, she goes through the Perils of Pauline! And it doesn't make any difference whether she's an up-timer or a down-timer."

The others in the teachers' lounge just laughed. But Maxine didn't think it was funny. None of her colleagues blamed the ongoing feud between Maxine and Veronica for the latest debacle. None of them thought that it was Keith's fault. Neither, of course, did Henry Dreeson.

Which didn't mean that other people didn't see it that way. There were a fair number of old hens like Veda Mae Haggerty going cackle, cackle, cackle, just as Keith had predicted.

Well, until Henry took Maxine out for Sunday brunch at Cora's. Then they got to twitter about something else. Most of them, at least.

Amberg, the Upper Palatinate

Keith still didn't have time to agitate himself about how all of this would affect Maxine and the folks back home. He was busy arranging decent funerals for Toby and Lambert.

Lambert's was easy enough, since he was Lutheran. The pastor at the *Frauenkirche* would do it, for a reasonable fee, and the church had a cemetery.

Toby was going to be harder, because he wasn't a church member. Keith didn't have the vaguest idea what to do, with no funeral home available.

And then he had to write to Toby's mother and Lambert's wife. There wasn't anybody else to do it. In one way, he wished that the radio wasn't out. He'd be able to get the news to Mary Lou and Lena sooner. In another way, he was sure that they didn't want to know. Mary Lou's other two kids were grown; Bruce, Jr., got married last year. Lena's little girl was just a baby. And she was pregnant again. She had written Lambert about it, just before the epidemic started. He'd been real proud and pleased.

Finally, he talked to young Böcler, who agreed to say a few appropriate words at a service right here in the *Schloss*. The words turned out to be more than a few, but they were suitable and didn't say anything about eternal damnation. Just that Toby had been a nice guy. Böcler compared him to a whole bunch of ancient Romans who had been virtuous pagans. All things considered, Keith thought, Böcler probably did about as good a job as anyone could have.

Duke Ernst took the opportunity to endow a civil cemetery

for the city of Amberg, just outside the city walls, that would henceforth offer a respectable resting place for people who were not members of any of the churches. It seemed a reasonable solution to the problem—better than just interring them in a potter's field. He also provided for the traditional potter's field at the rear. There were always vagabonds, transients, unidentified vagrants. The poor you have always with you.

Grantville, State of Thuringia-Franconia

"Why am I crying by myself?" Mary Lou Snell looked at her daughter-in-law. "Because nobody cares. I can't even have a funeral for him. They buried him down there. I don't have the kind of money it takes in this day and age to have him embalmed and brought home. And nobody cares, except you and Bruce and Anita. Everybody is talking about Mary and Ronnie. And about the war up north. Everybody hangs on the radio to see what Gustav Adolf is doing. And the Danes. And the French. And what's happening in the Netherlands. When a soldier from here is killed, it's all in the paper.

"Toby was a soldier too. But he just—died. Died of a stupid kid's disease. No blood or guts or glory. No monuments or memorials to a hero. He's just gone."

She put her head down and sobbed.

Lena wondered what would happen now. Lambert had been a good man. Now he was a dead man. Dead tinsmiths earned no pay. How was she going to take care of her little girl? Who would hire a pregnant woman with a small child?

The answer to that question turned out to be Annalise Richter, who appeared like an angel. She managed all the legal business with Huddy Colburn about terminating Lambert's rental agreement, hired Lena as a live-in janitress/caretaker, and installed her in an apartment above the second St. Veronica's Academy. The one in the new building, by the refugee housing, that had been built with an apartment on the second floor. According to the provisions of Henry and Veronica's marriage contract, the apartment would have been for Hans and his wife when he married some day.

It had been, perhaps, the only really nice empty apartment in Grantville.

All that Annalise said to Henry was, "It needed doing."

Henry recognized the phrase. Annalise had picked it up from him. He said it quite often.

The happiest man in Grantville—or, more precisely, some miles outside of Grantville, since he had chosen to built his local residence near his slate quarries—was Count August von Sommersburg. Not, of course, that he was indifferent to the fate of Mesdames Simpson and Dreeson. He had written appropriate notes to both the admiral and the mayor, in his own hand, expressing his concern and sympathy.

Nonetheless, that was all he could do in that regard, whereas the final report that he had received from Leopold Cavriani was a work of art, not to mention being of much more immediate concern to him.

It contained very little about mining and metalworking *per se*. It was comprehensive in regard to the who, what, when, where, how, and why of earth moving and rock removal in the Upper Palatinate. Names and addresses of contacts. Advice that this would be a most advantageous moment to offer a partnership to the owner of Clarence's Pump Corporation. Discussions on capitalization, particularly in regard to the rebuilding of locks and dams. Advice on what to reply if people kept harping on the 1609 survey.

In the report, Cavriani mentioned that he had greatly appreciated the bit of wisdom that Jack Whitney dropped one day in the Grantville Exchange—that in playing the market, the best principle was, "Don't invest in computer companies. Hardware and software will come and go. Presuming that you've decided that computers are a coming thing and likely to stay around, invest in the companies that make the wires that any computer manufacturer will need to use."

He had, Cavriani said, found it comforting that the up-time world had not lost sight of this eternal verity.

Cavriani's fee had been steep.

Count August's eventual profits were likely to be much steeper.

CHAPTER 35

Stipendia Pluria

Copenhagen, Denmark

It was a good thing, Mike Stearns reflected, that John Chandler Simpson was in excellent health for a man in his mid-fifties. Or else Mike would be worrying that the USE's premier admiral would soon be suffering a stroke or a heart attack—or just dropping dead from apoplexy. Simpson was a naturally pale-skinned man. At the moment, though, his complexion could best be described as "blotchy," with the color red prominently featured among the blotches.

Despite his sympathy, Mike had to restrain himself from smiling at the tableau in front of him. Not that Simpson was likely to notice, anyway, given that the admiral's attention was entirely riveted on the figure of the junior officer standing at attention before his desk.

The admiral's very vehement attention. One might even say, displeased and irate attention.

For his part, Lieutenant Eddie Cantrell was doing a far better imitation of a respectful junior officer than was his normal habit. Mike thought he might actually start vibrating in place, so rigidly was he standing at attention.

"I didn't ask you to tell me what was *impossible*, Lieutenant Cantrell," said Simpson, all but snarling the words.

Fortunately for Eddie, the admiral's son Tom intervened. The army captain was standing not far from Eddie. Because of his special personal connection to the situation, he'd been invited to the meeting along with General Frank Jackson. But, modestly, he hadn't taken one of the chairs available.

"Dad, c'mon. Stop glaring at Eddie as if he was a minion of the devil. Or a Bavarian agent. He's just telling you the plain and simple truth—and you know it yourself. You *can't* get those huge ironclads up the Danube. Even in our day and age, it wasn't really that navigable a river. That's assuming you could get them through the North Sea, part of the Atlantic, almost the whole of the Mediterranean and a portion of the Black Sea in the first place. Not to mention the small problem of starting a war with the Ottoman Empire on the way and having to blow your way through Vienna and the whole Austrian army. And even if you did, so what? You'd *still* not be within cannon range of Munich, which isn't on the Danube to begin with. It's—" he cocked at eye at Eddie "—how far?"

To Eddie's credit, he gave the answer without even gulping first. "The Bavarian capital is about sixty miles south of the river, at its nearest approach." He did gulp, here. "And I'm afraid, ah, sir, that the river that does pass through Munich—that's—"

"I *know* it's the Isar river, Lieutenant Cantrell," growled the admiral, "and I *know* that it's even less navigable than the Danube."

He glanced at his son, and the glare faded some. There might have been a time when John Chandler Simpson would have inflicted Tom Simpson with the same completely unreasonable ire he was heaping on poor Eddie's head. But not today, so soon after the father and the son had been reconciled after a long and bitter personal feud.

Tom was quite smart enough to know that himself, and Mike was sure he'd intervened just to lower his father's temper. As understandable as it might be, Simpson's fury at the situation faced by his wife Mary was not helping the situation.

Finally, thankfully, the mood broke. Simpson's shoulders slumped and he slowly sat down in the chair behind his desk. Then, wiped his face with a large hand.

"My apologies, Lieutenant," he said. "I realize that it's completely out of the question to use the ironclads against Bavaria." Bitterly:

"*Any* part of the Navy, for that matter. For all practical purposes, the damn country is land-locked."

Mike was about to say something—nothing practical, just something that would hopefully further lower the admiral's blood pressure. But, seeing the glance exchanged between Eddie and Tom Simpson, he kept his mouth shut. Say what you would about Eddie Cantrell's often rambunctious and sometimes downright reckless habits, the youngster had a very good brain. So did Tom, even if his thick skull, absence of a neck worth talking about, and football lineman physique often gave people the impression he was a dimwit.

"Well, not exactly, sir," said Eddie. "The thing is—me and Tom talked it over, with Prince Ulrik and his tech whiz Baldur Norddahl—the thing is, ah, well—"

Tom picked it up, seeing that Eddie was faltering. "The iron-clads can't be used. But that's not the same thing as using the guns themselves."

Simpson's head came up. "Explain."

Tom lowered his own head a bit, like a football lineman expecting the ball to be snapped. "Well . . . you aren't going to like this, Dad. But the fact is, you're about the only person left who thinks the *Monitor* can really be salvaged and made fit for duty again. The damage that—ah—"

It was his turn to falter. But his father just smiled. There was even a bit of humor in the smile.

"The damage that your new friends and cronies Prince Ulrik and Baldur Norddahl did to my fine ship, I believe you mean to say. Less than two months ago."

"Ah . . . well, yeah. And even if you're right and everybody else is wrong, not even you think the *Monitor* can be rebuilt in less than a year."

"More like eighteen months," growled the admiral. "And you needn't remind me that everyone thinks I'm nuts."

But there was no heat in the growl, and Simpson sat up erect. "I see your point, though. If we're willing to inflict still more damage on the hull, we could extract the guns."

"We just need the ten-inch guns for now," said Eddie. "Ah, sir. There's no point in removing the carronades for this."

Simpson nodded, his eyes now a little unfocused as he pondered the suggestion. "No, no, you're right. The carronades are simply anti-ship weapons. Not designed to reduce fortifications the way the ten-inch . . ."

He planted his hands on the armrests of his chair and swiveled to face Mike, who was sitting on a divan nearby. "Are you willing to authorize this, Mik—Prime Minister?"

"Sure—and I don't doubt Gustav Adolf will too. Maximilian of Bavaria might not be right at the top of the emperor's shit list, but he's awfully damn close. But is it really a practical idea?" Mike raised his hands. "I'm not arguing the point. I simply don't know. I presume what you have in mind is taking the ten-inch guns out of the *Monitor* and somehow—"

"We already figured that out, Mike," said Eddie eagerly.

"*Lieutenant Cantrell*," growled Simpson—there was heat in this growl—"you will desist from interrupting the *prime minister*."

Mike had to fight to keep from smiling again. But Eddie was suitably abashed.

"As I was saying," he went on, "somehow you'll try to get the guns down to Bavaria. It'll have to be done overland, of course. Which means—I don't doubt Eddie and Tom have figured out *how* to do it; I don't even doubt that whatever they've figured out, as cockamamie as it may seem, would even work. But *how long* would it take?"

Eddie and Tom exchanged glances again.

"Several weeks, Prime Minister," replied Tom. "Not less than a month, maybe six weeks."

His father snorted. "Junior officers and their eternal optimism—and they have the nerve to tell *me* I've got my head in the clouds." To Mike, he said, "Here's the basic rule, Prime Minister. If a junior officer tells you he can have something done in X number of days, or weeks, or months, add one or two more Xes to the equation."

He turned his gaze back to his son and Eddie. "So. Two months. Maybe ten weeks. Which is what my own estimate would be, now that I've started thinking about it. I think you two youngsters—so quick to point out my own over-optimism when it comes to salvaging the *Monitor*—are drastically underestimating how hard it will be to haul several enormous cannons from Denmark all the way down to southern Germany, given the conditions of seventeenth-century roads and rivers."

Eddie and Tom looked suitably respectful. "Well, you certainly have more military experience than we do, Admiral," said Eddie.

Simpson chuckled. "Will wonders never cease? A public admission from Lieutenant Cantrell that an old fart admiral might know more than he does. But it's not actually my military experience at work here, Lieutenant Cantrell. Mostly, it's my industrial experience. Moving really heavy pieces of machinery—even in a factory or refinery, with good surfaces to work on and plenty of modern equipment—is hard as all hell. Trust me. Still . . ."

He looked back at Mike. "How does eight to ten weeks look to you, Prime Minister?"

Mike shrugged. "I'm hoping to have a diplomatic resolution of the problem long before then, Admiral. But it certainly won't hurt my negotiating position to let that arrogant Bavarian duke know that the same guns that turned good parts of Hamburg and Copenhagen into rubble are headed his way."

All four of the officers in the room grinned at that.

Mike was thinking it through, still. "In fact . . ."

He looked back and forth between the Simpson, *père et fils.* "How about we put Tom in charge of the expedition? I think that might drive the message through Maximilian's thick hide even better. Ten-inch guns sent by Mary's husband, to be delivered—the shells from them, rather—by her son."

Both men looked pleased by the idea. After a moment, though, Admiral Simpson frowned. "Tom's only a captain, Prime Minister. An expedition like this amounts to a heavy artillery battery, operating as an independent command under special conditions. We really should have a major in charge, at least. A colonel would be better."

"No sweat," said Frank Jackson. The army general, who served as General Torstensson's special aide for anything involving up-time military tech, had been silent thus far in the meeting. "I'll have Lennart promote the fine lad."

But before he finished, Tom was shaking his head. "I'd just as soon avoid that, sir, if you don't mind. It'll look like special favors being applied, especially if you jump me up to colonel. Major would probably be okay—but my father's right. An independent command like this really should have a colonel in charge. What I'd suggest is that you give Heinrich Schmidt a promotion to colonel. He's way overdue, if you ask me. If he hadn't had to basically sit out the war guarding Becky in Amsterdam, he'd have gotten it by now."

"True enough," said Frank.

"He's a top-notch field officer," Tom continued. "He and I have worked together before and we get along really well. And the truth is, Heinrich has a lot more experience than I do commanding the size force this would take. So that's my recommendation, General Jackson. Promote Major Schmidt to colonel, put him in charge of the expedition, and then you could promote me to the major who serves as his staff officer. Nobody would squawk at that."

Tom gave Eddie another glance. "And—ah, if this wouldn't interfere with the lieutenant's marital plans—"

"Hell with that," said the admiral. "Lieutenant Cantrell is still on active duty. He's *engaged* to King Christian's daughter, that's all, with no wedding date having been set yet—and I can tell you the king is in no hurry to set it, either, as young as she is. So, yes, I agree it's a good idea. The Navy can send Lieutenant Commander Cantrell along as the special advisor for the big guns."

He grinned, for the first time Mike could remember since news came of Mary's captivity in Bavaria. "Sure, why not? May as well hand out promotions all around, while we're at it. Shove *that* up Maximilian's ass, too. Which"—the grin widened and grew positively evil—"if he doesn't come to his senses, will soon measure ten inches in diameter."

Naturally, Eddie being Eddie, he couldn't resist the temptation. "Well . . . the diameter of the shells isn't actually quite that—"

"Shut up, Eddie," hissed Tom. His own eyes grew a little unfocused. "I can tell you to do that, I think."

"Actually, you can't," grunted his father. "The army rank of major is roughly equivalent to the naval rank of lieutenant commander, so your relationship is that of peers, not commander and subordinate." He gave Eddie a very fish-eyed look. "On the other hand, I can demote the impertinent fellow as quickly as I can promote him. So that problem could be remedied."

At least, this time, Eddie had enough sense to keep his mouth shut.

After Eddie and Tom left, to start working on a detailed plan of action, Frank Jackson turned to Mike. "I hope I can make good my boast. But I'm pretty sure I'm right, that General Torstensson will approve the plan. It's his call, of course."

✧   ✧   ✧

As it turned out, Torstensson was delighted with the idea—but for reasons that hadn't even occurred to anyone else.

"Oh, splendid. On the way there, you can make a short detour and bring those guns before the walls of Ingolstadt. That ought to solve *that* problem, for sure."

Admiral Simpson did not look pleased at the idea. "General, that 'short detour' will take at least three weeks."

Torstensson waved his hand airily. "Nonsense. It won't take so much as a minute." He had a very evil sort of grin himself, when he wanted to put it on. "You don't know General Johan Banér like I do, John. The moment I let him know that we're sending the world's best siege guns down to help him reduce Ingolstadt, he'll move heaven and earth to make sure he seizes the city before the guns can even get there. Lest he have to share any of the credit with miserable fucking up-time artillery shitheads."

Mike chuckled. "Heinrich Schmidt's a down-timer, actually."

"Not the way Banér looks at these things, Michael," said Torstensson, shaking his head. "That man is to bigotry what the ocean is to wet. Practically its definition. Schmidt has supped with the devil, so he's a devil himself. And he'll be irate to begin with, once I let him know I'm sending some of my regiments down to lend him a hand."

Again, he made that airy hand-waving gesture. "So have no fear, Admiral. Your expedition won't have to deviate from its route so much as an inch. Banér will figure out a way to take Ingolstadt, be sure of it. He's an asshole, sure enough, but he's also quite a good general." He chuckled himself. "And a good thing that is for him, too. Or I think our blessed king and emperor might take Johan's own advice and remove yet another Swedish nobleman's head. His. Gustav Adolf finds him every bit as annoying as I do. But Johan's good at his trade, he surely is."

CHAPTER 36

Audacter Calumniare

Neuburg

Marc Cavriani was disillusioned by his first introduction to serious intelligence gathering. It seemed a bit deflating that instead of indulging in elaborate skullduggery, intrigue, and derring-do, they could have found out where Frau Simpson and Frau Dreeson were just by staying right here and reading this week's newspaper when it was delivered from Nürnberg.

His father just smiled. "I will point out that by being in Neuburg, at least we got the news two days before the paper came out, since the observer sent to Freising by Egli went to the expense of a special messenger. This allowed me to send another courier across the Danube to Duke Ernst. It also allows us two additional days of time to use for planning the best way to utilize the resources of *Cavriani Frères de Genève* in arranging a rescue."

The word "rescue" perked Marc right up. Leopold's smile broadened, almost became a grin. He could still remember the vigorous approach of youth to these things; even if, at his current age, he was firmly determined that the *operative* verb would not be "to rescue" but "to arrange."

Beyond that, Leopold said—life was frequently like that and the firm's other lines of work only rarely involved more gallantry and romance than did counting spools of drawn wire for Jacob

Durre in Nürnberg or estimating the cost of pumps for hammer mill operations in the Upper Palatinate. Marc should not in any way expect occasions for gallantry and romance to arise in the course of his duties.

Amberg, the Upper Palatinate

Julius Wilhelm Zincgref contemplated his latest assignment with some disbelief. Not that he hadn't expected Duke Ernst to order some propaganda about villains who kidnap intrepid ladies. He was, after all, the regent's paid publicity agent and public relations "spin doctor." He loved that up-time description. He just hadn't quite expected the items that he would need to include to be so complex.

There was, for example, the question of just whom to use for the villain. There were quite a few possibilities, none of them really good. Von Wenzin, the bailiff in Grafenwöhr, had continued tracking down the evidence of Kilian Richter's various activities over the past fourteen years with the tenacity of a little bulldog. Once that man got his teeth into something, he just didn't let go. A report arrived at Duke Ernst's office every morning. Böcler duly copied them and sent them on to Zincgref. Elias Brechbuhl, who figured that even with Veronica out of the picture, his children and sisters-in-law still had valid claims, kept working on Richter's various endeavors in the field of property misappropriation and sending the reports to Hieronymus Rastetter, who also provided them to the regent. Eric Haakansson Hand had people examining Richter's ties to Arndt and the crooked trail of Arndt's legal practice.

Brechbuhl also reported that according to his sister-in-law Clara's husband, Nicholas Moser and Dorothea Richter had appeared in Nürnberg. The two idiots (that was Matthias Schreiner's description, not Brechbuhl's) were eloping and had appealed to Dorothea's relatives there for a loan of money to travel the rest of the way to Grantville. Young lovers fleeing from a dastardly father; always an appealing motif. Fleeing the possibility that the girl might be Immured in a Convent by her villainous father; even better as Protestant propaganda.

Zincgref sighed. All of this still did not make Kilian Richter into a usable political villain.

Oh, he could have made him into a wonderful villain if he had been writing about the Richter family. He might yet, some day; he wasn't sure. A neo-Latin epic? A tragic play on the model of the ancients, with the protagonist finally destroyed by his own *hubris*? Possible, very possible. Except, of course, that Böcler said that his friend Harsdörffer in Munich was already beginning a neo-Latin epic on the subject of the abduction. That left a play. Oh, well. Not as prestigious in the literary world, but probably more profitable in the long run. Perhaps a Latin original text with translations made available for popular productions.

Unfortunately, if one were not writing a play, the truth appeared to be that Richter was just a greedy man. He had not collaborated with the Bavarians, as far as anyone could find out, for any motive more complicated than his desire to collect all of his father's properties in his own hands and then accumulate more wealth. He certainly had not collaborated with the Bavarians because he was politically opposed to the United States of Europe or to the up-timers, because neither had existed when he began his evil deeds.

And, above all, there was no motive, anywhere in all of it, for Richter to have included Mary Simpson in his devious machinations. For a good, rousing, denunciation, it was really not feasible to end with the sentence, "And by the way, the villains accidentally attacked Admiral Simpson's wife as well."

Not to mention that Duke Ernst and Hand said that the real lurking political villain whom Zincgref was to denounce was John George of Saxony, who was a Protestant and had no known connections to Kilian Richter at all.

Arrrgh. He had a very short draft.

Three days later, his mood brightened minimally. The regent and Hand had changed their minds as to the proper villain. He was to go through the draft of his pamphlet and change the name of John George, wherever it appeared, to Duke Maximilian. That made a little more sense. Kilian Richter as the tool of the venomous Bavarian. Zincgref started to write a longer pamphlet.

Eric Haakansson Hand kept gathering every morsel of information he could find on the attorney Arndt. There was quite a bit in it concerning his activities on behalf of the landgrave of Leuchtenberg.

In Grafenwöhr, von Wenzin followed up Wilhelm Bastl's passing comment and tied the two bargemen to families in Pfreimd. They were Leuchtenberger, both of them. The bailiff in Pfreimd sent information about the family of the one named Forst. It was large, he said. Moreover, one of the men who were of interest to the regent had a cousin who was working in Amberg, right in the *Schloss.* They might well wish to question her.

Except that, upon investigation, she had died in the epidemic. Hand closed the file.

Böcler, to provide raw material for his friend Harsdörffer's projected epic, sat down and read through everything in order. He saw the name of the cousin. Riffled through the accounts. Identified her with the chambermaid who had been assigned to clean the rooms of Mrs. Simpson and Mrs. Dreeson. Ha!

He dashed down the corridor, just in time to prevent Zincgref's eloquent but mistaken blast against Duke Maximilian from being taken to the printer. The day after that, the radio and newspaper reports in regard to the bargemen, the Landgravine Mechthilde, and the dumping of Mrs. Simpson and Mrs. Dreeson into her presence in Freising started to arrive.

Zincgref was rather relieved by these reports, since he had already spent several hours going through his manuscript substituting Leuchtenberg for Maximilian in all the appropriate places, and pointing out wherever possible, because he didn't want to waste the excellent diatribes against the duke of Bavaria that he had already written, that the landgrave was a client of Maximilian living in exile in Bavaria.

Eric Haakansson Hand, in a few spare minutes, read through the draft, grabbed a few intelligence reports, and pointed out that the landgrave had not been mentally or physically capable of villainy for quite some time. With a sigh, Zincgref, noting that the landgrave's sister was married to the villainous Maximilian's brother, went through the manuscript once more, substituting Mechthilde's name for that of her brother.

In that form, the propaganda pamphlet finally went out, a full week past the deadline that Duke Ernst had originally set him. Zincgref's final hypothesis that Mechthilde and Albrecht were, as the employers of the two bargemen, the immediate villains in the kidnapping and that they had been acting upon the instigation of Duke Maximilian, the malignant general of the Catholic League, would remain unkillable ever more because it was now in print. Certainly, this version of the events suited Gustav Adolf and Oxenstierna splendidly.

As Oxenstierna would later remark to Mike Stearns, only a tie to Ferdinand II or Richelieu would have been better, but a person couldn't have everything.

They saw to the pamphlet's wide circulation; the emperor sent Zincgref a generous bonus. Very generous.

None of the Bavarian controversialists who flocked to their duke's defense in the next few weeks were able to prove otherwise. Arndt was dead; the chambermaid was dead; Kilian Richter honestly did not know. Forst and Becker both did not know the truth in the first place and had subsequently so deluded themselves that their multiple depositions, given in perfectly good faith, were utterly misleading.

Future historians would discover that Mechthilde and Albrecht's surviving papers contemporary with the events contained no indication of such activity. Depending upon the viewpoint of the author, this only meant, as the debate went on, that they were innocent (a position mainly taken only by irredentist Leuchtenberger loyalists, who defended the former ruling family to the end); that Albrecht and Mechthilde destroyed the papers, or that Duke Maximilian's intelligence agents destroyed the papers to hide evidence of some even more diabolical machinations that they contained.

Some decades later, a radical young revisionist suggested the possibility that the whole kidnapping was an accident, a comedy of errors. Because he was so rash as to publish this conclusion without sufficient primary sources to support it, he failed to obtain tenure and was laughed out of academia.

Neuburg

Marc's mood brightened perceptibly when his father told him that he could come along to Munich. They left Neuburg on horseback, quite openly. They were still merchants. Not, however, from Geneva. Bavarian border authorities were quite picky about allowing Protestants into Bavaria's sacred precincts—almost as bad as they were about prohibiting the import of Protestant books and pamphlets. The Cavrianis, father and son, were now Italian cloth merchants who had been visiting a branch of the family firm in one of Switzerland's Catholic cantons and were returning home by way of Bozen—Bolzano to Italians—in the Tyrol, in order to consult with the firm's factor there.

Marc wished that they could have been disguised. Unfortunately, beyond a few minor items, disguise would have been pointless. Italian Catholic merchants looked remarkably like Genevan Calvinist merchants, with the addition of a religious amulet here and there and a neat little case containing a rosary fastened at one's waistline.

Every paper that they carried was impeccable. They were even as rubbed and shopworn as anyone would normally expect them to be after two months of being put into and pulled out of their wallets. Marc had spent one whole day, while listening to his father and his Neuburg factor, Veit Egli, make plans, putting those papers into a leather case and pulling them out again; unfolding them, refolding them, holding them close to a candle, dog-earing an occasional corner, rubbing a bit of dirt on the margin of one, flicking a couple of drops of water to give the impression that at some check point they had been presented on a rainy day, putting them into the leather case, pulling them out again. By far the best way to make a document look well-used was to give it the appropriate amount of use.

Marc didn't have to worry about aging the seals. They were both authentic and authentically worn, having been carefully removed from other papers issued to other Cavrianis at other times and other places. *Cavriani Frères de Genève* had quite a collection of these, both at headquarters and in the various branch offices; one never knew when they might come in handy.

Egli pointed out to Marc the importance of leaving such seals attached to their original documents until one actually needed them. In the event of such an undesirable phenomenon as a large number of some angry ruler's minions inspecting one's business premises, a drawer full of detached seals would excite suspicion. An unlocked, battered chest full of old business travel papers and expense vouchers would not.

"Once you take the seal off an old passport, burn the paper. Inspectors may also regard the spot with the removed seal as questionable. Keep the expense vouchers, though. You never know when you may need them."

Marc nodded solemnly.

For travel reading, Marc picked up several of the latest Bavarian propaganda pamphlets in regard to the situation in the Upper

Palatinate. He found their illustrations of Duke Ernst rather amusing, especially the woodcuts that depicted him with cloven hoofs, horns, and a forked tail.

The woodcuts had been recycled, of course. A discriminating reader could tell that Duke Ernst's head had been remodeled, and rather amateurishly at that. It seemed likely that the originals had, at some time, included a papal tiara. Marc found the manifestations of political and theological controversy that were aimed at the general public to be endlessly entertaining.

Bavaria, south of Neuburg

Maximilian Adam, oldest son of the landgrave of Leuchtenberg, knew that he was not at his best this morning. The hangover possibly had something to do with it. But the officers of his regiment were noted for their hard drinking, even as professional soldiers went, so he was used to hangovers. They were a quite regular part of his daily routine, so that could not be the problem. He was dressed to ride. Presumably he had dressed without thinking about it. Why had he been drinking, last night?

Oh, yes. He had learned he was not going to be assigned to the Ingolstadt garrison, as he had hoped. He had made strenuous representations to Duke Maximilian's *Kriegsrat* to the effect that he wished to be transferred to a different regiment, if at all possible. He had asked to be assigned to the fortress, where he could earn glory in the process of beating back General Banér's siege. He had not phrased his letters quite that way, of course. He had emphasized the increased opportunity for service to the cause of Catholicism, supported by the importance of having officers who were willing to share the deprivations that were inevitably suffered by the common soldiers in a closed city.

Or, more accurately, his father's chaplain had emphasized those things. The chaplain had actually written the letters. Composition had never been Landgrave Maximilian Adam's strongest subject. He could not remember that his tutors had ever described any topic of study as his strongest subject. More frequently, they had complained that his brother, although two years younger, made more progress than he did.

Not that he had ever studied more than they could make him.

He had received quite a few thrashings in his time from irritated pedagogues.

He had signed the letter, though, he thought with some satisfaction. His handwriting wasn't bad at all, at least not for someone whose tutors had pronounced it completely hopeless and never likely to be legible when he was eight years old.

The letters had not helped, though. The war council had refused the transfer, so he was still stuck out here at the Bavarian camp in the countryside south of Ingolstadt, supervising things like forage resupply.

Or, at least, getting on his horse and following for several hours every day a sergeant who understood things like forage resupply. And who kept trying to explain it to him. It actually would not be so bad if the sergeant didn't have this peculiar idea that he ought to learn about it himself. Surely, that was what the sergeant was for.

Leopold Cavriani drew up his horse. There was clearly a problem involving a damaged bridge floor and a carriage wheel that had plunged through it, plus, it would appear, three women with seven small children in the carriage. The coachman had managed to cut the horses free and lead them to the other side of the stream. He was standing there, looking at the carriage. The bridge was far too narrow for the occupants to get out on either side. The wheel kept sliding a little farther; then a little farther.

"We can lift you out the back," Leopold called as he dismounted. "Start by handing us the children, one at a time."

"The back is too high," one of the women squealed nervously. "And the bridge is narrow. There are no railings. If the children get out before we do, one of them might fall off the edge. Or stray away. Or be trampled by one of your horses. There is no way we can tell if they are well-trained."

"I want," one of the other women said, "to get out from the front. First. On the same side as our coachman, whom I trust. Then, when I am there, my sisters may hand over the children, one by one."

Leopold sighed and started to marshal his powers of persuasion.

Marc tossed the bridle of his horse to his father, swung himself hand-over-hand along the side of the bridge, and bounced up in front of the carriage. He then handed the first woman out, followed by the rest of the passengers. He looked mildly startled when the last of the women, before coming, passed him a picnic chest to carry to the bank. Then she climbed out; the women proceeded to unpack their lunch.

Marc looked at the coachman. The coachman shrugged.

"We can lift it, I think, up through the broken board, if all three of us work," Marc suggested. "You lift from the front. My father can lift from the back of the coach. I'll climb under the bridge and push up on the wheel."

"Too high," the coachman diagnosed. "No way you can reach the wheel from the creek bed."

"I can stand on one of the girders and push up."

"They don't look all that strong to me," the coachman said dubiously.

Marc pulled off his boots and stockings; then hopped down into the creek and shook them. "They'll last long enough for me to heave the carriage up so we can haul it off the bridge."

The one that he chose to stand on did last long enough. Just barely. The carriage was on a good part of the flooring before the girder dumped him into the water. Undiscouraged, if dripping, he climbed back up onto the bridge and pushed the broken wheel as far back onto the axle as it would go, anchoring it with a piece of the broken slat. Cautiously, the coachman and Leopold jockeyed the carriage to the far bank. Marc stood there, staring at the bridge thoughtfully.

Maximilian Adam of Leuchtenberg was not really watching where he was going.

"Keep your damned horse off the bridge flooring," was not something he was expecting to hear. Even though it possibly prevented him from putting the animal's leg through the hole and breaking it.

"Speak to your betters with a little more respect, lout!" he replied.

"Ah, Your Grace," the sergeant said, clearing his throat. "Perhaps we had better wait."

"It's not just the board. The girder went, too," came the disembodied voice from under the bridge. "I'm trying to shore it up, but if you put a thousand pounds of horse on it right now, the whole thing will go. I can prop up the bridge, probably, but I can't build you a new one from scratch."

✧   ✧   ✧

The picnic party was watching with interest. Leopold and the coachman were watching with concern.

Mark scrambled out from under the bridge.

"Why aren't you in the army?" the officer demanded.

"Ah, I'm not Bavarian, sir," Marc answered quietly enough. "I'm Italian. We are merchants. My father, across the stream, is carrying our papers."

The officer looked across the stream to where Leopold, who had also stripped to his shirt and slops, was pushing mightily while the coachman tried to fit the broken spokes back into the wheel rim. "If he is, he shows remarkably little respect for his station in life. And you even less."

Marc looked down at his feet. Mentally, he was biting his tongue; physically, he was biting his upper lip. The misbehaving curl slipped into the middle of his forehead as he looked back up.

"Sergeant, we shall dismount and cross on foot," pronounced the officer. "Tether the horses here. When the lout finishes his work, he can lead them across for us." The officer dismounted and looked at Marc—rather, looked *up* at him. "Bring them a couple of buckets of water, while you are at it."

Marc nodded.

The carriage repaired, at least enough to get to the next village, the coachman handed his passengers into it and proceeded down the road.

Two hours later, Marc estimated that the bridge was strong enough that he could lead the two army horses across it. Which he did.

The sergeant thanked him. The officer demanded to see his papers.

Leopold, who had put his stockings, boots, doublet, and hat back on as soon as the carriage drove away, brought the papers out of their case.

The officer eyed them. "You do not look much like father and son," he said.

"My wife assures me that we are," Cavriani replied with impeccable politeness.

The sergeant snorted.

The officer looked slightly bewildered. "I will remember you if I see you again," he said to Marc. "I am Maximilian Adam, son of the Landgrave of Leuchtenberg."

There seemed no particular purpose to that last sentence. But Marc let him get out of hearing before commenting on the matter.

CHAPTER 37

Sedis Apostolicae
Propositiones

Munich, Bavaria

The English Ladies received mail in the ordinary way, of course. In addition to that, they received mail through the Jesuit Order's own postal system. This was "just one of those things" in the ambivalent relationship between the Ladies and the Jesuits.

More than one officer of the Inquisition, over the past decade, had found this an exasperating state of affairs. In 1631, the cardinals had authorized a decree to the effect that the bishops of those territories in which the Ladies had foundations were to apprise the Inquisition of such details as where these "Jesuitesses" lived, under whose protection they stood, and whether they received letters from foreigners. If yes, the letters were to be intercepted, their contents checked, and reported to the Congregation for the Faith.

But.

Long before the current crisis, one frustrated Dominican had reported to his superior that, as far as the source of their correspondence was concerned, he had been told in confidence that the Ladies ordinarily got their letters from England by way of the Father-General of the Society of Jesus, but he had not been able to find out the specific Jesuits under whose names the letters arrived, because the letters were contained in the Jesuits' mail bag. He did know that since many of the Ladies from England were of good family, they received money in this manner for their own support and that of their schools. What was more, he himself found out all of this only through another member of his own order, who found it out from his sister, who found it out from some noblewomen who were in the confidence of the English Ladies.

This morning, the mail bag was full. Mary Ward distributed the regular mail. Those were mostly letters from family, many addressed to Father Edward Shiner, S.J., and redirected from him to Munich. Then she looked at the business letters, of which there were a number. Mostly bills. Even nuns need food, clothing, and shelter; not to mention books and school supplies. Among them, however, was also a bank draft from Cardinal Francesco Barberini.

Mary Ward looked at the amount in astonishment. No explanation. She put it aside.

There was a copy of a letter from one annoyed inquisitor to another complaining that in the Ladies' schools, they taught the more capable young girls the works of Saint Thomas Aquinas in, depending on the language of the region, Flemish, German, and English translations. Not to mention teaching the most capable girls Latin in addition to more appropriate subjects such as grammar and needlework, and then having them read the saint's treatises in the original. The author was practically spastic on the topic of the impropriety of teaching philosophy and theology to those who should keep silence in the church.

There was also a copy of a letter written two months earlier by Cardinal Saint Onofrio (Antonio Barberini, the elder) to the secretariat of the Holy Office. Saint Onofrio assured the father-general of the Dominicans that he was still "concerned"—he had been expressing this concern for the past three years without actually doing anything—by the fact that Cardinal Buoncompagni in Naples was pretending that he didn't know anything about the decree of dissolution and was permitting the Ladies there not only to accept new pupils, but also to accept postulants. According to the nuncio in Naples, Saint Onofrio said, Buoncompagni had been so oblivious, or so under the thumb of certain noblewomen, as to make the manifestly absurd protest to the Holy Office that he was under the impression that the pope was actually going to change his mind and confirm the Institute.

Mary Ward grinned to herself. When it came to playing dumb, few could outdo Cardinal Buoncompagni. A fact which Cardinal Saint Onofrio most certainly knew.

Of course, it was barely *possible* that Cardinal Buoncompagni in Naples really never had received proper legal notice of the decree dissolving the Institute. She had received good information that in 1631 Father Corcione, S.J., had pulled the official copy down off the door before anyone had a chance to read it.

But this was old news. Where were the letters from Rome? Surely *someone* would have written her about the attempt to assassinate the pope. Surely *someone* would have forwarded a description of what had led to the appointment of a cardinal-protector for the United States of Europe.

Ah—Cardinal Antonio Barberini the Younger. And a very, very, entertaining version of the events in Rome. She would read it aloud to the sisters during supper.

Finally, there was a large, closed, envelope. Not a folded letter, as most, with the address on the outside. A thick envelope. Opaque. Sealed. Nothing on the outside but her name.

Two letters inside. One from Father-General Vitelleschi. Rare, but not unprecedented.

The other was from the pope himself.

Mary Ward had been standing at her pedestal desk. She moved back, sitting down on a straight-backed wooden bench that stood against one wall of her office.

The English Ladies were to leave Munich.

That first sentence of the pope's edict was so shattering that she almost dropped the letter. To give up even the limited scope of activity that they had been allowed thus far?

It was very hard to pretend that a person had not read a letter from the vicar of Christ on earth. Especially when it was accompanied by one from the father-general of the Jesuit order and arrived in a Jesuit mail bag. His Holiness would know perfectly well that it had been delivered into her own hands.

Praying for the courage to obey, she read farther.

They were to go to—Grantville? Her heart started to pound; her hands shook.

Not to some polite prison where they would live henceforth in the shadow of the Inquisition? Next year, she would complete a half century on this earth. She was not well. She had not been well for years. But, if God were gracious, she would still have time to serve him.

She started to read the pope's letter again, from the beginning. They were to remove from Munich and go to Grantville.

There. That was clearly written. She had not been mistaken.

She could safely read farther. They were to remove from Munich inconspicuously, if possible surreptitiously. It might be the course of prudence for them to announce their intent of making a pilgrimage, but any other plausible reason would be quite acceptable. They would be observed by the Holy Office, of course; the Holy Office observed everything that the Ladies did. It was to be presumed that Duke Maximilian would not endorse their departure.

That, Mary Ward thought, had to be the understatement of the year. Everybody knew that the duke was infuriated by anything that had to do with these "monstrous men from the future" who had welded themselves to the cause of the Swede.

They were to go to Grantville, where the suppression of the Institute of the Blessed Virgin Mary would be reversed for purposes of its operation within the limits of the United States of Europe, under the sponsorship of the new cardinal-protector.

"You will have received a bank draft from Our nephew."

That accounted for the transmission from Cardinal Francesco.

"Father Vitelleschi will provide details."

The school run by the English Ladies announced that for purposes of allowing their pupils to participate more fully in the festivities associated with the marriage of Bavaria's gracious Duke Maximilian to Archduchess Maria Anna of Austria, after the girls had participated in the ceremony of welcome when the wedding procession reached the gates of Munich, classes would be dismissed for the entire following week. The Jesuits had extended a blanket invitation for the pupils of the school to participate as extras in the production of *Belisarius, Christian General* in the *Schrannenplatz* to celebrate the wedding. The girls would need to be available for costuming, rehearsals, and other incidentals.

The pupils were duly ecstatic.

Their parents, upon occasion, somewhat less so. It meant, of course, that during a week of uproar, they would have to keep an eye on their daughters themselves. However, they could hardly protest the decision without seeming disloyal to the duke. And girls could always help their mothers with the cooking, baking, and other activities at home when they weren't rehearsing. The parents made the best of it. There probably wouldn't be another wedding in the ducal family for a long time. If the Austrian became pregnant and bore a son, not for twenty years, at least.

Let the girls have their fun.

Father-General Vitelleschi's instructions had been meticulously detailed.

Arrangements in Munich would be made through Father Matthaeus Roeder. Mary Ward cocked her head for a moment at the spelling. Who? Oh, Father Rader. He was very old. But he had taught rhetoric for years. He knew *everybody*, including, because of his three-volume history of the duchy, everybody at court. And he had written famous plays himself, so he was certain to be consulted on the production being put on for the wedding. What a good choice, especially since the girls from the school had been invited to take part in the play.

Was that *why* the girls from the school had been invited to take part in the play? The English Ladies were never cloistered; they could move freely through the city in pairs. But this way, no one would be surprised to see them at the rehearsals, supervising the girls even though they were officially out of school.

Father Drexel would assist them. Jeremias Drexel was the rector of the Jesuit *collegium* in Munich; formerly head of the *gymnasium* as well. Also formerly Duke Maximilian's court preacher, although he had given up that responsibility more than a dozen years earlier, in 1621, after the duke's Bohemian campaign. He had retired to write a biography of the Duchess Elisabeth Renata and compose theological works. Conflict of interest? Not for a Jesuit; his vow of obedience was to the pope, not the duke. Father-General Vitelleschi must be *serious* about this.

Drexel had overall responsibility for the entire production of the play.

He would also be, perhaps, better able than most to give the Ladies advice on what might be happening in the United States of Europe. Born in Augsburg, he had originally been Lutheran. Father Drexel, as a convert, might have some insight into the way the Swede and his allies would look at the holy father's latest move.

Mary Ward decided to use Father Drexel's *School of Patience* for this evening's spiritual reading.

> We should think, as we gather riches, as we sit in positions of great honor, as we indulge in luxurious pleasures. All this only a dream, and moreover a short and frivolous dream. When we wake from it, there will be no riches in our hands.
>
> What, then is life? To be brief, the period for which human life lasts is only a point on a line, its very nature changeable, during which we see through a glass darkly. Our bodies are unreliable, our moods variable. Riches are a thorn, lust is a poison. Everything bodily is a running river that passes on. Life is a war; the stay of a guest in a foreign city; an existence full of suffering and effort. Great buildings and strong fortifications collapse; their strength does not help them. The hardest of stones erode. The greatest fame is forgotten after a man's death; the greatest worldly titles disappear like smoke.
>
> The most beautiful and praiseworthy thing a man can do before he dies is to devote his life to the untiring performance of virtuous acts, constantly seeking to practice prudence, justice, moderation, endurance; faith, hope, and unselfish love.

It seemed as though all of Munich was involved in preparing for the presentation of *Belisarius*. Of course, Father Drexel was fielding a veteran team. For the past three decades, Jesuit theater in Bavaria had assumed an increasingly laudatory function. It praised the piety of the ruling house and the martial glory of its duke. This was far from the first performance that was no longer confined to the yard of the *Wilhelmsgymnasium*, the secondary school named for Duke Maximilian's father, but rather staged in the *Schrannenplatz*. The city was the stage; the cast was huge. The casts of the Jesuit plays presented in Munich had been huge for a half-century, already. In 1575, about a thousand actors and extras took part in the presentation of *Constantine the Great*. *Esther*, with its crowd scenes at the court of Persia, required half again that many, or more.

Belisarius. *Belisarius* had armies. Scenes with armies required the maximum number of extras that the director could locate, cajole, persuade, or strong arm into appearing on a stage.

The costumes would be elaborate; the staging more so. Music had increasingly become an important element of the productions. The *Oratory of Philothea*, performed earlier in the year, had been more an opera than a play. In addition to the new prologue and epilogue, which Balde had sent from Amberg, they were adding music to the new production of *Belisarius*. That would require a couple of hundred additional performers, just for the vocals. Here a martial chorus of men; there a heavenly choir of angelic voices. It all added up.

The residents of Munich were becoming quite accustomed to seeing groups of heavily armed Roman soldiers strolling down the street, accompanied by Byzantine court ladies garbed in stiff robes and elaborate headdresses, not to mention an occasional angel. They were becoming used to hearing random explosions from the direction of the *Schrannenplatz* as the technicians experimented with the fireworks that would accompany the battle scenes. It was normal to observe portions of nearly full-sized ships (one side only, with braces behind them) being hauled through the streets on wagons, with much cursing by the teamsters as they had to negotiate through narrow *Gassen* to make their deliveries. There was constant hammering. The bleachers and pegs were saved from one performance to the next, of course; just placed in storage. Still, each time, they had to be fastened back together sturdily enough that there was no danger of their collapsing under the weight of those spectators lucky enough to obtain a seat.

The programs were at the printer. The play's dialogue would be in Latin, of course. However, the programs provided a German libretto, so that all the spectators could follow the action. There was little point in presenting such a spectacle if those in attendance could not understand the moral that it was all designed to impress upon them.

Mary Ward called upon Father Rader. Between them, they got the removal plans for the English Ladies under way. He agreed that announcing a pilgrimage might not be amiss, although that might also be considered something of a cliché. Perhaps such an announcement could be made more timely by linking it to the closing of the school for the wedding festivities. Perhaps the ladies were graciously doing this in order to make the space in their house available to the duke's important guests.

"Important guests," he said, "but not quite important enough to merit quarters in the *Residenz* itself. Or even in Duke Albert's old palace. I will give some thought to precisely who might fit into that category. Ecclesiastical guests, perhaps? In any case, we should represent it as being an act of generosity on your part. Since the Marian pilgrimage at Ettal has become so much more popular in recent years, particularly since Ettal is almost due south of Munich, we could try that. Your departure in that direction will scarcely raise immediate alarms in the mind of even the most zealous agent of the Holy Office."

While Father Rader had been expecting Mary Ward, he had not been expecting Doña Mencia de Mendoza. She begged a favor from him. She needed to send an important and confidential letter to her brother, Cardinal Bedmar, in the Netherlands. If he would be so kind as to include it in the Jesuit mail bag . . .

He agreed. And wrote a letter of his own to Father-General Vitelleschi. It might, at a minimum, he reminded the authorities in Rome, be prudent to alert the Jesuits at St. Mary's in Grantville to expect the arrival of the English Ladies, in order that they could arrange for appropriate housing, if nothing else. He understood that the up-time town had become very crowded in the past three years.

CHAPTER 38

Nova Confoederatio

Munich, Bavaria

The daily routine of the Bavarian court was greatly disrupted by the wedding preparations. Normally, over seven hundred fifty people lived in the *Residenz*. This week, there were twice that many. The cooks had brought in extra staff from the duke's other palaces. Still, they had been forced to hire temporary helpers. The usual residents had been relocated to less commodious quarters under the roof to accommodate important guests; the servants who normally slept under the roof were on pallets in the kitchens and cots lined along the back corridors. Even some of the administrative offices had been required to pack their papers in chests and vacate temporarily in order to provide additional lodging.

Servants of the important guests ran around demanding better rooms and special services for their masters and mistresses—hot water in the rooms, special ways to prepare certain foods, the need to borrow a seamstress, objections to the stabling provided for horses, even greater objections to the duke's mandate that the hundreds of carriages and baggage wagons, once they had delivered their passengers and trunks, must be parked outside the city walls to avoid clogging the streets. There were constant disputes about diplomatic precedence and protocol.

That didn't even count the guests who were not lodged in the

Residenz, but who had quarters in inns or private houses and came to the palace during the day for various ceremonial occasions. Nor the visitors who were not invited guests but had come to see the wedding anyway. Nor the vendors who had applied for special licenses, with their wives and children. Nor the day laborers who were heaving and hauling stands and booths into place.

Diplomatic guests objected strenuously to having their personal possessions searched at the gates in the usual manner. Some of them held written exemptions authorizing them to enter without such a search. Some of them did not have room in their assigned quarters for all the baggage they had brought, so their servants were constantly running back and forth to the wagons to fetch something that had been left behind.

Every church in town was holding special services. A mass of thanksgiving here, a *Te Deum* there, a chorale here, a morality play there. People who ordinarily attended their local parish church and had no reason to go farther from their homes than the nearest market square were running all over town to hear and see them.

The whole city was in complete chaos. Half the time, the regular guards had no idea who the people walking down a given corridor in the palace or street in the city were or why they were there. This made them nervous, but they were under strict orders not to offend if they could avoid it. This was a celebration.

The extra guards, the ones brought in from the duke's country palaces and borrowed from garrison regiments outside Munich, by and large didn't even recognize the usual and customary occupants of the palace. They had no idea whether the people on a street lived there or were strangers, although, usually, they could safely presume that those who were walking around looking at the civic buildings and churches, going "oooh" and "aaah," were tourists.

This presumption could not be made about those who were wandering around the walls and fortifications of the city going "oooh" and "aaah." Any one of them could be a spy for the Swede. These gawkers made the captain of the guards very nervous, but as long as they did not directly trespass, his men were not allowed to chase them away. The commander of the Munich garrison would be very glad when the damned wedding was over and things got back to normal.

✧   ✧   ✧

The day after the wedding procession arrived in Munich, Duchess Mechthilde filed formal charges of witchcraft against the two foreign women who were being harbored in Archduchess Maria Anna's household, thus confirming Duke Maximilian's growing suspicions of his brother's disloyalty.

Duke Maximilian was under considerable pressure from his privy council to do something about it. Not, of course, to do any one thing about it. Donnersberger wanted him to quash the charges. Others, particularly Richel, didn't. Richel also advocated, quite strongly, making the most of the women's presence. Although the duke had not, in fact, deliberately obtained them to use as hostages, Richel admitted, he also argued that since they were here, Maximilian might as well use them for maximum leverage. It was unlikely that the Swede himself would pay much attention to the fate of two elderly female commoners. However, perhaps that could be used to divide him from his demonic allies? Or, if the regent in the Upper Palatinate did display concern, possibly one could extract concessions? The status of Leuchtenberg? That annoying south-of-the-Danube enclave at Neuburg? Richel insisted that it would be imprudent to overlook any possible advantages to be obtained from the situation. After all, he pointed out, if it should be determined that they were witches and the duke ultimately decided to handle them accordingly, he could do so without any conscientious scruples.

Almost reluctantly, Father Contzen agreed with Richel. Whatever the duke might promise the Swede or the up-timers or Duke Ernst in return for concessions, there was, in fact, no obligation to keep faith with heretics. That was the most general conclusion of the moral theologians. It might be considered casuistry, perhaps, but that was the accepted position. If the duke agreed to remand the women to the United States of Europe in return for certain concessions—he would not incur eternal damnation if he changed his mind.

Father Vervaux cleared his throat. "The Dreeson woman, I believe, is Catholic."

Richel, on the basis of the personal experience of his wife, replied that during the course of time, a lot of Catholic women had been burned as witches if the judges determined that they were guilty. Adherence to Catholicism was not, in itself, an impediment to execution as a witch by a Catholic ruler, as demonstrated by the events in Bamberg, for example.

Most of the privy councillors wanted the duke to remove the

women from the custody of the archduchess and imprison them. Or, at the very least, immure them in a convent. Preferably, the nuncio and the deacon Golla suggested, in the convent of the Poor Clares. That had proven to be a very satisfactory solution when the Inquisition had demanded the imprisonment of Mary Ward, the head of the English Ladies.

Duke Maximilian raised one of his graying black eyebrows. Golla shuddered. When the duke did that, he bore a much greater resemblance to many images of Mephistopheles than to that of a proper champion of the Catholic faith.

"Let there be a formal hearing for the women."

That was that. When the duke said, "let there be," there was.

Item the First. Are these women actually who they say they are?

Item the Second. If so, why are they here?

Item the Third. Is there sufficient credible evidence to justify trying them for witchcraft?

(Item the Fourth. If not, why did Mechthilde bring the charges?)

The fourth would not go on the official agenda. It would, however, be very much on the duke's mind.

Duke Maximilian looked at the note with disbelief. Archduchess Maria Anna asserted that since she had taken the two women into her household and was therefore responsible for their *Schutz und Schirm*, she must be present at the formal hearing and be permitted to provide them with competent counsel.

He waggled the piece of paper at Dr. Donnersberger. At Father Contzen. At Richel. The first two looked very uncomfortable; Richel looked annoyed. It was, in fact, an uncomfortable and annoying meeting of the privy council throughout, especially in light of the exclusion of Duke Albrecht.

Since the letter arrived on his desk, Duke Maximilian had begun referring to his fiancée as *die Habsburgerin*. That was not a good omen. Before his first marriage, he had refused to accept any Habsburg bride.

The privy council, backed with numerous legal opinions from consulting jurists, determined, reluctantly, that the archduchess did in fact have the right to participate.

"Duchess Elisabeth Renata," the duke said, "never did anything of the sort."

That was most certainly true.

After the meeting, several of the less important members of the privy council discovered that they had urgent business on their country estates. Business that was too urgent to permit them to remain in Munich between now and the wedding. They would return the following week, they said. Several of the more important members of the council devoutly wished that they could do the same.

After all, "You have saddled me with a termagant," was not a promising statement for a bridegroom to make a week before his wedding. Neither was, "God is punishing me for listening to you when you tempted me to break my vow to enter a monastery." That sort of statement tended to be followed by adverse consequences for the luckless advisors.

There was a lot of excitement and gossip. After all, Bavaria now had two very prominent, foreign, accused witches right here in Munich. If they were found guilty after a proper investigation, and the duke so decided, the burning might even be part of the wedding festivities. People shivered; some with excitement, some with apprehension.

The hearing occurred. Maria Anna, on the principle of "begin as you mean to go on," participated fully in the discussions. Since formal hearings were open to the public, reporters were present. They took notes. And, the instant the hearing closed, headed for the post office, scribbling as they went. As did clerks from the various embassies.

The women were who they said they were.

More than enough members of the various foreign missions in Munich had seen Mrs. Simpson in Magdeburg to verify that; some had even been introduced to her at receptions and other official functions. Far fewer had previously seen Mrs. Dreeson.

Duke Maximilian, however, deemed the number of witnesses to her identity to be sufficient, particularly since one of those witnesses, who did not, however, appear on the stand, was his most important spy in Amberg. His spy had provided him with an extensive written narrative of what Duke Ernst's council appeared to know about the two women's disappearance, which was disappointingly little. None of the data that the regent had obtained in the Upper Palatinate itself appeared to clearly, much less conclusively, link their disappearance to Leuchtenberg. Indeed, the primary speculation there was that the kidnapping had been arranged by Duke Maximilian himself to obtain the women as hostages.

Maximilian pursed his lips. Dimwits.

The Amberg council, the spy said, appeared to be more confused than anything else by the accounts involving Leuchtenberg that had appeared in the newspapers. Maximilian found that disappointing. Since his own people were confused, he had hoped for clarification from the other party's intelligence.

There was insufficient evidence to bring an indictment for witchcraft.

In fact, Duke Maximilian noted, there was no evidence whatsoever to bring an indictment for witchcraft other than the completely unsubstantiated accusations made by the two bargemen, Forst and Becker. Upon repeated close questioning in Freising, it appeared from their subsequent statements that they had no evidence either; they had simply made an unsubstantiated assumption. No one could list any supposed *maleficia* committed by either of the women.

Moreover, Frau Simpson, when asked if she had ever worshiped the devil, had replied, "You've got to be kidding."

However—

There was also no reasonable explanation for their arrival in Bavaria.

Therefore, they would remain in detention pending further investigation. *Dekan* Golla suggested interning them in the convent of the Poor Clares. Archduchess Maria Anna of Austria suggested interning them with the English Ladies as an alternative. Golla glared at her.

Duke Maximilian took the alternatives under advisement. Pending a decision, the foreign women would remain in the official custody of the archduchess, thus satisfying the jurisdictional concerns of the prince-bishop of Freising, but would reside with the English Ladies. According to the formal minutes of the hearing, the duke determined that this was the most convenient solution in the short term, given that the Ladies had dismissed their pupils in honor of the wedding festivities and their house, therefore, would provide a peaceful retreat for Bavaria's unexpected guests, offering them a period of recollection and recovery.

Dr. Donnersberger was rather proud of that last sentence. He had drafted it himself.

Vienna

Father Lamormaini read the dispatches from Munich. He read the newspapers.

Marry her off to the right man, and soon.

He had tried. "Man proposes; God disposes." Duke Maximilian had his full sympathy.

Brussels, the Spanish Netherlands

"Fascinating," commented Don Fernando, as he laid down the report. "Don't you think so, Pieter?"

Rubens was not sure how to respond. Ruefully, he was reflecting that having a direct radio connection in Amsterdam—the prince of Orange and Rebecca Abrabanel were being most accommodating, in that regard—was not always a blessing. In times past, it might easily have taken weeks for this news to get from Bavaria to the Netherlands.

"What I mean is, Maximilian is by all accounts a formidable man," the prince continued. "He's sixty-one years old, to boot. And the archduchess *defied* him? On more or less the eve of their wedding?"

Rubens cleared his throat. "Well . . . I'm not sure 'defied' isn't too strong a term, Your Highness."

Don Fernando gave him a smile that bordered on a jeer. "Oh, stop trying to maneuver me. You know what I mean! I imagine you think of it as protecting me from youthful enthusiasms, yes?"

That was, in point of fact, exactly how Rubens perceived the matter.

The prince looked around the audience chamber. "Where did you hide the portraits, by the way? You know what I mean! Did you really think I wouldn't notice?"

Rubens sighed. "I'll have them brought out, if you insist. But I will point out again that there is simply no purpose—"

"Yes, yes, I know. Still, I'd like to look at it again."

"It," not "them." Worse and worse.

Fifteen minutes later, the portraits of the two Austrian archduchesses were back in the audience chamber, propped up on armchairs.

Don Fernando did not so much as glance at the portrait of Cecelia Renata. But he spent some considerable studying the portrait of the older of the two sisters.

To be fair, Rubens allowed, the artist who had portrayed Maria Anna had done a superb job. It was quite difficult—he knew from his own experience—to do one of these formal portraits without rendering the subject so solemn and stiff that all personality was leached away.

The portrait of Cecelia Renata was of that sort. Just a painting, of a pretty young woman in very expensive costume, looking . . . like a pretty young woman.

Maria Anna's portrait, on the other hand, had genuine intensity. The dark eyes looking out possessed obvious intelligence; and there was something subtle about the mouth that suggested a wry wit lurking beneath the slight smile.

"She's interesting," Don Fernando finally pronounced. "I mean, *she* is. Not her station."

Rubens ordered the servants to wrap up the portraits and return them to his chambers.

"Yes, I suspect you're right, Your Highness. What I am certain of, however, is that her father is Ferdinand II, Emperor of the Holy Roman Empire, and her soon-to-be husband is Duke Maximilian of Bavaria. An avalanche can also be described as 'interesting'—which doesn't make it any less impossible to stop once it starts moving."

"Oh, stop fussing at me, Pieter. Reminds me of my blasted tutors from the years in Madrid. Sour old men. I was just making an observation, that's all."

Munich, Bavaria

Mary Ward would have much preferred to have the two women from Grantville placed with the Poor Clares—or in any other convent in Munich that was not the house of the English Ladies on Paradise Street. Their presence put her in a considerable dilemma in the matter of following the papal instructions to leave Munich.

They could not use the first idea that Father Rader suggested, that they leave Munich without arousing any suspicion for several days by announcing that they were going on a short pilgrimage to Ettal while the school was closed for the wedding festivities. Ettal as a goal had the advantage of being in Upper Bavaria, about thirty-five miles south of Munich, not at all in the direction of any border that Bavaria had with the USE.

But they could not plausibly go on a pilgrimage and leave their unexpected "guests" unattended. Nor, for that matter, could they take them along.

They could still, of course, leave Munich "surreptitiously" and take their guests along when they left. It didn't seem likely that Frau Simpson and Frau Dreeson would have any objection to leaving Munich and going to Grantville.

The problem was that if they left the city without having announced a reasonable pretext, pursuit could be expected to follow much more quickly than under the original plan. Mary Ward was under no delusions. She lived under the shadow of the Inquisition. All of her movements were observed.

Additionally, several important wedding guests who had been scheduled to lodge in the English Ladies' house during the wedding festivities were now looking for other quarters. Assisted, naturally, by Father Rader.

At the moment, however, she was informed by the cook that Benno, who delivered produce, was engaged in a bitter dispute with Korbinian, who delivered fish, and who now asserted that the week before, Benno had collected the larger payment that had been owed to the fishmonger and now refused to make restitution of the portion that was not rightfully his. In this vale of sorrows, questions of great policy were frequently punctuated by extremely mundane interruptions. She proceeded to the kitchen, settled the matter, and then stood with her hand on the door jamb, looking out the back door into the alley at the shabby lean-to shed that had been built onto the back of the house on the other side.

CHAPTER 39

Peregrinatores Suspiciosi

Munich, Bavaria

München. Unlike many German cities, it was not named for a castle, nor a mountain. *Monacum*, the town of the little monk. Leopold Cavriani paused long enough for Marc to take a good look.

Munich was impressive, even compared to Nürnberg. Over the past couple of years, Marc had become accustomed to measuring every other town and city by the standard of Nürnberg—its population of forty thousand people, its churches, its civic buildings, its guild halls, its music. Jacob Durre was, passionately, a Nürnberg local patriot. He had managed to share part of his love of his adopted city with Marc. From his perspective, one of the greatest blessings that the coming of Grantville had brought to the Germanies was that in this world, the battle of the Alte Veste had not resulted in the deaths of about two-thirds of the population of that city and the equally harsh devastation of a wide swath of the hinterland around it.

The capital of Bavaria wasn't as large, of course. Its population was less than half that of Nürnberg, probably not much over eighteen or nineteen thousand, if you counted only the citizens and their households. In Munich, though, a person would have to add the people living at the court and the far larger numbers of clergy. And, of course, the beggars. Duke Maximilian had issued a strict ordinance regulating the poor just a few years previously. Still, though, even with those, it was only about half as big as Nürnberg.

According to his father, if life were fair, Duke Maximilian of Bavaria ought to be just as grateful to Grantville as Jacob Durre was. Even the very general descriptions of Gustav Adolf's 1632 campaigns in Bavaria that were in the history books that came back in time made it clear that the Swedes had devastated the duchy in that other world. In this world, after the Alte Veste, with the exception of leaving Banér in the Upper Palatinate and Horn in Swabia, the Swedes had withdrawn to the north. Bavaria was still, in this summer of 1634, except for Ingolstadt, essentially untouched by the war's destruction, its great abbeys and convents intact and its castles unburned.

Maximilian was prepared for war, though. Munich's fortifications were impressive. Marc had been expecting the church towers. He had seen the old view of the city, from about seventy-five years before, in a book about the cities of the world, while he was in Nürnberg. That book proclaimed that Munich excelled and out-dazzled all the other seats of German princes in its "elegant cleanliness." Since then, around and outside the old medieval walls, smooth curtain walls in a sort of irregular egg-shape, the dukes of Bavaria had constructed another set of modern walls with every imaginable innovation. The arrow-shaped extrusions almost looked like they were weapons themselves. Marc was hoping that he would have time to get a good look at them.

They were coming in on the *Augsburger Strasse*, from the southwest. Leopold had cut directly south from Neuburg until they intersected it. He said that arriving from that direction would attract less attention than coming from the northwest on the *Nürnberger Strasse*, since entering there led visitors directly past the *Residenz* itself, where security would certainly be highest. The view lacked the drama of Nürnberg, where the old medieval fortress stood high above the rest of the city. The walls were impressive enough without it.

Leopold had been giving considerable thought to where they should stay. *Cavriani Frères de Genève* did not have a factor conveniently located in this most Catholic of Catholic cities. The first question was "inside or outside the walls?" Either had its advantages and disadvantages. If they stayed outside the walls, they would not be trapped within the city when the gates closed at night. That would give them somewhat more flexibility. Also, because of the wedding, lodgings inside the city would be hard to find, as well as expensive. While Marc looked at Munich's walls, his father looked at the parking area where the baggage-wagons for the duke's guests had been collected. He looked even more closely at the constant stream of servants going back and forth through the gates to the wagons.

It was that, finally, that decided him. He would not have begrudged the money that an inn inside the walls would have cost, but staying outside would work better. They would be in a camp in which, basically, almost nobody knew anybody else, so no one would be in a position to watch them doing something they "shouldn't" or keeping a routine that they "oughtn't." He turned his horse toward the baggage wagons; Marc followed. Renting a place to stake their horses and put out their pallets at night took less than a half hour.

Marc was still feeling a little deprived. At the very least, he thought, they should have needed to sneak around, peeking into dungeons and making secret signals, until they found the damsels in distress whom they had come to rescue. Well, not *damsels*, precisely. At any rate, until they found Frau Simpson and Frau Dreeson. Instead, the newspaper had announced the duke's decision that they would be interned in the house of the English Ladies. It had even conveniently provided the name of the street on which the house was to be found.

His father said that the first order of business was to become familiar with the city and its streets, before they went anywhere near that house. Munich wasn't all that large. An energetic man could walk across it, north to south or east to west, in fifteen minutes. The bridge across the multiple channels of the Isar River was on the east, opposite to where they had entered the city through the Neuhäuser Gate, leading from the *Salzburger Strasse* past the Jesuit *collegium*.

They were being tourists, though, like a couple of thousand other people who were wandering around the city this morning, so they hadn't taken the short route. They had first passed the old palace, built by Duke Maximilian's grandfather Albert, as they came in. Leopold said, quite seriously, "We are very fortunate.

Through certain informal connections, my factor in Pfaffenhofen was able to obtain tickets for us to view the late Duke Albert's collection of antiquities tomorrow afternoon. It is too bad that Duke Maximilian does not permit public access to his own collections. They are said to be very extensive—tapestries, jewels, paintings. Unlike France, where the royal palaces are virtually open to the public and the king's own bedchamber may be viewed by the curious when he is not in residence, the duke keeps his own apartments and chapel very private. Even the court nobility have limited access, and that by invitation only."

They crossed over to the south side of the *collegium* and walked along the main street through the "Beautiful Tower." They looped around the *Frauenkirche* with its two round-topped towers. It was almost in the center of town, facing onto the *Schrannenplatz*. St. Peter's church, *der Alte Peter*, was on a line with it. Marc had never seen a city with quite so many churches and monasteries. Back on the main street, they walked northeast through the chief marketplace, past the parliament house where the Bavarian Estates met, and the city hall.

"The Estates," Leopold commented, "have frequently not been happy with the cost of all this ducal splendor. In 1571, the ducal household was up to more than eight hundred and fifty people. Just Duke Wilhelm's investment in music, Orlando di Lasso, Andrea Gabrieli, sixty-odd singers and instrumentalists, plus a boys' chorus, was incredibly expensive. The extravagance of it all was why, in 1597, the Estates compelled Duke Wilhelm to abdicate in favor of his son. A lot of Duke Maximilian's efforts during the first years of his rule went to getting a grip on the financial situation. Even now, though, when the total number of court personnel is smaller, most of it comprises the duke's own household: the hunt, the stables, the cellar, the kitchens, the bodyguards; painters, sculptors, craftsmen, tailors. Duke Maximilian's 'strictest economy' has only reduced the court personnel to about seven hundred and seventy. Less than a fourth are engaged in the administration of the duchy, from the highest member of the privy council down to the most junior clerk. And, of course, Duke Albrecht has his own household, with his own major domo and steward. As will the new duchess."

It was fairly easy, most of the time, to guess which of the people in the street were residents of Munich and which were visitors. Munich women wore hats with high crowns and the ubiquitous aprons, many of them colored. The men wore the same style of hat.

Duke Maximilian's officials attempted to enforce the 1626 sumptuary ordinance regulating "unnecessary and superfluous costliness" in the clothing worn by his subjects, the *Kleiderordnung*, quite strictly in this, his capital city. Woe to the farmer who had his wife's shoes sewn on a last or the ordinary workman who expended his money on a pair of knit stockings with satin garters! The ordinance divided the duke's subjects into classes and prescribed the acceptable clothing for each, the man and his family alike: farmers, day laborers, menial civil servants, and common soldiers; ordinary citizens of a town and artisans; merchants and civil servants of higher rank, such as court clerks; patrician families in the cities; knights and the lower nobility; lawyers and university professors; counts and barons.

Leopold's factor in Neuburg had a copy of the pamphlet. He and Marc were wearing clothing entirely suitable for a merchant of modest means and his son, without satin trimming. The lace on their collars was carefully narrower than a joint on the middle finger, but not in the Munich local style. They were, after all, here as foreign tourists.

"If Duke Maximilian had been born English," Leopold commented softly, "he would have made an excellent Puritan. I have read a commentary by a visitor from Holland, written already twenty-five years ago, in which he stated that the members of the duke's court were 'all temperate, strict in morals and upright; every vice is banned at this court; the prince hates drunkards, rascals, and idlers; everything is directed to virtue, temperance, and piety.' It is a pity, in a way, that he is Catholic. He would make a much better Calvinist than the late Stadtholder Maurice of Nassau ever did." More loudly, he commented, "Tomorrow is Thursday. We should be sure to observe the weekly religious procession of all the court officials."

They didn't go all the way to the Isar Gate. Rather, after viewing the city hall, they turned north. Much of the northern portion of the city was taken up by the *Residenz* and the pleasure garden associated with it. They stopped and looked at the more-than-life-sized statue of the Virgin Mary that had been installed in a niche on the facade of the *Residenz* in 1616.

They stood quietly. Any observer would have assumed, respectfully as well, although nothing could have been more alien to Genevan Calvinists. Mary crowned as Mother of God, standing on the sickle of the new moon, a scepter in her left hand, the Christ Child held on her right arm. The child raised his hand as if to bless everyone who entered the city from the nearby Schwäbinger gate. A perpetual flame burned beneath the image.

There was a Latin inscription: *Sub tuum praesidium confugimus, sub quo secure laetique degimus.* Leopold told Marc to translate. There was never any point to getting out of practice with a language once one had gone to the trouble of learning it.

Marc looked at it again and said, a little hesitantly, "'We flee to your protection' or, maybe better, 'we place ourselves under your guidance.' That's the first half. Then, 'beneath which we live safely and happily' or, maybe, 'beneath which we exist securely and joyfully.' Then, at the bottom, '*Patrona Boiariae.*' That's 'patroness of Bavaria.'"

"Not bad. It seems as though your teachers earned their money." Leopold paused, considering the implications of Bavarian Mariology for European politics. "Shall we move on?" They walked as far as the Würtzer Gate, then turned to make a circuit of the inner walls. By the time they finished, Marc was urging that it was time to stop at a streetside grill and get some sausages on buns for lunch. Or something for lunch. He was starving.

They spent some time observing the house of the English Ladies on Paradise Street.

"Why," Marc asked, "couldn't we disguise ourselves as delivery men, like those two?" He gestured at the back alley, where Benno and Korbinian were once more in dispute.

"Why?" Leopold asked. "Because at least one of them, I would presume, is a spy for the Inquisition. Which makes it probable that the other one is a spy for someone else. Possibly the duke; possibly some party in the city whose interests do not run entirely parallel to those of the duke. Who? I could not say yet. Possibly the Jesuits have placed an observer to keep an eye on the other people observing the good ladies. In any case, people would notice if the faces of the deliverymen changed, even in a week in which the local world is turned as nearly upside-down as this one."

"Then," Marc asked, "what do we do?"

"I think," Leopold answered, "that tomorrow I should walk up to the front door and ring the doorbell. I should explain that since we were traveling to Munich in any case, we were asked to bring them some letters that had been forwarded from Perugia to Constance."

This was quite true. In a way. The letters had indeed been passing through Constance on their way to Munich when they were subjected to a small detour in the best interests of *Cavriani Frères*. Also, the letters, if anyone had inspected his luggage and confiscated them at an earlier stage in the trip, were not only genuine, but also quite harmless. The postal clerk had checked.

CHAPTER 40

Schola Cordis

Munich, Bavaria

"If I do not make friends with Duchess Mechthilde, my position in the Bavarian court will be impossible." Maria Anna looked at Countess Polyxena, barely smothering her annoyance. "Trust me, this is true. I am not sufficiently foolish as to deliberately make an enemy of my sister-in-law."

"But," Polyxena protested, "she is only a landgravine." Polyxena was not the most brilliant of the ladies-in-waiting. She owed her position to her father's influential position and her husband's astonishing wealth rather than to any scintillating intellectual qualities of her own. She was extraordinarily status-conscious.

"I," Maria Anna pointed out, "am only an archduchess of Austria. Which did not prevent my sister-in-law Mariana, who is an *infanta* of Spain itself, from taking the trouble to become my friend. So I shall model my conduct on Mariana's and do my very best to live in harmony with Mechthilde." Maria Anna's eyes twinkled. "Even though it may be more difficult."

Everyone knew what she meant. Mariana had come to Austria as the bride of the heir; Maria Anna had been brought to Bavaria to bear a child who would displace the current heir. Who was Mechthilde's husband. And to displace her sons in the succession. It would be harder.

Maria Anna looked at Polyxena, a little sadly. "The difficulty does not mean that I will not try. Don't be a fool. She is older than I; she has had years of experience in this court."

"Naturally," Freiherrin Lukretia wrote to her husband, "the attitude of the archduchess is greatly to be commended for its charity and generosity of spirit. I consider it to be, however, somewhat impractical. There is no reason for her to anticipate anything but continued enmity from Duchess Mechthilde. Nor do I myself see any reason why Duchess Mechthilde *should* feel any other sentiment towards her."

Impractical it might be. Nonetheless, Maria Anna continued to grant Duchess Mechthilde the precedence due to Bavaria's first lady—which she was, of course, and would be until Maria Anna's wedding had been blessed and successfully consummated. Maria Anna sent her an invitation to come to her apartments in the *Residenz* for a private viewing of the Golden Rose.

Mechthilde accepted. As she said frankly to Duke Albrecht, "I can't very well not, without appearing hopelessly ungracious and boorish. Which, given the tense conditions at court right now, we cannot afford."

To her own surprise, Mechthilde found that while she could not bring herself to speak with the archduchess on any basis but that of strict courtesy as demanded by the protocol of the court, she did enjoy the acquaintance of Doña Mencia de Mendoza. They had several very pleasant conversations following that first visit.

It was the third conversation before Doña Mencia subtly sounded Mechthilde out about her motives for bringing the witchcraft charges against Frau Simpson and Frau Dreeson. From Duchess Mechthilde's response, which was oblique and unspecific, Doña Mencia picked up an underlying sense that she was primarily concerned about the position of her sons. The charges seemed to be a ploy on her part to try to get rid of what she perceived as a threat to her, and through her to them—a threat that the bargemen had created by tying the abduction of the two women to Leuchtenberg. Mechthilde reiterated to Doña Mencia that she was convinced that her brother had nothing to do with the kidnapping, was pretty sure that neither of his sons did, and was damned well sure that she herself didn't.

Doña Mencia also picked up hints that Duchess Mechthilde would not be at all sorry to see the two women mysteriously disappear from Bavaria, which would make an end to the immediate problem. These hints led naturally to Mechthilde's mention that she had been, temporarily, serving as patroness of the English Ladies, where Mary and Veronica were staying, since Duchess Elisabeth Renata's death. She asked whether is would be the archduchess' pleasure that she continue to do this, or whether, since it was generally known that the empress took an interest in the Ladies' schools for girls, Maria Anna would prefer to assume this role when she became duchess.

Doña Mencia and Duchess Mechthilde conducted an extensive and mutually beneficial exchange of opinions, as diplomats tended to put it.

Potentially, a mutually profitable one. Immediately, however, they concluded that it would be appropriate for Maria Anna to call upon the English Ladies and officially assure them that as duchess she would continue to extend the court's protection to them, just as the late Duchess Elisabeth Renata had done.

Incidentally, of course, while she was there, she would be able to converse with Frau Simpson and Frau Dreeson, who were, after all, still members of her household.

Maria Anna had not planned on doing it. Spontaneously, during her formal visit to the house on Paradise Street, she invited Mary Ward and the English Ladies to come to the *Residenz* for a private viewing of the Golden Rose.

Their charges, naturally enough, were not free to come. Doña Mencia volunteered to remain with Mary and Veronica during the visit.

Duke Maximilian, upon hearing of this occurrence after the fact, requested the *Hofmeister* to inform Archduchess Maria Anna of his strong preference that the family apartments not be opened to outside visitors. The members of this order, while they came from Catholic families of good social standing in England, were not of a rank that justified their admission to the future duchess' parlor, much less her bedchamber and oratory.

Maria Anna was far from being in the confidence of Uncle Max. She had not had a private conversation with him since arriving in Bavaria. She had not really had a public dialogue with him since the hearing. Still, other people told her things. One of those things was the increasing influence of Dr. Richel in the privy council. Supposedly, which was probably the reason that someone brought the rumors to her attention, he had made statements in regard to Frau Simpson and Frau Dreeson who, although now residing with the English Ladies, were still formally under her protection. Richel continued to urge upon Duke Maximilian the principle that there was no obligation of conscience to keep the faith with heretics.

Father Vervaux had again reminded him that the Dreeson woman was a Catholic. Richel retorted that she was married to a Calvinist whose country was allied with the Lutheran Swede. Second, he added, since the conversion of the Upper Palatinate in the 1620s had been more or less compulsory, it was entirely possible that she was only a Catholic of convenience and not a Catholic at heart. This would be a situation no different, in essence, from that of the secret Jews and Muslims of Spain, with whom the Most Catholic Monarchs had kept no faith at all. There was, therefore, he concluded with some satisfaction, a precedent.

In less than a week, she would be married to Uncle Max. In the hierarchy of being, he would as her husband be unto her as Christ was to the church, as the sun was to the moon; he would be her lord. She would be obliged to bow to his opinions in all things, including the handling of the two women.

She arranged to meet Father Vervaux through Duchess Mechthilde. She told Mechthilde how unhappy she was at not having confessed since leaving Austria; Mechthilde had mentioned that her sons' tutor had performed this office for the late Duchess Elisabeth Renata.

Surely, Maria Anna thought, Uncle Max could not, then, take offense if she requested that Father Vervaux confess her. He was, clearly, qualified to perform this office for a duchess of Bavaria. There could be no anonymity in such a relationship, of course; all her life, she had known who her confessor was, and he had known her. This was standard, in all courts.

It was after confession that she asked him about the rumor. Uncle Max, she heard, in opening the daily session of his privy council, was omitting the rosary of thanks for the pope's safe deliverance from the assassination attempt. She said that she thought that this report could not be correct. Father Vervaux confirmed that it was.

He also told her that Father Contzen had come down with a serious gallstone attack, sufficiently debilitating that he was not, for the time being, able to participate in the privy council discussions or perform his duties as confessor for the duke, who had sent for a temporary replacement.

"Is this confidential," Maria Anna asked, "or will it be generally known who the replacement is?"

"It is no secret," Vervaux answered. "It is Father Forer."

Maria Anna almost gasped, but checked herself. Father Lorenz Forer, S.J. He was a famous controversialist, a protegé of Heinrich von Knoeringen, the bishop of Augsburg, a bitter, unremitting, and unrelenting opponent of the Lutherans and all other heretics. This choice was not a good omen for peace. The faculty at the University of Dillingen, the institution of higher education in the Diocese of Augsburg, were generally well known for advocacy of refusal to compromise with the heretics and insistence that in no way should toleration for the Calvinists be included in any treaty provisions aimed at ending the war.

After her second confession, Maria Anna asked Vervaux the same question that she had asked Father Lamormaini, about the temporal possessions of the church *vs.* losing one's soul. Vervaux temporized. Obviously, rulers had a moral obligation to re-Catholicize a region when possible. He talked briefly about his experiences in the Duchy of Saarwerden in 1631. On the other hand, in instances where this was not possible...

Vervaux's voice trailed off.

Maria Anna waited.

"Your Grace, you must realize that what I am going to say next is my opinion. There are many, even within my own order, who do not share it."

"Granted, Father Vervaux."

"If it is necessary, in order to bring peace to the empire, I do believe that the emperor and the church should agree to the unconditional transfer of former one-time Catholic dioceses and abbeys to the Protestant territories that already are in effective possession of them. I believe, that in the interests of peace, the Edict of Restitution should be revoked."

"And the Calvinists?"

"There is no possibility for peace if they are not included within the provisions of the Peace of Augsburg."

The seamstress removed the heavy, formal, court costume, all sixty pounds of it, leaving the archduchess in her shift.

"Frau Stecher," Maria Anna said.

"Yes, Your Highness."

"I am extraordinarily tired. Since you say that you are entirely finished with all the last-minute work for the dress I will be wearing to dinner, complete the fittings for my ladies-in-waiting somewhere other than my private apartments. Go. All of you. Find some other place. Doña Mencia will remain with me until it is time to dress. I must get some rest."

Dinner, at the Bavarian court, took place strictly and regularly at mid-day. At mid-day in July, Munich could be very hot. Today, it was.

Frau Stecher looked profoundly offended, but was not in a position to defy a direct order. "Yes, Your Grace." Then, "Susanna, if anyone is using the empty room in the next corridor, tell them that I have need of it." She gathered up her notions and her apprentices, backing out of the room after the young noblewomen as Doña Mencia brought Maria Anna a loose, lightweight, robe.

Maria Anna sighed with profound relief. This was the first time since entering Bavaria that she had been alone with Doña Mencia.

Doña Mencia was thinking the same thing in reverse. It was the first time she had been alone with the archduchess. For the past weeks, private conversation had been almost impossible. Perhaps it was just the unavoidable crowding when traveling, perhaps the strict protocol of the Bavarian court. She suspected, however, that Ferdinand II had instructed any of several members of Maria Anna's household to prevent them from being alone with one another. Especially that perpetual and incredibly annoying chatterbox, Countess Polyxena. They couldn't very well throw her out of the room. The Holy Roman Emperor, perpetually strapped for cash, owed her husband too much money.

She had to start the conversation immediately. She had a lot to say and it was far from impossible that one of the other ladies-in-waiting would return as soon as her fitting was completed rather than staying to gossip and giggle with the rest. *Start it some way.*

Doña Mencia drew a breath. "I have received a reply to your question, Your Grace."

"Which question?"

"The one that you had me send to my brother, Cardinal Bedmar."

"Please be so kind as to share it with me."

Doña Mencia pulled the letter from her pocket. "You are welcome to read it all."

"The answer to the question first, please."

"Many people would like to have their cake and eat it too. This is rarely possible in life. There is no question that if we must take a bargain, either the right to make our best effort to save souls or the right to keep ecclesiastical power and property as they have accrued in the centuries since the conversion of the Emperor Constantine, the only morally acceptable choice is that we opt for the salvation of souls. Otherwise we have no right to call ourselves the disciples of the savior who died for us."

Doña Mencia folded the letter and put it back in her pocket. "He has provided citations from the church fathers and canon lawyers for his conclusion."

Maria Anna reached out her hand for the letter. Doña Mencia gave it to her.

"You realize, Your Grace, that you are not the only one who is asking this question. Nor are you the only one who is asking similar questions, as this war drags on. My brother is advising Don Fernando in the Netherlands. Some resolution must be reached there and it cannot be a legalistic reading of the 1555 Peace of Augsburg, which gave only the Lutherans rights within the Holy Roman Empire along with the Catholics. Don Fernando must deal with Fredrik Hendrik, who is indubitably a Calvinist. As are his subjects in the north."

"Papa will never agree to extend the terms of the Peace of Augsburg to cover more Protestants. He wishes to make it ever narrower."

"Your Highness." Doña Mencia paused. "Your Highness, it is possible that the emperor's intransigence may lead to the signing of separate peace treaties between various German princes and the Swede. Without his concurrence. Which in turn . . ."

Maria Anna nodded. Her brother Ferdinand had reached that conclusion also. "Which in turn may ring the death knell of an empire that has, however imperfectly, endured for eight hundred years. And with its death, of course, the Peace of Augsburg would lose effect. It is possible that Papa may be the last Holy Roman Emperor. That my brother Ferdinand may never be elected King of the Romans before Papa dies." She lifted her chin. "Ferdinand is considering what to do if that happens. And much of the Hungarian leadership is also Calvinist."

She didn't have the right to say any more than that.

Doña Mencia was a little surprised that the emperor's two oldest children had actually discussed the possibility openly, even with one another.

Then Maria Anna said, "I do not believe that Uncle Max would be at all happy if the electoral vote for which he fought so long and hard turns out to have no meaning. He will be very angry if he never gets to exercise it after Papa has given it to him. If there are no more elections, then it will also be meaningless that his brother in Cologne holds an electoral vote. If there is no longer a Holy Roman Empire, the position of *die Habsburgerin* in the Wittelsbach court will not be an easy one."

Doña Mencia really had not intended to do it. She reached into her pocket again, and brought out the other item that had been in the bag the courier gave her just before she reached Passau. The rather obsolete note from Don Fernando in which he wrote in his own hand that a marriage with Archduchess Maria Anna of Austria would be his first choice.

Then, after Maria Anna had read them, she took back both of the letters. "I am sorry, Your Highness. But I do not believe that you have any secure place for these. The other morning while you were eating breakfast, Susanna Allegretti had reason to enter your oratory, to return the kneeler that you sent for repair. There was someone in the room, in the livery of one of the footmen, flipping through the pages of your Book of Hours, as if looking for hidden notes or letters. She didn't recognize him; there was no way to know whether he was sent by the court of Vienna or by the duke or . . ."

Maria Anna finished the sentence. "Or by the Bavarian ecclesiastical council. Or even by the Holy Office. I do not have the standing in the Bavarian court that Aunt Elisabeth Renata held. Or that Mama has at home. I have not earned the status, the prestige. I do not have the support from Uncle Max that will keep me out of the shadow of the Inquisition, now that I have offered my patronage to the English Ladies. Not even Carafa, not even the nuncio, would be able to prevent them from taking an interest in me. Not even if he tried."

Doña Mencia greeted the emissary from *Dekan* Golla. She apologized. She was sorry to inconvenience the friar, who was representing the man who had administrative authority over all of Munich's churches, but the archduchess was at prayer. If she could be of assistance in any way . . .

"I wish," the emissary said, "to see the archduchess at prayer, to confirm that this is indeed the case. Just to see her; I do not need to interrupt her meditations. Not, of course, that I doubt your assurances. However, a question has arisen in the confines of the Holy Office in regard to the archduchess' contacts with the foreign witches."

Doña Mencia was well aware that Duke Maximilian had determined that there was insufficient evidence to bring an indictment against Frau Simpson and Frau Dreeson for witchcraft. She did not, however, think it was prudent to bring that up at the moment. Beckoning Countess Polyxena to accompany them—as stupid as the girl seemed to be, Polyxena was one of those she suspected of having been placed in Maria Anna's household at the behest of Father Lamormaini—she led the Capuchin into the archduchess' bedchamber, across it, and silently opened the door to the smaller cubicle that had been intended to serve as a dressing room.

The archduchess had arranged it as an oratory, containing her prie-dieu and several of her favorite votive pictures. She was kneeling; there could be no question that it was she, since she turned her face toward the door when it opened. She was halfway through a rosary; the golden rose lay on the reading pedestal where she would ordinarily place her Book of Hours; that lay closed on a small table beside her.

Doña Mencia stood quietly while the Capuchin watched; he then nodded his head and withdrew.

"Would you care to schedule an appointment with the archduchess? I am sure that she would be willing to receive you."

"Thank you, gracious lady, but I do not believe that it will be necessary." He withdrew into the corridor.

"What was that all about?" Countess Polyxena asked.

"I don't know," Doña Mencia answered. "I can only suspect. As, probably, you can as well." She did not define her suspicions.

Maria Anna completed the interrupted rosary; then folded her hands and bowed her head. Thus far, her meditations had led to only one conclusion.

She had to make an important decision. She was the only person who could make it.

She realized that this was the first time she had ever been in this position. For the entire quarter century of her life, every important decision in regard to her existence had been made by someone else; by Papa and Mama; by her tutors; by the privy council.

She had dreamed that some day she would become a formidable Habsburg regent. What justification did she have for that dream? A regent had to assume heavy responsibility; a regent issued orders that affected not only herself, not only her immediate household, but the people of the territory entrusted to her care. How could you make wise decisions for others, when you had never made a decision for yourself? What good did the preparation do, the training in the names and functions of monarchs, magnates, and important counselors? What good, if you had never in fact made an important decision and accepted the consequences. Had never, on many days, even decided what to wear. Had rarely decided what to eat. Had never decided who your attendants would be.

She could request certain ladies, but she did not control their appointments. Had never decided where she would live or what rooms would be assigned her. She kneeled, stripping herself one by one of every delusion she had ever had in regard to power and authority.

The decision she must make would not just affect her. It would affect—she paused. Papa, certainly, and through Papa, Mama; her sister and brothers, her sister-in-law and nephew. Uncle Max; no, call him by what he was now, her betrothed husband. Don Fernando, her cousin, in the Netherlands; through him, his brother of Spain. Her own ladies and the other members of her household; the advisers and counselors of all the others; from there, in a dizzying spiral, other political powers, the Swede, Wallenstein. She pulled herself back from that abyss before its confusion could swallow her.

She looked at the golden rose lying before her. It would affect the pope and the church itself.

She looked at her folded hands. The easy decision was to stay. That was the decision that had already been made for her, of course. But if, this day, she made a conscious determination to follow the path that others had laid out for her, that would still be a decision. Because, now, there was another possibility. She had a chance to reach out, to grasp that prepared path, to make it her own.

She thought of her conversation with the Spanish courtier Saavedra and judiciary chancellor Abegg. A path along which accused witches would burn if she were not fertile.

She bowed her head. She faced a life in which the husband who had been chosen for her turned his face away. In another world, according to the *encyclopedia* articles that Don Fernando sent, Aunt Elisabeth Renata had lived one more year. It had been a hard, bitter year during which she had been relentlessly attacked by the cancer. A hard, bitter year during which Uncle Max, although grieving, had made his farewells and, if he had not welcomed, had at least accepted that it was a mercy when God granted death to end his wife's suffering. In this world, Elisabeth Renata had been taken so fast. Uncle Max would not easily forgive his advisers for thrusting a second wife upon him before he had a chance to mourn the first.

Nor would he easily forgive his second wife, if at all, if ever, for being alive when Aunt Elisabeth Renata was dead. There. She admitted what she had known in her heart for these past weeks; what she had known since the ceremony at Passau.

It would, according to the *encyclopedias*, be a long marriage. Uncle Max was sixty-one now; he would live for eighteen more years.

Papa had not mentioned that. It was impossible to believe that Papa had not known. Father Lamormaini had not mentioned that. It was impossible to believe that he, too, had not known.

She could not rely upon those she had trusted. If they believed that withholding the truth would make her more malleable to their wishes, they would withhold it. That was a thing that she knew. She could not know why they did it, whether for good motives or for ill. She could know *that* they did it. This was something that she knew.

The other possible course of action . . .

Father Drexel's words came back to her. "If you are assigned the role of beggar, then play that person slyly and artfully." What role had God assigned her in this world that was a stage?

"The most beautiful and praiseworthy thing a man can do before he dies is to devote his life to the untiring performance of virtuous acts, constantly seeking to practice prudence, justice, moderation, endurance; faith, hope, and unselfish love." Presumably, it was the best thing a woman could do also. How could she best serve the church?

Maria Anna bowed her head in prayer; her eyes focused again on the golden rose that lay before her. She took out her rosary.

It was expected that everyone in the *Residenz* be in bed by ten o'clock in the evening at the latest.

Doña Mencia sent the ladies-in-waiting to bed; she, herself, continued watching. At midnight, she replaced the archduchess' candle; she performed this small service twice more during the night.

Just at dawn, Maria Anna rose stiffly from her prie-dieu, walked out of the oratory, and put her hand gently on Doña Mencia's shoulder, shaking it.

"Dress me for mass, please. And try to create some time, today, for us to speak privately again. We must make our plans."

CHAPTER 41

Sursum Corda

Munich, Bavaria

Through her chief attendant, Doña Mencia de Mendoza, Archduchess Maria Anna expressed a wish to spend some time viewing the
duke's formal gardens. This was not surprising; her stepmother,
Empress Eleonora, was known to be an enthusiastic gardener. The
Hofmeister arranged it promptly. He had been ordered to extend
every reasonable courtesy to the future duchess. The duke had
not rescinded those orders in spite of the reprimand he had sent
her in regard to the visit by the English Ladies.

Maria Anna announced, to the great joy of the gardeners,
that she had been highly pleased with the excursion. She would,
if possible, walk in the gardens for a half hour after mass each
morning, granted that the weather permitted.

The *Hofmeister* saw no reason why this would not be possible.
The gardens were well-secured and he had been notified by his
counterpart in Vienna that the archduchess was fond of outdoor
exercise. He arranged this also. It was not the sort of task for which
he needed to consult the duke or the privy council, after all.

After their conversation in the *Hofgarten*, Doña Mencia set out
to mastermind the escape plot. In very short order, the archduchess' household was effectively divided into two categories: people

whom Maria Anna trusted and those whom she did not trust at all. With a few in the middle concerning whom, despite her shrewdness, her opinion wavered. However, by consulting Doña Mencia and, for the lower servants, Susanna Allegretti, she drew a line. Her advisers were firm; those about whom she wavered must, necessarily, be included among those whom she did not trust. Maria Anna made that decision.

Her personal escort was large. After all, marrying into Bavaria was just like moving next door. Her father had not expected to have to pay the expenses of a long journey to bring her household home again when they were replaced by Bavarians of Duke Maximilian's choosing, so he had been generous.

Freiherrin Lukretia was within her circle; Countess Polyxena was not. Frau Stecher most definitely was not. It largely fell to Doña Mencia to think up ways and means to occupy those outside the circle somewhere else. Errands; lots of errands.

Within the circle, protocol fell by the wayside. It was hard enough to plot without trying to insist that everyone strictly abide by court etiquette at the same time.

"In all the plays," Susanna said, "the princess disguises herself as her maid. Then the maid takes her place." She made this contribution to the discussion with considerable self-satisfaction for having thought of it.

Maria Anna looked at Doña Mencia and then at Susanna. She raised her eyebrows.

"Oh," Susanna said.

Neither of them qualified as a double for the archduchess: Doña Mencia was more than thirty years older; Susanna was about eight inches shorter.

For that matter, Maria Anna pointed out, none of the noble ladies-in-waiting whom she trusted qualified as a double. Freiherrin Lukretia, for example, was several months pregnant. Freiherrin Helena was blonde. It wasn't as if modern court ladies went around with their heads and faces swathed in yards of cloth, like a nun back in the period the humanists called the *media aeva* that had happened between the glories of the ancients and the modern revival of learning. She had been on public display every day since her arrival in Bavaria, surrounded by her ladies-in-waiting. That was what ladies-in-waiting were for at public events. They stood in a bevy around their mistress, looking decorative, so the people of the court or city, town or village, could admire their clothes. By now, a large number of Bavarians had seen the faces of all of them. Some from a distance, such as the people who lined the procession route; others, however, up close, such as the chambermaids in the palaces at which the entourage had stopped overnight. Duke Maximilian's guards had seen their faces many times. As had his prominent officials, courtiers, their wives, and the waiters who served their meals.

"There is something to be said," Doña Mencia said, "in favor of disguise in plain sight. Like playing 'hide the thimble.'"

"The *Hofmeister* has spoken to me," Maria Anna said to her ladies-in-waiting. "These are, after all, guest quarters—not where we will be living after the wedding. He wishes to consult with us about our preferences. For this duty, I have detailed Doña Mencia; the constant standing during official functions is, in any case, a hardship on her." She smiled affectionately.

"Thus, for the purposes of such functions, I need to appoint one of you as her deputy."

She looked around the circle. Officially, this would be a great honor for one of them. Practically, it would keep one of them from snooping.

"Countess Polyxena, you will please assume this duty for the time being."

The countess nodded. "Of course, Your Highness. Thank you." It was the kind of request that she couldn't refuse. Not even if she had wanted to. She didn't want to. It was only temporary, of course, but possibly a stepping-stone to greater things, to a permanent position as chief attendant if Doña Mencia chose to request permission to retire.

"Freiherrin Lukretia, in view of your condition," Maria Anna smiled, "please be so kind as to assist Doña Mencia with the housing arrangements. The constant standing cannot be easy for you, either."

Countess Polyxena smothered a smile. The other obvious candidate to succeed Doña Mencia was also being pushed to the side.

"Fräulein Ward," Duchess Mechthilde said. "I believe that you may place confidence in Archduchess Maria Anna. And in Doña

Mencia de Mendoza. If they bring to your attention a method by which Mary Simpson and Veronica Dreeson might be privately removed from your custody and returned to the United States of Europe, there is no reason for you to be afraid that this is a trap."

Mechthilde sighed. "All things considered, I will also be glad to be rid of the Grantville women. The allegation that my brother supposedly had them kidnapped is not making my position easier. If it were true, which I am sure that it is not, it would have been very imprudent of him."

"How," Mary Ward asked, "can the archduchess and Doña Mencia arrange to have them taken them out of this house without our being held culpable?"

"That," Mechthilde answered, "is their problem. Not mine."

She thought for a moment, finally realizing what the other woman had meant.

"Of course, if they do not think of a way to do it that absolves you and your sisters from complicity, then it will certainly still be yours. The Inquisition would be all too happy to have one more reason to doubt your orthodoxy and obedience."

Mary Ward sat quietly for a moment. Then, "Your Grace?"

Mechthilde inclined her head.

"I am speaking to you in the greatest confidence."

"As long as you are not speaking outright treason, I will keep your words private."

"The pope has directed us to leave Bavaria. We were planning our removal before Mrs. Simpson and Mrs. Dreeson were placed in our custody. I have been comforted by your efforts to obtain the archduchess' patronage and benevolence for our school, and truly grateful. I have also been, privately, a little upset that you were, without knowing it, further risking your credit with the duke on our behalf. He will not be happy when we leave. Your kindness and charity to us will be one more source of trouble for you."

"Thank you for the warning." Mechthilde paused. "I must, I think, mention your plans to leave to Doña Mencia de Mendoza. If she and the archduchess have already made a plan to smuggle these women out of Bavaria, then it needs to be coordinated with your departure. If the Grantville women leave first and it is discovered, then you will be trapped in Munich indefinitely. Probably not in the comfort of your own house, but as guests of the Inquisition."

✧   ✧   ✧

Doña Mencia felt a little confused, for a moment. She had been making plans, true. But not plans to smuggle Frau Simpson and Frau Dreeson out of the house of the English Ladies.

To Duchess Mechthilde, she said only, "Thank you for letting me know the Ladies' plans."

"Just take them with you." Doña Mencia looked at Mary Ward. "Take them *with* us?"

"Yes. Don't announce a pilgrimage to Ettal; don't announce anything. It wouldn't be reasonable while these women are your 'guests.' Just let everyone assume that you have no plans at all to do anything unusual. You have no other guests to complicate things, since those whom Father Rader had planned to lodge in this house during the wedding have been put somewhere else.

"Just, on the day of the production of *Belisarius*, leave. The whole city will be in chaos; the gates will be opening early in the morning; people will be going in and out, around and about, in costume; the town will be full of tourists and other strangers. Just walk out of the gate and onto the *Nürnberger Strasse* dressed as ordinary working women. Not dressed, as you usually do, befitting your rank, as if you were the wives and sisters of prosperous merchants or lower nobility, with high hats and capes. Dress as the wives of butchers and rope-makers, the wives of carpenters and shoemakers. Dress as women who might well be employed to go out to the camp of baggage wagons to bring in things needed at the last minute. Just add your involuntary guests to your group."

"Where would we get this clothing?" Mary Ward asked.

"This, I think, Duchess Mechthilde can provide. She has a large household with many servants. A Munich household, with servants from Munich, who dress in the local style."

Mary Ward smiled. "The more I think about it, the more I like the idea. Father Rader and Father Drexel can still help. And, if Duchess Mechthilde can't obtain clothing without arousing suspicion, they can help with our 'costuming' as well. You are quite right; there is not going to be any day that gives a better chance for quite a few people who are, ah, not quite themselves, to be moving around the city unobserved. Not that we are a huge group, but there will still be a dozen or so."

✧   ✧   ✧

Marc Cavriani was repairing a wrought iron fence. The fence surrounded a small garden; the small garden, not more than four feet wide, was in front of a town house on Paradise Street. The owners of the town house had rented it to several parties of travelers for the wedding festivities; they, themselves, had gone to the country for two weeks. There was nobody to raise questions about who had hired someone to repair the fence, or whose journeyman was doing it. In any case, the whole city was being repaired and prepared for the festivities. The owners were lucky to have found someone to do the work this week.

What was more, the fence needed to be fixed and, thanks to Jacob Durre, Marc was perfectly capable of fixing it. Barefoot, wearing a loose-necked unbleached shirt that had seen better days and tan leather knee britches in the same condition, he occasionally glanced up from his work to observe the people who entered by and left through the front door of the English Ladies house.

If he ran out of fence—he glanced up—the wrought iron grilles on the windows could benefit from some attention also. That, of course, would require a ladder.

He had not seen Mary Simpson and Veronica Dreeson; that was scarcely to be expected. They were interned. They wouldn't be coming in and out.

If he had a ladder, however, he might be able to glance into the windows on the upper floors. He took another look at the ornamental bars on the windows, then walked down the alley and looked at the grilles on the side windows. The owners of this house had really let it run down. He clucked disapprovingly.

Leopold Cavriani toyed with his quill pen. He could make very little sense out of Marc's reports. That the archduchess had made one call, in the company of Duchess Mechthilde, made sense. That her attendant, Doña Mencia, had called repeatedly made some sense, if there were still negotiations regarding the custody of Mary Simpson and Veronica Dreeson going on.

Leopold himself had delivered the letters he was carrying. He had been admitted only to the vestibule; there had clearly been no way that he could contact Mary and Veronica if they were in some other part of the house. They did not come to the school rooms, of course.

Marc could not abandon his post and follow when the English Ladies themselves left the house. He, himself, could only follow one pair at a time. To play rehearsals; to the Jesuit *collegium*; to market; to play rehearsals; to the apartments of Duchess Mechthilde.

The whole pattern made very little sense. Or, more precisely, and worse, he could not determine the pattern. Nor had he found a way to contact Mary and Veronica.

He was sure of very little. He was quite sure that both the produce man and the fishmonger were spies. The produce man, almost certainly, for the Holy Office; he had traced him to *Dekan* Golla's office more than once. The fishmonger was more careful. After leaving the house on Paradise Street, he merely continued his deliveries for the remainder of the day.

Leopold thought. Possibly, he was not taking information out. Possibly, he was bringing it in. But, if so, from whom, and why?

He rearranged the order of the names in front of him.

Susanna Allegretti went back and forth from the *Residenz* to the house on Paradise Street several times. Once, to measure the ladies, including their feet. Then, after she had taken the list of sizes to Duchess Mechthilde, with a box of clothing from the store of servants' discards that the duchess had gathered for donation to charity. Again, after she had been to the play costumer with a note from Father Rader, with more clothing, including several plain doublets with pointed fronts in the style that market women wore.

Then again.

Marc Cavriani watched her come and go.

She watched the iron smith who was repairing the house next door to that of the Ladies, also. She shouldn't; she knew that. It wasn't at all proper. But she peeked.

After the fourth trip, Mary Ward gave her a key to the back door of the house on Paradise Street. The girl had her own duties in the archduchess' household; the hours when she was not required by her mistress were erratic. With a key, she could come and go with the various boxes and satchels even when the cook had returned to her own home for the night and the Ladies were performing their offices.

The produce man reported to the Inquisition only what he learned from the cook: that a girl was frequently coming back and forth, bringing costumes for the school's pupils who would be taking part in the play.

That was true, as far as it went. The costumer saw no reason to waste an additional volunteer who had been sent by Father Rader.

The day before the play, the English Ladies sent each student's play costume home with her.

"You will leave in the morning on the day of the play," Doña Mencia said to the twenty-three people gathered around her, "those of you who will not be expected to attend it. Draw your straws from the blue cup.

"The rest of you, in the evening. After the play. Draw your straws from the brown cup.

"You will not let anyone else know which group you are in. Beyond what we all know, that all of you will leave Munich that day, each group of you will determine how, when, and what direction you will go, from which gate, and under what guise.

"Do you understand me? You will not, absolutely not, tell anyone else here who will be going with you or the route that you plan to take after you leave the city."

She held out the cups. Some of the parties would be all women; the archduchess naturally had more females in her household than males; some would be mixed; the number of people in each varied from three to five. The chances were very high that most would try to go directly to the Austrian border. Some, perhaps, would have more imagination.

Maria Anna was not going to know that, either. She had made the decision that it was safer for them if she did not know. She was practicing making decisions.

Naturally, somebody told somebody. One of Freiherrin Lukretia's laundresses, a thirtyish woman named Edigna, had been courted rather assiduously since her arrival in Munich by a prosperous fishmonger named Korbinian. She could not bear to part from him without saying goodbye and giving him her father's address. Hope sprang eternal.

She did, at least, only tell him that *she* would be leaving. She personally. She didn't even say that her mistress would be leaving, much less that a larger exodus was planned.

Korbinian, naturally enough, informed Duchess Mechthilde.

This was, after all, the kind of information for which she paid him so well. He kept the address; he found Edigna to be a *very* attractive woman. Not the daughter of a fishmonger, of course, but almost worth marrying out of the guild. Maybe worth marrying out of the guild. Almost certainly worth marrying out of the guild, given her court connections.

Mechthilde reflected for some time. Why would one of the archduchess' servants be leaving the city? Mary Ward had not informed her of this. Why not?

Of course, Korbinian never told her that the English Ladies were planning to leave the city, either. He didn't know. It was easy enough to miss a detail or two when you were a wagon driver getting your information from a cook. Fräulein Ward had been sufficiently prudent to continue her advance orders, essentially unchanged, for the next couple of weeks, just as usual.

Possibly, therefore, Mary Ward did not know that the archduchess' servant was leaving. If one was leaving, was it possible that others would also be leaving? Mechthilde thought that she should mention this to Fräulein Ward; this might well be a complication to the English Ladies' plans.

"I am not fully in their confidence," Duchess Mechthilde admitted.

Mary Ward did not panic. It was against her principles. If she had permitted herself to do so, she would have panicked right now. She stared at Duchess Mechthilde.

"What is going on? Do you know?"

"All I definitely know, at the moment, is that when I hinted to Doña Mencia that I had heard about their own departure plans—not, as I had suspected, plans to remove the two Grantville women—they called in the laundress, who admitted to Freiherrin Lukretia what she had done. The freiherrin herself has now publicly announced plans to leave. She states that she believes that she has estimated the due date for her child wrongly and that she should return to Austria now. That isn't bad, actually. It will cover the laundress' statement very well, if she said anything to anyone else, other than the fishmonger. Which I do not believe that she did."

Mary Ward thought a moment. "The freiherrin? Short-sighted, with spectacles?"

"Yes, that's the one. She came with the archduchess although she was pregnant. She thought that, at six months, she would have plenty of time to see her mistress through the wedding and then return home."

Mary Ward snorted. "Estimated wrongly? I have seen her. Celibate that I am, I would say that she is at least six weeks farther along than that. What odds that the freiherr urged his wife to nudge the calculations a little, so that she might have the honor of attending the archduchess to her wedding? But, perhaps, I am being unfair. Perhaps she is carrying twins."

Mechthilde, all too well aware of the constant jostling for position among her own attendants, smiled sourly. "The question is—are others among the archduchess' attendants leaving? If so, why? I think that I need to have another chat with Doña Mencia."

"Why are the archduchess' other attendants planning to leave?" Mechthilde asked.

"We have some concerns," Doña Mencia said slowly. "The other afternoon, a representative of *Dekan* Golla called upon the archduchess while she was at prayer, in connection with her meetings with the English Ladies. He demanded—courteously enough, but demanded—to confirm with his own eyes that she was at prayer. The archduchess is concerned about the safety of her household. She has decided that those who can be spared should return to Austria now, to the protection of her father."

Doña Mencia watched to see how this would be received. Not with full acceptance.

"And why the secrecy?" Duchess Mechthilde raised her eyebrows.

Doña Mencia swallowed. *In for a penny, in for a pound*, she thought. Then—in a crisis, why does a person's mind always fill up with proverbs? Because the same idea has come to so many other people? Because proverbs embody useful, generally applicable, principles? Mental shorthand? "I have concerns for the safety of the archduchess herself."

That should be ambiguous enough. Let the other woman draw her own conclusions.

Mechthilde thought. From Albrecht, she knew what had been going on in the privy council. Duke Maximilian's dissatisfaction after the formal hearing . . . *die Habsburgerin* . . . That the archduchess might actually be considering fleeing from Munich and returning home to Vienna was almost beyond belief. But, if she was . . .

My sons, my sons. This was not something that she could tell Albrecht. Not now. Not ever. Albrecht was a very loyal brother.

"If . . . If you have reason to believe that these concerns are serious, Doña Mencia, I . . . By no means do I wish any harm to come to the archduchess. Perhaps you are being overly cautious. Nonetheless . . . Possibly, because of my greater familiarity with the situation here . . . If you believe that she is in need of assistance . . ." Mechthilde realized that she sounded half-incoherent; her mind was moving much faster than her mouth.

Doña Mencia nodded gravely. *Swallowed, hook, line, and sinker.* Now if she could only maintain Mechthilde's assumption that the archduchess would be returning to Vienna . . .

"No, I haven't seen either Frau Simpson or Frau Dreeson yet. But, certainly, they have not been removed from the English Ladies' house by daylight. I don't think that they have been taken out at night either. I'm not sure what is going on, Papa," Marc said. "There is much more activity than usual. But no special anxiety, if that is what one would want to call it. It is possible, of course, that the play may explain it. The girls from the school come to have their costumes fitted; the sisters go with them to the *Schrannenplatz*, but I have a funny feeling."

Leopold looked at his son. This was a fine thing. Funny feelings—*informed* funny feelings—were among the firm's most valuable assets.

"Is there any way that you can arrange to sleep inside the gates? Not just anywhere at random. Somewhere you will not be noticed, but from which you can observe the house on Paradise Street?"

"Well, I can't very well settle on the street itself and pretend to be a beggar. Too many people in the neighborhood have seen me for too many days." Marc thought a moment. "There is a lean-to against the back of the house across the alley. I don't know what use it is meant for, but I've never seen anyone go into it. It's locked, but the hinges are just leather." He grinned. "Which leads me to suspect that the contents are of little value to their owner. The day always comes when an old leather hinge finally splits and lets a gate or door sag."

He thought again. "It's not expensive for the owner to repair, either. Not as if I broke the lock."

"Even knowing that it will happen the day of the production of *Belisarius* is too much. I don't," Duchess Mechthilde said, "want to know any more about it. At all."

Doña Mencia felt that this was an admirable decision. She smiled.

"However," Mechthilde continued. "If someone should be intending to stay behind to give, for as long as possible, the impression that the archduchess is still in her apartments?"

Doña Mencia nodded.

"If the person chose to stay behind partly because of a sense of responsibility to her mistress, but also, partly, because her knees will not permit her to walk the roads of Bavaria with any briskness and she fears that her presence with them would endanger the others?"

Doña Mencia nodded again.

"It might be possible, when discovery is imminent, for that person to seek sanctuary in Duke Albrecht's household. Coming through the back way, through the servants' corridors. Until such time as we next go to one of the rural palaces for hunting, perhaps? There are always numerous attendants with us. From someplace like Schleissheim, it is far easier for people to come and go unobserved than from here at the *Residenz*."

"That is very generous of you, Your Grace."

Doña Mencia had become quite resigned to the likelihood that her loyalty to Maria Anna—her loyalty to her brother, Cardinal Bedmar, as well, of course—would cost her her head in the foreseeable future.

That she might keep it was . . . an interesting possibility.

CHAPTER 42

Effugium Admirabile

Munich, Bavaria

"Yes, I am."

"No, you are not."

"Am."

"*Not!*"

"*Am!*"

Doña Mencia sighed. These morning walks through the *Hofgarten* severely stressed her knees, especially when the archduchess became agitated and started striding at full speed. "With all due apologies, Your Grace, you are being foolish. Someone *must* remain in your apartments to carry through with the cover story of your illness."

Maria Anna's expression could only be described as mulish. "I am not leaving you behind."

"You are. You will. Or you will greatly endanger not only yourself, but all of the other members of your household who have supported you and who are leaving to make their way back home." Doña Mencia made her voice as firm as she could while still keeping it soft enough that no one else could hear her.

Maria Anna looked at her. *It is your clear duty. It is God's will.* The voices that had surrounded her all her life were not gone. The only difference, it seemed, was that now they lived in Doña

369

Mencia rather than in Papa, Mama, and Father Lamormaini, her tutors and her governesses.

"They will arrest you. And . . ."

"It is to be hoped," Doña Mencia said, "that they will not. And that is all you need to know, Your Grace. Just carry that hope in your heart."

It was so close to the time to leave, Maria Anna thought, that she could risk offending Frau Stecher. More than, for some reason, her very existence appeared to offend Frau Stecher.

As the dressmaker adjusted the high, stiff, lace-edged collar for the dress she would wear to attend the play, Maria Anna suddenly threw her head back.

"Ouch! Frau Stecher, that was not called for."

"What was not called for, Your Grace?"

"You poked me. And hard."

Frau Stecher began to protest that she had done no such thing.

"Leave the room. At once!" snapped the archduchess. "Let Susanna Allegretti remain behind to complete the fitting. Her hands are more delicate."

Maria Anna had never before had the joy of giving in to an unreasonable temper tantrum, but she thought that she was doing it rather well. Especially since, if she didn't manage to do it perfectly, everyone else would just put it down to pre-wedding nerves. Three more days to the wedding.

"Everyone else, too. Out!"

Doña Mencia remained behind.

"That means you, too! And close the door behind you."

Doña Mencia left.

Such a responsibility! From the archduchess herself!

Susanna's hands shook as she inserted the pins at the base of the collar. They had to be just right if the stitching was to cause it to stand at the correct angle, framing the archduchess' face.

"You do understand?"

"Yes, Your Grace. I understand. When I join the others in the group of which I am a member, I am to tell them that we do not leave Munich right away. We are to wait, somewhere that we ourselves decide. We are to wait until Doña Mencia cannot keep up the deception any longer. Then we are to make sure that she gets away safely. Upon our most sacred honor."

"That," Maria Anna said, "is definitely the general idea. If you have trouble persuading the other members of your group, show them this." She grinned down at the tiny girl; then handed her a note.

"Susanna, have you ever read any of the books from Grantville?"

"Ah, no, Your Grace."

Maria Anna's grin grew more reckless. "I have. The few that have been brought to me, that I have been able to obtain, in spite of how carefully I am watched. One was a fascinating book. I left it behind in Vienna, with the cloth merchant who helped with the masque costumes. Just as well, since you found that man in my oratory here, leafing through my prayer book."

She threw her head back. "The author was named Benjamin Franklin. Doña Mencia says that she has hope. But, perhaps, hope can be given a stronger foundation. *God helps those who help themselves.*"

Maria Anna decided. To this girl, she would say what no one else but Doña Mencia knew. All the others believed that she was returning home. She leaned down, whispering. "Save Doña Mencia, for me, Susanna. And do not go to Vienna, then. Come to Brussels. Come to me in Brussels and join my household there."

This was the day. Mary Ward looked at them. "We are going now and taking the risk that we may be captured. I will not hide that possibility from you. We could have delayed here as long as possible, until the day when we were arrested. Those were our choices, given what Bavaria is becoming this summer. And we are obeying the will of the pope, to whom, I hope, we may shortly be permitted to make a vow of special obedience."

She had not kept the summer's news away from the other sisters. All of them nodded.

Or from Mary and Veronica. Mary Simpson, thinking of the pope's change of policy toward the United States of Europe, also nodded. She was mildly nervous. She tried to hide it by remarking on the similarity of their plight to the circumstances under which Martin Luther's future wife had gotten out of her convent. Hidden in a grocery wagon, accompanied by her aunt and fellow-nuns.

Winifred Wigmore looked at her disapprovingly.

Veronica pulled the pouch out from under the front of her dress and further disguised herself by taking out her teeth again.

Someone giggled, a little shrilly. Everyone in the house on Paradise Street was feeling rather high strung this morning.

Mary Ward opened the front door. It was not yet quite dawn; they would be at the gate shortly after it opened. The gates were opening early today, because of the play.

Marc heard noise.

Unexpected noise. At this hour of the day, the English Ladies should be chanting one of the liturgical offices. He admitted to himself that he didn't have the slightest idea which one. He was, after all, a Calvinist. Maybe he should learn; he might need to know some day.

He sat up. He couldn't stand in the lean-to; the roof was too low. It hadn't been a bad night, though; his only companions had been some old lumber, a small pile of bricks that matched the ones that paved the courtyard, and a few bugs.

Cautiously, he forced his way through the uncomfortably small gap that breaking the upper hinge on the door had left; then he set it back in place, with only a small sag to show that the hinge had broken and that the door's weight had stretched the lower one.

The English Ladies were leaving their house.

All eight of them. No, ten of them. No, nine and a man. No. Eight English Ladies. They never wore nun-habits, but they were not wearing their ordinary ladyish clothes. They were all dressed like ordinary Munich women. Each carrying a worn satchel. A ninth English Lady. No, Veronica Dreeson, also with a satchel. A serving man. No. Mary Simpson, wearing a shirt and slops. Her hair was still short, though he supposed that she had last had it cut before the left Grantville in the spring, far too short for her to present herself as a down-time woman. Or, at least, as anything but a down-time prostitute who had recently had her head shaved.

Involuntarily, he smiled at the incongruous image of the precise and gracious Frau Simpson as a lady of easy virtue. Frau Simpson was pushing a wheelbarrow.

That was the noise he had heard.

Thanking God profoundly that he was barefoot, he followed them.

✧   ✧   ✧

They were almost to the Schwäbinger gate now; Mary Ward had decided that if they were going north, as a group, they could not afford the delay of going out one of the other gates and around the walls. First, the inner gate. Then, the space between the two sets of walls. Then, the outer gate. Then crossing the narrow bridge over the moat. A long time, to be watched by guards.

Through the inner gate. There was a constant stream of people coming in. Those going out had to move to the right. Coming down from the direction of the *Hofgarten*, a tall, brunette, young woman, her hair tied back with a kerchief. Also dressed in a Munich woman's working clothes; a white blouse; a brown skirt with a wide waistband; rough shoes. Pushing a gardener's wheelbarrow.

"Wait for me, *Tante* Maria. Mama says that I am to go with you." The German was as coarse as that of any market woman.

Mary Simpson gasped.

"Now." The guard pointed his lance at them. "Move along through the outer gate while there's this break in the crowd. Don't dilly-dally."

The younger woman broke into an energetic run, catching up with the rest of them without much trouble.

The guard was watching her bosom jiggle. It was a very impressive bosom.

He didn't pay any attention to her face.

Marc had no idea who the younger woman was. As soon as he got through the gates—he had to wait longer because an entire circus appeared to be coming in—he dashed for the baggage wagons to tell his father that Frau Simpson and Frau Dreeson were outside the gates.

Without either of the Cavrianis having done a thing about it, which he found rather disheartening.

Leopold, more practically, asked where they were going.

"North on the *Nürnberger Strasse*, the last time I saw them." Quickly, Marc described how they were dressed. Then he paused. "But they were all carrying satchels."

"By now, you are implying, they could be dressed quite differently?"

"Well, not by now, I think. The road is too busy. But probably they don't intend to look like *Münchnerinnen* tomorrow."

"That makes sense." Leopold stood up. "I'll take my things and follow them. Here's a purse. I'll leave the camp here, with your things. You go back in. Keep working on the house next door to the one on Paradise street. See if anyone comes to it; tries to go in, tries to go out. If nothing happens today, stay tomorrow. Sleep here, as usual. If nothing has happened in three days, come on north. Don't try to catch me; there's no way I can predict which way the English Ladies are going and if I leave directions for you, Duke Maximilian's men might find them. Just head for Pfaffenhofen; if I'm not there, for Neuburg. I'll find you there."

By the time he had finished talking, Leopold was packed and ready to go.

"Papa," Marc called after him as he rode away. "There was a younger woman who came later. She went with them, too." He wasn't sure whether or not his father had heard him.

Marc looked at the camp. Papa had said to sleep here tonight. But, just in case something happened, he had better pick up. He rolled up his pallet and packed his things into his rucksack; then, wrapped them all in the oiled canvas that they had in case of rain.

The young iron smith arrived at work a little late. No one noticed. But if anyone had observed, he would not have been particularly surprised. The traffic was terrible this morning.

A half mile outside the walls of Munich, something occurred to Mary Ward. Two empty wheelbarrows would attract attention to their group. They would just have to lose some time. At her direction they turned back, skirting the city walls until they came to the baggage wagon park. They lined up the wheelbarrows neatly, next to a couple of dozen other wheelbarrows.

By the time they got back on the *Nürnberger Strasse*, they were behind Leopold Cavriani.

Maria Anna could scarcely believe how lightweight and comfortable these clothes were. Somewhat coarse and scratchy against the skin, but still very comfortable. That was good. Under the skirt, on the left side, between her petticoats, she was carrying a rather heavy purse. It didn't have much money in it; she didn't have much money. It did have her prayer book and rosary. On the right side—thank goodness that Doña Mencia had wrapped it in flannel; even through the bundle and two petticoats, its leaves poked her—was the golden rose.

At the last minute, she just couldn't bear to leave it behind.

The archduchess had attended six o'clock mass, as usual. She had gone for her walk in the *Hofgarten*. Nobody actually saw her return, but Doña Mencia and the other two ladies-in-waiting who had accompanied her requested a light breakfast, as usual. For themselves only. Doña Mencia remarked that the archduchess was not feeling well and had decided to rest until time to dress for the mid-day meal and the play.

An hour later, Doña Mencia requested one of the servants to bring two hot bricks, wrapped in towels.

An hour after that, Doña Mencia announced that the archduchess was suffering from a severe case of the cramps and would be forced to miss the play.

The privy council met. This was a bad omen. With the wedding in two more days, this distressing timing, however natural the phenomenon, would complicate the issue of consummation of the marriage. Consummation was necessary for a canonically valid marriage. The discussion became physiologically detailed. Duke Maximilian excused himself from the remainder of the meeting.

Doña Mencia called for more hot bricks.

There was great public disappointment that the archduchess was too ill to attend the presentation of *Belisarius*, particularly since Duke Maximilian had taken the excuse of her illness not to attend either, but was staying in his office to catch up on paperwork.

He was also discussing with Richel and Forer the insanity of the pope's action in appointing a cardinal-protector of the USE. Both of them heartily agreed with his outrage.

This did not keep the festivities from going on. Duke Albrecht, his wife, and their sons did the public honors. The archduchess' ladies-in-waiting, with the exception of Freiherrin Lukretia, who was on her way back to Vienna, were present.

Well, also with the exception of Doña Mencia de Mendoza who had, naturally, remained with her mistress.

Everyone agreed that Countess Polyxena's gown was magnificent. Somewhat more magnificent than was allowed to a countess under Duke Maximilian's sumptuary laws. Of course, her husband was a *Reichsgraf* ennobled by the emperor in Austria, not a *Graf* from one of the German principalities. The rank of imperial count might make a difference. Then again, it might not. There was a lot of discussion. In any case, those court personnel who were not watching the play were watching Countess Polyxena. She was highly gratified.

Belisarius was a wild success.

"After all this effort," Father Rader said, "it is almost a pity that there is only one performance. It is too bad that we can't do it over again tomorrow."

Father Drexel just looked at him.

After the play, but before the banquet scheduled for the evening, the remainder of Maria Anna's loyal household members left, in small groups, just as planned. By twos, threes, and fours; some on foot, some on horseback.

When Countess Polyxena returned from the play, Doña Mencia reported to her that the archduchess was seriously ill.

"Don't so much as whisper it to anyone else," Doña Mencia said. "I certainly don't wish to cause a panic, with so many people in the city, coming and going. But I am not sure that it is a simple case of the cramps. If she is not better in the morning, I will ask the duke to send the court physician."

Countess Polyxena didn't need to have it spelled out for her. When people spoke of "seriously ill" in those hushed tones, it could only mean plague.

She did not go anywhere near the archduchess' bedchamber.

"I," *Dekan* Golla said after the banquet, "find this illness rather astonishing. We have all been assured that *die Habsburgerin* is, whatever else she may be, abundantly healthy."

"I have read the reports from Frau Stecher in some detail," Duke Maximilian's physician said. "They contain no information whatsoever that the archduchess is prone to suffer from cramps. Or related ailments. Moreover . . ." He paused, looking at the other men. "While we know that the cycles of women are prone to be overset by excitement and anxiety, which is a natural consequence of their weak and fallible nature . . ."

"Come to the point," *Dekan* Golla said.

"It is the wrong time of the month for the archduchess to be having cramps. We took that into account when we scheduled the wedding date." He grimaced with distaste. "Along with, of course, her horoscope. And that of the duke."

Someone knocked on the door. Father Forer rose and opened it. Frau Stecher was standing outside.

"I thought you might want to know," she said, "that according to Countess Polyxena, Doña Mencia has expressed some concern that the archduchess is more seriously ill than cramps could normally account for."

Countess Polyxena had thought, "plague." However, she had not said it when she spoke to Frau Stecher; the possibility had not occurred to the seamstress. There were, just at present, no known plague cases in the city. Not that there probably wouldn't be after the wedding, with so many people coming and going from so many different places.

Plague did not occur to the four men, either. The first thought that came to each of them was the same, and quite natural. *Poison?* The implications of that possibility distracted them for quite some time. By whom? For whose benefit?

By the time that the physician made his way to Maria Anna's hushed and darkened apartments, Doña Mencia informed him that the archduchess was now sleeping quietly. She spoke of a day marked by stomach pains, fever and restlessness; she commented on the nature of the illustrious patient's bowel movements and provided him with a sample she had saved; she described the pain in the joints and headache that the archduchess had experienced. She promised that if there was no improvement in the morning, she would summon him at once.

CHAPTER 43

Decisiones Abrogandas

Munich, Bavaria

Susanna joined the rest of her group early on the morning of the play. The random draw of the straws had, oddly, made three of the four men—two husky stablemen and one footman—the other members. There was an extra person, unexpected: Doña Mencia's elderly personal maid, Guiomar, who spoke neither Italian nor German and who had not been in the group that drew straws at all.

Nep Baier, one of the stablemen, had appointed himself their leader. He was holding the group's purse. As soon as Susanna came downstairs, he shouldered his rucksack and said, "Let's go."

"No," Susanna said. "We can't go yet."

"And just why not, Miss High and Mighty Seamstress?" That was the other stableman, Honorato, Susanna thought his name was. She was actually rather glad to see him. He spoke Spanish as well as German, which meant that they could, in a roundabout way, explain things to Guiomar.

"Because the archduchess said not."

"Just why," Nep asked, "would the archduchess be talking to you?"

"She does, you know. Talk to Susanna, I mean." That was Jindrich Horschiczy, the footman. "I have seen her do it. Especially when they performed the masque before Lent back home. But here, also. Think about that. The archduchess talks to her."

Susanna looked from one man to the other. There had to be problems here that she knew nothing about—problems that had existed long before today. But she didn't have time to worry about them.

"Truly, we cannot leave yet," she insisted. "The archduchess told me that the group I joined was not to leave. Not until we saw Doña Mencia safe."

Honorato turned and said something quickly to old Guiomar, who looked somewhat happier than she had previously.

Nep continued his protest.

"She gave this to me, just in case you would not believe." Susanna pulled out the note that the archduchess had scribbled.

Nep clearly did not want to believe it. But he had to. She had showed it to Jindrich first.

Susanna took the note back. The piece of paper was very small. The note had served its purpose. Maybe she was being too dramatic. But she tossed it into her mouth, chewed, and swallowed.

"Go back to the stables." That was to Nep and Honorato. "Be seen. I know that most of the horses had to be left behind. Tend them. Do what you would do on any ordinary day."

She gained the ascendancy. Reluctantly, they left. Susanna watched them go. *Lazy bums*, she thought. Probably, they had looked at all of this as a way to get out of an honest day's work.

"Now," she said. "Come back to the archduchess' rooms with me."

Guiomar looked at her blankly.

Susanna took her hand. Jindrich followed

Doña Mencia was not happy to see them come back.

Susanna, fortified by the knowledge that she had the archduchess' own written authorization, even if she had eaten it a little prematurely, simply said that they had orders from the archduchess to stay throughout the day and they were staying.

Duke Maximilian's physician had not appeared. A boy came with an apologetic note. Father Contzen had taken a serious turn for the worse; Duke Maximilian had directly ordered him to stay by his confessor's bedside, night and day if need be.

As the day went on, Doña Mencia became more reconciled to having the other three there. Jindrich went up and down to the kitchen, bringing hot bricks and other comforts to the supposedly incommoded archduchess—although why, Susanna wondered, even a supposed invalid would want hot bricks on a day as miserable as this one was a mystery.

Susanna moved around, here and there, inside the apartments. Occasionally, someone from the staff of the *Residenz* opened the outer doors of the apartment and looked in. There was always someone in view; sometimes a lady-in-waiting, reading a book by the window, or a lady's maid just crossing the open door to the bedchamber, a chambermaid cleaning the grate, a different lady-in-waiting standing at the foot of the archduchess' bed. Susanna got to change clothes quite a few times; if it hadn't been for Guiomar, she couldn't have done it. The fastenings of even the simplest clothing worn by court ladies were far too complicated. She also helped Guiomar change twice. Given that most of the ladies-in-waiting and their personal attendants were known to be attending the production of *Belisarius*, it must have seemed to the people looking in that the archduchess' quarters were quite normally populated. At least, Susanna hoped so.

Doña Mencia, of course, remained in her own clothes, in her own role, in case anyone asked to speak with her. Which several people did.

Just before dusk, Susanna heard a quick rapping on the back entrance to the rooms, off the servant's corridor. She opened it. Nep and Honorato were both standing there.

"The physician's coach just pulled into the stable yard. You are all going to have to get out of here. Now."

Doña Mencia nodded. This was as far as the deception could go. "Go with them, quickly," she said to Susanna.

"No," Susanna protested. "We are here to see you safe. That is why the archduchess sent us back. You have to come with us."

"I made my own plans; I am expected."

Susanna turned to the men. "Get in here and close that door! I am going with Doña Mencia. The city gates won't be closed yet; they're staying open late tonight to accommodate the playgoers. Take Guiomar with you and get out." She put her hand in the middle of the elderly maid's back and pushed her toward the two stablemen. Honorato took her arm and began to talk.

Susanna turned. "You, too, Jindrich. With them. Out. Out the front door. Go down the main corridor and out. Out the side way. Not the back through the stables. Wait for me just outside the Würtzer gate. I will come as quickly as I can."

The four left.

"We," Doña Mencia said. "We go the back way. As I was told to do by Duchess Mechthilde. Child, you are a fool to stay here and be brave."

Susanna shook her head. "The archduchess told me." She started to pull Doña Mencia out the back door of the apartments into the servants' corridor.

Doña Mencia protested, "Wait." She smiled a small, malicious, smile and tucked a note, as if carelessly used as a bookmark, into the book on the side table that the "lady-in-waiting" had been reading that afternoon. Then she allowed herself to be pulled.

There was nothing in the corridor with which to block the door. Success would depend on keeping out of sight. Susanna, by herself, would have run. With Doña Mencia, she had to walk. Slowly.

At various times, three other people saw them. Two women walking slowly, one elderly, raised no alarm. Doña Mencia occasionally spoke a quiet sentence. "The second turn, here. At the fifth branch, there is a staircase to the first floor. Soon, we will come to an alcove; turn to the right at the first corridor beyond it. The correct door will be marked with a pungent herb."

Susanna just didn't know how long they had. How long would it take for the physician to reach the archduchess' empty bed? How long would it take him to summon the guards? How long for him to notify anybody he had to notify? How long for her to get Doña Mencia to her refuge?

How long before all the city gates would be closed?

Their progress was painfully, agonizingly, miserably, slow. Especially on the stairs. Narrow steps, steep risers, without railings. Doña Mencia could never have descended them or climbed them without help.

Going out the front corridor of the wing, Nep and the others realized how very little time it was going to take to set the hunt in place. As the physician came in, they, as servants, politely turned their faces to the wall, in order that they need not be noticed by their betters. When the medical party was past, they started to move in a hurry.

The uproar began on the second floor corridor that they had just left.

Nep had an option that was not open to Susanna. As he heard the first party of guards coming, he hefted Guiomar over his shoulder and started to run. He was a big man. Honorato and Jindrich, even unimpeded by a burden, could barely keep up with him. He plunged down a side corridor on the first floor, into the stable yard, and threw Guiomar onto a beautifully harnessed mule that was tethered next to the entrance.

They were out of the yard and heading toward the Isar gate when the first of the guards came around the corner of the *Residenz* and saw them. Saw a small woman dressed in black, riding on an elaborately caparisoned mule, attended by three men. He stopped, hesitating as to whether he should pursue or notify the captain. Notifying the captain won. He turned back, waving urgently.

"Doña Mencia," he called. "I saw her fleeing, with three men accompanying her." The rest of the troop speeded up. Behind them, someone yelled, "Halt!"

Obediently, they halted.

"Where," the huffing footman who was following them cried, "is Messire Carafa's mule? What have you done with the nuncio's mule?"

The guard captain looked at him with astonishment. One could not smite the papal nuncio's footman. No matter how sincerely one might wish to smite him. One could think it, though. Smite, smote, smitten. So there. Arrrgh. He turned. "After them." With a flurry of uniform livery and flourishing swords, the guards returned to the pursuit.

Only to find that another messenger from the *Residenz* had gotten to the Isar gate first. It was firmly, solidly, closed. The lieutenant in charge absolutely refused to reopen it without authorization from the duke. When pressured, he drew his own sword. He pointed out that the colonel from whom the messenger had come considerably outranked the captain.

The captain looked at him grimly. "Have you seen . . . ?" he asked.

"Yes," the lieutenant said agreeably. "They came through just before the duke ordered the gates closed. They were heading for the Isar bridge. We had no instructions to halt anyone leaving the city this evening."

The captain left half of his troop at the gate, just in case someone might see fit to open it and let them through. Then he turned, hoping that the march back to the *Residenz* would be long enough for him to get control of his tongue before he spoke to the colonel.

"We have to leave the damned mule," Jindrich said insistently.

"But the old lady can't keep up with us," Honorato protested.

"It's *white*," Jindrich replied. "It will stand out like a beacon at night. What's more, it's *stolen*. Use just a little bit of common sense."

Seppi the market gardener was very surprised the next morning. In the place of his common donkey stood the most beautiful mule he had ever seen. His first thought was of a divine miracle, a gift from Our Lady. His second thought was more prosaic. He called the watchman.

After that, Honorato and Jindrich let Nep give the directions and set the pace. Guiomar sat on the donkey's back, clutching its collar and moaning to herself. Shortly before dawn, Jindrich asked, "What about the seamstress?"

Nep just looked at him. "The bossy little snip can take care of herself. No way was I going to spend last night trying to sneak along the walls of Munich from the Isar gate down to the Würtzer gate and camp outside it in hopes she would come out this morning. Good way to get us all hanged. Forget her. We're halfway to Altötting and we're pilgrims. *Don't* forget that. We get this one back to Austria and we collect our reward for a job well done."

The guards were searching the archduchess' apartments.

At first, it seemed as though nothing at all was missing. There was even a neat, small, stack of bricks and towels on the hearth in the bedchamber.

Frau Stecher, quickly summoned, stated that none of the archduchess' wardrobe appeared to be gone. The dress she had worn to mass the previous morning was lying carelessly on a chair near the window—the shoes, stockings, shift, petticoats, cuffs, collar. Everything pertaining to the outfit was there. Her robe was on the bed.

One of the guards picked the shoes up. Soft, composted leaves and a little fine gravel were stuck to one of the heels by a bit of mud.

"Oh, that," Frau Stecher said. "A nuisance; she was terribly careless of her clothes. Didn't really appreciate them, after all the work I do. She insisted on walking in the garden every morning, even on a day like today, when the ground was soft from rain the night before." Frau Stecher took the shoe. "Look," she said accusingly. "Look how the mud is staining that heel. She didn't even bother to send it for cleaning right after she came in. It will be ruined. Is ruined."

The guard captain asked, slowly, "Did she come in? Did you see the archduchess come in?"

Frau Stecher shook her head. "I didn't see her all day."

There was a slight disturbance at the door. *Dekan* Golla had arrived, accompanied by a small man in a gray habit. A Capuchin friar. The captain bowed.

"What have you found?"

"They tell me that nothing appears to be missing."

The man in the gray habit walked past the guards, through the bedchamber, into the oratory. He looked around.

"Who tells you that nothing is missing?"

The captain gestured. "Frau Stecher. The seamstress who came from Vienna with the archduchess."

"Ah," the little man said. "Yes. It would appear that Frau Stecher failed to mention that a few things are missing from the oratory."

"I have never," Frau Stecher said rather defensively, "been admitted to the oratory. There was never any reason for me to be there."

"More to the point," *Dekan* Golla intervened, "what is missing?"

"The archduchess' prayer book. Her rosary, quite a beautiful one." The little man looked around; walked forward, first placing his hand on the pedestal of the prie-dieu, then on the table next to it. "And the golden rose; the papal rose. Those I can see, at the very least."

He left the oratory. "Secure the room. Leave a guard at the door. I will wish to look at it again in the morning, in daylight."

He came into the bedchamber; paced around it twice, finding nothing of interest. He moved to the antechamber, repeated the pacing, and paused by a small table with a book lying on it. Almost reflexively, he riffled through the pages of the book, drawing out the bookmark.

Father Drexel's *Schola Patientiae*. Not a book he cared for. Irenic; gently ironic. Too much focused on the penitent, too little on the impenitent. It was, he had been told, popular as spiritual reading even among the Protestants. The king of Denmark supposedly owned a copy and read it. That, by itself, should be sufficient evidence that it was doctrinally unsound.

He looked at the note. Nodded his head slowly. In this life, unfortunately, double agents were not uncommon. Greedy people, who collected money for informing each side about the other.

He looked at the seamstress. "Frau Stecher," he asked, "would you be interested in explaining this to me? Here? Or would you prefer to wait for judicial questioning?"

Frau Stecher backed up a few steps. "Explain what?"

"Why," the little man said, "this note to you from Countess Polyxena. I find it quite fascinating. She thanks you very graciously for providing the archduchess with the clothing that she wore this morning when she left Munich."

"She does, does she?" Frau Stecher knew that there were some things which could never, in the eyes of the Inquisition, be adequately explained. "Well, the damned little bitch!"

Finally. Susanna had reached the proper door with Doña Mencia. Carefully, she removed the small sprig of pungent sage that someone had bound to the latch, to guide the archduchess' attendant in case the corridor was completely dark. Carefully, she pushed it open and looked around. It was just a small room.

"Where are we?" she asked rather anxiously.

"In the old nurseries for Duchess Mechthilde's sons," Doña Mencia replied. "This is the room in which their wet nurse slept. No one comes here, any more. The young dukes moved to larger rooms a long time ago. They have their own household already, tutors, governesses. They are much too old for nursemaids and toys."

Susanna looked around. There was a carafe of fresh water on the table; a plate of fruit. She lifted the cover of the bowl. Cheese. A basin and pitcher; a towel; a commode. A clean shift on the small bed; fresh sheets. A small prayer book on the stand next to it. Doña Mencia was expected.

"Your Ladyship," she said. "I hate to leave you. But you are safe here. As safe as we can make you."

Doña Mencia reached out. "Stay with me, child."

Susanna shook her head. "Duchess Mechthilde offered her protection to you; not to me. It will be hard enough for her to hide one person; two double the risk. Also, the others will be waiting for me, and every minute that they wait is dangerous for them, too." She led Doña Mencia to a chair, placed a hassock under her feet, and backed out into the servants' corridor.

Susanna had no intention of retracing her steps. She was already in a different wing of the *Residenz*, on a different floor from where the archduchess' household had been staying. She walked along briskly. Into a third wing, then up a set of stairs; up another, into the lofts. Through the servants' quarters, into another loft. Down again. Into the kitchens, where dozens of temporary helpers were sleeping in every available corner. Into the herb garden; into the pleasure garden. It was still the late, late twilight of summer; a few couples were walking along the paths, unaware that anything unusual was happening in the palace. It was a very large building, with multiple courtyards and wings.

Out into the street. Turn north. That should lead to the Isar gate; from there she could go outside the walls to where Nep and the others were supposed to wait for her. People coming back from the gate; guards; people being turned back. She stopped, turned with the flow of traffic, listened to what they were saying. The gates were closed for the night. She couldn't get to the others until morning.

She kept walking. A man and wife with several children were just in front of her. She walked as if she were with them, trying to think. She was on her own. Really on her own; that had never happened before. In a strange city. Well, most of it was strange, certainly. Since coming to Munich, she had never, except for coming in with the wedding procession, been anywhere except the *Residenz*, to the *Schrannenplatz*, and to the house of the English Ladies. She didn't have any money; Nep had the purse.

Where could she go? Not back to the *Residenz*, certainly. Not to the *Schrannenplatz* on a festival night. Even in a city as well policed as Munich, it was bound to be full of drunk, boisterous, men. She felt in her pocket. The key to the house in Paradise Street. It would be empty. She could take refuge for the night there and think again in the morning.

Early in the morning. Before the cook arrived to find the Ladies gone and turn in an alarm.

CHAPTER 44

Amicitia Plena

Munich, Bavaria

Susanna knew where she was, even though it was starting to get dark. The next street would be Paradise Street. She turned into the alley behind it, intending to take a shortcut to the back door of the house.

"Fräulein," a man's voice called softly. "Fräulein, don't."

She looked up. It was the young iron smith she had been noticing for several days. Up on a ladder, working on a grille on one of the back windows of the house next door.

"Why not?"

Marc wondered what on earth he could say to persuade her that he was one of the "good guys," as Toby Snell would have called them.

"The Ladies left this morning. I saw them go. But since then, men came. Guards. Two friars. They went into the house. They haven't even posted a notice on the door. I think that they are waiting to see who comes. To arrest anyone who comes."

Susanna stopped.

"What am I going to do now?"

Marc climbed down the ladder. They weren't speaking loudly, but he wasn't certain that the house on which he had been working was still empty. Everyone lodging there had left in the morning for the play. He hadn't seen any of them return, or heard them, but he had been working in the back. Better to be safe.

"Right now, you can sit right here. Under the ladder, in the corner next to the cellar entrance. Once it gets full dark, I know a place where you can hide. But not until then. It's where somebody inside the Ladies' house, looking out the kitchen window, could see us. And I'm pretty sure that there is somebody standing there."

Susanna sat. Mark climbed back up the ladder and continued working until he couldn't see properly any more. It was a very long hour. It was another long hour before he thought that it was safe for them to go into the shed.

As he pulled open the loose hinge, he whispered, "Not the stuff of stories, where there are always gaily decorated tents or sylvan bowers available. But I've spent the night in here before. I can at least promise that there aren't too many bugs."

They each took a corner. About midnight, it started to rain. The lean-to was not built on a foundation; the boards just met the ground. The roof leaked; not a lot, but some. Steady drips. The water draining off the cobblestones in the alley was worse; first a few trickles. Then little rivulets.

"Move over a little," Mark said. "I'll pull these boards down and make a platform to get us up out of the puddles. It won't be comfortable. There aren't many of them." He managed to stack three short ones at each end and find two that were long enough to reach most of the length of the shed—all four feet of it.

Susanna sat on her board, pulled up her knees, and wrapped her skirts around her legs.

"It could be worse, you know," she said.

"It could?"

"Yes. It could be October or November and the rain could be so cold that it was just almost freezing, but not quite."

"Yeah. Right."

"You." Susanna shook Marc's shoulder.

"Unnh?"

"You. Don't we need to get out of the shed before it starts to get light? Unless we want them to see us when we climb through the door?"

"Lord, yes. Ooof. I can't believe that I actually went to sleep.

Wait a minute. I need to stack these boards back." He was feeling of them, matching wet end to wet end. "No sense in leaving evidence that someone's been in here. If someone just glances in, maybe he'll just think that they got wet from a leak if it's all turned on the same side. At least the leather hinges will have gotten soaked last night, so nobody will see at first glance that the rip is new."

He finished stacking the boards, wriggled out through the open space, and held it for her. They quickly crossed to the other side of the alley; hugging the backs of the houses, they went out into the street.

"What next?" Susanna asked.

"At this hour? Get something to eat. It will start getting light in a little while. Vendors will be setting up, to catch the workers coming to tear down the bleachers and clean up the sets and stuff like that. I don't think we look too bad. Not sodden wet or anything. Maybe you should tie your hair back again, though." Marc paused, trying to gather up the essence of all the wisdom his elders had been trying to teach him the last few years. It seemed to amount to this. "Whatever you're going to be doing, always try to eat first. Things always look better after you've eaten. Let's get over to the market."

Susanna shook her head. "I don't have any money. None at all."

"I do. Not more than a workman should have, but enough to get some breakfast. So let's go."

By the time they got to the marketplace, the first food sellers were setting up their stands. He ordered two equal portions and water.

Susanna ate half of hers. Marc ate all of his and was now demolishing the rest of hers. He practically inhaled food. She smiled. "No dainty morsels, either."

"What?"

"In the stories. When knights and ladies have gaily decorated tents and sylvan bowers, the food is always dainty morsels, too. Never pork sausages on rye buns, with kraut on the side."

Marc managed to swallow the bite in his mouth before he laughed.

The sausage vendor looked at them. *Young people*, he thought enviously. *They never have a care in the world.*

✧　　✧　　✧

"Next," Marc said, "we've got to get out to where I'm camped. Through the gates. Better try the Schwäbinger gate. I've been coming in and out for several days. If the regular guards are on, they'll sort of know my face."

"I ought to go out the Würtzer gate. I told my . . . friends . . . to wait for me there."

"What if your friends are on the guards' list of people they're looking for, too? Are they?" Marc asked.

"Yes, probably," Susanna admitted.

"Then I hope that if they got out last night, they had the sense to keep going. And if they did, you'll never find them. You'll just be standing outside the Würtzer gate by yourself with no money. Stick with me."

He headed for the Schwäbinger gate.

Susanna fretted. "There are going to be a lot of people trying to go out this morning. More than they were planning on. I was by the Isar gate last night when they closed it up. Lots of people were turned back. It was probably the same at all the others. If you look around, an awful lot of the people look like they slept on somebody's floor or in the streets. So the crowds will be bigger than they were expecting. We'll just have to get in the lines."

They didn't have any problems, aside from having to wait. Marc didn't look a thing like any of the people the guards had been warned to watch out for. Susanna's name was actually on their list, way down. But the description was only, "small woman, light brown hair." That covered at least ten percent of the women in the crowd; possibly more, since it didn't say anything about her age.

There's only so much that a guard company can accomplish overnight.

The stuff was there. It was also, owing to Marc's prudence with the oilcloth the previous morning, dry. He shook out the oilcloth and laid it down for Susanna to sit on.

"Next," he said, "I have to sell the horse."

"What?"

"Papa and I rode down from Neuburg. He took his horse when he left. Mine's still here. If we take him with us, it will draw attention; a horse is fine for a prosperous merchant, but not for someone dressed like I am right now. We can't just leave him here, either. Ordinary people don't go off and leave their horses behind. It's the sort of thing that will be noticed. Besides, we're going to need the money. Just stay sitting here until I get back. You'll be safe enough. The duke's inspectors have kept the camp really well policed, clean and safe. If anyone does, er, accost you or something, just yell. A watchman will turn up in no time."

He sold the horse to the manager of the camp, explaining that his father had bought a cart with a team that was used to working together and he didn't want to bother leading this one behind it. The manager wasn't surprised. Unlike a lot of noblemen, who spoiled their horses, a merchant mainly just thought of them as a way to get his goods from here to there; bought one when he needed it, sold it when he didn't. They dickered a bit, but it wasn't a transaction worth a lot of dickering. Marc got about what he expected; the manager paid about what he thought the beast was worth and told a boy to go move it from the private tethering to the common paddock.

"Harness?" he asked.

"What was on him when Papa bought him. Plain bridle; the saddle is pretty well fitted. Decent saddle blanket, no holes."

The manager named a sum. Marc took it, stuffing the coins into his purse.

Susanna sat on the oilcloth, thinking. She hadn't been accosted. If she was, she couldn't really yell. That would attract a watchman, sure, but then he might think that she was a fugitive and turn her over to the guards. She saw Marc coming back. She wondered what he was planning next.

"That's that," he said. "Next, we need to pack this stuff and try to catch up with Papa."

Susanna looked up. She felt vaguely comforted. Never once, not in a single book she had read or play she had seen, had a villainous seducer started his campaign against the heroine's virtue by announcing his intention to consult his father about the matter.

Not that the young iron smith seemed like he would be a villainous seducer. He would probably be sort of nice about the whole thing. But respectable girls didn't let themselves be seduced, not even by nice young men. When respectable girls were old enough, they got betrothed and then married, which involved parental consent and marriage contracts and dowries and stuff.

Seduction led to having a baby and losing your place at court and spending the rest of your life spinning rough flax in an institution for penitent magdalens and never, ever, getting to make beautiful clothing of velvet and satin, damask and brocade, again.

"What's your name?" she asked.

"Marc Cavriani. Who are you?"

"Susanna Allegretti." She let out a torrent of Italian. "I'm a seamstress. I'm apprenticed to Frau Stecher. I'm from Florence but my parents are working in Tyrol."

"I'm from Geneva. My father is a merchant. I was traveling with him. I have four little sisters."

Marc looked down. Little sister. That was a really good idea. He would treat her as a little sister; he could handle little sisters. If he didn't treat her like his sister, well . . . That sort of thing led to carnal temptation which led to fornication, which was definitely a sin, and fornication led to having a baby and having to get married years before Papa and Mama planned for you to, so that you couldn't finish your training, and some of the guilds wouldn't want your son for a member and other families looked at you funny and wouldn't want their sons to marry your daughter and, well, bad things. Plus, she was a Catholic. Had to be, going back and forth to a house where nuns lived. Even if they weren't very nunnish.

"I'm an only child. And it's my stepfather, really. My own father died when I was a little girl."

Susanna knew that she was chattering. Bad habit. She knew that. While she chattered, she was thinking. Geneva? That was Calvinist. He was a heretic? Well, why should she be surprised? After all, he had been watching the house where the two Grantville women had been held, and all the newspapers said that Grantville was a nearly demoniacal mix of every imaginable religious faith, most of them heretical.

Marc could follow what she was saying, sort of, but the dialects of Italian that they spoke were even more variant than their German dialects. Her Italian was very Tuscan; his highly French-influenced. After a few minutes, they lapsed back into German.

"Let's pack. We've got to get going."

✧   ✧   ✧

Some distance down the road, Marc spotted a hedge. A nice, thick hedge that would screen anybody behind it from the road. He steered Susanna to it.

"We can't go on the way we are. Not far. Not if they're looking for you. And I think that they are."

"I don't have anything else to wear." Susanna shrugged.

"We are," Marc said firmly, "or we will be, a journeyman and apprentice. A newly qualified journeyman. A new, very young, very junior, and not very adept apprentice. An apprentice who is a boy," he added, suddenly remembering that Susanna actually was an apprentice. There weren't that many trades in which girls apprenticed. "At least, when they ask what we are, we'll both be telling the truth."

"I do not," Susanna pointed out, "have any boy's clothing."

"Oh, lucky for you, I do. It won't fit, of course, but that's all to the good. Very junior apprentices are usually clothed in hand-me-downs that are droopy in some spots and hitched up with belts in other spots."

He started digging around in his rucksack. Some of these things, he had brought along from Neuburg in case it rained. Marc's mother had always just hated for him to get his good clothes wet. Even now, supposedly all grown up, if he knew, or even suspected, that he was likely to get caught out in a downpour, he simply put on the oldest things he had—or, at least, the oldest things he had that still fit him. That could get tricky at times, remembering what was what. He was supposed to remember to give his clothes to the poor when they no longer fit; most of the time, however, he just stuffed them in the bottom of his chest. One old shirt (shapeless); one old pair of trews (droopy); one slouch hat. His razor. He rubbed his chin. No way was he going to try to shave without hot water. And a mirror. Papa took the mirror.

"Sit," he said. "Take your hair down." The resulting haircut was just as bad as that of almost every other apprentice in the world—a fully satisfactory result. He tossed the hair that he had cut off well up into the branches of a nearby tree, hoping that nesting birds would find it and be grateful for the treasure trove, while simultaneously removing one more clue by which they might be traced. "Take these and go change."

"What are we going to do with my clothes?" Susanna asked.

"Good question. If we leave them here, it will be like painting a sign saying which way we went. If we take them, though, and anyone finds them in our sacks, we'll have an accusation of theft against us at the very least. Plus, somebody might investigate and figure out that you're a girl."

"Double back into the city," she suggested. "A fair number of the people who came into the city for the wedding will still be there. They'll be busy all day taking down the sets and bleachers. With all the costumes, no one will be surprised to see people putting clothes into one of the prop bins."

"Done. Now get changed before somebody comes along."

They had no trouble getting into the city. None at all. The guards were fully occupied with examining the people who were leaving. Or trying to.

On the theory that one attracts the least attention by being quite obvious, Marc walked down the street with the set of women's clothing folded over his left arm. Within a quarter hour, they were close enough to the *Schrannenplatz* that they could see stagehands from the previous day's entertainment moving around, taking down the sets. Calmly leaving the clothing on a rack and dropping her dainty little shoes into a bin, he moved on, skirting the square, Susanna behind him.

Then he stopped. "This isn't going to work. Not for going out through the gate again."

"Why not?"

"Your feet are too small. It's all right for me to be walking barefoot. My feet look like a man's feet. But yours don't and you don't walk right." He leaned back against the wall of a house, digging in his rucksack again. "These are my oldest shoes. You're going to have to stuff them and they won't be comfortable, but you've got to put them on. I've got some extra stockings, too."

"Yes. And I'll clump. The way boys clump." Susanna clumped down the *Gasse* right beside him.

Funny, Marc thought. I didn't really notice how gracefully she moves until she started clumping.

What he said was, "Let's stop and get something to eat before we go back out. It has to be close to lunch time."

The crowds were a lot thinner. The guards examined Marc's rucksack. There was nothing in it that was even vaguely interesting.

The apprentice just stood there like a dolt, drawing pictures on the ground with the toe of his shoe and gnawing the last little bit of pulp off the core of his apple.

"Where are we going?"

"Papa went after the English Ladies. The last time I saw them, they were on the *Nürnberger Strasse*, heading north. So I guess we go that way. No telling that they won't have turned off somewhere, though." Marc paused. "You were going in and out of their house. Do you have any idea where they were headed?"

"I heard one of them say, to Grantville. Well, *over*heard," Susanna admitted.

"Right general direction, at least. I guess the best plan is, we'll try to catch up with Papa. If we can't, I was supposed to meet him at his factor's office. If we can catch him in Pfaffenhofen, that's only about seventy miles. Even if he isn't there, his agent should be and we can get some more money and find out what's going on. If we miss him there and have to go on to Neuburg, about another fifty-five."

Susanna calculated. "That's not bad. When I came from Florence to Bolzano, Bozen in the Tyrol, that is, it was about two hundred fifty miles. Last fall, when I went from Bolzano to Vienna, it was about three hundred fifty. It shouldn't take us more than a week to get to Neuberg."

But the roads going north were clogged with soldiers, far more soldiers than there had been when Marc and his father came south toward Munich. The privy council was moving every man who could be spared toward Ingolstadt. They moved very cautiously, also trying to avoid the hungry dogs that were rapidly going feral.

Munich, Bavaria

The captain of the guards motioned for one of his men to hold the back door of Archduchess Maria Anna's apartments in the *Residenz* open for *Dekan* Golla and the Capuchin friar who accompanied him; he permitted them to precede him.

Dekan Golla looked up and down with some dissatisfaction. "While the duke's servants are certainly to be commended for their zeal for cleanliness, just in this instance it would have been nice to have some dust. Containing a few footprints, perhaps."

The floors, alas, were immaculate.

"Let the servants be questioned," the Capuchin said. "Not, at present, under torture. Just to determine whether any of them passed through this corridor at about the time the physician made his report. Only the footman was in the rooms during the day, according to what I have heard thus far. No one saw the archduchess' male servants walking through the main corridors toward these rooms, so they must have come in this way."

Three servants admitted to having passed through the corridor shortly before the alarm was roused. All three denied having seen any men. They maintained these denials even under strict questioning, which was very disappointing.

One stated that she had seen two women, but had not particularly noticed them. In any case, they had not been near the door to the archduchess' apartment, but had been walking, quite slowly, close to the far end. She had only seen them from the rear.

"Two women?" one of the guards asked. "If they came from here, which two?"

"No way to tell." His companion shook his head. "Only a few people came into the archduchess' apartments during the day. Doña Mencia de Mendoza was certainly present, but we know that she escaped with the three men. All we can say, really, is that they may have been two of the archduchess' female attendants who are not still here. If, of course, they were not just two tired servants, walking slowly at the end of the day."

It was scarcely feasible to question every servant in the *Residenz* about every corridor. It was a large building; with the wedding preparations, there had been a great deal of coming and going that did not follow the ordinary daily routines.

It was early in the morning, even for a meeting of the Bavarian privy council. "Is this really all that they have been able to find out?" Duke Maximilian was clearly displeased.

Duke Albrecht, who had been recalled to the privy council meetings more or less on sufferance, looked very uncomfortable. "Yes."

"We are not pleased."

They were interrupted by a soft knock at the door. The duke's secretary motioned for a servant to open it. The court physician stood there, holding his hat. Impatiently, Maximilian beckoned him in.

"Your Grace. I would not be here if it were not important. I am very sorry to inform Your Grace that Father Contzen did not survive the night. If Your Grace could direct the *Hofmeister* to coordinate with the Jesuits in regard to the requiem mass and whether there shall be a procession?" His voice trailed off.

The duke looked at his secretary. "Let it be done." The secretary left immediately. Maximilian stood up.

"This meeting is adjourned. I am retiring to my oratory and do not wish to be interrupted. By anybody, for any reason. Father Forer, I will have you called when I need you. The rest of you may leave."

The funeral was elaborate. Duke Maximilian ordered that all of the food prepared in expectation of the wedding be presented to the poor in Father Contzen's honor. That the clothing prepared in expectation of the wedding festivities be sold, and the proceeds given to the poor in memory of Father Contzen.

He attended the obsequies in the role of chief mourner. The next day, he directed that the apartments that were being prepared in the *Residenz* for a new duchess and her household were to be permanently walled off from the remainder of the building. They were to be occupied by an order of fully cloistered contemplative nuns, whose time was to be devoted solely to prayer for the repose of the soul of the late Duchess Elisabeth Renata.

The news from Ingolstadt was not good. Colonel Farensbach had been detected in communication with the enemy, with an intention to betray the fortress to General Banér. Since he had been the duke's personal choice as the new overseer of the garrison and the town's security, this was, to say the least, embarrassing. It certainly had not improved Maximilian's overall mood.

CHAPTER 45

Momentum, Utilitatum, Pretiumque Communicationis

Banér's Camp, outside Ingolstadt

"He rode up to a sentry, holding his hands out," Mark Ellis said. "All weapons sheathed. Said that he had important messages to send to the USE and needed permission to use General Banér's radio."

"And you are telling me," Dane Kitt asked, "that he's just been sitting in your tent ever since?"

"Well, I tried to get him in to see Banér's adjutant, but I haven't had any luck. I thought that maybe you would do better. And he doesn't speak English." Mark Ellis shrugged.

"I'll see what I can do." The two of them paced across the camp toward the adjutant's shelter.

Dane had managed to talk their way into the adjutant's tent. Not without promising, on his parents' behalf, a few things about weapons that he was not by any means sure that they could come up with on the proposed time schedule.

"Look," Mark was saying with frustration. "He's not going to sabotage the radio. We can make sure of that. He's not even going to lay hands on the thing. He's going to be saying the message out loud. The operator—our operator—is going to be sending it to some other USE government operator. Someone at that end will be deciding whether or not the information is good. What's the damned hang-up?"

Finally, the adjutant agreed to see the man.

"Look on the bright side," Dane said. "At least, he came into the camp at noon. This is as fast as the operator would have had a window to transmit, even if he'd been welcomed right away. Good thing that it didn't drag out any longer, though; we'd have had to wait until tomorrow morning."

Once in the presence of the person who could authorize use of the famous radio, the messenger started to talk.

He had been sent by Herr Veit Egli, who was a merchant's factor in Neuburg. He was authorized to say that.

The merchant for whom Herr Egli was a factor was Herr Leopold Cavriani. He was authorized to say that.

"Hey, wait a minute," Dane said.

Mark nodded. "Cavriani. That's the guy who was in Amberg this spring with Keith Pilcher and them, negotiating about iron. He really is as thick as thieves with a lot of the people up in Grantville, and that includes Ed Piazza. This could be for real. Let's just hope that our dear old principal is awake and around."

The adjutant nodded to the radio operator, who started transmitting.

The messenger wished to make it known that he was merely delivering this information and did not take any personal responsibility for its content.

Grantville, State of Thuringia-Franconia

Ed Piazza intervened personally in the transmission. "Kitt, Ellis, are you there?"

"Yup, both of us."

"Is there somebody standing over this man with a sword and a threatening expression, looking like he might carve his guts out any minute?"

"Two of them, actually. But one has a pistol."

"Well, tell them to back off and let the man talk. I have a feeling that he's afraid that they're inclined to kill the messenger. Which makes me hope that the news isn't bad."

❖   ❖   ❖

Ed got home, took his shoes off, grabbed a sandwich, and went upstairs to sit on the bed with his feet up, so he could undertake his analysis of the transmission at leisure. First, four quick phone calls, to two sets of parents, a wife, and a fiancée, with assurances that Dane and Mark had been on the radio from Ingolstadt two hours ago and they were both just fine as of that date. Then, try to make sense of the message from Ingolstadt in a little more comfort than his office provided.

(1) In Munich, the English ladies had left their house. Nobody knew why, or whether they were elsewhere in the city or had left it. This was generally known and would probably appear in the newspapers and diplomatic dispatches within one or two more days.

Ed mentally corrected "ladies" to "Ladies." They weren't directly relevant to Grantville, so why had Cavriani's factor listed them first? Mary and Veronica had been interned in their house in Munich, but . . . Wait a minute. Back when he took that adult class in church history, when he first took over the CCD classes at St. Mary's, St. Vincent de Paul as it had been then, he'd heard something about English Ladies.

"Annabelle," he called.

His wife trotted up the stairs from the kitchen where, finally, at nine o'clock at night, she had started to wash the dishes.

"Do you remember anything about English Ladies from that 'how to run a CCD program' class that we took?"

"Just that they were mentioned. Why?"

"Not sure. But I think that this could be important. Could you try to find out something about them for me?"

"I could call Elaine Bolender and see if she could meet me at the State Library."

"They exist in the here and now. You might try the rectory, too."

"I'll do what I can." Annabelle abandoned the dishes. They could wait. They had already waited for two days. Not that there were many. She had been so busy that they were living on sandwiches and fruit or take-out from Cora's. She had been sturdily resisting the idea of getting a maid, but one of these days, she was going to have to give in. There were just too many other things to do for her to keep this house in shape.

Upstairs, Ed moved on to the next point.

(2) The two Grantville women who had been interned with the English Ladies were also gone. It was not known whether

they had left with the Ladies or separately; it was not known whether they had left the city or remained inside it. There was no indication that they were in the hands of either the duke or the Inquisition.

Ed looked at that. He was really glad that Stearns had this. And Nasi, which amounted to the same thing. He had it sent on as soon as it came in. Stearns could tell Simpson. Simpson hadn't been taking all of this very well. In his world, men were supposed to go out and fight wars, leaving their wives safe and secure at home. Mary had been turning his whole world topsy-turvy this summer. Ed couldn't really blame Simpson. He knew how he would feel if Annabelle were out there, somewhere, in trouble, and he couldn't do a thing about it.

So what was he supposed to tell Henry and Annalise? In a way, it had been more comforting to have Mary and Ronnie locked up with the English Ladies guarding them. Even if it was a polite form of being in prison, at least people here had known where they were. Now they were back to not knowing.

(3) Archduchess Maria Anna of Austria, who had come to Munich to marry Duke Maximilian, had disappeared from her quarters in the *Residenz*, along with about half of her household.

Ed's mind filed that away as potentially important political information, but not directly relevant to the matter at hand.

(4) Most of this would be publicly known within a matter of two or at most three days. This part of the message read: *I was instructed by Cavriani to make every effort to inform you that you might have the most timely notice possible. I am doing this upon my own authority, since I do not currently know where Herr Cavriani is, other than probably in Bavaria. Sincerely yours, etc. Egli.*

Ed picked up the phone, about to dial Henry Dreeson. He heard the front door open.

"Ed, Honey, can you come down?" That was Annabelle.

He pattered down the stairs in his foam-lined, utterly decrepit, brown corduroy house slippers. Annabelle was at the door with Father Kircher and—yes, the Englishman. Smithson.

"Father Kircher met Elaine and me at the library. I've got quite a bit of stuff about the English Ladies. They were the ones that wanted to be Jesuitesses. I remembered once he mentioned it. They were suppressed in our world, well, here, too. The ones who wanted to run schools for girls. But that's not what is so exciting."

Ed smiled. Annabelle was bubbling. He loved it when Annabelle bubbled.

"Father Smithson actually knows Mary Ward. Their superior. And they are coming here. To Grantville."

Father Kircher was smiling, too. Annabelle did that to people.

Ed raised his eyebrows.

Kircher explained. "In this world, the pope has seen fit to revoke the suppression of the English Ladies' order. He has directed them to come to the USE and operate under the protection of Cardinal-Protector Mazzare. We have been instructed by Father-General Vitelleschi to make them welcome. According to the latest information that we have, they should be somewhere between Munich and the Danube."

Ed's ears pricked up. "Between?"

Father Smithson nodded. "Yes. We received a letter from Father Rader in Munich in this afternoon's mail bag. The Ladies left Munich early in the morning the day that the play was performed; they should be well on their way by now. And, I suppose it would interest you to know, Mistress Dreeson and Mistress Simpson left Munich with them."

Ed thanked them profoundly. And put his shoes back on. If the radio was still up, this needed to go to Mike Stearns. If not, it would have to wait until morning and there wouldn't be a thing that he could do about it.

And he had to ask Mike whether or not he could tell this last bit to Henry and Annalise.

Ed knew that Mike was back in Magdeburg for a few days, fortunately. The radio connection to Magdeburg was a lot more reliable than the one to Copenhagen.

Mike said not to tell them. Not that Mary and Ronnie were with the English Ladies and out of Munich. It was okay to pass the rest on, since Egli said that it was going to be in the papers in a couple of days, anyhow.

Magdeburg

Mike Stearns looked around the room with some exasperation. Being fair, most of his ill humor was not the fault of anyone in the room. It was simply due to the fact that Mike didn't like to fly, had never liked to fly—even in late twentieth-century commercial aircraft, much less Jesse Woods' World War I-era equivalent of a tiny down-time air force—and had just had to make another flight from Copenhagen to Magdeburg to deal with pressing Prime Minister-type affairs.

To make things worse, he was fretting over Becky's medical condition. Her pregnancy was far enough advanced now that she'd decided to leave Copenhagen and return to Amsterdam. He'd wanted her to come to Magdeburg to have the baby—Grantville would have been better still—but Becky insisted that she'd be in good hands in Amsterdam, with Anne Jefferson in the city. And she needed to be in Amsterdam, able to talk readily with Don Fernando and Fredrik Hendrik, given the way the diplomatic situation was developing.

Mike had conceded, since he couldn't really argue the point. But given the mood he was in, the last thing he needed was to have a brand new development dropped on him the moment he got back to Magdeburg. It didn't help his mood any that Francisco Nasi was in a snit. And a damned childish one, in Mike's opinion.

Francisco had been scooped. Rumors that Duke Maximilian was not entirely pleased with his prospective bride—yes, he had received those, and had passed them on. But nothing that would have escalated the difference of opinion to the point that the bride returned to Austria. After all, nobody required the spouses in important political marriages to be personally compatible.

He was not made happier by Landgrave Hermann's question. "Do we know that she is returning to Austria?"

Sattler said, "Presumably. Where else would she go?"

That led to a long and meandering discussion. Don Francisco was not happy that he could not provide a definitive answer to the question. He was in a mad scramble to get more intelligence and anxiously awaiting the arrival of the diplomatic pouches.

Finally, Mike interrupted. "The answer is, we don't know. Let's just table it until we do know something. Now, as to Mary and Ronnie."

Don Francisco was also not happy that the Jesuits had known more about their whereabouts than his agents did. Overall, Don Francisco was not happy with the state of his operations in Bavaria. He expressed his exasperation that two such important, but unrelated, events had happened more or less simultaneously, so the few informants whom he did have in the duchy were having their attention pulled in two different directions.

"Are you sure," Landgrave Hermann asked, "that they are unrelated?"

"At present, I do not see any reasonable causational relationship. Nor any clear link. In the reports on the archduchess' daily activities—" he paused and thumbed through them "—she did pay one formal courtesy visit. The English Ladies paid one formal courtesy visit to her apartments. That is all." Don Francisco sighed. "Of course, I may be missing something. I certainly do not have enough agents in Bavaria that I could have her entire household observed."

"Is there anything," Hermann asked, "that we should be doing in regard to Frau Simpson and Frau Dreeson. And the nuns?"

"Well, at a minimum, if they really are headed for Grantville—which we do not know for a certainty, but have only the Jesuits' word for it—we should notify Duke Ernst and Banér of the possibility that they may attempt to cross the Danube into the Upper Palatinate. But we have no idea where."

Just in case somebody might be getting fancy ideas, Philipp Sattler warned, "And there's no point in having us send somebody to look for them. Not in a territory as large as Bavaria."

"Damn," Mike said. "I wish that I had some idea what Cavriani is doing. And once this news gets out, Frank Jackson is going to start driving me nuts, the way he'll pester me for news of Diane in Basel."

He cocked an eye at Francisco. The Sephardic nobleman shrugged. "There is nothing new there, Michael. And Basel is hardly close enough to Munich for these latest developments to have any impact on Diane's situation."

"Famous last words," said Mike darkly.

Nasi chuckled. "Michael—please. How could Basel get involved in this?"

"Who the hell knows?" Mike replied irritably. "But I'm telling you—mark my words—any situation that involves Mary Simpson and Ronnie Dreeson being kidnapped and hauled down the Danube in barrels and a princess of Austria decamping from her fiancé's capital on the eve of their wedding—going who knows where, and for what reason—and with Mary and Ronnie escaping from captivity at the same time—by who knows what means or with what end in mind—can wind up damn near anywhere."

After a moment, he added gloomily. "Do we have any agents in China? Or Timbuktu? If not, maybe we should send some. You never know, with something this screwy."

Nürnberg

Veit Egli had underestimated the growing German press corps. A daredevil reporter left Munich the morning after the news of the disappearances became known there. He made it to Ingolstadt in a remarkably short time, bribed the owner of a small boat to ferry him across the Danube, and hitched a ride north on an army truck. The special edition came out in a day and a half. The reporter deposited his very large bonus in his bank account and had the nerve and energy to go back to Bavaria.

The disappearances made the papers in Magdeburg and Frankfurt am Main two days after that—with the stories datelined Nürnberg. The publisher gleefully informed the public that the court in Vienna had attempted to suppress one entire issue of the Vienna newspaper, but that the "entirety" had not been fully successful. The edition had been reprinted in Prague and smuggled into Austria in large quantities.

Grantville, State of Thuringia-Franconia

Ed Piazza inspected the collection of newspapers in front of him with some bemusement. The news articles, *per se*, weren't that bad. The reporters didn't know much, so kept them short and stuck to what they did know. The Case of the Disappearing Archduchess got the most play, with Mary and Veronica a close second. The English Ladies were barely on the horizon. The paper from Frankfurt am Main gave their departure from their house in Munich a two-inch notice at the bottom of a column on page three.

The editorials were another matter. Speculation, on a level that amounted to fantasy, was running rampant, especially in France and Venice. Ed's personal favorite was the one which stated that the archduchess, forbidden from following a true religious vocation by the depraved political ambitions of her father, had been saved by the personal intervention of the Virgin Mary, who had transported her to a cloistered convent on the borders of Transylvania, where her diligent prayers would henceforth prove to be a bulwark of Christian civilization against the marauding Turk.

Not bad. Maybe a bit hard to reconcile with the more succinct version that asserted that the archduchess had secretly converted to Calvinism and was known to be making her way to Geneva, but not bad.

A batch of them were sentimental—the archduchess had eloped with, take your pick, a valiant Austrian revolutionary, a member of the lesser nobility who was not of equal birth, or a former tutor. Alternatively, one could have a bit of gruesome. This writer considered it likely that the archduchess had been murdered by Duke Albrecht and Duchess Mechthilde in order to prevent a marriage that would bar their sons from the Bavarian succession.

Ed folded up the pile, wrote "archives" on a piece of paper he put on top of it, and tied the bundle with red tape. Historical documentation. Not of what had happened, but good primary evidence for what people were guessing.

USE army camp, outside Luebeck

"I don't believe this shit," grumbled Eric Krenz. Sourly, he studied the battery wagon he'd be riding from the army camp outside Luebeck on the Baltic all the way down to Bavaria. More precisely, one of whose horses he'd be riding, since there was no way a man could ride on the limber for that great a distance. Leaving aside the fact that doing so was against army regulations, he'd probably have a broken back by the time he got there. An injured back, for sure. The suspension on the limber's axle, such as it was, had been designed for metal, not flesh and bones.

Eric didn't like horses much, and he hated riding them.

"Oh, stop grousing," said his commanding officer, Lieutenant Thorsten Engler. "Look on the bright side. Once we get into the *Thueringerwald,* and from there south except parts of Franconia, the roads are so lousy that you'll probably have to walk most of the time anyway."

Krenz wasn't mollified. He gave the officer's insignia on Engler's uniform a look that was every bit as sour as the one he'd given the battery wagon.

"I can remember you being a friendly and sympathetic fellow, back when you were a mere sergeant."

Thorsten snorted. "Not on this subject. Your memory's rotten. I never had any sympathy for your idiot refusal to learn to ride a horse properly. I warned you back in training camp that you'd come to regret it."

Krenz didn't argue the point, since . . .

Well, it was the plain and the simple truth.

Instead, he shifted his grousing elsewhere. "And that's not all that's rotten about the situation," he whined. "We're supposed to be heroes. Basking in the glory of our triumph at Ahrensbök. Since when does 'basking' last only a few weeks?"

Grinning, one of the other members of the flying artillery battery gave the inevitable reply. That was Olav Gjervan, one of the gunners. "It's called 'the army,' Eric. Not 'the fairy tale.' "

"I still say it's lousy," insisted Krenz. "Unfair. Unjust. Let one of the green regiments go down there to Bavaria."

"Which syllable in 'the ar-my' don't you understand?" demanded Engler.

"See!" Krenz pointed an accusing finger at the silver bar on Engler's shoulder. The army of the United States of Europe had wound up adopting the rank insignia used by the now-dissolved army of the New United States—now also dissolved, into the State of Thuringia-Franconia—which, in turn, had been taken from the army of a United States of America located in a different universe.

"Back when he just had chevrons like the rest of us grunts"—that word was English, one of many American loan terms adopted by the new Amideutsch dialect that was becoming the common language of the USE—"he wasn't that sarcastic."

"Like the lieutenant says," jeered Olav, "your memory's rotten. Thorsten never suffered fools gladly."

Engler was looking sour himself, now. "The promotion wasn't my idea, anyway, Eric. As you damn well know. They forced it on me."

Krenz's usual good humor returned. "Well, sure. Who can blame them? What could be more silly than 'Sergeant the Imperial Count of Narnia?' "

Everybody laughed at that. Even Thorsten.

CHAPTER 46

Servus Mori

Dr. Donnersberger was the first member of the privy council executed. He was not the last. Abegg was gone, too. Both chanceries were in chaos.

Duke Maximilian concluded that those most responsible for the debacle were the members of the privy council who had at first been inclined to oppose his remarriage, but had subsequently changed their minds. They were guilty of not having provided a counterpoise to those who directly urged him to remarry. They were guilty of not having made him listen to the words of his own vow.

The formal charge was misprision of treason.

Their estates, of course, escheated to the duchy, after payment of court costs.

Dr. Richel had performed some rather deft footwork to bring the duke to this point of view. He was now generally regarded as the most influential among the lay councillors, second only to Father Forer. The duke was known to be listening to the Spanish ambassador, as well.

In the week that led up to Dr. Donnersberger's execution, quite a few of the lower nobility who held seats on the privy council sent their families out of Munich, to their country estates. Followed, as quickly as they could make arrangements, by themselves.

Duke Maximilian told the colonel of the garrison and the captain of the guards not to worry about it. They could take care of the problem later, at leisure. There were more immediate and important tasks.

It was clear, Duke Maximilian concluded, that Ferdinand II, from the beginning, had intended to make a fool of him. He ordered the members of the archduchess' household who had remained in Munich interned; questioned; then ordered them executed.

With due attention to protocol, of course. Countess Polyxena and the other three ladies-in-waiting who had remained behind were beheaded; the remainder, Frau Stecher among them, hanged in the *Schrannenplatz*. The seamstress had protested to the last that she had been a faithful informant to the Inquisition and had no part in the departure of the archduchess. This was manifestly contradicted by the note from Countess Polyxena that *Dekan* Golla's associate had found. The countess had first denied writing it, as was to be expected, but had later admitted it under torture.

Their heads were sent to join those of the privy councillors, lining the outer walls of Munich, above the gates.

Vienna, Austria

"Mama," Cecelia Renata asked anxiously. "What are we going to do? Papa is practically apoplectic."

Empress Eleonora looked at her stepdaughter wearily. "I know. I have used every soothing and cooling potion that I know, but they are not doing him any good. Not even the poultices. I have had snow and ice brought down from the mountains, but even so, it is clear that every day his humors are a little more choleric."

Mariana leaned over and kissed her cheek, giving her a comforting hug.

"I can't nurse him. But I can, and have, written to my Ferdinand. Telling him that he needs to come home from the Hungarian border now. Whether Papa and the privy council authorize him to or not."

She leaned back on the bench in the empress' private garden. "If only it weren't so hot."

"Maximilian has done this, you are telling me, in spite of Our official assurances, sent to him in the diplomatic pouch, that these members of the archduchess' household were personally loyal to Us?"

"Yes, Your Majesty."

"They *were* personally loyal to Us, weren't they?"

Father Lamormaini looked very unhappy. "Most of them, certainly. With the exception of a few, such as Countess Polyxena. I don't believe she was disloyal, as such, if only for the reason that no sane person would have attempted to use *her* as an agent or informant. Though we could not avoid including her among the appointments, given how essential her husband is to the proper operation of the imperial treasury."

Cardinal Dietrichstein nodded. "She was completely useless—not a thought in her head beyond clothes and getting a high-status position at court. Little idiot. Pretty, though."

"Is it true that We do not have any information at all in regard to the archduchess and the remainder of her household?"

The emperor had ceased to refer to Maria Anna as his daughter.

"Yes. Freiherrin Lukretia, who left Munich a couple of days before the disappearance to return to Vienna for her expected confinement, has taken refuge with the count of Ortenburg. She is afraid to proceed on to Passau, for fear of being arrested by Maximilian's agents, which is not unreasonable, under the circumstances. Ortenburg sent a courier to Archduke Leopold Wilhelm. According to the Freiherrin, all the other members of the household were going about their usual tasks at the time she left."

"Is that all she knows?"

"It is all the information that was in the letter that the courier brought."

"Is there ambivalence in your sentence?"

"Freiherrin Lukretia is far from being a pretty little idiot. It may well have occurred to her that as long as she stays in Ortenburg, Maximilian cannot question her—but, then, neither can we."

Munich, Bavaria

Carafa prudently withdrew from Munich to Passau. From there, he went to Vienna. As Richel noted, it still had not been explained just how the nuncio had happened to leave his mule so conveniently tethered that it had been readily available for use in Doña Mencia de Mendoza's escape from the archduchess' apartments.

The Spanish ambassador did not miss the opportunity to point out to Duke Maximilian that the withdrawal of the nuncio necessarily gave rise to a suspicion that Urban VIII might have been in league with the Austrians. Ungrateful wretch that he was, not to appreciate all that the duke had done for the papacy and for the cause of the church.

The duke was inclined to listen to this theory, especially in view of the pope's recent appointment of a cardinal-protector for the heretical United States of Europe. One of the up-timers, no less.

A cardinal-protector from Grantville. Which is where the two damnable women with whom Mechthilde of Leuchtenberg had saddled him came from. He needed to look into that more deeply. It would have been easier if Landgrave Wilhelm Georg had not finally died the week before.

It was entirely proper that Albrecht and Mechthilde, with their sons and much of their household, had left Munich to attend his funeral and arrange for the transportation of his body to Pfreimd, where it would be interred in the family crypt. It would be a normal courtesy for Gustav Adolf's regent to permit the transport of the coffin through the Upper Palatinate to reach it.

It was not entirely appropriate that they had left Munich for Johann Franz Hörwarth von Hohenberg's estate near Planegg a week ago and had not yet returned. Hörwarth, the son of Dr. Donnersberger's predecessor as the administrative chancellor of the Bavarian government, had been, for some time now, the landgrave's rather unwilling host.

The Leuchtenberger, no matter what Mechtilde said, were the ones who had saddled him with the Grantville women. Possibly witch women. Certainly servants of the Swede.

Maximilian ordered the extension of questioning to those of his brother's servants who remained in Munich. Not, at first, strict questioning.

Even without strict questioning, one of the maids provided very troubling testimony. She stated that beginning the day of the archduchess' disappearance, she had been instructed to deliver food, clean towels, soap, and various other amenities to the unused rooms that had served as nurseries for Duke Albrecht's sons. This had continued until the day that the household left Munich, when she was told that they would no longer be needed.

"Surely," Dr. Richel said, "they cannot have been keeping the archduchess imprisoned."

The question returned to Duke Maximilian's mind. "Who would benefit most?"

He ordered one of the guards to bring the maid back. Under a repetition of questioning, still without torture, the maid stated that she had never seen the woman who was apparently staying in the rooms. Whenever she brought supplies, except for the first day, she had left them in the outer nursery. The woman must have been in the small room once used by the wet nurses.

"You are sure that it was a woman?" Father Forer asked.

"Yes, sir." She provided some explanation of the different types of supplies and food that gentlemen and ladies often used. At request, she made a list of everything she had delivered. And everything that she had removed.

"In the brushes, were there curly, black, hairs?"

"No sir. The only hairs that I saw were straight; some were black, others gray. Very long, even for a woman."

"Gray." Richel was thumbing through the list. "What are 'wraps'?"

"Strips of cloth, sir," the maid answered.

"Strips of cloth?"

The court physician leaned forward. "They are often used by people who have injuries or pain in their joints. Bad ankles. Bad knees. They provide some support. In the case of rheumatism or arthritis, they can reduce the swelling somewhat."

"Good God," Richel exclaimed. "Doña Mencia."

"But she was seen to escape," Father Forer exclaimed.

"An old woman dressed in black was seen to escape. No one has heard of her since." The Capuchin frowned.

"But what connection would there have been between Duke Albrecht and Doña Mencia?" Richel meant it as a hypothetical question.

Dekan Golla answered. "The English Ladies. Who stand in the shadow of the Inquisition. Duchess Mechthilde was serving as their patron; the archduchess Maria Anna offered to become their patron. There must have been a taint of heresy in both households. And in Vienna, as well; it is widely known that Ferdinand II supports them."

Dr. Richel opened his mouth, then closed it again. This was

not a suitable occasion to mention that Duke Maximilian himself and the late Duchess Elisabeth Renata had also supported them. Times had changed.

"Not to mention," the Dominican said, "that many of the families of Munich's patriciate—a class of which Dr. Donnersberger was a member—sent their daughters to the school that the English Ladies conducted. It may be desirable to widen the scope of your investigation."

The Capuchin suggested, on the basis of information received from the man who delivered produce to the English Ladies, that it might be prudent to question their cook.

The guard stood quietly behind the maid, listening to the entire conversation. They had forgotten to order him to take her from the room.

He completed his shift on duty and said to his sergeant that he thought he would drop by St. Peter's for vespers. It was something that he did regularly.

The sergeant waved him away.

He went to St. Peter's for vespers; then, on his way back to the barracks, stopped at his mother's house. Where he gave his brother a note and urged him to take it to Duke Albrecht in the country right away.

The English Ladies' cook could not be found. Neighbors stated that she and her family had not been seen for a week. The Inquisition noted that as a suspicious circumstance.

Many of the families who had sent their daughters to the English Ladies' school could be found. They were questioned, as were their daughters.

They confirmed the reports of the Inquisition's agents. Both Doña Mencia de Mendoza and Duchess Mechthilde had been visitors at the house of the English Ladies with some frequency. Upon several occasions, their visits had overlapped.

The Inquisition began an extensive investigation of suspicion of heresy within many of the city's most influential families. It was expected to take some time. The affected families were placed under house arrest. This did not prevent four of them from admitting their guilt by fleeing from the city.

✧   ✧   ✧

Duke Maximilian signed the charges against his brother and Mechthilde. Conspiracy to commit treason. That would suffice for the time being. *Dekan* Golla was preparing charges that would provide a basis for an investigation in regard to heresy and witchcraft.

He dispatched four full companies of troops to Freiherr Hörwarth's residence near Planegg. That should be more than adequate; he was informed that they had taken only the usual complement of household guards when they left Munich.

Their first task was to secure the boys and bring them back to Munich. Bavaria still needed heirs; he had no others.

CHAPTER 47

Ad Extrema Descendere

Planegg, Bavaria

Duke Albrecht gave the guard's brother a reward. A substantial one.

Then he took the information to Mechthilde, whose first thought was that Maximilian would try to take her sons.

Albrecht started to protest; then agreed.

"It's so damned frustrating, Tilda. A lifetime of loyalty, erased as if it meant nothing! He hasn't even *asked* me if there might be some other explanation than the one Richel is giving him. Every order he issues just feeds into another. But even if he arrests all of us, there's no evidence that could lead to a conviction. None."

"There is my connection to the English Ladies." Mechthilde gestured to the note that the guard's brother had delivered. "They can build on that; will build on that."

"It's not enough."

"There are the two women from Grantville."

"He can't prove a connection."

Mechthilde lifted her chin. "I provided refuge in our apartments in the *Residenz* for Doña Mencia de Mendoza. From the night the archduchess' disappearance was discovered; she came that evening. I had a place prepared for her. She remained for some time."

Duke Albrecht choked.

"She remained until we came to my brother's funeral. She came with us. She is here."

He looked at her, frozen. Then, "It is far too late for turning her over to Duke Maximilian to do us any good now. The game is too far in play. Why in hell did you do it?"

"I didn't assist the archduchess to leave. But I knew that she planned to. I *wanted* her to." She gripped his wrist fiercely. "For the boys, Albrecht. For the boys."

He issued orders. Tomorrow, the ducal party would hunt. The day after, they would return to Munich.

The servants started packing.

He consulted with the chief huntsman. He wanted to take the boys along, he said, so he would prefer small game. A reasonable number of beaters.

Guests?

"No, I don't think so. Not so soon after Landgrave Wilhelm Georg's death. Just a private family party. But a nice one. The duchess will accompany us. A picnic lunch, please. Plan on a full day."

The carriage for the duchess?

"No, she will be riding with us. But, yes, bring the small carriage. Some of the ladies-in-waiting may not wish to ride."

So it was decided. They were going. The question was, where? Which way? He sat down to figure that out.

Austria was not possible. Not only would it be hard to get there—most routes between Bavaria and Austria involved mountain passes at which Max's troops could cut them off—but also they would not be particularly welcome when they got there. Ferdinand II was not happy with Maximilian at the moment, but he wasn't particularly happy with any Bavarians.

Additionally, if they went into Austria, that would put Doña Mencia de Mendoza into the emperor's hands. They could not hide her forever. The simplest solution would be to have the old woman strangled, but he was incapable of ordering that.

Letting the old woman fall into Ferdinand II's hands would be equivalent to ordering her strangled. Except that Ferdinand, without doubt, would have her questioned first.

If he ordered her strangled, to be just, he would have to order

Mechthilde strangled. She was far more culpable. And she was his wife.

The old woman, he was certain, knew what had happened. Where the archduchess had gone, and why. He had not asked her; it was something that he did not want to know. She knew that Mechthilde had been at least marginally involved. If they went to Austria and Ferdinand II had Doña Mencia questioned, it would have the same eventual effect as if he ordered Mechthilde strangled himself. Or as if they just stayed here and let Max arrest and imprison them.

Austria was impossible.

Tyrol was too far; same problem anyway—mountain passes. The same for Salzburg.

Passau, no good. First, Max's troops could cut them off at the choke point; second, the bishop was Ferdinand II's son.

To Dachau. Then over to the Isar, through Freising and Landshut. To the Danube. Across. Into that neck of the Upper Palatinate that reached down toward Passau. Across it; into Bohemia.

Wallenstein. The king of Bohemia. Right now, Wallenstein offered the only possible sanctuary. The only one within reach. There was no time to feel him out first; no time to make an offer and receive a counteroffer.

He could only hope that Wallenstein would consider that having all of Bavaria's heirs within his control was a sufficiently important diplomatic edge that he would leave them alive.

Albrecht had no illusions. If Wallenstein did not consider it important enough, they might all die at the end of that route, too.

The hunting party rode out. A half hour later, all of Duke Albrecht's household guards rode out, as well. And waited.

Two hours later, the hunting party arrived where the guards were waiting. They had not yet reached the copse where the beaters had been setting up the hunt.

Albrecht looked at Landgrave Wilhelm Georg's head huntsman a little apologetically.

"I can't leave you and your men here. I'm sorry."

The huntsmen were completely unprepared; the guards made short work of the business.

"Leave their bodies here. Perhaps their deaths will spare their

families back on the estate the attention of my brother's troops."
He was not counting on that, though. Not at all.

They headed northeast, down the Isar. Bishop Gepeckh's men
let them through. That saved a lot of time.

The hunting carriage, never built to take the punishment of
traveling so far at so fast a rate, had to be left outside of Landshut.
The guards commandeered a sturdy market cart with two good
horses. It was better than nothing.

"They weren't there. We arrived at the estate and they were
gone. Hunting, the steward said. Hörwarth isn't home, of course.
He's been called to Ingolstadt to serve as one of the official witnesses to Farensbach's execution. Duke Albrecht's servants were
packing their baggage, to come back to Munich the next day. At
first, the captain thought it was routine enough. They'd ordered
a picnic; the beaters had been called out. First, the captain just
told us all to dismount and wait, so we did. It was when we went
to take the horses to the stables that we noticed."

"Noticed what?"

"All the horses that Duke Albrecht's guards ride were gone.
And so were the guards. The sergeant went to tell the captain.
And they didn't come back."

Richel was having unusual difficulty in thinking clearly. "Didn't
come back?"

"From the hunt. Not Duke Albrecht or his wife or his sons.
They're gone. And some of their household, plus the guards."

When the beaters came in, the captain questioned them about
the planned route of the hunting party. The next morning, they
traced it out. Only to come upon a local *Pfleggerichter* and his
men investigating six corpses. A local farmer's dog had given the
alarm. Freiherr von Hörwarth's huntsmen.

It was little comfort to Duke Maximilian's captain that everyone
present except himself and his men—the *Pfleggerichter*, the village
mayor, the local peasants—seemed to assume, without question,
that a contingent of the duke's troops on their way to reinforce
Ingolstadt had just happened to come across a group of lightly
armed men out in the open, found them annoying in some way,
and killed them for the hell of it. Because they could.

The mayor said, "They do it all the time. We're less than nothing to them, and this was just a little country estate, belonging to the Freiherr. They weren't in a fancy livery or anything, to show that they worked for someone powerful. Just countrymen."

Which provided no answer to the question of where the remainder of the hunting party might be. The captain sent a rider back to Munich.

The *Pfleggerichter* had suggested the possibility that hostile raiders, perhaps out of Regensburg, had kidnapped Duke Albrecht and his family and were taking them into the USE as hostages. The captain conscientiously reported this theory, but added that he did not think that this was the case. Although the ground was hard, there was no indication that there had been a large number of horses at the scene. Not more than would be accounted for by Duke Albrecht's household and guards.

Large numbers of horses, stopped in any one place for any length of time, left traces of their presence other than footprints.

Most of the local farmers were standing around looking at the corpses.

One young man, the oldest son of the village mayor, was making his way to Regensburg. The family had relatives there. They had not always been Catholic; some uncles had left rather than give in to the late Duke Wilhelm's conversion campaign. They kept in touch.

Munich, Bavaria

"Pursue them," Duke Maximilian ordered. "Prepare the men to ride as fast as possible, as little extra weight as possible on the horses. And bring me my armor."

"Your Grace," Richel exclaimed. "You cannot. What if..."

"Do you think that I have not ridden with my men before, Dr. Richel? Or that I am no longer capable of doing so?" The graying black eyebrow went up.

"Er, well, no, Your Grace, of course not, but..."

"But you are afraid that if I am killed, then you will have to face Duke Albrecht. Which you will. But there is one other thing that you need to think of, if you plan to keep the position into which you have clawed yourself."

"What?"

"There is only one person in Bavaria who outranks Albrecht. He is still the heir. He has not been indicted for any crime; we have merely lodged charges against him. Not tried; not convicted. Which means that if someone is going to countermand any order that Albrecht has given, I am the one who must do it."

Maximilian moved his arms so the valet could help him put the armor on. "Are you thinking, Richel?"

"Yes, Your Grace, most certainly."

"Then think that I am the only person in Bavaria who can order my brother's execution, if it should come to that. Remember that he can order yours. And ask yourself if you really want to dissuade me from riding after him."

Amberg, the Upper Palatinate

Duke Ernst looked at Eric Haakansson Hand. "What do you make of it?" The information that came into Regensburg had been relayed to them by Brick Bozarth, the UMWA man who was dealing with the city council there.

"By itself, not much. With all the other information that has been coming out of Bavaria, actually, I'm inclined to believe it. What Duke Maximilian has been doing is like a witch hunt that isn't a witch hunt. It's not impossible that it has expanded to take in his own brother's family and not impossible that they would be running, if they got wind of it in time."

"Witch hunt that isn't a witch hunt?"

"It's working the same way. That's how the persecutions go. They start with one or two little things, minor, a lot of the time. Then some local official decides that they are serious enough to merit an investigation, so he questions some witnesses and turns in some reports. Mostly, it never goes beyond that. But, sometimes, someone at a higher level picks it up. The witnesses and the accused are questioned again, under torture, until they name others. Accomplices, other witches. Then those are arrested and investigated and indicted and tortured. It can keep expanding and expanding until hundreds of people are involved. That's what seems to be happening in Munich, as far as I can follow it. Except, I think, that no one at all seriously believes that Veronica Dreeson is a witch, much less Mary Simpson. But it's growing the same way, and coming from the highest level, the duke himself. He's the one who is weaving all the separate threads together, seeing patterns. Or, perhaps, Richel or Forer or Golla, which amounts to the same thing. The impetus is coming down from the very highest level of the duchy's administration, so there's no one who can put a stop to it, no one who can call a halt. A witch hunt without witches."

"Anything to the report that they appeared to be coming this way?"

"Dashing down the Isar, he said. He last heard that they had passed Landshut. Unless, when they get to the Danube, they all climb into a boat and head for Passau, they have to be coming this way. And if they were heading for Passau, there wouldn't be any reason at all for them to go so roundabout. They're mounted."

Hand looked at Duke Ernst, considering for a moment. After all this time, nearly two years now, he still wasn't sure that he had the man's measure. "What are you thinking about doing?"

Duke Ernst smiled. The leprechaun smile. "I believe that they are headed for Bohemia. I'm going to let them through."

"*What!*"

"Unless you, as the king's, ah, emperor's cousin, veto me." He winked. "You have read the up-time fable also, I am sure. 'All animals are created equal, but some animals are created more equal than others.' Or something to that effect. The cousins of kings or emperors are always just a little more equal than ordinary dukes." He paused. "Not that it hasn't been a pleasure working with you, Colonel Hand."

Hand decided not to comment on this. "How do you plan to let them through?"

"Warn the boatmen and the *Grenzjaeger* that they are coming; have them watch the most likely crossing points, let them cross, make sure that they keep moving, and that they keep on a northeast course, which will land them in Bohemia rather than Austria. Herd them a little, if they seem to be veering to the south."

Duke Ernst reached up and rubbed the back of his neck. "I certainly don't want to end up with them here. Let Wallenstein deal with the political headaches. I have too much else to do."

Hand thought about it. "Not a bad solution."

He thought again. "What if Maximilian sends pursuers across after them?"

Duke Ernst smiled again. "Then we will see what our boatmen and *Grenzjaeger* have learned during all of their training."

✧   ✧   ✧

It was well after dark, but the moon was approaching the full. Duke Albrecht was cursing. There were supposed to have been more boats; he had sent two of his guards ahead to Isarmuend, riding fast, to arrange for boats. But the rest of them had been slowed down; an officious bailiff at Dingelfing. God be thanked that Maximilian had not sent riders ahead of them. He had managed to pull rank, of the "I am the duke's brother and *you* are going to be sorry about this" type. But they had lost two hours; some of the boats had left the meeting point.

Which meant that they were not going to be able to take everything across. He had planned on putting the carriage, or cart, now, with its team, on the large raft that the guards had procured. They would have to leave that behind, in favor of taking more of the horses. Even then, they left some of the horses behind. And a half-dozen guards. Not enough to check pursuers, but enough to make a lot of noise and disturbance; maybe even slow them down a little.

Under the circumstances, the crossing went better than he had expected. On the north shore, he rearranged the riders; some of them would have to double up, others follow on foot and attempt to delay any pursuit. Fifty miles, more or less, to the Bohemian border.

Doña Mencia, knees and all, was going to have to get on a horse. Well, be put on a horse. Two of the guards lifted her on; then tied her there. They put a protesting Sigmund Albrecht up in front of her; his father had to swat him to get him to cooperate. Vervaux, the tutor, on another horse; Maximilian Heinrich in front of him. Duke Albrecht told Vervaux to keep hold of Doña Mencia's reins; Sigmund could hold on to the pommel. The rest of the women were told to take children in front of them, starting with the youngest. There were only a half dozen women in addition to Mechthilde and Doña Mencia; not a lot of children, but enough to slow them down. Better to risk them on the flight than to leave them behind, he had concluded.

Pursuit would come from behind; Duke Albrecht put only a couple of guards to the front; then the women and children. Moon or not, it was not safe to gallop. They started out cautiously.

On the south bank, there were shots. Maximilian's troops must have been gaining on them all day. He could count on their being across very soon. Somewhere, they would find boats.

They continued along the road. It was starting to get darker. The moon was still out, but now occasional clouds had started to scud across its face; then more and more, until it was cloudy more of the time than they had moonlight. The changes made it harder for their eyes to adjust.

The guard who was taking the lead pulled up his horse. Planted at a fork in the road, there was a board, whitewashed. Turned to face the moon. With large letters, and an arrow. "That way to Bohemia."

Duke Albrecht grunted. "It seems that we are expected. I hope that they are telling the truth."

The guard pulled up the signboard and turned it face down.

"They're across. Duke Maximilian's men." One of Duke Ernst's boatmen slid into a group of *Grenzjaeger*. "They had to go downstream about a mile, but they found where the boats that didn't wait for Duke Albrecht were tied up. Right outside Isarmuend would you believe, fastened to the piers just like it was a perfectly ordinary night with nothing going on. Rousted them out and came across. Now they're trying to figure out where Duke Albrecht landed, just by riding upstream toward Deggendorf."

"Too bad they didn't ride downstream towards Aich. Quirin, you, go down to Aich and bring back the men we left there. Wish we were allowed to cut them up a bit."

"Not here. Not unless or until they get too close to the first bunch. The fighting will be farther up. Some guys get all the fun."

"Want us to stove in their boats while they're gone?" the boatman asked hopefully.

"Hell, no. Duke Ernst doesn't want to *keep* them. He hopes they'll give up and go back where they came from."

One thing that the *Grenzjaeger* had not counted on was that a couple of Maximilian's men were from this part of the Upper Palatinate. Maximilian had combed through the soldiers he had in Munich, before he left, looking for such men. One of them knew a shortcut. Not an easy one, but the pursuers were not having to take women and children into account. They bypassed the road fork where the sign had been posted and those of Albrecht's men who were not on foot had been waiting to delay them. After two hours, the men realized that something was wrong; they started to follow Duke Albrecht again.

CHAPTER 48

Haeredes Bavariae

Duke Albrecht looked back. He thought he heard something.

The guard farthest to the rear was waving a white handkerchief, easy to see since the moon was out again, for a moment. Maximilian's troops had caught up with them. He turned back to position himself with the guards.

The pistols weren't doing much good. Not with the clouds coming and going. It was mainly swords. Quiet, for a fight. The road was dusty; there was grass growing on the edges. Old leaves. His guards were more than holding their own.

A horse peeled back from the front of the column. Oh, please God, not Karl Johann Franz. Too old, too big, to be doubled up with another rider. On his own horse, with his sword out, plunging into the thick of the fight. Not quite sixteen, and nowhere nearly as skilled as he thought he was.

"Karl!" his father shouted. "Get back! Get out of there. Go back where I left you; back where you belong."

Too late. The boy was down, his mount running.

Duke Albrecht spurred his horse, trying to reach where his son had fallen.

Toward the front of the column, a shriek of fury. Mechthilde. She had turned; she had seen Karl fall. No, no, no. He watched helplessly.

Mechthilde, spurring her horse at the Bavarians, riding into the melee. Unarmed in any conventional sense, using her horse itself as a weapon. She had always been a fierce rider in the hunt. She rammed her mount into the side of the one ridden by the soldier who had unseated Karl; knocked them hard enough that the Bavarian's horse slipped on the dewy grass and fell. Rearing up, she brought her own horse's front hoofs down on the man.

Several of the Bavarians turned toward her. One of Albrecht's men tried to grab the reins of her plunging horse. She pulled away. Albrecht desperately tried to reach her.

A moment of moonlight. The oncoming rider was clearly visible. The armor. Maximilian himself? Oh, surely not, but so recognizable, so very different from the standard issue of the regular troops. Mechthilde, screaming, screaming, driving her horse toward him.

Reflexively, Duke Maximilian brought up the lance mounted at the side of his horse. She impaled herself on it and fell.

Johannes Vervaux had passed this way before on one of his trips to the *collegium* in Amberg. He recognized it, even in the imperfect light. He could not predict the outcome of the fight; his responsibility was to his pupils and to the future for which they were destined. Gathering up the reins of the horses carrying himself and Doña Mencia, he turned off the path that the group had been following. Not northeast, but west. He pulled them away to safety as two of the guards anxiously hurried the other women and children along the determined path, as fast as they dared.

"What do you want to do about it?" one of the *Grenzjaeger* stationed along the side road that led toward Regen asked anxiously. "This wasn't covered in our orders."

"Stop them and take them back to the rest? Duke Ernst doesn't want to keep Duke Albrecht's party."

"Right into the middle of that cut, hack, and slash? A priest, an old lady, and two kids?"

"Priest?"

"He's got priest clothes on. I could tell that, even by just the moon."

"No point in sending lambs back to the slaughter. Let 'em go. What difference can it make?"

"Second thought."

"Yeah?"

"We're not doing anything else here. Let's make sure they get away."

"Hey, Franz."

"Yeah."

"It's starting to rain."

"I noticed."

After Mechthilde fell, the Bavarians pulled back, briefly. Maybe it was the sudden dark again; maybe the rain starting up. Albrecht decided to take advantage of it. "Turn and ride. Keep up a rear guard fight if we have to, but our main concern is getting across as fast as we can."

The guards followed him. They were almost a half mile behind the lead party, which eventually came to a white sign that read, "Turn here to follow the Kleine Regen." A guard pulled that and laid it face down as well. Yet another sign directed them to the pass. The signs were telling the truth. The next town that they reached was Suzicz.

Duke Maximilian halted his horse and looked down at Mechthilde. She was dead. He had seen enough dead people to know.

"Your Grace." A very young rider.

"During the fight, Your Grace. A priest took the young dukes and an old lady away from the rest. Sir, when you sent us to the landgrave's estate the first time, you said that the young dukes were the most important. Sir."

The duke looked at him. "You are to be commended for good thinking." He gestured. "Lieutenant. Take five men and go after them. They can't have gotten far."

Maximilian looked down again. Two of the young dukes. Karl, like his mother, was dead.

"Wait here," he directed the rest of his men. "The most important thing is to ensure that I have control of Bavaria's heirs."

A half hour later, the lieutenant was back. With three men and two lamed horses.

"There are wires across the path in the dark, Your Grace. And traps on the road. I don't see any way that the priest could have set them. They were, ah, professional. If I do say so myself."

"Do you have an explanation of why the priest and the young dukes did not encounter these supposed wires and traps?"

"Ah, Your Grace, I suppose that they must have been put up after they passed by."

Maximilian glanced up. It was still raining, but the clouds were patchy. The moon was coming out, a cloud sliding away from it. In the sudden light, there was a flight of arrows out of the trees on either side of the road. Aimed at the horses. Several neighed and reared; none down, but some would be lame.

Then, from behind them, a volley of shots, also aimed at the horses. These brought some of them down.

The moon disappeared again; the rain gathered force.

"Those of you with horses, head back to the boats in good order. Those without, follow us as best you can."

He turned his own horse; his two regular bodyguards appeared at his side.

Duke Albrecht's guards who had been coming up the path on foot evaporated into the woods; the *Grenzjaeger* let them. Once the Bavarians were out of hearing, the guards returned to the path and started to follow Duke Albrecht. The *Grenzjaeger* permitted that, as well. Duke Ernst did not want to keep Duke Albrecht's party. The lieutenant of the *Grenzjaeger* was very pleased that the guards had not seen any of his own men.

Half of the boats were gone. Not as bad as it could have been, since nearly half of the horses were gone, as well. Maximilian's men loaded them and pushed out into the river.

Duke Ernst's boatmen looked after them wistfully. Maybe it had been against orders. They had been told not to destroy the duke's boats, but nobody said, well, not directly, that they shouldn't just hide them.

"Wish the main fight up there had lasted a little longer. We could have disappeared them all and had some fun here while they milled around."

The scout from the *Grenzjaeger* slid in among them again.

"Don't go into mourning too soon, Matzi. There's a batch more coming on foot."

The boatmen settled down to wait. To finish the business. Leaving half of Matzi's men behind to clean up, the scout led the rest northeast to find the others.

✧   ✧   ✧

At dawn, the *Grenzjaeger* came out of the woods, onto the scene of the skirmish. You couldn't call it more than that.

"What do we do?"

"With the soldiers? Just collect their weapons and armor, clothes, shoes, knives, anything useful. Then start digging. A couple of you see if any of the horses are worth saving. If not, put them down. I'll send Heinz the knacker and his boys to collect them. I hope he appreciates the bonus."

"Good. I don't want to think about digging graves that size."

"What about them?" The first man gestured toward the woman and young boy.

"Hell, I don't know."

"Sarge?"

"Yes, Matzi."

"I've seen her before. She wasn't so old, then. But it's the land-gravine. From Leuchtenberg, up by Pfreimd. I'm sure of it."

"What in hell was she doing with a bunch of Bavarians?"

"Married one of them. You know, how they marry off princesses. The family picks somebody important and she doesn't have a bit of say about it."

"Damn. Wish it was that simple with my daughter Anna. Mule-headed, determined that she's going to have Endres the fisherman or nobody."

"Nothing really wrong with Endres. Better let her have her way, or she'll make your life miserable. So what do we do with them?"

"If they really do belong up at Pfreimd, we'll send them there. Fancy family, they'll have a tomb or a crypt or something to put them in. Go to that town up to the west and call a teamster to bring a couple of coffins out."

"Tell him to bill it to Duke Ernst."

Vervaux had been moving slowly, saying a rosary of thanks that, apparently, no one had seen them leave the fight. Now it was getting light. There was a town ahead. Doña Mencia and the boys were too exhausted, from the flight and the fight, to ride through to Amberg. They needed to eat, to stop and rest. He had enough money for an inn, though innkeepers were more used to having people show up at dusk rather than dawn.

They lost their way. Always a good, reliable, excuse. How to travel? The boys weren't wearing anything fancy, just hunting clothes, thank goodness, but still they were obviously from a very wealthy family. The old ploy of a man traveling with his elderly mother and two young sons clearly would not do, if only because he himself didn't have any secular clothing.

Simple, Johannes, simple. Two young men on their way to the *collegium* in Amberg, accompanied by their grandmother and their tutor.

Which was, in fact, where they went.

Jakob Balde notified Duke Ernst of their arrival. And of their identity.

Ernst Haakansson Hand howled with laughter. "Remember what you said. 'I certainly don't want to end up with them here. Let Wallenstein deal with the political headaches. I have too much else to do.' So much for plans that are all too clever."

"How did they get here?" Böcler asked. He scribbled a note to himself: *interview all involved.* His *Historia Ernesti Ducis*, he thought, was coming along very well. If only people kept on doing such interesting things for a while longer, eternal fame would be within his grasp. Plus, since Duke Ernst was only thirty years old, there should be a second volume. At least.

"A little self-help and initiative. On the part of Vervaux," Hand answered. "And a certain tendency to interpret their orders freely by some of our *Grenzjaeger*, I'm afraid. Who didn't have the slightest idea who they were, of course, so I decided not to discipline them too hard."

"Have you heard anything about Duke Albrecht?" Duke Ernst asked mournfully.

"Yes, he did make it into Bohemia with the rest of his party. But he didn't realize that his sons were missing until dawn, and he still doesn't know where they are."

"So all we have to worry about are the boys."

"Well, not exactly." Hand grinned and handed over a piece of paper.

"Cardinal Bedmar, in the Netherlands, would appreciate it very much if we would reunite him with his sister. This wish is endorsed by the cardinal-infante. Or the prince formerly known as the cardinal-infante. Don Fernando, in any case. Accompanied by a personal communication from my illustrious cousin asking us to do just that."

"Bedmar's sister?"

"The old lady Vervaux brought in with the boys."

Duke Ernst rested his chin on the tips of his fingers. "Archduchess Maria Anna's chief personal attendant?"

"Got it."

"She had rheumatic knees, I've heard."

"I have it on the best authority that Grantville is sending a diesel truck."

Böcler took notes steadily.

Part Seven

August 1634

And I again am strong

CHAPTER 49

Triumphata Conscientia

Landshut, Bavaria

Duke Maximilian called his privy council and his close advisers, both civilian and military, to Landshut. He ordered the rest of the court establishment to remain in Munich, since he intended to return there shortly. Upon their arrival, he announced that young Duke Karl and his mother, *die Leuchtenbergerin*, had been killed during the pursuit.

The duke did not describe the circumstances of the deaths. Enough of the troops who had accompanied him into the Upper Palatinate had seen the events, though, that rumors were flying wild.

He formally announced that Duke Albrecht and the other two young dukes had escaped, but said no more than that. It was left to rumor, again, to circulate the information that while Duke Albrecht had achieved his goal of Bohemia, the two boys had been taken in another direction.

The most widespread rumor was that the removal of the two young dukes was the result of a conspiracy between, ah, someone, and Duke Ernst, with the intention of handing them into the power of the Swede. There was no other explanation of the undoubted fact, to which any number of the troops who had accompanied Duke Maximilian were willing to testify, that the regent in the Upper Palatinate had men in place with the intent of preventing Bavarian pursuit.

This being so, and since they had been taken from their father by their tutor, the Jesuit Vervaux, who had been sent to Bavaria by the duke of Lorraine . . . speculation went wild. It was a conspiracy that involved the French, possibly Richelieu, but more likely Monsieur Gaston, who was married to the duke of Lorraine's sister. The Jesuits, for unknown motives, were conspiring with the French against Bavaria.

At least, some of the Jesuits. Father Forer made it very plain that he did not in any way endorse the action of the renegade Vervaux. He stated that he had appealed to Father-General Vitelleschi to do something about it. Demand that Vervaux, wherever he was at the moment, be arrested and handed over. If not to Duke Maximilian, then at the very least to the bishop of Augsburg, or to a trustworthy emissary of the father-general, or to . . . someone, at any rate. As soon as they definitely found out where he was. And if, he added mentally, there was anyone trustworthy left in the world.

The formal announcement did not include any information in regard to Doña Mencia. Neither did the rumors, since none of the common soldiers had recognized her in the darkness of the night. In any case, Maximilian himself did not know that she had been the old woman drawn away from the escape party by Vervaux or even that an old woman had gone with the boys.

Richel sat next to the duke, taking notes. Personally, he expected Doña Mencia to surface in Bohemia any day now and be returned to Austria in a flamboyant gesture of magnanimity by Wallenstein. At which time they would have evidence, when Ferdinand II received her honorably, that he had been part of a conspiracy to humiliate Duke Maximilian from the moment he agreed to the marriage project. What the Bavarians really needed to determine, now, was why the Austrians had done it.

And do something about finding *die Habsburgerin*. Wherever she might be. Having her in custody would give Duke Maximilian a considerably greater amount of leverage against Austria.

This was not included in Duke Maximilian's statement to the privy council. Which did not mean that it failed to have a prominent place in Richel's instructions to the duke's intelligence staff, along with the disappearance of the Grantville women. The question of where the English Ladies might be led back, of course, to the question of the renegade Jesuit, Vervaux, who had confessed the archduchess. Even if not formally, Mary Ward's sisters were *de facto* Jesuitesses. They had maintained close contacts with the *collegium* in Munich, which led naturally to a suspicion that more of the Jesuits there had been involved in the conspiracy that had now deprived Bavaria of its heirs.

The next item of business, was the siege of Ingolstadt. Again, the news from Ingolstadt was not good. The Swedes showed no sign of giving up now that their plot with Farensbach had been discovered. They were not making much progress, but they were not giving up.

After the formal announcements, the duke dismissed the majority of the privy councillors, sending them back to Munich.

Munich, Bavaria

Father Forer was finding life very difficult. Heinrich von Knoeringen, the bishop of Augsburg and his own former penitent, the man who had once investigated the fitness of Gepeckh to become prince-bishop of Freising, formally demanded an investigation into the orthodoxy of the Munich Jesuits. Father-General Vitelleschi—probably as a delaying tactic, Forer thought—had responded by requesting that Ferdinand II permit Father Lamormaini to conduct a visitation of the Munich house. The Holy Roman Emperor had the impudence to issue him the necessary passports to travel to Munich.

Duke Maximilian, of course, had refused. One did not invite a conspirator to investigate his own fellows. Maximilian's objections were vociferous. He appealed to the pope; then from the pope badly informed to the pope better informed.

Forer himself desired, certainly, that the Catholic church be utterly uncompromising toward heretics. He also suspected, more strongly with every passing day, that at least some of his fellow Jesuits were somehow mixed right into the thick of the departure of the English Ladies. Duke Maximilian's net was widening. The Inquisition's investigation of heresy associated with the house on Paradise Street spread farther ever day. Reluctantly, Forer warned his fellow-Jesuits at the Munich *collegium* and the *Wilhelmsgymnasium*.

Father Drexel left Munich, taking the elderly Father Rader with him. Forer did not want to know where they were going.

Several other Jesuits whom the Inquisition might possibly consider to be tainted also left. Father Forer did not want to know that, either, but he suspected that they were going to Tyrol.

He was beginning to think, at least to suspect, that the father-general had supported Urban VIII in the appointment of the Grantville priest as cardinal-protector of the USE. If that was true, what was his own obligation of conscience? Had he sworn a vow of obedience to a heretical pope? Did he stand under the command of a heretical father-general? Had he allowed the formal obligation of oaths he had taken to them to lead him from the path of strict orthodoxy? Had he, in warning the other Munich Jesuits, permitted heretics to evade correction?

Night after night, after completing his duties to the duke and in the privy council, he went through Loyola's *Spiritual Exercises*. Had the formal oaths taken his conscience captive? Were they leading it in chains, as if it were loot captured in a military campaign, paraded under a triumphal arch by a conquering Roman emperor? He prayed.

Amberg, the Upper Palatinate

Duke Ernst ordered that Doña Mencia be transferred out of the Jesuit *collegium* in the dark of night. The order was accompanied by the direst of threats about what would happen to anyone who leaked the slightest bit of information about how she came to be in Amberg at all. His most sincere hope was to have her make a public reappearance in Grantville as if miraculously translated there by divine intervention. Plus, of course, a diesel truck. Certainly without any rumors that someone, anyone, of interest to the wider political world might have been or ever be in Amberg.

Which was why his secretary Böcler and his publicity agent Zincgref found themselves walking along the cobblestones of Amberg at four o'clock one morning, carrying a litter with a recumbent form on it. Dressed as gravediggers; the recumbent form covered with a shroud. The truck would have attracted far too much attention if it had been brought into the town. Not to mention that it was too large to pass through any of the gates.

By the time they reached the truck, it was starting to get light. Doña Mencia found the vehicle fascinating. She was particularly enchanted by the amenities provided in the rear portion. Of those, the "recliner" that had been firmly fastened to the floor was, by far, the finest. She had never envisioned such a thing. She stroked the leather. The teamster who had brought the truck said that the chair had been loaned, just for her, by Grantville's mayor, to whom it belonged. She had heard of the city's wealth; she revised her estimate of it upward.

It even had straps that were somehow mounted beneath the floor and fastened across the chair, so that if bad roads caused the truck to ride unevenly, she would not be thrown out. If she were younger, she would have liked to look underneath to see how the device was made. At her age, however, she would simply accept that some ingenious mechanic or engineer had created it. All through her life, such men had been demonstrating new marvels.

She had been prepared for a torturous trip across the Germanies, from the Upper Palatinate to join her brother Cardinal Bedmar in the Spanish Netherlands. Now, at least from Amberg to Grantville, she would ride more comfortably than if she were in the most luxurious bed ever made. All a gift of the king of Sweden.

With company, although the others would not ride so easily. The remainder of the chairs placed in the "bed" of the truck were much more Spartan. There would be several of Duke Ernst's young soldiers, going to be trained to operate the "radio" of which the regent was so proud. Herr Pilcher would also be traveling to Grantville in this truck. As soon as she was safely inside, the "recliner" screened from view, Pilcher would bring the iron men with whom he had signed contracts to view the truck. Duke Ernst believed that this would impress them all with Pilcher's importance, that Grantville would send such a grand vehicle to return him home, and make them less likely to renege upon their agreements. Not to mention providing an answer to curious questions about why the truck had come to Amberg.

So he would travel with her, as would two coffins. That was the other announced reason for the presence of the truck outside Amberg's walls. After some negotiation, Pilcher had arranged for the bodies of a young up-time soldier and a tinsmith who had served as his own translator to be disinterred and embalmed as expensively as if they were the bodies of fallen kings being returned to their native countries from a crusade in the Holy Land. They would be returned to Grantville for burial.

Doña Mencia did not mind sharing the truck with them. The coffins were sealed and death was a part of life.

Banér's siege lines outside Ingolstadt, the Upper Palatinate

Johan Banér, his full portliness completely unabated by the effort of personally managing the siege of Ingolstadt for three months, arose from his chair. Immediately following Doña Mencia's departure, Duke Ernst and Eric Haakansson Hand had left Amberg. Immediately as in, their horses had been saddled and waiting when the truck drove off down the *Goldene Strasse* toward Nürnberg.

"What," he asked, "in the name of every demon in the lowest depths of the inferno, is going on?"

"Madness," Duke Ernst answered. "Madness that we must, I think, take advantage of. If we possibly can, we should avoid extending the siege into the winter. This is the time to launch a final assault."

"Just how, and with what?" Banér's frustration was plain in his voice. "I do not have any more resources this week than I did last week."

"They're coming," Hand said. "Five regiments from Torstensson's army of the Baltic."

"CoC troublemakers!" Banér sneered.

The emperor's cousin shrugged. "Perhaps so. But I will point out they did very well for themselves at Ahrensbök. Two are already in Nürnberg and are resupplying. Three more have reached Bamberg and are marching fast."

"The other issue, General, is 'from where?'" Duke Ernst answered. "A siege from the north bank has not succeeded; all the boats we put on the river have not been able to prevent resupply of the garrison. Which you yourself have reported to me often enough. You are dealing with The Bridge That Will Not Die. Mosquitoes, those little boats; skipping through the channels and around the islands in the river like flocks of gnats in a swamp."

"I know. You don't need to tell me. What do you expect me to do about it?"

"With the disappearance of the archduchess, with Duke Albrecht's

flight, with Duke Maximilian's purge of his best advisors..."
Duke Ernst paused. "I believe that we should invest Ingolstadt
from the south, as well. Cross the river; cut off the supplies. In
addition to—"

"In addition to what?" Banér was abrupt.

"The USE military administrator in Franconia, Colonel Blackwell, tells me that he is having increasing difficulty in persuading
the commander of the mercenary forces that the emperor sent to
him in hopes of managing the Ram Rebellion more effectively to
restrain his desire to kill people. According to Colonel Blackwell,
the commander has little interest in limiting what the up-timers
call collateral damage. He does not wish to worry about civilians.
Rather his view of these things is 'bomb them all to bits, kids
in the town, we don't worry about no stinkin' kids, let God sort
out the pieces.'"

"I," Banér responded, "can see the commander's point of view.
Especially when it is a matter of winning or not winning."

"Ah," Duke Ernst said. "I thought as much. In Franconia, however,
the administration seems to be of the opinion that it is not trying
to win a war, but to establish a peace. So I have suggested that,
since the peasant revolt seems to have dwindled to a faint shadow
of what it was in the early summer, that Colonel Blackwell send
the commander and his restless mercenaries on to you, who will be
delighted to give them an opportunity to shoot at Bavarian soldiers,
since they seem so anxious to shoot at someone."

"They may," Banér reminded his superior, "be a lot less anxious to shoot at well-trained Bavarian soldiers. Those tend to be
heavily armed and shoot back."

"You can't have everything. You *can* have two more regiments
from Franconia, in addition to the regiments from the Baltic. If,
and that is a definite condition, *if* you are willing to control
their depredations against the civilians on this side of the river
and if, that is also a definite condition, *if* you are willing to cross
to the south bank."

Hand smiled coldly. "Keep in mind, General Banér, that if
you don't control those Franconian soldiers, the CoC regiments
from the Baltic are very likely to do it for you. They have not
much patience with undisciplined mercenary forces. None, at all,
I should say."

Banér stared at Hand, his eyes practically bulging. Clearly, the notion that some units—supposedly under his command—would cheerfully attack other units—also supposedly under his command—was a concept he was . . . grappling with.

Duke Ernst cleared his throat. "Colonel Blackwell tells me that the Franconian troops are ready to march. We can have the first of those units here in one week, about the same time as the first of the Baltic regiments; the second, which has been scattered into garrisons in northern Franconia, in two."

"If Franconia erupts again the instant that the regiments are gone, will they call them back?"

"It isn't their plan. They intend, I believe, to rely as much as possible on the assistance of Margrave Christian of Bayreuth in that case."

"Stinking ordure of wilting violets!"

"I am aware," Duke Ernst remarked, "that you consider the margrave's allegiance to Gustav Adolf to be somewhat wavering; that you find his commitment to be less than complete. Nonetheless. Do you want two more regiments and will you cross the river?"

"Yes. And yes. What is the actual strength of the regiments? Both the CoCs and the mercenaries?"

"The Franconians won't be much better than at half-strength. As usual with mercenaries. The Baltic units, on the other hand, are a lot closer to paper strength than we have come to expect," Hand answered. "Plus, one of those regiments is an artillery unit, which apparently distinguished itself at Ahrensbök. What they are calling, sometimes 'light artillery' and sometimes 'heavy weapons.' With the five regiments from the king and the two from Blackwell—let us say at least another eight thousand effectives. Possibly as many as ten thousand, if they are spared from disease on the march."

"Logistics, then," Duke Ernst said. "How many additional boats will you need?"

Banér smiled. "I have no intention of trying to cross by boat, Your Grace. We will cross at Neuburg first. On the bridge that is there, to occupy, garrison, and fortify that city. Then, the next day, on the bridges that will be there."

"Bridges that will be there?"

"The young civil engineer from Grantville, Ellis his name is, has taught mine a few tricks. We can build temporary bridges, of course. We do pontoon bridges fairly often. But it takes time. It is something that we can't prevent the enemy's spies from finding out. It gives them time to prepare. This young man, with his telescope and calipers, his droplines with sinkers, his 'soundings,' all very tedious when he explains it, has introduced us to the concept of 'prefab.'"

Banér smiled. "We have three more bridges, Your Grace. On sledges, here in the camp. I am assured that once we gather enough draft animals to move them upstream, toward Neuburg, each can be constructed in a day; less if things go well, but the young engineer is quite superstitious, believing in something that he calls 'Murphy's Law.' We plan to build them at intervals of two and a half miles, more or less, between Neuburg and Ingolstadt. Our forces cross them in the night; the next day, parallel to the river, from Neuburg to Ingolstadt, we throw up temporary fortifications. That will give us a 'secured supply line' from Neuburg to Ingolstadt. Invest Ingolstadt from the south and east; turn around and throw up a second set of earthworks against the Bavarians. We should be nearly done by the time that Maximilian realizes that we are there; certainly done by the time he can concentrate his forces against us."

Duke Ernst smiled back. "So. My question, then, should have been, 'How many additional draft animals will you need?'"

"'Prefab,' I take it," Hand commented, "is the reason that the closer we rode to Ingolstadt, the fewer trees we saw and the more stumps. Until we came within eyesight of the city and the river bank, at which point the forests were again undisturbed?"

"Damned right."

"With your permission, Your Grace," Hand said, "I believe that I would like to remain with General Banér rather than returning to Amberg with you. I would like to see 'prefab' in action."

Duke Ernst nodded. "You are taking precautions, I hope. If we can march south on one of these, then, if things do not go well, the Bavarians can march north on them, too."

Banér laughed. "Not if the bridges act as the models do. Let me show you." The room to which he led them was full of sluices and troughs through which water was flowing; sometimes slowly and lazily, bringing debris; sometimes pumped with great force. Many of them containing model bridges.

"Test them, Your Grace. Push down. See what load they will bear."

Duke Ernst complied. The spindly looking bridges were astonishingly strong.

"Now," Banér said. "Now."

Moving to the bridge that Duke Ernst had just been testing, a young man wearing glasses reached into the trough and grasped a string; pulled it. Almost at once, the bridge became sticks, floating away down the trough, piling up against a wire barrier at the end so that they did not float away. A teen-aged boy ran to seine them out of the water.

The young engineer smiled. "It isn't *quite* that easy with a full-sized bridge, Your Grace," he said. "But not much harder, either. I have advised the general to guard the ropes very carefully."

But Duke Ernst had wandered away. On a table next to the end of the trough, the teenager was rapidly putting the bridge back together. Every piece, every interlocking miniature support and plank, was numbered.

Erik Haakansson Hand leaned over and said to Banér: "There's other help coming as well. The emperor ordered the big guns taken out of that ironclad that was half-sunk outside Copenhagen and sent down here. Those ten-inchers will make the world's most ferocious siege guns, you know. They're an independent command under a certain Colonel Schmidt. A very promising and upcoming young officer, apparently. Should have the walls of Ingolstadt reduced in no time, once they get here. That'll be a while yet, of course."

The look of anxiety on the Swedish general's face was downright amusing.

Planegg, Bavaria

Duke Maximilian walked through the empty rooms of the castle on the Hörwarth estate, followed by his secretary and the owner's steward. He had felt obliged to come. He had known Dr. Johann Georg Hörwarth von Hohenberg, the father of the present Freiherr, well. Dr. Hörwarth had died several years before, in 1626. During his lifetime, he had held many offices. He had led the joint finance committee of government and Estates which brought about the abdication of Duke Wilhelm V when the state was threatened with bankruptcy in 1597; he had been at Maximilian's side during the hard years thereafter. He had led several investigations when high officials were suspected of corruption.

Now, however, Maximilian was beginning to wonder if, all those years, he had been misled. The warning signs had been there. Hörwarth had not only been a bureaucrat, but also a scholar, with wide-ranging interests. History and classical philology. Those were usually safe enough. Also, though, astronomy and mathematics. His *Tabulae Arithmeticae* were, Maximilian understood, high valued by the kind of people who valued such esoterica. Additionally, although Maximilian had chosen to ignore it at the time, Hörwarth had, for years, carried on an extensive correspondence with Johannes Kepler. He had encouraged the Holy Roman Emperor Rudolf to employ the man, had recommended his promotion. Had, although Hörwarth was Catholic and Kepler was Lutheran, in spite of the difference in faith, served as godfather to one of Kepler's daughters.

Duke Maximilian was afraid that he had been too trusting. Hörwarth's son had provided hospitality for Landgrave Wilhelm Georg of Leuchtenberg. Albrecht and Mechthilde had been here just before they fled.

He wandered into the magnificent library and thought wistfully of the wonderful Heidelberg library that Tilly had captured in 1622. More than eight thousand volumes belonging to the counts Palatine; it would have been a wonderful addition to the seventeen thousand or so books that the dukes of Bavaria had already collected. Briefly, in 1623, it had passed through Munich; he would have loved to keep it, part of the Wittelsbach heritage, just as the Palatinate's electoral vote was part of the Wittelsbach heritage. He had even ordered bookplates printed, enough for each of the books. His heart had been heavy when the papal nuncio had insisted that he send those magnificent manuscripts and printed books on to Rome.

He looked around Hörwarth's library again. The man who collected it had, possibly, been sympathetic to heresy; his son, Freiherr Johann Franz von Hörwarth, who now owned it, could be reasonably suspected of treason.

"Pack it up," he ordered the steward. "Send it to Munich, to the ducal library."

CHAPTER 50

Negotiationes Et Resolutiones

Grantville

The truck rumbled into Grantville. Someone had bent the rules about motorized vehicles; it was allowed to come directly to the presidential office. Followed, naturally, by any number of curious people who were wondering why the exception had been made.

The ramp came down. First, the soldiers who would be trained as radio operators. Fully outfitted as soldiers, at the moment. Duke Ernst was quite thrifty; they had served as the guards on the way. Not that guards had been needed; the drive had been monumentally uneventful.

Then Keith Pilcher, escorting an elderly woman. A down-timer. Not someone whom any of them recognized. Ed Piazza, coming out to greet her. Very respectfully. An influential down-timer, then.

The truck pulled away, toward the funeral home lot. Cora, in the coffee shop, got on the phone. Maxine, first; then Mary Lou; then call the second St. Veronica's to notify Felser's widow.

Annalise answered the phone.

Annalise Richter, as it turned out, was just the person that Doña Mencia wanted to talk to.

"Since I was coming in any case, you know. The Amberg Jesuits understand from Herr Hieronymus Rastetter, Frau Dreeson's lawyer, that the granddaughter holds a full power of attorney. And, of course, I should personally thank Mayor Dreeson, if possible, for the use of his chair. A true miracle of comfort. Not just the back that retreats. Not just the footrest that comes up. But, above all, the lever that lifts the seat beneath me when I must stand once more. I owe him great gratitude."

"Henry will be delighted to hear it," Ed Piazza replied. "He likes the chair himself."

"It is a settlement offer in regard to the land upon which the Amberg *collegium* is partly built," Doña Mencia explained. "In short, Fräulein Annalise, your grandmother wants the value of the land, they think. The land itself would do her very little good, since the former building was razed. The *collegium*'s dining hall sits directly above where your grandfather's printing business was once located; its library on the floor above that."

Annalise nodded. She had seen a lot of redevelopment. Grantville had been undergoing constant redevelopment almost since the day she arrived.

"It was the library that gave them the thought," Doña Mencia continued. "The other lady, Frau Simpson, talked a great deal about schools while the trade delegation was in Amberg. I did not meet her there . . ." Doña Mencia was very precise in her use of words; not for nothing was she the sister of a diplomat.

"I did not hear what Frau Simpson had to say about schools during her visit to Amberg, that is. However, it is generally understood that both your grandmother's schools, the St. Veronica's Preparatory Academies, and this 'normal school' that Frau Simpson wishes to found are in the greatest need of books. Not so much for the children, but as training for the teachers? Am I correct?"

"You are," Annalise said, "right on the spot."

"The Jesuit order teaches. That is its primary function, though it also does many other things. Its members have written many pedagogical works, suitable for the training of teachers. They are, however, all in Latin; thus, not suitable for people who are teaching very young children and village schools, people who often have no Latin at all. For whose training you do not plan to make Latin a requirement?"

Annalise inclined her head. "We feel that while Latin will be a great advantage to the students, for the time being, it would be counterproductive to require all the potential teachers to acquire expertise in it. If we had suitable pedagogical works, they can teach many subjects at that level in German."

"So." Doña Mencia segued into the subjunctive. "Would it be possible to reach an accommodation by which the Jesuit *collegium* in Amberg retains title to the land on which it is built, recompensing your grandmother by translating all of the pedagogical works of the order into German and printing them for the use of your schools in training their teachers?"

Back into the verb forms of normal discourse.

"It so happens that at present the Amberg *collegium* has an unusually high number of fathers in residence and an insufficient number of pupils to occupy them. In other words, they have a lot of spare time right now. That means that they could produce the translations quite quickly."

"By September?" Annalise asked. "That is when Mrs. Simpson wanted to open the normal school. If so, I will accept the settlement offer."

Doña Mencia knew where they were, now. This was a young woman who knew her own mind. Decisive.

"In hopes that we could reach an understanding, two of the fathers have already begun translation of the titles most useful for understanding the ways in which small children learn. Only three, but that should be sufficient for a beginning. Those three can be ready by September."

"How many different books in all? For what age groups?"

"I understand that the wife of Admiral Simpson was finding some difficulty in locating space for this school in Magdeburg."

Annalise raised her eyebrows. How had the Amberg Jesuits found that out? Through the grapevine, presumably. She had noticed, as a faithful member of St. Mary's, that the Jesuits who now provided most of its staff seemed to have a really healthy grapevine, roughly the diameter and height of Jack's beanstalk. Or maybe Mrs. Simpson had told Duke Ernst when they were talking about it.

"I am not directly involved with the normal school project," she said rather carefully. "But, yes. I understand from the members of the committee in Magdeburg that there is no affordable space in the city. They had hoped to use part of the *Gymnasium* building this first year, but it is already over-enrolled. We would have to consult the committee there for further information."

"Which, presumably, we can do, this very evening, using the radio?" Doña Mencia smiled at Ed Piazza. "You see, I have brought a second offer. And I rode from Amberg to Grantville, in the mayor's wonderful chair, in the company of a half dozen young men who wish to become radio technicians. They are all very enthusiastic about their newly chosen trade. I found myself becoming greatly enlightened about how radio works. And when it works."

Magdeburg

"It isn't," Carolyn Rush pointed out, "what Mary Simpson planned. On the other hand, Mary isn't here, she hasn't been here for several months, and nobody knows where she is. 'Last heard of in Bavaria' isn't much help."

"Exactly what does this offer that Annalise Richter radioed up to us involve?" Vanessa Clements asked.

"Well, back to money."

The rest of them nodded. Carolyn always had her priorities straight.

"Mary went off to try to pry some funding out of this Duke Ernst, Wilhelm Wettin's brother. Apparently she made some impact on him, at least. According to this offer that Doña Mencia de Mendoza brought to Annalise, and it's in writing, mind you, Duke Ernst agrees to provide funding for a normal school, but only on condition that it is located either right there in Amberg, where he is being Gustav Adolf's regent now, or somewhere in the Saxe-Weimar hereditary lands, rather than Magdeburg. 'So he can take a more personal interest in it,' he says."

"Will a normal school in either of those places work?" Livvie Nielsen asked.

"The real estate costs are likely to be a lot more reasonable than they are here in Magdeburg," Carolyn answered. "Even without the sweetener."

"What sweetener?" That was Tiny Washaw.

"There's a Jesuit college there in Amberg with more room that it needs. Annalise has negotiated a deal for the normal school to use their extra space for five years, with access to their library as well. There's a young man running it, right now." Carolyn paused to leaf through the sheets of transcribed Morse code that had been delivered to her that morning. "Balde, that's his name. Annalise says that he swallowed pretty hard when she stipulated that the normal school would be co-ed and they had to let female students into the library on an equal basis. Not to mention that it was nondenominational and they had to let Protestant students into the library. And all that stuff."

"Mary wanted something glorious," Livvie said. "Not a sort of cobbled-together thing that's located in a very provincial city about as far away from here as a person can get and still be in the USE."

"There is nothing to say," Vanessa said rather slowly, "that the USE will only have one normal school as time goes on. And, since we can't get in touch with Mary, we have to decide. She also wanted the normal school to open this fall. I think we all know that before this deal dropped in our laps, it just wasn't going to happen. No matter how hard we had been working on it. Nobody ever claimed that Fairmont State was Harvard, but it managed to educate most of the people in Grantville who have college degrees."

Carolyn frowned. "Mary can work on glorious when she gets back. We've done the best that we can, without her political influence and without her contacts with the powers that be. If Gustav Adolf decides that he wants to have a normal school in Magdeburg once the war is over, he can provide the funds for it. For that matter, if the USE parliament as a whole decide that they want one in Magdeburg, *they* can provide the funds for it. Some day. Right now . . ."

"Right now," Tiny interrupted, "it looks to me like a bird in the hand is a bird in the hand, and I don't see any bushes."

"Very well," Vanessa said. "I think we have reached a consensus, so are we ready to vote?"

The formalities taken care of, they got down to work. Recommended library holdings, course offerings, curriculum organization, lesson plans. Everything, all the things that they had worked on all summer. To be copied and sent to Duke Ernst as fast as possible.

"Hey," Carolyn said suddenly.

"What?"

"Who's going to be running this operation?"

Rome

Father-General Vitelleschi looked rather disbelievingly at the contents of the mail bag from Amberg. Which, he noted from the routing, had *not* been sent through the provincial house in Munich.

A non-Catholic establishment for the training of elementary school teachers, male and female, to be located within the walls of a Jesuit *collegium*, was not something that he, or the Jesuit order as a whole, had planned for. It appeared to be something that, henceforth, they would have to deal with. He had better bring the matter to the attention of Cardinal Barberini; and Cardinal Barberini; and Cardinal Barberini. Not to mention to the attention of the pope.

Grantville

Keith and Maxine Pilcher were hovering a little anxiously. Jeff Adams was examining Doña Mencia's knees, shaking his head. "We just don't have anything that would help. No cortisone. We can send aspirin with her, for the pain. It will also reduce the inflammation somewhat."

"Y'know Doc," Annabelle Piazza said. "I don't like to hear that."

"I don't like to say it, either. It's just the way things are."

Keith looked at Adams as he finished with Doña Mencia. "When is one of those likely to hit Grantville, Doc? A diphtheria epidemic, I mean. Do we have quarantine plans, something like the lazarette that the Jesuits set up in their *collegium*? If it hits here, we can't be bringing contagious people into Leahy. Half the other patients won't have had it. Do you know what someone said to me at Cora's yesterday? 'It wasn't even plague.' Where does he get off saying, 'It wasn't even plague?' What do they mean when they say, 'It wasn't even smallpox?' We were burying two or three kids every day, plus a bunch of adults, for nearly a month. Amberg is not that big a town. Not as big as Grantville is, these days."

"Okay, Ollie," Keith said. "That's it. The cartel is down; this is the list of the masters who want to open and rebuild; this is the technology they're going to need to make it profitable again; these are the proposed investment agreements that I've negotiated. Wish I could have done more, but that epidemic took a good chunk out of the middle of it, and then Cavriani and his kid hared off hunting for Mary and Veronica, Felser died, and I just had to sort of muddle through at the end."

"Don't worry about it. All anybody can do is the best he can."

"Max," Keith said to his wife. "I just don't see what you're getting so bent out of shape about. There's no point in tying your underwear in knots. Just because I'm the only person who went out with the trade delegation who has come back. Well, except for Toby and Lambert and I guess you're not counting them. So some sort of odd things happened. So what? I got things started so that the iron will be coming back into production. That's what Ollie wanted. That's why I went."

Munich, Bavaria

The news was waiting for Maximilian when he returned to Munich. The Swedes had crossed the Danube near Ingolstadt. In force.

"Hörwarth!" Duke Maximilian exclaimed. "We should have known that Farensbach could not have been acting alone, or only with a few subordinates. Hörwarth must have been involved, as well. And he is there. What an irony that we sent him to act at the execution of his co-conspirator. Order his arrest, at once."

Even though Duke Maximilian consistently dismissed most of the privy councillors from the meetings before he proceeded to a consideration of the situation at Ingolstadt, this did not keep them, and the lesser members of the official staff of the Bavarian government, from thinking about it.

If nothing else, the intensified assault there provided them with something to think about other than the fact that Duke Albrecht was in Bohemia and any one of them who had ever supported Duke Albrecht in any privy council discussion was now, very likely, in a precarious political position.

Something to think about other than where Duke Albrecht's sons, the heirs to Bavaria, might be. If in the hands of the Swede, as

suspected, and if he chose to have them reared as Protestants . . .
Oh, dear. Duke Maximilian could not live forever.

Something other than where *die Habsburgerin* might be and
why she had failed to go through with the wedding. How many
of them had been seen talking to her politely at the various festivities that took place while the wedding procession had been en
route and after its arrival in the city? Would this be interpreted
by the duke as opening the possibility that they had been part
of a conspiracy leading to her escape?

Other than the fact that several of them had daughters who had
attended the English Ladies school, so it was to presumed that
the inquisitors simply had not yet gotten around to interviewing
them yet. But that an inquisitorial interview lay somewhere in
the near future.

Better to think about Ingolstadt. Every available soldier in
Bavaria who could be pulled from other duty was now crisscross-
ing the duchy on his way to Ingolstadt. The duke's commanders
were recruiting again, but at present the duchy was so hemmed
in that recruitment, at least of veterans, was hard. Which meant
that the heretics might succeed in taking the fortress in spite of
their best efforts. What would the Swede do then? Ingolstadt was
fifty miles from Munich. Fifty miles was by no means far enough
for comfort. The up-time histories said that in 1632, the Swede's
forces had reached Munich.

Better to focus one's mind on facilitating the movement of
troops, providing them with fodder and horses, allotting forage
districts to the various regiments, dealing with bitter complaints
from the residents of the forage districts, than to think of the
multiple, multiple reasons why a man might be losing his own
head. Not to mention, his regular job.

Ingolstadt

Johann Cratz von Scharffenstein watched the soldiers taking young
Hörwarth out of Ingolstadt, toward Munich.

Arrested. For treason. On grounds that were . . .

"Flimsy" was the mildest term he could think of.

So far as the commander of the Ingolstadt garrison could determine, the charges against Hörwarth came down to no more than

two, both of them completely circumstantial. First, the poor fellow had offered—none too willingly, by all accounts—to provide the Landgrave of Leuchtenberg with a comfortable resting place for his last months of life at the Hörwarth family estate at Planegg. Secondly, Duke Albrecht and his now-dead wife Mechthilde had used the same estate as a staging ground for their escape.

But they had done so in Hörwarth's absence, and the murder of the estate's huntsmen by Albrecht's guards would surely seem to indicate that they did so without Hörwarth's complicity. As for the supposed "conspiracy with the Landgrave," the charge was almost laughable. Georg Wilhelm had been *senile,* for the love of God.

"Flimsy"? It would be better to call the charges "insane."

A term which, the more von Scharffenstein learned about Maximilian's ever-expanding purge in Munich, seemed appropriate to apply to the duke of Bavaria himself. For whatever reason—peculiar, on the face of it, since the duke had seemed quite indifferent to his new bride-to-be—Maximilian had reacted to the archduchess of Austria's flight with almost insensate fury. He'd even had the young woman's entourage executed, despite the vehement protests from Vienna.

Insanity indeed, especially from a military viewpoint. Bavaria had been badly stretched as it was, fending off the Swedes here at Ingolstadt. Now, Duke Maximilian had severed his ties to his closest and most reliable ally. For what? The faithlessness of a young woman he didn't care about in the first place?

Cratz von Scharffenstein was now inclined to believe the rumors he'd heard, that the death of Duchess Elisabeth Renata had unhinged her husband's mind. Of course, it was the iron mind of an iron ruler in his sixties, so it had taken some months for the madness to become manifest. It was like watching an ancient dam, finally crumbling.

Crumbling it surely was, though—and Cratz von Scharffenstein himself might be caught in the ensuing flood. It was time to consider all his options. As the commander of the Ingolstadt's garrison, those options were . . .

Not flimsy. Not flimsy at all. And, unlike Farensbach, whose head had been removed along with the "von" from his name, Cratz von Scharffenstein was not incompetent. There hadn't actually been anything wrong with Farensbach's scheme, as such, if the bastard hadn't bungled the matter.

❖ CHAPTER 51 ❖

Multiformis Atque
Multimodis

Bavaria, south of Ingolstadt

Leopold Cavriani considered himself a practical man. When the troop of Bavarian cavalry stopped him and confiscated his horse, he made no more protest than an Italian merchant ought reasonably to have made. Demanding a receipt, stating that he would be sending a request for compensation to the duke's officials.

The captain, after finding his papers in order, had said, "Be my guest. There's a long line." They had left him his purse, so the duke was not yet so desperate for funds that his soldiers were authorized to strip foreign merchants. Nor so desperate for men that his officers had lost control. On this day, there was still discipline in the Bavarian army; a fact to be filed away.

So he had walked into Hohenkammer, where he now stood fuming. There was not a decent horse for sale in the entire region; the Bavarian troops were taking them all. Plus fodder, plus food. The Bavarian army was foraging all through the duchy between Munich and Ingolstadt. Not just through the duchy, either. They had ended all pretense of respecting the jurisdictional boundary between Bavaria and Pfalz-Neuburg. From what he heard here, Bavarian troops were foraging all over the southern and western portions of the enclave.

Possibly over more of it than that, but thus far he had only heard reports of what was going on in the southern and western portions. There weren't a lot of refugees on the roads yet, trying to get south against the stream of troops, but there were a few. They said that the Bavarians were treating Neuburg as enemy territory, enforcing the *Brandschatzungen* and such that went with foraging. He had the names of three villages that had been burned out already.

So here he stood in Hohenkammer. Twenty miles in two days. Miserable time, but he had been moving slowly, asking discreet questions, looking for a party of women on foot whom he had not found.

Where could they be? Which way next? He had planned on going to Reichertshausen, then through Ilmmuenster and Pfaffenhofen to Reichertshofen; from there he could go north to Ingolstadt or northwest to Neuburg as seemed most convenient.

Suddenly, he laughed. Twenty-five years ago, he would have relished this. What had Ed Piazza's wife said when she described them to him? He spoke English with Mrs. Piazza. "Middle-aged, middle-class, and middle-brow." She had laughed; she considered it a joke. He, once she had explained "middle-brow" to him, had found it very apt. Succinct and graphic, an excellent aphorism.

So here he stood, middle-class, middle-aged, and middle-brow himself, wondering if he should not have stayed home and sent out someone else. He laughed at himself.

Ah, no, Leopold my friend. You are not ready to stay home in Geneva. Not yet, not quite yet.

The inns here had not yet been stripped of their provender. People were walking up and down the street, chewing on sausages. He might as well get something to eat.

Pork *Schnitzel*, by a miracle. *Nudeln* to go with it. Fresh fruit. "No bread today," the innkeeper apologized. The last group of soldiers had taken it all. Bread kept. Of the things in his larder that spoiled easily, they had only eaten their fill and then moved on. They lieutenant had even given him a chit for the cost, not too bad an estimate, either. If the treasury honored it.

Leopold took his wooden plate out to the picnic tables at the side of the inn and sat down where he could watch the road.

Mary Ward stood by the side of the road, frowning, as a cavalry company rode past them on its way north. Thus far, they had not been molested. Older women mainly, poor to judge by their clothing, several of them together, one thin, feeble old man. The passing troops had a goal, to get to Ingolstadt. None had paused to harass them. They had been moving much more slowly than she had thought they would, because they left the road so often to let faster groups go by, to get out of the way of teams pulling cargo wagons.

They also needed to let Mrs. Simpson nurse the blisters that were causing her to limp so badly, to appear so feeble. She did not complain, but the only shoes they had been able to find for her were very poorly fitted and her feet had no calluses at all. Mary Ward had never seen such delicate feet before. Even the archduchess—that is, even her "niece" Maria Anna—had harder feet than the up-time woman. They could not let Mrs. Simpson wear the shoes she had when she was brought to them. Those, they had to leave in Munich. Sturdy, well-made, but so different! They would have attracted surveillance like a lighthouse beacon.

Mary Simpson had not let them go to waste, though. She had given them, with many other things, to their cook who worked at the Paradise Street house, days before they left. The cook had agreed to hide it all.

The cavalrymen were still riding past, not even looking at them. When they got closer to Ingolstadt, though . . . Ingolstadt was another thirty miles. If, closer to the fortress, the army was already encamped, if the troops were out foraging in small groups? They might not be so indifferent, she thought. She kept worrying. She was far from sure that the plan with which she had left Munich was going to work. She was supposed to find the brother of the cook. He would agree to take them to the left bank of the Danube, the north side, under cover of the fleets of small boats that set out every night to resupply the fortress.

What was happening at Ingolstadt? Why were all the troops on the move? The siege had been going on for months, now, without reaching a crisis point. Why now?

The mounted company was past. They might as well go on into Hohenkammer. They would be safer in even a small town than out here, on an open road. They were not vagrants; they would be allowed to spend the night, at least.

Perhaps she could find bandages, salves.

Maria Anna took the "old man's" arm. "Papa," she said. "Papa, we need to walk on."

Veronica pulled her lips back between her bare gums. She missed her teeth, but she couldn't wear them. No old woman in Bavaria had teeth as perfect as hers. If she wore them, they would attract attention.

"Papa." If a "Papa" the size of Mary Simpson had begotten Maria Anna, he would have had to marry a giantess. She started to make up a story to entertain herself, this one of a weakly grocer's apprentice who successfully courted the oversize daughter of a miller.

Perhaps, she thought a little grimly, once they managed to return to Grantville—if they did—she would write it down. Sell it to the despised printers of Harlequin Romances. Make some money and send Annalise to college. God knew, nothing else that she had done this summer had made the slightest progress toward that goal. All outgo, no profit. She was worse off than she had been to start with.

At least, the story kept her mind off where she was and what she was doing.

Another creek. They would have to wade. The ford was churned up, muddy from the horses that had recently crossed. She looked at Mary Simpson. Her feet inside the rough shoes, the open sores. What might be in that water? What "germs" that would lead to what "infection"? She had listened to Dr. Abrabanel just as carefully as anyone in Grantville. More carefully, since she was the mayor's wife and had to set a good example. It was still at least a mile until they could rest at Hohenkammer. The wet shoes, muddy water squelching inside them, would be rubbing against the open blisters.

She stopped on the bank and said: "No." Stubbornly refused to go on. Until Maria Anna broke the impasse by simply picking "Papa" up and carrying "him" across.

For the first time since the young woman had joined the group, Veronica said, "thank you." She did not want to. She had no charity for the nobility in general, and even less for the Habsburgs in particular. But, "pretty is as pretty does," so thanks were in order, however grudgingly given.

Mary Ward sighed. The old *Oberpfälzerin* was a problem. One expected village women to be ignorant, superstitious, often poorly instructed in their faith. But this one! Catholic, she said. The wife of a prominent man in this Grantville, of the mayor. Far from ignorant, not at all superstitious. But never, ever, in a half century of life, had Mary Ward met a purportedly Catholic woman who was so poorly instructed in her faith. Or so stubborn in refusing instruction.

She didn't even know the rosary.

She didn't even *have* a rosary. They had not noticed, in Munich. There had been plenty of rosaries available in the house on Paradise Street and the two interned women had not participated in the Ladies' liturgies.

No rosary. That could be repaired. Not elegantly, right now, but repaired. As they walked, Mary Ward plucked small twigs, sliced them up into bead-sized lengths with her dinner knife, and poked the soft pulp out of the center with one of the large needles from the sewing kit in her pocket. A length of thin grapevine was functioning as the string. One length of twig forced through another for the cross. Unblessed. Good enough, as a teaching tool. Until the instruction began to take hold, perhaps unblessed was preferable. It would avoid any possibility of blasphemy if the old woman treated the beads disrespectfully.

Hohenkammer, finally. An inn ahead, with benches and tables. People were eating. A place to rest.

And the *Oberpfälzerin* was running.

Actually running to the inn. Mary Ward started after her, then stopped.

She was running up to a man who sat there, eating. Speaking to him. Not a high-born gentleman, by his dress, but certainly a prosperous merchant.

Almost, Veronica started to greet him as an equal. Then remembered how she was dressed, where she was. That she had no teeth. Instead, she forced herself to curtsey humbly, as a servant to an employer, or to a friend of her employer. "Herr Cavriani. Ah, I am grateful to have found you at last."

All that Leopold could think at first was, "How did they get behind me?"

Then, when he recognized the younger woman who was assisting the old man, he realized that he had been thinking of putting his adventuring days behind him much, much, too prematurely.

One of the waiters at the inn saw the old woman run up to the merchant, noted the other women who were following her, and the old man. As requested by a "beggar" who had, for the past several years, paid him a modest weekly sum for providing information on events in the Pfalz-Neuburg enclave to the duke of Bavaria's bailiff in Schleissheim, he duly noted their presence in Hohenkammer. Two days later, when the "beggar" made one of his regular stops at the inn to request a handout, the waiter sent his weekly report, which the bailiff received the next morning.

And put at the bottom of his inbox. He was very busy. Like every other local official north of Munich, his time was fully absorbed right now by the need to move troops to Ingolstadt—demands for forage, fodder, food, supplies, transport, cash; complaints from farmers, complaints from townspeople, edicts from Munich. Schleissheim, since one of Duke Maximilian's favorite rural hunting lodges was located there, was busier than most. Almost a week after it arrived, the bailiff extracted the report, combined it with other reports he had received concerning women moving through the area, and forwarded it to the chancery in Munich.

Munich, Bavaria

In the Munich chancery, the report from Hohenkammer arrived on the desk of a minor official assigned to collate the various reports in regard to women traveling in Bavaria, where it joined many others. Many, many, others. In a jerky, disjointed, unsystematic manner, greatly complicated by the troop movements, surveillance went on.

The minor official who received the report felt overwhelmed already—partly by the reports and partly by his concern that, since he had previously worked under the unfortunate Dr. Donnersberger, neither his tenure in office nor his life would be particularly secure if he did anything to bring his existence to the duke's attention. It was very hard to be sufficiently inconspicuous when compiling reports for the duke's own eyes. And there were, certainly, a plenitude of reports. Surely not every woman in

Bavaria could be traveling, the hapless bureaucrat thought wearily. Surely, it only seemed that way.

Of course, one could always count on pilgrims. There were so many shrines and pilgrimage sites. One old woman on a decrepit donkey, accompanied by her son and two nephews, on her way to Altötting to pray for relief from some unspecified physical ailment. Nothing suspicious there. Pile one.

All groups of two to four women. Possibly suspicious, especially if they appeared to be fairly prosperous. Pile two.

Groups of more than four women. Unless they contained the same number as the English Ladies, pile one. It was, after all, coming on to harvest season. Farmers and estate managers all over Bavaria were hiring seasonal laborers right now; seasonal laborers were out looking for work.

Discerning just who a suspicious group might be was a different matter. Possibly members of the archduchess' household? Pile two-A. Possibly members of Duke Albrecht's household in Munich or possibly people from Duke Albrecht's rural estates? Pile two-B. Possibly former servants of the late Wilhelm Georg of Leuchtenberg? Pile two-C. Possibly members of the households of various Munich patrician families? Pile two-D.

Why could the duke not have addressed these problems one at a time? At the moment, there were far too many women whom one could presume to be sharing a single thought: let's get the hell out of Bavaria.

He was a cautious man. The times were uncertain. His wife and daughters were currently *en route* to Tyrol.

He did his best to make his summaries dull.

On the twentieth of July, the district administrator in Vilsbiburg reported that a group of women representing themselves to be pilgrims returning from the shrine at Altötting had transversed his district. According to the innkeeper in Mühlburg, there were seven in the group; they were said to reside in Landshut and to have letters of approval from their own parish priest. There was no indication that this group of women were of interest to the Inquisition. In any case, since both their purported place of origin and the destination of their pilgrimage were outside of his own jurisdiction, he did not consider it a judicious use of his budget to expend monies to observe them farther.

The city clerk of Landshut, upon inquiry by the chancery, sent confirmation that a group of local women had indeed left two weeks earlier to undertake a pilgrimage to Altötting. This group included the wives of the baker Adolf Blum and the sausage maker Veit Haller. All of the women regularly attended their local parish church and none of them were delinquent in their annual obligation to receive Easter communion. The city clerk did not understand why this pilgrimage was of interest to the Holy Office, particularly since the distance to Altötting from Landshut was less than forty miles.

The chancery sent a query to the city clerk in Landshut asking him to ascertain, when the women returned home, whether they had at any time during their pilgrimage deviated from the route they had been expected to take, or whether, at the time they returned, there were more people in their party than when they had left.

The city clerk in Landshut reported that when the group returned home, there was one less person in their party than when they left on the pilgrimage. They asserted that this was because one of the women, an unmarried sister of the teamster Adalreich Pfister, remained behind temporarily to visit her grandmother in Dingolfing.

The mayor in Dingolfing reported that a woman who could be the missing individual from the Landshut pilgrimage to Altötting had been observed in Dingolfing, the prior Sunday. According to the nephew of the priest, she accompanied to mass a woman whom she asserted was her grandmother. Local informants confirmed the identity of the grandmother and stated that she did indeed have an unmarried granddaughter residing in Landshut. It was said that the visitor intended to return to Landshut within a fortnight.

The bureaucrat rubbed his aching temples. The district administrator in Vilshofen reported that four women were staying as guests in the household of Count von Ortenburg, which was not, of course, under his jurisdiction. Prior to arriving in Ortenburg on the previous Wednesday, these women had supposedly made a trip to Freising, in order to see the duke's wedding procession. They had a carriage and were accompanied by a driver and a footman. He had not been able to confirm that they had indeed visited Freising, nor where they intended to go upon leaving Ortenburg. In a tavern in Ortenburg, the driver indicated that they intended to take their leave on Tuesday next and proceed to Passau. Thus far, however, they had not left Ortenburg.

Pile two-A, with follow-up.

The chancery clerk anxiously requested further details on the four visitors to Ortenburg, particularly as to whether these might possibly be some of the English Ladies who had left Munich and who were of interest to the Inquisition.

The district administrator in Vilshofen replied that he did not believe that these were English ladies, since they had been overheard speaking German to one another.

The frustrated clerk replied that he was not asking about English *ladies* but rather about English Ladies, members of the Institute of the Blessed Virgin Mary, a religious order that had been dissolved by papal decree and whose members were of interest to the Holy Office.

The district administrator from Vilshofen replied that he did not think so, because one of the ladies was advanced in pregnancy and was accompanied by a ladies' maid and a laundress. The fourth appeared from her clothing to be a gentlewoman of high standing.

The chancery clerk wrote, *Why didn't you say that one of them was pregnant before?*

The district administrator answered, *Nobody asked me.*

More summaries. Dull, think dull. Very, very, dull.

The district administrator in Vohburg reported that three women in religious habits had passed through his district two weeks before. They stated that they were beguines from a house in the city of Cologne, and they were traveling on passports issued by the archbishop-elector of Cologne. They presented papers indicating that they were traveling to Salzburg.

Pile one.

The district administrator in Vohburg added in passing that during the past week, two or three groups of women had been observed traveling toward Neuburg, and one to Reichartshofen.

Pile two.

The district administrator in Mühldorf reported that three women in religious habits had passed through his district a week before. They professed to be beguines from Cologne. He did not know where they went after they left Mühldorf, although they had stated that they were on their way to Salzburg.

The district administrator in Aichach reported the arrest of four vagrant prostitutes, one a young girl. One of the older women asserted that the girl was her daughter; two professed to have been born in Tyrol; the woman and her daughter in Augsburg. There was no indication that they were heretics, although all four were very poorly instructed in the tenets of the Catholic faith. They had been remanded to a *Spinnhaus* for repentant magdalens, from which the girl had already made an effort to flee.

The district administrator in Abbach reported that he was keeping close watch on all efforts made by groups of women to enter the portions of the Imperial City of Regensburg on the south side of the Danube.

The bailiff in Griesbach reported that his wife, while shopping in Vilshofen the previous week, saw three well-dressed women whom she did not know. Since his wife was personally acquainted with every woman in Vilshofen who could afford to dress well, he believed that he should report this, although nobody had asked him about it. The women were wearing dresses in the current style, one green, one blue, and one deep red. These dresses were trimmed with silk and made in the modern style with wide arms. Two of the women wore broad collars in the French style. All of the women wore caps, embroidered with silk, and hats. They claimed to be on their way to a spa, where they intended to take the curing waters. The *Amtmann* reported that he did not know of any popular spas in the general direction in which they were traveling until one reached Karlsbad in Bohemia.

Frantically, the chancery clerk requested follow-up to this sighting. Four days later, the bailiff reported that he had ascertained that this party of women, which was on horseback and accompanied by two grooms, had passed the border into the diocese of Passau.

On behalf of the prince-bishop, an administrator in Passau replied to the Bavarian inquiries that he had not seen such a party of women. This was quite literally true, which did not mean that he did not know who they were, one of them being both his own cousin and a former lady in waiting of Archduchess Maria Anna. It also did not mean that he had not issued orders to expedite their travel through Passau to their homes in Austria.

A low-level clerk in the Passau chancery sent duplicate copies of these orders to Munich, accompanied by an invoice for his services.

The Bavarian chancery clerk did not know whether or not to hope that this meant that the archduchess and the two witches were out of Bavaria and out of his hair. Pile two, though; definitely pile two.

He kept reading reports, of which those he had already extracted and summarized were only a small sample. The unsummarized pile, no matter how steadily he worked, grew inexorably. They kept coming in daily.

The bailiff in Schleissheim reported that one of his informants stated that a group of about a dozen women and one man, dressed in the ordinary clothing of rural workers, had come into Hohenkammer, where they had been met by a merchant, presumably their employer, who was waiting for them at an inn. The group had continued north, walking, in the company of the merchant, who was also walking. This was not a suspicious circumstance, since the man had eaten at the inn and complained to the host that a cavalry troop had confiscated his horse that very morning. The informant assumed that these were migrant laborers, hired for the harvest season. The Schleissheim bailiff concurred. Pile one.

The official sighed. He wished that he had received more reports from the region between Munich and Ingolstadt, but with the troop movements there, it was probably too much to hope for.

In any case, he had received a letter from his wife. His family was safe in Tyrol. He closed up his desk. Times were very uncertain in Bavaria. Someone else would have to deal with the rest of the reports. He was leaving for Tyrol.

Salmading. So far, so good. Reichertshausen. The whole town was in chaos because of Bavarian foraging parties. Ilmmuenster. The flow of refugees heading south was becoming a stream. Pfaffenhofen. Only ten miles again today, but they would have to stop. There was no possibility that Mrs. Simpson could walk farther.

Refugees. Sources of information.

Banér's army was pouring across the Danube at Neuburg. Some had forded, but the great majority was crossing on the bridge. First, he had sent across scouts; then squads that secured the perimeter of the town on the west and south; then they had secured a route to the south of Ingolstadt.

From Neuburg to Ingolstadt, no one could reach the Danube without crossing a well-secured line of Swedish and USE regulars.

Refugees. Carrying with them as much of their worldly goods as they possibly could. Willing to sell some of them for hard cash. Not a lot, from any one group. Plus, the English Ladies still had some things in their satchels. Others, he had traded for them.

Miss Ward was a reasonable woman. When he explained what he had discovered, she agreed readily enough that crossing at Ingolstadt would be impossible. They would try for Neuburg. They could all stay with Veit Egli until the southward traffic on the bridge slacked off. Then they could cross and go on to Grantville.

Refugees. One sold him a sedan chair. Mary Simpson was no longer a crippled old man but rather an old woman, her short hair hidden by an old-fashioned, capacious, matron's cap, her shoeless feet swathed in bandages. Sores from gout, they could tell anyone who asked. Two day-laborers, happy enough to find paid work that would take them away from the presence of Bavarian troops, were carrying her.

Leopold felt considerably relieved. He considered himself an enlightened enough man, but the Bible itself forbade women to wear men's clothing. He understood that in Grantville, certain forms of trousers were defined as women's clothing; so be it. Undoubtedly, however, when the women found him in Hohen-kammer, Mary Simpson had been wearing men's clothing. Down-time men's clothing. The kind of thing for which the Catholics of Bavaria would burn a woman, if they discovered it.

Be fair, Leopold. The kind of thing for which the Calvinists of Geneva would burn a woman, if they discovered it.

He looked at Mary Ward. Mrs. Simpson had been dressed in those male clothes with the consent of a Catholic. A nun, the superior of a Catholic religious order, no matter how troublesome a one. It was all very disturbing.

In any case, he was far happier now that Mrs. Simpson was dressed as a woman again.

Pfaffenhofen. Several days in Pfaffenhofen. It was as secure as Neuburg and refugees were still coming south steadily. There was little point in trying to move farther north. Leopold had not spotted anyone observing them. He was rather surprised that the surveillance, thus far, appeared to have been so lax. Happily surprised, but surprised.

Pfaffenhofen and, at the end of the week, a Neuburg newspaper.

Dramatic Flight of the Heir of Bavaria and His Family. How providential. That might account for some of the surprisingly thin surveillance. No clue, however, as to the goal of their flight. Or, for that matter, the reason for their flight.

Another day. Another newspaper, a week old, carried by a refugee, who sold it to the innkeeper. Who wouldn't let it out of his hands, although, for a fee, he would read it out loud to people in his dining room.

Duke Ernst and General Banér Mount Intense Attack on Ingolstadt.

"Gee, whiz. As if we hadn't guessed," Mary Simpson said later that evening. It was safe enough to speak English in their own rooms, Leopold thought.

Well, it *was* a Nürnberg newspaper. But it scarcely came as new information to people who were sitting here in Pfaffenhofen in the middle of a region that was not just ankle deep in military types but, by now, practically neck deep.

Two more days. A special edition of the Augsburg newspaper, brought in by a runner who was risking his neck to make a lot of money. Between the arrival of the last newspaper and this one, Duke Maximilian had issued a proclamation forbidding the importation of all foreign printed matter. *Duchess Mechthilde and Duke Karl Killed During Escape from Bavaria. Mysterious Disappearance of the Younger Bavarian Dukes.* The innkeeper wasn't reading the papers out loud any more, but he had bought a half dozen and resold them surreptitiously and for a highly inflated price.

The reporter whose dispatch had reached Augsburg had apparently based his lead story on talking to the man who provided the wagon and coffins to transport their bodies to Leuchtenberg. The story only went that far. There was no information as to whether Duke Albrecht had reached Bohemia.

Maria Anna read though the meager information in the Augsburg paper over and over, as if she could force the printed columns to provide her with more information than they contained.

The only consolation she had found was what was not there. No headlines saying that Doña Mencia had been captured. No headlines saying that Father Vervaux was dead. Not even the most minute notice at the bottom of the sixth column on the fourth page.

No news from Austria. Why was there no news from Austria? Never had she been in more need of the *School of Patience.*

CHAPTER 52

Excursio Culpae

Bavaria, south of Ingolstadt

The stream of refugees was slacking off. Those who were still passing through Pfaffenhofen were mainly, they said, going to stay with relatives. The body of the Swedish army was on the south bank of the Danube now. They had invested Ingolstadt itself from the south and constructed a body of counter-fortifications to keep the Bavarians at a distance. There had been two sizable battles, both to the east of Ingolstadt, when the Bavarians had tried to force their way through. The attacks had been repulsed.

The Bavarians took the two day-laborers whom Leopold had hired to work on fortifications, so he re-sold the sedan chair to a family going south with a sick woman.

He asked what was happening farther to the west, toward Neuburg. The answer was that the Swedes had built fortifications all along, the whole dozen miles from Neuburg to Ingolstadt. A "secured supply line," they called it.

To the east, the Bavarians were massing at Manching and Ernsgaden. Nobody knew for sure, but it was generally assumed that since they could not break through at Ingolstadt itself, they would drive west, south of the "secured supply line," and try to break through at Neuburg. Nobody—well, no ordinary person—knew precisely when they planned to move, but it had to be soon. There was hardly anyone still in the expected path. The reason that the stream of refugees was slowing down was that Weichering was empty. So were Zell, Obermaxfeld, the villages and hamlets around them. Schrobenhausen had taken in so many refugees that there was, literally, room for no more. Even the villages farther to the south had driven away any livestock that the foraging parties had left them and the people were prepared to run if the armies swung a few more miles to the south than people expected.

At Neuburg itself, though, the Swedes were permitting traffic to pass in and out of the city.

Leopold was inclined to stay in Pfaffenhofen, he said. To wait and see.

Privately, he was beginning to worry. Marc had not caught up with them, even with the pause, and there was no indication that he was ahead of them.

Mary Ward was not inclined to wait and see. He learned something about determination. Although he did not learn that she had addressed the College of Cardinals in Latin in defense of her order and her orthodoxy, he learned something about the personality that had permitted her to do that without flinching. Learned that she had, in her pocket, a letter from the pope that ordered her to Grantville.

He could stay, or he could come, she said, but the Ladies were making a run for Neuburg and the bridge before an army marched between them and it. Twenty-five miles. Mrs. Simpson's feet were largely healed. They would make a run for it. With him or without him.

He came.

Cavriani wanted to go through Reichertshofen. He was quite insistent on it.

No way was Mary Ward going to take the time to go to Reichertshofen. Not even if the detour would be only five miles. Through Pörnbach to Pobenhausen, to Weichering, to Zell, to Neuburg. Straight through.

Mary Simpson's feet were not as well-healed as Mary Ward had hoped. At Pörnbach, scarcely six miles out of Pfaffenhofen, they started to slow down. Leopold said that he would detour to

Reichertshofen, talk to his agent there, and catch up with them at Pobenhausen. By then, certainly, Mrs. Simpson would have to rest.

Mary Ward did not like it, but neither did she have any authority over the man. "If you do not catch up with us by tomorrow morning," she said firmly, "we will go on without you."

"I wish," Veronica said, looking at Mary Simpson rather anxiously, "that we had kept the sedan chair. Four women could have carried you, easily enough."

She was on her knees, unwrapping the bandages.

"Look here, Miss Ward. None of the new skin has broken yet. But it will, if she walks any farther, for all of your bandages and salves. And for all of your rosaries. Damned Bavarians. Take your Ladies and go on. I'll stay here with her. When Herr Cavriani meets you at Pobenhausen, tell him where we are. The whole village is empty. We can find a barn or a shed, somewhere to stay."

"Impossible," was Mary Ward's response.

"Believe me," Veronica answered, "it will be better accommodations than an ore barrel. Just come and look at her feet and then try to tell me 'impossible' again."

"I cannot permit—"

"You cannot permit?" Veronica stood up, swelling to her full, if not very impressive, height. "You cannot permit. Who are you to tell me what I may and may not do, Madam Lady, so Superior?"

Startled, Mary Ward backed up a couple of steps.

Mary Simpson looked up at the two of them, then around. Someone was missing.

"Maria Anna," she called. "Maria Anna, where are you?"

Everyone had been paying attention to the argument.

"Maria Anna!" Veronica's voice, schooled by the handling of Gretchen's collection of orphans, managed double the volume of Mary's.

"Just calm down." The answer came from behind a cattle stall.

Oh, well, then. Not an emergency. Just, presumably, a call of nature.

The archduchess reappeared around a corner, trundling an empty wheelbarrow in front of her.

"I thought of it when you said 'sedan chair,'" she explained. "That there might be one in the stall."

"Since when," Veronica asked, "do high-born gracious ladies

have occasion to think that there might be wheelbarrows in cow byres?"

Maria Anna looked at her mildly. "Since they, or at least this one, last accompanied her Mama when they inspected the dairy barns back home in Graz. Which was only, though it seems much longer, last summer. I didn't spend all my growing-up time in Vienna, you know. Now, if you're done with those bandages?"

Mary in the wheelbarrow, Maria Anna pushing it, they proceeded on their way.

After two miles, Maria Anna began to wish that someone else would offer to take a turn. The wooden handles were rubbing her hands raw; she had no gloves. Soon her palms would be as badly blistered as Mrs. Simpson's feet. The right handle kept causing the golden rose underneath her skirt to bang against her thigh. Impatiently, she twitched the drawstring from which it was suspended a little to the side.

It would help if she could wrap her hands in some of Miss Ward's bandages.

Miss Ward did not offer. She was profoundly offended.

Nobody else offered to push, either. Except, for short stints, Veronica, who was determined, but not strong enough to manage the heavy, awkwardly balanced barrow for very long.

The English Ladies were, after all, Englishwomen of good family. Gentlewomen by birth. Far more conscious of what they owed to their status in society than people who weren't, well, English. Miss Ward had heard that the wife of Duke Hermann of Hesse-Rotenburg, now the USE Secretary of State, made cheese in the barns at their country residence, right along with her milkmaids, and claimed to be proud of it.

Germans! Disorderly, the lot of them, and Austrians were worse.

Austrians being farther from England, that was only natural, of course. That was probably why Ferdinand II had welcomed the school they established in Vienna so heartily. He realized, presumably, that his nation needed English schoolteachers if it were ever to become properly organized.

"You are sure?" Leopold Cavriani said anxiously to Egli's agent in Reichertshofen.

"Yes, Herr Cavriani," Lothar Mengersdorf said. "I have remained here because I was expecting you. And him. He certainly has not come. And, I do not mind saying, I am very anxious to leave. I sent my family into Neuburg two days ago, already. This is not a good place to be. There is no one here at all except me and the runner I retained."

Leopold looked at him. "You have a runner? Here?"

"Yes," Mengersdorf said. "He is very good, accustomed to taking messages *à diligence*, whether by foot or by horse."

"I need to use him," Cavriani said abruptly.

"Of course. Naturally he is at your disposal. You pay him, or Egli does so on your behalf. He is the man who takes your messages across to General Banér's radio."

Cavriani was not aware of any specific messages that he had sent to General Banér's radio, but he did not question divine providence. The runner was shortly on his way. Two messages. No, three. One to Egli, asking him to arrange safe-conducts across the Neuburg bridge for the English Ladies. An additional, very private, message, to be taken to Banér's radio, for Ed Piazza, to be forwarded to Prime Minister Stearns. One for the man to leave in some obvious spot asking the English Ladies to wait for him.

Mengersdorf looked anxious. "Herr Cavriani, I really do believe that we, too, should leave now. There is nothing to be gained by staying. Nothing at all."

"A couple more hours cannot hurt," Cavriani answered. "Just in case Marc comes."

They were interrupted by a "Halloo!" from outside. Mengersdorf ran to the door. A young man stood there.

"Zobel!" he exclaimed. "What?"

"The Bavarians will march from Manching before dawn, to invest Neuburg from the south and west. From Ernsgaden, they will try to force through the 'secured supply line,' breaking it. They have a company of engineers with them there, sappers. And this run has earned me what you promised to pay me for warning you."

"If you keep running," Cavriani said, "to warn Neuburg and the Swedes, you will earn far more. Whatever General Banér gives you, I will double. And if Banér should give you nothing, I promise you triple what Mengersdorf paid you for the run from Manching to here."

He reached into his doublet. "Take this letter. At Neuburg it will get you through the gate to Egli. Egli can get you the commander of the city militia and to Banér's staff."

Pobenhausen, finally. Thankfully. A light rain had started an hour before. Not a good kind of rain; enough that they left footprints on the dirt of the ruts, but not enough to wash them away. They had moved to the side of the road, walking on the grass, so as not to leave tracks marking their passage. Any group of Bavarian soldiers passing this way would necessarily be curious about a group of people moving north.

Pobenhausen was totally deserted. One set of tracks in the ruts. Recent; a runner headed toward Neuburg. No Cavriani.

Why stay in a barn if you could find some better shelter? Mary Ward sent Winifred Wigmore to investigate just how tightly the inn was locked up.

Very tightly. The landlord clearly believed in locks, bars, and sturdy shutters fastened from the inside.

Tacked to the door, a short note. "C. is behind you; wait." No signature. Sister Winifred brought it back to her superior. So it would be the barn shed by which they were standing. The boards on the door were so shrunken that they could reach between them and slowly slide the bar back. A roof. If they were lucky, straw.

"Somebody," Maria Anna said, "has to stay outside to watch the road. Otherwise, he won't know where we are. And I'm not inclined to tack another note onto the inn door describing our location to any group of passing strangers. This is just . . ."

She looked around. It was the silence that bothered her. Villages were never silent. There were always chickens clucking, children crying, women calling to one another, cattle lowing in the pastures outside. Here, there was nothing. A few wild birds in the trees, a few insects. "Eerie."

"It's not raining all that hard," Veronica said. "If I stand under that tree, I'll be dry enough. So I'll watch. The rest of you go in and get some rest."

She watched. She was dry enough. The rain slacked off. In any case, she was an old hag of a camp follower. She had been out in worse rains, and she had found a protruding root to sit on, so her feet were resting. Surely, he would come pretty soon.

The sun was setting. It wasn't high summer any more, but the dusk would still be a long one. If he came pretty soon, they could still try to make Weichering this evening.

Mary Simpson came out of the shed. They sat next to one another. It got a little darker.

Maria Anna joined them. "The Ladies are about to start the vespers liturgy," she said. "I will watch for a while, if you wish to join them."

Veronica was feeling a little guilty for having been rude earlier in the day. Old hag of a camp follower she had been. Not proper abbess of Quedlinburg style at all. The Englishwoman meant well. She couldn't help what she was. She nodded and slipped inside the shed, her fingers groping at her waist for the twig-and-grapevine rosary that Miss Ward had so patiently made for her.

"Don't you want to go, too?" Maria Anna asked.

Mary Simpson shook her head, smiling, "I am not Catholic."

Maria Anna nodded. "True. I understand that many of the people in Grantville are not. Lutheran? Calvinist?"

"No. I am Unitarian."

A new word. "What is that?"

Mary explained.

Maria Anna stood transfixed, looking down at her. A Socinian. Common enough in Poland, where the sect had been tolerated in decades in the past century. She knew what the Socinians were. They . . . they denied the divinity of Christ. They, since they denied His divinity, did not honor His mother. Nor Anna, the mother of the Virgin. Neither of her patron saints. Although, oddly, the woman's name was Mary. It had never occurred to her that a Socinian might carry the name of the Virgin Mother.

"Oh," she said.

"I will not hide what I am," Mary said. "If you tell them"—she gestured toward the shed—"I will understand. I won't try to predict what they might do about it. Herr Cavriani knows, perhaps. But I am not sure. It is no secret, but there is no Unitarian church in Grantville. My husband does not share my beliefs, nor my son. They are Episcopalians, Anglicans, Church of England. English Protestants, of the same faith as the current king, as Archbishop Laud." She smiled a little. "Rather high church Episcopalians, by ordinary up-time American standards, especially my son Tom. Very like Archbishop Laud, oddly enough."

She shrugged.

The archduchess looked at her. "I will . . ." she said. Then she stopped. She stood quietly.

Processing her reaction to this heresy, Mary presumed.

What would the girl do? Mary could think of several things, starting with finding a representative of the Inquisition and turning her over to it. The archduchess was, after all, a product of Counter-Reformation Catholicism. Daughter of Ferdinand II, the Holy Roman Emperor, who was one of the most unrelenting persecutors of Protestantism in all of Europe. Clearly, from her participation in the prayers that the English Ladies recited on such a regular basis, a pious and devout young woman, completely sincere in her beliefs.

Maria Anna stood under the tree. Silently. Mary estimated that at least fifteen minutes had passed since that, "I will." She thanked her lucky stars that no man was there. No man who would leap into the middle of it, lobbying, arguing, attempting to persuade. Men tended to do that. Even the best of them.

She blinked. When John proposed, she had not said, "This is such a surprise." They had, after all, been dating seriously for almost a year. She *had* said, "Please give me time to think. Not about whether I love you, because I do. But about whether I have what it takes, or can learn what it takes, to be the wife of a man who has chosen the Navy for a career. It's not what I ever, before I met you, thought that I might do."

He'd answered, "As long as it takes." Which had almost caused her to accept then and there. Instead, she had walked around like a zombie for a week, thinking about it. Death, injury, captivity, all part of your husband's job. By the time she said "yes," she had accepted what she was doing.

This way, at least, whatever conclusion the archduchess might reach, she would "own" it. Whether she called off the whole project of the escape and went running to the nearest Catholic church for sanctuary rather than travel in the company of a Socinian, or worse. Worse from Mary's perspective, at least. Or if she decided to continue traveling with them. Whatever she did, if she decided for herself, she would not feel that she was pushed into it, would not be resentful later.

It was a long quarter-hour.

"I will . . ." Maria Anna said again, "I will get up a half hour earlier than is my custom every day for the remainder of my life, to say a rosary for your salvation. I will also dedicate two novenas per year for that purpose, as well as performing the Stations of the Cross for this purpose during Lent."

Whatever Mary had expected, it was not that. Her shoulders sagged a little; she put one hand against the tree trunk for support.

A little tremulously, she answered, "That is a big commitment of time for a prominent political figure to make. I do know who you are, you know. Not Miss Ward's niece who was told by her mama to come along with us. Knowing that you are doing that, going to so much trouble over me, will give me a very bad conscience, every time I think about it."

Maria Anna smiled triumphantly, "That's what it's *supposed* to do."

Maria Anna was far from sure that her decision was the correct one. She knew that Papa would not think so, certainly. Nor Father Lamormaini. *Conscientia triumphata.* Not conscience triumphant, but conscience being paraded, like booty in an ancient Roman triumphal procession, by her conquering affections. It was all too likely that she had allowed her growing liking for this up-time woman to take her conscience captive, against the requirements of strict duty and clear obligation. If that was the case, nonetheless, she had made the decision. She could discuss the matter with her confessor later, if she ever again got to a place where she could confess. Which seemed by no means certain at the moment. She let her right hand drop, feeling the flannel-wrapped golden rose that she wore beneath her skirt.

She looked down the darkening street. "There is Herr Cavriani," she said.

He was running toward them smoothly, followed by another man who was not running with anything like the same ease.

"We have to go," he said. "There is no more time. A messenger came to Reichertshofen just as I was about to leave; that delayed us, a little. The Bavarians will be marching out at first light, before full dawn. If we aren't in Neuburg by then, they will overtake us. We sent him on, cross-country, to notify the Swedes. The USE. General Banér's forces, in any case. With a request that as a *quid pro quo*, he is to beg that Neuburg opens its gates to us if we manage to arrive ahead of the Bavarians. Which means, essentially, if we arrive before sunrise. If, of course, they let him in to deliver the message. Or if he can find a patrol outside the walls that will believe him."

Mary Ward, reluctantly, cut the vespers liturgy short. After Cavriani had said several things that were just what she would expect of a man who did not appear to be at all devout. He carried a rosary case, but she had never seen him open it.

Neither Mary Simpson nor Veronica had seen fit to enlighten the mother superior about Cavriani's background. Some things just were not necessary.

The pudgy little man with Cavriani was still panting when they started down the road towards Weichering. Mengersdorf, he said his name was.

They had been on the road for four hours when Mengersdorf fell. They had not even reached Weichering.

He was just lying on the ground. Floppy.

Maria Anna let loose the handles of the wheelbarrow, noticing that some of her skin stuck to them. Mary Simpson climbed out. Looked at him. Felt of him.

No fever—if anything, he was chilly. He didn't speak any English, nor did he appear to understand her German. Painstakingly, through Cavriani, she asked questions. No chest pain. No headache. But his limbs were like jelly, his whole body floppy.

She stood looking at him, frowning. Thinking. Trying to remember. Tom, when he was about seven or eight. Always such an energetic boy. A day when he had been running and climbing, nonstop. They had been in the country, a creek with a swimming hole. Jump from the bank, splash, wade to the shore, run up the bank again, jump, repeat.

Just before supper, he had fallen like this. What had the pediatrician said? "He has just used up all of his blood sugar. Give him something to eat; a couple of teaspoons of sugar, if you have it. Put him in a warm tub, keep the arms and legs moving so he doesn't stiffen up. He should be all right in a couple of hours."

It had seemed such an unfeeling thing to say to a mother whose only child had collapsed. But she did it, and in a couple of hours, Tom had been ready to run again.

"Ask him," she said to Cavriani, "when was the last time that he ate."

"Ate?" Mengersdorf looked bewildered. "Ah. I sent the food that was in the house with my family. When I sent them to Neuburg. I expected to follow them much sooner. Ate? Two days ago, I guess. Three days, counting this one."

"Are you accustomed to taking this much exercise?"

"Exercise?" Cavriani was puzzled.

"Does he usually run, walk, like this, for hours on end?"

"What? Oh," Mengersdorf said, "no, no."

No sugar. No hot bath. Some food, though. She gave him a little jerky, some water, and said, "No help for it. He goes into the wheelbarrow and I walk." They hefted him up from the ground.

"He's quite a bit heavier than you are," Cavriani said. "Let me push it for a while." He grasped the handles; felt the stickiness, let loose again.

"Your hands," he said sharply to Maria Anna. "Are they blistered? Are the blisters breaking?"

She held them out; then realized that it was too dark to see. "They are raw; much of the skin is gone."

Cavriani swore. "How long have you been pushing this by yourself?"

"Veronica helped."

"How long have you been pushing it?"

"Since Pörnbach, most of the time. But we rested in Pobenhausen, waiting for you. You know that. You found us. They weren't quite so bad, then."

Cavriani shook his head. Then, to Mary Simpson, "If you have enough water, a little to spare, perhaps you could wipe off these handles. And pour a little on her hands, to rinse them. Who has the salve and the bandages? We don't dare make a light; do the best you can by feel."

Past Weichering. Darker than ever, a steady drizzle. Without a moon, no way to guess how much time had passed. From Weichering to Neuburg, only seven miles. The Bavarians would be sending out patrols before the bulk of the army marched; mounted patrols, moving much faster than people on foot. The English Ladies made no complaints; neither did anyone else. They trudged on steadily.

Hoofbeats, behind them, following the road. It was still dark, just the slightest hint of a false dawn. No way to get the wheelbarrow out of the rut and out of sight. Mengersdorf looked, Cavriani thought, dead enough to pass for a corpse. The patrol wouldn't risk a shot; if one of them paused to spear him to make sure—well, they would have traded one life for a dozen. The rest of them hid.

The lead horse slowed a little; the patrol walked single-file around the wheelbarrow, in the other rut. They didn't bother moving it from the road; neither did they bother examining the apparent corpse.

I hope, Mary Simpson thought, *that they go back another way.* She could feel the new, tender, skin on her feet breaking through again, the gauze of the bandages grinding into the soles.

Cavriani went back to pushing the wheelbarrow.

Dawn. A little village, to the left. "Zell," Mengersdorf whispered. Two and a half miles to the Neuburg gates, perhaps.

Hoofbeats again. Not the same patrol. Muffled, this time, slower. Closer than the first patrol had been when they heard it. No time to disappear; they moved to the side of the road. Stood. Just refugees.

We are not worth your time, we are not worth your time, Mary Simpson thought. *We are not worth your time.*

Cavriani pushed her forward. It was a man with a horse and cart, whom Cavriani seemed to know.

They abandoned the wheelbarrow. She, Mengersdorf, Veronica, Sister Winifred with her bad ankle, got onto the cart. The man turned the horse. The rest of them ran, trying to keep pace with it.

"Tell me, Veit," Cavriani gasped, "how did you do it?"

Egli looked at him in some surprise. "Your runner arrived last evening, just before dark, so I knew you were coming. I bribed the gatekeeper—this is his cart. Let's hope that he stays bribed."

He had. Scarcely a testimony to the Neuburg city militia's tight security procedures, but nonetheless welcome.

Egli did notify the Swedes about it. After the people for whom he felt immediate responsibility were safely at his house.

Neuburg

"I am not," Maria Anna said, "going to Grantville."

Mary Ward looked at her. "You are my responsibility."

"You are not," Maria Anna retorted, "my Mother Superior. Or, for that matter, my aunt. Nor am I your responsibility. I have traveled with you. I am grateful that you allowed me to. It has made my trip thus far a lot easier."

Easier? Mary Simpson looked at the archduchess' hands. As bad as her own feet. She wondered exactly what Maria Anna had been expecting when she left Munich.

"It is perfectly clear what you should do," Mary Ward insisted.

"You have instructions from the pope. Obey them." Maria Anna paused. "They do not include me."

"I am sure," Mary Ward said, "that if the holy father had the slightest idea that you would be leaving Munich with us . . ."

"The fact remains," Maria Anna answered, "that he did not. Nor am I sufficiently arrogant to believe that I can gauge his intent and desires when he is in Rome and I am in Neuburg. Once again. Your instructions do not include me. Is that clear?"

Narrowing her lips, Mary Ward said, "I will check on Sister Winifred. And on the unfortunate man who came with us." She left the room.

Veit Egli rested his chin on his hand. His house was not large. Four rooms, which included the kitchen. Two up, two down. And, at the moment, very full, not that all of Neuburg was not very full. Right at the moment, he wished that he were somewhere else. There were all too many strong-minded women in one small space. "I believe," he announced, "that I will take a walk. See if there is anything to see at the perimeters."

"Please check at every entry point," Cavriani said pleasantly. "You know what I mean."

"Enjoy yourself," Mary Simpson said pleasantly.

Veronica's contribution was, "Don't get shot. There are a lot of stray bullets going up. You'll be just as dead if one falls on your head by accident as if somebody deliberately aims one directly at your chest."

"Just a little ray of sunshine, this morning, aren't we?" Egli retorted. He was seriously thinking about eating lunch out. Perhaps supper as well, if Herr Cavriani did not need him, of course. Cavriani had gone to the bridge, to see if anything could be done to expedite the safe conducts for the English Ladies. The runner whom he had sent ahead had arrived and delivered the message, but had not been seen since. Egli hoped that he had crossed the bridge and had reached Banér's radio. He had no real way of knowing. No one would admit having seen the man after he left Egli's.

✧   ✧   ✧

At the moment, they had Egli's office to themselves.

"Why not?" Mary Simpson asked.

"Why not what?" Maria Anna returned the serve.

"Why not go with them?"

"I do not trust the Swedes. The Swede. The usurping so-called emperor."

Mary nodded slowly. Sometimes, she almost forgot that this energetic, shrewd, practical young woman, knowledgeable in the ways of gardens and dairy barns, was also the daughter of Ferdinand II, Holy Roman Emperor. It occurred to her that Maria Anna probably never forgot that.

Maria Anna was talking, rather slowly. "At the moment, I hope, General Banér does not know that I am with the English Ladies. In all of the newspapers that we have bought, there has not been any speculation at all that I left Munich with them. Some seem to believe that I have already returned to Austria but am being, as you say, kept under wraps. If I am not in Hungary praying for the defense of the border. Or somewhere else. If Herr Cavriani has not told the general . . . somehow, I do not believe that he has told the general. Then, in any case, there is no reason for the Swedish commanders here to take a special interest in one more refugee from the countryside."

"Honestly," Mary said, "I don't think that Mike—that Prime Minister Stearns—would agree to an effort to hold you against your will. I don't think that the people in Grantville would let anyone imprison you, if you came to them voluntarily."

"Why not?" Maria Anna asked simply. "In a way, they are holding Princess Kristina hostage, aren't they? No matter how politely and gently? Even if she spends time in Magdeburg and joined her father for the Congress of Copenhagen. Bars are bars, even if they are woven of spider silk rather than cast of steel. And I am not a young child, who is accustomed to having adults such as your future Imperial Countess of Narnia molding and forming her actions, limiting where she can go and telling her when, happy enough if her cage is fairly large. I am an adult, with a place I need to go and a task to complete. A place and a task that, I think, the Swede would try very hard to find out. He would, I think, feel obliged to put me under much tighter constraints than you have done to Princess Kristina, knowing that I ran from Munich. In the last analysis, the prime minister serves the emperor. Not the other way around."

Mary looked down.

"No, you have no reason to be embarrassed. I don't bear *you* any grudge, for it. It is just the reality of political power. If I put myself within Gustav Adolf's control, he would be a fool not to grasp the chance to use my presence as leverage against my father. Against . . . never mind. And the king of Sweden has demonstrated, quite consistently, that he is no fool. I will go into the USE only if I am taken captive here in Neuburg and carried there. Tied as tightly as you and Frau Dreeson were tied when the Leuchtenberger dumped you out of the barrels before me."

"Then," Mary said, "you will not go there. Wherever you go when you leave here, I will go with you. Not on to Grantville with the English Ladies. As—as a kind of guarantee of our good faith."

"As, I will," Veronica added. "We cannot leave you alone. I will stay too." She cast around for a reason that would not make her seem a sentimental fool. "Henry would certainly not approve if I left you here alone." Then, more slowly, "If Annalise were here, I would not want everyone else to go away and leave her by herself." She shook herself. "And, of course, I can't leave Mary by herself, either. I'm sure that both Mike and Admiral Simpson would be quite irritated with me if I did such a thing."

"Ronnie," Mary said, "I hate to tell you this, but you do not have the 'dutiful and compliant down-time woman deferring to the menfolk' act down anywhere near as pat as you have the abbess of Quedlinburg when you need her."

"Abbess of Quedlinburg?" Maria Anna asked.

Since Mary Ward still had the rest of the English Ladies upstairs, they started reminiscing about Magdeburg. The Hesse-Kassel soiree. Princess Kristina. The abbess of Quedlinburg. And, somehow, the women's college that would be opening there.

Mary Simpson had serious doubts that Maria Anna, if and when she returned to some variety of being an archduchess, would be inclined to fund a college located in a Lutheran *Damenstift*, but the general principle of serious fundraising was that one just never knew. And, after all, there were also Catholic convents within the borders of the USE. She managed to get in a few words about the proposed normal school, as well.

Cavriani came back with a packet of safe conducts. For Mary Ward and the remainder of the English Ladies, only.

That was fine, of course, since they were the only occupants of Egli's house who would be crossing the bridge today. But a little surprising. How did he know it?

Mary Ward did not want to leave the archduchess behind. She did not want to leave Frau Simpson and Frau Dreeson behind.

As formidable as she was, in the ensuing test of wills, Maria Anna prevailed. Hitting below the belt, possibly, by reminding the mother superior that one of the things that the Jesuitesses would have to take, if they were to be true Jesuitesses, was that additional vow of obedience to the pope, so they had better start practicing. But, then, it would be a pity to waste her own Jesuit education. She was aided, of course, by the deadline for crossing contained in the safe conducts.

Mary Ward had simply expected to cross the bridge carrying their papers and start walking toward Nürnberg. With all the attendant hazards that might involve, if the Swede was sending still more troops south to reinforce Banér. Which she did not know. If he was, it had not been reported in any of the out-of-date newspapers they had been able to find.

Of all things, she had not expected to see Father Rader and Father Drexel waiting for her. Father Rader looked exhausted; he was not a young man. "We have come," Father Drexel said, "somewhat the long way around. By way of Regensburg and Amberg." He handed her a piece of paper. A radio message, he said. From Grantville.

"*You are expected. Kircher.*"

That was all. It was enough.

Father Drexel smiled. "He sent the wagon and team, as well. Prepaid. With a sufficiently large number of certifications signed by people in sufficiently high places that not even General Banér has dared to requisition them. So. Shall we be on our way?" He backed the team and wagon from where it had been halted, rather skillfully. As he did so, he handed a newspaper to Leopold Cavriani. "The most recent I have been able to purchase on this side of the bridge. I thought that you might appreciate it."

Father Drexel looked at his left hand with surprise. He was still holding something. A small packet. Carefully, he placed it inside his robe.

✧   ✧   ✧

Cavriani obtained a copy of a newspaper from Frankfurt am Main. Frankfurt was much more cosmopolitan than Nürnberg, so the paper had a lot of international news. The lead article was on the Spanish Netherlands. The cease-fire was holding. The emperor was negotiating.

Cavriani took a closer look at the article. Somewhere behind this reporter, there was a fairly sophisticated military analyst. The level of Gustav Adolf's weaponry—more advanced than anyone else's to be sure, but still not enough, in terms of his main forces, to end any siege quickly without the ironclads and their guns. Evaluation of the flashy weapons that he did have, such as airplanes, being not enough to make a decisive difference. Someone had been reading about the American Civil War and knew that sieges took a long time then, also.

Then some discussion of whether Gustav Adolf would have anything to gain by such a series of sieges. The reporter, or the man behind him, concluded that Gustav Adolf had already, in regard to Denmark and France, gained his major objectives. Denmark had been forced into a new Union of Kalmar. There would be, in time, a marriage between Princess Kristina and Prince Ulrik.

Ah, Cavriani thought. That would, what did Ed Piazza say, oh, yes, *frost* Axel Oxenstierna. *Frost him but good.*

The French had been decisively defeated at a place called Ahrensbök, near Luebeck. As soon as the news arrived, Gustavus' administrator in Mainz had struck west, largely on his own initiative. The emperor said that he considered Nils Brahe second only to Torstensson as a strategist among the Swedish officers. Bernhard of Saxe-Weimar had pulled his regiments back into Alsace and the Breisgau. Brahe had gone all the way to the border of Lorraine. The USE had a new Province of the Upper Rhine. West of the Rhine. There was little question that Gustav Adolf would force a punitive treaty on the French, with huge reparations.

The reporter asked whether, in view of the above, the Swedish king really had any desire to let Don Fernando drag him into a long, slow, bloody and protracted campaign in the Netherlands. Particularly in view of the big problems looming for the USE to the east. The article ended with a rhetorical question. Was it not likely that the king/emperor would like to settle the conflict in the Netherlands as soon as possible?

Yes, Cavriani thought, it seemed likely. He wondered who had planted the article. Nasi? Stearns? If so, Mike or Rebecca? Don Fernando himself? Fredrik Hendrik?

Leopold re-read the article. What had Ed Piazza called him once? A "foreign policy junkie."

"To the Spanish Netherlands," Maria Anna said, as they waited for Cavriani to come back. She looked down at her bandaged hands. Sore, so sore. She was sitting in Neuburg. Hundreds of miles to go. Not much of her money left. On the strength of a note that Don Fernando had written months ago. How much of a fool was she making of herself?

Mary and Veronica just looked at her. That was—um, a long way to walk. Farther, somehow, than either of them had expected when they promised to stay with her.

How did she intend to get there, anyway?

And why was she going?

Leopold put his foot down. He was not leaving Neuburg right away. *They* were not leaving Neuburg right away. Any of them. Maria Anna's hands had to heal. One of them was slightly infected and inflamed, and required regular cleaning with boiled water. Plus, he thought, considerable prayer, if the infection were not to spread into the arm. If it did . . .

He watched it very carefully; so did Mary Simpson. They both wished that they had some sulfa, chloramphenicol, anything. Frau Simpson's feet also had to heal again.

And, he declared, they would ride, not walk; ride if he had to bring horses from fifty miles away. Veronica accepted this dictum with minimum good grace.

They *would*, he said, wait at least a week before trying to move out of Neuburg. In spite of all the risks of the war around them. In spite of Maria Anna's anxiety that General Banér might find out that she was there.

Which, since he had been forced to used Banér's radio, he shared to some extent. The very private and personal message his runner should have transmitted to Piazza and Stearns by way of Banér's radio had been so vague, though, that he wondered if Ed Piazza himself could make any sense of it at all once he deciphered it, much less anyone else.

"The other three are with the rest. I am with them. L." That had been, of course, the message that he had sent from Reichertshofen. It had been the only way he had of letting them know that Mary and Veronica, the archduchess, and the English Ladies had escaped together and that he was traveling with them.

He was sure that the packet he had sent with Drexel would make them less happy. The news that although the English Ladies were *en route* to Grantville, the other three were at present remaining in Neuburg for some time. Even ciphered, he would not risk that going through Banér's radio.

Not, Leopold was sure, that the general was not a fine man. But he fought to win. The archduchess would be a tempting prize.

Mary Simpson had cleaned Maria Anna's left hand again. For the last two days, she had been feverish, the red streaks starting to expand from her hand up her lower arm.

Cavriani risked one more radio message. The runner took it to Banér's camp again.

"Packet of sulfa powder needed ASAP. Will wait. L."

The runner brought it back; Ed Piazza's radioed reply had instructed the young medic from Grantville who was with Banér's army to make it available to him at once; some of the precious chloramphenicol as well. No questions asked.

Meanwhile, Leopold and Egli continued their patrols of the gates; their conversations with sentries; their casual questioning of refugees from different villages along the route from Schleissheim to Neuburg. No one had see him. There was no sign of Marc.

Cavriani sent the runner north again; three days into the week, the runner came back. He had been called to Nürnberg, he said. The response to Herr Cavriani's message, through General Banér's operator, had been only: "Go to Nürnberg and wait." He assumed this meant that there were additional messages for Herr Cavriani there that the senders did not want transmitted through General Banér. He had traveled both ways *à diligence*. He had not needed to wait long. Cavriani paid him accordingly. The packet was unusually thick. The runner brought the current Nürnberg newspaper, too.

Something for everyone. An envelope for each of them. Ed Piazza had understood him. Both times. And more sulfa powder, a few more doses of chloramphenicol.

Mary Simpson cleaned Maria Anna's hand, sprinkled it with the powder, rebandaged it, made her take one of the pills. Cavriani didn't give her the envelope until that was done.

Maria Anna looked at her two messages. Who would be radioing her from Grantville? Who, there, knew that she was here? And how? She eyed Cavriani with considerable suspicion. Open them, open them.

"The hills are alive."

She gasped. Doña Mencia! The identifier they had agreed upon between them, one evening when her attendant had been wrapping the lumps on her swollen, bumpy, knees.

"In Grantville." Was she a prisoner, a hostage?

"Going to my brother." So, no. Maria Anna sighed with relief. Now, the other message.

"Go to Basel. Spanish Road. F."

She looked at it, a little confused. How was Don Fernando able to use the USE radio? Well, he was negotiating with Gustav Adolf through Fredrik Hendrik in Amsterdam. Everybody knew that. It had been in the last newspaper, the one that Father Drexel brought, a long report. But the negotiations had been stalled.

Nonetheless, she felt better. She was *not* a fool, after all, to have relied on that months-old note. He expected her to come; if she got to Basel, he would somehow arrange safe travel to the Spanish Netherlands via the Spanish Road. That made sense.

She looked at the others. "When we leave, we will go to Basel."

The news in the Nürnberg paper did not make her feel better, though.

Serious Illness of the Holy Roman Emperor. Inflammation of Choleric Humors Feared.

Maria Anna excused herself. While the others discussed their messages and the news, she prayed. With tears, clutching her prayer book. "Papa, Papa."

Finally, she found some comfort. "The Lord giveth and the Lord taketh away; blessed be the name of the Lord." O, *Papa. Mama, why can't I be there with you? Papa.*

"Leopold," Mary Simpson said the day before they were planning to leave, "you are worrying. What is bothering you?"

Cavriani smiled. Not cherubically, as was his custom. Rather sheepishly.

"I appear to have misplaced Marc. My only son. In a duchy in which the duke is running amok, a war has broken out around the appointed rendezvous points, and, in general, there is chaos." He drew his brows together. "I really don't know what my wife Potentiana is going to say about this. She is very fond of Marc."

For the first time since Mary had met him, Cavriani seemed less than fully sure of himself. "For that matter," he added, "so am I."

CHAPTER 53

Lux Veritatis

Magdeburg

"I am very glad to see you." Mike Stearns meant it.

"I hopped a ride in the truck bringing Doña Mencia," said Ed Piazza, "since it was coming by way of Magdeburg in any case. We haven't built any improved roads that make it easy to get from Grantville to the Netherlands on a diagonal; it pretty much has to follow two sides of a rectangle. We dropped her off at John Simpson's house."

"Simpson? Not the palace?"

"She seemed a little queasy about the palace, even if Gustav Adolf isn't in residence at the moment. Bedmar is her brother, but I get the sense that she hasn't had any way of knowing just how close we are to getting a settlement of the situation in the northwest. There's no one there to entertain her, in any case."

"What's your sense of her?"

"Shrewd." Ed paused for a minute. "Very much tending to keep her mouth shut, at least with us. Not at all forthcoming about the extent to which she was, or maybe was not, involved in the archduchess' decision to abandon the Bavarian match. Even less forthcoming about future plans."

"Of course," Francisco Nasi commented, "as you say, she is not aware of how far the negotiations have come."

487

"What does she know?" Mike asked.

"Since she crossed out of Bavaria with Duke Albrecht, no more than any other member of the public who buys a newspaper now and then," Ed answered. "It has been several weeks since she has seen the archduchess. Except, of course, she knows perfectly well that Vervaux brought the young dukes of Bavaria to Amberg and that, as of last week, they were still in the *collegium.*"

"I am honestly very surprised," Don Francisco commented, "that Duke Ernst has been able to hold that information quiet. I myself do not know exactly who is aware of it. But few people, very few people."

"Until you just said that," Ed said, "I did not *know* it myself. Surmised it, true. But I did not know."

Nasi looked at him. He hated being trumped.

Duke Hermann of Hesse-Rotenburg smiled at Sattler. Who now owed him a bet.

Mike waited them out. It was Ed who changed the subject. "Well, catch me up to date, will you. Grantville is a bit off the beaten track, these days. How are things coming with the Prince Formerly Known as the Cardinal-Infante? Whatever he is calling himself these days?"

Mike leaned back, stretched his arms, hunched his back. He had been sitting at this desk too long. "We're getting there, I think. A re-united Netherlands should come out of it, if they ever bring the negotiations to a conclusion. Rebecca and Fredrik Hendrik go back and forth, back and forth. Consisting basically of what in our world was the Netherlands, what you call the United Provinces, as well as Belgium. What we knew as Luxemburg. Meaning that Don Fernando's going to swallow the prince-bishoprics up there, Liege for a certainty. He can't afford not to have its industry. With maybe some territories in the immediate proximity added as well."

"What does that leave for Fredrik Hendrik?" Ed asked. "Anything?"

"Oh, hell yes," Mike said. "Particularly since East Frisia and Bentheim have petitioned to join the United Provinces rather than be absorbed into the USE. Gustav Adolf is in an impossible military situation facing Don Fernando, who has his army positioned on the defense in excellent fortifications. But Don

Fernando is in just as impossible a one facing Fredrik Hendrik, who has his army holed up in Overijssel in fortified positions that are every bit as good. With the USE controlling those three northernmost provinces, the *Stadtholder* has a friendly rear area. Even with help from Spain, which isn't likely to be arriving given the current situation along the Spanish Road, Don Fernando could never manage to dig him out. There's simply no way, even if the USE never gets involved directly in the fighting, that he could overrun the Dutch up there. And with an ongoing USE naval presence in the Zuider Zee, he has no hope of winning the siege of Amsterdam either."

"But," Don Francisco interrupted, "consider the other side. Fredrik Hendrik faces an equally impossible situation. He has no hope of driving the Spanish out, either. And if they settle for a division of the Netherlands based on who controls what, then he winds up being the ruler of a dinky little country with no major cities or ports except Amsterdam, which is isolated from the rest. Unless the emperor agrees to let East Frisia go peacefully—Emden isn't a major port, but it's not a bad small port. Don Fernando winds up with almost everything in the Netherlands that counts. Fredrik Hendrik will have good agriculture, but no industry and not much industrial potential."

"Stalemate." Ed nodded. "So what are they aiming at?"

"If they can reach a good political settlement, Fredrik Hendrik can get as many concessions from Don Fernando as possible and wind up being one of the most influential figures in a new reunited Low Countries. So. Fredrik Hendrik will officially surrender. Don Fernando will immediately confirm him as the prince of Orange, highest ranked nobleman in the new political entity. He will agree to sweeping political concessions, including some form of freedom of religion. Not a carbon copy of our up-time version, but a real one nonetheless. With, I suspect, a considerable component of, 'Don't ask, don't tell.' Also guarantees for the established political liberties of the Dutch provinces, and at least a willingness to see them extended throughout the Netherlands—at least, if Gretchen Richter and her CoCs can make it stick."

"How sour will those pickles be?"

"Not as sour as the last one," Nasi said. "Gustav Adolf will relinquish the Dutch provinces he took. That's a meaningful concession on his part. Except that at Admiral Simpson's insistence, he will insist on keeping the port of Harlingen, so that the USE Navy has direct access to the Zuider Zee."

"I don't think," Ed said, "that either of the Netherlandish gentlemen will like that. But, who knows? It may give them a common interest in the long run."

Mike looked at him. "Nobody has said that before, as far as I know."

Ed thought for a minute. "What 'political entity'?"

"Aye, therein lies the rub," Duke Hermann said. "We have a truce; we have a cease-fire. But we do not have a peace treaty. Gustav Adolf wants some guarantees that the Spanish Netherlands will become, in effect at least, an independent nation. In essence, he's insisting that the Habsburgs have to agree to yet another split in their dynasty. There would now be three branches of the Habsburgs, not two. Naturally, the Spanish and Austrian Habsburgs are not keen on the idea at all."

"Well," Ed commented, "the Austrians may not be enthusiastic, but given the pickle they are in at this point, there isn't much they can do except sputter. From everything we hear, Ferdinand II is on his last legs and there is no prospect at all that his son will ever become Holy Roman Emperor. If there ever is another Holy Roman Emperor."

Nasi nodded. "Yes, that too. Which does lead us to the question. Where is Archduchess Maria Anna?"

Ed smiled. "I was beginning to think that you would never ask." He reached into his breast pocket and pulled out a little packet. "Special delivery from Leopold Cavriani, via the Jesuit grapevine. Drexel, formerly of Munich, brought it when he drove the English Ladies into town."

"What English ladies?" Nasi asked.

Ed stared at him. Well, nobody could be a hundred percent up to speed on everything, all the time. Nuns were probably pretty low on Don Francisco's list of things to think about.

"The teaching sisters. Mother Superior Mary Ward's Jesuitesses. The pope has revoked the dissolution of their institute and moved them into the USE to work under Larry Mazzare. The first batch arrived the day before yesterday; more to come, probably. Drexel picked them up at Neuburg about a week ago. And this from Leopold. I guess he didn't want to risk the news to the radio."

"Ed," Mike said painfully, "what news?"

"That Archduchess Maria Anna is currently in Neuburg. Presuming that the sulfa and chloramphenicol have fixed her up, she is about to set out, in the company of our friend Leopold, not to mention Mary and Veronica, for Basel. From which point she is going to the Spanish Netherlands to marry your friend Don Fernando."

Deadly silence. Then, "What sulfa and chloramphenicol? And why?"

Ed grinned. "By the way, that leads up to a question of my own. Since when are Rebecca and Fredrik Hendrik transmitting radio messages for Don Fernando? From Amsterdam, bouncing through Grantville to Nürnberg to be transcribed and delivered to his lady love in Neuburg. Or, if not his lady love, his intended wife, at any rate?"

"Ah," Mike said. "Ah. I didn't know that they were."

"Well, they are. Were. Did." Ed checked around in his pocket. "This wasn't in the packet from Cavriani, but Kircher gave me a copy when he came over to bring the other. According to the Jesuits, Don Fernando has already been negotiating with Rome for all the necessary dispensations. Breaking Maria Anna's betrothal to Maximilian, allowing first cousins to marry, the whole thing. He finds Urban VIII favorably inclined."

"Holy smoke." Mike sat back.

Sattler looked shocked; then went back to Mike's first question. "Why sulfa? Why chloramphenicol? Plague?"

Ed smiled. "Infected hands from pushing a wheelbarrow. Don't ask. It gets complicated. Mary Simpson was in the wheelbarrow with blistered feet."

From the other side of the table, Frank Jackson, who had been sitting quietly, a sardonic look on his face, suddenly exploded. "Basel? Basel! Damn it, Mike, *Diane* is in Basel. Those old . . . biddies . . . are going to dump a goddamned major political crisis right on top of Diane!"

"We absolutely have to keep this under wraps," Mike said. "For their safety, if for no other reason. Ed, who all knows this?"

"That she was in Neuburg as of last week? All the English Ladies who left her there. Say, ah, eight or nine women. I didn't exactly count them."

"Two can keep a secret," Frank said.

Ed nodded. "If one of them is dead. But as for the rest, how many know where she is going? Well, I don't know whether any or all of the English Ladies do. Don Fernando and his advisers, presumably. Rebecca or Fredrik Hendrik, since one of them has to have sent out the message—or maybe both of them. The pope and how many other people in Rome I can't guess. Them—the archduchess, Mary, Veronica, Cavriani. Some of the Jesuits, at least."

Frank grunted. "Too many. I do not want that fucking madman Maximilian chasing after your blasted archduchess into Basel. If it leaks out that she's on her way to Basel, somebody is going to end up dead."

Don Francisco nodded.

"Frank isn't taking this very well, is he?" Ed asked after supper that evening.

Mike looked down at his beer. "To be perfectly honest, neither is John Simpson. I hate to think what he's going to say when he hears that Mary was as close as Neuburg. That she had a chance to come home and went haring off again after a political chimaera. Which is how he's going to see it."

"It would bother me too. If Annabelle were off somewhere, like that. If . . ."

"If you couldn't take care of her." Mike grinned.

"Didn't it bother you—Becky penned up in Amsterdam? All that? Even if you did manage to sneak in a couple of visits?"

"Well, of course. I missed her like hell. But I *did* know in advance that I was marrying Daughter of Super-Spy. That makes a little bit of difference, I guess. But, still. Yeah, it's hard to swallow. What about Henry?"

"He loaned Doña Mencia his recliner for the rest of the trip to Brussels. Just told the driver to bring it back safe. Otherwise, he seems to be bearing up under the weight of the orphans."

"Is *she* married? Doña Mencia?" Mike asked.

"I really don't know. If there was a husband, he must be dead. I've never heard one mentioned, but with the way the Spanish set up their names, it's hard to tell. Cardinal Bedmar, as far as I can tell, is Alfonso de la Cueva y Benavides Marques of Bedmar. Which might lead a person to suspect that Doña Mencia de Mendoza was a married name. But don't count on it. Mama is Elvira Carillo de Mendoza y Cardenas, and any of the kids has a perfect right to use any of the multiple surnames that mom and dad tag along with them, just as suits their fancy, as far as I can tell. She has a sister who is a de la Cueva y Mendoza, but she's married to a Carillo de Mendoza; another sister who goes by de la Cueva y Benavides; a couple just use de la Cueva. I *really* don't know. But family that counts for Doña Mencia is made up of her mother, brothers and sisters, nieces and nephews. Whether they worry about her, I don't know either.

"No kids. Doña Mencia, I mean. But she *is* very fond of the archduchess. Quite genuinely. That came through when we were talking in the back of the truck, on the way up here." Ed frowned a little. "Leopold didn't say directly that Mary and Veronica like her, but I get that impression, somehow. They refused to let her go on from Neuburg by herself. They were fussing over her when she was sick."

"A Habsburg?"

Ed nodded. "I don't think that we can count on all of the Habsburgs being stamped out on the same die. People tend to think of the one with which the Spanish line died out, feeble minded and multiply handicapped. We couldn't find anything in the encyclopedias about Maria Anna other than that she got married and had children; same for her sister. But both of the brothers seem to have been pretty competent."

He finished his wine. "It may be a case of 'be careful what you wish for.' If we've wished too hard to get rid of Ferdinand II, his successor could be more of a problem. He will succeed in Austria, you know; he's already king of Hungary. Depending on how we handle it, he could be more of a problem. More reasonable, a better politician, and a lot, lot, brighter than dear old dad."

"I wonder," Mike said, "how he and his oldest sister get along. If they do. Nothing in the library, I presume."

"Not a thing. But Doña Mencia says that they are very close. He's also married to Don Fernando's sister, you know. Ferdinand and Mariana; Fernando and Maria Anna coming up. Brother and sister; brother and sister—and now all of them brothers- and sisters-in-law."

"I suppose," Mike said finally, "that we ought to radio Basel. Just to let Diane get prepared for visitors. Let's see if somebody can raise up Tony Adducci."

Ed nodded. Then, grinned. "And you'd better get a message to Heinrich Schmidt and Tom Simpson. They were still fighting to get those huge cannons over the Thueringerwald, when I left Grantville, and cussing a blue streak even over the radio in Morse code. I hate to think how they're going to react to this news."

Mike stared at him. Then, realizing what Ed meant, he rolled his eyes. "Oh, Lord. I think I'll let Frank Jackson handle that one." Piously: "I mean, even though I'm the prime minister, I think it would be improper for me to interfere with the established chain of command. Over something like this."

Ed kept grinning.

Mike shook his head stubbornly. "That's my excuse, and I'm sticking to it."

Somewhere in the Thueringerwald

"They have *got* to be kidding," said Tom Simpson, after his commanding officer explained the new developments. His eyes went to the nearest wagon, which was hauling one of the carronades.

Had been hauling the carronade. The right rear wheel had dug into a furrow in the road—the miserable misbegotten excuse for a road—and that had caused the axle to break.

Again.

Colonel Heinrich Schmidt smiled. "It's not so bad as all that. First, who knows? As cockamamie as this whole situation is, for all we know the women will turn up in Paris next. Maybe Madrid. Maybe Moscow."

Tom was still glaring at the wagon, where Lieutenant Commander Cantrell was hollering orders at a small mob of artillerymen. "Swell. We're supposed to rescue globe-trotters. With an artillery train that moves slower than a tortoise. When it moves at all."

"Ah, but you're missing the second point. Whatever else, we no longer have to go to Munich. Such a relief. I've been there. It's the most boring town in Europe. For anyone, much less a spry young soldier like me."

That drew Tom's attention from the sight of the broken wagon. "Huh? I thought Munich was supposed to be Germany's party town. *Oktoberfest,* all that."

Heinrich sneered. "Maybe in that world you came from. In this world, it's the most pious pisshole you can imagine. Priests and monks everywhere you look. More churches than taverns—and a ghastly dearth of friendly women."

The scowl finally left Tom's face. "I'm married anyway. Besides, what do we get in exchange? *Basel?* Somehow I doubt it's the Fort Lauderdale Spring Break of our times."

"Whatever that string of incomprehensible English syllables means. Who cares? It can't be worse than Munich." Heinrich gave Tom a look of profound sorrow. "There's something downright unnatural about a husband faithful on campaign."

Tom even chuckled at that, despite the hours of labor they had ahead of them getting the wagon fixed and the artillery train back underway. "Leave that aside. Don't forget what has to happen before we can possibly celebrate anything."

"That is?"

"We have to rescue my *mother,* Heinrich. Hardly the person I'd bring to a wild and woolly party."

Colonel Schmidt looked vaguely alarmed. "But . . . surely she wouldn't be paying attention to *my* doings?"

Tom grunted. "Depends. If she gets the idea into her head—no matter how unlikely it may seem—that you might be a source of income for one of her pet charities or projects, she'll seize your leg like a mastiff and never let go." He shuddered. "It's a horrible, sight, it really is. Watching a man being pulled down and his wallet ripped to shreds by high society dames in a fund-raising frenzy. They hunt in packs, you know."

He thought about it some more. "Not to mention that Gretchen's grandma will be with my mother. You know her, don't you?"

Heinrich's eyes seem to bulge.

Tom grinned. "Oh, yeah, that's right. Of course you know Veronica. She's also Annalise's grandmother. How could I forget?"

Yes. They *were* bulging.

"You remember Annalise, I'm sure. Gorgeous sixteen-year-old girl—no, I think she'd be seventeen, now—Gretchen's younger sister—they say Gretchen knifed that one Spanish mercenary for ogling Annalise too much—the one who has the hots for you."

Heinrich said something. Tom thought it might have been "urk."

CHAPTER 54

Personae Consecratae

Grantville

The last leg of their trip, Mary Ward assured Athanasius Kircher, had been very pleasant. She knew that soon enough he would be debriefing her about the first part of it, all of which would be included in a "Jesuit relation" and sent off to Father Vitelleschi.

"What have you heard from Cardinal Mazzare?" she asked.

"The cardinal has, with papal approval, as well as with Father-General Vitelleschi's support, authorized the Institute of the Blessed Virgin Mary to operate throughout the USE; to use the Jesuit rule; and not be bound by oaths of stability; nor to be enclosed."

Mary Ward bowed her head.

"To be a parallel order, not an associated order. I am sure that you are aware that the Jesuit rule forbids us to undertake the spiritual direction of women's orders."

"Of course."

"Which will not mean, however," Father Kircher continued, "that we will not be available for consultation informally, as has been the case in the past."

Mary Ward smiled.

"But you must find your confessors among ordinary diocesan priests. That is a recommendation, by the way; not a command, but it would seem preferable. Representatives of almost any other religious order are likely to start pressing for enclosure. Parish priests, by contrast, tend to be somewhat more realistic. Not often scholars, perhaps, but more practical. Grounded in the needs of their flocks.

"I have," Kircher said, "some people whom I would like you to meet." He was not one hundred percent sure about this, himself. Miss Ward was a woman of very strong personality. So was Bernadette Adducci. So were all of the Grantville women with whom he had been meeting in regard to the organization of a religious order, of whom there were now five. The Spanish teacher at the high school—one of them, Guadelupe di Castro, her name was—had been coming to the meetings that he had recently held with the others. She said that she had concluded that the need for the high school to have two people teaching modern Spanish in a world where no one spoke it was pretty small. That there must be something else for her to do.

"The ultimate question," Mary Ward said, "is whether you wish to found your own order, to become a part of ours, or of some other that already exists. Although I do not believe that any one of you has a vocation to a life of enclosure and contemplation. At the moment, to the best of my knowledge, the English Ladies are the only approved active order for women. The Sisters of Charity are not, will not be, quite the same. And they are, at present, only French."

She smiled. The former name of Grantville's Catholic parish was becoming something of an in joke. She wondered how long it would be before Vincent de Paul himself found out. He had a reputation for being utterly oblivious to anything but his causes.

A stocky woman, sitting at the back of the room, stood up. She had not come to any of these meetings before.

Mary Ward and Bernadette Adducci motioned for her to speak. Simultaneously.

Father Kircher smiled. Two *very* strong-minded women.

"I'm not here to think about being a religious. Don't have a vocation now, never did. Besides, I'm too busy. I teach the CNA and LPN courses at the Tech Center. My name's Garnet Szymanski, by the way, Miss Ward. I don't think we've met before. But I heard people talking about this—saying the same thing, that you're the only act in town. And it isn't true."

She walked forward and laid a book on the table. "This belonged to my grandmother. That's why it's in Polish. Which I can't read, by the way, but I know more or less what it says. Gran didn't die until 1984; I was thirty-two years old by then. She was born in Cracow, and she had an older sister who stayed there. Joined a religious order, lived through both the world wars, into the Soviet occupation. She died in 1963." She paused. "Tough old bird," she added.

"But, anyway. The book is about Gran's sister's religious order. This lady, her name was Zofia Majciejowski. Or Zofia Czeska; she was a widow. She did just about what you have done, Miss Ward, except that she didn't try to make it a Papal Institute. And it lasted. Educating girls, especially poor girls, orphans. Preparing them for life. There's a time line here. See. She started it in 1621. Got it approved by the bishop of Cracow in 1627. Confirmed by the nuncio in Poland in 1633. Approved by the king of Poland the same year. Under the bishop; spiritual guidance provided by the Jesuits." Garnet swallowed.

"She's alive, you know. Unless something awful has happened that we don't know about. There's not a lot of news from Poland, here in Grantville, so I'm not sure if all these things have gone off on schedule. But I hope she's still alive. In our world, up-time, I mean, she didn't die until 1650. So there's at least one more around. She even picked a name a lot like yours. The Virgins of the Presentation of the Blessed Virgin Mary. More approvals. By the pope in 1658 for the constitution, the statutes. Again in 1660 by another bishop of Cracow. It's, sort of, something that's just in the air."

Father Kircher nodded. "This is true," he said. "In France, Father Nicholas Caussin, formerly the king's confessor before he came out on the wrong end in the efforts to bring about a reconciliation between the monarch and the queen mother, is working on a life of the Blessed Isabelle. Neither married nor cloistered. Living a life of Christian piety while active in the world. A devout princess of the thirteenth century, true. But it will be read by many, we think—Father Caussin is a Jesuit—as a challenge to the efforts of both the ecclesiastical and civil authorities to restrict women's freedom to follow their consciences. As was done to the Ursulines. As was done to the Visitandines. We are not quite sure how Cardinal Richelieu will receive it. If the Father-General grants permission for it to be published. We are not sure about that, either. It may be deemed too sensitive, given the present political situation. Still . . ."

The meeting went on. And on.

The doorbell rang. Annalise went to answer it. A young man stood there, his arm around the shoulders of a young woman. A little older than herself; pregnant. Otherwise a near mirror image. She stepped back, a little startled.

"Annalise Richter?" the man asked.

"Yes, that's me."

"Your grandmother sent us to Grantville. She said that we could marry here. Thea is Catholic, I'm Calvinist. It's a problem at home. My name is Nicholas Moser."

"Yes, you can get married here. Maybe in either church, depending. Certainly at city hall. Henry can tell you how. Do you have a place to stay? Won't you come in?"

The girl shook her head. "No. That is, I mean, I think I had better say something first. I'm your cousin. Dorothea. My father had your mother murdered; tried to have all of your family killed. But they've probably hanged him by now."

"Oh," Annalise said. "Oh," again. She held on to the doorknob hard.

"In that case, I guess you had better come in. It sounds like you've had a hard time of it."

"I don't see," Andrea said, "why we shouldn't just teach school. Gina teaches school already, anyhow. Aside from the fact that we don't know Latin . . ."

"I do," Guadelupe said.

"You *do*? Why aren't you teaching that, instead of Spanish?"

"Because I speak Latin with a Spanish accent. None of the Germans whom they have hired to teach Latin like it. I am from Bolivia, you know. I was only to be in Grantville for a two-year exchange, then go back home. Besides, the down-timer academics, whom they have hired to teach Latin, will not believe that I have a Ph.D. Some things they will believe about up-time, but not that a woman could have an advanced degree. But I do. There, in Bolivia, I teach, I taught, in a women's college. Not a high school."

"Why not start a women's college? The four of us."

"Andrea!"

"Why not? A full-fledged Catholic women's college? If they're making Lutheran ones, why not one for us? We wouldn't even have to put it in Grantville, if we didn't want to. Would Würzburg be better? Or some other town in Franconia? There are more Catholics down there than there are up here in Thuringia. A lot of parents might be happier if they could keep their daughters closer to home. Not send them here. We're as good a faculty as they're going to find. I'm low man, or woman, on the totem pole, and I was just about to get my B.A. There are two master's degrees, here. Honest, guys. We could do it. If we just had enough guts."

Rome, Italy

The proposal ended up on Mazzare's desk. Which was inevitable. The buck stopped there, these days.

He looked at it. Franconia. Secular clothing, no habits, just an identifying badge.

Down-timers in Thuringia; up-timers in Franconia. Girls' school in Grantville; women's college in Franconia.

Mary Ward and Bernadette Adducci. Both serving the church. Not in the same house. Not in the same city. Not even in the same organization. The idea started looking better and better.

He had a feeling that in this world, Catholic women's religious orders were going to develop on different lines than had been the case up-time. Rather rapidly.

Grantville

The letter came by regular mail, addressed to Miss Mary Ward, in care of the parish. She read it, then looked at the telephone in the rectory office with some trepidation.

Was a woman who had spoken before the college of cardinals to be intimidated by a mere machine? Firmly, she picked up the receiver and poked the numbers in order.

"Miss Adducci. May I speak with you? Privately."

"Why yes, of course. I will come right over."

"No, not here. I am at the rectory. Too many people. Is here any place private at your office? Truly so?"

"If you don't mind sitting in an interrogation room."

"Interrogation room?"

"Where we question prisoners."

"Ah." In spite of the time she had spent under investigation by the Inquisition, Mary Ward had never experienced even the *terratio verborum*, the first level of interrogation in which the executioner merely explained what each instrument of torture was and how it functioned. One at a time. In detail. She had heard that for many prisoners, however, that by itself was quite sufficient to impel them to confess their crimes. Holding a meeting in an interrogation room?

Bernadette seemed to realize that Miss Ward had spent a long time under surveillance by the Inquisition. "Just a plain room, painted white, with green chairs and tables. Nothing more."

"Oh. Oh, well, yes, then. Thank you."

"You have a nephew named Tony Adducci, who is in Basel?"

Whatever Bernadette had expected, it wasn't that.

"Why, yes."

"Can you contact him? With this radio?"

"I could, I guess." Bernadette was a little doubtful. "I wouldn't ask Ed Piazza for permission to use it, though. Not unless it was a real family emergency. Not just casually."

"This isn't casual, I think." Mary Ward paused. No one had told her not to mention that they had traveled for some time in the company of the other three women. She had decided for herself that it would be more discreet not to mention it. Had directed her sisters not to mention it. Now, though . . .

"You are acquainted with a Mrs. Simpson? The wife of the admiral?"

"Mary Simpson. Yes. Where? Do you know where she is?"

Mary Ward handed over a letter. "When she wrote this to me, she was in Neuburg. But about to leave."

"In Neuburg. Where you were? What on earth? Was Ronnie Dreeson there? Why didn't they come home?"

Mary Ward paused. "Their task, I think, was not yet complete. It is best, perhaps, if you read the letter." She handed it across the corner of the table.

Bernadette read through it. "Yeah," she said. "This probably does rate asking Ed for permission. I think he's back from Magdeburg. Let me give him a call and see if we can use the radio if it comes up this evening. See if somebody can raise up my nephew Tony in Basel. Just to let Diane get prepared for visitors."

She looked at it again.

"I absolutely do not believe that Mary just dropped this little bombshell into the regular mail, COD. Even though a lot of the mail we get these days is still COD, in spite of the new stamps."

"It arrived," Mary Ward pointed out. "How else could she reach us? And it had not been tampered with. Trust me, I would know. Even if it had been opened by an expert, I would know. A lot of my mail has been opened before it reached me, these last few years."

CHAPTER 55

Vultures Culturae

Neuburg

"We cannot," Leopold Cavriani said, "even get out of Neuburg on the south side of the river. The city is, at the moment and until something decisive happens at Ingolstadt, more or less completely invested by the Bavarians. Not only can't we get out, but it would be insane for us to try to go through the lines. The only sensible thing to do is to cross the bridge to the north bank and follow it at least as far as Donauwörth."

Maria Anna had no desire at all to be on the north bank of the Danube. That would put her inside the USE; at the mercy of the Swedes, if they should find her. Not even as far as Donauwörth. Not even for twenty miles. She said so emphatically. She would rather risk the Bavarians. Even her will, however, eventually had to bow to reality. They could not get out of Neuburg on the south bank.

Not, of course, that Leopold had been trying very hard to arrange it. He hadn't even asked Egli and Mengersdorf to see what might be done. Personally, he had no desire to spend any more time among the Bavarians than he had to and he certainly didn't want to risk Mary and Veronica inside Bavaria again.

What the archduchess didn't know wouldn't hurt her. He hoped. He had done his best to ensure that Banér's Swedes had no suspicion at all that she was within their grasp.

Besides, it would be easier for him to get horses on the north shore. Not easy, but easier. The only horses in Neuburg now were military horses. Not that they had necessarily been military horses a few weeks ago, but they were now. Requisitioned. "Contributed," as the down-timers put it. The former owners, if they were lucky, held chits for reimbursement.

"You know what?" Mark Ellis asked Dane Kitt that evening.
"What?"
"I was over in Neuburg, today, at the bridge. Looking to see the way the down-timers put in those footings. Might be able to learn something from it.

"Now that the bridge isn't filled up railing-to-railing with Banér's soldiers going south, as many people as possible are trying to get out of the city. Get over to this side, find someplace to stay, I guess, away from the siege. Lots of women with children, old people. Don't want to risk getting penned up, I suppose. At least, I keep thinking that if we managed to cross to the south, what's to prevent Maximilian from trying a crossing to the north, some-where to the west, between here and Donauwörth, and trying to pen us up in Neuburg the same way we've penned his garrison; then come over and cut Neuburg off from Ingolstadt. He grabbed Donauwörth at one point, you know, even back before this war started. I expect he's not a bit pleased that the Swedes took it back and are letting it be an imperial city again. Well, sort of, at any rate; they have a pretty big garrison in it and I don't think that the city council has much right to talk back to the colonel.

"Anyway, there were a couple of old ladies crossing, with their family, I guess. Them, a couple of men, a younger woman. But if I didn't know better, I would have sworn that it was Mrs. Simpson and Mrs. Dreeson."
"Naaah," Dane said. "What would they be doing here?"

Between Neuburg and Donauwörth

Egli had crossed first, to try to find horses. Mengersdorf crossed the bridge with Cavriani and the three women. The two factors would be going back, of course. Business was business and it didn't stop just because there was a siege going on. *Cavriani Frères* would go out of business fairly promptly if the money from its ordinary commissions ceased to flow into its bank accounts.

Egli apologized. His best efforts had resulted in the purchase of only two horses. At least, he thought, these two might possibly, just barely, each manage to carry a rider as far as Donauwörth before the knacker had to be called. Even so, the price had been exorbitant. At Donauwörth, perhaps, Herr Cavriani might have better luck.

Veronica smiled triumphantly. "I," she announced, "will walk." She was feeling much better about life now that she thought it was safe to wear her false teeth again. As long as she kept her mouth closed most of the time so no one started to wonder about their perfection, they were probably safer there than in her pouch.

Mary, obviously, would ride. Her feet were still very tender, although she had bought new, well-fitting, shoes in Neuburg. Not to mention several pairs of stockings, the softest Veronica could find in the shops. She was shocked by the cost, but Cavriani had insisted that they were a good investment and he was sure that the Herr Admiral would be happy to reimburse *Cavriani Frères* when he had a chance.

That left the second horse. In the end, Cavriani rode. He had overcome Maria Anna's will in the matter of an impossibility such as leaving Neuburg to the west on the south bank of the Danube. When there was a possibility, however . . . and, in all truth, her argument was not bad. His German *was* far more cultured than the gutter German she had learned from laundresses and gardeners in the *Schloss* at Graz. If something happened that they had to speak extensively, she would make a far more convincing maidservant than he would make a manservant. So. A merchant traveling with his wife and her two maids. The merchant's "wife" looked quite a bit older than he did, but that was not uncommon in this day and age.

The sky was bright blue, with a few feathery white clouds. Egli had insisted that they all wear broad-brimmed pilgrim's hats.

Their progress toward Donauwörth was slow. It was only twenty miles, but what should have taken one day was going to take two. The road was clogged with cattle and sheep, their drovers, wagons hauling grain.

General Banér had decided that his army had to eat. While

he had been profanely delighted—as nearly ecstatic as he ever became—to find that a cattle drive from Hungary had arrived at the *Ochsenschlacht* island in the river south of the fortress only two days before his troops did and several hundred steers were penned up there, next to the slaughtering facilities, when his first troops arrived, that would not feed a regiment for very long. Banér had inspected the earthworks along his "secure supply line" from Neuburg to Ingolstadt. He was far from sure that it was as secure as a prudent commander would want it to be. He was getting as much food inside the earthworks along the old Sandrach channel of the Danube south of Ingolstadt as he could, while he could.

Within, of course, the limitations of how much fodder was available to keep the animals alive until they were eaten. Sieges were always a problem, especially when the besiegers themselves were penned in, as his forces on the south bank were. Moreover, there was a limit to how much he could draw from the communities on the north bank, even if he paid for the provisions. Farmers had this habit, nasty and inconvenient from the viewpoint of military leaders, of wanting to feed themselves and their families and save seed grain for the next season.

As Duke Maximilian was finding out. There was said to be considerable unhappiness in many districts of *Oberbayern* in regard to the new exactions and contributions associated with his current troop movements. It would not be surprising if some of Bavaria's rural folk broke into outright rebellion, before too long.

Well, Cavriani thought, once they got to Donauwörth, it would just be another two hundred miles to Basel. As the crow flies. In reality, up and down hills, across creeks, along river banks, and trying to get through Swabia without meeting either the Swedes or Bernhard of Saxe-Weimar.

He wondered if Don Fernando was aware just how limited in size Maria Anna's escort really was.

Maria Anna had far too much time to think, walking along like this. She was not even, Herr Cavriani had said, to pray her rosary as she stood at the side of the road waiting for the drovers and shepherds to pass, here on the north shore, in Pfalz-Neuburg. Although there were many Catholics in the region since Wolfgang Wilhelm had converted in 1613, one did not wish to draw

unnecessary attention to oneself. The papers Cavriani was carrying now said that they were from Geneva. All of them. Genevans
did not say rosaries.

It was hard to pray without it. She was accustomed to the beads
slipping through her fingers, one by one. A focus of concentration,
an *aide-memoire*. Pray without it, count on her fingers, tapping
the nails. An Our Father for Papa, a Hail Mary for Mama. An
Our Father for Ferdinand and Ferdinand the Most Recent—he
would have grown so much by now. He might even be walking
and starting to talk. A Hail Mary each for Mariana and Cecelia.
She remembered each member of her family. But then her mind
came back to where it had been before.

Her loyal household. Where were they all? What had happened to them because of her? Had they escaped or had they
been caught up in Duke Maximilian's madness? One of the
newspapers had contained a list of those executed. An Our Father
for Dr. Donnersberger, who had been a faithful servant. A Hail
Mary for Countess Polyxena, who had been a pretty little fool,
untrustworthy, but had surely done nothing to earn a beheading
in the *Schrannenplatz*. A whole rosary of thanks for the safety
of Doña Mencia.

Susanna. What had become of little Susanna? Surely, if Doña
Mencia was safe and on her way to Brussels, Susanna was with
her. After all, she was with the party that Maria Anna had sent
back to see Doña Mencia safe. But why hadn't Doña Mencia
said so? It would have only taken one word, or two. The radio
could do that. A rosary for the safety of little Susanna, so bright
and perky, so cheerful and chatty. So brilliant a designer. A Hail
Mary for Frau Stecher, who had seen this and envied the girl so
deeply, realizing that one day, not so far in the future, she would
be supplanted.

Maria Anna jumped back a couple of steps to avoid a sheep that
was trying to run off the edge of the path. The golden rose banged
against her thigh under her skirts. Prayers for the church.

Prayers for Papa; prayers for his health; prayers for his recovery.
Prayers that, if need be, he would have a good death.

Three hours on the road from Neuburg, Cavriani called a
halt for lunch. They hadn't even gotten to Rennertshofen. Then
they would have to wait to cross the Ussel. It would be amazing
if they got to Marxheim before dusk. Then they would have to

cross the Lech. Lunch was bread and . . . olives? Cavriani laughed. "Egli says that the Swedes, apparently, do not care for olives. They were one of the few things that the Neuburg grocer still had in abundance, not marked up." They had plenty of water; Maria Anna ate olives with abandon.

While they waited at the Ussel, Mary got down to walk for a short distance. She was trying to toughen her feet again. Maria Anna stood, holding the horse, watching her.

A man standing near the ford looked up, glanced at her casually. Looked again. *Surely not.* But so like, so very like the missing archduchess.

Captain Raudegen was not especially happy to be holding water buckets for horses. A captain of cavalry should have risen well above such a duty. Colonel von Werth had sent him, with five men, to scout north of the river to find out whatever he could. But he was not to do it by riding rapidly through the countryside. If such a raid was to come, it would come later. Instead, Raudegen had been instructed to stand at fords, counting the men and animals going past them. Among other things. Colonel von Werth had not mentioned his intentions, but the possibility of a raid in strength north of the river, against Banér's camp outside Ingolstadt, was certainly a good one.

Raudegen did not like Colonel Johann von Werth. He respected his abilities, but he did not like him at all. "Von" Werth, to start with. Everyone knew that he had been born a plain "Jan van Wierdt" in a village up around Cologne, about 1591. The Low German of the region, like Dutch, did not use "van" as a designator of nobility, but just to say that a person was "from" here or there.

The colonel spread the story of a family tradition that once upon a time, in Friesland, the family had been knights, driven out after the Reformation for its unshakable Catholic faith. But he admitted that he and his eight brothers and sisters had worked in the fields, that he himself as a boy had herded swine, and that after his father's death he had worked as a hired man on farms owned by others.

So Jan van Wierdt joined the army when he was nineteen—yes, it was said, starting as a water boy for horses, performing the same service that Raudegen was performing now. As he rose from the ranks under General Spinola, he modified his name into the High German form. With all of the associated implications. "Von Werth" or, depending upon the document, von Wörth, Werd, Weert, or even, in the French form, de Weerth. Within ten years, he had made captain; in another ten, colonel in the Bavarian Eynatten regiment.

A water boy from a village on the lower Rhine. Raudegen was ambivalent. The son of farmers. What did it say about the hierarchy of society? After Pappenheim, von Werth had been the second most effective cavalry commander in the service of the imperial forces—certainly the most effective in the service of the Bavarian forces. It was a matter of judgment, at any given time, just how closely the Bavarians and the emperor were allied with one another. At the moment, Werth was in command of Duke Maximilian's cavalry south of Ingolstadt.

What did it say about Raudegen's own prospects? There was no noble predicate preceding his name, either. It was, in fact, a military alias. So who knew how high the son of a village farrier might rise? That Raudegen was the son of a village farrier was the reason von Werth had assigned him to this scouting mission. He, too, knew how to stand at a ford and water horses, with none of the danger that a noble captain might run of breaking out of character.

There were all sorts of stories going around in the army, coming from the books of Grantville. That in another world than this, in May of this very year, von Werth had played a significant part in a great Catholic victory at Nördlingen; that as a reward, Ferdinand II really had made him a Freiherr, whatever ambiguities his social status may have had before. That Maximilian had promoted him. *Feldmarschalleutnant und Generalwachtmeister*. Lieutenant field marshall and major general.

In this far less favorable world, von Werth was in a stinking camp south of Ingolstadt. Champing at the bit, wanting to do something, anything, to move against Banér.

Raudegen finished his task and walked downstream to where five other Bavarian cavalrymen in plain clothes were waiting for him. They had expected nothing more exciting from this day's work than a count of sheep and oxen being driven toward Neuburg and Ingolstadt. Only one went back across the Danube, carrying a message to von Werth and his commander, General

Franz von Mercy, whom Duke Maximilian had borrowed from the Lorrainers. Raudegen himself took the others and headed back to Rennertshofen, profoundly wishing that they had horses. They had left their horses on the south bank. If he was wrong, he was making a laughing stock of himself. If he was right . . .

They were across the ford. Walking again, next to Mary's horse, Maria Anna thought that she might as well start now. She would begin a novena, for the salvation of Mary Simpson's Socinian soul.

She told her so, as they ate their supper. There were no rooms to be had in Marxheim. Cavriani had bought a salad of peas from a vendor and fresh bread; they had a place to camp and tether the two horses in the fenced courtyard behind the bakery.

"Oh, into guilt tripping, are you?"

Some explanation followed. What a lovely concept, Maria Anna thought. She rested her chin upon her knee, meditatively.

"To think," she said, "that I have been 'guilt tripped' all my life and no one ever told me. I am not embarrassed to 'guilt trip' you. People do it all the time." She gestured at Veronica, who was pulling a bucket of water for the horses from the cistern on the other side of the yard. "Just as Mother Superior Ward's making the rosary of twigs was to give Frau Dreeson one. Which it did."

They had a rather nice discussion of tactics and techniques. Not, Mary pointed out, manipulation. It was nicer to consider it under, well, some other word. But it had to be done. Otherwise, if one did not bring people to some common focus of purposes, there would be no schools, no operas.

"Opera? You like opera?" Opera had not entered the conversation as long as they were traveling with the English Ladies. "Have you ever heard this?" Maria Anna started humming; Mary laughed and started singing along.

"I saw the original production of *The Sound of Music*."

In the back courtyard of a bakery in Marxheim, plans for the expansion of Europe's commitment to opera, generously defined, began to arise; then spread to ballet. In the course of it, Maria Anna and Mary each discovered that the other would really rather converse on these matters in excellent literary Italian, or in French, rather than in somewhat fractured German. Their conversation rapidly became more voluble. The discussion moved to contemporary artists of the Netherlands, and to the interior decoration of state buildings in national capitals.

Veronica, who did not know a word of either Italian or French and had no desire to learn, looked at them sardonically, curled up, and went to sleep.

Leopold Cavriani smiled into the dark. "Culture vultures," Annabelle Piazza had called such people. Idly, he wondered for a while about the best way to put the phrase into Latin. When he had a chance, he would have to ask Marc's friend Böcler back in the Upper Palatinate. Then he went to sleep as well.

Raudegen was uncertain. The younger woman certainly had an uncanny resemblance to the archduchess. But he could scarcely believe that an archduchess of Austria would walk while permitting another woman to ride. There could be no other woman in this part of the Germanies who outranked her. But now that he had seen the other two women with her, he was nearly sure. He had been there, that day in Freising, when the "witches" were dumped out of the barrels. Possibly, just possibly, an archduchess might walk and permit the wife of the up-time admiral to ride, given the way that the war between the Swede and the League of Ostend had gone.

He would risk following them for another day, at least. He had come up through the ranks; he had not gained his commission through mental timidity any more than he had gained it through physical cowardice.

From Donauwörth to Ulm

Egli had been right in both of his predictions. The two horses he had bought at Neuburg reached retirement age by the time they got to Donauwörth. But there, more horses were to be found, not to mention another factor employed by *Cavriani Frères de Genève* and, thereby, access to more money. Cavriani bought four decent horses, whether Veronica wanted to ride or not. He obtained clean clothing, not new, but of good enough quality to justify the horses, from a secondhand dealer. They kept Egli's broad-brimmed hats.

✧　　✧　　✧

Four horses. That meant that the group had the money, obviously, to purchase them. Plus different clothing. The younger woman's stance on horseback was very like that of Archduchess Maria Anna.

Raudegen sent a second man back to Ingolstadt with another, more urgent, message.

The next day they made Höchstädt by noon. The town had plenty of amenities, naturally, since the counts of Pfalz-Neuburg had a residence there and the customary service businesses had grown up around the palace. They had a pleasant lunch.

Cavriani bypassed Dillingen altogether. No sane and reasonable Calvinist wanted to go near the seat of Heinrich von Knoeringen, prince-bishop of Augsburg.

Lauingen was Pfalz-Neuburg again, another residence of the counts; a short day, but a safe place to spend the night. The southerly road that forked off before Lauingen would have been easier, but Gundremmingen and Offingen were subject to the prince-bishop of Augsburg. Cavriani preferred to avoid them, just as he had avoided Dillingen.

Captain Raudegen was seriously disappointed. He sent the third of his five men back, this time to Dillingen and then to continue to Ingolstadt. He told the man to get a horse from the lieutenant and come back, with information on what Werth said. He was becoming concerned; he should have received *some* response from Werth before this.

They could have made Gundelfingen today easily enough, just another mile and a half. But that was over the border into another jurisdiction. Better, Cavriani thought, to stay where they were. Going through Gundelfingen and its check points in the morning would suffice. After that, Günzburg and an unavoidable crossing to the south bank; there were no more passable roads on the north shore of the Danube along here. Günzburg. *Voerderoesterreich.* Austrian. One of the widely strewn Habsburg possessions in Swabia. Günzburg; one of the archdukes—Karl, Cavriani thought—had actually resided there twenty or so years ago, for quite a while. He checked with Maria Anna.

"Yes," she said. "It was Archduke Karl. The son of the one who obstinately married the Augsburg girl, Philippine Welser. She was rich and beautiful, but not noble. Her two sons, therefore, were not eligible to inherit any hereditary Habsburg titles." She smiled. "We are, though, sufficiently proud of ourselves that we did not leave them commoners, but gave them other titles. This Karl first married an Italian commoner who bore him children; he had none by his second wife, a Cleves duchess who was of equal birth. He died in 1618. His sons are called von Hohenberg."

The vagaries of Habsburg genealogy were not Cavriani's concern. Before they started out the next morning, he asked, "Is there anyone in Günzburg who would be likely to recognize you?"

Maria Anna pursed her lips. "I don't think so. It is a long way away from Vienna or Prague, and Günzburg has been administered from Tyrol since Archduke Karl died. If any official stationed here has ever seen me, it would have been when I was a child or young girl, probably." She frowned. "Unless, of course, it might be one of the military officers. Or even an ordinary soldier. They come and go."

Leipheim; good enough. Nersingen and a thorough examination of their travel papers by officials of the prince-abbey of Elchingen. They were passed through. So were Raudegen and the two men he still had with him.

Ulm

Ulm. Beautiful, beautiful, Ulm. Cavriani had never been so happy to see an imperial city in his life. This had been their longest day since leaving Neuburg, and an uneasy one.

Never so happy until the next morning. Leaving the women at the inn where they had slept, he went to look up some business-men of his acquaintance, bought a newspaper, and checked with the money changer who served as the firm's banker here.

All of them were unanimously in agreement. Going farther into Swabia now would be the act of an insane man. Even if Cavriani had urgent business at home in Geneva, he should plan to stay in Ulm for quite some time. No one in Ulm knew precisely what Bernhard of Saxe-Weimar planned to do next, nor, above all, why he was carrying out his current course of action, but the rumors were running wild.

Half of Bernhard's army was still in the Franche-Comté, the Sundgau, and Alsace. It was still employed by the French, but the French were not moving. Given the crushing defeat they had suffered at Ahrenbök, how could they? The other half—at least half, maybe more—was marching into southern Swabia. No one knew why. Certainly, however, he had cut the Spanish Road.

Horn had thrown a strong garrison into Ehingen, a dozen miles or so up the Danube; the roads were secure that far, at least, although there were foraging parties throughout the countryside collecting "contributions" from the villages.

Past Ehingen, tomorrow? Or the next day? Who knew? No one had heard from Munderkingen for three days; the great monastery at Obermarchtal had burned already in the spring of 1633; each side, Bernhard's troops and Horn's troops, accusing the other of having done it. Either seemed equally probable, the way the war in Swabia had been conducted. The magnificent organ had been a great loss; even a Lutheran city councilor in Ulm would admit that. In any case, he would be well-advised not to try the south route. The northern road, however, past Lauterach and Reichenstein, was in very poor repair for at least five miles before it intersected the main road again, and there were reports of attacks on travelers.

In any case, Horn had occupied Riedlingen, one of the five Austrian cities along the Danube. That was five days ago. Anywhere Cavriani went, past Ulm, he would be in the presence of troop movements. Which meant that, almost certainly, some of those troops would confiscate his horse.

Nobody had reliable information on the current situation beyond Riedlingen. The monastery at Inzigkofen, too, had been burned, the previous fall. That, it was fairly certain, had been done by Bernhard. After all, he and his troops, although in the service of France, were mainly Protestants. In many villages that before the war had sixty or seventy households, there were perhaps six or seven remaining. The other farmers had fled, some into the walled cities with which they had sanctuary contracts, some into Switzerland. At one point, Horn had invested the Austrian towns of Mengen and Sigmaringen, which he would have to pass, but he might have pulled those troops away to face the new threat from Bernhard. There was no way to tell. The monastery at Beuron had also gone up in flames last fall; the abbot and monks had fled into Switzerland.

The valley of the upper Danube had suffered greatly since the autumn of 1632, everyone said. Mühlheim had been repeatedly occupied by the opposing forces, first Bernhard's and then the Swedes. In one attack there in 1632, two hundred Swedes had been killed; he would see the mass grave as he passed by. The little town was no longer really significant since the moving of the road from Lake Constance to Rottweil to run through Tuttlingen, but still, before the war, it had nearly a hundred households. The last Cavriani's informant had heard, there were fewer than thirty. The rest had fled, starved, or fallen victim to the plague. All of which meant that if he insisted on leaving Ulm, he would find no safe stopping point before Tuttlingen, at the earliest.

Cavriani came back to the inn in full sympathy with Duke Ernst. He sincerely wished that General Banér were available to say what he was thinking. They had been lucky, thus far. Now he was facing ninety miles between Ulm and Donaueschingen—more if they had to detour around scenes of military action—through nearly two dozen different official political jurisdictions, none of which had any authorities effectively in charge because of the war, on insecure roads in the midst of major troop movements. In the company of three women who would make extremely valuable hostages for Bernhard or, in the case of the archduchess, possibly for Horn also.

If, of course, anybody bothered to identify them and did not simply kill them first.

CHAPTER 56

Vita Brevis

Bavaria, south of Ingolstadt

"This," Marc Cavriani proclaimed, "is completely insane."

For the past three days, he and Susanna had spent more time in the fields, sitting or lying concealed behind or under bushes, than they had spent walking. They had spent one entire afternoon in a pear orchard, up in one of the trees, avoiding soldiers. At the moment, they were lying in a drainage ditch, about a half mile outside Hohenkammer. There were three or four inches of water at the very bottom from the recent rains. In the spring, it probably ran full, eighteen inches or two feet before the water would spill over into the low-lying portion of the planted fields and drown the young crops.

Marc's impression was that every soldier in Bavaria must be moving in the direction of Ingolstadt. That had to be wrong, of course. Duke Maximilian might be pulling men from the eastern border, against Austria. Out of the garrisons, even though that would be risky, considering how strongly the local administrative districts had been objecting to quartering and contributions during the past year. Bavaria was poised on the edge of a peasant revolt; the demands of the military were more than its people could meet. Surely, however, the duke was not pulling away the ones who were looking west, toward Swabia?

In any case, wherever they came from, Marc certainly did not wish to join them. The last thing that he wanted to be was a Bavarian soldier—which he was likely to become, being a young man and able-bodied, if any of these units saw him. He did not have much confidence that an Italian passport would save him. That was the last thing he wanted, not just because of personal distaste, but because he was responsible for Susanna.

Susanna. If they were taken by a military company, there was no possibility that she could disguise the fact that she was a girl for long. When that happened . . .

No. It was plain and simple. They *had* to keep out of sight. It would be nice to be invisible. He thought wistfully of the stories of the ancient *Tarnhelm*. More prosaically, they were constantly hiding.

That was easier than it usually would have been. The villages were basically deserted and unpopulated; the fields untended. It would have been a good harvest, after the miserable one of the preceding year, but the soldiers were carelessly riding or tramping the grain down as they passed. Another grievance for the peasants. The region between Munich and Ingolstadt would be very restless once this autumn campaign was over and the armies had to go into winter quarters.

Marc and Susanna hadn't gone into the villages. Soldiers were in all of them, looking for food and loot. They had stayed on the outskirts; even better, in the hay meadows. The cattle were all gone from the grazing lands, either driven off by their owners or confiscated by the army. Any hay that was to be made this year had already been made and was in the barns. A bit of stubble was left. There was not much new growth coming up through it this late in the season, not in this heat. There was little in the hay meadows to interest passing troops. Marc hoped that the soldiers would continue to graze their horses on the pasture land that had not been put to hay this season.

The unit passing now was unusual. It had to be the retinue of some extremely important officer, with his staff. The duke was sending someone very significant to confront the Swedes south of Ingolstadt. Who? Marc wondered. From what he had heard of the Bavarian army in this year of 1634, the only commander who would rate that kind of retinue, short of Maximilian himself, was Franz von Mercy.

A troop of riders made a lot of noise, but he could hear a dog, probably one of the half-starved ones left behind in a nearby village, over the hoofbeats and rattles. It was baying. By the sound of it, the cursed mutt was running across the field directly toward them.

A shadow fell over him from behind. "A couple of deserters, Captain," somebody said.

Marc rolled; stood up. Susanna rolled, sat up.

Two men. One an officer.

Definitely the wrong officer to see him here.

"My," the captain said. "Not deserters, I think, Sergeant. If it isn't our supposedly Italian repairer of bridges? Lying here beneath a bush, spying perhaps? With an apprentice spy to help him. A runner perhaps, who takes the information he gathers to his paymaster? Both unarmed, as it would appear. Secure them."

It was a drainage ditch, after all. For generations, the farmers of the village had been tossing rocks into it, to slow the loss of soil caused by the flow of the water after the rains. Susanna's left hand closed on a fine, solid, rock. She threw it into the face of the sergeant's horse, followed by a right-hand throw of a rock in the general direction of the captain's horse.

The horses were trained, but this was not a battle. They were not expecting this. The sergeant was half-dismounted when the rock hit; his horse spooked and headed in the direction its horsy brain thought might be home, at a flat out run. This required it to jump the drainage ditch. The sergeant was lucky, in a way; he managed to pull his foot out of the stirrup; he was not being dragged across the countryside by one leg. He was unlucky in another. The landing on the rocky lower bank smashed his left wrist to a pulp. The right one was broken, but cleanly. He moaned in pain. Susanna wobbled out of the ditch, her footing uncertain on the loose, rough dirt of the upper bank, a rock in each hand.

All Marc could think was that the captain must not be allowed to get a shot off. A shot would bring a dozen men, at least. The captain was drawing his sword. Marc thanked God for the training that the man's tutors had drilled into him from childhood. A noble. His first response to danger was to go for his sword, even when a pistol would be more effective.

The captain had been wrong in his assessment. Marc was not completely unarmed; he had his dirk on his belt, hidden under his loose shirt. He leaped forward, slashing at the thongs that attached the rider's saddle-bags, pistols, helmet, any thong he could reach. He was hoping for the saddle girth, but missed.

The captain started to bring his sword down. Susanna threw another rock. She was aiming at the horse again, because horses were big. She missed the horse but she did hit the man. The down-slash of the sword missed Marc and went against the side of the horse. With the flat, not the blade. The captain was good at this; he had managed to turn it at the last instant. He raised the sword again. Marc was jumping back, trying to get out of its reach. Susanna threw her last rock. Without waiting to see where it went, she scrambled back into the ditch to get more.

Marc slashed another thong. The captain's elaborately inlaid and engraved steel helmet rolled under his horse as it landed; it bounced once. One of the horse's hooves came down on it, caught it a glancing blow, shot it to the side. It came to rest by the ditch.

Marc ran around the horse's head, dirk out; came in on the other side before the rider could turn; plunged it into the horse's neck, where it stuck. He couldn't get it back out. The horse faltered; Marc backed off again. The captain jumped clear, dropping his sword to get it out of his own way. Susanna threw another rock, hitting him in the back. He stumbled forward a half step rather than bending to pick up the sword. Marc grabbed him around the neck, pulling him away from the sword. Marc would far rather wrestle an unarmed man than face an armed, skilled, swordsman. Any day. Especially today.

Marc was down. Underneath. That had to be bad. Susanna looked around. The helmet. Grasping it by the chin strap, she ran toward the two struggling wrestlers and brought it down against the back of the head of its owner just as hard as she could, with an overhead swing, a two-handed grip.

His hold on Marc faltered a little. She swung it again, just as he turned his head. Her swing connected with his temple.

Marc was unconscious. The man had been strangling him. But he was breathing.

Susanna looked down. She could not be sure how long the captain would be out. She looked at his sword. She was not sure that she had the strength to kill him with it. Even cutting up a tough old hen with a butcher knife took a lot of strength. She knew; she had done it.

But he was right on the edge of the ditch. The bank sloped down. She wouldn't have to lift his weight. She pulled him down to the bottom and held his face in the water.

Maximilian Adam, the elder of the two surviving sons of the landgrave of Leuchtenberg—now himself, for a few brief weeks, the landgrave of Leuchtenberg—drowned in a drainage ditch south of Hohenkammer.

Susanna looked at her hands and let out a little sob.

"Are you hurt?" Marc asked.

"No. But my hands are ruined. So rough, so callused; the fingernails and cuticles are all snagged. When I do get back to the archduchess, it will be weeks and weeks before I can work on delicate fabrics. Hands like this would ruin silks, satins, and velvets. Not to mention chiffons and fine lace. I will have to soak them in olive oil and keep them inside kid gloves for a long, long, time. Buff them, smooth them. I hope that she will keep me in her *Hofstaat* that long, while I can't work. Her allowance is very limited, you know. She can't afford to pay many super-numeraries."

Susanna considered it more prudent not to tell Marc that she had drowned the captain deliberately. He might worry about it. After she was sure that the captain was dead, she just climbed out of the ditch and shook Marc until he woke up. Then they just left everything there—well, except that Marc took the weapons and ammunition, the ones he would be able to carry on foot, in his pack, without anyone's seeing them. The horse with his own dirk in its neck had run away. They also took the food that was in the captain's saddle bag—the one that Marc had cut off—and came back to the herdsman's shelter at the side of the hay meadow.

Marc looked at her with concern. She was so cute, like a kitten. Not a fluffy one; a skinny orange and cream tabby that needed to drink more milk. So little and defenseless. Sitting here, in the middle of a war, worrying about her hands. He had to take care of her.

They had both lost interest in watching more soldiers ride past, for today, at least. They ate the captain's food. It had been meant for today; it wouldn't keep.

The official record, written up after the body was found, stated that the young landgrave had been killed in action while participating in the siege of Ingolstadt. The sergeant died that night, of shock, during a field amputation of his left arm. Searchers from Leuchtenberg's unit had not found them until evening, well after dusk; by then, the sergeant was not coherent. In any case, he could not have explained exactly what had happened. He had been lying face-down in the ditch since he fell.

Part Eight

September 1634

Another race hath been, and other palms are won

CHAPTER 57

Distrahere Dolor Tale Dulcis

Bavaria, between Neuburg and Ingolstadt

General Franz von Mercy leaned forward in his saddle, squinting at the enemy forces that had just come in sight on the road ahead. "That looks . . ."

His subordinate, Colonel Johann von Werth, finished the sentence. "Like the new light artillery the Swedes used at Ahrensbök. Yes, sir, I agree. The ones that are said to have devastated the comte de Guébriant's cavalry charge."

Von Werth's head swiveled from side to side, assessing the terrain with an experienced soldier's eye. "And this ground is as bad as you could ask for. The river hemming us in on the right, those woods on our left. No room for cavalry to maneuver, and a good field of fire for artillery on the defense."

Facing them from the other direction, also squinting into the distance, were two young officers of the USE's flying artillery regiment.

"What do you think, Thorsten?" asked Lieutenant Markus Reschly.

The lieutenant next to him made a face. "Well, we certainly aren't going to charge them. Not with only four out of six batteries."

He swiveled in his saddle, looking back down the road. The last two batteries of their company had encountered problems with broken equipment. Their commanding officer, Captain Carl Witty, had stayed behind to deal with the matter while he sent the other four batteries ahead under the command of his two lieutenants.

Thorsten didn't really expect the other batteries to arrive within less than an hour. As fast as the flying artillery had been moving since the assault across the Danube began, they'd outpaced their supply train. It wasn't likely that Witty and his handful of artificers would find wheels and axles that fit the gun carriages in any of the nearby Bavarian villages—and even less likely they'd find a blacksmith or a wainwright. The villages were completely deserted. No civilians in their right mind wanted to remain in an area about to be turned into a battleground. Or anywhere in the vicinity of an army—enemy or "friendly," it hardly mattered—that was on campaign.

Lieutenant Reschly grunted humorlessly. "I wouldn't be any too keen on charging them even if we did have a full company. That'd be playing cavalrymen at their own game, I think. No, better we just take defensive positions across the road and keep that Bavarian cavalry pinned down, until we get reinforcements."

Thorsten wasn't about to argue the point. Certainly none of the battery's sergeants would, either. Those noncoms, with the experience of the Baltic campaign under their belts, already had the guns spreading out and setting up to cover the entire field.

"Right you are," he said. "We'll just wait and see what the Bavarians decide to do."

From the set expression on his face, Colonel von Werth knew his commander had decided that, bad as the tactical situation might be, they simply had no choice. They had to break that artillery, before the noose could close any further around Ingolstadt. No matter how severe their own casualties.

"I don't believe we have any choice," said General von Mercy. "Colonel, I'd appreciate it if—"

He broke off, hearing the sound of a horse galloping up from behind them. Swiveling in their saddles, the two officers saw a courier racing up.

"General! General von Mercy!" The courier was waving his hand in a vigorous manner. Almost a frantic one, even.

"We may as well wait until we see what this is about," said von Mercy.

A few seconds later, the courier drew up next to them. "Ingolstadt is taken," he said, half-gasping the words. "Given up, rather. That stinking traitor Cratz von Scharffenstein surrendered it to Banér not more than an hour ago."

Von Mercy set his jaws grimly. Von Werth leaned over his saddle. "You're certain?" he demanded of the courier. "No possibility this is just a rumor?"

The man had his breath back. "It's certain, Colonel. I was there myself when it happened. If I hadn't been warned by a friend in the garrison—those bastards didn't raise so much as a peep of protest—I'd have been caught by the Swedes pouring in. As it was, I just managed to escape in time to bring you the news."

Von Werth nodded; then, looked at von Mercy. Seeing the expression on the general's face, the colonel turned back to the courier and pointed a bit off to the side.

"Your horse will need water. There's a stream over there."

Once the courier was gone, von Werth turned his eyes back to von Mercy. By now, the two officers were quite good friends, as well as soldiers who trusted each other in professional terms—and this was now, clearly enough, a matter between friends.

"What are you thinking, Franz?" Von Werth's lips twisted into a sardonic smile. "Aside from the obvious fact that we will not be charging the enemy, after all."

The general's expression was every bit as sardonic. "To say the least. Our soldiers are now our sole asset. Yours and mine, I mean—and fuck Bavaria."

Von Werth drew in a long, slow breath. By the standards of the war, he and Franz von Mercy had both been somewhat unusual—in terms of being loyal to their employers, even more than their skill. It was not a reputation that von Werth wanted to give up lightly.

"You really think Maximilian . . . ?"

"Don't fool yourself, Johann. The duke's behaving insanely. It doesn't matter that Cratz von Scharffenstein betrayed Ingolstadt to the enemy, not us. You can bet everything you own that Cratz will no longer be within the duke of Bavaria's grasp. Which leaves you and me—the two most prominent officers left who were assigned to defend Ingolstadt. Maximilian will have our heads off within a day after we get hauled into Munich."

Von Werth didn't really doubt von Mercy's assessment. The arrest and execution of young Hörwarth—so transparently innocent of the charges against him—was enough to prove that Maximilian's fury was insensate, no matter how cold it might seem.

He pursed his lips. "You realize that if we flee, he'll strip us of all our possessions."

Von Mercy shrugged. "True. The ones in Bavaria, at least. Which, granted, is most of what either of us owns. But"—here he tossed his head back, indicating the large force of cavalrymen behind them—"we still have our most precious asset, as professional soldiers. Our men."

Von Werth glanced back. "An even split, more or less? That's what it will be, if you allow me to keep the companies I raised." Honesty compelled him to add: "Well . . . I'd actually have a bit more than half, I think."

His friend smiled. "You'll need them, if I'm guessing right. Bernhard of Saxe-Weimar is a friend of yours. I presume that's where you'll go, yes?"

Von Werth nodded.

"Then you have a tougher road ahead of you than I do," said von Mercy. "You'll have to skirt the Swede's forces in Swabia as well as the Bavarians. But . . . in this chaos, I think you'll manage. Take the troops with my blessing, Johann."

His friend and subordinate cocked his head slightly. "And you? I'm sure the Swede would hire you."

Von Mercy grimaced. "I don't think I'm quite cold-blooded enough to actually switch sides in the middle of a war. Besides, it could be awkward. I might run into Cratz von Scharffenstein over there—and it would be hard not to shoot the swine down."

"Vienna, then."

The general nodded. "That's what I was thinking. I've met young Ferdinand, who looks to be inheriting the Austrian throne before too long. I think he'll hire me, especially if I bring a sizeable body of cavalrymen with me. And from here to Austria is an easy enough march. Even if I run into some Bavarian troops, I should be able to bluff my way through."

That was it, then. There was no time to dally. Von Werth leaned over and extended his hand. "It has been a pleasure to serve under you, Franz. Hopefully, some day we may serve together again."

There was no point in adding that, given the nature of the war that had engulfed Europe for the past sixteen years, it was just as likely that someday they'd find themselves on opposite sides of a battlefield. Such was the nature of a professional soldier's trade.

The two men shook hands. Then, began trotting their horses toward their cavalrymen, shouting orders as they went.

They'd get no quarrel from the troops, of course. First, because their soldiers were mercenaries also, and went wherever their paymasters told them to go. And, secondly, because any mercenary is delighted to learn that he'll be going *away* from a battle, thank you very much.

"What are they doing?" demanded Mark Reschly. "Their maneuvers make no sense."

Thorsten Engler hesitated for a few seconds, before answering. "I think they're retreating."

"But . . . why?" The young lieutenant from the Moselle was frowning. "I can understand why they'd decide not to charge us. But they ought to be setting up their own defensive lines, then. Keep us from moving on to Ingolstadt."

Engler shrugged. "Maybe they know something we don't."

"Could they . . . be planning to move away and come back on our flank?"

"Possibly. But with these woods—not to mention all the marshland—that'd take them a while. By then, we'll have reinforcements. Not just Captain Witty and the two batteries, either. Within two hours, the whole regiment should be here, along with at least one of the infantry regiments."

He spotted one of the sergeants giving them a quizzical look. Thorsten waved his hand, trying to make the gesture seem as relaxed as possible.

"Just keep having the men dig in!" he shouted. "We're not going anywhere for a while."

Ingolstadt

Erik Haakansson Hand didn't think he'd ever seen Johan Banér in such a jolly mood. The Swedish general was practically prancing in the headquarters of the fortress he'd just captured.

"Ha! Ha! Taken without a single one of those CoC assholes within ten miles of the place! And those useless oh-so-precious world's-best-siege-guns and those fucking snotty up-timers can kiss my rosy Swedish ass! They're still mired somewhere in Franconia!"

None of it could be denied, of course. True, seizing a fortress by suborning a treacherous garrison commander was hardly what anyone besotted of martial myths would consider a splendid feat of arms. But neither Gustav Adolf nor any of his top officers were prone to such nonsense, anyway. It was just a fact, attested to by the long history of warfare, that most sieges were won by that method.

For a certainty, none of General Banér's own troops would begrudge him the honor of having seized Ingolstadt without needing reinforcements. They'd been able to march into the city through its own open gates, without a drop of blood spilt in the process. A good portion of them were already guzzling beer in the taverns and eyeing the waitresses.

The waitresses and tavern-keepers wouldn't even be too worried about the situation, themselves. Troops who captured a city without a fight were usually in a decent enough mood, and not prone to atrocities. Not so long as they remained sober, at least—and by the time they started getting drunk, Banér would have military police units in place. The general was a shithead, sure enough, but he was a competent one. He'd not want Ingolstadt to become a problem instead of an asset.

So, it was time to do the honors, and no stinting. "My congratulations on a splendid triumph, General Banér," said Colonel Hand, bowing.

Banér eyed him intently.

Hand managed not to smile. "I shall send a dispatch to my cousin Gustav immediately, informing him of your success. The king and emperor will be most gratified."

Banér grinned. "Have a drink first! It's dry work, writing long dispatches."

Hand planned the dispatch to consist of not more than two sentences. Three, at most. What more was needed?

But a beer sounded good, actually.

A bit later, halfway through his first mug, the grin that seemed fixed onto Banér's face thinned a little. Not much.

"Only problem now is that I've got to figure out what to do

with that fuckhead Cratz von Scharffenstein. He insisted on a job, the greedy swine, as well as a bribe. Don't suppose you'd want him?"

"For what?" Colonel Hand shook his head. "I really don't have much in the way of a military retinue, you know. My cousin mostly uses me for . . . ah . . ."

This could get a bit delicate.

"Special assignments." Hopefully, Banér was too full of his jolly self at the moment to press for details. *Special assignments like keeping a watch on intemperate and overly ambitious generals, for instance.*

"Too bad." Banér took another swig. "I'd love to fob him off onto Torstensson, but he's a canny one. Maybe Horn will take him."

Hand shrugged. "I really can't see where it's a big problem, Johan. If you'd like, I can add a sentence or two to my dispatch, asking the emperor if he has a garrison command available somewhere."

"Better make it somewhere far away from any possible action," sneered Banér. "The treacherous louse."

Hand smiled. "Oh, I'm sure there's something. The garrison at Stralsund, perhaps. He can study the glorious waters of the Baltic all day, keeping an eye out for fish with evil ambitions."

Somewhere in Franconia

Major Tom Simpson and Lieutenant Commander Eddie Cantrell studied the radio message that their commander Colonel Schmidt had just passed over to them. They were standing outside the tent that the radio operator had set up for the night.

"Well, fuck. I guess it's Basel after all."

Eddie kept studying the message; as if, by some magic brought on by intense scrutiny, the contents might change. Tom looked up and glowered at the artillery train. The great, huge, heavy, ponderous, unwieldy, break-your-back-before-breakfast-and-rupture-you-by-lunch artillery train.

"Fuck," he repeated. "It seemed like a good idea, a couple of months and a few hundred miles ago."

Schmidt shrugged. "It's the nature of war, that's all. Most of what a soldier does winds up being a waste of time and effort, in the end."

"Please, Heinrich. Don't go all philosophical on me."

"Don't be silly. That's just common sense. It stands to reason that most of war is a useless waste, since it's a wasteful business to begin with. 'Philosophy' is that mess you fall into when you try to come up with a logical reason for war in the first place."

"I said. Cut it out. All I know is that by the time I see my globe-trotting mother again, I'm likely to be smaller than I was when she brought me into the world. More wrinkled, too, and squalling worse than I did then. All squished down by unending toil and wailing from endless trauma."

"Now you're being ridiculous. I'm sure you'll be no smaller than you were at the age of ten. True, you'll be wrinkled. True also, you'll be sobbing like a babe."

He retrieved the message from Eddie and stooped to enter the radio tent. "I shall inform our esteemed superiors—oh, so very far away from here—that we shall be off to Basel on the morrow."

"Moving as fast as we can't," muttered Eddie.

"Well, fuck," said Tom.

Army camp on the Danube, west of Ingolstadt

"What do you mean, they won't let us into the city?" demanded Eric Krenz. The gunnery sergeant's face was filled with outrage. He flung his arms wide. "They couldn't have taken it without us!"

Mildly, Lieutenant Thorsten Engler replied, "Actually, we didn't fire so much as a shot, Eric."

"Well, sure. That's because those gutless Bavarians were terrified, the moment they heard we were coming. I'm telling you, Thorsten, without us that fat Swedish bastard would still be on the outside looking in."

"That's as may be," said Engler. "But legitimate offspring or otherwise, Banér's in command—and he insists there aren't enough billets in Ingolstadt for us. So here we camp, until we get new orders. Just the way it is."

"Well, fuck," said Krenz.

Munich

It was touch and go, for a few days, but eventually Richel decided he'd escaped the headsman's ax.

Probably.

Duke Maximilian was in a cold rage, and much of his fury was being leveled on the man who'd wormed his way into being the duke's new principal adviser by arguing for a hard line on every question. No proposed execution had failed to gain Richel's immediate support. Many of them he'd proposed himself, in fact.

But . . .

Even Maximilian had to finally recognize the new reality he faced. He'd severed his ties with Austria, lost Ingolstadt, and had just seen his two best cavalry commanders abandon him for other service. Not even the iron duke of Bavaria could afford to keep executing everyone around him who incurred his displeasure.

Not any more. Not with the Swede's troops pouring across the Danube and a peasant rebellion spreading through the southern districts of the duchy.

Richel had no idea how to handle the first problem. But he had an instant solution for the second.

Behead the peasant ringleaders, of course.

However, it would be prudent not to raise that proposal for another few days, he thought. Any reference to the headsman was probably not a good idea still, around Maximilian.

CHAPTER 58

Pericula Varia

Neuburg

Marc Cavriani was not sure whether he should be glad or sorry. He was glad, certainly, without any doubt at all, to hear that his father had come safely to Neuburg. He was very sorry that his father was already gone.

They were staying at Egli's house. That made Marc a little nervous. He had not let even Egli know that Susanna was a girl. He was afraid that if Egli knew, he would refuse to let them go on, wherever they decided to go next. He had actually been rather reluctant to let even Egli know that he had someone with him, but he couldn't leave Susanna by herself at an inn and Egli would get curious if he, himself, did not stay at his house in Neuburg. So they were in the loft of Egli's house, in two of the "servants' rooms." Not that Egli had any servants, other than a cook who came in on a daily basis and a woman who came once a week to clean. He found the loft to be handy, however, for the many couriers who passed through bringing letters from the businessmen whom he represented in the city.

It was too early to get up. Marc sat at the window, drumming his fingers on the window sill. His father had arrived with a dozen women. His father had left with three women. From the descriptions, he assumed that his father had caught up with the English

Ladies and taken charge of Frau Simpson and Frau Dreeson. He could not imagine how his father came to be accompanying the archduchess. Egli was no help on that; Herr Cavriani, he said, had not explained the matter.

At least Marc could stop thinking about the English Ladies. Egli said that they were on their way to Grantville or, perhaps, already there. He had received no news.

The sensible choice, Marc was inclined to think, would be to cross the river; to head for Nürnberg and Jacob Durre. A short distance, little more than sixty miles, in friendly territory that was reasonably well policed. There wouldn't be any armies, except, perhaps, some USE troops coming down to reinforce Banér. Friendly troops might be to some extent preferable to hostile troops, at least within the USE's own boundaries. Durre could advise them what to do next.

Marc thought, very, very, strongly, that Nürnberg would be the sensible choice. The other direction, following his father to Basel, was two hundred miles, much of it through territory as chaotic and war-torn as what they had just experienced between Munich and Neuburg. Not something he wanted to repeat, particularly since there was no guarantee that he would catch up with Papa even there.

It did not make any sense at all for them to try to go to Basel, especially since he was running out of money. Then it occurred to him that he could simply ask Egli for a bank draft. He had a right to. Which lost him one good argument.

Susanna was crying. Marc could hear her, through the thin boards that partitioned the servants' rooms in the loft of Egli's house. Not loudly. Quietly, the way his sister Idelette had cried after old Muffin, their mother's little dog who had been part of her life since the day she was born, had died. Into her pillow, not wanting anyone to hear.

He wished that he could go comfort her.

He did not dare.

A few weeks before, when he and his father rode to Munich, he had not even known that she existed. He tried to remember what it had been like, living in the world then, before he knew that Susanna Allegretti was in it. Now, he thought, every hair on his head knew that she was alive and in the next room. Separately and individually. Each hair on his arms as well.

No way did he dare put those arms around a crying Susanna. Not if he was to remain an honorable man.

He thought that this was the first time he had ever described himself, to himself, as being a man. Not a boy; not a youth. He was a man.

There were still Catholic churches in Neuburg, just as there were in the Upper Palatinate. Wolfgang Wilhelm had forced them on the people; the counts of the *Junge-Pfalz*, taking their guidance from Duke Ernst's policies, had neither confiscated them nor expelled their clergy. They received no revenues other than those voluntarily donated by the parishioners, but some were still there, holding services.

Susanna said that she had to go to confession. Marc blinked. He had a very unfavorable view of going to confession. Not that one should not confess one's sins, of course. But not to a priest. Not in the darkness of a Catholic church with candles and graven images and ... well, awful, papist, sorts of things.

But she *was* a Catholic. He knew that. Maybe she was used to it.

He went along, anyway. Standing in the entrance, halfway in and halfway out. Waiting.

"I killed a man, Father."

"Do you sincerely repent of this, my child. Do you come to God with contrition?"

Susanna paused for a moment. She was in the presence of God; she could not lie.

"No, Father. The man was a soldier. He was trying to kill someone, someone whom I, well, someone who is very dear to me. No. I am sorry that I had to kill him. But if I were put there again today, I would do it again. I would make the same choice. So I cannot say that I am sorry. Not truly."

She bowed her head, the tears streaming from her eyes, falling on her hands.

The priest sighed. He had no idea who this penitent was. Not one of his parishioners, certainly. Anonymity or not, he usually had a fairly clear idea of who was kneeling before him, if only because he usually had a fairly clear idea of what the members of his flock were doing.

This war, the soldiers. A woman; young, from the sound of her voice. A refugee, possibly. Most of the people from the surrounding Bavarian villages were Catholic; some had come into Neuburg instead of fleeing to the southwest. But her accent was not local; Tyrolese, if anything he recognized. The war. Plundering, thieving, raping, both sides alike. Whom had the soldier threatened?

"Did you plan this in advance, my child. Finding a weapon and concealing it?"

"No, oh, no. The man who, who was guarding me, was down. I threw rocks. Then I saw the soldier's helmet. I hit him with it. At the end, though . . ." She confessed about the ditch. The water. Her premeditated action.

He believed she was contrite. The tears told him so. Her heart was not hardened. She had told him only the truth. If she had to make the choice again, she would make the same choice. That was not a lack of sorrow. Merely the harsh realism of living in this world. He reminded her that she was shedding tears; asked her if these were the first.

"Oh, no, Father. Every evening, in my pillow. At least, since we came into Neuburg and have a safe place to stay. While we were still outside the walls, I did not have time to cry."

A penance. Not to be performed immediately, since she probably couldn't do so. A pilgrimage to *Maria-Hilf* on the Lechfeld, when she had the opportunity. South of Augsburg. Not so far away that an ordinary family could not afford to send her there. Managed by a monastery of his own Franciscan order. New, as pilgrimage centers went; only thirty years old. For now, prayers. And, probably, more nightly tears. He reminded her that we live in a vale of sorrow.

When the priest left the booth and looked around the half-darkened church, he saw no sign of the penitent to whom he had been speaking. Probably she had gone into one of the side chapels. One of the front doors was half-open, letting a bright oblong streak of sunshine into the vestibule. Outlined against it, at the door, there was a boy, speaking to a young man.

"I have to go back," Susanna was saying to Marc. "I forgot something."

"What?"

"I forgot to confess that I have been wearing men's clothing."

"Let it go for this time," Marc answered. "You're going to be wearing those clothes for quite a while longer. Might as well take care of it all at once, later on."

Susanna was in no mood to listen to sensible arguments about going to Nürnberg. She wanted, she insisted, to follow her mistress the archduchess. She informed Marc that Maria Anna had told her to come to Brussels and rejoin her household there. She had no idea whether, if she went to Nürnberg, she would ever be allowed to go to Brussels. Or how. The Spanish Netherlands were, after all, at war with the Swede. Nürnberg was his ally.

Listening to her, Marc started to realize that Susanna had not just been an errand girl. She had been one of the archduchess' confidants in the escape from Munich. When she mentioned going back to see Doña Mencia safe, he started to think that Susanna might actually be in specific rather than just generic danger. That she might really be someone whom not only the Bavarians but also the Swedes would like to interview.

She pointed out that the archduchess could have gone to Nürnberg, but did not; that the archduchess could have gone to Grantville with the English Ladies, but did not. That, for whatever reason she had chosen not to do so, Marc's father and Frau Simpson and Frau Dreeson had apparently concurred with her.

They spent quite some time talking and speculating. Why hadn't the others persuaded her? There must, Susanna insisted, have been a good reason.

He tried to put his foot down on one thing. No way were they going to some pilgrimage church twenty miles south of Augsburg at a dinky little village called Untermeitingen so she could do a penance. Not even if she cried about it. He insisted firmly that she could not possibly have done anything that she needed to be so penitential about; after all, she was just a girl.

Finally, he heard himself say something strange. He would take her to this place. This *Maria-Hilf* on the Lechfeld. After all, there was a direct road from Neuburg through Augsburg to the place.

Even that, though, did not move her to agree to do something as sensible as agree to go to Nürnberg. She pointed out that Untermeitingen was in the opposite direction from Nürnberg. She managed to argue that from there, it would make more sense to go to Ulm. In the upshot, Marc and Susanna agreed that they would go to Ulm, not that Marc thought it was a good idea, at all.

Egli, somehow, was left with the impression that Marc and the boy were going to Nürnberg. He fully concurred with this decision. He saw them across the bridge to the north bank of the Danube. After he went back, they returned and left Neuburg again through the southern gate. At least, now that Ingolstadt had fallen, a person could get in and out of Neuburg again. There were a lot of perfectly ordinary people going in the general direction of Augsburg. Very few soldiers, however, which was a considerable relief to Marc.

Ulm

To think that he had been considering settling down; becoming staid and middle aged. It was all a matter of predestination, of course, Leopold Cavriani realized. Clearly, God did not want him to become a respectable Genevan homebody yet.

He gave the ladies a summary of what he had heard. Ulm, he reminded them, was a really beautiful city. Yes, they could go sight-seeing and shopping for lightweight items for which they felt an impelling need. Not, however, until he arranged for them to have a couple of husky escorts, which he could and would arrange. The city was packed with refugees, which meant that there would also be a good supply of criminals hoping to prey upon shoppers. Tourists were, under the circumstances, in very short supply.

He was going to take a few days to plan. That had been the whole problem with the escape from Munich: no one had given him a chance to plan it. He had had no opportunity to coordinate anything, which had resulted in blisters and the absurd possibility that an archduchess might contract blood poisoning and die from pushing a wheelbarrow without gloves on her hands. He was still indignant about that, when he stopped to think. What was a facilitator for, if not to facilitate the projects of others? No, they had all made their own plans, leaving him to chase after them, without Marc.

He worried briefly about Marc. Then, reminded himself firmly that these things were in the hands of a just and merciful God.

This time, though . . .

The old pilgrim route to Santiago de Compostela in Spain, the

Jakobsweg, would be a possibility. Going south from Ulm; Oberdischingen, Biberach, Bad Waldsee, Weingarten, to Constance; seventy-five miles, more or less. They could cross the lake by boat and then continue on the pilgrimage route to Basel. It had certain advantages, the main one being that it was forty or so miles farther east of Bernhard and Horn's current theaters of operation than either of the others. The disadvantage, of course, was that it was also that many miles closer to Bavaria. Although Duke Maximilian was probably focused on Ingolstadt at the moment, he was undoubtedly capable of thinking about more than one thing at the same time.

Hmm.

Leopold started with the thought that Ulm was packed with refugees and travelers, many of whom undoubtedly, like himself, would rather be somewhere else because they had relatives, or business, or . . . Many of whom, undoubtedly, the Ulm city government would rather have go somewhere else, so that the city's granaries would not have to feed them during a siege, to reduce the risks of disease that came with overcrowding.

Surely, it should be possible to bring these common interests together. Not himself, of course. One did not wish to be conspicuous. But if one just mentioned something, here and there. He set out on another set of visits to his business colleagues. There were a few lunches and suppers at which possibilities were mentioned. Common interests emerged. Occasionally, he would insert a concrete suggestion.

Sunday, of course, was a day of rest. A day for attending church; for family dinners to which, of course, men might invite their friends. If their friends were also business associates, why, that was only natural. If some of those business associates held positions on the city council, that was how city government worked.

By noon on Monday, Cavriani was feeling much better.

The convoy left on Tuesday morning, with an ultimate goal of Strassburg. It included approximately three hundred civilians who had found themselves in Ulm but who really wanted to be in various locations to the west and south of Ulm. Civilians, many of them well-armed, who could afford to pay to get there. There were approximately two hundred more refugees who could not afford to pay, but whose departure was aided by a generous grant from the city council, which also gave each of them three days' worth of rations. Not generous or luxurious rations, but adequate, and certainly far less than those people would have eaten if they had remained in the city all winter. About fifty commercial freight wagons with their drivers, some with private guards. Safe-conducts from the imperial city for everyone concerned. Three full, reliable, companies of professional guards—those had been the largest expense, the reason why the fee for each paying civil-ian was comparatively high. They were not all trained to work with one another, but the men were experienced. Overall, it was a sufficiently large group that occasional small military compa-nies moving through Swabia to forage would not be inclined to attack it.

Raudegen was now the captain of one of these guard companies. He still believed that he recognized the archduchess. He still did not understand why he had received no replies to his urgent mes-sages. His military experience, however, more than qualified him for this simple job when he outlined it to the caravan organizer. He merely omitted his latest employment under Duke Maximilian from the resumé he supplied.

Cavriani was not the organizer of the convoy. All that he had done, as far as the public was concerned, was pay the necessary fee for himself and his relatives to travel with it. This, he thought to himself with great satisfaction, was precisely as it should be.

He paid their way to Donaueschingen. They might need to con-tinue on to Strassburg, if it turned out not to be feasible to reach Basel; but, if so, he could pay the extra later. He could always ascribe a change in plan to news received in Donaueschingen.

He intended to spend those travel days thinking about the next stage of the trip. The time spent in Ulm had delayed them, certainly, but in the long run, planning was almost always a good investment. Improvisation could sometimes bring quite flashy results. His cousin Giuseppi was good at improvisation. Leopold preferred advance planning, given the chance. It was a matter of temperament, perhaps.

Cavriani was feeling reasonably pleased with himself when the convoy moved out of Ulm. Five miles down the road, less than half way to Ehingen, he was less so. Maria Anna, drawing her horse near to his, spoke softly. And in Italian.

"Herr Cavriani. I am concerned about the captain of one of the guard companies. The one riding foremost now. He looks very much like a Bavarian military officer I saw several times during the wedding procession, between Passau and Freising. I cannot guarantee that it is the same man. I am by no means certain. But I believe that I have seen him before, since we left Neuburg. Once in Rennertshofen. Once since then. It may be coincidence. He may just be traveling in the same direction that we are. But I thought that I would at least mention it."

Cavriani had no way of knowing. At Ehingen, however, shortly before noon, he advised Maria Anna, Mary, and Veronica to drop back towards the rear. Then, in the midst of the town, they turned into a side street. By that time, the front of the procession, with the captain of whom Maria Anna was suspicious, was well out of sight in the turns and twists of the streets. Circling a few blocks within the walls of the town to let the remainder of the convoy clear out, they left by the southern rather than the western gate, cut down to Biberach, and stayed there for the night.

From Biberach, they followed the valley of the Riss, the old pilgrim route, to Constance. Passing through Weingarten, they spent the second night in Ravensburg. Cavriani was developing a positive affection for well-fortified imperial cities. Although a sincere Genevan patriot himself, he had often tended to regard other city-states as nuisances, impeding trade as much as they advanced it with their stubborn guildsmen and obstreperous city councils. For travelers, though, a conveniently located series of cities was certainly a blessing in these troubled times.

The third day, in the afternoon, they sold the horses and caught a fishing boat. The fishermen agreed to take them across Lake Constance, not directly, but to Kreuzlingen. *Fischers Fritz fischt frische Fische*, the man who bargained with them joked: "fisher's Fritz fishes fresh fishes," a classic tongue twister of the *Bodensee*. From Kreuzlingen, they walked along the south shore of the lake via Ermatingen, then cut over toward Schaffhausen, where Mary and Maria Anna greatly admired the waterfalls of the Rhine.

They were not hurrying, since they had to take Mary's feet into consideration. It was, basically, just a matter of walking the rest of the way to Basel, along the Rhine, through the cantons of the

Swiss Confederacy. The route was not strenuous; the remaining distance was only sixty miles. Cavriani heaved a sigh of relief.

In Donaueschingen, Raudegen was swearing mightily to himself. The woman whom he thought to be the archduchess had disappeared from sight the first day out. He did not know precisely when or where she and her companions had turned away, or which direction they had taken.

And the news, brought by courier from Ulm, was that Ingolstadt had fallen. His only choice was to go on with the convoy. It was, at least, a paying job, and it might eventually lead him to another, more lucrative, one.

CHAPTER 59

Augusta Vindelicum

Kloster Lechfeld near Untermeitingen

Marc was thinking about Augsburg. In 1629, the Bavarians and imperials had forced most of the city's Lutherans into exile; their churches had first been closed and then pulled down. In 1632, the city had been held for Ferdinand II by a Colonel Bredau, with four thousand five hundred men. Gustav Adolf had taken it in April. Chancellor Oxenstierna's cousin Bengt, backed by Count Georg Friedrich von Hohenlohe as the Swedish regent of the Swabian Imperial Circle, did the same to the Catholic citizens before the USE constitution instituted a policy of separation of church and state in the fall of 1633.

Neither set of overlords had tolerated Calvinists or smaller religious groups, of course, and Swabia was not yet a province of the USE. It wouldn't be until it had been, as Chancellor Oxenstierna had phrased it at the Congress of Copenhagen, "pacified." Augsburg was still under Gustav's direct administration. Marc wasn't precisely sure what the religious situation might be. According to the newspaper he had bought the night they spent there, the Augsburg city council was now floating suggestions that the two confessions should be granted parity—that the council's right of *cuius regio* should include the legalization of both at once. That would mean that both Catholics and Lutherans would have the same rights in every aspect of life. Neither group was talking about the rights of Calvinists, even now. He made a little face.

Susanna looked at him. "Stop it. You have been muttering and grumbling and making faces ever since we left Neuburg."

"I don't like the fact that by going south to Untermeitingen, we are only forty miles west of Munich. Too close for comfort. Pilgrimage or no pilgrimage."

"We're almost there. The complex of buildings down the road ought to be the Franciscan monastery. It has a hostel where the pilgrims stay."

Susanna stood on tiptoe, looking down the road, trying to see a little farther. It was all very flat. This was the *Lechfeld*, of course, where so many battles had been fought over the centuries; where Charles Martel had turned back the Hungarians. A nice open space where men could fight.

"Isn't it exciting to visit *Mariahilf*—a place where the Virgin Mary helped someone so recently? There could still be people alive who remember it. It was just over thirty years ago. Maybe the coachman. Do you suppose that if there is, he would be here to tell the pilgrims about it?"

She looked up at Marc, who was raising one of his eyebrows rather doubtfully. "Why," he asked, "would a coachman be likely to remember it? Whatever it was."

Susanna was scandalized. "Don't you even *know*?" she asked. She reached into her doublet and brought out a pamphlet.

"I bought this in Neuburg, to study, so that I could get the most benefit from the pilgrimage. The lady of the castle at Untermeitingen was the widow of the mayor of Augsburg. His name was Raimund Imhof. Her name was Regina Bämlin, from a family at Reinhartshausen. She was traveling at night and lost her way on the Lechfeld. That was in 1602. Naturally, in the dark, off the road, she was afraid that they might accidentally come into a bog or slue, or even into the river itself. So she made a prayer to the Virgin. She vowed that wherever she first saw the lights of her home, there she would build a chapel." Susanna nodded her head firmly. "She was very pious, of course. And just then, she saw the lights and ordered her coachman to stick his whip into the ground, to mark the exact place."

Susanna turned a page. "So she set out to build her chapel. There were all sorts of permits and things that she had to get, of course. There always are. But the bishop of Augsburg, Heinrich von Knoeringen, did give permission to build a chapel in honor of Our Dear Lady, and they laid the foundation stone on April 7, 1603."

Marc heaved a sigh. "Why don't we sit down on the bank?" he suggested. It looked to him like Susanna was prepared to read the whole pamphlet.

She was. She had thrown herself heart and soul into her pilgrimage. "Then the son of the foundress, his name was Leonhard Imhof and he was a knight of the Order of St. Stephen, had shortly before come back from a trip to Rome. He suggested that the chapel could be built like Santa Maria Rotonda, the Pantheon it is also called, in Rome. A round building, not the ordinary rectangular or cross shape. So the foundress hired an architect in Augsburg, named Elias Holl."

Marc did frown now. "Elias Holl is a Lutheran. Always has been. I know that, for sure. He's famous. He was one of the Augsburg Protestants driven into exile by the emperor in 1629."

"I don't know about that," Susanna answered. "Anyway, this was a long time before we were born, when the Catholics and Protestants got along better, maybe. And the man had to make a living, I guess, so he took the job and designed the chapel, even if it was Catholic. He designed it, they built it, and it was dedicated on June 3, 1604. That was Trinity Sunday. The high altar is designed in accordance with three visions that the foundress had in dreams, at night. And now we get to the good part."

"What do you call the 'good part'?"

"The miracles, of course," Susanna answered. "The first one happened already while the chapel was being built. There was a peasant named Veit Müller from Großkitzigkoven. He had a little daughter named Agatha, not even a year old, who had suffered in agonizing pain for six weeks and nobody had been able to relieve her, even though they had asked for advice from the doctors. Finally he made a vow to go to the new chapel and promised to make an offering as soon as it was finished. And from that very hour, the child got better."

Susanna smiled brilliantly. "Isn't that wonderful?"

Marc said, "Ummm."

"Then so many pilgrims came that the priest in Untermeitingen could not take care of them all and asked for help. So in 1606,

Observant Franciscans from the Province of Strassburg came to establish a hospice. Those are the buildings we were looking at, where we will stay while I do my penance."

"I would much rather," Marc said, "camp outside."

"That," Susanna countered, "is where we will stay." She turned a page. "Soon, the little round chapel was not big enough to accommodate all of the pilgrims. So in 1610 they added an outside pulpit, so more people could hear the homilies at once. They also added a tower with a cupola, which has a lantern burning in it always. Frau Regina Imhof paid for that also, so it would be a permanent beacon for people traveling on the *Lechfeld*."

Marc observed, with considerable thankfulness, that Susanna was coming to the last page of the pamphlet. It was the standard, cheap, eight-page popular type.

"There have been lots and lots of miracles; the monks keep records of them all. The most important ones are listed here. I'll lend you the pamphlet, so you can read about them while I'm doing my penance. And now, even during the war, so many people come that they will have to enlarge the church again, as soon as they can," she finished triumphantly. "Donations are welcome."

Marc was not at all sure that he wanted to read the pamphlet while Susanna was inside. Of course, it was good to be reminded regularly that Susanna, however adorable, was an unquestioning adherent of papist superstitions. It was one of those things that assisted him in restraining his impulses. That was a project on which he needed all the help he could get.

"I think," Marc said, "that the sensible thing to do is to go back to Augsburg and take the trade route to Ulm. Actually, I think that the sensible thing to do is go back to Neuburg and then to Nürnberg."

"Not that again." Susanna stuck out her tongue. She was feeling greatly relieved in spirit since completing her penance, which tended to show itself in a certain argumentativeness. "We already agreed that we were not going to Nürnberg. And why can't we go on south? From Landsberg am Lech, we could go to Memmingen, and then follow the Iller to Ulm. If we're going anyhow, we might as well see some new things."

Ulm

"We're too late, again. Papa's friends say that he and his 'relatives' left with a convoy a couple of weeks ago. They had paid their way to Donaueschingen. Then it, the rest of the convoy, was going on to Strassburg. He told them that he had business in Basel."

"When is the next convoy going out?" Susanna asked.

"Not this week. Or next, as far as anyone here in Ulm knows. The last one got to Donaueschingen safely—they do know that much. But beyond, about halfway between there and Freiburg, things were pretty desolate. One of the mercenary companies hired to guard the convoy that Papa went out with tried to loot its own clients. The other two companies rallied to the defense of their employers and put the attempt down, but not without consider-able loss of property and several deaths, both of guards and of civilians. The noise, the shooting and other racket, attracted the attention of a detachment of Bernhard of Saxe-Weimar's troops. The news is that Bernhard has detained the entire convoy, so nobody is in the mood to try it again."

"So what do we do now?"

"Head for Donaueschingen, I suppose. Without a convoy. I wouldn't put it past Papa to have intended to go on to Strassburg and just paid the fare part way to throw people off his trail. So that's the only place we're likely to be able to find out whether he really did turn off for Basel. Or to find out which way he went from there. I don't like it, though. It's ninety miles to Donaue-schingen and it will be tricky."

Swabia, Bernhard of Saxe-Weimar's Camp

"So that's it," Raudegen said. After the debacle with the convoy, he had switched into Bernhard of Saxe-Weimar's service. "That's why I took service with the convoy. It's only a suspicion, Your Grace. None-theless, I was sure enough to take the risk of following them."

"If it is the Austrian archduchess, the admiral's wife, and the mayor's wife," Duke Bernhard answered, "it's more than worth risking a few men to lay hands on them. Take your three men—I'll give you a few more—and start back toward Ulm. Try to get back on their track. Before you leave, interview everyone in the convoy who is interned here. Try to find out the last time anyone saw those four people. Once you find out where they left the convoy, track them from there."

From Ulm to Donaueschingen

Every time that Marc and Susanna saw soldiers, they took to the fields again. That was, if they saw them, or heard them, soon enough to get into the fields without being seen themselves. The morning that they crossed paths with Raudegen and his men, they didn't have time. The riders were moving fast.

Being seen running attracted attention. Marc had impressed that on Susanna. It gave people the idea that you had some reason to run. This time, the two of them had just moved to the side of the road to let the cavalrymen going the other direction move past.

Susanna turned her face away from the road. Marc noticed that her hair was starting to grow longer. Not that much time had passed since they left Munich, but he really ought to cut it again. She looked more like a girl when she had hair. Should he cut her hair while he was thinking about the girl-ness of her? Maybe not. Probably not. Definitely not.

Once the riders were well out of sight and hearing, Susanna said, "The captain. He was with the guards in Bavaria for the wedding procession. I remember him."

"He didn't seem to recognize you. He just glanced; he wasn't really paying attention."

"I wasn't a boy then." Susanna sniffed. Then she frowned. "He was very careful, though. Always watching. He never just sat on his horse like some of the soldiers. His eyes went back and forth, all the time. Checking people along the streets. Checking where the group or horses or carriage next in front was going to stop to look at a display. Looking back to see if the procession was starting to bunch up. It could be, after he thinks about it a bit, that he might remember me."

"All right, then," Marc answered. "It's back to the fields."

A half mile later, he regretted his idea. They couldn't get beyond where they were without fording a good-sized stream; they couldn't get to the ford because a bunch of men, not upstanding farmers but rural louts, were lolling around at a water hole just above it on this hot autumn afternoon, drinking and splashing.

Mark looked around. They took refuge in a hay shed to which, presumably, the louts were supposed to be bringing the cut hay that was in the field. Marc climbed the ladder to the loft. It was already full; no reason for the louts to come up there, even if they did eventually start hauling hay.

Hay was not as comfortable as it looked. It was not the straw. Susanna had slept on straw mattresses all her life. However, that straw had been stuffed inside heavy hempen ticking and, usually, crumpled or softened through use. This hay could not have been in the loft more than a few weeks. It was stiff and prickly. It had weeds and a variety of other stiff and spiky things mixed with it. If she turned one way, it poked her left cheek; if she turned another way, it poked her right forehead. She gave up and sat up.

Marc was looking at her.

"Have they gone?" she whispered. "Can we move on?"

"No, they are still there. Still drinking. Disgustingly drunk, but not dead drunk."

Susanna peeked out through a crack that had opened in the daubing. The five men were still sitting by the river, wasting a perfectly good afternoon. She wished that their employer would come. She wished that his wife would come. She wished that his son would come. She wished that his steward would come. She wished that *someone* would come and drive them back into the fields to gather up the hay shocks or back to whatever else they certainly should have been doing. Lazy, worthless, servants—that was what they were.

Marc leaned over her shoulder. "You might as well sit back down. I think that they're going to stay."

Susanna looked back. The sun, coming in through the cracked daubing, made a stripe down his face, focusing on the left eye, which he was using to peer out.

Suddenly, the unfairness of life was too much for her. She flopped down on the crude planks of the floor and sobbed. "Why?"

"Why what?" Marc asked with pardonable bewilderment.

"Why does God do it? Look," she sat up and leaned toward him. "Look at my eyelashes."

Marc looked. "Yes. So? I mean, they're there."

"But they're *plain*." Susanna would have wailed, if she hadn't had to whisper. "They're light brown, and they're thin and they're straight and they're short."

Marc backed away a half-step, looking a little apprehensive.

"Marc," she asked. "Have you ever looked at your eyelashes?"

"Well, no," he admitted. "At least, not in any detail."

"They're black. They're thick. They are long and curly and *wasted on a boy*." Except, she thought, really, they weren't wasted. They were very attractive right where they were, even if their possessor didn't appreciate them properly. "Do you know how much any girl would like to have lashes like that? Do you know how we paint and darken and crimp the poor things trying to get that effect?"

Marc thought at moment. "We could," he suggested, "try to exchange them. Since we're here anyway."

"*Exchange* them?"

"Yes. Here. Like this. You stay there." He sat down next to her, facing the other direction. Carefully, he folded his arms behind his back. Then he leaned forward and fluttered his eyelashes against hers. Left eye to right eye; right eye to left eye.

Startled, Susanna pulled back a little. Still, it wasn't an unpleasant sensation. She leaned forward and tried it again. It was perhaps ten minutes later that she folded her own arms firmly behind her back. And ten minutes more before she felt compelled to say, "I don't believe that it's working."

Marc looked at her. "No," he said judiciously. "I don't believe that it is."

They sat for a few moments. "Your eyelashes are perfectly fine the way they are, you know. They go with the rest of you. It's all sort of cute, the way it fits together."

"Thank you." She might have said more, but there came the sound of someone opening the door to the barn below. As quietly as possible, they slipped into their respective, separate, piles of hay.

Raudegen and his men stopped at noon to eat something and rest the horses. He was frowning. There was something. It had been bothering him all morning. No, not all morning. Just since they passed the man and boy. Nothing about the man. He had never seen him before; he was sure of that. The ridiculous curl that fell down in the middle of his forehead made him easy enough to remember. The boy, then. He chewed on his bread, thinking.

He was looking for the archduchess. If the sight of the boy was bothering him, then it should have something to do with the archduchess. "Just stay here for a few minutes," he said to the others. Sometimes, looking in water helped him remember; using it like a mirror, letting the reflections carry his mind. He hated to let other men see him doing it; they would think him a fool. He led the rested, cooled, horses down to the brook, standing quietly as each of them drank.

Passau, he thought. Passau, at the edge of the pavilion. In the archduchess' household. A girl, standing on her very tiptoes, straining to see to see the ceremony. The line of the neck, the ears. The boy. Neck. Ears. Archduchess. Not a boy; a girl. She had not been traveling with the other four, as far as he knew. But it was worth splitting the party—and *he* would follow the girl. He sent his corporal and one of the men on toward Ulm, with a copy of the questions they were to ask, and turned back towards Donaueschingen.

"I know it isn't safe to travel at night," Marc said, "but we have to keep moving, I think, as late as we possibly can, every single day. If you recognized that captain, then, if he crossed the convoy that Papa was with, coming this direction, maybe he recognized the archduchess and the other ladies. Maybe they are riding to get assistance. We *have* to catch up with Papa, now, as fast as we can. Even if we do things that are riskier. We have to warn them."

Donaueschingen

"Nobody here saw Papa when the convoy from Ulm went through. Or any of them."

"Maybe they were keeping out of sight," Susanna suggested. "This town does belong to Count Egon von Fürstenberg. He's an imperial commander. Sometimes under the Bavarians and sometimes under Tilly. But he's been in Vienna, sometimes for weeks on end. He would certainly recognize Archduchess Maria Anna if he saw her. So would quite a few of his staff, I think. He isn't someone she would want to meet while she is running away." She paused. "He's not someone I would want to meet."

"Would any of the count's people have been in Bavaria? For the wedding procession, that is, or in Munich? Could they have seen Frau Simpson and Frau Dreeson, also?"

"Maybe. It's not as likely, but it's possible. Count Egon is a powerful man, the right kind of wedding guest for Duke Maximilian to invite."

"Well, we can't just stay here. We have to make up our minds. Let's just figure that Papa did what he planned. It's still pretty decent weather. Better, really, than it was earlier in the summer; not so hot. Let's turn south tomorrow morning and go on to Basel. If he isn't there . . ." Marc paused, mentally reviewing Susanna's demonstrated history of being able to finagle him into doing things that he didn't think were the best ideas available. "If he isn't there, I'm taking you straight to Geneva and letting Mama deal with you. I have four sisters. She's used to girls."

CHAPTER 60

Magnus Dies

Basel

The bright mid-morning sunshine of a perfect autumn day did not improve Diane Jackson's mood, which had been very bad for several weeks. After all the trouble she had gone to, coming to Basel to let this son of Gustav Adolf's ally inspect an up-timer for himself, she had hardly spoken to Margrave Friedrich V of Baden-Durlach. Or, more precisely, he had hardly made time in what he asserted was a very, very busy schedule to speak to her. She did not regard guided tours of the Basel region as an adequate substitute, even though her guide was doing his best.

"So then, Your Excellency," Johann Rudolf Wettstein said, "my father and his brother came to Basel from a little place called Russikon in the administrative district of Kyburg in the canton of Zürich and started to rise in the world. Father became the business manager of the *Spital*. From what you have told me of your world up-time, that would be a kind of combination of an orphanage, a retirement home, and an assisted living center. He did well. When I was sixteen, in 1610, he applied for both of us to become members of the vintners' guild."

Diane blinked. When she had agreed to become an ambassador, she had not realized that almost everyone she met would substitute "Your Excellency" for her name. She still had to pause and remember that people were talking to her.

"How did managing a hospice lead to manufacturing wine?" Diane asked. "Was he starting to sell supplies to this hospital?"

"Oh, we were not vintners. We had never been vintners; we will probably never be vintners. I was studying to become a notary public, a chancery official. But in Basel, to qualify to participate in city politics, you have to be a member of one of the guilds, and the vintners' guild is the most influential. He could afford the fee, so that's the one we joined. Some people are members of more than one guild, to qualify them to be members of different sections of the city council. For instance, for some you need to be in a merchant or finance guild; for others, you need to be in a craft guild. In this city, you do not have to work at either one. Guild membership is, you might say, a figment of the imagination. Of the political imagination. It is not an occupation, not a profession. One does need to be Protestant, of course. The city turned Protestant over a century ago. It threw off the prince bishop of Basel's claims to lordship and exiled the Catholic families of the old medieval patriciate, so the bishop no longer has rights in the city and hinterland—only in his own territories."

"And you have continued to rise in Basel politics ever since your father joined this vintner's guild?"

"Not, ah, entirely smoothly. It is not easy for outsiders to enter the Basel political system and many still consider our family outsiders. Not really part of the oligarchy. In spite of the fact that Basel accepted Protestant refugees from France, Flanders, and Italy as residents, it has not admitted many of them as citizens. The government of the city is still largely in the hands of the leading guilds. For all practical purposes, because the merchants and bankers can purchase membership in more than one guild, in a craft guild also, leadership has stayed in the hands of a small number of wealthy, influential, elite families."

"Oh," Diane answered. "Yes, like the book that I read once. *Animal Farm*, it was called. The pig says that all animals are created equal, but some animals are more equal than others. This is always true. In Grantville, the UMWA members like Mike and Frank now are somewhat more equal than others, no matter what they say. Not according to the law, but really." She looked at Wettstein. "I will ask them to send me the book. For you."

"When I was in my early twenties," Wettstein continued, "after a slight difficulty, I entered the Venetian military service for a while—nearly four years." He looked a little abashed. "It was there, with the Venetians, that I met some persons from the kingdoms of eastern Asia. So when you came to Basel, the city council decided . . ."

"That you would be a 'perfect liaison.'" Diane sniffed. "Then you find out, when I point to spots on the great globe in your city hall, that I am from a place you never heard of. But it is too late, so you must still play guide."

Wettstein smiled down at the cynical little woman. Asiatic ambassador sent by the king of Sweden, absurd as that might be. He rather liked her. Although he had more than enough to do in his current job as district supervisor of Riehen, Basel's territory on the right bank of the Rhine, he had still learned a great deal during their tours. That made them worthwhile for a man with political ambitions. Someday, when his title was, perhaps, mayor of Basel; perhaps, who knew, even ambassador in Magdeburg. These weeks would have been well-enough spent, even if his colleagues were laughing at him behind his back because he had been assigned to watch her. Nothing ventured, nothing gained.

"Escorting you is a refreshing change from considering customs and tolls, which are the main concern of the district administrator of Riehen, Your Excellency," he said. "Or from calculating budget projections for procurement of provisions. The citizens of Basel eat a great deal and the council has no intention that they should starve in case of adverse political events."

"In case the French should attack you?" Diane asked.

"I would prefer not to be too specific," Wettstein replied. "But certainly, it is always possible that *someone* might attack the city. It would be a mistake to focus solely upon the French. If you look here, for example," he gestured to a series of stones mounted in the ground, "this is the boundary between Basel territory and that of Austria, here on the right bank of the river. Basel never thinks of the Austrians as being far away, in Vienna or Prague. We always think of them as being next door. Always. Uneasy neighbors." He paused. "Some day we Swiss will be legally free of Austria. Not just effectively free of Austria. That is my goal."

He shook his head. He tended to tell this little woman more than he should. Damn, but she was shrewd. Not articulate, in the way one ordinarily expected of envoys, but clever and observant.

"In any case," he continued, "that is about all there is to see here in Riehen. Tomorrow, I think, if the weather remains fine, we will drive upstream along the Rhine to see the Roman ruins at Pratteln."

Diane nodded her head. She seemed to expect very little from Roman ruins.

Margrave Friedrich V of Baden-Durlach was reading his mail. Because he ran the Baden-Durlach government-in-exile for his father, here in Basel, he got a lot of mail, some of it through the postal system and some through private courier. For the predictable number of urgent but brief messages, he kept a pigeon loft. So, as far as he knew, did every major bank and commercial firm in the city.

The current letter had arrived by pigeon. The signature at the bottom had nothing to do with the sender's real name. Margrave Friedrich smiled. He appreciated ambitious young men. Ambitious enough to take risks; young enough to take some really stupid risks. Talented, carefully sheltered young men with prosperous middle-class parents who provided them with tutors and Latin schools and university educations in law or in political economy.

He stood up and thumbed through his files. Johann Freinsheim, also known as Ioannes Freinsheimius. Age twenty-five, he confirmed. Born in Ulm. Most recently at the University of Strassburg studying history and German literature under Professor Matthaeus Bernegger until he decided to make a journey to France as part of his grand tour and somehow managed to enter the royal household there as a secretary in the interpretation service. In which capacity he met Bernhard of Saxe-Weimar who was, although a traitor to the king of Sweden, nonetheless the brother of Wilhelm Wettin. And of Duke Ernst in the Upper Palatinate, whose secretary, Heinrich Böcler, had also studied under Bernegger, at the same time as Freinsheim, it so happened. Through which connection, Freinsheim came into correspondence with Margrave Friedrich's father, who was in the service of Gustav Adolf and who had managed to ship the young man a small crate of pigeons who believed that Basel was home. And thus into correspondence with Margrave Friedrich.

It was astonishing how much a simple secretary in the French interpretation service could learn. It was also gratifying, given the proximity of Baden to Alsace, which until very recently had been the secondary focus of Duke Bernhard's military operations. Secondary, at least, until Bernhard's recent abandonment of the Mainz front and probe into Swabia. Margrave Friedrich was very concerned about what Duke Bernhard was doing in Swabia.

The problem had distracted him terribly from what he should have been learning from the up-time ambassadress, Frau Jackson. Or trying to learn. The woman was very close-mouthed. He had been quite gratified, however, to discover that he was considered sufficiently important that the Grantville general had sent his own wife.

Pratteln

Basel was a natural focus for trade. It had been for four centuries, since the bishop built the first bridge across the Rhine at the site of the city. The road from the bridge ran across the Gotthard Pass into Italy. The city had papermaking and printing; a major university. It traded in ideas as well as in goods. Having a university, it naturally had students of antiquity. For the excursion to Pratteln, Herr Wettstein had acquired a guide.

Herr Professor Buxtorf. Professor Buxtorf, junior. Professor Buxtorf, senior, an eminent Hebraicist, had been dead for some years. Professor Buxtorf, junior, who had accompanied them this morning, was a slightly less eminent Hebraicist. Naturally, a Hebraicist also knew Greek and Latin and took a scholarly interest in classical antiquities. He did not, however, know English. He and the ambassadress found one another's French mutually incomprehensible, so Wettstein was translating.

Diane was receiving far more secondhand information about Roman ruins than she had ever wanted to know. She had looked at her watch several times. Unfortunately, Wettstein thought, it had not stopped. Time really did move that slowly in the company of Professor Buxtorf. He was only in his mid-thirties, but he had "pedantic" down to an art form.

Wettstein's mind wandered. Buxtorf was becoming quite famous in his own right, not just as his father's son, due to his extended academic controversies with a French Huguenot scholar on the topic of whether or not the vowel points and accents in contemporary printed Hebrew had existed in ancient Hebrew. Buxtorf took the position that they must have, at the time that the Old Testament manuscripts were first recorded in writing, since by definition the text was divinely inspired and completely unchanged. Louis Cappel's argument for the modern origin of vowel points and accents, which he had published in 1624 contrary to the advice of the older Buxtorf, if it were accepted, would make it much more difficult for Calvinists to argue that the Bible was infallible because it had been handed down from the earliest ages without the slightest textual alteration.

Well, Buxtorf was becoming famous in a limited sort of way, Wettstein admitted to himself. Only a certain number of scholars had strong feelings about the issue, although it did have interesting theological implications, more for Protestantism than for Catholicism. If the whole doctrine of the verbal inspiration of scripture should be undermined by this controversy on Hebrew punctuation, what would be left to keep the Protestants from splintering into endless sects? How many sects had Her Excellency told him coexisted in this little town of Grantville alone? Had, at some point, Cappel's views prevailed over those of Buxtorf?

Wettstein pulled his mind back to the matter at hand.

The two up-timers from the USE embassy guard who never left Diane Jackson's side when she was out of the embassy building itself were looking impatient. Lee Thomas Swiger, one of them was named. About fifty. He was here, Her Excellency had told Wettstein, because he had "served with Frank in Viet Nam." Wettstein had not pursued the matter, but was of the opinion that Swiger was a dangerous man—dangerous, at least, to anyone who might threaten General Jackson's wife during this mission. James Dean Gordon was the other one. "National Guard," Her Excellency had said. Something like militia. Younger than the other man, perhaps thirty-five. Physically abler than Swiger, but less threatening. A half-dozen down-timers, all armed.

From the road, somebody calling. "Diane! Thank goodness. Diane!"

Every one of the embassy guards had his gun out at once.

Johann Rudolf Wettstein was beginning to think that this trip had been a bad idea.

The woman who had called out the first time yelled again. "Swiger, Gordon, don't shoot at us, *please*. That's all we would need, getting this far and then being shot by our own people."

The older up-time soldier dropped the muzzle of his rifle, putting on the safety. The others followed him.

The woman ran toward them; she and the ambassadress embraced one another.

Diane Jackson turned to Wettstein. "The embassy has guests," she said. "I have been notified to expect them. Just not right here. Nobody said anything about Pratteln."

The first woman had been joined by three other people. Another woman, another embrace. A third woman and a man; no embraces.

The man and Professor Buxtorf? A few words about kinship, or at least connections, through the Curio family. Buxtorf's mother was a Curio, of course; it appeared that the man's—Cavriani, was it?—wife's uncle was married to a Curio. Wettstein was no longer surprised. The Italian Protestant emigrant families in Switzerland were closely intertwined.

Her Excellency extended her hand to the man—Leopold Cavriani—whom she appeared to have met before. She was looking at the third woman with some puzzlement on her face, as were the embassy guards.

Diane turned again. "Herr Wettstein, this is Mary Simpson, Admiral Simpson's wife. This is Veronica Dreeson, Henry Dreeson's wife. He is the mayor of Grantville This is Leopold Cavriani. He does a lot of business in Grantville." Then she turned to the others. "This is Johann Rudolf Wettstein. He is on the small council of the city of Basel, so he is important. He is not rude. Margrave Friedrich of Baden has been very rude. I told Frank and Mike so. At least, Tony Adducci told them so for me. And I do not know your guest."

Mary, Veronica, and Leopold looked at one another. Mary drew in a rather deep breath, then turned to the younger woman. "Your Highness," she began, "permit me to present to you Mrs. Diane Jackson, ambassadress of the United States of Europe to the city of Basel, and Herr Wettstein of the Basel city council."

The tall, tanned, brunette smiled graciously. Mary continued. "Diane, Herr Wettstein, this is Archduchess Maria Anna of Austria."

Lee Swiger and Jim Gordon grasped their rifles rather harder than they had before. Mary looked at them. "Thanks, but we've managed to get this far without shooting anybody." She turned her head. "Diane, I do think that all of us would be a little bit easier in our minds if we could get into embassy property, now that we've announced ourselves. Just because of diplomatic immunity. We were sort of wondering the best way to come through the city gates, but if we can come in with you and your escort..."

"Oh," Diane answered. "Gosh, yes. Welcome, Your Highness."

"Yes," Wettstein seconded. "Welcome to Basel, all of you. I do think it would be best that you go into the embassy before anyone else, officially or unofficially, knows that you are here." His mind was very busy, sorting through the implications.

Basel

"I wish," Veronica said, "that Leopold was staying at the embassy."

"He had a point," Mary answered. "He isn't a USE citizen, after all, so he might make, as he said, an 'uneasy guest' for Diane. And the embassy is a perfectly ordinary town house. It's already full of people right up into the attics."

Diane Jackson nodded.

"And, as he said, he has business to catch up on, so it makes more sense for him to stay with Professor Buxtorf. At least, he managed to get a bank draft so Maria Anna can get some clean clothes. You've given him a draft on the embassy account to pay him back for what he loaned us to get some stuff when we were in Neuburg and Ulm, haven't you, Diane? And for the lodgings. The bill came to quite a bit, once we counted it up. He says he sold all the horses that came and went on the trip for more than he paid for them, so we don't owe him anything for those."

"Yes, I pay him already. Or Tony did. Tony does the money here," Diane answered.

"But that's why we arrived without any more than we were carrying," Mary said. "We left Munich with just what we were wearing and there was never any point in buying a lot. Not just because we were having to borrow money, but, after all, we did have to carry it all. That explains, I'm afraid, why we are all rather dirty."

"We do," Veronica said, "have clean underwear and socks. Since Neuburg, at least. We looked like tramps when we came to Neuburg. So did the English Ladies. We got a few more things in Ulm. Linen towels, for washing our faces and feet. And the shops there already carry baking soda and toothbrushes. We each got a set. Even me, for the false teeth. And scarves to go under the pilgrim hats, to keep dust from our hair. Better clothes. One set each. But that is all."

"The archduchess, too?" Diane's voice clearly indicated her disbelief.

"Yes," Mary Simpson answered. "Maria Anna, too."

"Perhaps some of my things will fit you," Diane offered rather doubtfully.

"Veronica, maybe. But I am five inches taller than you are. And Maria Anna . . ." Mary's voice trailed off.

"She is much taller," Diane said. "And twice as wide. But it is not safe for her to go shopping. Also, I do not want to let a dressmaker into the embassy. For good reasons. We try to keep strangers from coming in, as much as we can. It is not easy here, right now. The Basel people are nervous. This Margrave Friedrich, who wanted to see an up-timer, is nervous. I said he was rude. Maybe not rude, but he pays no attention to me."

"Then," Veronica said practically, "let's just wash the clothes we have on. We can sit around wrapped in sheets until they are dry. And make a list. You can send one of the men shopping."

"Tony will go shopping," Diane said. "Tony does the money here. It was not in his job description, but I put it there. It is a big waste to make him a soldier just because he runs the radio."

News. All three of them were starving for news. They had been walking out in the countryside for a week with no news to be had. Diane updated them with the latest she knew in regard to the three-way negotiations between Gustav Adolf, Fredrik Hendrik, and Don Fernando.

Maria Anna looked at Mary and Veronica. Without saying anything, she raised her eyebrows. Mary nodded.

"Perhaps, Your Excellency," she began, turning to Diane, "I should explain why I am here. And where I am going."

When Cavriani arrived to have supper with them, he brought even more news as well as his banker's complete collection of newspapers from the past month. They were only on loan, he pointed out conscientiously.

"I really should write Potentiana," Cavriani was saying. "I need to explain to her, I think, that I do not know where Marc is."

"Why?" Veronica asked.

"Well. Because I need to tell her that I have misplaced our only son."

"So because you feel guilty, you will write a letter and make her worry." Veronica banged the haft of her knife on the table. "What good will the letter do? She cannot go find him. You do not know for sure that he has problems. Only that he has not caught up with you."

Veronica was frowning at Cavriani fiercely. "It is bad enough to *know* that your son is dead. Or your grandson. If you do not *know* that it is so, making her worry about it is cruel."

"But . . ."

"Write her. Tell her that you are in Basel. Tell her the last you know for sure. But do not say that you are afraid for him. If you say that, then she will be afraid for him, too. Each day has troubles enough of its own. If he is dead, she can grieve when you know it is true."

Tony Adducci powered up the Basel radio system. It was one of the down-time radios that had been built from up-time parts—the best that Frank Jackson had been able to get hold of to send along with Diane. On the average, he was able to communicate with Grantville about four hours a day. He could also communicate reliably and consistently with Amsterdam. He could not communicate directly with Magdeburg at all. It was something to do with the length of the jumps.

So. This was certainly the most exciting information that he had sent out in a long time. Who got it first?

Tony was a prudent young man. A member of the USE army, to be sure, but still a prudent young man.

Mary Simpson, Veronica Dreeson, and Archduchess Maria Anna said that the first person to get the news was to be his Aunt Bernadette, who was to tell a nun named Mary Ward that they were safe in Basel.

Diane Jackson had ordered him to tell Mr. Piazza first, to send it on to Magdeburg.

The minute he managed to raise up Tanya Newcomb, he sent a message that she should get both Mr. Piazza and his Aunt

Bernadette into the same room as the radio, right now, please, if she could.

She could, she said. Mr. Piazza had just gotten back from Magdeburg that afternoon and was still in his office going through mail; she would phone Bernadette and have her there in a jiffy.

As soon as she signaled back, Tony sent off the messages. Simultaneously. For the first time since they left Neuburg, somebody in a position of authority inside the USE knew exactly where Maria Anna, Mary, and Veronica were.

Grantville

Bernadette Adducci dashed for St. Mary's rectory, where, as soon as she had talked to Father Kircher for five minutes, she picked up the phone and asked Mary Ward to come over.

Ed Piazza left it to Tanya to radio Magdeburg. He would rather be out of the room when the message went through, if only because if John Simpson might be in Magdeburg for the conference. The admiral would never be rude enough to yell at Tanya. He might very well, however, yell at Ed—and Simpson was fully capable of yelling in Morse code if he was sufficiently provoked. Ed told Tanya to call him back if Mike or anyone else in Amsterdam wanted him.

Then he went back to his own office and grabbed the phone to notify Henry and Annalise that Veronica was safe, although, for a reason that he was not yet authorized to share with them, in Basel. Yes, Switzerland. Basel was okay, he assured them. Basel was neutral, like the rest of Switzerland. Some way, from Basel, Ed promised, they would manage to get her back home.

At St. Mary's, Bernadette told Mary Ward that Maria Anna, Mary, and Veronica were in Basel.

Mary Ward reached through the slit in her skirt and pulled out the separate pocket she wore. Opening the drawstring, she pulled out a small packet wrapped in oiled cloth. She broke a seal, unwrapped the cloth, and handed a folded piece of paper to Bernadette. "For you," she said. "From Archduchess Maria Anna of Austria."

Bernadette read it. She looked at Father Kircher. "If the two of you will excuse me," she said, "I need to get back to the radio room before Amsterdam closes down for the evening."

Basel

Tony Adducci fully expected that radio messages would be coming and going until the window of opportunity closed down. He had not expected to hear from the Netherlands, but something from Becky Stearns or the Stadtholder, Fredrik Hendrik, was not completely beyond the normal. They kept the various embassies updated on the progress of negotiations, so the ambassadors could be at least a *little* ahead of the newspapers. Not much, given the wild expansion of journalism in the past couple of years.

There was one from them. From Becky, rather. Another from Mike Stearns. In Amsterdam? What was Mike doing in Amsterdam? Of course, they were in the middle of negotiations, but they had gotten bogged down by Gustav Adolf's demand for some kind of guarantees from Don Fernando.

He read everything as it came in, of course. He had to. Becky said thanks for the information sent via Grantville and Magdeburg.

Amsterdam

Mike Stearns was in Amsterdam because there was a truce. Because it had occurred to him that he could gain some brownie points by personally delivering Doña Mencia to her brother. Because he badly wanted to see his wife. Because Gustav Adolf had agreed that he could go. The arrangements had been rather complicated.

He watched. Becky and Fredrik Hendrik were having fun writing a note to Don Fernando. Finally, it said:

> We know exactly where your intended bride is. We will tell you if you agree to declare yourself ruler of the Spanish Netherlands and make a formal break with Spain, whether the rest of the Habsburgs agree or not. Fish or cut bait. For further information, contact Becky or Fred. Love.

It was accompanied, of course, by a far more formal communication which said the same things in diplomatically suitable language. The short note would probably only be read by Don Fernando himself. Well, also probably by Rubens, Cardinal Bedmar, who was now his chancellor, and Doña Mencia.

Becky had written another note to Doña Mencia. Just, *She is safe. She is well*, in her own hand, with Mike's co-signature at the bottom.

Attached to it was a copy of a radio message from Grantville: *Most honored cousin. If you receive this, I have arrived at the destination you named. We owe patronage to the English Ladies. Maria Anna.*

Fredrik Hendrik was hand delivering both notes to Don Fernando's headquarters at this very moment. Mike and Rebecca were enduring some sarcastic remarks by Gretchen, who was far from impressed by the apparent intention of Gustav Adolf and the USE to compromise with a younger brother of the king of Spain on several of the minor points.

Don Fernando read through the three notes and smiled at Fredrik Hendrik. "She is in Basel, then, so I do not need you to tell me. Although, to be sure, I would appreciate knowing 'exactly' where in Basel." He rose. "But, nonetheless. I had intended to delay a formal announcement. But we are certain of my aunt's approbation. We are as prepared, here, in Brussels and in Antwerp, even in Liege, even in Luxemburg, as we ever are likely to be."

He turned to Pieter Paul Rubens. "So let us do it now." Then to Cardinal Bedmar. "You have it?"

"Yes, Your Majesty," Bedmar said smoothly. "The latest clean draft treaty proposal received from the king of Sweden's negotiators. And five exact copies. Six exact notarized copies of Infanta Isabella Clara Eugenia's will."

Don Fernando looked at Fredrik Hendrik. "It will be faster if I come to your quarters."

Basel

Intended bride? Tony blinked a minute and then made the connection. Maria Anna, the archduchess. She was going to marry Don Fernando? But he was a cardinal, wasn't he?

Another message incoming. Reception was fading, but it was

short. "Done." *Stearns, prime minister, for the emperor; Fernando, king in the Low Countries; Fredrik Hendrik, Stadtholder, for the United Provinces.*

King in the Low Countries? Probably not a cardinal. Not any more. *Politics.* It was none of Tony's business, of course, but he disapproved. The church shouldn't operate that way. He wished he could talk to Larry Mazzare about the stuff that was going on.

The message would have to be short, of course, Tony thought. The window of opportunity would be closing for Amsterdam, too, and they would be trying to get it out to Emperor Gustav Adolf, wherever he was; to Mr. Piazza in Grantville; maybe to Chancellor Oxenstierna in Stockholm before things shut down. He copied out the two notes and handed them to Diane. She read them; then got up and went out into the anteroom where the archduchess, Mrs. Simpson, and Mrs. Dreeson were waiting with Mr. Cavriani.

Not just truce. Peace. At least in one corner of Europe, for the time being, until the Spanish decided what to do about it. And the French, if the French were in a position to do anything about anyone right now, given what Gustav Adolf was doing to them.

It was probably about as good as they were going to get. Tony started packing up the radio gear. There wouldn't be any more news until morning.

Maria Anna sat, looking at her copy of the last message from Amsterdam. Somewhere inside her, there was a feeling of quiet satisfaction that she would be marrying a king after all. She noticed this. Pride, certainly; perhaps even arrogance; she would need to mention it at confession.

But she would *much* rather, she admitted to herself, be married to a king than to a plain duke. She really would. But she would not say so to Mary and Veronica.

Herr Cavriani, she suspected, already knew. And would not be surprised.

CHAPTER 61

Epistolae Diplomaticae

Basel

As soon as Tony Adducci set up the radio before dawn the next day, the messages started coming in. The most urgent was from Frank Jackson in Magdeburg, via Grantville, to Lee Swiger. "Get Diane and the rest of the staff out of there as soon as you can. Reasons to follow."

Tony looked out the window. He would pass the message on to Swiger, but none of them were going anywhere any time soon. An "honor guard" from the Basel militia surrounded the whole building, as it had since the previous evening.

There had been more important information to send out the night before, so he hadn't informed Grantville or Magdeburg about the "honor guard." Now, on his own initiative, he wrote up a short message describing its presence and sent it out.

He was sort of glad that Mike or Mr. Piazza would have to tell Frank. *He* sure wouldn't want to be the one who did it.

Every now and then, he wondered whether he should really start thinking of these men he had known all his life, friends of his dad's, as Mr. Stearns and General Jackson, now that they were important. Mr. Piazza had always been Mr. Piazza, of course. He was the high school principal.

The archduchess turned up in the radio office. Tony thought that she seemed to be a pleasant, polite, sort of lady, not at all what he would have expected Emperor Ferdinand II's daughter to be like. She had authorization to send messages, signed by Diane. Okay.

The first one went to Amsterdam, to be given to Don Fernando.

"Most honored cousin. Congratulations on new status. What about dispensations? Yours from vows? Mine from Bavarian betrothal? Ours for first cousins to marry? If you have them already, we owe Cardinal Bedmar a favor. Not to mention the pope. Maria Anna."

Tony sent it off. Thanks to his Aunt Bernadette's dinner table conversation, he even pretty much understood it. The archduchess seemed to be a practical sort of lady. In fact, she sort of reminded Tony of Aunt Bernadette. He wondered if Don Fernando knew what he was getting himself into. Pleasant and polite or not, if Tony ever got married, he didn't intend to pick a wife who reminded him of Aunt Bernadette.

The second one went to Amberg, to Duke Ernst.

"Thank you for your kindness to Doña Mencia. Maria Anna Oe."

No problem there.

The third one to Amsterdam again, for Doña Mencia de Mendoza.

"Where is Susanna? Maria Anna."

Tony sent it, wondering who on earth Susanna might be and how she was involved in all of this. Code? None of his business, he told himself sternly.

Johann Rudolf Wettstein looked at the gathered city council of Basel and thought, *the whole lot of you have gone utterly insane.* What he said was, "Gentlemen, I am not persuaded that the course of action suggested by my honored colleague is the most prudent one that the city could adopt. Certainly not without full prior consultation with the other cantons."

Of course, he had notified the council of the arrival of Archduchess Maria Anna and her escort after he had safely seen them inside the walls of the USE embassy. He had not expected—really, really, had not expected—that any member of the city council would suggest holding the archduchess hostage as a pawn in negotiations to obtain Austria's legal recognition of the independence of the

Swiss Confederacy from the Habsburgs. Not that independence wasn't a laudable goal. He fully intended to work toward it himself. It was one of the things that, he hoped, could be achieved in any final peace treaty when the current war finally dragged to an exhausted close.

He had expected even less that once the nitwit had suggested interning the archduchess, or at the very least preventing her from leaving Basel, the council would surround the USE embassy. Nor that now, the next morning, the entire small council with both mayors and the two guild chairmen would actually be sitting here, discussing it seriously rather than immediately dropping it into the cesspit of bad ideas where it belonged. The council had been called into session at dawn. Now, at noon, there was a motion on the floor. The fools were considering trying it. They were actually considering trying it.

Lee Swiger looked at the special edition of the Basel newspaper. It had what amounted to a glaring black headline by down-time journalistic standards: eighteen point type across two columns of the front page.

Nobody knew who had leaked. Somebody, without the slightest doubt, had leaked. Suspicion lay in the direction of the Basel city council. It simply had too many members for successful secret-keeping.

> *Archduchess Maria Anna in*
> *USE Embassy in Basel.*
> *Wife of Admiral Simpson and*
> *Wife of Grantville Mayor with Her.*
> *Future Plans Unannounced.*

Since the Basel newspaper had it, that meant that every stringer in the city would have sent out a copy of this, plus whatever gossip he could pick up, to his own paper. Which meant that the shit had hit the fan.

The other two columns of the front page had a considerably smaller headline.

> *Peace Between United States*
> *of Europe and Netherlands.*

Don Fernando Becomes King.
Stadtholder To Receive
Position of High Honor.

Diane had issued a press release the night before. Too bad that the treaty had been demoted to second in importance, but naturally the readers in Basel would be more interested in news with a local focus.

"I feel," Margrave Friedrich V of Baden-Durlach said rather stiffly the next afternoon, "that in view of my position as a loyal ally of Emperor Gustav Adolf, I should have been provided with this information in a timely manner by the embassy of the United States of Europe. Certainly, I should not have been left to read it in the newspapers."

"We sent a note about the treaty," Diane Jackson answered. "A courier brought it to you yesterday. He got receipt from your doorman. You read it in the paper first only because you read the newspaper before you open your mail."

"And in regard to the archduchess?"

"It was not my news to tell you," Diane said stubbornly. "They did not told me to tell you. Mike did not told me to tell you. Frank did not tell me. Ed Piazza did not tell me. Nobody telled me to told you."

If the margrave had been polite to her this past summer, Diane thought, she would have been nice to him. She would have spoken French, a language that he knew. However, he had been rude, so she spoke English to remind him that she was an up-timer from Grantville.

In moments of stress, even after all these years, she still tended to lose control over English verb tenses, particularly when the verbs were themselves irregular. At the moment, this seemed to be causing the margrave's translator some confusion. But she thought that he grasped the gist of the matter.

"The ambassadress had not received instructions, Sire," he said to his employer.

Margrave Friedrich was fairly sure that whatever the ambassadress had said, it amounted to more than that. There had been several personal names in her statement.

He cleared his throat. "Ask her," he said, "if she has received instructions from Gustav Adolf in regard to the archduchess."

"I have not," Diane said, "seen any."

This was quite true. She had come to the radio room that morning as soon as she heard Tony opening the door, even before he had time to set up the gear. She had been waiting.

The expression on his face as he read the incoming message had been quite horrified. After he had given her a short verbal summary of Frank's latest news from Horn about the placement of Bernhard of Saxe-Weimar's troops and the emperor's belief that Bernhard would attempt to coerce the Basel city council into turning the embassy's "guests" over to him, she said, "I do not wish to see this."

Then: "Send it to Mike now. Ask him what to do. Do not tell Mary. Or anybody. Not Lee Swiger. Nobody. You understand me, Tony? Nobody else at all. When you are done sending to Mike, put it in the box." She pointed to the container where he kept less urgent messages that he would transcribe during the day. "Put it at the bottom. Do not have time to get to it."

Tony understood her. He nodded.

"Do not have time to get to it until Mike sends the answer. Maybe tonight. Maybe tomorrow morning. Not until then."

Now she looked back at the margrave. She had spoken with him very little. She was not sure whether he would be friend or foe. But, surely, if it had nothing to do with the archduchess, he would be told about the troops.

"I did hear from the office of Emperor Gustav Adolf," she said, picking up a message. She handed it to Tony Adducci to read on her behalf.

"Already in June, at the Congress of Copenhagen, Prime Minister Stearns developed a suspicion that Bernhard of Saxe-Weimar was no longer, or no longer only, a mercenary in French employ. We have been watching his operations carefully since then. As of the date of this transmission, Bernhard is bringing the main strength of his army toward Basel. He has left only the smaller part of his infantry in the Franche-Comté. You can expect his full forces to be on the right bank of the Rhine within a week."

Margrave Friedrich nodded. This was good information, so the ambassadress was not trying to mislead him. He had received the same news from other sources.

She was frowning at him. "This I warn you. I tell you that I warn everyone fair. I tell Wettstein, also, for the city council."

"Perhaps," Margrave Friedrich suggested, "I should be the one to contact the council. They are more likely to accept the authenticity of the warning if it comes from the son of one of the Protestant generals than from . . ."

Diane smiled. "Than from a foreign woman about so high?" She held up her hand. It didn't come far above her seated head. "I say it wrong again? Not I *will tell* him. I *told* him already. I told Herr Wettstein. It is done."

She looked at him. "Now we talk about those guards that the city council put around the embassy, no? We talk about 'diplomatic immunity.' If you want to help, I speak French. If not, I speak English."

"Let us," Margrave Friedrich said, "speak French. As a beginning."

"They are completely insane," Wettstein said to Cavriani and Buxtorf. "We are facing invasion by a man who is completely ruthless and who . . ."

"Who," Buxtorf said pragmatically, "can easily overrun Riehen, which is the part of Basel for which you, specifically, are responsible."

"Well, yes. That is why, if you have had a chance to look at the bridge for the past several days, the elderly, the women, the children of Riehen have been crossing it onto this bank. In two more days, I believe, only able-bodied men will be in Riehen. I wish that there would be more able-bodied men in Riehen, but the council refuses to send the militia across. Should Bernhard of Saxe-Weimar appear, they are content to meet him at the river. I am not."

"Have they authorized you to resist him on the right bank?" Cavriani asked.

"I have not asked for authorization," Wettstein admitted. "But that is not what we are talking about. At least, not what I was trying to talk about. Why, in the name of all that is sacred, staring a very real peril in the face, does the council still spend its time talking about this archduchess. If Bernhard comes into the city, believe me, even if they somehow get her into their hands, which I do not believe that they can, she will very rapidly be removed. Bernhard will not care a fig for how she might be used to negotiate the independence of the Swiss Confederacy. He will have his own purposes. There are a half-dozen ways that he could use her as a counter against the Swede or against the Austrians."

"A half dozen?" Buxtorf said. "Surely not that many."

Cavriani started counting on his fingers. "One. Marry her and through the marriage gain a hereditary claim, or some color of a hereditary claim, to the Habsburg territories here in Swabia, where he is trying to build his power base. Two. Turn her over to the Spanish to hold hostage against Don Fernando, in return for Spain's recognition of his position in the Franche-Comté. Three. Turn her over to Gustav Adolf in return for his recognition of Bernhard as an independent ruler in Swabia. Four."

"Never mind," Buxtorf said.

"All of which," Wettstein said, "involve his either persuading the council to violate the grounds of the USE embassy and turn her over to him, or his invading the city and removing her by force."

"Where," Cavriani asked, "is General Horn?"

"I would dearly love to know," Wettstein answered. "Which is why I am here. I am hoping that you can find out."

"The banks are doing all they can," Cavriani assured him.

"I'm an academic. A scholar. Not a politician. Certainly not a soldier," Buxtorf protested.

"I still think you can assist us in finding out," Wettstein said. "You do know Professor Wilhelm Schickard, don't you?"

"Of Tübingen in Württemberg? Well, of Tübingen when the university there was still functioning, before the war closed it down. Yes, of course I do. An excellent mathematician. Also something of a mechanical tinkerer. The late astronomer Kepler used his calculating box in preparing the tables when he published some of his observations. Really, of course, Schickard was a professor of Hebrew. His professional association with my father and myself has been in that capacity. We correspond regularly, even though he is Lutheran and I am Reformed. He is in Magdeburg, now, working for . . ." Buxtorf looked up. "For Duke Hermann of Hesse-Rotenburg, the USE Secretary of State, in regard to the establishment of a mapping service."

Leopold Cavriani inclined his head. "I believe that you also know a young man named Johann Heinrich Böcler?"

Buxtorf thought a little longer. "Yes, or I have heard of him, at least, from Matthaeus Bernegger. Böcler was one of Bernegger's students. Very promising, he said. Böcler is now, umm, the secretary of Duke

Ernst of Saxe-Weimar in the Upper Palatinate. I believe that the duke is in Ingolstadt, isn't he, arranging for a new city government?"

Cavriani nodded. "With quite a few soldiers, to the best of my knowledge, although the newspapers predict that General Banér will be moving his main forces now that the siege has been successfully completed. And with a radio."

Buxtorf's mind was going off on an apparent tangent. "Of course, Bernegger is a good friend of Schickard, also. Bernegger translated Galileo's work from the Italian vernacular into Latin, so it would be accessible to scholars, and published it at his own expense. Thus frustrating simultaneously both Galileo's effort at one-upmanship and the *Index Librorum Prohibitorum*. It was a great service to the scientific community."

"Why is it important that Bernegger is a friend of Schickard?" Wettstein sounded a trifle impatient.

"Your pardon, Councilor Wettstein. I am thinking like a teacher, I am afraid," Buxtorf said. "Bernegger has more former students than just Böcler, you know. Many of them will know of the friendship between the two men. Since Schickard is now in the service of the USE, that might predispose them to cooperate with requests they receive from him. Bernegger maintains close touch with the alumni of his department, you know. Almost, as with young Freinsheim, in a fatherly manner." He smiled. "I believe he has some reason to assume in that particular instance that he may well become the young man's father. Or, at least, his father-in-law. But that is a digression. Although Strassburg is an imperial city, it is, still, in the midst of Alsace. There must be some concern there, in the city council and at the university, about what would happen—just how long it could maintain its independence—if someone with the temperament of Bernhard of Saxe-Weimar governed all the lands surrounding it and if..."

"If what?" Wettstein asked.

"If there were no longer a Holy Roman Empire to be at least the symbol to which it owed its allegiance. If there were no longer a Holy Roman Emperor, which likely there will not be after Ferdinand II dies. Strassburg must be concerned, just as Nürnberg worries whether the city can maintain sovereignty against the State of Thuringia-Franconia and the USE."

"So if the Strassburg council is more alert than that of Basel, you are thinking, they may be taking measures?" Cavriani interjected.

"If not taking measures, at least gathering information." Buxtorf rested the tips of his fingers against one another. "Bernegger's students have been placed in chanceries all over the German states. There is at least one, Freinsheim himself, in the French service."

"The future son-in-law? That," Wettstein said, "I did not know. But it is all to the good. Can you give me a list of these students, and where they are?"

"I *don't* want to know precisely what you plan to do with it," Buxtorf said. "My position, like that of my father, is delicate enough because our academic specialty more or less requires us to stand as intermediaries between Basel's Jewish community and the council. That introduces a certain element of, shall we say, precariousness into our lives. I was certainly old enough to know what was going on when the council jailed my father for attending the circumcision of the son of one of his linguistic assistants. I do not want to provide it with any more reasons to look at me with doubt, although things have been better these last three years."

"I am sure," Wettstein agreed, "that having the head pastor of the Reformed churches of Basel as your brother-in-law does provide great spiritual support."

Cavriani smiled again. "Though it might have a rather damping effect on the conversations at the family dinner table."

"Oh," Buxtorf said, "Theodor Zwinger is not a difficult man. No older than I am. He came into his office very young after several older pastors died of the plague, one after another. And quite well-traveled you know, Leopold, should you ever need to consult him."

"Need to consult him?"

"In connection with these up-timers," Buxtorf said. "During his student years, he did not just spend time in Heidelberg, Leiden, and Geneva. He went to England."

"Herr Wettstein," Mary Simpson said. "How kind of you to pass through the barricades out there to come calling upon us here." She looked out the window. "But was it wise?"

"Probably not," Wettstein admitted. "But I do need to speak with Her Excellency if I may. I consider the matter to be rather urgent."

Mary took him to Diane's office.

"Tony can't sent your messages now," Diane Jackson said. "It is technical. Very complicated. It is about bouncing sound off the sky. Tony says it works like this."

She reached into her pocket and pulled out a tiny ball. "Here, I am a radio. The ball is the sound. The ceiling is the sky. I throw the ball to the ceiling. It bounces down to you. At least, if you are in the right place to catch it." She gave the little ball a toss toward the ceiling; Wettstein caught it.

"Me, I do not understand radio. But I believe what they tell me about it, just as religious people have faith in things they do not see. Can you come back just before the sun has set? Will set?"

Wettstein shook his head. "I have to attend a special meeting of the small council." He was examining the little ball carefully and bounced it once or twice on the floor. "Can I just leave the messages here? Can this 'radio' send them without my presence, if I write them down? Or must I be with them, just as I must be in a room to sign a letter?"

"Tony can send them and say that they are from you. But I will ask him questions. Who do they go to? What do they say? And he will tell me. See, I tell you the truth."

Wettstein nodded absentmindedly. "What," he asked, "is this ball made of?"

"Oh," Diane said. "That is rubber. It is not just for toys. Very useful. Lots of things are made of rubber. You can borrow it, if you want. Bounce it at your city council to impress them."

"Wettstein sent what?" Mary Simpson asked.

"A half-dozen messages," Tony Adducci said. "The main one was to a guy named Böcler. I put out that to two locations, Duke Ernst's radio in Amberg and General Banér's, if he's still around Ingolstadt. No way to tell which one will reach him first. Just a short message, no outgoing information, so to speak. It was a couple of questions with a list of a dozen or so more men to whom he was to send them on. Same message to Grantville, to be forwarded to Professor Schickard. Him I met before we left Magdeburg this year. Another half-dozen names to send the questions on to. A couple to Amsterdam, to be sent on to guys at the university in Leiden. A couple more to Mainz, to go to the university of Heidelberg. They're to get the answers back here, somehow, preferably by way of any radio set-up they can reach, with copies of everything to General Horn and a plea for him to get himself down to Rheinfelden just as fast as he can scamper. Plus, anybody who can is supposed to notify a guy named Freinsheim—I never heard of him—to get out of France."

✧   ✧   ✧

"I can't go into the USE embassy now," Wettstein said a couple of days later. "Given the position the council is taking, if I went in, it would be interpreted as a declaration that I am changing my allegiance from Basel to Gustav Adolf. I can't do that. I have to stay to organize the defense of Riehen. That is where my duty lies. I have done all that I can to assist the ambassadress."

"The last time I tried to go in," Cavriani said, "the council's guards told me that I was not authorized, because I have no diplomatic credentials."

Johann Buxtorf fingered his beard. "I will see what I can manage."

Theodor Zwinger delivered Wettstein's final warning about the city council's intentions. Not even the guards posted by the council itself would turn back Basel's head pastor if he chose to call upon a foreign embassy.

The embassy staff already had armaments in place, even before the warning. The ambassadress herself was occupied; Frau Admiral Simpson received him. He gave her Wettstein's letter. She offered him a cup of the novel "coffee" beverage; he accepted. After his first sip, she mentioned that some people preferred it with cream and sugar. These were on the tray. He accepted again, although he noticed that she drank hers without them.

They discussed potatoes for some time. Zwinger's father had been one of the earliest European scientists to provide a thorough description of this new world plant and its medicinal properties, particularly in the prevention of scurvy. Zwinger had heard that in this "up-time" it had become a staple food, almost as much in use as grains?

The Frau Admiral introduced him to Frau Mayor Dreeson. They discussed the ecclesiastical policies of Duke Maximilian of Bavaria in the Upper Palatinate during the 1620s and found themselves to be of one accord, which was quite gratifying, although he found her frequent use of the phrase "damned Bavarians" somewhat distasteful in a woman.

Thus he stayed long enough to be polite. He did not see the Austrian archduchess, but then he had not expected to. The city council's guards closed their barricades behind him when he left.

CHAPTER 62

Benedictiones Multiplex

Donaueschingen

"Marc," Susanna whispered. "Marc, wake up." She shook his shoulder. "Marc!"

He turned his face in the other direction.

"Marc, wake up. Wake up now." She looked around the stable loft, spotted an ancient bridle hanging from a peg, and flicked his shoulders with it.

"Whaaaat?"

"Wake up. Now, Marc. Right now."

He sat up.

"Susanna, it's still too dark to start out. What on earth?"

"I had to go downstairs, Marc. To use the latrine, before any of the stablemen come around. Behind. There are more stalls than we saw last night, behind where the ladder comes up here. They have horses in them. One of them is the horse that Bavarian captain was riding when he passed us when we were on the way here, I think. I'm not sure. It was just a sort of ordinary horse."

Marc frowned. "A roan gelding. Very distinctive markings and a nice gait. Old scar on the left shoulder, but no sign of crippling. The way he moved I wouldn't mind riding him myself."

"Well, go and look, then. Maybe you will be surer than I am."

Marc climbed down the ladder sleepily and reluctantly. He climbed back up a lot faster.

"You're right."

"We had better get our stuff and get out of here," Susanna said anxiously.

"That's the last thing we want to do. Let him leave before we do."

Two hours after dawn, the roan horse was still in the stall. Reluctantly, Marc concluded that the captain had business in Donaueschingen. He and Susanna headed for the southern gate.

Raudegen was sitting on a bench that evening, catching his breath as he talked with the last of Donaueschingen's various innkeepers.

He had been asking about the two all day, the man with the curl of black hair falling on his forehead and the nondescript boy. People said that they had been making the rounds of the inns in Donaueschingen just the day before, asking about a man traveling with three women. Two older women and a tall, young, brunette.

Raudegen asked about the party of four also. The answers were still what they had been the first time he came through Donaueschingen. Nobody had seen them. That's what they had told the man and boy, also, everyone said.

The man and boy? No, they had not stayed at any of the inns the night before. It was not likely that they had left the city so close to dark, though, the host at the *Silver Star* said. It had been nearly dusk when he talked to them.

Raudegen went back to his own inn. Too late to make the rounds of the gates, tonight. He would talk to the guards at each of them tomorrow. Once he knew which way they had gone, he would have some idea. But if the archduchess and her party had not been here, how would they decide how to go?

At supper time, he was cursing himself. His man reported that last night the two had been sleeping in the stable loft behind this inn—the one where they were staying themselves. With the slightest luck, he could have caught them.

"This isn't going to be easy walking," Marc warned. "We'll have to cross the high hills of the Black Forest to get into the Wiesental. Then we can just follow the Wiese River down to Basel.

They're not like the Alps that you had to climb when you went to Balzano and then to Vienna, but more than enough hills, and some of them steep. The guard I talked to at the gate yesterday told me how to get to Hüfingen. He's worked there, he said. It's belonged to the count von Fürstenberg since 1620 and there's an administrative district headquartered there. We'll be all right that far, and can ask someone there how to go on to Löffingen. Someone is bound to know. It has nearly five hundred people and it belongs to Fürstenberg, too."

"Being anywhere that's in the jurisdiction of the count of Fürstenberg," Susanna said, "does not make me feel better at all. Let's walk fast and try to get out of it."

"Yes," the guard said to Raudegen, "I talked to the man yesterday. He was asking about directions to Hüfingen."

"We are," Susanna said, "completely and totally lost."

Marc looked around. "Not lost, exactly. Just on the wrong path. It's pretty. Look at all those layers of rock. But there is no way that anyone has ever managed to bridge that gorge in front of us. We'll just have to turn around and go back to the other road."

"How much time have we wasted?"

"Two or three hours coming, I think. So it will be that much again, going back. Most of a day."

The leaves were turning. He reached over, broke off a couple of small branches, put them on her head, and looked at the effect.

"You look good in autumn leaves. Some day, you ought to make yourself a dress that color. If you were a bride in golden yellow and orange-red, you would put all the rest of the girls to shame."

Susanna pulled the twigs out of her hair. There wasn't any point in keeping them. The leaves would turn brown before she could press them. She tossed them down, but first she looked at them carefully, memorizing. She almost never forgot a color. Matching colors, she knew, was one of her strengths as a designer. Even if she went to a store without a swatch, she would return with a length of fabric that perfectly complemented the one left behind at the palace.

"That has to be where we made the wrong turn." Susanna started to run. Marc put his hand on her shoulder to hold her back.

She frowned. "What is the matter?"

"I smell iron."

"Iron?"

"Ore. In the ground. Either there are mines, which I have never heard of in this place, or it is close to the surface."

"What difference does it make?"

"We must be coming into the Wiesental, now. That has to be the Feldberg, over there. I don't see how we missed seeing it this morning when we made the wrong turn that ended up next to the ravine. If there is iron here, I need to take notes. For Papa and for Jakob Durre, my master. Where there is a little iron, there may be more. If there is enough to make it worthwhile and if they can get options on the right to open mines . . . I wonder who this valley belongs to? Who has jurisdiction, that is. I'm sure we're out of the Fürstenberg lands by now."

"Todtnau, boy," the old man said. "This village is called Todtnau. We belong to the archdukes of Austria, here. For a long time. Since the time of the grandfather of my father's grandfather. That's as far back as I know. There was a big battle, people say, and after that we were Austrian. Not that a lot of people wouldn't like to turn Swiss." He gave an impudent, if toothless, grin. "Wouldn't mind it myself."

Their talk wandered off onto the topic of iron ore. It was around, the old man said.

"You ought to talk to the smith. He never buys a pig of iron. He works it out of the ground himself, just on the forge. Slower, he says, but cheaper, too. What else does he have to do when he doesn't have any customers?"

The two of them wandered away from the road, in the direction of the smithy. The smith, the old man said, was his niece's husband.

Susanna was getting impatient. She would have liked to talk to the old woman, but she could not understand her accent at all. The people spoke Swabian German around here. *Schwäbisch*. It was almost a language in itself. She wandered to the side of the house. She was looking at the herb garden when she heard the hoofbeats. She sank down behind the trellises, peeking through.

Apparently the Bavarian captain could not understand the old woman, either. He raised his quirt in a threatening manner. She called into the house; a middle-aged woman came out. She repeated the old woman's answers. Susanna could understand her words.

The two men rode on. Susanna got up and came around to the front of the cottage where the two women were still standing.

"Thank you," she said. "I am very grateful. I do not know why you lied for us, but thank you very much."

"She did not lie," the younger woman said. "She has not seen the young man pass through the village, because he has not passed through. He has gone to the smithy with my husband's father. She has not seen a boy with him, because you are a girl. The man knows that you're a girl. You must have heard him say so later on. But when he asked the question, he asked my mother-in-law if she had seen a boy with the curly-haired man. She has told the precise and exact truth because it is never good when someone on horseback is looking for someone on foot. Especially not when he carries a whip and raises it against old women. We in this village are among those who go through life on foot. Would you like some fresh cheese? We have perry to drink, also."

"At least," Marc said, "we are behind them."

"This may not help," the old man said. "He will be asking in every village. In Gschwend; that comes next. Then in Schoenau, which is about five miles from here. In Zell. If they all say that they have not seen you, he may turn around and retrace his steps. Then you will be, perhaps, meeting him on the road. The road through this valley is not so wide that you can easily go to the side of it and hide yourselves."

"We have to get to Basel," Marc said.

"Not today," the younger woman answered. "Spend the night here. My husband has gone south, to find out where the soldiers are. You should wait until he comes back."

Marc looked at Susanna, who was sitting at the rough table, blinking rather slowly. She had not known that she should cut the perry with a lot of water. She was not used to it. Even though there would still be a couple of hours of daylight, maybe they had better stay. Then the word "soldiers" struck him.

"Soldiers?"

"Yes. There are soldiers between here and Basel. My husband has gone to the *Amtmann* to find out which ones. If they are friends, that is, if they are in the Austrian service, perhaps things will not go too hard with us. Mostly, they will just take things that they need, as soldiers do. But if they are French or Swedes, the villages along the road will need to move as much as possible up into the hills, because they will burn and kill as well as steal."

The old man frowned. "It is bad having soldiers come in the fall. It is worst when they come after harvest. In the fall they can steal everything after we have done all the work, leaving us to starve through the winter while they feast on our chickens and cabbages."

Someone knocked on the door. It was the smith and a younger man whom Marc did not recognize.

The younger woman put her arm around Susanna's shoulders and laid her down on a bench next to the fireplace. Then she put her mother-in-law to bed.

The four men started talking about iron and soldiers; soldiers and iron. The younger woman came back and sat with them at the table.

Her husband had been quite a way to the south. Soldiers, he said. Bernhard of Saxe-Weimar was occupying all the Austrian territories in the Breisgau, or that was the story. Most people had not decided whether or not it was true that he had abandoned the French, but it was quite true that he was here.

There wasn't anything that they could do about the soldiers tonight. The man and wife went to bed. Marc and the smith sat up late, talking about iron. There was some iron here at Todtnau, the smith said, but not a lot. There was far more a few miles to the south, at Hausen.

Susanna winced. Her head hurt when she woke up and the sunlight seemed miserably bright. The old woman laughed, gave her a big drink of water and a piece of dry rye bread, told her to keep walking, and advised her not to drink any more perry. "You being such an innocent little thing and all that, which I was not sure of when you first came here wearing those trousers and a boy's shirt."

The smith came with them as they walked south from Todtnau to Hausen. He and Marc talked about iron as they walked, and talked even more about iron after they got there. The smith had trained in Lörrach, a little piece of territory that belonged to the margraves of Baden in between the Austrian lands. The Baden *Amtmann* there knew that there was iron in these hills; he had sent reports to the margraves. The *Amtmann* believed in iron. Gold, he said, was pretty and all that, but mankind could not live without iron. Everybody needed iron. If there were mines here, iron would bring wealth to the valley. Even to the farmers, who had a hard time wresting a living from these rocks. Miners would need vegetables. The high pastures supported cattle; miners would need meat and cheese. The forests would provide charcoal.

"Everyone else thought that he was a dreamer," the smith said. "Everyone else said that no one would invest the capital that it would take to bring mines to the valley during these decades of war. Certainly not the exiled margrave, who has served the king of Sweden for more than a decade now. Probably not his son in Basel, either. He has no money; it takes money to open mines."

At Hausen, they left Susanna with a cousin of the smith's first wife and went up into the hills. After the noon meal, the Bavarian captain came into the village from the south, asking questions.

The people of Hausen, Susanna found, were tellers of truth, very like those in Todtnau. The only strange young man any of them had seen, they said earnestly, had come this morning with the smith from another village to see about some iron. In any case, they continued, they did not have time to worry about strange young men, because they had received notice that Duke Bernhard's soldiers were moving through the land not far to the south. That would mean that villages would be burned, the terraces for the grape vines destroyed, the fields trampled. And disease, certainly disease. Disease followed a soldier as if it were his twin brother.

The Bavarian captain raised his quirt.

"You can hit me," the woman who was speaking to him said. "But you cannot make it otherwise."

Shortly after that, Marc and the smith returned. The smith went back toward Todtnau; Marc and Susanna started walking south again.

"Do you really *like* iron?" Susanna asked with real curiosity.

Marc looked at her. "Yes. Yes, I do," he answered. There was some surprise in his voice. "I didn't, particularly, when I started apprenticing with Jakob Durre, but I do now. It's really interesting. And challenging. Just look." He motioned toward the Wiese with its shallow, rocky, channel. "To bring iron out of here in any quantity, either this stream would have to be fitted with a series of locks and dams like the ones I saw on the Naab in the Upper Palatinate last spring, or else a canal would have to be dug parallel to it. That might be best, because with a deeper draft, the water could power the wheels and the mills."

He turned around and pointed back toward Hausen. "Did you notice, while we were there, that the villagers have already cut a partial channel, a short one, to run their sawmill and the grist mill? To make the most of these shallow mountain creeks, you really have to harness them. Have you ever seen the Pegnitz at Nürnberg?"

"No, I've never been to Nürnberg," Susanna answered. She listened carefully. If Marc really *liked* iron, then there must be something more to the matter than she had ever thought. She would find out what it was if she listened. Even if she didn't ever like iron, she liked having Marc talk to her. The better she listened, the more he would talk to her.

Between Hausen and Todtnau, Raudegen pulled his horse into the shelter of a small thicket, gesturing for his man to do the same. "We will wait here," he said, "and see what may be learned from the two men who are supposedly interested in iron."

He was quite interested to see that only one man was walking north toward Todtnau.

The smith from Todtnau resisted Raudegen's questioning for quite some time. By the end, however, the captain had the information he needed. Although he did not yet quite comprehend just how a young man with an apparently profound and sincere interest in iron ore had come to be involved with Archduchess Maria Anna's servant.

He did not bother to kill the smith. If the man managed to drag his way back to Todtnau, he might even heal, in time. It was not likely, though, that his hands would ever again swing a hammer.

Raudegen was mildly annoyed. He didn't enjoy this sort of thing, the way some men did. It would be easier if civilians would just provide soldiers with the information they needed, straightforwardly and without evasions. He wished he could make an example of the lying women in Todtnau and Hausen, but he could not afford the time right now. He turned south again. The pair who might lead him to the archduchess could not be far ahead of him.

✧   ✧   ✧

Just above Schopfheim, Marc and Susanna took to the trees. Soldiers. A good-sized detachment, riding north. Foragers, probably. Marc thought that they were Duke Bernhard's men. They waited for them to pass, then started running.

Schopfheim, when they got there, was nearly burned out. Susanna stared. The smith had told them that this town had walls and gates; they had planned to spend the night. The walls and gates themselves were smoldering, where they had not been broken down. The party of soldiers they had passed on the road farther north was not large enough to have destroyed this town, which meant that there must be others, many more, quite near.

There was nothing they could do. There were no survivors here, outside. Inside, the embers were still far too hot for people to go in. They hurried around it as fast as they could, trying to ignore the smell. If Schopfheim was burned, there was no reason to expect that the smaller places the smith had mentioned, Steinen and Brombach, would still be standing. It would be ten more miles to Lörrach, where the Todtnau smith had trained. They started running, occasionally slowing to a walk to catch their breaths; then running again, as fast as they could for as long as they could.

Then Lörrach came into sight. "Oh," Susanna said. "Oh, no."

Raudegen recognized the lieutenant commanding the foraging party with some relief. If Harsch were here, that meant that Duke Bernhard was somewhere fairly close.

"Yes," the lieutenant said. "The main force of the army is not much more than ten miles to the south. The duke has taken headquarters in Lörrach while the rest of the army catches up to the vanguard."

"So that is as far as I got, Your Grace," Raudegen said. "The two men I sent on may have found information about where the four left the convoy, but I took the risk of following the girl once I realized that she was in the archduchess' household. I assume full responsibility for the decision."

"It wasn't all that bad," Duke Bernhard said, leaning back in his chair. "You have, of course, been back in the hills for quite some time." He tossed a copy of the Basel newspaper across the table.

"You are clearly correct," Raudegen answered after a moment. "I am seriously behind the times, according to this. My apologies, Your Grace."

"No apologies necessary. I am impressed, in fact, that you came so close to the truth. Your alertness ensured that I remained in the vicinity of the Swiss border. I am, in fact, currently on the way there in hopes of making the archduchess' personal acquaintance. Peacefully, if possible; martially, if necessary. The Basel city council having been so kind as to immobilize her, I propose to reap the fruits of their misguided efforts. 'Swiss independence.' What an absurdly inadequate use for a presumably fertile imperial daughter. I am just as much in need of a wife as the prince formerly known as the cardinal-infante."

Duke Bernhard stood up. Raudegen took a step a back.

"Take a dozen men, captain. Continue your pursuit. If this girl, whoever she is, was a part of the archduchess' household, as you say, she may yet be of considerable value to me if you can catch up with her. A bargaining chit, perhaps, if the archduchess is inclined not to cooperate with my plans."

"Yes, Your Grace."

"Hear me, though. Right now, I do not want any incidents with Basel. We are in the midst of some rather critical negotiations. If you can take them this side of the border, use whatever means necessary. If not, it would be more loss than gain to me, right now, to have a diplomatic incident."

"Yes, Your Grace."

"If they should try to double back, though, into Austrian lands . . ."

"Yes, Your Grace?"

"Pursue them. I no longer recognize Innsbruck's lordship over the Habsburgs' Swabian territories. Over the former Habsburg territories in Swabia, I should say. I quite anticipate having some interesting discussions with the duchess-regent of Tyrol on the topic in the not-too-distant future."

"Yes, Your Grace."

"Ah. Don't kill the girl. Don't even risk it. She would do me no good under those circumstances and it might well irritate the archduchess if she ever found out. Some women become attached to their servants."

"Yes, Your Grace."

"Very good. I am delighted to have staff who clearly understand my instructions. *Colonel* Raudegen."

✧   ✧   ✧

"You know," Marc whispered. "After these past few hours, I don't think that I'll ever take a fun vacation in Lörrach. I think that was what the stories call 'being in dire peril.'"

"That," Susanna answered, "is a really sensible decision. Never again in Lörrach. But at least we are through it now. It can't be much farther down to Riehen. Not more than three miles." She poured the pail of water she had been carrying into a leather bucket.

"Not," Marc said, "more than several thousand *more* soldiers to sneak past once we get out of this corral. Since Riehen is the Basel border and all that. Though I have to say that your idea of grabbing a couple of halters that were already on remount horses and sticking ourselves into a long line of other guys who were leading remount horses by halters wasn't a bad one."

"At least none of the soldiers between here and there will know us. Maybe we could find somebody's armor and put it on," she said a little hopefully. "Disguise ourselves, you know. I've designed lots of costumes for masques and pantomimes. That's part of what a seamstress does, you know."

"You can think about costumes now? Here?" Marc was sloshing two buckets of water for every one that Susanna managed.

"I can think about costumes anywhere. Anytime. That's what I do. Sort of like you thinking about iron ore."

"Oh." Marc was going to have to think about that when he got a chance. "Well. We might find some armor that fits me. But not you."

"Maybe I could disguise myself as a stableboy or something. Since we're in the place they pen up the cavalry horses."

"You *are* disguised as a boy. You have been for weeks, now. Stableboys aren't any different from the rest of them, really."

"Oh. Yes, that's right. I'm getting used to it, I suppose. Being a boy. So I keep forgetting that I am one, a lot of the time. Did you ever give me a boy's name? I don't think so." Susanna looked around. "But I was wrong, I think."

"About what?"

"When I said that at least none of the soldiers between here and Riehen would know us. Look there, by the tent. It's the Bavarian captain and he definitely seems to be looking for someone. Us, maybe."

"Us," Marc said. "Ten to one, us. A hundred to one, us. Run."

"Don't run," Susanna said. "Steal a horse." She looked at him. "You can ride, can't you?"

"I can ride, but . . ." Marc was going to say that he didn't think that this was the best option, but it was too late. Susanna was mounted. So he stole a horse, too.

At least, the captain was on foot. He would have to find a horse. They would have a head start. Maybe this hadn't been such a bad idea.

The Riehen militia was patrolling the marked boundary stones. So far, none of Duke Bernhard's troops had violated the line. The news was that the duke was negotiating with the city council; that he had promised that if they turned the Austrian woman over to him without incident, he would not invade the city's territory.

"Riders," one of them called.

Two riders. Behind them, not more than the width of the market square in Basel behind them, came a dozen more. Not shooting, though one of them was speeding up, trying to cut the boy off.

The Riehen militia stood silently, motionless, until the riders passed the boundary stones. Both riders reined up, or tried to. The man stopped and dismounted. "Get off!" he yelled at the boy, who was having more trouble reining in. He finally slowed the horse, turned it, came back, and jumped off.

The man slapped the rumps of both of the beasts, sending them back across the border. "Just borrowed!" he cried at the soldiers who had been in pursuit, and who had now come to a halt. Apparently, the soldiers did not intend to violate the boundary line. "No offense meant!"

The oldest militiaman looked at them. "What is this all about?" he asked.

"I was supposed to be meeting my father," Marc said. "In Basel." That was safe enough to say. It was also true, which he found vaguely comforting. "We had a little trouble getting through Duke Bernhard's camp around Lörrach.

"Things are sort of upset, right now."

"Really. We hadn't noticed," Susanna piped up. At the look Marc gave her, she closed her mouth again.

"What do we do with this smart-mouthed kid, Matti?" a younger man asked.

"They're the *Landvogt's* problem. Both of them. That's obvious. We can hold them for a few days. Maybe a boundary violation, maybe a customs violation, even though they sent the horses back. They don't have their baggage, so they probably don't have passports. If they have undeclared foreign money, it could be a currency violation. If they've been with the army over there, it could be a quarantine violation. The city council doesn't want plague being brought in."

"But Herr Wettstein is in Basel."

"They're still his problem. Take them down to the administration building and put them in a corner, somewhere. He won't have time to see them right away."

"If he's in Basel, why not send them across into the city to him?"

"Bridge closed. The council closed it at sunset. It's not going to reopen until they finish negotiating with Duke Bernhard."

"We haven't had time to declare any currency," Susanna protested. "You haven't even asked us to."

Marc was pulling a case out of the inside pocket of his doublet. "We do have passports," he said.

The oldest militiaman was still unmoved. "You're still Herr Wettstein's problem. Not ours. You'll just have to wait until all this is over."

CHAPTER 63

Potentiam Concupiscere

Lörrach

"I simply do not understand," Duke Bernhard said, "why all of them seem to be so surprised. I left the service of Gustav Adolf after his great insult to my honor, my reputation, after all. What caused them to expect that I would remain permanently in French service if a different course of action became, for some reason, more appropriate?"

Johann Freinsheim stood quietly, listening to the duke's meditations. He sincerely hoped that Duke Bernhard didn't ask for his opinion. He was not here to give his opinion. He was here to deliver a message from Margrave Friedrich V of Baden-Durlach.

On the one hand, Duke Bernhard's analysis seemed to be accurate. As far as Freinsheim could tell, "all of them" did appear to be surprised. "Most of them" at least. They also appeared to be disapproving. Certainly the French had been very surprised, not to say disapproving, when the duke had pulled his regiments away from their assigned position across from Mainz. He knew that definitely, having been working in the chancery when it happened.

Freinsheim realized that he was in no position to know Gustav Adolf's mind, but the king of Sweden's administrator in Mainz had certainly not hesitated to take advantage of the opportunity that Bernhard had offered to him, whether or not he was surprised by it; whether or not he approved of it.

Margrave Friedrich, certainly, was both surprised and disapproving. Freinsheim had come to the margrave at once, as soon as he succeeded in getting out of France. He felt obliged to him as well as to Professor Buxtorf for the timely warning he had received. Warnings, to be more precise—they had arrived by several ways. If he had stayed much longer—well, suspicion of collaboration with Duke Bernhard would have been almost certain to fall upon a German working in the translation division of the royal chancery. Under Cardinal Richelieu, it was common for suspicion to be followed by prompt action.

Whereas, Freinsheim thought righteously, he had not been collaborating with Duke Bernhard at all. But now Duke Bernhard was looking at him impatiently. "Well?" he asked.

Apparently the duke did want his opinion. "Margrave Friedrich's father has been unswervingly loyal to the Protestant cause," he began a little uncertainly. "Perhaps this has led him to cultivate a certain admiration for steadiness of purpose and for, ah . . ."

His voice trailed off. *Keeping your word once you have given it . . .* might not be the most appropriate thing for an emissary to say to the duke right now.

"Consistency in pursuit of one's goals," he finished.

"I have been quite consistent in the pursuit of my goals," Duke Bernhard said blandly. "From beginning to end. I would advise Margrave Friedrich to devote some consideration to what my goals are. If he is able to clarify that matter in his mind—which I doubt, if the letter you just delivered is a typical example of the way he thinks—then he may be moved to submit some slightly more acceptable proposal to me."

Duke Bernhard rose. "You may inform him that I do not regard his suggestions as an acceptable basis for beginning negotiations. If you care to wait, I will have my secretary draft a letter, so you may deliver a signed version, in writing."

Freinsheim inclined his head. "Thank you, Your Grace."

Basel

"The USE embassy is not really under siege," Diane Jackson said. "That is not the right way to say it. I told Frank so, this morning. Even though Swiger and Gordon act like we are under siege. We are just as comfortable as we were before the city council's 'honor guard' showed up. They let the grocer and the butcher deliver food every day." She nodded her head. "Sometimes they even let visitors come. If they have diplomatic credentials. Like you."

She nodded at Margrave Friedrich V of Baden-Durlach who was sitting at the foot of the table. There was a member of his staff at his right. The margrave had brought a copy of the note which the duke had sent in response to his suggestion for negotiations.

Diane read the note, listened to the margrave, and answered rather drily, "Duke Bernhard has a point. It is not normal for the man with the biggest army to go away because someone else tells him that he should play nice. Maybe he did not pay attention to his kindergarten teacher."

Margrave Friedrich looked at her, wholly baffled. Then at the others around the table. It made him rather uneasy that he was the only man present, other than his secretary and a young up-timer called Tony who was also taking notes, as well as sitting next to Frau Dreeson and whispering in her ear. A vague echo of the Scots pastor's pamphlet *First Blast of the Trumpet Against the Monstrous Regiment of Women* drifted through his mind.

These four. Frau Simpson's presence, he could understand. Somewhat. The archduchess, perhaps, although she certainly had no official status among the up-timers, since much of the focus of the negotiations was upon her person. But Frau Dreeson? He had not brought along the wife of the mayor of Basel to the discussion.

Frau Admiral Simpson smiled kindly. "Diane is referring to an up-time book, Your Grace, about the importance of what children learn during their earliest years. Our schools for small children are called kindergartens, which is a German word, but which does not yet exist in 1634."

Margrave Friedrich nodded. Certainly, everyone realized the importance of molding a child. Even the Bible spoke of it. "Bring up a child in the way he should go, and when he is old he will not depart from it."

"You think that Duke Bernhard was badly brought up?" he asked.

"I understand," Mary Simpson said, "that he was the youngest of a very large family of boys. He was really just a baby when his father died. Rulers or not, they did not have much money. I have spoken to Wilhelm Wettin, more than once. Duke Bernhard's allowance from the Saxe-Weimar lands, under their father's will, was much less than the annual salary of a colonel in one of the regiments that your father commands, Margrave Friedrich. Nor were the sons to have separate lands of their own. They were to govern Saxe-Weimar as a committee, so to speak, with Wilhelm, as the oldest survivor, serving as CEO—chief executive officer, that—or chairman of the board. I am not sure if there is a down-time word quite equivalent."

"And why," Margrave Friedrich asked, "do you see that this has caused Duke Bernhard to betray first one *Kriegsherr* and now another? 'War lord?' Would that be the correct word?"

"Literally, yes," Mary answered. "But 'war lord' has different connotations for us. It sounds more, well, feudal. Old fashioned. Obsolete. Or third-world, such as the conflicts in Somalia. A *Kriegsherr* is really something more straightforward. A ruler who employs a military contractor. Your problem with the ethics of Duke Bernhard is that he does not fulfill his contracts. Not that he violates some kind of mystical oath of fealty."

"He *has* broken oaths," Margrave Friedrich said rather stiffly.

"That is true," Mary answered. "But what we are talking about this morning, I think, is not that he has broken oaths, but why he has done it. He challenged you to understand why, didn't he? If I understand this letter correctly?"

"At first, when he pulled back from Mainz," Margrave Friedrich said, "my father's assumption was that it was part of a wider movement of French troops, no matter now improbable that might have seemed after the crushing defeat that Torstensson inflicted upon them outside of Luebeck. My father predicted that some other regiments would move into the Mainz front through Lorraine. He expected that Bernhard would make a major movement against General Horn here in Swabia; perhaps that he would probe through Württemberg against the USE frontier, possibly against Thuringia-Franconia itself at its most vulnerable point."

Veronica Dreeson spoke up for the first time. "That was what Henry thought, too, and the other men in Grantville. They sent everyone they could spare down to that point earlier this summer. They even called up a lot of the reservists like Jack Whitney and sent them down to Horn."

The young man, Tony, next to her, put her words into spoken French at the same time he was noting them down in the minutes.

Margrave Friedrich felt obscurely comforted. Though why it should be comforting to hear that the opinions of an experienced military leader and diplomat such as his father were shared by the mayor of a small city was not clear to him.

"But Bernhard did not attack the State of Thuringia-Franconia," Maria Anna pointed out. "He sent most of his troops back into Alsace and into the Franche-Comté—except for the ones here, under his personal command. Now he has moved into the Breisgau and the rest of the Austrian lands in southern Swabia. He has not, in truth, moved against General Horn this summer. If they meet on the battlefield this season, it will be because Horn seeks him out."

"There was another book, up-time," Mary Simpson said. "I am not sure whether Grantville has a copy any more. I had one, but it was left in Pittsburgh, of course. I can check with the library after I get home, if anyone is interested. It was written by an Englishwoman. The title was *A Room of One's Own*, or something similar. Margrave Friedrich, I think that you might, possibly, ask Duke Bernhard if he intends to obtain a room of his own. I am sure that he would prefer not to hear the option presented in those exact words, of course. It might be more prudent to ask him if all his moves have been calculated to bring him an independent principality of his own."

Freinsheim looked up, startled.

"Perhaps," she continued, "since he was always the 'baby brother' in his own family, a principality larger than any lands that the older Saxe-Weimar sons have any reasonable prospect of ruling."

Diane Jackson reached behind her. "Lee Swiger drew me a map," she said. "It is not big enough, but this is the biggest piece of paper that the printer had. This is three of the biggest pieces of paper the printer had. No tape here, down-time, but I put flour paste from the kitchen on strips of paper and glued them together from behind." She rolled it out on the table.

"We are here, in Basel. This is the Rhine River. Here are Becky and Gretchen, in Amsterdam, at the other end. This, on this side, this is what was last year. This, on the other side, this is what is now."

✧   ✧   ✧

Maria Anna understood the implications of the two drawings first. She stood up, pointing with her finger. "Duke Bernhard has occupied a lot of territory on the Upper Rhine. It's almost as large as the Swiss Confederacy itself, without conflicting in any way with the Confederacy's cantons. It draws almost equally from what were French lands and what were the lands of the Holy Roman Empire. That is important, yes. A new principality within the empire. Mary's 'room of one's own.' But also . . ." She pointed. "Along here. Your cartographer has not drawn it, Diane, but along here is crucial. If he holds this, he will have broken the Spanish Road from Italy to the Netherlands. That means . . ."

Everyone started to chatter at once.

"Diane," Maria Anna said. "I will write for you what I see here. It is very important. I will give you a copy. Tony, you must send radio for the whole window tonight, I think, without stopping. I will do this if you agree to send it to Amsterdam, that they give it to my cousin, to Don Fernando, and to the king of Sweden at the same time. Not first one and then the other. Together."

She turned to Margrave Friedrich almost fiercely.

"And both of them must have it *before* you send your envoy back to the duke and tell him what we have seen. Do you understand that?"

The margrave nodded.

Maria Anna continued. "Whether he can hold it for long? That is hard to predict. There are so many things which might contribute, both for and against, and I am only starting to think. If my brother and Duke Maximilian combine against him, here in the south, they might be able to drive him out of the lands on the right bank of the Rhine, at least. But there is no way, any more, that they could coordinate with Spanish coming from Italy to create a victory such as Nördlingen was, up-time. Not until after he has been pushed back very far."

"You know about Nördlingen?" Mary Simpson asked.

"Oh, yes," Maria Anna said with some surprise. "Last winter, before all this began, at home in Vienna, I was thinking about what I had read about the Battle of Nördlingen in that other world of yours, and how proud Papa had been of Ferdinand. I think I have studied all the things that your *encyclopedias* said about this war. And some of the books. Father Lamormaini did not want me to have all of them, of course, because I am a woman. But I am also a Habsburg. The Jesuits could not refuse to obtain the things for my brothers and they shared them with me. And with Cecelia, of course. We have to be prepared for our responsibilities."

Mary nodded.

"And, of course, there are more problems. First, of course, the way the map is at the moment, General Horn is here." Maria Anna drew an oval with her forefinger. "That means that my brother and Duke Maximilian could not even *reach* Duke Bernhard without somehow going through, or around, General Horn's forces. Going around is not possible, politically." Her finger draw two quick arrows on the second version of the map. "Not through the Swiss Confederacy; not through the State of Thuringia-Franconia. Either would mean a major escalation of the war. Duke Maximilian cannot afford one, just now. My brother, I believe, although I have not been able to speak with him since last spring, will not want one.

"Even if he did," the archduchess flashed a smile, "somehow, I do not think that the king of Sweden will wish to withdraw General Horn so that others may pass here," she drew her finger along the northern border of the Swiss Confederacy, "to confront Duke Bernhard, do you? There would be too much of a possibility that they might change the direction of their campaign." She drew another arrow with her finger, this one curving north through Baden and Württemberg at Mainz and the Rhine Palatinate.

"No, I suspect—suspect only, you understand—that in the long run, the king of Sweden will find the opening of the gap in the French defenses at Mainz and the cutting of the Spanish Road to be sufficiently great gifts to him that he will swallow his pride and allow Duke Bernhard his independent principality. If he agrees to play nice in his corner of the kindergarten sandbox. Even if he pretends to agree to play nice."

Margrave Friedrich nodded. He was thinking, of course, about what this reconfiguration of the map might mean for Baden.

Maria Anna was looking at the others. "But I will not be his tool, you understand. I will not let that heretic use me against my family. I will not be a brood mare through whom he can strengthen his children's claims to the lands he has won."

Margrave Friedrich nodded.

The archduchess looked at him fiercely, but phrased her next

statement diplomatically. "You will be so kind as to let Herr Wettstein know this, please, as he speaks with the city council. And,
if possible for you, Herr Cavriani as well."

Freinsheim mumbled something.

"Don't mumble," Diane Jackson said sharply. "It is not polite."

Startled, Freinsheim said, "If Wettstein knows it, it's damned
sure that Cavriani will, too."

The ambassadress smiled. "Much better. It is not polite to mumble.
They teach that in kindergarten, too. I know. I had three sons about
your age, before we came here. They were left up-time."

Freinsheim looked down at his notes, a little embarrassed.

Margrave Friedrich was more than a little startled. It had never
occurred to him to inquire as to whether or not the up-time general
and his exotic wife had children. As to whether the up-timers in
general had families, or how they lived among themselves when they
were not upsetting the political and confessional map of Europe.

General Horn's Headquarters, Swabia

"Overall," Gustav Horn said, "I preferred commanding Finnish
troops in Livonia to commanding USE troops in Swabia. Of course,
Christina was alive then. I preferred my life when Christina was
part of it, even if it did mean that I had Axel Oxenstierna for
a father-in-law."

"Perhaps," Burt Threlkeld said, "you ought to get married again.
If you found a really nice wife, maybe she could help your daughter
get over her nightmares about the way she was treated three years
ago and how her little brother died. My wife Debbie could help
match you up with someone, if you don't think your wife has to
be a Swedish noblewoman. You know. A nice child psychologist
or something. You're not like General Banér. You've been to the
university and everything. It would probably work out fine."

General Horn glared at his up-time military adviser.

"It doesn't do you any good to ignore it," Burt persisted. "Shit
happens when you're in the army. They taught us that back when
I was in. You thought your wife was getting better, so you went
back to the king's headquarters and then she died. You trusted a
junior officer to take care of your kids, but he made off with the
money you provided to him and left them to die in a wet cellar.

Your son did; the girl was tough enough to live and tell about it. You're going to have to deal with it. That much, at least, I got out of all the counseling they made us sit through in reserves.

"But not this minute. The rest of the staff is coming, so you're facing a meeting and you've got to decide what to do."

He moved to his customary position behind Horn. Whatever he had expected he might end up doing when he was sent down from Grantville to be the general's liaison with Grantville, psychological counselor had not been in the job description. He prepared himself for another protracted, indecisive meeting.

The long and short of it was that General Horn did not like to fight battles. General Horn liked maneuvering around, keeping the other guy off balance. Especially when the other guy was Duke Bernhard of Saxe-Weimar, whom he just couldn't stand anyway. As far as Horn was concerned, having a large, powerful, army available was an important piece on the board, in and of itself. A battle would risk this; especially an all-out battle with Bernhard. Bernhard might smash his pieces, take them off the board. Bernhard really was a damned good general once he managed to close against the other guy in a battle.

What was more, by refusing to fight a battle, Horn infuriated Bernhard. He seemed to think that scored him points, somehow. So, for two years now, they had been marching and countermarching, first in one place and then the other, all over the map of Swabia, Baden, Württemberg, leaving disease and destruction in their paths, but never coming to grips.

Burt gave Horn credit. For most of those two years, he had succeeded in keeping Duke Bernhard occupied. The Swabian front, the way Horn handled things, had never been an immediate dire threat to Gustav Adolf while he dealt with the League of Ostend and never a big drain on Sweden's resources. Since the king couldn't just wave his hand and make Duke Bernhard go away, that was probably a good thing.

Now, Burt knew, Horn had direct orders to proceed to Rheinfelden as fast as possible and confront Bernhard, who was threatening Basel.

Would he?

All he could do, Burt supposed, was wait and find out. Gustav Adolf was not likely to fire the man who had been Oxenstierna's son-in-law. There certainly weren't enough up-timers here to conduct a mutiny, even if they wanted to. Aside from the two kids, Kyle Bourne, the radio operator, and Bob Barnes, the EMT, who spent most of their time training down-timers to do their jobs at a pinch, there were only four besides himself. Three were veterans; two just reactivated from the reserves when things started to heat up down here—Jack Whitney, who had grown up in Morgantown even though he had relatives in Grantville and had married Jessica Ellis; Johnnie Sloan—Johnnie, like Jack, had been in the Gulf War.

Then the two who had been here as long as Burt. Gerry Pierpoint, a peace-time warrior. A techie, too. He didn't sit in on policy sessions; he talked to miners and sappers and artillery guys. Plus Marty Thornton. Marty? Well, as a soldier, he was very good at carrying a clipboard and keeping track of things like schedules for the sentries. Armies needed those, too, although why Horn's army needed Marty was beyond Burt's comprehension. Horn had hundreds of down-timers who could keep track of sentry schedules.

That was all, in an army of eight thousand, plus baggage train and camp followers. Not very much leaven for a very large loaf. The up-timers definitely did not call the tune in Swabia.

Basel

The city council meeting had been very long. The *leitmotif* of the majority appeared to be a desire to avoid destruction of Basel's resources. That, naturally, meant that the council would have to avoid having Duke Bernhard of Saxe-Weimar's army occupy the city's territory. Definitely avoid having it occupy the lands on the left bank; he must be dissuaded from crossing the Rhine.

They could, if necessary, sacrifice Riehen. Temporarily, of course.

Johann Rudolf Wettstein advanced passionate objections to this course of action, on the grounds that if Duke Bernhard ended up in possession of the rest of the right bank of the Rhine, he was unlikely to prove sufficiently accommodating to return Riehen to Basel.

Someone pointed out that Wettstein, as the *Landvogt* in Riehen, was possibly not completely dispassionate in his analysis.

Wettstein replied that the Riehen militiamen, who had stayed to defend Basel's interests, were, after all, the subjects of the city council. He also mentioned in passing the customs revenues that the right bank holdings generated.

Unfortunately, someone else commented that Duke Bernhard's demands could be met fairly easily, thus sparing Riehen from all the anticipated tribulations. The duke was not even asking that Basel itself violate the diplomatic immunity of the USE embassy; merely that the city council not offer opposition to his sending a limited force across the bridge to take custody of an embassy guest. A guest who was not, it should be noted, a citizen of the USE.

Gustav Adolf, someone said, would look rather ridiculous if he tried presenting himself as the appropriate champion of the interests of a Habsburg archduchess.

Actually, Wettstein thought, that had turned out to sow a nice amount of confusion, since at the mention of the term "Habsburg," the discussion veered off into the issue of whether the presence of the archduchess might offer sufficient leverage to obtain the legal independence of the Swiss cantons, and one of the guildmasters pointed out that if they let Duke Bernhard abduct her from the USE embassy, that opportunity would dry up.

Margrave Friedrich V of Baden-Durlach requested permission to address the council on behalf of his father.

The council refused.

He requested permission to address the council on behalf of the emperor of the USE.

The council refused.

They adjourned without a decision. Wettstein talked to Buxtorf.

Maria Anna tried very hard not to show her exasperation. It was almost dark. Margrave Friedrich V had called, telling Diane that the council had refused to hear his arguments. Pastor Zwinger, the Calvinist, Professor Buxtorf's brother-in-law, had brought information that the council had decided nothing—and that the date stated in Duke Bernhard's ultimatum, the date when he would cease to negotiate, was now less than a week away.

The soldiers inside the embassy would not let her close enough to the windows to get a really good look at what was happening outside. Sergeant Swiger appeared to be afraid that someone would shoot her, which he said was not going to happen on his watch. The ambassadress would not reverse his decision.

In fact, since the Basel city council was no longer permitting Cavriani and Wettstein to come into the USE Embassy, she was getting almost all the information she received from Mary Simpson, who herself was getting it only secondhand from Diane through Tony Adducci, as well as the radio.

She was a guest, with no more status than any other guest, she thought with frustration. But—she reached into her pocket.

Frau Ambassadress Jackson had authorized her to send four messages. The other morning, she had only sent three.

This was the time of day when Tony sent radio messages again. Mentally writing as she walked, Maria Anna headed upstairs to his office.

Tony confirmed it. Diane had authorized four messages; the archduchess had only sent three, so she could send another.

> *Most honored cousin. Basel trying to hold me hostage. Basel guards around USE embassy no longer permit visitors. Duke Bernhard on the border with army, trying to get permission to abduct me. Would prefer not to become the so-called guest of either. Should I run again? If so, which way? Maria Anna.*

CHAPTER 64

Sceptrum Tenens

Munich

"Duke Maximilian's reaction to the news of Archduchess Maria Anna's arrival at the USE embassy in Basel was not at all favorable," Bartholomaeus Richel admitted to Father Lorenz Forer. "In addition to threatening to dismiss all of the prominent officers who were commanding his forces at the time Ingolstadt fell in disgrace, he now is including in his disfavor everyone in the diplomatic service who has ever negotiated with either Baden or Basel. He counts them as being among the individuals whom he suspects of having participated in an Austrian-Bohemian conspiracy against him."

"One could wish," Forer commented, "that General Pappenheim were not a native-born Bavarian. That fact by itself is causing the duke, the more he considers the matter, to doubt the loyalty of Bavaria's native families. There were enough difficulties right after the general threw in with Wallenstein and became duke of Moravia. Now that Wallenstein has granted sanctuary to Duke Albrecht since Duchess Mechthilde's unfortunate accident..."

"There is no way to present it as an accident," Richel said. "Duchess Mechthilde was killed during a fight. We admit that. We merely avoid all reference to the agent through whom her death came about."

"If you say so," Forer said dubiously. "It would be better for Duke Maximilian's spiritual and mental rest if her death had been an accident."

"His reaction to the news was not at all favorable." Richel resumed his theme. "Duke Maximilian has ordered several arrests and has summoned the judges to issue indictments and hold another round of hearings under strict questioning. Beginning tomorrow."

"What is the reaction among the members of the Estates?"

"Unfavorable," Richel admitted reluctantly. "They did not care so much when his anger was falling on the army. Its commanders are, of course, mainly either foreigners like Mercy or both foreigners and commoners, like Werth. Even the execution of Hörwarth did not offend most of them, since his father was from Augsburg, not a Bavarian. This, however, affects many of Bavaria's own nobility directly, so their response is likely to become more unfavorable. Many of the leading families have members included in the current round of accusations. Several leading noblemen have submitted requests that the duke summon a meeting of the Estates."

"The duke's response?"

"He refuses, of course."

Vienna

The news arrived from Amberg, of all ridiculous places, by way of a Jesuit mailbag, Father William Lamormaini wrote, in his report to the father-general of the Jesuits.

The rider had galloped all the way. Archduchess Maria Anna was in Basel, residing in the embassy of the United States of Europe. Voluntarily, which made it worse, from his own perspective. Almost, he had considered withholding the information from the dying emperor. It would have been, he felt, an act of mercy.

Unfortunately, someone else had sent the same news, from the same city, directly to the imperial family. That *someone* being the Swede's regent, Duke Ernst of Saxe-Weimar, at the request of Doña Mencia de Mendoza, who had requested this favor through means of the radio. Doña Mencia was in Amsterdam. The courier sent by Duke Ernst handed it over to the Empress Eleonora.

That much, Lamormaini wrote to Father Vitelleschi, he knew.

He also knew that the empress had taken it directly to the king of Hungary, Ferdinand—who was likely to inherit the Austrian throne at any moment, given his father's health.

So Ferdinand was here now, in Vienna!

Lamormaini's hand shook, making a blot on the paper. The king of Hungary's Spanish wife had been so impudent as to recall him, without so much as asking permission from the privy council. Bishop Leopold Wilhelm, the youngest son, had arrived from Passau, as well. They never left the dying emperor alone. Whenever Father Lamormaini went to his room, one of them was there—the empress herself, the Spanish Mariana, or one of the three children. Always, at any hour of the day or night. Not even his physicians were permitted to see him alone, much less his confessor.

The empress had the impudence to tell him that the emperor wanted them there. The woman took too much upon herself. But when Lamormaini had ordered her to leave, the emperor had taken her hand, refusing to let go of it.

Father Lamormaini was not the only person who insisted on speaking to Ferdinand II.

"He is too ill," Empress Eleonora said. "Can't you let him die in peace?"

"I don't *want* to pressure him, Mama," Ferdinand III said, "but there are some things that I simply have to try to persuade him to do before he dies. Things that *only* the Holy Roman Emperor can do. He will understand that. He has never flinched from doing what he saw as his duty. He will not expect me to flinch from doing what I see as mine."

"Can't these things wait until you succeed him?"

"I will be able to take whatever steps are needed—well, whatever needed steps are politically feasible—within the hereditary lands. With the cooperation of Leopold Wilhelm, which I have. We don't have to bother Papa about Austria or Hungary. However, Papa signed the Edict of Restitution. I will probably never be elected emperor, since the electors have not even consented to designate me as King of the Romans. I can't revoke the edict. Only Papa can revoke it."

"At least," the empress said, "take it to the privy council first."

✧   ✧   ✧

His own impassioned opposition, Lamormaini reported to Vitelleschi, had been futile. The privy council consented to having Ferdinand III take the matter to the emperor. He himself was still not permitted to speak with the emperor privately. He hoped that the father-general would not interpret the tone of his report as an embittered complaint. He had been excluded from the meeting at which the heir presented his wishes to the emperor and the emperor had signed. Reluctantly, he heard, very reluctantly, but he had signed. He had consented to the loss of the church lands taken by the Protestants since the Peace of Augsburg in 1555, revoking the Edict of Restitution, after all the effort that Lamormaini had made to get him to issue the edict in the first place. The heretics would shortly be dancing with glee.

But, Lamormaini wrote, the next was almost worse. Ferdinand had requested that his father revoke the 1628 grant of the Palatine electoral vote to Duke Maximilian of Bavaria. In part, at least, on the grounds that Duke Maximilian was now clearly insane. His informants told him that Ferdinand had been so ill-advised as to tell his father that, perhaps, Archduchess Maria Anna's flight from Munich might have been the result of her realizing that she was about to marry a madman. But that had been only in passing. Mainly, Ferdinand had argued that the other electors had opposed the grant in the first place, that the grant had caused the emperor considerable political difficulty when it occurred, and that this was an opportune time to redeem a mistake.

At least, Lamormaini continued as he moved to the thirty-seventh page of his report, although Ferdinand II had agreed to revoke the grant to Duke Maximilian, he had at least refused to restore the vote to the young Count Palatine Karl Ludwig. That would have given the Protestants an additional vote. Rather, he had placed it in abeyance until the young elector came to his majority, to be restored to him on condition that at that time he freely and voluntarily embraced the Catholic faith. And, at the same time, the emperor had placed the Bohemian electoral vote in abeyance, thus depriving the current so-called king of Bohemia of the right to vote in any future election to choose a successor as Holy Roman Emperor, however unlikely such a vote might be. So he had reduced the theoretical number of electors to five, the three Catholic ecclesiastical principalities and two Protestant secular principalities.

Additionally, Father Lamormaini wrote, closing the relation with his most bitter grievance of the day, the empress and the other children had persuaded the emperor to dictate and sign a letter to his ungrateful and insubordinate daughter Archduchess Maria Anna, saying that he still loved her. He had that information directly from the emperor's private secretary, who had been called in to prepare the letter.

Only after all that was done had they permitted Father Lamormaini to confess the emperor and administer the last rites. He had been inclined to refuse absolution, on grounds that the emperor had not expressed penitence for his most recent actions and had refused to invalidate them. However, the king of Hungary had threatened that if he did not absolve the emperor, then Queen Mariana's confessor, the Spaniard Quiroga, would do so.

Rather than permit a Capuchin to have the honor of administering the emperor's last rites, Lamormaini stated, he had granted the absolution.

"That completes the arrangements for the state funeral," the *Hofmeister* said. "The emperor himself particularly requested the performance of the *Te Deum* as set to the music of Franz Josef Haydn's *Austria*."

Empress Eleonora inclined her head graciously. "Everyone has been most kind and helpful," she replied. "Please let our thanks be conveyed to Nuncio Carafa for all of his assistance."

"Yes," Ferdinand III said, "let our most sincere thanks be conveyed to you, and to all of the members of the *Hofstaat* as well. Let the plans that you have prepared be carried out." The *Hofmeister* bowed.

Ferdinand III continued. "Also, let a supper be prepared for the members of the family in the empress' private apartments tonight. Let the guards know that those whom I have summoned, who will appear separately, each carrying a note written in my own hand, are to be admitted after we have eaten. The *Hofmeister* has permission to leave our presence."

"In the midst of death," Archduke and Prince-Bishop Leopold Wilhelm said, "we are in life."

"Isn't that backwards?" his sister Cecelia Renata asked him.

"Not if I understand this evening's agenda properly," he answered.

"Ferdinand and Mariana have had their heads together ever since he got back from the Hungarian border. Who is finishing the inspection for him, anyway?"

"The younger landgrave of Leuchtenberg. Rudolf Philipp, his name is. Papa was lucky to get him onto our staff and Ferdinand has really enjoyed working with him. Everyone says that he's a lot brighter than his older brother, the one in Bavarian service."

She blinked. "Papa . . ." Cecelia Renata faltered.

Her little brother, now taller than she was, put his arm around her shoulder. "Hold up a bit longer, Sissy," he said. "You can cry for Papa after we get through the funeral."

First things first. The men whom he had invited were all those who long been of his own party, the "peace party," in the Austrian privy council. They would now become his most important advisers. Outside, of course, of the family. That was why they were here.

"I intend," he said, "to take the style of Ferdinand III, even if I am never elected as Holy Roman Emperor. I am already king of Hungary, and am the third Habsburg named Ferdinand to be king of Hungary. It will cause far less confusion than if I choose some other style. It will do."

They agreed.

"I intend to publish, at once, the draft peace proposal that we have discussed for so long, even though I am not emperor and there is no *Reichstag* in session to which I can present it. I certainly will not present it to the Swedish upstart's parliament, but if we simply circulate it under our signatures, it will function as a counterpoise to any sweeping proposal that Gustav Adolf may make for the Germanies. Nothing ventured, nothing gained."

"Open to all of the Germanies?" Leopold Wilhelm asked.

"Yes."

"Including the Calvinists?"

"Yes."

"Including the, ah, up-timers?"

"Yes."

"Wallenstein?"

"Wallenstein," Ferdinand III said, "is not in the Germanies. The proposed treaty will not be open to the usurper who is now calling himself the king of Bohemia. Let us first try to obtain a settlement in the Germanies. If we achieve that basic goal, then we can worry about handling the empire's peripheral territories."

"Peripheral?"

"The Swiss, of course," Leopold Wilhelm said. "That is one running sore that finally needs to be cauterized."

"And," Empress Eleonora added, "the Spanish Netherlands as well as Bohemia."

With Ferdinand III's advisers gone, only the family was left. A servant quietly brought in several dishes of sugared almonds, then withdrew. Leopold Wilhelm spoke quietly to the guards and pulled the door to Empress Eleonora's private sitting room shut.

"What else do we have to talk about?" Archduchess Cecelia Renata asked.

"Maria Anna," her sister-in-law answered. "Which means, according to what Carafa has told us about the petition to Rome for multiple dispensations, my honored brother Don Fernando. Which leads us to my brother in Spain, which leads us back to Duke Bernhard of Saxe-Weimar, who has perched himself across the Spanish road to the Netherlands."

"Not to mention," Leopold Wilhelm grimaced, "that he has seized half of the Habsburg holdings in Swabia, as well."

"That's more Duchess Claudia's immediate problem, since they have been allotted to our cousins in Tyrol for a long time."

"Habsburg problems," Ferdinand III said, "are Habsburg problems. Family is family. There is something that we may be able to do to assist Claudia in regard to Duke Bernhard, depending on whether we are willing to use the prince-bishop of Speyer as a pawn in negotiations. Given that Sötern's subjects are revolting against him because of his pro-French policy and the Swede has occupied his lands on the right bank of the Rhine, we should keep it under consideration, since Speyer is certainly in Duke Bernhard's area of interest. An imperial garrison in left-Rhine Speyer would be very useful."

"Since the duchies of Luxemburg will be part of Don Fernando's new 'kingdom in the Netherlands,'" Empress Eleonora said slowly, "then he will be in the position of a natural protector of the prince-bishop of Trier, as well."

"And that is Sötern, too," Leopold Wilhelm interrupted. "He holds Trier as well as Speyer. He is in no position to resist pressure brought to bear on either of his dioceses. An imperial garrison in Trier would be a good thing. According to the up-time *encyclopedias* that I have studied, we took Sötern prisoner in 1635 and locked him up for more than a decade. Perhaps we could bring that to his attention."

"Why stop at Trier?" Empress Eleonora asked. "The French have occupied the dioceses of Metz, Toul, and Verdun, as well, for three-quarters of a century. It seems to me far more appropriate, when I look at the map, that they should be regarded as Habsburg protectorates. If Don Fernando can manage it, of course."

"Those are properly Lorraine. Should we ally with Lorraine?" Cecelia Renata asked. "Should we try to take advantage of the fact that the Swede has crushed the French to restore Duke Charles, since it was the French who forced him out?"

"If we ally with Lorraine . . ." Ferdinand III paused. "Duke Maximilian borrowed Lorraine's general, the one he is so angry with for the fall of Ingolstadt. Duke Charles is not happy with the way that Maximilian has treated Mercy, whereas we have taken him into our employment. There are possibilities there."

"I don't suppose there's anything to be done about Cologne right now," Leopold Wilhelm said.

Empress Eleonora shook her head. "The *encyclopedias* say that Archbishop Ferdinand did not die, will not die, until 1650, so there does not appear to be any immediate possibility of reducing the Bavarian foothold there. However, if Maximilian's power and influence continue to be greatly reduced, then at the next election there may not be a Bavarian successor."

"So one Catholic elector is definitely pro-Bavarian," Cecelia Renata said. "But Archbishop Anselm Casimir of Mainz is not, and he has thus far managed to elude falling into the Swede's hands as well. If we and Don Fernando can influence Trier, then the two Protestant electors, Saxony and Brandenburg, have no love of Gustav Adolf. Four votes of five, the way Papa set it up. Four votes of seven, even if Bohemia and the Palatinate cast ballots and insist that they are valid. Brother, dear, it may still be possible for us to get you elected as the Holy Roman Emperor Ferdinand III. It certainly couldn't hurt to try."

Ferdinand looked at the younger of his two sisters. "Sissy, have you read about your marriage in the other universe?" he asked abruptly.

She nodded solemnly. "I married the king of Poland. A practical match, of course. The *encyclopedias* say that it was a disastrously unhappy marriage. They do not say why, but apparently it was so unhappy that people remembered the fact for three hundred and fifty years."

Her eyes filled briefly with tears. "I won't complain. I know my duty. But Papa was always so *nice* to our mother, and to Mama." She jumped up and gave the empress a kiss. "And you and Mariana like each other."

"Actually," Mariana said, "I love him quite dearly."

"I think," Ferdinand III said firmly, "that in this universe we can rule the king of Poland out, Sissy. I'll think of some other way to handle Wladyslaw. That doesn't mean, of course, that any other marriage we find for you would necessarily be happier. But as I think about it, there is a place where you might be very helpful."

Cecelia Renata raised her eyebrows.

"Duke Bernhard of Saxe-Weimar is now sitting directly on top of the Spanish Road. If he manages to hold that territory, then some time in the next two or three years, a marriage alliance might appear to be prudent. Not to mention helpful to Duchess Claudia in regard to the Swabian possessions."

"If you were prepared to deal with being married to a heretic," Leopold Wilhelm said. Being a bishop, however unwillingly, he did feel obliged to bring the matter up.

"Of course," Ferdinand III said to his younger sister, "Bernhard is not a king. He is only a duke, and a younger son, if that matters to you."

Cecelia Renata rested her left elbow on the polished table; then rested her chin on the palm of her hand. "The Bavarian was a duke and Papa betrothed Maria Anna to him," she said placidly. Then she gave him a wicked grin. "Nor, for that matter, was our honored cousin Fernando a king. Not until last month, that is."

Ferdinand III opened his mouth; then closed it again. "It's a fascinating possibility," he said. "If, of course, Hungary and the Turks do not demand all of our resources. The Ottomans can never be far from Austria's mind. If Austria falls, then Europe falls."

CHAPTER 65

Tu, Felix Austria, Nube

Magdeburg

Mike Stearns looked up in response to the knock on his office door. People rarely interrupted when Don Francisco was briefing him.

"It's Ed," Claire Hudson said. "Finally."

"Well, just send him on in. What happened?"

"Track delays." Ed Piazza sat down in the softest available chair. "Those benches in the cars are really hell on a middle-aged rear end when there's a rough ride. Five hours of track delays. Can't you do something to make the trains run on time?"

"If I could, I would. 'What's the news of the day, good neighbor, I pray?'"

"No balloons up to the moon. At least not yet, but if we don't get a handle on these lighter-than-air enthusiasts, I wouldn't be surprised. Actually, I have the latest installment in the Gospel According to Annalise—and her cousin Dorothea."

"So?"

"The Richters are spreading out. One of Ronnie Dreeson's step-daughters married a Nürnberger as her second husband, so she isn't leaving. Two of them and their husbands are going back to Grafenwöhr to handle the Richter property up that way. Brechbuhl is staying in Amberg and bringing his children back. Rastetter bought out Arndt's old practice and can use a partner. Brechbuhl can make a much better career there than he'll be allowed to by the Lutherans in Nürnberg, now that Duke Ernst has officially promulgated the religious toleration policy."

"Any specifics on that?"

"Full public toleration for Lutherans, Calvinists, and Catholics, with the Lutherans as 'first among equals,' more or less. Tacit toleration for everything from Jews and Anabaptists to Socinians, Moravian Brethren, and Mormons, on the presumption that they don't make waves or do the ecclesiastical equivalent of yelling 'fire' in a crowded theater."

"Which concurs with the reports that I've received. I don't have a copy of the document itself, yet, but that pretty well covers the situation in the Upper Palatinate, as far as I've heard from Jake Ebeling, too. With the wrap-up at Ingolstadt, since things are still quiet with Wallenstein, Duke Ernst can focus on administration, which is what he does best." Francisco Nasi folded his hands.

"It won't last," Ed Piazza predicted. "Once Wettin becomes prime minister, he'll pull Ernst out of the boondocks and make him Secretary of Education for the USE. He'll want him in Magdeburg, not Amberg."

"The USE doesn't have a Department of Education. Just to be practical," Mike said.

Ed shook his head. "It will under a Wettin administration. If only because Ernst is Wilhelm Wettin's brother. Ernst will do for the USE what Wolfgang Ratichius is doing for the SoTF—take the best of down-time reform ideas and combine them with certain elements of what Grantville brought along. Not with everything that Grantville brought along, by any means. I just don't see that the balance between church-sponsored schools and secular public schools is going to tip any time soon. Not even in the SoTF and Magdeburg Province. 'Soon' meaning 'in my lifetime.' Ernst won't want it to, any more than Wolfgang does. Gustav certainly won't be leading any crusade for replacing Lutheran schools with nondenominational ones. In any case, nobody has the money to scrap the existing system and start over. The way I see it, the secular public schools will be a supplement, giving educational opportunities to kids who don't fit the Lutheran or Catholic—or Calvinist—molds."

Mike grimaced with disgust. No matter how, well, *unfeasible* it was, he would rather see the old USA model exported to the entire continent of Europe, "given his druthers," as his grandma would have said. "Will he move the normal school to Magdeburg, then?"

Ed shook his head. "Not with the sweetheart deal it has in Amberg. It isn't an *either-or* situation. He'll see to it that there's funding for another one here. There's plenty of demand and teacher education isn't all that expensive. It's not all that glamorous, either, but it sure is cheap compared to engineering or medicine. And we all know that Gustav is going to spring for Imperial Colleges for those in Magdeburg."

"Duke Ernst can clone the normal school. Can he clone those two boys? It's pretty sure that *either* Maximilian's nephews stay in Amberg *or* Gustav decides to move them somewhere else. Somewhere farther from Bavaria and Bohemia." Nasi reached up and pushed his new reading glasses up his nose. Four years of serious, practically nonstop, reading of mostly handwritten reports and relations had taken their toll on his eyes.

"You need to get those frames fitted better the next time you get down to Grantville," Ed said absently. "Have your secretary make an appointment with McNally."

"About the young dukes of Bavaria," Nasi said. He was not about to be distracted.

"I think the USE should leave them where they are for the time being." Ed glared at Mike, even though it was Francisco who had spoken. "They've been through enough, losing their mother and their home. Being separated from their father. I wouldn't recommend taking them away from a tutor they like and from a school where they're just starting to settle in—not at all. They're not just pawns on someone's political chessboard, you know. They're two boys. Real, live, people. Young Maximilian will be thirteen in October. Sigmund just turned eleven. Kids, still."

"Sometimes, the fact that you've spent most of your life as a professional educator just shines through."

"Can't help it, Mike. I did. That's what I *am*. Time enough to move them if you see some kind of a real threat. Right now, I don't see that Duke Maximilian is in a position to do anything serious. Any major effort would take money and their father is living on Wallenstein's charity. Leave them alone."

"I'd be happier if they were someplace more central. Like Magdeburg."

"If Wettin's smart, and he is, he's having Ernst make friends with them—between now and when the new administration comes in. Figuring the election and the transfer-of-power protocol we've written into the new constitution, that's eight or nine months. Ernst can bring them, and Vervaux, to Magdeburg when he moves. Which makes me hope that by then Larry Mazzare has a Jesuit collegium here to receive them."

"Not a bad solution. Just as long as Duke Ernst can keep them safe between now and then."

"He can. As well as anyone can. I've watched him in action, probably more closely than you've had time to. And I've talked to Duke Johann Philipp about his future son-in-law. Don't underestimate him."

"So much for the Upper Palatinate, from personal soap opera to high policy, then." Mike dismissed one concern.

Turning to Nasi, he raised the next one. "What do you think Austria is going to be doing?"

"Thinking about what princesses they have available to marry to those two Bavarian boys in a decade or so."

"God, Francisco. They're just kids." Mike winced at his involuntary echo of Ed's argument.

"You know the proverb. 'Let others wage war; you, happy Austria, wage marriage.' I don't think that Ferdinand III will want to hold his other sister off the marriage market for several more years just to make a Bavarian marriage—especially since there's a lot less of Bavaria now than there was five years ago. The daughters of Claudia de Medici, the archduchesses of Austria-Tyrol, are just about the right age and background to pair up with them. They aren't very closely related, either, the way the upper nobility sees these things. For that matter, the way my own people see these things."

Mike frowned.

"Not everyone is 'into' this maddening American preference for exogamy," Francisco said mildly.

"Do you really think that Gustav will let those boys go back and rule Bavaria?" Ed asked.

"The hereditary principle is still very strong. It's the best solution—once they've been given a reasonable education and character formation on the USE model."

"What about Wallenstein's girl?"

Don Francisco raised his eyebrows above the top rim of his glasses.

Ed looked at him. "Well, now that his wife is pregnant again—if the child is a boy and survives, his daughter becomes not the heiress of Bohemia but just an incredibly wealthy and influential bride-to-be. And Catholic. Why wouldn't she make a decent wife for one of the Bavarian boys?"

"She could. She might. It would depend on how firmly Wallenstein keeps control. We should factor her in as a variable, though. Maybe one of the Bavarian boys with an Austrian wife; the other with a Bohemian. That would leave the Austrians with Claudia de Medici's youngest girl still to put into play. . . ."

"Will Tyrol fall in with Vienna's plans, or go its own way? Given the actions of Duchess Claudia in connection with Kronach—and now she's sent those three doctors of hers off to Bernhard of Saxe-Weimar."

Nasi steepled his fingers. "There just aren't that many different eligible Catholic possibilities." He thought a minute. "It's my guess that Ferdinand III will pull his brother out of the church and marry him off. I've heard rumors that the up-time history books have put an end to the proposed Polish match for Archduchess Cecelia Renata. They'll still want to maintain the dynastic ties with Poland, though, so it would be only logical to marry Leopold Wilhelm to Wladyslaw's half-sister."

"Konstanzia Vasa? I'm always a little disconcerted, still, when I have to think of Polish Catholic Vasas. I've gotten the notion of Swedish Lutheran Vasas so firmly in my head. Not to mention that I have to deal with the Swedish Lutheran ones on a daily basis." Mike grinned. "Even though the emperor's ambition is basically limitless, I have a problem with 'Gustavus Adolphus, King of Poland and Defender of the Catholic Faith.' It just doesn't ring right. Not that Gustav would draw the line at swallowing up the Polish-Lithuanian Commonwealth, if he could manage it."

"If Wladyslaw manages to hang on, it's not likely to happen. Rest your mind," Nasi advised. "But I do think that Vienna is going to want a Polish marriage, and that's the only one on the drawing boards at the moment. Which leaves Anna de Medici for Wladyslaw."

"And still leaves Ferdinand III with his second sister to dispose of—advantageously."

"Well, there is Don Carlos."

"Don Carlos is dead." Ed frowned. "I was in a play about it, once, in college. Schiller. In an English translation, of course. I played the evil Philip II. Our drama professor, who was directing it, said that the history in the play was really lousy. The real Don Carlos was a nut rather than a hero and the real Philip II did his country a favor by offing him before he could turn into a real-life mad king."

"Different Don Carlos," Nasi said. "This one is Philip IV's next younger brother, between him and Don Fernando—not his oldest uncle."

"Never heard of him."

"Philip III didn't put him into the church, the way he did Don Fernando. Kept him as the spare to the heir. He's the grand admiral of Spain. That's just a title, of course. I doubt that he's ever been to sea."

Piazza grinned. "Even if he is the 'ruler of the king's na-vee.'"

Nasi's eyebrows went up again.

"Gilbert and Sullivan. Next time you're in Grantville, I'll have Annabelle put some on the stereo. It's nineteenth-century English, though, so you'll probably miss a lot of the patter that makes the lyrics funny. Even most twentieth-century Americans couldn't follow it. People who put the plays on had to put explanations in the programs. But, anyway. To repeat myself. Never heard of him."

"That's probably because he's eminently forgettable. Or he was, in your world, since he would have died a couple of years ago without having done anything much. He's in his mid-twenties, now. Said to be pleasant. Amiable. Inoffensive. But there may be more to him than that, given how hostile Olivares is to his influence on his brother. Olivares keeps maneuvering to separate the two of them. Since he isn't dead, the king is bound to start maneuvering to marry him off."

Ed leaned back. "Why are you only suggesting Catholic marriages for the Austrians? And Wallenstein's girl?"

Nasi sputtered. "Well . . . um . . . because . . . champions of Catholicism and all that."

"The first time I met Cavriani, he told me that Lutherans are half-Catholic. So's the Church of England in a way, I suppose. They have bishops and all that, which is why the Puritans are so irritable most of the time. So—look at it this way. The grand dukes of Tuscany wouldn't have any interest in the Upper Palatinate, really. But given the geography, wouldn't Wallenstein be just as happy to see his little girl married to Karl Ludwig and safely installed next door in an Upper Palatinate that offers freedom of religion to Catholics? As happy as he would be to see her married to a second son in Bavaria, I mean. Maybe even happier to have her married to the heir rather than the spare, given how Mechthilde of Leuchtenberg ended up this summer. It might upset the Calvinists, but the Catholics there would be glad enough to see her coming, I should think."

Mike shook his head. "Rebecca doesn't foresee any developments along those lines, any more than Francisco does. Maybe Wallenstein might consider it—he was born a Protestant, of course. But not the Austrians."

"The Winter King had thirteen children. Ten of them are still alive. Throw them into the equation and everything changes." Ed smiled. "Give copies of a children's biography of Rupert of the Rhine to some little princesses and watch them start to sigh. They're about the right ages to marry Claudia de Medici's children, too, without stretching it to the ridiculous age differences that some royal matches have had."

"What about Duchess Claudia herself? And her sister?" Mike asked.

"The sister's dead, according to the latest dispatches from Tuscany. Which everyone more or less expected—she's been an invalid for years. Everybody expected her to croak when she got sick last December." Nasi was clearly proud of his mastery of that idiom. "Claudia, though . . ." He paused.

"Thirty years old. Redhead. Good looking. Six children from two marriages, and five of them alive and healthy. That's pretty much what you could call a proven track record in this day and age. Odd that Don Fernando didn't snap her up when he had a chance." Mike looked thoughtful.

"Someone will. You can bank on that."

"If she were willing to marry a Protestant . . . What would be her bottom line?" Ed asked.

"Duchess Claudia's bottom line is the bottom line in Bozen's account books. She's a descendant of the grand dukes of Tuscany, but never forget that the Medici were bankers long before they were princes."

"Who's available? Fredrik of Denmark, but he's definitely second-string now that Ulrik is betrothed to Princess Kristina. Charles I in England, since Henrietta Maria's death. Umm . . . Wladyslaw, if he doesn't go for her niece Anna?"

"Duke Bernhard."

All three of them laughed.

"At least we don't have to worry about Lorraine," Mike inserted. "What a bunch of flakes. Chaos-creators. What's it called? Forces for entropy? But unless someone's spouse dies, they're like the French. Out of the running until they produce a new generation."

"And in this world, Monsieur Gaston hasn't waited for permission from his big brother and Richelieu to start sleeping with his Lorrainer wife. The newspapers say that she's pregnant. Ye gods, it's a damned epidemic." Ed looked at Mike. "How's Becky feeling, by the way?"

Madrid

"King in the Low Countries," Philip IV of Spain said, his voice tight with anger. "Just what does he mean by 'king in the Low Countries.'"

"I believe, Your Majesty," Count Duke Olivares said, "if I read the communication from Cardinal Bedmar correctly, that by being king 'in' the Netherlands, he claims that precedence only when he is within his own territories, and when foreign monarchs call upon him there. If, however, it should chance that he had some reason to make a state visit to Spain, he would come as an infante of Spain and Your Majesty's younger brother. It is a fine distinction, perhaps."

"Fine or not, it is a declaration of independence."

"*De facto*, yes. But not quite *de jure*. Considering that, officially, the Spanish Netherlands are still governed by your aunt. The situation may well change upon the death of *Infanta* Isabella Clara Eugenia."

"Why," Philip IV demanded, "did Urban VIII grant the dispensations?"

"Because our envoys were not able to prevent it," Olivares said frankly. "Nor did we have military forces close enough to Rome to send them there promptly enough to persuade the pope that his decision was not at all wise."

"We will remember his action."

"Yes, Your Majesty. That is a given."

"Ecclesiastically, you say, the dispensations are impeccable?"

"I am quite persuaded that Urban set the very best of his canon lawyers to studying the matter," Olivares answered.

"Fernando's children then, by Maria Anna, will be impeccably legitimate, from a dynastic point of view?"

"It would be almost impossible to get any other interpretation of the situation accepted. Barring, of course, denying the legitimacy of Urban VIII's election as pope." Olivares paused. "Nor am I sure that, in the long run, it would be to the interest of the House of Habsburg to make the attempt."

The king looked at him.

"I have provided you with the information, Your Majesty. In that other world, the queen died ten years from now. Your subsequent children by her, born in those ten years, were girls—although that is not to say that this will be the same in our new future. Still, we cannot rely fully on the hope of additional sons. Don Balthasar Carlos died, two years after her death. You remarried. The son born to your second marriage was incompetent to rule, incapable of begetting children. And Spain fell to the Bourbons."

"France." Philip IV looked at his chief minister. "Anything but France, Gaspar. Anything but France. And Balthasar Carlos, according to the information you have brought me, died of smallpox. Introduce these up-time measures against smallpox into Spain. Now. We have a dozen years to ensure that, by the mercy of the holy mother, her son, and all of the saints, Balthasar Carlos does not die."

"Yes, Your Majesty."

"And there is still my brother Carlos. The grand admiral still stands as a buffer between Fernando's offspring and Spain. We should be grateful for the arrival of Grantville, I suppose, since the political complications prevented our planned trip to Barcelona. It was in Catalonia that he contracted typhus, even though he died after our return to Madrid. Damned Catalans. Too many forget Carlos."

Olivares tightened his lips. He and the king's next younger brother, second in line for the throne after the little prince Balthasar Carlos, were political opponents. He needed to say something neutral. Inoffensive. Philip IV had grown up with his younger brothers as his primary companions. They had studied together.

Hunted together. There was a—camaraderie—there, with both of them, that he found difficult to overcome. "In that other world, Your Majesty, Don Carlos died young. Two years ago, of typhus. Not quite twenty-five years old. The authors of the encyclopedias in Grantville appear, almost, to have forgotten him."

"This world, perhaps, will remember him better." The king of Spain rose from his chair, smiling thinly. "In any case, Gaspar, whatever your personal opinions, we must thank God that he is still alive and begin serious negotiations for his marriage. Under the circumstances, our cousin Cecelia Renata would be the best choice. However, there are others. Wladyslaw's half-sister in Poland. Anna de Medici. Let one of the court painters begin the process of obtaining portraits."

Olivares nodded. "Velasquez would be the best choice. Since we have learned that Rubens undertook this office for the 'king in the Netherlands,' it would be disadvantageous to Spain's royal prestige not to utilize a Spanish artist with equivalent prestige to undertake the preliminary contacts. Not that we can disguise the purpose of his efforts for long, in any case."

"Let it be Velasquez, then. In the interval, in regard to my youngest brother, it is clearly too late for us to enforce my father's will. If Fernando will not become a priest to say masses for the soul of Philip III, then at least let him breed Spain heirs that are Habsburg rather than French. But we will deal with Urban VIII, who permitted this while he had broken off diplomatic relations with us, supposedly over the problems in Naples. Had intentionally broken them off, I am sure, to enable him to permit this. If, in fact, he did not instigate it."

Rome

"I am not sure," Urban VIII said, "that I care for radio as a means of communication. Every morning, every evening. These messages are like having a drummer constantly beating a rhythm in one's bedchamber. The worst is that the operators acknowledge to one another that they have received the messages as well as sent them. Which means, of course, that one cannot pretend, when convenient, that a letter must have been delayed in the mail."

"What is the decision of the canon lawyers?" Cardinal Francesco

Barberini asked. "Are these messages valid dispensations, or must Don Fernando and Archduchess Maria Anna wait for paper copies?"

"I sign the dispensations," the pope answered wryly, "*before* the radio operators send their versions bounding and bouncing through the air. The question, therefore, does not come up. Naturally, we will forward the signed paper copies, but the signature becomes valid when I place it on the document—not when the document arrives at its destination."

"Naturally," Cardinal Francesco admitted.

Father-General Vitelleschi said. "Cardinal Mazzare tells me that up-time it was literally possible to have this radio beating a rhythm all the time. Father Kircher has confirmed this. A town did not just have one receiver, as the up-timers do here. Every carriage, every home, had these receivers. The broadcasters, if they had nothing significant to say, played music. Bad music often, and very loudly."

"Whether you wanted it or not?" Cardinal Antonio Barberini the younger asked.

"It was possible to 'turn it off,'" Vitelleschi answered. "I am sure that I shall shortly understand it all better, when we open our own broadcasting station. Almost, I am tempted to travel to Germany, just to listen to it. Or, perhaps, if we are successful with Loyola University of the North and its radio, we could build one here in Rome."

Urban VIII blanched.

"Or possibly, just outside the borders of Venice. It might be quite useful in explaining to the republic's citizens that their rulers do not tell them 'the truth, the whole truth, and nothing but the truth.'"

"Surely," Father Vitelleschi persisted, "we will want more than one."

"Speaking of the mail," Cardinal Antonio Barberini the elder interposed, "I have received a very outraged letter from *Dekan* Golla in Munich. He informs us that Archduchess Maria Anna definitely did not leave the golden rose behind in her oratory when she left the Munich *Residenz*. He demands that the holy father write her and insist upon its return."

"On the theory that marriage to Don Fernando is likely to be considerably more of a pleasure for her than marriage to Duke Maximilian?" Cardinal Antonio the younger asked. "Fernando is actually not bad looking. Certainly less prunelike."

Vitelleschi looked at him.

He looked down.

"The rose was bestowed," Urban VIII said, "for extraordinary services to the church. Perhaps we should bide our time in the matter. If, of course, it has not simply been lost. Or stolen and melted down."

❖ CHAPTER 66 ❖

Facinus Magnum Ac Memorabile

Headquarters of Fernando, King in the Low Countries, outside Amsterdam

Don Fernando's entire privy council had spent the previous evening discussing the question that Maria Anna had sent from Basel. Should she try to escape again? If so, which way should she go?

"We have to get one of the radios in Brussels." His Majesty, still ordinarily addressed as Your Highness or simply as Don Fernando by his staff, got up from the table. "The one the up-timers placed in Antwerp is useful for the Wisselbank, of course, but Antwerp is not my capital. I feel as pinned to this camp by Fredrik Hendrik's radio as a butterfly must feel pinned to a display board in a cabinet of natural curiosities. I should go back to Brussels. For work, to Tante Isabella Clara Eugenia. Yet I remain here, waiting for the latest message that they deign to share with me. I can't bear to be a hundred twenty miles away from their radio. My secretary must talk to the Jesuits at Loyola University of the North as soon as possible."

"The up-time words," Cardinal Bedmar said, "are 'information junkie.'"

Don Fernando scowled at him. "Where is everybody else?" he asked.

"You're early."

"When I arrive, it's time to start."

"Your Highness, you are pacing."

"Well, of course I am pacing. I have made a decision and I need to tell them about it."

Eventually the remainder of his council made their way into the conference room. Don Fernando took his seat at the head of the table, looked at them, and asked a question. "What was the deciding event in the rise of the Habsburg dynasty?"

"Your Highness?" Rubens said.

"When you look at our history, what one event turned a family of minor south German and Austrian nobility into a dynasty that ruled much of the continent of Europe? What captured people's imagination?"

"Emperor Maximilian's ride?" suggested his military adviser tentatively.

"Very good, Miguel," Don Fernando answered. "A hundred fifty years ago. Now, where did Maximilian ride, and why?"

The one woman in the council answered immediately. "Across the continent, from Austria to the Netherlands, to save his fiancée, Mary of Burgundy, from being forced to marry the heir to the French throne," said Doña Mencia.

Don Fernando smiled at her. "I knew it was a good idea to add a female mind to this group."

"If you will pardon me, Your Highness," said her brother, Cardinal Bedmar, "I do not believe that I care for the direction in which this discussion is moving."

"I know that I do not," said Miguel de Manrique.

Don Fernando ignored them. "Now," he gestured dramatically, "at another crucial juncture for our dynasty, I face a problem similar to that of my great-great-great grandfather."

"Is that the right number of greats?" the secretary muttered under his breath as he took notes.

Rubens glared at him but Don Fernando seemed merely amused. "Of course it's the right number of greats." The young Habsburg prince waved his hand. "If there is anything our tutors insist that we learn, it is the family's genealogy."

"Very well. Three greats."

Rubens cleared his throat. "To get back to the point. Archduchess Maria Anna is besieged in Basel."

"Not," Miguel de Manrique muttered, "by the French."

Don Fernando waved his hand again. "A mere bagatelle. She would probably be besieged by the French if it were not for the fact that the king of Sweden has Louis XIII's few remaining forces fully occupied. In any case, being besieged by Bernhard of Saxe-Weimar, even if he is no longer in French employ, is an adequate substitute. In no way will I let him get custody of her. Therefore, obviously, a mad romantic dash to save my bride is clearly in order."

Don Fernando's military adviser buried his face in his hands, moaning dramatically.

"That will take quite a while," Cardinal Bedmar pointed out. "It is over four hundred miles."

"Not to mention a few problems in the way," added Rubens. "From a military standpoint, that is—not just pure transportation."

Don Fernando ignored that also. "Time is of the essence," he proclaimed. "My plans will be turned upside down if either Duke Bernhard or the Basel city council get their paws on my bride. In Bernhard's case, unfortunately, that might be a quite literal description of the outcome and the political complications would be really distressing."

"You cannot just wave your hand and make the either the distance or the problems go away, Your Majesty."

"No," Don Fernando said. He beamed at them. "However, the solution came to me while I slept."

"Whatever it is—" the cardinal began. He had become all too familiar with his ruler's moments of inspiration. "—it is too risky."

"Now there's a comprehensive warning," Don Fernando said. "However, now that we have a treaty with the Swede . . ."

"Yes, he may give us free passage through Mainz and the Palatinate, through the parts of the Rhine that he holds," Miguel responded. "But that still does not mean that we can move enough men, fast enough, to dislodge Bernhard from the position his army has taken up north of the Swiss border. Not even if we could afford to remove them from the Netherlands for that long."

"No, no," Don Fernando said airily. "That is not the plan."

The military adviser was beginning to get that sinking feeling in his stomach that came all too often when he dealt with his commander-in-chief.

"I shall speak to Fredrik Hendrik today," Don Fernando said, "and see if he can arrange for us to borrow one of the marvelous airplanes. And a pilot, of course. Then I shall simply fly over the heads of all these obstacles, save Maria Anna from the bunch of villainous dastards, bring her back her to the Netherlands, and once again capture the imagination of all Europe. Just think of the songs. The poems. The Harlequin Romances."

"Oh," Rubens said. "Dear God, no!"

"Oh," Don Fernando answered. "Oh, yes."

Amsterdam

"If he marries an Austrian Habsburg archduchess," Rebecca said, "the *bona fides* of what amounts to the new dynasty he will create will be impeccable. And if he rescues her from the clutches of Bernhard of Saxe-Weimar, even the Habsburgs will have a face-saving way to agree to it. I certainly cannot imagine that the Habsburgs would ever consider accepting the marriage of one of their archduchesses to a heretic upstart—which, in their view, Bernhard most certainly is."

"If he goes off to rescue her, it certainly would be cutting the Gordian knot for him," Mike mused.

"No. He cut the knot when he signed the treaty. But he has to make it work. It is this planned marriage that really makes the treaty and the new title of 'king in the Low Countries' feasible for him. Without it, his brother is almost certain to offer far more strenuous opposition. And with Maria Anna as his wife, he can perhaps tell his Austrian Habsburg relatives to 'take a hike,' too. The Austrians can't do anything about it. The Spanish Habsburgs don't begin to have the military strength to *force* Don Fernando to do anything, any more. They cannot dictate to him. But if he marries Maria Anna, they can all pretend that they don't need to."

"Which brings us back," Fredrik Hendrik said, "to this astounding request. Will Gustav Adolf agree?"

Mike smiled. "Actually, I think he'll be quite charmed by the idea. And even if he isn't, I am well-nigh certain that King Christian would be."

Everyone stared at him. Mike's smile became positively seraphic. "The constitutional situation with the new Union of Kalmar is still vague, in many respects, but one thing is definitely established—Denmark's military remains under the direct control of Denmark's king, not the High King of Kalmar. And King Christian has insisted on establishing, formally, his own Danish air force. To be sure, it's an air force with neither planes nor pilots."

"But—" Rebecca said. Mike continued right on.

"*But*—you were there, yourself, sweetheart, when they cut the deal—it was agreed that until such time as Denmark could develop its own air force, the High King of Kalmar would place one of the USE's planes, with a trained pilot, at the disposal of the king of Denmark. Should he happen to need it. And Christian immediately took advantage of the offer, just so he and his future daughter-in-law could have joy rides, if nothing else. One of the Gustavs has been stationed at the airfield outside of Copenhagen ever since, with a pilot always present. Jesse Wood still hasn't stopped grousing about the waste of precious resources."

"But . . ." said Fredrik Hendrik.

Mike shrugged. "Look, folks. Everybody including Christian IV understands that this is mostly a face-saving measure, and that if he were to try to use his official power against any real military interest of Gustav Adolf, there'd be all hell to pay. But Christian could certainly argue that this was no military matter at all, simply one monarch doing a favor for another in a purely personal matter."

Rebecca, normally quite imperturbable, practically spluttered. "Purely 'personal' matter! We are talking about the formation of a new European dynasty, Michael!"

"Sure. So what? All that matters is that Christian *would* have a formal excuse—and both he and Gustav Adolf would know perfectly well that what's really involved is an arm-wrestling match to see exactly where the power of Denmark ends and the power of the Union of Kalmar begins."

Rebecca sat back in her chair, her expression clearing. "Oh. I see."

A moment later, Fredrik Hendrik leaned back also, adding a little laugh into the bargain. "Michael, you are wasted on a republic. Machiavelli himself would say you are the perfect model of his prince."

Mike gave him a grin. "Oh, that's silly. I think republics provide much more of an interesting challenge, when it comes to political skullduggery." In a more serious tone, he added: "The point is, Gustav Adolf is no dumber than Christian IV. So I think he'll agree right off, if for no other reason than just to avoid the arm-wrestling match with the Danes."

After a moment, with his best *butter-wouldn't-melt-in-my-mouth* expression, Mike added, "Especially once I point out the danger to him."

The answer from Copenhagen came almost as instantly as Mike predicted.

Do it, said the message from Gustav Adolf. *Use Colonel Wood himself.*

The Spanish siege lines, outside Amsterdam

The negotiations involved a great deal of risk assessment. Not just the obvious risk that the plane might fall out of the air. Neither Don Fernando nor his advisers really minded that. He would not be in more danger of falling out of the air than he would be of dying in a military action on the ground. Those things were in the hands of God.

No. There were other risks. They had to negotiate the plane's point of departure and where it would arrive. Nobody mentioned the Saint Bartholomew's Day massacre out loud, but it was certainly at the back of almost everyone's mind. That, too, had involved a treaty, a wedding, Catholics and Calvinists. There were still those who called for revenge, a half-century later. Might the Dutch use this device to entice Don Fernando into their clutches? If he landed in the midst of General Horn's army, which would be necessary, would the Swede's men allow him to leave again? Would they wait until he rescued Maria Anna from Basel and then hold them both? Don Fernando's diplomats were nervous.

Except for Cardinal Bedmar. Since he realized, with some resignation, that his master was going to get into an airplane and fly off in the company of one of Gustav Adolf's pilots, he concentrated on making it happen. At least, the "Gustav" plane that the up-timers suggested could carry four persons, rather than only two. The pilot said that on the trip out, Don Fernando could be accompanied by two aides. Bodyguards, if one wanted to think of them that way, as long as they were fairly small ones. Bedmar was sitting in his chair studying a "cheat sheet" on cargo capacity.

Somebody started talking about a chaperone for the archduchess. Rebecca sighed, remembering that the men around Don Fernando were, after all, mostly from Spain rather than Holland or Germany, where women had so much more freedom of movement.

"You could," Mike said to Don Fernando, "rescue Mary Simpson and Veronica Dreeson at the same time. Since you're going to be in the neighborhood, so to speak. Mary Simpson could fly back with Maria Anna as duenna, since you seem to think it is necessary. She will be wanting to rejoin her husband, in any case, and he is working up at Harlingen, now. Not to mention, of course, that she is probably aching to visit the Netherlands and recruit a few artists. Vacuum up as many as she can, and at least meet the others, even if they don't agree to move to Magdeburg. She would give her eyeteeth to talk to Rembrandt, for example. Horn could arrange to get Ronnie back to Grantville."

Bedmar pursed his lips. Don Fernando had not cared for the aspect of the treaty that led to Simpson's presence in Harlingen. He was building a naval base there that would, in effect, allow the USE Navy to close off the Zuider Zee in the event of a renewal of hostilities. Gustav Adolf, of course, was in possession of the town—along with all three of the northernmost Dutch provinces, Friesland, Groningen, and Drenthe, as a result of his successful summer offensive. Possession was one thing. Legal acknowledgment of that possession in a treaty was something else. Don Fernando had not had to give up anything he held; indeed, not anything that he had ever held. Looked at one way, the treaty had simply formalized the situation—and the USE had actually returned most of the lands as a compensation. All they insisted on retaining was the town of Harlingen itself. But it always hurt a Habsburg to give up a land claim. Any land claim.

"I would like to remind you . . ."

Bedmar looked up from his "cheat sheet." That was the pilot speaking, Colonel Wood. He had been at Harlingen and had come down to Amsterdam in a truck. Bedmar had enjoyed inspecting the truck; it was not quite like the one that had brought his sister from Amberg to Brussels, but very interesting.

"I would like to remind you that the carrying capacity is limited.

We have agreed to your stipulation that His Majesty be accompanied by two military aides on the flight to Basel. However, if I have the archduchess and Mrs. Simpson in the plane on the return flight, that means that the aides will have to remain with General Horn and make their own way back to the Netherlands by more traditional means."

More technicalities followed.

"The landing field is easy," Colonel Wood said. "We can use the same one just outside the city that you built a few months ago, that I used to fly in our prime minister. We'll convoy the fuel in from Harlingen; there's a stockpile there now. Refuel at Mainz, both ways. The field there is reliable. And have somebody prepare a field at the other end. Which means on the German side of the border. I have a feeling that the city of Basel isn't going to lay out a landing strip for me. The land on that side of the river is pretty hilly, anyway."

Mike looked at Rebecca.

"I am sure," she said, "that Gustav Adolf will be willing to direct General Horn to move into place and prepare a landing field. Do you have a preference as to location, Colonel Wood?"

"He'll find a suitable spot somewhere near Rheinfelden. I'll give him the coordinates."

"How do you know?" Don Fernando asked.

"There was a huge air force base at Rheinfelden, up-time. I flew in and out of it more than once."

Swabia

"It is a direct order, General."

Gustav Horn looked at the message with distaste. "I know. Is Gustav Adolf aware that if I move my forces to Rheinfelden, I will be confronting Bernhard directly? Something that I have worked very hard to avoid?"

"He must be of the opinion that in this case, the gain is worth the risk."

"Bernhard may try to force a battle. He is that kind of an opportunist."

"It is a direct order from the king, General."

"I know. Give the orders to move. First priority to the miners, sappers, engineers, and anyone else who may be able to assist with the preparation of this 'emergency landing field.' Cavalry ahead; dragoons. Infantry and baggage train to follow as fast as they may. I had not been planning to go into winter quarters on the Swiss border, but it looks as though I may have to, if we cannot pull out before autumn changes to winter. And Knut . . .'"

"Yes, General."

"Start drawing up contingency plans for a fighting retreat, if need be."

"Fuel convoys are already starting from both Mainz and Grantville, in the general direction of Rheinfelden. Once we know exactly where the army will be located after the advance forces arrive there—once we know where the landing field will be, that is—we will need to notify them. The hope is that at least one of them will arrive soon enough to refuel Colonel Woods' plane for take-off as soon as Don Fernando's party arrives from Basel with the ladies. Weather permitting, of course."

Horn grimaced. "Then send the radio and its operator with the advance forces. And tell the king that you have done so. That way, he will stop using it to send me orders. Because he will have to. Until I catch up with it, at least. And Knut . . ."

"Yes, General."

"Start drawing up contingency plans for what to do if the fuel does not arrive. Or if the weather holds the plane on the ground and we have to stand Bernhard off for a week or more."

Gustav Horn was a pessimistic man.

The Spanish siege lines, outside Amsterdam

"Would you like to see the radio?" Rebecca asked. "You could hand the message to the operator yourself."

"I would, very much," Don Fernando replied. He looked around the table. "However, I do not think my advisers want me to come into Amsterdam right now. Not, at least, without a rather substantial company of bodyguards."

Rebecca glanced at Fredrik Hendrik. "Would you mind?" she asked.

"Oh, no, not at all. What are a few Spanish troops in Amsterdam, after all?"

There may have been some sarcasm underlying the stadtholder's statement, but Rebecca chose to take it at face value.

"It would be also interesting," Don Fernando said rather wryly, "to see the famous Gretchen Richter again. The Trojan Amazon. I have Rubens' painting of her hanging prominently in my head-quarters, you know. In fact, I have purchased a copy of it from his studio for my office in Brussels."

"Er," Mike said in a rather strangled voice. "Why?"

Don Fernando looked at him calmly. "As a reminder that if I do not succeed, she is waiting." He smiled. "And, of course, she has a very impressive bosom."

Thus all of them, Fredrik Hendrik, Mike and Rebecca, Gretchen and Jeff, managed to crowd into the radio headquarters and watch Don Fernando send out his reply to Maria Anna.

Most honored cousin. Stay put. I'm coming. Be there day after tomorrow. Fernando.

CHAPTER 67

Nuntius Optatissimus

Basel

"Day after tomorrow?" Mary Simpson asked.

"How?" That was Maria Anna.

Diane handed her a piece of paper. "Tony says. This is what Don Fernando sent to you. It is the first that came this evening. There is more coming, that Mike sent to me. Tony will write it all out as soon as the radio window closes."

"How?" Maria Anna persisted.

Diane shrugged. "We wait and see. What else?"

"There is no way he can come that fast from Amsterdam," Veronica proclaimed. "Not unless he flies. Young fool. He must be as reckless as Hans."

"Flies? How would he get hold of a plane and a pilot? The treaty was just signed last week," Mary said.

"How long did it take him to capture back most of the Dutch?" Diane asked. "Fast worker, that boy."

General Horn's headquarters, outside Rheinfelden

Gustav Horn was scarcely pleased to be preparing a full military welcome for the cardinal-infante. For the infante who had formerly been a cardinal and was now "king in the Low Countries." Whatever he was calling himself these days, Don Fernando was still a Habsburg and still the brother of Philip IV of Spain.

Horn did it, though. On the orders of Gustav Adolf. As well as he could, given the harum-scarum nature of his headquarters at Rheinfelden. The airplane taxied in and halted. Horn's scraped-together ground crew, consisting of anybody in his army who had ever been at any other USE air field and had at least once before seen a plane land, ran forward with chocks and a ladder. Two men climbed out, taking stations at either side of the foot of the ladder; then the guest of honor.

As soon as the Spanish prince reached the ground, he turned and looked at the people waiting for him. Spanish? By his looks, he might as well be Swedish or German. Or Dutch. Waving his hand in a quite dramatic gesture at his two bodyguards, he called out—in German first, then in a half-dozen other languages, including English.

"These are the only troops I have brought with me, gentlemen! Who else would like to write his name on the pages of history by being part of the rescue of Archduchess Maria Anna?"

Horn restrained himself from groaning. "Not another one," he muttered under his breath. "Not another Essence of Captain Gars. The European stage has no need of a second flamboyant, exuberant, overwhelmingly self-confident monarch."

Standing behind him, the up-timer Whitney spoke, just loudly enough that only Horn and his immediate aides could hear: "We call it charisma. And, believe me, I don't like it one bit better than you do. Particularly since this kid is fifteen years younger than Gustav Adolf. Has to be. Where's a nice plague epidemic when you need it?"

Every one of the up-timers assigned to Horn bounced to the front at once and volunteered. Every up-timer in sight, Horn noted sourly, including Whitney, no matter what his personal opinion of Don Fernando might be.

Somehow, Horn was not surprised. The up-timers appeared to have a strong tendency to volunteer for quixotic undertakings. Idly, he wondered if Cervantes' novel had been part of the ordinary up-time school curriculum. He would have to ask someone, when he had the time.

With the exception of the pilot, of course, who had gotten out of the plane at last and was now gathering up the impromptu ground crew for what looked likely to be intensive training. Perhaps getting the plane off the ground was more difficult than landing it appeared to be. That seemed only reasonable.

Plus, there were a lot of other volunteers. Practically every cavalry officer. A good half of the infantry officers. A scattering of others.

"Do you have *any* contacts at all inside the city?" Don Fernando's aide asked.

"Not since they closed the bridge," Horn answered. "Naturally, there are businessmen in Basel who have been selling to the army, but that does not mean that they wish to be involved in this. Nor can we reach them at the moment, even if they did."

"Does this mean that we are going in blind?"

"Well, there are people available who know the city," Burt Threlkeld answered. "The militia on this side, in Riehen, the place is called, have been watching Bernhard's people. They sent messages over to the general and said they will be glad to help. Their *Landvogt* got caught in the city; he's a member of the city council, too. I have no idea how they plan to get in touch with him, though. The bridge has been closed off for several days."

The aide was looking very dubious.

"Give orders to saddle up," Don Fernando said. "I promised her 'day after tomorrow.' This is 'day after tomorrow.'"

Basel

"I see them," Cavriani said. "This is a pretty good telescope." They were standing on the roof of the building that the University of Basel used for an astronomical observatory.

"Augsburg manufacture," Johann Buxtorf answered. "The very best we could get outside of the Netherlands. It cost the university a pretty penny, too, so don't drop it if you get excited, Leopold. Or you pay for the replacement."

"And you were right, Wettstein. Your Riehen militia are with them."

"Not *all* of the Riehen militia, I hope. I hope very sincerely.

Most of the Riehen militia should still be watching the boundary stones, ready to signal if Duke Bernhard's troops start to move. I do love those up-time police whistles. Such a simple technology, once one has thought of it. Such a delightfully piercing sound, much louder than most fifes. But the dot-dot-dash light signals that we used last night are nice, too. It would have been much more difficult for me to keep my men informed and instructed, without them. Words are so much more flexible than just a set of codes."

He turned around and looked at Buxtorf. "Are the students in place?"

"Yes, on either side of the bridge." Buxtorf smiled. "I must say, they appear to be happily astonished by their discovery that I am a subversive. Or at least, they are happily astonished by their mistaken belief that I am a subversive. I would certainly not consider myself one."

Cavriani raised one eyebrow.

"I am sure that I am a conservative," Buxtorf said firmly. "I am quite positive that I am a conservative. I believe that the proposed action of the city council in holding the archduchess hostage would be profoundly unsettling to the *status quo*. There must be far less disruptive ways to go about achieving the goal of Swiss independence. So. Truly, Leopold, the Lord himself taught us to pray, 'Lead us not into temptation.' I am merely preventing the city council from succumbing to the temptation to do something outrageous, by assisting in the removal of the source of temptation from the city."

"Undoubtedly, the members of the city council will be very impressed with that bit of sophistry," Cavriani commented.

"I cleared it with the pastors," Buxtorf answered.

"Not the same batch of people at all." Cavriani raised the telescope again. "Here they come." ·

"Don Fernando and his party?"

"The students. Behind the city guard at the bridge, causing a disturbance to pull them back and away. Don Fernando's party is still some distance. Wettstein, take a look. You are more familiar with the landmarks and terrain over there than I am."

"About a quarter-mile; no more than that. And riding fast."

"Any sign of Duke Bernhard's people?"

"None."

They stood, sharing the telescope amicably, until Wettstein said, "They're through."

"Put the telescope back in the case and return it to the room where it belongs, then," Buxtorf said. "We have to get downstairs. The Basel militia seems to be getting rather irritated with the students. Luckily, I thought to ask for any students who had close relatives among the city militia officers to volunteer to stand in the front ranks. That may keep them from ordering to shoot before we get there, but I would not count on it. And there is still the 'honor guard' around the embassy to be dealt with."

"I'll go that way," Wettstein said. "I am a member of the city council. If you see either of the mayors, Buxtorf, tell them they are needed at the USE embassy. You two handle the problems around the bridge."

"What is going on?" Diane Jackson asked. She was sitting in a chair in the reception room. In the middle of the reception room, far from any windows, somewhat to her chagrin.

"A lot of yelling," the down-time corporal who was looking out answered. "A pretty well-disciplined good-sized company of cavalry."

Gordon left Diane's side and went for a look. "Some guy wearing a mortarboard hat, looking like he's about to graduate or something, arguing with some other guy who is wearing a great big ceremonial chain around his neck. I wish Cavriani was here. He might have a better idea of who's who."

"The Basel city guards who have been standing around this building are moving away. The guy with the ceremonial chain waved them off. The cavalry is moving towards the front."

"Whose cavalry?" Lee Swiger asked pragmatically. "The ones we're expecting, or Bernhard's?"

"Mostly down-timers. I don't recognize the banners, but then I wouldn't," Gordon answered. "Corporal, do you recognize the banners?"

"Not the fancy one in front. Never seen it before. But the next one after that is General Horn's personal ensign. The general is not with them, though. I have seen him before; I would recognize him."

"If Duke Bernhard had managed to take Horn's banner, we would have heard about it. Even cooped up here."

"One of them has a foghorn. He's trying to say something to us. Damned walls are so thick, I can't hear a word."

"Open up the window," Diane ordered.

The corporal, paying no attention to the weapons trained on it from front and back, opened the window.

"*Swiger, open up the fucking door!*" the man holding the foghorn shouted.

"That's Burt Threlkeld. These are our guys."

"Open up the door," Diane said. She got out of her chair, holstering her gun.

Don Fernando was right at the head of the incoming company. *Impulsive again*, his advisers would have moaned to themselves, if they had been there to observe. Once inside, however, he stood back.

"Prepared for battle, were you?" Burt asked, as he looked around. The reception room was bristling with various implements of mayhem.

"More or less," Lee Swiger admitted. "Just in case we had any trouble. I doubt we could have stood Bernhard off for very long, if he broke through the walls, but we thought that we could probably discourage the Basel city militia."

"Where are the damsels in distress?"

"Various spots. We made the archduchess stay upstairs with Mary Simpson. They both have guns, but Tony has orders to keep them away from the windows, like we did with Diane here. Ronnie is back in the kitchen. Except that there were two of us and one of Diane, but there's one of Tony and two of them, so at least one of them was probably looking out. Mrs. Simpson, if you want my guess; the other girl is used to having heavy security around her."

Diane turned. "Corporal, take someone back to get Mrs. Dreeson. Then go up and tell the other ladies they can come down."

Jack Whitney followed the corporal, who motioned at a door and then started up a set of back stairs. He looked into the embassy kitchen. Ronnie Dreeson was sitting on a three-legged stool next to a double-barreled shotgun the size of a small cannon, which was pointed at a ground-level window. The window was covered with iron bars, but they looked a little rusty and shaky. She looked quite prepared to shoot anyone who tried to pull them loose and come in through it.

He stopped a minute. He had helped Dan Frost with quite a lot of the firearms training in Grantville. He was a veteran of Ronnie's epic refusal to carry a gun. She was no better a markswoman than Rebecca Stearns, so they had given her a small shotgun. She had taken it home, cleaned it just as she had been taught, oiled it, and locked it away unloaded, first in Jeff's gun cabinet in the trailer and then, presumably, after she got married, in Henry's gun cabinet, where it probably still was unless someone else in the Dreeson household was using it at present.

Why was she willing to carry a gun now? he decided to ask.

"I am *not* carrying it," she answered logically. "The barrel is resting on a sawhorse. The stock is resting on the table where the cook chops vegetables. Those heavy candlesticks hold it in place very well. I do not have to carry it at all—just take off the safety and pull the trigger if someone comes. I do not mind shooting people with a gun if I need to. But carry one all the time? No, I will not. It weighs many pounds. It does not fit in my tote bag. If I try to carry it on my back, with a strap, it keeps knocking down the bun." She motioned at her hair.

Jack Whitney suddenly realized that communication between English-speakers and German-speakers in Grantville during the early days after the Ring of Fire had been far from perfect. She had literally been trying to tell them that she did not want to *carry* such a heavy, awkward weapon, day in and day out.

"Oh." Maybe, he thought, they ought to consider revising the manual for basic firearms training. Possibly even implement some standard other than pure marksmanship as the basis for deciding what type of gun to issue to whom.

Maria Anna led the way into the reception room.

Mary Simpson paused to watch from the door. The two of them were such a contrast. Don Fernando, like so many of the Spanish Habsburgs—it still came as a surprise to her—was a blue-eyed strawberry blond, rather fine boned and with delicate features, in spite of the heavy lower lip. Now that she saw them together, Maria Anna was as tall as he was, possibly even a little taller. With the brunette looks of her Wittelsbach mother—black hair, dark brown eyes—and rather full-bodied, the two made a striking couple.

With a flourish of his feathered hat, he bowed at the same time that the archduchess curtseyed.

The bow seemed to make a most favorable impression on Maria Anna. Of course, it would be such a contrast to the stiffness of Duke Maximilian. Mary knew perfectly well that Don Fernando's other main attraction—being twenty-four years old instead of sixty-two years old—was something that Maria Anna had known about in advance. The archduchess had even told Mary, once, on the long trek to Basel, about her youthful hopes for a bride-groom who would die in a timely manner so she could become a formidable regent, joking that she would be willing to make an exception to this requirement in the case of her cousin.

Maria Anna, in turn, seemed to be making a most favorable impression on her fiancé. Mary could guess what he was thinking. *Healthy.* He would have heard that often enough, but it would be something else for him to see it for himself.

Don Fernando was indeed thinking. Not only *healthy* but also *and with all her component parts in the right slots.* And laughing at himself—*here I am, already thinking to myself in terms of that horridly tedious treatise on interchangeable parts that I have commanded myself to master before I command my subordinates to master it. And that is—um—a really magnificent bosom. Nearly of Richter-like proportions.*

He took her hand as she rose. "Most honored cousin," he said. "I very much regret to tell you that just before we left Amsterdam, we received news of the death of the Holy Roman Emperor."

"I was afraid," she said. "The newspapers said that Papa was very ill." Automatically, her other hand felt for her rosary.

He reached out and embraced her.

"I will not go." The expression on Diane Jackson's face was a triumph of stubbornness. "I will not abandon this embassy. My job is not over. Margrave Friedrich has just started to talk to me. I need to finish."

Jack Whitney and Burt Threlkeld just looked at her.

"Duke Hermann, the one with the complicated name, from Hesse. He has not told me to go. Ed Piazza has not told me to go. Tell Frank they are my boss."

Neither Jack nor Burt really wanted to be the man who told Frank Jackson that. Frank had made it very plain that he wanted them to yank Diane out of Basel.

"I'm staying with her, then," Tony Adducci said. "She'll need the radio. Besides . . ."

"Besides, what?" Whitney asked.

"He is my mouthpiece," Diane said.

"Mouthpiece?"

"Like the lawyer, in gangster movies. He talks for me. He speaks English. He speaks French, which is even better. He can take notes when I speak French with the margrave. He says that he took two years of French because he did not want to take Spanish. Then he took two more years because he was sorry for Mrs. Hawkins. He thought she might lose her job if not enough students took French. Then, after the Ring of Fire, he learned German. Also, he learned Latin from Father von Spee. And from his grandparents, he remembers a little Italian. So he is my mouthpiece."

"'Spokesman' might be better," Whitney suggested.

"Mouthpiece, spokesman, all the same. I am the ambassadress. I need him. He stays."

"I really sort of think," Tony said, "that we ought to try to do some fence-mending with the Basel city council after the way you all came barreling over the bridge and through the gates. Figure out some way to help them save face. The margrave will probably help, and Freinsheim. Plus anything we can do to keep them from firing Wettstein would be all to the good."

"Maybe 'aide-de-camp' would be a better description," Whitney said, looking at Tony. The Grantville kids, the ones who had been in high school or younger when the Ring of Fire happened, were adapting to this world with a speed that sometimes made their parents and grandparents dizzy. It even made him dizzy and he was more "older brother" age. Especially in regard to the traditional American reluctance to learn foreign languages, which they simply seemed to have weighted down and dropped into a pond somewhere.

"Anyway," Tony said, "I'm not going unless Diane does."

Swiger, Gordon, and the rest of the embassy staff turned out to be of the same opinion.

"This Duke Bernhard is still out there," Diane said. "Tony will send radio to Ed Piazza. They will tell me what to do about him."

"Ah, Diane," Burt Threlkeld said. "I don't think that Mike and them really expected you to try to handle anything that high-level when they sent you down here."

"No," Diane admitted. "It was just that the rude margrave wanted to look at an up-timer. But I am here and they are not. So I handle. You want him to go away, don't you?"

Burt Threlkeld emitted a slightly gurgling sound from the back of his throat. "I am sure," he said, "that General Horn would be delighted to have him go away."

"Fine," Diane said. "I stay. You go now. He goes later."

There did not seem to be much more to say. There was certainly no point in spending more time in Basel than they had to.

Their march through the streets of Basel was rather tense, with everybody thinking that something was going to go wrong at the last minute, but they made it across the bridge and into Riehen district, followed by Cavriani, Wettstein, Professor Buxtorf, and a sizable contingent of university students, all of whom were having prudent thoughts to the effect that the Basel city fathers were going to be really, really, annoyed about this, might possibly try to vent their feelings on anybody handy, and should be allowed to simmer down for a while before life went on.

CHAPTER 68

Rosa Mystica, Redux

General Horn's Headquarters, Rheinfelden

"It looks like they pulled it off," Jesse Wood said.

"I don't see them bringing any wounded."

"We didn't hear any shots, either."

"Swords are always an option. Arrows. Clubs. Rocks."

"Get back to work, guys," Jesse said. "Since they are here this afternoon, we'll have to get the Gustav ready to climb off the ground in the morning."

"If the fuel comes."

"Sure, if the fuel comes. One or the other of the convoys is bound to make it."

"Tell the infantry to take position," Horn said, "between here and where we know Bernhard to be. Don't go into Riehen. I don't want to cause unnecessary controversy with the Basel city council. Between Rheinfelden and the Riehen boundary markers. Knut has the diagrams for all the emplacements we worked out."

"How much baggage?" Jesse Wood asked. He was trying to calculate whether he could possibly get back to Mainz the next day even if neither of the fuel convoys appeared. "I hope you warned them that there's not a lot of room. Mary Simpson should know that, anyway."

"They don't have any," Jack Whitney said.

"Two women with no baggage is beyond belief."

"They walked into Basel with the clothes they were wearing, Diane said. Plus, each of them had some extra underwear, socks, and towels in a little satchel. They rode out the same way. She spent some embassy money to get them better clothes. The ones they were wearing when they got there had sort of bit the dust while they were riding and walking from Ulm to Basel. Those outfits are what they are wearing now, but they rode out of the town without much more than they walked in with. And tomorrow morning they plan to leave everything they aren't actually wearing with Ronnie Dreeson. Mrs. Simpson says she can give it away. Or whatever."

Jesse eyed the sky. "Lord," he said, "I do most sincerely ask your pardon for having ever doubted that miracles still do happen."

Landvogt's Office, Riehen, outside Basel

"Do you suppose that this Herr Wettstein is ever going to show up?" Susanna asked, for the eighth time that morning.

That was a record, since they had not yet finished their break-fast. The first repetition had been before she even ran her hands through her hair.

"I have no idea at all," Marc answered, also for the eighth time. "All we can do is wait. We're warm, we're dry. You have a bench to sleep on. I have a nice wood floor to sleep on. It is not a damp, dank dungeon. They're feeding us. No one is chasing us. Once things calm down, we can go into Basel and get some more money from Papa's banker."

"But we don't have anything to do," Susanna wailed.

Marc had been waiting for that. "Oh, yes, we do," he said cheerfully. "I spent what money I did still have to buy a ream of paper, two pens, and some ink from one of the *Landvogt's* clerks last evening. Clean paper. Last night, after you settled down on your bench, I started writing up a report on iron ore in the Wiese valley. I kept at it until it got dark. Now that it's light again, I'll go back to that and you can start making five clean copies. A ledger a day keeps boredom away."

Susanna looked at him, poised between objecting that she didn't want to make five copies of a report on iron ore and really wanting something to do other than look out the window and whine.

"Be nice and do it," Marc said winningly. "Sit on the floor and use the bench as a desk. Think of it as a birthday present. I'm fairly sure that this is the thirtieth day of September. If so, I am nineteen."

"Why do you get presents on your birthday?"

"Well, because I do. At least, we do in my family. And something good to eat. Something special."

"What do you do on your saint's day, then?"

"Saint's day?" Marc asked.

"The festival of your patron, in whose honor you have your baptismal name. Mine, Susanna, is from the Apocrypha. Susanna and the Elders. Your name, I suppose, is for the apostle."

"No. Mine is for Mama's uncle, Marco Turettini. Calvinists don't have saints."

She looked at him, scandalized. "Surely you must have a patron saint. Who watches over you? Who protects you from harm?"

"God," Marc said. "And my parents. It's enough."

General Horn's Headquarters, Rheinfelden

"Not everyone reads Cervantes, then, Mrs. Simpson, if I understand you correctly. But he was still well known as an author in your world." Gustav Horn looked down the table, to make sure that he was not ignoring his other guests. He was having an unexpectedly good time at the supper he was hosting. His profession did not often bring him into association with people who were truly interesting conversationalists with a wide knowledge of literature. His acquaintance with the admiral's wife was a genuine pleasure.

"That is quite correct, General," Mary Simpson said. "Although I think that it is safe to say that probably more people in our country became familiar with *Don Quixote* through . . ." She suddenly stopped, caught her breath, and clapped her hands.

Everyone else interrupted their conversations, turned, and looked at her.

"I have it," she said. "Your Majesty," she said to Don Fernando. "Your Highness."

"Maria Anna," the archduchess said. "For you, Mary, I am still and will always be Maria Anna. What do you have?"

"The perfect wedding present from the United States of Europe. I know how much you enjoyed *The Sound of Music*, and I am sure that you will arrange to have it produced in your new home. But there is something else. It will take a little time, but I know we can do it. From Magdeburg, I will arrange, rehearse, costume, and send you the world premiere production of *Man of la Mancha* for the Brussels theater."

She turned back to Horn. "Thank you so much, General. Without your literary interests, it would never have occurred to me."

"All I really want," Veronica said, "is to go back home. To Grantville, not to Grafenwöhr."

Leopold Cavriani nodded his head solemnly.

"Henry's hip was bothering him before we left and not one single person who has sent a radio message has said anything about Henry's hip. That certainly means that it is much worse and they simply are not telling me."

"Perhaps it is perfectly all right, so there is nothing they need to tell you."

Veronica snorted. "What did I tell you about writing to your wife about Marc?"

"Not to worry her unnecessarily."

"Did that mean that the news was not bad?"

"Ah, no."

"So. There is certainly something wrong with Henry's hip, which they are not telling me. Also, they have said nothing about the schools. I have wasted a whole summer, spent a lot of money traveling, and gained nothing. I still have no money for tuition to send Annalise to college at Quedlinburg. There are still no books to train my teachers at St. Veronica's academy. The Jesuits in Amberg are still eating dinner on top of Johann Stephan's print shop. Undoubtedly they will appeal any judgment in the family's favor all the way to the *Reichskammergericht*. Which is sitting where, now, the cameral court? In Wetzlar, I think. So if the case is heard there, there will be more travel expense. I shall have either to start with another lawyer, who knows nothing about it, or pay Rastetter his expenses to go there and file our briefs. Not to mention food and lodgings while he waits."

"Just a little ray of sunshine this morning, aren't we?"

"And Jack Whitney found me ready to shoot a gun out of the kitchen window of the embassy. Which means that when I get home, everybody will start nattering at me again to carry that shotgun they gave me. There were almost three years from when they gave it to me and when Mary and I were kidnapped. I never needed a gun in those three years. I went to Magdeburg and back twice without needing that shotgun. I have been to Badenburg many times; to Rudolstadt; to Jena. I never needed a gun. But they will start again. They will expect me, every step I take, to carry one of the things. Or, if I will not carry it, they will try to stop me from going places. It is too dangerous, they will say, as if I am an idiot child."

"In general, I perceive, the world is not your oyster."

She looked at him. "Do you carry a gun everywhere you go?"

Cavriani shook his head. "I carry a pistol, sometimes, when I think that I may need one. Also a sword, but it isn't quite the same for a woman. You aren't expected to wear one on dress occasions. How about a nice dirk?"

He pulled one out from under his doublet. "Efficient, inconspicuous, but above all lightweight and easy to conceal. Overall, I have always felt, there is really nothing like a dirk when it comes to personal weapons."

Rheinfelden Air Field

"I want Mary in front with me," Jesse Wood said. "She's not a trained pilot, but she'll still be of more help to me than either of you, if we run into any kind of trouble. I know that you sat in front on the way down, Your Majesty, but that was simply because you wanted to and neither of your aides would have been any more use than you could be. At least, as it turned out, you don't get air sick."

"I have no objection to the arrangement," Don Fernando said.

"I'm sorry, Your Highness," Jesse said to the archduchess. "Perhaps if there is a really calm stretch of air, you and Mary can change places so you can enjoy the view for a few minutes."

Maria Anna looked at him. "I think that just *knowing* that I am up in the air with nothing underneath me except a thin floor will be quite sufficient. Without seeing it with my own eyes while it is happening."

"It's quite fascinating, really," Don Fernando said, "and not at all frightening. Almost like looking down on a map that has been colored to match reality, showing the trees and buildings. Perhaps we can show you another time. Some day, I really must have one of these machines for myself."

By then, of course, Bernhard of Saxe-Weimar's spies in Basel had reported the situation to him.

"What should we do?" asked one of his officers. "We might be able to shoot down the airplane, if we used a massed volley. That's said to be the way the Danes brought down Richter's craft at Wismar."

Bernhard glanced around the small circle of officers standing with him on the field outside Basel. His eyes came to rest on the newest addition to the circle.

"What's your opinion, Johann?"

Colonel von Werth took a deep breath. "Ah... I'm really a cavalry officer, Your Grace."

"Your opinion, Johann."

Von Werth was still trying to get accustomed to the young duke's somewhat peculiar ways of being a ruler. He and Bernhard had known each other for some time, and been on good terms, true enough. But this was the first time he'd ever served under him as a commander.

Bernhard was... difficult. Also brilliant. And often unpredictable. But one thing Johann had concluded was that, beneath the Saxe-Weimar duke's frequently arrogant and sometimes even abusive manner, lay a mind that expected—no, demanded—that his subordinates speak honestly to him. He might snarl at you for contradicting him, but he would not punish you. He *would*—instantly—dismiss an officer or adviser he decided was not saying what he really thought.

So, von Werth's hesitation didn't last for more than the time it took to exhale the breath.

"I can think of few things more ill-advised, Your Grace—given your delicate political situation—than to be seen by all of Europe as the man who murdered a prince and princess of the Habsburg family. Especially a prince so bold and a princess so captivating."

Bernhard smiled. "My thoughts exactly, Johann." He gave the officer who'd advanced the idea no more than a glance. The fellow avoided his eyes.

"No, gentlemen, we shall simply let them make their escape. If the plane crashes, it will be no fault of ours."

He shrugged, then. "It was just a ploy, after all. As the up-timers say, you win some and you lose some. Never a good idea to become so taken by the charms of a maneuver that you lose sight of the campaign."

In the event, when the plane appeared, Bernhard did no more than give the occupants a salute with his drawn sword.

They probably didn't see the gesture, thought von Werth. But if they did, he imagined that the young Habsburg prince—perhaps even the young princess—would understand the sentiment.

"What a marvelous player he'll make in the game," Bernhard commented, after he sheathed his sword.

"A dangerous opponent, though," said Johann.

Bernhard smiled. "True. But who's to say he can't be an ally? And whether he turns out to be friend or foe, he's already done me something of a service."

Von Werth cocked his head, inviting an explanation.

"Oh, come, Johann. I should think it would be obvious. It is entirely to my advantage for Europe to get accustomed to—perhaps even to cherish—bold young princes, is it not?"

En route from Rheinfelden to Amsterdam

The space in the back of a Gustav was not precisely roomy. At present, it was occupied by two healthy young adults, one male and one female, both in their twenties, tucked under a large pile of thick furs to fend off the cold, who were eying one another with the normal curiosity of two people who know perfectly well that they will be having sex, if not in a matter of hours, certainly in a matter of days, and that they will probably never again be this close together between now and then.

Maria Anna found his interest rather flattering.

"What," Don Fernando asked, "was that?" His exploring hand had just encountered a rather sharp and pointy object.

Maria Anna reached through the slits at each side of her skirt, where her pockets were tied around her waist, and felt for the drawstring. She untied it; then snaked up her skirt and the top petticoat until she could shake the package loose.

"I haven't taken it out since Doña Mencia wrapped it for me the day I left Munich. I hope it is not bent or dented." Carefully, she unrolled the flannel. The golden rose lay on her lap, undamaged. After a few minutes she said, "I suppose that I should wrap it up again. It isn't mine to keep, I am afraid."

Don Fernando picked it up, held it against her nose, and said, "Sniff."

"How strange. It almost seems to have an aroma."

"Ah, Herr Colonel Woods," Maria Anna asked. "Is there any way that you can tell when this plane will cross the border into the Netherlands?"

"More or less. It isn't as if the borders are marked on the land. Why?"

"It is protocol, you know. When a bride enters the land of her new husband, she is stripped of the clothing she is wearing and reclothed freshly with garments from her new home."

"I am afraid that we will have to forego it," Don Fernando said rather apologetically. "I did not bring any Netherlandish clothes with me." He leaned back as far as he could in the cramped seat, lifted the pile of furs, and looked at Maria Anna from head to toe. "However, I would be quite willing to conduct the first half of the ceremony, if you think that would help," he offered brightly.

"Will anyone be waiting with another set of clothes when we land?" Maria Anna asked pragmatically.

"Not as far as I know. I forgot all about it, we were in such a rush to leave."

"It is not exactly warm in this airplane. I think that I will keep my clothes on right now, thank you. If I do step out and we find some great noblewoman standing at the foot of the ladder with her arms full of fabric, that will be time enough."

CHAPTER 69

Monita Paterna

Landvogt's Office, Riehen, outside Basel

"It is Herr Wettstein, finally. It has to be." Susanna had her nose pressed to the window pane. "A man arrived on horseback, and just the way the other men here are gathering around him and talking to him, he has to be the boss."

"Don't get overexcited. We're probably not the first on his list, by any means," Marc said stoically. "It may be a couple of days before he gets around to thinking about us."

It would have been, normally. But Wettstein's clerk happened to mention that he had sold a ream of ledger paper to a young man, Cavriani, and would need to order a replacement from Basel, since they would be running short fairly soon.

At the name, Wettstein raised his head. "Where?" he asked.

"In the reception room. They weren't really prisoners, even though the militia brought them in. We didn't have anyplace else to put them."

"They? Them?"

"Cavriani. And the kid he has with him."

The conversation did not last five minutes. Realizing that Horn had, by placing a substantial portion of his army between the landing field and Bernhard, also placed it between the two members of the Cavriani family, Wettstein issued safe-conducts, assigned a guide, accepted an IOU for food and lodging, and shooed them off. Not that he wouldn't have enjoyed getting to know Leopold's son under other circumstances, but at the moment he had a very full schedule.

"Who's the boy?" he asked idly.

"Don't think I ever heard his name," the clerk answered.

General Horn's Camp, outside Rheinfelden

"Papa!"

At the sound of this urgent cry, Cavriani turned quickly away from Frau Dreeson and her incessant grumbles. Two young men, escorted by a couple of members of the Riehen militia and followed, or possibly chased, by two of Horn's soldiers, were running toward him. He ran toward them.

"Papa, what luck to find you still here. Herr Wettstein was afraid that you might already have left. I'm completely out of money; I spent the last of it on paper to draw up my report on iron ore in the Wiese river valley. Wettstein's clerk didn't charge a lot for it."

Marc handed his father five neat copies of the iron ore report which he compiled while stuck in the *Landvogt's* office in Riehen, but didn't stop talking. "I was almost out of money before I bought that. We had already figured that between where we were when the Bavarian captain started to chase us—that was before, somehow, the Bavarian captain started to chase us again with part of Duke Bernhard's army helping him—and when we got to your factor's house in Basel and could draw an advance, we wouldn't be eating much that we couldn't find growing along the roadside. If we ever had time to stop and eat, that is."

Marc was tanned, dirty, disheveled—and abundantly alive and healthy, totally unharmed. Leopold embraced him heartily, with a kiss on each cheek.

"And, I see, you have found a companion in your mischief." He gestured toward the other young man—boy, really, at closer range.

Marc squared his shoulders. "Ah, yes. Papa, this is Susanna. Susanna Allegretti."

Leopold Cavriani had spent enough time in Grantville to be fully aware of why "A Boy Named Sue" was considered to be a joke. There weren't any boys named Sue. Or Susanna. He turned.

"Frau Dreeson," he called. "Veronica."

Veronica became somewhat distracted from her catalog of grievances. What she said was, "See, I was right. No need for you to write your wife and make her worry. None at all."

Marc was not sure what might be coming next.

"A fascinating tale of adventure. But such a sad absence of chaperones," his father said at dinner, after Marc and Susanna had narrated their way through everything that had happened since Munich, usually in turn, but sometimes in chorus. "Two unrelated young people, boy and girl, scampering every which way through the countryside. Presumably, we should now remedy the situation by marrying you off to each other."

"That's fine," Marc said.

"No," Susanna said at the same time.

Marc looked at her a little reproachfully. In response to Veronica's urgent note, sent back via the Riehen militia and Wettstein, Diane Jackson had checked through her closet for clothes she could spare and sent Tony Adducci across the bridge to Riehen with a package. Wettstein had forwarded it to Horn's camp by courier. Susanna was dressed as a girl again. Sort of. Marc had never seen anything even vaguely like a turquoise satin *cheong sam* embroidered with red and green dragons before. He had never even imagined that such a garment existed, but he certainly appreciated the effect when Susanna wore it, as she was doing for the evening meal. The cream-colored turtle-neck sweater and the blue jeans embroidered with butterflies on the back pockets were rather nice, too. Diane did not go in for down-time fashions.

"No?" Leopold Cavriani raised an eyebrow.

"No. I like Marc, but I won't be married to him and go to some Calvinist city where everybody wears black broadcloth. Or black gabardine. Maybe with a white linen collar if they are feeling very cheerful. Not even if they would have me! We didn't do anything wrong. We don't have to marry each other. I got this far. Somehow, I can get to the Spanish Netherlands. I will go back to my lady and make beautiful clothing with velvet and satin and brocade and lace . . ."

"Ah. Professional pride, I see. That is understandable. Certainly, we can see to it that you arrive in the Spanish Netherlands safely. Perhaps Potentiana's cousins in Lyons . . ."

"At least, girl," Veronica said, after they had told the men good night and gone to find the tent that General Horn had assigned to them and go to bed, "you are thinking about the problems. Which is more than Dorothea and her young man were doing last spring. That only means, of course, that they will have to deal with it after they manage to get married."

She scowled ferociously and added with her usual level of cheer, "If, of course, they managed to get to Grantville. If they were not killed by bandits along the way. If neither of them has died from some ordinary disease. If Dorothea does not die in childbirth—it is her first, and that is always the riskiest one. Indeed, if the two of them did not starve to death during the trip. Mary and I were kidnapped before I could arrange a bank draft for them."

"Who is Dorothea?" Susanna asked.

"My late husband Johann Stephan's idiotic niece. After marriage, it is certain to be more awkward. When they look at one another across the baby's cradle, for example, and *then* start discussions about whether the baptism will take place in a Catholic or Calvinist church, which, if she does not die and the baby is born alive, they will do before Christmas. You are quite right. It is undoubtedly difficult to yoke a Catholic and a Calvinist together in marriage. Though, of course, Dorothea is such a little fool that she may not have strong opinions about the matter. She may just change over if her husband tells her to."

"I," Susanna said firmly, "would never do that. Not ever."

Veronica smiled, even if somewhat sourly. "Precisely what I thought. Although, child, believe me, having a Calvinist and a Catholic united in one marriage cannot possibly be as awkward as playing host to a Calvinist and a Catholic united together in your own mind, soul, and body. Damned Bavarians. Not that Duke Maximilian was responsible for the fact that I host a Lutheran to keep them company, I admit. The counts Palatine managed that without his help."

Susanna had never thought about that problem. She looked at Veronica a moment and said so.

Abruptly, Veronica asked, "Since you seem to recognize the problems, why are you even thinking about marriage to the boy?

Though at least you did have enough sense to refuse his father's suggestion."

Susanna's eyes flew wide. "Because I want to kiss him. I really do. I've been thinking about kissing him since the first time I saw him. Maybe not quite since the first time I saw him, but even when he was just an iron worker repairing the house next to the English Ladies on Paradise Street, I was thinking . . . Oh, well, at least, definitely, since the first time I really looked at him. And, well, other stuff."

She blushed. "I have dreamed about it. I never really wanted to do that with any other man I've ever seen in my life. I couldn't even imagine really *wanting* to do those things when the other seamstresses talked about it. It was just something, I thought, that you had to put up with in order to get married. Then I looked at Marc in the baggage park outside of Munich and I started to think about it all. When I was a boy, it was a very peculiar feeling. But he never gave me a boy's name. When we were alone, he always called me Susanna, and when we were with other people, he never called me anything at all. And he did say, once, that he thinks that the way that all my parts are put together is cute. And he doesn't mind that my eyelashes are short and straight and blond. That's a good sign, don't you think?"

Stop it, she told herself. *You are chattering to this dried up prune of an old lady who is part Calvinist. She will not approve of you at all if you say such things.*

"Did you have to agree quite so fast to sending her on to the Spanish Netherlands?" Marc asked after Veronica and Susanna had left the supper table. "I've known you all my life, Papa, so don't try to look innocent. You could have thought of something to keep her here, if you wanted to."

"But you did nothing wrong?" Cavriani's eyebrow was up again.

"We did nothing wrong. We did not even come close to doing anything wrong." Marc smiled rather ruefully. "Papa, I am afraid that all those lessons that I was given by all those tutors whom you hired actually did have an effect. I find, when I examine my conscience, that I disapprove of fornication and adultery and—umm—almost all the other things that the ministers hope that a young man will grow up to disapprove of. Adultery, Apostasy.

Arrogance. Flattery, Fornication, Freemasonry. I could compile a whole alphabetical list." Now he grinned. "Which is a shame, honestly, considering that Susanna really is the loveliest girl I have ever met, and doing something wrong would have been a lot of fun. Especially in the fornication area."

Cavriani laced his fingers across his chest, leaned back, and contemplated his son. He saw that the incorrigible curl had escaped once more and was hanging down right in the middle of Marc's forehead. That rebellious curl would remain—if Marc was, by the grace of God, granted a long life—until a receding hairline took care of the problem.

He contemplated Susanna with his mind. Blondish, but really light brown, straight hair, a little wispy—check. Eyes of no particular color, somewhere between gray and hazel—check. Nose present, but rather narrow in the bridge—check. Teeth present, but if she had been an up-timer, she would have been given "braces"—check. Mouth quite a bit wide for the rest of the face, smiling readily, but the lips were thin rather than full—check. Clear skin—check, and remind Potentiana's cousin to bring up the topic of seeing a physician in the Spanish Netherlands for one of these new vaccinations with catpox to ward off the smallpox. Tiny in both height and girth. If a Grantviller were to rate her buxomness on a scale of one to ten, possibly a two, if the man doing the rating were in a generous mood.

There were, he thought, a couple of possibilities. The first was that Marc was not fully in the possession of his senses, to categorize this as, "the loveliest girl I have ever met."

Cavriani did not believe for an instant that his son was not in possession of his wits.

The second was that this was the girl whom, Catholic seamstress of luxury clothing or not, Divine Providence had predestined to become his daughter-in-law. God, therefore, had providentially instilled in Marc a due appreciation of God's gracious gift of a good wife, whose worth was above that of pearls and rubies.

Clearly, it would be more prudent to act, for the time being, on the basis of the second hypothesis. Cavriani thought the parents of Romeo and Juliet had behaved in a remarkably stupid manner ever since the first time he saw the play.

"Susanna has explained to us," he began, "why she is not currently enthusiastic about the idea of marrying you. However, if you listened carefully, none of her reasons contained any objection to you, as a person. Merely to the circumstances. Also, you are both still very young to be considering marriage—given, which I will grant as a presupposition, that you have done nothing wrong and there is no urgent cause for you to take precipitous steps."

Marc was listening intently.

"We have closed no doors. You mother's cousin will have her address, once she is safely brought to the Netherlands. There is no reason why you could not write to her. I gave her our firm's main address in Geneva. For business reasons, clearly. Still, there is no reason why she should not address a letter to you there, if she should wish to do so. I am sure she is aware that it would reach you, eventually. I gave her no reason to think that I am inclined to behave like an irrational parent in a tragic play, I hope."

Marc caught the reference. "I don't think," he commented, "that anyone has ever considered relocating the site of 'Romeo and Juliet' to Geneva. Or to the Tyrol, which is where Susanna's parents still were the last she heard from them. Papa, you should send them a message to say that she is well. And maybe mention what a fine young man I am?" He winked.

Cavriani assumed a supremely dignified expression, ignoring the interruption. "Since she has explained her reasoning about not wishing to live in a Calvinist city in a quite coherent manner, then perhaps we should make the effort to find out whether it would be possible for you to live in a Catholic city, or if it would cause you unbearable discomfort. Or, at least, if such an arrangement were to be permanent, whether you could settle in a city in which the majority of the population was Catholic and the predominant forms of dress and public display were formed by that fact and would allow Susanna the suitably-paid exercise of her talents. Without causing you unbearable discomfort. On condition, of course, that such a city granted Calvinists liberty of worship."

Cavriani pursed his lips. He had not explained the logic of his thought processes as clearly as he might have wished. "Surely, within the next five or ten years, there should be several such cities to choose among. If things go as we hope."

Hope had become the dominant expression on Marc's face.

Cavriani continued his musings. "Or, possibly, living in the Netherlands, it will dawn upon her that Fredrik Hendrik and his courtiers do not limit their wardrobes to black gabardine with white linen collars. The court maintained by the House of Orange does not dress quite as flamboyantly as that of Savoy, for example, but there is still quite a lot of satin and lace present. However, we should not rely too heavily on that possibility."

Cavriani rose and looked out the window. "The Americans have a lot of lovely proverbs to be added to the classical store that we find in Aesop and others. One of my favorites is, 'God helps those who help themselves.' So, after we have been to Geneva and allowed your mother to assure herself that you are in splendid health, I will arrange for you to experience living in a Catholic city. Events in Naples have not been developing as quickly as I had hoped. I think—indeed, I am sure—that you should plan to spend the next year, or perhaps two, in Naples."

Part Nine

October 1634

Of splendour in the grass, of glory in the flower

CHAPTER 70

Mars gravior sub pace latet.

General Horn's Camp, outside Rheinfelden

There were safe-conducts for the whole Rhine from Basel to the Netherlands; a whole file of safe-conducts. For the Upper Rhine, one from the margrave of Baden-Durlach. One from the Basel landvogt in Riehen. One from General Horn. The last one, improbably enough, from Duke Bernhard of Saxe-Weimar. Marc had seen it for himself as his father placed it in the passport case. What's more, they were all quite authentic. Once the boat reached the Main, Frau Dreeson would leave Susanna to join her husband in Frankfurt. For the Middle Rhine, there were safe-conducts from the duke of Lorraine and from Nils Brahe in Mainz.

And a couple of French ones, probably not quite so genuine, that Freinsheim had produced when Margrave Friedrich asked him about it. Papa had once more reminded Marc never to look gift horses in the mouth. On the other hand, they might possibly be real. Richelieu had sent a minor diplomat, who rejoiced in the rather excessive name Michel l'Esclavon, duc d'Espehar, marquis de Choses-sans-Valeur, vicomte de Lavion, seigneur de l'Haleur, chevalier Sanscourage de Contre-Ours, to Basel to make a very stiff diplomatic demand to Margrave Friedrich V for the return of Freinsheim. Espehar had managed, by following Wettstein out of the city, to finagle a position inside Horn's camp from which he had actually seen, close up, the Gustav take off carrying Don Fernando and the archduchess. He might have been sufficiently impressed to thank his impromptu guides by signing a couple of documents.

There was a wagon, also, to take Susanna and Frau Dreeson to the boat, and guards. Duke Bernhard had offered to provide the guards, on the pragmatic grounds that the first part of the route would take them through territory that he held—and held firmly. Horn, Swiger, and Gordon had agreed only on condition that the two women had an equal number of guards from the USE Horse Marines at the embassy. Marc looked at the captain of the guards uneasily, then suspiciously. It was the same Bavarian who had chased them so relentlessly.

Raudegen looked down at him, and smiled thinly. "I'm a professional, boy," he said. "I cut my teeth on the Hungarian frontier. I'm in the duke's service now. When he says capture her, I try to capture her. When he says protect her, I use everything I know to protect her. Not just until your relative from Lyons joins her. All the way to Brussels. Advantage is advantage. If Duke Bernhard can't use her as a pawn for exercising pressure on the archduchess, he will harvest whatever gratitude there may be for delivering her safely to a mistress who values her services. He has no truck with cruelty for its own sake. Nor, for that matter, do I."

For traveling, Susanna was wearing the cream-colored turtleneck sweater with a pencil-slim, ankle-length, mahogany brown velvet skirt. The side of the skit was slit to above the knee, which would allow for such functions as walking or climbing into carriages. She had her left hand thrown back, carrying a matching jacket over her shoulder. The sweater outlined her tiny breast. Marc tried conscientiously to keep his eyes focused somewhere in the region of her nose.

He took her right hand. "Ah, good-bye. Good wishes. It has been a pleasure make your acquaintance." He tried again. "I hope it all works out well for you."

"Kiss him." Marc heard Frau Dreeson's voice coming from the wagon. "See if it's worth all the speculation you've been devoting to the matter. If it isn't, it will save you a lot of bother in the long run."

Susanna looked at her, startled. Then she dropped Marc's hand, stood up on tiptoe, threw both of her arms around his neck, pulled herself up a little farther toward his face while bending his neck down a bit, and kissed him.

Their noses bumped, but they managed to rearrange things. After a while.

"Enough," Veronica interrupted. "There's your food for thought, girl. Time to get going."

Margrave Friedrich V of Baden-Durlach managed to persuade both the Basel city council and Duke Bernhard that he should be allowed to move freely between the city and General Horn's headquarters. Gustav Adolf had kindly sent both Duke Bernhard and the city council a formal letter pointing out that the younger margrave's father, Georg of Baden-Durlach, was now the USE's administrator for the Province of Swabia. The amount of public respect that Margrave Friedrich was getting had rapidly ratcheted up several notches.

By noon, he and Leopold Cavriani were having a nice chat about development funding for the iron ore in the Wiese Valley. Margrave Georg was, after all, the legal overlord of most of the iron-bearing seams that Marc had identified—if Duke Bernhard went away again, now that he had so conveniently removed most of the Austrian garrisons from the region and was no longer serving the French.

Leopold gave him a copy of Marc's report before forwarding two on to Jacob Durre. One through the regular post; one by special courier. One, of course, he had left with his regular banker in Basel.

He took the last one along when he and Marc left for home the next day.

Thinking all the while that it was very much too optimistic to hope that Duke Bernhard would go away.

Grantville, State of Thuringia-Franconia

Ed Piazza worked his way through a long radio message that had just come in from Jack Whitney, reporting from Horn's headquarters.

I know you are buddies with Leopold Cavriani, Whitney said in the message, *so I thought you might want to know that he and his son left for Geneva right after lunch. Cavriani mentioned, sort of casually, that you might be interested in knowing that he's going to send the kid to Naples for a couple of years.*

Casually? Leopold never did anything casually. *Naples?*

Ed jogged down the hall toward the radio room. Mike needed to know this. Preferably yesterday.

France

"It is not," Louis XIII said, "that we currently have any options. Not that there is anything that France is in a position to do about it. Of course, it is in the interest of France to have the Netherlands divided from the other Habsburgs."

"Possibly not in the long run, Sire," Cardinal Richelieu replied. "Not if the two of them have a dozen healthy children. Don Fernando is calling himself 'king in the Low Countries' and 'Netherlands' is a quite expansive concept. Much of the coastline of northern France is quite low-lying."

"The coastline of northern Germany," the king of France pointed out, "lies even lower. Consider the actions of Ostfriesland. Oxenstierna made it very clear at the Congress of Copenhagen that the Swedes were not happy about that. Personally, I consider it inspired on the part of Count Ulrich to have petitioned for admission to the United Provinces even before his dear cousin Gustav's army got into his territory. Of course, both of their mothers were sisters of the old Lutheran prince-bishop of Bremen who's being supplanted by Prince Frederik of Denmark now. I certainly hope that the thought of the low-lying coast of his new 'Province of Westphalen' keeps Gustav Adolf awake at night, damn his hide."

Somewhere in Swabia

"Well, fuck," said Major Simpson.

"That's getting to be a distressingly common expression in your lexicon," said his commanding officer, Colonel Heinrich Schmidt. The tone carried more in the way of amusement than reproof, though.

Tom ignored him, as did Lieutenant Commander Eddie Cantrell. Both of the young up-time officers were too intent on glaring at the radio transcript.

"Fuck a *duck*," was Eddie's useless contribution. He looked around almost wildly at the countryside. Then, his eyes came to rest on the artillery train.

The great, huge, heavy, ponderous, unwieldy, break-your-back-before-breakfast-rupture-you-by-lunch-and-put-you-in-a-grave-by-nightfall artillery train.

"You mean to tell me we've dragged these fucking cannons halfway across Europe for *nothing*?"

"It was your idea in the first place," pointed out the colonel. "The two of you both. I was an innocent party to the affair, brought in only after the fact."

Tom ignored that too. "Now what?" he demanded.

Heinrich grinned. Seeing the expression, Eddie winced. Then he leaned over and rubbed his leg just above the peg that supported it. "Oh, my aching foot-and-pegleg. Don't tell me."

The colonel shrugged. "We can hardly leave the valuable things just sitting here somewhere in Swabia, after all. No, gentlemen, I'm afraid it's back we go—and we'd best not dally, either, or winter will be upon us. Imagine having to haul these monsters through snow drifts as well."

"Well, fuck," said Tom.

"Maybe something will turn up," said Eddie, ever the wild optimist.

Something *did* turn up, to everyone's surprise. A miraculous intervention by the emperor himself, in the form of a radio message that came the next morning.

Pointless to bring them back to Luebeck. Even the admiral has now given up salvaging the Monitor *for more than parts and the steel. Take the guns to Ingolstadt. I might want to use them against Maximilian, before too long. Or against Austria, perhaps. There are many possibilities down there. So best to keep them in place.*

"Ingolstadt's not so bad," mused Eddie.

"Still be a back-breaker," cautioned Tom. But he was clearly in a much better mood. No matter how you sliced it, getting from Swabia to northern Bavaria was a lot better proposition than returning the guns to the Baltic.

"We might even make it before the first snowfall," was Heinrich's sardonic contribution, such as it was.

USE *army camp, outside Ingolstadt.*

"It's an outrage!" complained Eric Krenz. "Just when that fat swine Banér agreed to let us at least take liberty in the town."

Hands on hips, he glared around at the tent camp that had been set up by the artillery regiment. "And now! Pack all this up and march to Magdeburg."

"Give it a rest," said Thorsten Engler. "It's the army, Eric. What do you expect?"

Give it a rest and *Eric Krenz,* of course, never fit well in the same sentence, if Krenz had a grievance.

"Exactly my point!" he insisted. Piously: "In *military* terms, we should stay right here. In case the war with Bavaria flares up again."

Thorsten would normally have satisfied himself with a simple, sarcastic retort, but he actually found himself interested in the military equation. Willy-nilly, whether he'd ever intended it or not, having been promoted to officer rank had caused a subtle change in his attitudes. He couldn't help it. Thorsten was a natural foreman, and although he had no craving for a position of authority, once he found one given to him, he simply *had* to take it seriously.

"Well . . ." The lieutenant scratched his chin. "At a guess, I'd say the emperor has decided that Maximilian poses no threat for at least a year. Not with his court in disarray, large parts of his army vanished—and certainly not if the rumors we've heard about the farmers' revolt are even half-true."

"So?" demanded Krenz. "Now's the time to jump on the bastard, then."

Engler shook his head. "You're not thinking clearly, Eric. Even if we succeeded in taking Bavaria, then what? We'd have a farmers' rebellion on our hands—and probably a rebellion in most of the towns, too. We'd have to keep an army there for years, before everything settled down."

"Quarters in Munich," said Krenz. "Years of that don't sound too bad."

Thorsten couldn't help but smile. "Sergeant Krenz, you are to far-sighted vision what a hog is to scenery, when there's a full trough in front of him. 'Oblivious,' is the most polite term I can think of. For the next year, at least, the emperor is far more concerned with Saxony and Brandenburg—and who knows how far east?—than he is with Bavaria."

He waved a hand at the camp. "So let's start packing everything up. Concentrate on the task of getting ourselves back to Magdeburg before the first snowfall, shall we? Instead of pining pointlessly about whatever comforts—or lack thereof—we might find in Munich."

Krenz still had his hands on his hips. He leaned forward slightly and gave Thorsten an accusing glare. A sneer came with it, too.

"You don't fool me, with your new-found—ha! you, a farm boy!—military sagacity. *You* just like the idea of Magdeburg because *Caroline's* in Magdeburg."

Engler saw no reason to dignify that charge with a direct reply. Especially since there was some truth to it.

Quite a bit, in fact. His fiancée was in Magdeburg, after all. And while Caroline Platzer was an enthusiastic supporter of the German custom of *fenstering*, she was still an up-timer in most regards. So she saw no reason to require her betrothed to climb through a window just to get into her bed. She'd have the door open for him, instead, with herself smiling in the doorway.

"Get a move on, Sergeant!" he commanded brusquely.

CHAPTER 71

Cor Ad Cor Locquitur

Amsterdam

"Overall," Rebecca said, "I am rather proud of our handiwork. They make a handsome couple."

"They are leaving tomorrow?" Fredrik Hendrik asked.

"Yes," Rebecca said. "They want the wedding to take place as soon as possible, naturally. Don Fernando wants very much to be married at the cathedral in Brussels. I think that he wants, even more, to present Maria Anna to the *Infanta*, to Isabella Clara Eugenia, since everyone thinks that the time remaining to her is very short. Indeed, many people are astonished that she has lived this long. Since it is a hundred and twenty-five miles, even though they will be traveling with minimal pomp and almost no luggage, just the necessary staff personnel and a really big security detail, it will take several days for them to make the trip. That allows time for the great nobles of the southern Netherlands to get to Brussels, though scarcely time for any of them to get new clothes."

"The death of Ferdinand II, of course, provides Fernando and Maria Anna with every excuse for marrying quietly, since the bride will be in official mourning. The extensive formal processions and such can come later," Fredrik Hendrik said.

"True," Rebecca replied. "And Gretchen gave them advice on how to get married in a hurry."

The *stadtholder* raised his eyebrows.

Rebecca winked. "Borrow the dress."

Mike laughed raucously.

"That is exactly what Maria Anna plans to do. Gretchen and Jeff gave her a wedding present, too. I didn't expect Gretchen to do that, given her grumbling against nobility in general and Habsburgs in particular."

"Dare I ask?"

"Jeff went shopping and bought an Indian sari in the oriental imports section of the Amsterdam marketplace. It is red chiffon sprinkled with gilt stars and a fancy gilt border. Practically transparent. The color should look great on Maria Anna, she's so brunette. That would have been okay by itself, but Gretchen did some minimal stitching and turned it into a sort of regency-style nightgown. Gathers over the bosom and floating panels. No seams down the sides below the high waistline. It's really, ah, very . . ." Rebecca paused.

"Victoria's Secret?" Mike completed her sentence.

Rebecca looked blank.

"The kind of thing to inspire a husband to go shopping in the oriental bazaar."

"Precisely." She looked down at her swollen belly. "After the baby is born, of course. Which Anne Jefferson tells me should be almost any day now."

Mike looked slightly relieved at the reminder that his wife would be giving birth with an up-time nurse present. There was no way, of course—not at this late stage in the pregnancy—that they could fly to Grantville. The baby would have to be born right here in Amsterdam. For the same reason, they wouldn't be able to attend the upcoming wedding in Brussels of Don Fernando and Maria Anna.

Rebecca was sorry for that, since she would have enjoyed being there for the occasion. But she was also privately amused by Mike's attitude. Anne Jefferson herself thought that the down-time and very experienced Dutch midwife would handle the matter just fine. Probably better than she could, in fact.

"I might," he said, "just do that. Now that you have brought the matter up."

Brussels

There had been several busy, but comparatively quiet days. Contrary to protocol, Fernando and Maria Anna had ridden side by side during the trip to Brussels. He had justified this by saying that he did not really have enough guards along to provide two separate details. Doña Mencia had contributed a request that her brother be allowed to share the carriage, which gave Maria Anna an opportunity to volunteer to ride—and Don Fernando the chance to give her a really gorgeous horse as a first wedding present.

"Given that you are coming to me without a sixty-eight clause treaty protecting your interests, dower, and everything else," he said frankly, "I might as well start making it very clear to your brother that you will receive from me, voluntarily, every perquisite that normally it would have taken our diplomats months to negotiate."

"I doubt that it's been the first thing on his mind lately," Maria Anna said. "But, of course, it will be one more item that he *doesn't* have to worry about, so he will be properly grateful."

Without pomp was a relative concept, of course. They had created time for two noon meals with local nobility, regional officials, and municipal officers, one at Utrecht in the new kingdom's northern provinces, the second at Antwerp in the old southern provinces, so neither could claim to have been disadvantaged. There had been a third formal meal today, after their arrival at Brussels. Don Fernando had reserved the afternoon for catching up on paperwork; the evening, he had kept free for an unofficial dinner with the members of his privy council. Maria Anna had spent the afternoon being fitted for a trousseau. That left the twilight.

Doña Mencia, was, it had to be said, dozing. Perhaps even sleeping—certainly, her chin had dropped somewhat, although it would have been unkind to describe her breathing as a snore. Don Fernando's secretary, making the most of an autumn evening in the Netherlands, was writing at his desk in the back of the room, next to the windows that faced onto the street.

"Shall we walk along the terraces?" Fernando asked.

"That would be nice. It seems to have stopped raining." Maria Anna picked up her shawl.

The first traverse along the arcades, which covered almost a quarter of a mile facing the gardens, was devoted to the day's events. At the end, they noted that Doña Mencia still appeared content, while the secretary had lit a lamp to supplement the fading light of the sun.

The second traverse through the colonnades was devoted to Don Fernando's request for an update on the escape from Bavaria and Maria Anna's intervening adventures, along with what they might mean. "Somewhat more open than you have felt it possible to give me when a half dozen other people were listening," he specified.

"I had a lot of time to think," Maria Anna said. "Walking and riding for so many weeks, that is almost all that I did. Think and pray. My information is not good, of course. I really only know what I read in the newspapers, so you must forgive me if some of my premises are incorrect."

"Of course," Fernando said. "That is understood."

"The most important for us, in the long run, should be that there were two betrayals this summer—the one at Ingolstadt against Duke Maximilian and then that by Bernhard of Saxe-Weimar against the French."

"You see them as linked?"

"Not in their origins, I believe. But in the way that the pamphleteers will show them. For both Colonel von Farensbach and Duke Bernhard were, at one time in the past, in the employ of the Swede—and the traitor Cratz von Scharffenstein has now done the same. Someone who does not see them as simple opportunists can discern a whole pattern, deeply laid, by which Gustav Adolf has been employing double agents, infiltrating them deeply into the councils of his opponents—the French, the Bavarians, our own. In the case of Farensbach, since his family is from the Baltic, a writer might well argue that the roots go far back in time, a decade or more before the Swede intervened in the German wars. Mary Simpson says that they called such writers 'conspiracy theorists' up-time."

Fernando nodded.

"The most important reaction immediately, I think, will be in France. Duke Bernhard's action in opening the lines across from Mainz will give Monsieur Gaston and his supporters opportunities for endless publicity. Especially coming on top of the disaster this summer at Ahrensbök." She smiled. "I could almost write the pamphlets myself, if they employed me to do so. 'Bernhard's joining the French was a feint all along.' That would be the first section. Then, depending upon the pamphleteer's preference, either, 'Richelieu fell for it, which means that he is incompetent and must be replaced by a minister who will better serve Louis XIII,' or, 'Richelieu knew it all along, which means that he is a traitor, Louis XIII was duped by him, and he must be replaced by those who will serve the king more faithfully.' Either of those, of course, can be capped by a call to place Monsieur Gaston as his brother's chief minister, with Gaston's supporters filling the privy council."

What a keen mind, Fernando thought. How trenchant her observations are. How clear and to the point. How marvelously . . . *political* she is! He glanced down briefly. And a bosom, too.

They moved on to the question of more specifically family politics. Vienna, first; then Madrid.

"As things stand," Maria Anna said, "I believe that Ferdinand, my brother, will not expect to be able to call a *Reichstag* at any time soon. That may change, of course, once there is peace in the Germanies." She squeezed Fernando's arm. "I am so glad that you provided me with the copy of the alternate peace treaty draft that he is distributing. He has worked on it so hard and so long. We loved Papa so much, but he simply could not understand that things had to change now. Not so much would not as simply could not."

"I know the problem," Don Fernando said. "We find it in the Spanish branch of the family also, often enough."

"Without a diet, there is no way he can be elected as Holy Roman Emperor to succeed Papa. I do not think it likely that he will quietly just not be an emperor, however. We can read *encyclopedias* as well as anyone. Before I left Vienna, when Papa sent Ferdinand to inspect the defenses in Hungary, Mariana and I were already talking. I love Mariana; your sister is so darling and I am so glad that Ferdinand married her. But we were talking that if the Swede can simply name himself an 'emperor' in the Germanies, then there is no reason that Ferdinand should not be emperor of an 'Austro-Hungarian' empire as happened many years later in that other world. It would be a balance."

Fernando nodded again. "A very good balance."

"It also makes sense. Austria's primary responsibility will always be to hold against the Turks. Always. No matter what happens in the Germanies, Austria must look toward the Balkans."

"Perhaps," Fernando said, "some day he and I will meet with our armies and win a great victory. Not at Nördlingen against the Swede, as we did in that other world, but against the Ottomans. A united Habsburg initiative against the Turks, bringing Spain's resources into play on that front and thus reuniting the family."

"That would be wonderful. It is just too bad that Papa could not live to see such a victory," Maria Anna said rather wistfully. "Although, of course, he is in heaven with the saints and angels, so he will see it if it happens. But I know that Mariana had her confessor translate the parts about Nördlingen that we found in the *encyclopedias*, so maybe he had time to read those before he died. Maybe he knew, even if it won't happen the same way." She blinked. "But what about your brother?"

"The exact status of my relationship with my brother of Spain is unclear right now. 'Tense' is not adequate to describe the situation. But I bear him no ill will and I will attempt to demonstrate that in every way possible."

Fernando frowned. "Tante Isabella's old court physician was impossible. He attended her for years. The man was so obsessed with his hatred of the Jesuits that, as far as I can tell, he spent most of his time intriguing against them and had little time for medical practice. He left a legacy of that attitude to his successors. I have cleaned out the whole nest of them. I have also sent several shipments of cats, on different ships. Kittens sick with cat pox, pregnant females expecting kittens, all in the same cage. With letters to explain it all. Clearly, it was a dispensation of divine providence that the Spanish Netherlands is the core place in all of Europe where this remedy is to be found. Perhaps, this time, Balthasar Carlos will not die young, at least not of smallpox. My brother has to be concerned. He has too much sense not to be. We cannot let Spain fall to the French."

"Clearly," Maria Anna said, "the Habsburgs need more heirs. Healthy ones."

Fernando glanced down at her bosom again, his eyes lingering somewhat. "I will be quite happy," he said, "to devote my most vigorous efforts to siring a third, abundantly healthy, Habsburg family line."

Maria Anna looked at him. First down; then up at his face. "Your efforts to make this project sound like a prim dedication to familial duty are falling rather short." Then she added, rather mischievously, "Or, possibly, quite the reverse." She moved a little closer to him and tucked her hand into the crook of his elbow.

Fernando devoted the third traverse to a briefing on the situation in the Netherlands, both north and south, an assessment of Frederick Hendrik, the momentary potential for revolutions, and what measures he might, he feared, be called upon to take. As they once more glanced into the reception room, noting no change in the status quo, he added a little ruefully, "Of course, if the ruler has the choice between being feared and loved, it is certainly more secure for him to be feared. But, still . . ."

A watery full moon broke through the dispersing clouds, as they prepared for a fourth traverse of walkway. "Ah," she said, "but there are two of us, so perhaps we can have both. Not at the same time for each, of course, but, as you say, still . . . Let me tell you about this wonderful game that I learned from Tony Adducci while I was in Basel. The Americans had almost developed formal rules for it. It's called, 'Good cop, bad cop.'"

"I think," Maria Anna said after Fernando had gone to sup with the privy council, "that I am in love. Or, at least, falling in love. Truly, I always thought that Mariana was perhaps a little peculiar for falling in love with my brother Ferdinand at first sight. Of course, there is nothing romantic about Ferdinand, as far as I can tell. He has a double chin. He did even when he was a child. And even though he is very athletic, he is developing a paunch. My honored cousin does not have a paunch. And his hair is so pretty."

Doña Mencia smiled benevolently.

Maria Anna looked at her a little doubtfully. "Do you think that I could get him to love me?"

"He is a young man," Doña Mencia answered. "According to my brother Bedmar, he has been chaperoned right up to the tip of his nose ever since reaching puberty, because of his father's intent to have him take priestly vows. If he is anything like his brother . . ." Doña Mencia paused a moment, considering Philip IV's growing gaggle of illegitimate children by several different women. This certainly was not an opportune moment to bring them up. "Well, that's neither here nor there. At the moment, Don Fernando appears to be rather enthusiastic about the whole matrimonial project. My brother says that he has been showing a distinct, if thus far theoretical, interest in female bosoms. Happily, you are quite well endowed. Cheerful cooperation on your part, Your Highness, ought to be quite adequate to nudge him over the edge into personal as well as political alliance."

"Cooperation?"

"If he kisses you, kiss back. Repeat that at each stage of the subsequent events, no matter how peculiar or improbable they may seem. Some of them will seem very peculiar at first, I am afraid. Your sound knowledge of horse breeding will not be much help, because men and women do it rather differently. Try to ignore the official witnesses on your wedding night; their presence is a necessary confirmation of the canonical validity of the marriage. They are there for your protection, after all—think of all the claims that Henry VIII raised in England in regard to the consummation or nonconsummation of his various marriages. After the first time, they'll be gone."

"Do you suppose that, maybe, Fernando might be interested in arranging the palace here the way Papa and Mama did? So that they had apartments that opened into one another and out on the private garden, I mean? So that everyone in the corridors won't be marking down every time he comes to my rooms to couple?"

"Marking the record is important, my dear, when a royal pair rarely couple. In that case it is necessary in order to validate the wife's pregnancies. Can you imagine the furor that would ensue if the queen of France suddenly announced that she was pregnant, given the circumstances of that marriage? But it is not really necessary when the spouses are known to couple regularly.

"Don Fernando is Spanish, of course. He may be old-fashioned about this, but you might suggest a more modern arrangement." Doña Mencia thought a moment. "If he does much paperwork by candle light in the evenings, having adjoining apartments would really save him time. They would be quite convenient. Not to mention avoiding chilly corridors while he is dressed in his nightshirt, which is more of a consideration here in the Netherlands than it would be in Spain. Yes, I see nothing wrong in suggesting a more modern arrangement."

She smiled. "Particularly if you suggest it while you are wearing the nightgown that Gretchen Richter gave you. I do not recommend wearing it on your wedding night, although it is very becoming, Your Highness. Even though you may really, really, want Don Fernando to see you in it. Even though I am also sure that he would be favorably impressed, it is probably not the course of prudence for you to wear it in front of the rest of the court. There are some things that the official witnesses do not need to see.

"And, of course, there would be political implications if you wore a gift from *die Richterin* on your wedding night. Later on, everyone will know you wear it, of course—maids do gossip—but knowing and seeing are two different things."

Rome

"And what is the news from Brussels?" Urban VIII asked. "Has the radio at the USE embassy received messages from Amsterdam or Antwerp, that is?"

"The wedding took place without any further impediments, Your Holiness," Cardinal Francesco Barberini said. "The infanta Isabella Clara Eugenia commanded that she be dressed in the habit of the Order of Poor Clares, placed on a litter, and taken to the cathedral that she might be present at the nuptial mass. To almost everyone's surprise, she survived the experience."

"I was greatly relieved by the news that the bride had been safely retrieved from Basel. I am even more relieved to hear this." The pope inclined his head. "I wonder whether I will live long enough to see the miracle of an airplane for myself. Father-General Vitelleschi, do you have any additional news?"

"I have been asked to transmit to you a request from the bride and groom. As a special favor upon the occasion of their marriage, they would appreciate it very much if you do not require the English Ladies still in the Spanish Netherlands to remove to the USE. Rather, they ask that you extend the reversal of the dissolution of the Institute of the Blessed Virgin Mary to all of the dioceses of the new kingdom and permit them to resume their valuable labors unhampered."

"Your sense is?"

"While the Jesuit Order is forbidden by its rule to accept the spiritual direction of women's orders, we of course are prepared to provide the English Ladies with advice and counsel in ways that are appropriate under the rule."

"I think," the pope said, "that we might as well let the queen in the Netherlands keep her golden rose."

November 1634

Though nothing can bring back the hour

Prague

Duke Albrecht of Bavaria looked at the letter that had just arrived. So now Rudolf Philipp, Landgrave of Leuchtenberg, was dead also. Mechthilde's last surviving nephew had been considerably brighter and more competent than his unfortunate late older brother, Maximilian Adam. Rudolf had stayed behind to complete the inspection tour of Austria's defenses against the Turks when Ferdinand III was called back to Vienna. He had been killed in a random minor skirmish on the Hungarian border, no different from any of a dozen others that occurred along the border with the Ottomans every day.

He crossed himself. Contrary to all reasonable expectation, his own sons, wherever they might be and please God they were still safe and well, would now unite Leuchtenberg with Bavaria—if, of course, they could expel the Swedish occupiers from Leuchtenberg. And if they some day inherited whatever might be left of Bavaria by the time Maximilian died.

At the moment, it seemed highly improbable that Maximilian would remarry. Duke Albrecht looked back, reflecting on the irony of it all. The situation could probably have been saved if they had simply permitted Maximilian to abdicate when he wanted to after Elisabeth Renata's death.

Cast of Characters

Adducci, Bernadette   Former nun, policewoman and social worker in Grantville; aunt of Tony Adducci in Basel

Adducci, Tony, Jr.   Radio operator and "mouthpiece" for Diane Jackson in Basel

Allegretti, Susanna   Apprentice seamstress at the Austrian Habsburg court

Arndt, Augustin   Lawyer, agent of Landgrave Wilhelm Georg of Leuchtenberg in the Upper Palatinate

Austria, Ferdinand II of   Habsburg, Holy Roman Emperor

Austria, Cecelia Renata, Archduchess of   Younger daughter of Holy Roman Emperor Ferdinand II; sister of Archduchess Maria Anna

Austria, Maria Anna, Archduchess of   Older daughter of Holy Roman Emperor Ferdinand II

Austria, Leopold Wilhelm, Archduke of   Younger son of Holy Roman Emperor Ferdinand II; brother of Maria Anna

Austria, Ferdinand III of   Son of Holy Roman Emperor Ferdinand II; married to Mariana, infanta of Spain; brother of Maria Anna

Baden-Durlach, Friedrich V of   Margrave, oldest son of Margrave Georg of Baden-Durlach; running his father's government-in-exile in Basel

Baden-Durlach, Georg of	Margrave, staunch supporter of Gustav Adolf; father of Margrave Friedrich of Baden-Durlach in Basel
Banér, Johan	Swedish general, commander of Gustavus Adolphus' troops in the Upper Palatinate
Barberini, Maffeo	See Pope Urban VIII
Barberini, Antonio	Cardinal, nephew of Urban VIII
Bavaria, Albrecht, duke of	Younger brother and heir presumptive of Duke Maximilian
Bavaria, Maximilian I, duke of	Ruler of Bavaria; member of the Wittelsbach family, childless in his first marriage to Elisabeth Renata
Bavaria, Sigmund Albrecht of	Third son of Duke Albrecht and Mechthilde of Leuchtenberg
Bavaria, Maximilian Heinrich of	Second Son of Duke Albrecht and Mechthilde of Leuchtenberg
Bavaria, Karl Johann Franz of	Oldest son of Duke Albrecht and Mechthilde of Leuchtenberg
Bavaria, Ferdinand of	Brother of Duke Maximilian; Archbishop-Elector of Cologne
Bedmar, Alfonso de Alonso de la Cueva y Benavides	Marques of Bedmar, Cardinal, adviser of Don Fernando
Bidermann, Jakob	Jesuit, playwright, formerly resident in Munich
Böcler, Johann Heinrich	Private secretary of Duke Ernst of Saxe-Weimar
Bourne, Kyle	Radio operator, soldier with Horn in Swabia
Brechbuhl, Elias	Accountant, in exile from the Upper Palatinate to Nuernberg, widower of Veronica Dreeson's stepdaughter Elisabetha Richter
Buxtorf, Johannes the Younger	Professor of Hebrew at the University of Basel, Switzerland
Cantrell, Eddie	Lieutenant Commander, USE Navy

Carafa, Carlo	Papal nuncio in Munich
Cavriani, Marc	Son of Leopold Cavriani; apprenticed to Jacob Durre
Cavriani, Leopold	Genevan Calvinist merchant, associate of Ed Piazza
Cavriani, Idelette	Daughter of Leopold Cavriani
Contzen, Adam	Jesuit, confessor of Duke Maximilian of Bavaria
Cratz von Scharffen- stein, Johann Philipp	Commander of the Bavarian garrison at Ingolstadt
Donnersberger, Joachim	Chancellor of Bavaria
Dreeson, Henry	Mayor of Grantville
Dreeson, Veronica	Widow of Johann Stephan Richter; wife of Grantville's mayor Henry Dreeson; step-grandmother of Gretchen Richter
Durre, Jacob	Merchant of metals in Nuernberg; associate of Leopold Cavriani; master to whom Marc Cavriani is apprenticed
Ebeling, Jacob "Jake"	USE military liaison to Duke Ernst in the Upper Palatinate
Egli, Veit	Factor representing Leopold Cavriani in Neuburg
Ellis, Mark	Grantville engineer, with Banér at Ingolstadt
Engler, Thorsten	See Narnia, Imperial Count of
Ernst, Duke	See Saxe-Weimar, Ernst, duke of
Farensbach, Wolmar von	Bavarian officer at Ingolstadt
Felser, Lambert	Tinsmith in Grantville, goes to Amberg with Keith Pilcher
Forer, Lorenz	Jesuit, confessor to Duke Maximilian after Contzen's illness
Forst, Afra	From Leuchtenberg, maid to Mary Simpson and Veronica Dreeson during their stay in Amberg, Upper Palatinate

Forst, Valentin   From Leuchtenberg; cousin of Afra Forst and Emmeram Becker; employee of Augustin Arndt

Freinsheim, Johann F.   Secretary in the French interpretation service; agent of Margrave Friedrich V of Baden-Durlach in France; future son-in-law of Matthias Bernegger

Guiomar   Elderly maid of Doña Mencia de Mendoza

Golla   Ecclesiastical official (Dekan) in Munich, Bavaria

Gonzaga, Eleonora   Empress, second wife of Holy Roman Emperor Ferdinand II

Gordon, James Dean   Military escort of Diane Jackson in Basel

Hand, Erik Haakansson   Swedish colonel serving under Duke Ernst of Saxe-Weimar in the Upper Palatinate, son of an illegitimate cousin of Gustavus Adolphus

Hanf, Jacob   Nephew of Veronica Dreeson; son of Karl Hanf

Hanf, Karl   Cooper in Grafenwöhr, Upper Palatinate; stepfather of Magdalena and Margaretha Herder; brother-in-law of Veronica Dreeson

Hanf, Thomas   Nephew of Veronica Dreeson; son of Karl Hanf

Helena, Baroness   Lady-in-waiting to Archduchess Maria Anna of Austria

Hell, Caspar   Jesuit, rector of the Collegium in Amberg

Herder, Magdalena   Niece of Veronica Dreeson, in Grafenwöhr

Herder, Maria   Niece of Veronica Dreeson, in Grafenwöhr

Hesse-Rotenburg, Hermann Landgrave of Hesse-Rotenburg; half-brother of Landgrave Wilhelm V of Hesse-Kassel; now Secretary of State of the USE

Horn, Gustav   Swedish general commanding Gustav Adolf's forces against Bernhard of Saxe-Weimar in the Swabian region

Hörwarth, Johann Franz   Bavarian nobleman and official, executed by Maximilian

Jackson, Diane	Wife of Frank Jackson; envoy to Margrave Friedrich of Baden-Durlach in Basel
Jackson, Frank	USE general, husband of Diane Jackson
Kircher, Athanasius	Jesuit in Grantville
Kitt, Dane	Grantville engineer, with Banér at Ingolstadt
Krenz, Eric	Sergeant, USE Flying Artillery Regiment
Lamormaini, Wilhelm	Jesuit, confessor of Holy Roman Emperor Ferdinand II
Leuchtenberg, Rudolf Philipp of	Second son of Landgrave Wilhelm Georg of Leuchtenberg
Leuchtenberg, Mechthilde of	Landgravine; sister of Landgrave Wilhelm Georg; wife of Duke Albrecht of Bavaria
Leuchtenberg, Maximilian Adam of	Oldest son of Landgrave Wilhelm Georg of Leuchtenberg
Lorraine, Elisabeth Renata of	Duchess of Bavaria, wife of Duke Maximilian (deceased)
Lukretia, Baroness	Lady-in-waiting to Archduchess Maria Anna of Austria
Manrique, Miguel de	Military adviser to Don Fernando
Maximilian, Duke	See Bavaria, Maximilian I, duke of
Mazzare, Lawrence	Cardinal-Protector of the USE
Medici, Claudia de'	Regent of Tirol, widow of Archduke Leopold of Austria-Tirol
Mendoza, Doña Mencia de	Chief attendant of Archduchess Maria Anna of Austria; sister of Cardinal Bedmar
Mercy, Franz von	Bavarian general, from Lorraine
Moser, Nicholas	Town clerk in Grafenwöhr
Mossberger, Lorenz	Notary, in exile from the Upper Palatinate to Nuernberg, husband of Veronica Dreeson's stepdaughter Hanna Richter
Narnia, Thorsten Engler, Imperial Count of	Lieutenant, USE Flying Artillery Regiment

Nasi, Don Francisco	Director of intelligence for the USE
Olivares, Count-Duke of	First minister of Philip IV of Spain
Orange, Fredrik Hendrik of	Stadtholder of the Netherlands (United Provinces)
Oz, Caroline Platzer, Countess of	Fiancée of Lieutenant Thorsten Engler
Palatinate, Karl Ludwig of the	Elector Palatine in succession to his late father, the Winter King; now in Spanish captivity
Piazza, Ed	Former principal of Grantville high school, later Secretary of State of the NUS, later president of the SoTF
Pierpoint, Gerry	Soldier from Grantville, in Swabia with Horn
Pilcher, Maxine	Grantville elementary school teacher, wife of Keith Pilcher
Pilcher, Keith	Grantville machinist working for Ollie Reardon; commercial representative to the Upper Palatinate; husband of Maxine Pilcher
Platzer, Caroline	See Oz, Countess of
Polyxena, Countess	Lady-in-waiting to Archduchess Maria Anna of Austria
Rastetter, Hieronymus	Lawyer employed by Veronica Dreeson in Amberg
Raudegen	Mercenary captain in the Bavarian service; later transfers to that of Bernhard of Saxe-Weimar
Reschly, Mark	Lieutenant, USE Flying Artillery Regiment
Richel, Bartholomaeus	Lawyer, deputy to Joachim Donnersberger as chancellor of Bavaria, diplomat
Richelieu, Armand du Plessis de	Cardinal, first minister of France under Louis XIII
Richter, Anna Elisabetha "Annalise"	Younger sister of Gretchen and Hans Richter

Richter, Kilian	Resident of Grafenwöhr, younger half-brother of the late Johann Stephen Richter and brother-in-law of Veronica Dreeson
Richter, Maria Margaretha "Gretchen"	Organizer of Committees of Correspondence; sister of Hans Richter; wife of Jeff Higgins, now in Amsterdam
Richter, Johann Stephan	Printer in Amberg, Upper Palatinate; first husband of Veronica Dreeson (deceased)
Richter, Maria Dorothea (Mossberger)	Wife of Kilian Richter in Grafenwöhr, sister of Lorenz Mossberger
Richter, Hanna	Veronica Dreeson's stepdaughter, married to Lorenz Mossberger
Richter, Anton	Son of the late Johann Stephan Richter; father of Gretchen, Hans, and Annalise (deceased)
Richter, Hans	Pilot, hero, step-grandson of Veronica Dreeson (deceased)
Richter, Margaretha	Veronica Dreeson's stepdaughter
Richter, Clara	Veronica Dreeson's stepdaughter
Richter, Dorothea	Daughter of Kilian Richter; fiancée of Nicholas Moser
Richter, Hermann	Son of Kilian Richter
Rothwild, Johann	Nephew of Johann Stephan Richter
Rubens, Pieter Paul	Painter; diplomat and adviser to Don Fernando
Rush, Carolyn (Leek)	Associate of Mary Simpson in Magdeburg, working on normal school project
Sartorius, Petrus	Steward of Landgrave Wilhelm Georg of Leuchtenberg in Pruefening
Sattler, Philipp	Swabian, personal liaison of Gustavus Adolphus to Mike Stearns
Saxe-Weimar, Bernhard, Duke of	Brother of Wilhelm and Ernst; traitor to Gustavus Adolphus
Saxe-Weimar, Ernst, Duke of	Brother of Wilhelm IV, duke of Saxe-Weimar, now Wilhelm Wettin; regent for Gustavus Adolphus in the Upper Palatinate (Oberpfalz)

Saxe-Weimar, Wilhelm IV, duke of	See Wilhelm Wettin
Scaglia, Alessandro	Diplomat from Savoy, adviser to Isabella Clara Eugenia
Scharffenstein	See Cratz von Scharffenstein
Schmidt, Heinrich	Colonel in the USE army
Schreiner, Hanna	Sister of Matthias Schreiner; wife of Wilhelm Bastl; in Grafenwöhr
Schreiner, Matthias	Husband of Clara Richter
Schreiner, Clara	Brewer in Grafenwöhr, aunt of Matthias Schreiner
Schuster, Casimir	Brother of Veronica Dreeson (deceased)
Schuster Hans Florian	Brother of Veronica Dreeson
Schusterin, Jakobaea	Sister of Veronica Dreeson (deceased)
Schusterin, Veronica	See Dreeson, Veronica
Simpson, John Chandler	USE Admiral
Simpson, Mary	USE socialite and charity activist; wife of USE Admiral John Chandler Simpson
Simpson, Tom	Major, USE Army; son of John Chandler and Mary Simpson; husband of Rita Stearns, Mike Stearns' sister
Sloan, Johnnie	Soldier from Grantville, in Swabia with Horn
Snell, Toby	Grantville military radio operator accompanying the commercial expedition to the Upper Palatinate
Snell, Mary Lou	Mother of Toby Snell
Spain, Don Fernando of	The cardinal-infante; younger brother of King Philip IV of Spain; now king in the Low Countries
Spain, Isabella Clara Eugenia of	Infanta; daughter of Philip II; half-sister of Philip III; widow of Albert of Austria; regent of the Spanish Netherlands; aunt of Don Fernando

Spain, Mariana of	Infanta; married to Archduke Ferdinand III of Austria; sister of Don Fernando of Spain
Spain, Philip IV of	King of Spain, brother of Mariana and of Don Fernando
Spain, Balthasar Carlos of	Infante, son of Philip IV
Stearns, Rebecca (Abrabanel)	Wife of Mike Stearns; USE envoy in Amsterdam
Stearns, Mike	Prime minister of the USE
Stecher, Frau	Chief seamstress at the Austrian Habsburg court
Sweden, Gustav II Adolf of	King of Sweden, Emperor of the USE, High King of the Union of Kalmar
Swiger, Lee Thomas	Military escort of Diane Jackson in Basel
Tanzflecker, Caspar	Iron/metalworker, entrepreneur in the Upper Palatinate
Thornton, Marty	USE soldier from Grantville, in Swabia with Horn
Threlkeld, Burt	USE soldier, with Horn in Swabia
Torstensson, Lennart	Swedish general, in command of USE army
Troeschler, Thomas	Purchaser for ore barges and ore barrels
Turenne, Henri de la Tour d'Auvergne, vicomte de	French general
Urban VIII	Pope
Vervaux, Johannes	Jesuit; confessor of the late Elisabeth Renata of Lorraine, duchess of Bavaria; now tutor to the two younger sons of Duke Albrecht of Bavaria
Vitelleschi, Mutio	Father-General of the Jesuit Order
Wallenstein, Albrecht Wenzel Eusebius	Former imperial general, now king of Bohemia
Ward, Mary	Former Mother Superior of the English Ladies, or "Jesuitesses"

Washaw, Carol Ann	Associate of Mary Simpson in Magdeburg, working on normal school project
Wenzin, Thomas von	Bailiff representing Duke Ernst's interests as regent of the Upper Palatinate in Grafenwöhr
Werth, Johann von	Bavarian cavalry colonel, from the lower Rhineland
Wettin, Wilhelm	Formerly duke of Saxe-Weimar, now leader of the opposition party to Mike Stearns in the USE parliament
Wettstein, Johann Rudolf	Basel official, administrator of Riehen
Whitney, Jack	USE soldier from Grantville, in Swabia with Horn
Wigmore, Winifred	Member of the English Ladies
Witty, Carl	Captain, USE Flying Artillery Regiment
Wood, Jesse	Colonel, in command of the USE air force
Zincgref. Julius Wilhelm	Propagandist and public relations specialist for Duke Ernst of Saxe-Weimar
Zwinger, Theodor	Head pastor of the Calvinist churches of Basel, Switzerland; brother-in-law of Johannes Buxtorf the Younger

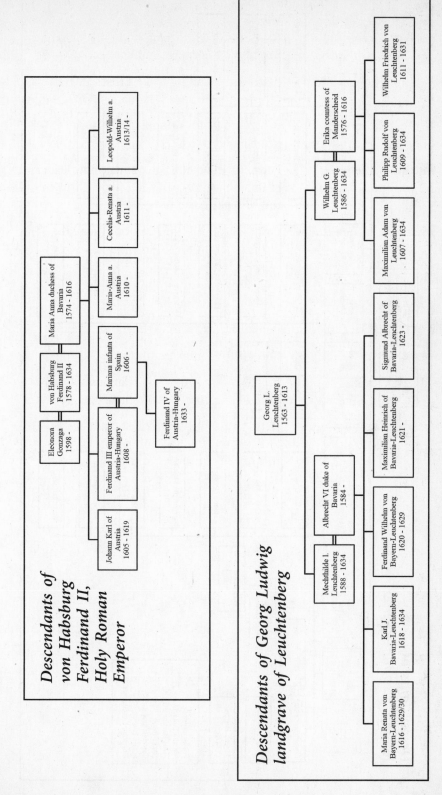

Descendants of
von Habsburg
Ferdinand II,
Holy Roman
Emperor

Johann Karl of
Austria
1605 - 1619

Eleonora
Gonzaga
1598 -

von Habsburg
Ferdinand II
1578 - 1634

Maria Anna duchess of
Bavaria
1574 - 1616

Ferdinand III emperor of
Austria-Hungary
1608 -

Mariana infanta of
Spain
1606 -

Maria-Anna a.
Austria
1610 -

Cecelia-Renata a.
Austria
1611 -

Leopold-Wilhelm a.
Austria
1613/14 -

Ferdinand IV of
Austria-Hungary
1633 -

Descendants of Georg Ludwig
landgrave of Leuchtenberg

Georg L.
Leuchtenberg
1563 - 1613

Mechthilde I.
Leuchtenberg
1588 - 1634

Albrecht VI duke of
Bavaria
1584 -

Wilhelm G.
Leuchtenberg
1586 - 1634

Erika countess of
Manderscheid
1576 - 1616

Maria Renata von
Bayern-Leuchtenberg
1616 - 1629/30

Karl J.
Bavaria-Leuchtenberg
1618 - 1634

Ferdinand Wilhelm von
Bayern-Leuchtenberg
1620 - 1629

Maximilian Heinrich of
Bavaria-Leuchtenberg
1621 -

Sigmund Albrecht of
Bavaria-Leuchtenberg
1623 -

Maximilian Adam von
Leuchtenberg
1607 - 1634

Philipp Rudolf von
Leuchtenberg
1609 - 1634

Wilhelm Friedrich von
Leuchtenberg
1611 - 1631

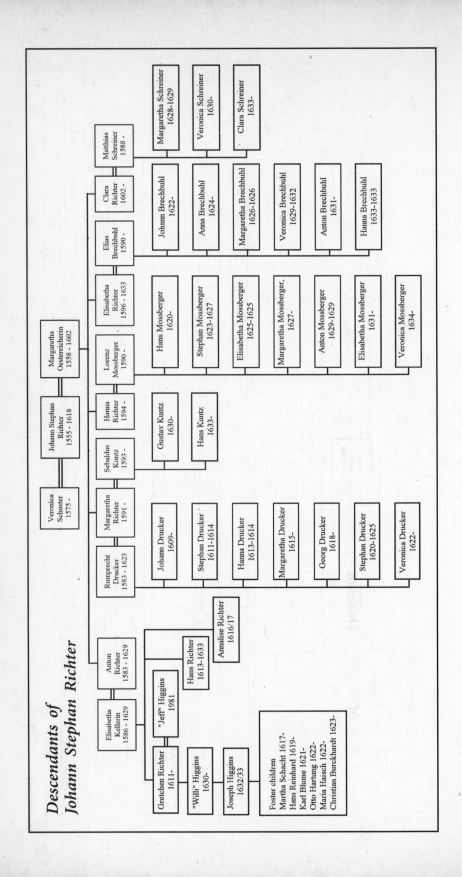

Descendants of Johann Stephan Richter